VORTEX

Sweeps The Critics Away!

"One rousing read . . . Bond's storytelling is superb."
—*Cleveland Plain Dealer*

☆ ☆ ☆

"*Vortex* swirls with wartime thrills."
—*Boston Herald*

☆ ☆ ☆

"Larry Bond has done it again! A tense, provocative, suspenseful story with a plot so good and gripping that putting this book down is almost a physical impossibility. Simply put, it's a classic of the genre."
—Pete Earley, bestselling author of *Family of Spies*

☆ ☆ ☆

"Sustains interest from first page to last and confirms Larry Bond as a highly capable storyteller. . . . Gives an excellent sense of the problems—and limits—of power projection in an underdeveloped theater."
—*Publishers Weekly*

☆ ☆ ☆

"Fast-paced and well written."
—*Houston Chronicle*

☆ ☆ ☆

more . . .

"This knowledgeable evocation of the spectacle of modern weaponry and international conflict will reward new and old admirers of military action."

—Library Journal

☆ ☆ ☆

"A big, sweeping novel full of action and suspense."

—Washington Times

☆ ☆ ☆

"Well-done battle scenes . . . a detail-rich treatment of a multifront war. . . . Armchair warriors should find considerable satisfaction."

—Kirkus Reviews

☆ ☆ ☆

"*Vortex* draws you in. . . . Reads fast . . . readers will wish it had been longer."

—Flint Sunday Journal

☆ ☆ ☆

"Bond displays a firm grasp of how the national security bureaucracy in Washington goes into action and how the military deploys."

—Navy Times

☆ ☆ ☆

"Bond takes us from one hot spot to another. . . . Cleverly woven . . . it has some scary—and quite real implications."

—Dayton Daily News

☆ ☆ ☆

"Remarkable. . . . *Vortex* is a finely tuned drama combining intrigue, romance, weaponry, politics, deceit and history of a region many Americans don't really understand."

—Baton Rouge Sunday Advocate

☆ ☆ ☆

"Interesting and original. . . . [Tom Clancy] has some real competition on his hands."

—Bookpage

☆ ☆ ☆

"For lovers of military strategy, especially in a current-day context, this novel is a must."

—Orlando Sentinel

☆ ☆ ☆

"Action aplenty. . . . Bond's attention to detail—especially military detail—is remarkable."

—Florida Times-Union

☆ ☆ ☆

"A massive work. . . . a frighteningly realistic scenario for a possible world war."

—Richmond Times-Dispatch

☆ ☆ ☆

"Compelling . . . dramatic . . . colorful. . . . The military strategies and tactics, the political machinations, the historical backgrounds of the country, and the realistic character portrayals combine to make *Vortex* a powerful presentation of possibilities."

***—Sun-News* (Deland, FL)**

☆ ☆ ☆

"A man of many talents . . . Bond struck out on his own and produced *Red Phoenix*, a highly acclaimed first novel. Now, for the second time in as many tries, Bond has delivered a good military adventure with *Vortex*."

—Ocala Star-Banner

☆ ☆ ☆

Also by Larry Bond

RED PHOENIX

Published by
WARNER BOOKS

LARRY BOND

VORTEX

A Time Warner Company

A signed first edition of this book has been privately printed by The Franklin Library.

WARNER BOOKS EDITION

Cover design and illustration by Peter Thorpe
Book design by H. Roberts
Map by Giorgetta Bell McRee

Warner Books, Inc.
1271 Avenue of the Americas
New York, NY 10020

Printed in the United States of America

Originally published in hardcover by Warner Books.

First Printed in Paperback: June, 1992

10 9 8 7 6 5 4 3 2 1

Dedicated to our brothers and sisters,
Mary Adams and Jim Bond, Erin Larkin-Foster,
and Colin, Ian, Duncan, and Christopher Larkin.

ACKNOWLEDGMENTS

We would like to thank Jim Baker, Jeff Bowen, Greg Browne, Jerry Cain, Jeff Cavin, John Chrzas, Col. Terry Crews and Grace Crews, Dan and Carmel Fisk, Bill Ford, John Goetke, Bill Grijalba, Peter Hildenrath, Jason Hunter, Dick Kane and Presidio Press, Don and Marilyn Larkin, John Moser, Deb Mullaney, Bill Paley and Bridget Rivoli, Tim Peckinpaugh and Pam McKinney-Peckinpaugh, Jeff and Deena Pluhar, Jeff Richelson, Dick Ristaine, Michael J. Solon, Bruce Spaulding, Steve St. Clair, Thomas T. Thomas, Chris Williams, and Joy Schumack of the Solano County Bookmobile Service.

Special thanks to Steve Cole and his newsletter, *For Your Eyes Only*, and Steve Petrick, for their assistance in reviewing the manuscript.

For Your Eyes Only was very useful in writing *Vortex*, and I recommend it as a way of keeping up with military and conflict issues around the world. Write to Tiger Publications, PO Box 8759, Amarillo, TX 79114-8759.

Finally, we would like to thank two men without whose constant and invaluable aid and advice this book could never have emerged from our word processors: our editor at Warner Books, Mel Parker, and our agent, Robert Gottlieb of William Morris.

AUTHOR'S NOTE

Though Patrick Larkin's name does not appear on the front cover, *Vortex* is his book as much as it is mine.

This is the second book that Pat and I have written together, collaborating from start to finish. In a process that lasted nearly eighteen months, we helped each other over literary hurdles, argued politics, tactics, and strategy, and spurred each other on as the deadline approached. Like all good teams, we believe our work together reinforces our individual strengths and skills.

We hope you enjoy the story we've tried to tell.

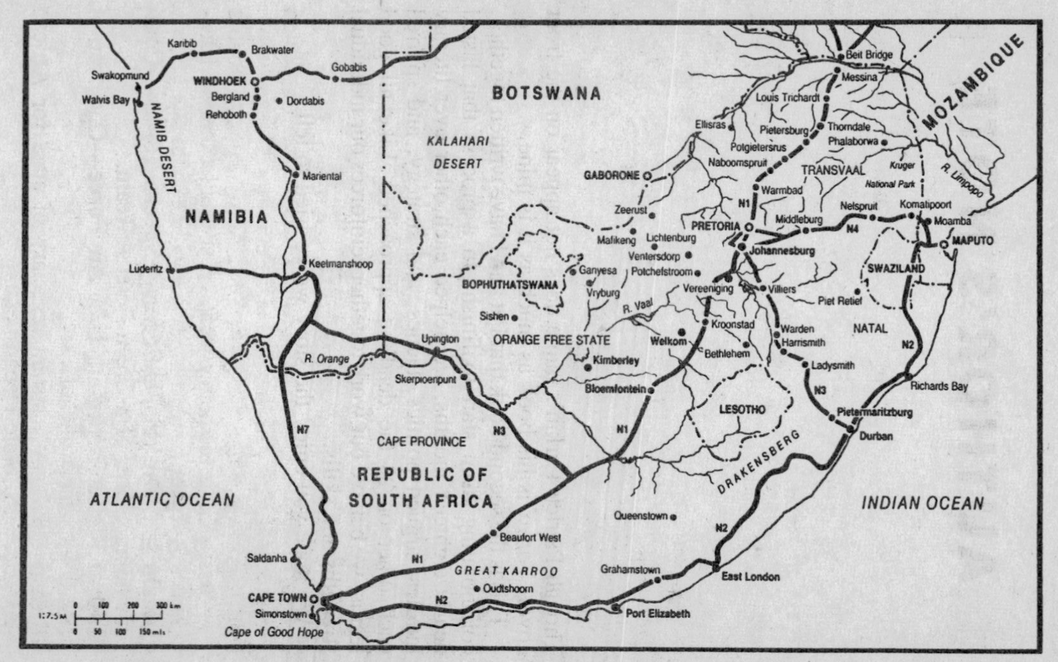
BOTSWANA
NAMIBIA
MOZAMBIQUE
KALAHARI DESERT
NAMIB DESERT
Swakopmund
Walvis Bay
Karibib
Brakwater
WINDHOEK
Bergland
Rehoboth
Dordabis
Gobabis
Mariental
Keetmanshoop
Luderitz
GABORONE
Zeerust
Mafikeng
Lichtenburg
Ventersdorp
Potchefstroom
Ganyesa
Vryburg
BOPHUTHATSWANA
Sishen
Ellisras
Naboomspruit
Potgietersrus
Pietersburg
Louis Trichardt
Messina
Beit Bridge
Thorndale
Phalaborwa
TRANSVAAL
Kruger
National Park
R. Limpopo
Warmbad
N1
PRETORIA
Johannesburg
Middleburg
Nelspruit
N4
Komatipoort
Moamba
MAPUTO
SWAZILAND
Piet Retief
Vereeniging
Villiers
Kroonstad
Welkom
Bethlehem
Warden
Harrismith
Ladysmith
NATAL
N2
Richards Bay
N3
Pietermaritzburg
Durban
R. Vaal
ORANGE FREE STATE
Kimberley
Bloemfontein
LESOTHO
DRAKENSBERG
Upington
R. Orange
Skerpioenpunt
N7
CAPE PROVINCE
REPUBLIC OF SOUTH AFRICA
ATLANTIC OCEAN
INDIAN OCEAN
Queenstown
Beaufort West
GREAT KARROO
Oudtshoorn
Grahamstown
East London
Port Elizabeth
Saldanha
CAPE TOWN
Simonstown
Cape of Good Hope
1:7.5 M
0 100 200 300 km
0 50 100 150 mls

DRAMATIS PERSONAE

AMERICANS:

Lieutenant Colonel Mike Carrerra, U.S. Army—Commanding officer of 1/75th Ranger Battalion.

Lieutenant General Jerry Craig, USMC—Commanding officer of the 2nd Marine Expeditionary Force and later the Allied South African Joint Task Force.

Lieutenant Nick Dworski, U.S. Army Special Forces—Executive officer for Jeff Hawkins's A Team.

James Malcolm Forrester—Vice President of the United States, chairman of the National Security Council.

Staff Sergeant Mike Griffith, U.S. Army Special Forces—Assigned as the heavy weapons specialist for Jeff Hawkins's A Team.

Captain Jeff Hawkins, U.S. Army Special Forces—Commanding officer of a Green Beret A Team.

General Walter Hickman, U.S. Air Force—Chairman of the Joint Chiefs of Staff.

Edward Hurley—Assistant secretary of state for African Affairs, U.S. State Department.

Lieutenant Jack "Ice" Isaacs, USN—A Navy F/A-18 pilot.

Captain Peter Klocek, U.S. Army—Operations officer of the 1/75th Ranger Battalion.

Sam Knowles—Ian Sherfield's cameraman.

Captain Thomas Malloy, USN—Commanding officer of the Iowa-class battleship *Wisconsin*.

General Wesley Masters, USMC—Commandant of the U.S. Marine Corps.

Christopher Nicholson—Director of the Central Intelligence Agency.

Lieutenant Colonel Robert O'Connell, U.S. Army—Acting commanding officer of the 1/75th Ranger Battalion, later commander 75th Ranger Regiment.

Hamilton Reid—Secretary of commerce.

Ian Sherfield—An American journalist assigned to South Africa.

Brigadier General George Skiles, U.S. Army—Chief of staff of the Allied South African Expeditionary Force.

Rear Admiral Andrew Douglas Stewart, USN—Commander of the carrier group including the Nimitz-class carrier *Carl Vinson*, later commander of Allied naval forces operating off the South African coast.

Major General Samuel Weber, U.S. Army—Commanding officer of the 24th Mechanized Infantry Division.

SOUTH AFRICANS:

Captain Rolf Bekker, South African Defense Force (SADF)—Company commander, 2nd Battalion, the 44th Parachute Regiment.

Brigadier Deneys Coetzee, SADF—A close friend of Henrik Kruger, now assigned to Army staff headquarters in Pretoria.

Brigadier Franz Diederichs, Security Branch, South African Police—Special military commissioner of Natal Province.

Major Richard Forbes, SADF—Executive officer of the 20th Cape Rifles.

Frederick Haymans—President of the Republic of South Africa.

Colonel Magnus Heerden, SADF—Head of Military Intelligence Branch of the Directorate of Military Intelligence.

Constand Heitman—South African minister of defense in Vorster's cabinet.

David Kotane—ANC guerrilla leader commanding the Broken Covenant strike force.

Commandant Henrik Kruger, SADF—Commander, 20th Cape Rifles.

Colonel Sese Luthuli—A senior officer in Umkhonto we Sizwe, the military arm of the African National Congress.

Helmoed Malherbe—South African minister of industries and commerce in Vorster's cabinet.

Gideon Mantizima—Leader of Inkatha, the Zulu political movement, and chief minister of KwaZulu, the nominally independent Zulu tribal homeland inside South Africa's Natal Province.

Major Willem Metje, SADF—Assigned to Military Intelligence Branch of the Directorate of Military Intelligence.

Erik Muller—Head of the South African Directorate of Military Intelligence.

Riaan Oost—A South African farmer acting as a deep-cover mole for the ANC.

Colonel Frans Peiper, SADF—Commanding officer of the 61st Transvaal Rifles, the battalion guarding South Africa's Pelindaba Nuclear Research Complex.

Fredrik Pienaar—South African minister of information in Vorster's cabinet.

Sergeant Gerrit Roost, SADF—Capt. Rolf Bekker's headquarters sergeant.

Andrew Sebe—An ANC guerrilla and member of the Broken Covenant strike force.

Matthew Sibena—A Xhosa resident of Johannesburg assigned as a driver for Ian Sherfield and Sam Knowles.

Jaime Steers—A fourteen-year-old fighting as part of the Transvaal Commando "Goetke."

Major Chris Taylor, SADF—Executive officer of a Citizen Force infantry battalion based in Cape Town.

Emily van der Heijden—Only child of Marius van der Heijden.

Marius van der Heijden—Deputy minister, South African Ministry of Law and Order, in Vorster's cabinet.

Colonel George von Brandis, SADF—Commanding officer of the 5th Mechanized Infantry Battalion.

Karl Vorster—South Africa's minister of law and order and later president of the Republic of South Africa.

Corporal de Vries, SADF—Capt. Rolf Bekker's radio operator.

General Adriaan de Wet, SADF—Chief of the South African Defense Force.

CUBANS:

Senior Captain Victor Mares, Cuban Army—Executive officer of the 8th Motor Rifle Battalion in Namibia, and later commander of the First Brigade Tactical Group's reconnaissance battalion.

Colonel José Suarez, Cuban Army—General Vega's chief of staff.

Colonel Jaume Vasquez, Cuban Army—General Vega's chief of intelligence.

General Antonio Vega, Cuban Army—Commanding officer of Cuban forces in Angola and later in the South African theater.

MOZAMBICANS:

Captain Jorge de Sousa—The Mozambican officer assigned to serve as a liaison between Vega's forces and the Mozambican Army.

BRITISH:

Major John Farwell, British Army—Commanding officer, A Company, 3rd Battalion, the Parachute Regiment.

Captain David Pryce, British Army—Troop commander, 22nd Special Air Service Regiment, attached to the Quantum assault force.

ISRAELIS:

Professor Esher Levi—An Israeli nuclear scientist familiar with South Africa's nuclear weapons program.

PROLOGUE

MAY 22—THE TULI RIVER VALLEY, ZIMBABWE

The sky demons came in the dark hours before dawn.

Joshua Mksoi saw them first only as a faint flicker on the horizon and turned away without knowing what he had seen. Joshua, the youngest of his father's four living sons, had never had any schooling and couldn't waste time or energy in studying the black, star-studded sky or the waning moon. He had to drive his family's cattle up the dry river valley to their grazing lands before sunrise. It was a task that had consumed every day of nearly half his short life.

The small boy trudged wearily along the trail, herding the long-horned cattle with the sound of his voice and the tip of his hardwood staff. Cowbells clanked and jangled in the quiet night air. Everything was as it had always been.

Then the demons came—flashing close overhead with a howling roar that drove everything but fear from his mind. Joshua stood frozen in terror, sure that these monsters of darkness and air had come for his soul. He wailed aloud as his thin, tattered shirt billowed up, caught in their clutching, sand-choked breath.

And then they were gone—fading swiftly to mere shadows before vanishing entirely.

For long seconds, the boy stood rooted in shock, waiting helplessly as his pounding heart slowed and his arms and legs stopped trembling. Then he started running, chasing frantically after the maddened cattle as they stampeded away into the darkness.

For as much as Joshua understood them, the Puma helicopters, turbine engines howling, might as well have been demons. Filled with malign intent and of fearsome appearance, they certainly fitted the definition. And they were totally uncaring of a small boy's fears.

It was the smallest of the many tragedies that would strike Zimbabwe that day.

STRIKE FORCE, COMMAND HELICOPTER

The lead Puma helicopter shook violently, caught in a sudden upward surge of air, and then nosed over—following the winding, northward trace of the Tuli River valley. Four other camouflaged helicopters followed in staggered trail formation. The group flew so low they were almost skimming the ground, at two hundred kilometers per hour.

Aboard the lead Puma, Rolf Bekker bounced against the shoulder straps holding him in his seat. He leaned forward and craned his head to see past the machine gunner crouching in the open door. A black, uneven landscape filled his limited view.

After a moment, he looked away from the door and sat back. He'd seen it too often in the past few years to find it very interesting.

Bekker was a tall, lean man with a rugged face. His tanned features were covered with streaked black and green camouflage paint. The African sun had bleached his short-cropped, blond hair almost white. His camouflage uniform carried only the three stars of a captain on twin shoulder boards and a unit patch on his right sleeve. The patch bore the emblem of South Africa's 44th Parachute Brigade.

He pulled the Velcro cover off his watch and checked the time. Just minutes left to the LZ. Bekker looked up and met the wide-open, frightened eyes of the informer, Nkume.

The black was a tall, thin Xhosa tribesman sitting as far away from the open door as the seating arrangements would allow. He looked out of place among the fourteen heavily armed paratroopers who were the helicopter's other passengers. He was unarmed, dressed in worn civilian clothes. The soldiers wore helmets, camouflage gear, and carried compact and deadly assault rifles. They looked very sure of themselves. Nkume did not.

The South African officer scowled. He didn't know the black man's full name and he didn't care. Though he realized that the success of this mission depended in large part on this cowardly kaffir, he didn't have to like it. Bekker's right hand closed around the trigger guard of his rifle and he nodded to himself. If Nkume endangered the mission or Bekker's men in any way, the black would soon be begging for death.

The helicopter pilot's voice filled his earphones. "I'm in contact with the pathfinders. LZ is clear. Two minutes."

Bekker looked back at his men and held up two fingers. As they started checking their weapons and gear one last time, he unbuckled his seat straps and moved forward to stand behind the Puma's flight crew. He stared through the cockpit windscreen.

He would not see the landing signal. Only the copilot's infrared goggles could spot the light marking the drop zone. Instead, he studied the terrain, a mixture of patchy grass and brush.

The copilot said, "I have it," and pointed. Bekker held on to the doorframe as the Puma banked sharply, turning to the new heading.

They were approaching a relatively open spot, clear of scrub and hidden from their objective by a low, boulder-strewn hill.

The helicopter dipped lower still and Bekker felt the jar as it touched down in a swirling, rotor-blown hail of dry grass and sand. He swung round and jumped out onto the ground, followed in a rush by the rest of his men. Two more troop carriers landed seconds later, followed by the last helicopter, a gunship. Soldiers emptied out of the transports, ducking low beneath slowing, still-turning rotor blades.

Assault rifles held ready, the first South African paratroopers were already fanning out into the surrounding brush. A figure detached itself from the shadows and ran to meet them.

Bekker waved the soldier over to him. They shook hands.

"*Kaptein*, I'm glad you made it." Sergeant van Myghen was as tall as Bekker, but thicker, and much dirtier. He and his pathfinders had parachuted in hours earlier to secure the landing zone and scout their objective.

"Anything stirring?" Bekker asked.

"Nothing." The sergeant's contempt for their opponents was audible. "But I've got Kempler posted to keep an eye on the bastards all the same. We're about twenty-five hundred meters from the edge of town."

"Good." Bekker looked around the small clearing. His troops were assembled, ready to march in a spread column of twos with scouts and flankers thrown out to warn of any ambush. Two burly privates stood on either side of Nkume, each within easy knife reach. And nearby, the three lieutenants of his stripped-down company waited impatiently for orders.

He nodded to them. "All right, gentlemen. Let's get going."

Teeth flashed white in the darkness and they scattered back to their units.

The column started moving, threading its way through the tangled vegetation in silence. There were no voices or clattering equipment to warn of their approach.

South Africa's raiding force was nearing its target—one hundred and sixty kilometers inside the sovereign Republic of Zimbabwe.

STRIKE FORCE COMMAND GROUP, NEAR GAWAMBA, ZIMBABWE

Bekker lay flat along the crest of a low hill overlooking the town of Gawamba. His officers and senior NCOs crouched beside him.

The soft, flickering light of a waning moon bathed Gawamba's houses and fields in a dim silver glow. Bekker smiled to himself. It was perfect. They would have enough light to kill by.

He scanned the valley floor. Small plots of corn, wheat, and cotton spread outward from the town, with cattle enclosures and storage sheds scattered between them. A single main street, paved with asphalt, ran straight through the center of Gawamba itself. Narrow, unpaved alleys broke rows of low, tin-roofed homes and shacks into blocks. Two large buildings dominated the north end of town—the police headquarters and the train station.

Bekker checked his watch again. They had less than three hours to get in and get out before the sun rose. He rose to his feet. "Right. No changes to the plan. We've been given a good start, gentlemen, and I'm depending on you to make the most of it."

Bekker met the eyes of the lieutenant commanding his first assault section. "How's the black? Still holding up?"

Hans Reebeck was a little keyed up, but kept his voice even. "Nkume's unhappy, sir, but I'm afraid my men aren't too sympathetic." He forced a grin.

"Just watch the kaffir, Hans. Remember, he knows this country well."

Reebeck nodded.

Bekker turned to his other officers. "On your way then, boys. Send them to hell."

Der Merwe and Heitman saluted sharply and loped back to their units. Bekker and Reebeck followed suit and took their places at the head of the column as it started moving—flowing silently up over the crest and down toward the town.

Without any spoken orders, the column split into thirds.

One section of paratroops moved north, toward the police station. Another angled south, slipping quietly into a cornfield. Both were out of sight within minutes, invisible among the shadows.

The rest of the force trotted ahead, spread out into an arrowhead formation with Bekker and a radioman at the point. It was aimed straight at the raid's primary objective.

The objective—code-named Kudu if it had to be mentioned on the radio—was a two-story concrete building one block off Gawamba's main street. Its ground floor was occupied by a small, family-owned grocery store. But the top floor was an operations center for guerrillas of the ANC, the African National Congress.

The existence of the Gawamba operations center hadn't even been suspected by South Africa's security forces until recently. In fact, they'd first learned of it from Nkume, an ANC guerrilla who'd been captured while trying to run a shipment of arms across the border with Zimbabwe. In return for his freedom, and probably his life, Nkume had spilled his guts about this ANC headquarters inside Zimbabwe.

Bekker scowled. Zimbabwe and the other border states had agreed to prevent the ANC from operating on their soil. The lying bastards. He didn't care whether the ANC was operating here with or without the connivance of the Zimbabwean government. Blacks were blacks, and none of them could be trusted to keep an agreement or leave well enough alone.

Now they would learn that defying Pretoria meant paying a high price.

Bekker and his troops reached Gawamba's outskirts and started working their way down a garbage-strewn dirt road, weapons out and ready. Houses lined each side of the narrow street, one- or two-room shacks with rusting metal screens covering their windows. A dog barked once in the distance and the South Africans froze in place. When it was not repeated, they moved on, staying in the shadows as much as possible.

One block to go. Bekker felt his heart speeding up, anticipating action. His radioman leaned closer and whispered, "Sir, second section sends 'Rhino.' "

Good. Der Merwe's men were in position—covering the north end of town, including the road, the rail line, and the police station. He kept moving, with his troops close behind.

Suddenly, they were there.

Bekker and his men found themselves facing the side of the building, a whitewashed wall that had no windows. Nkume's information was right, so far. The radioman whispered another code word in his ear. Heitman's third section was in place to the south.

Bekker checked his rifle, took a quick breath, and scanned both sides of the street. No movement, at least not yet.

He gestured, and the team crossed in a rush. Hopefully any observer would not recover from his initial surprise until it was too late and they were all out of view. Once across, his men took up covering positions while Bekker headed for the rear of the building. Nkume, flanked by his two escorts, followed.

Reebeck met Bekker at the rear and pointed to the back door. It was solid steel, set in a metal frame, and had no lock or handle.

"A little much for a small-town grocery, *Kaptein,*" Reebeck observed in a low, hoarse voice.

Bekker nodded abruptly. It was the first direct evidence that this building was more than it seemed.

"Wire it," he ordered.

While a private laid a rope of plastique around the edge of the door, Bekker heard a low rustling as the rest of his men readied their weapons. Sergeant Roost, a short, wiry man with a craggy, oft-broken nose, crouched nearest the entrance and looked as if he couldn't wait for the chance to go through it. Bekker waved him back and took his place.

The private with the plastique finished working and moved away. Bekker nodded to his radioman. The man spoke into his handset, waited a moment, then gave him a thumbs-up. Everybody was ready. Bekker motioned to the soldier holding the detonator and buried his face in his arm.

An enormous explosion lit the street for a split second, punctuated by a solid *clang* as the building's steel door blew inward and landed somewhere inside. Bits of doorframe and concrete flew everywhere.

Bekker felt the concussion rip at his clothing. Even as he held his breath, the blast's acrid smell filled his nostrils. He dove through the still-smoking opening, followed by half the men of his first assault section.

He found himself in a single, large room. Canned goods from spilled stacks, smashed boxes, and shattered glassware littered the floor. He was expecting, and saw, a stairway leading up. Seconds were precious now.

"Two men to search this floor!" he shouted, and bounded up the stairs. He took them two at a time and coughed as the exertion forced him to breathe smoke-filled air.

A wooden door blocked the stairs. Without stopping, Bekker fired a long burst into it, then hit the door with his shoulder. Shredded wood gave way and he landed on his side, rifle pointing down the length of the building.

Nobody in sight. He was in what could only be an office, a room crowded with tables and desks. Doors in the opposite wall opened into other rooms and corridors. His mind noted a picture of Marx prominently displayed over a desk in the corner.

Bekker kept moving, rolling for cover behind a desk and making room for the men behind him. He rose to one knee and leveled his weapon just as a black man carrying an AK-47 came running into the office. Bekker fired a short burst, heard the man scream, and saw him crumple to the floor.

Sergeant Roost crashed into the room in time to see the kill. He raised an eyebrow at Bekker, who pointed to the open door. Roost nodded and with a single, smooth motion, tore a concussion grenade off his webbing, pulled its pin, and lobbed it through the doorway.

The sergeant dove for cover as his grenade exploded, sending a mind-numbing shock wave pulsing across the room. Both Roost and Bekker were up and running for the open door before the explosion's echoes faded.

Roost was closer and made it first. Jumping over the dead man in the doorway, he flattened himself against one side while Bekker took the other. Roost took a quick breath, then snapped his head and rifle around the doorjamb. Bekker heard a startled shout from down the corridor—a shout that ended in a low, bubbling moan as the sergeant fired a long, clattering burst.

Bekker leaned out and saw Roost's target lying twitching in a spreading pool of blood, hit several times by point-blank fire. The dying guerrilla had been caught coming out of the nearer of two other doors opening onto this corridor.

Footsteps sounded behind him. The rest of his men had cleared the stairs. Keep moving, his mind screamed. Obeying combat-trained instincts, Bekker stepped carefully out into the corridor and covered by Roost, slid slowly along the wall toward the closest door.

He was halfway there when another black leaped out, swinging a rifle around at him. Bekker, close enough to tackle the man, threw himself prone instead.

Even before he hit the floor, he heard gunfire and felt bullets whipcracking overhead. The guerrilla's eyes opened wide in surprise and pain, and stayed open in death, as the force of Roost's fire threw him back against the wall. Bekker had time to notice the man's bare chest and bare feet before fear and surging adrenaline brought him upright again.

He dove over the bodies and into the doorway as he heard Roost running down the corridor. He felt exposed, knowing nobody could cover him but wanting to move quickly.

Then he was through the door, rolling clumsily over the tangled corpses into a small room, and scrambling for any cover he could find. There wasn't any within reach.

Bekker fired blindly, scanning for targets behind the hail of bullets tearing up walls, mattresses, and bedding. There weren't any. The room was empty.

Roost crashed in behind him and the two men took a hasty look around.

They were in a small bunk room filled with five or six neatly arranged cots and footlockers. Militant political posters decorated all four walls. A wooden weapons rack, empty, stood in one corner.

More gunfire and grenade bursts echoed down the hall from other parts of the building. Roost paused just long enough to replace the magazine in his assault rifle and then dashed back out through the door. Bekker picked himself up and with one last look for concealed guerrillas, followed his sergeant.

Dense, choking, acrid smoke swirled in the air. Bekker's nose twitched. Even after more than a dozen firefights, he still couldn't get used to the smell. He looked around for his radioman. It was time to start getting control of this battle.

He found Corporal de Vries crouched next to a desk in the outer office, watching the stairwell.

"Any word from der Merwe or Heitman?" Bekker asked.

"Second section reports activity in the police station, but no . . ."

They both heard ringing and turned around to stare at a phone on one of the desks. Bekker looked at his radioman, shrugged, and picked it up.

The voice on the other end shook, clearly shocked and more than a little frightened. "Cosate? What's going on down there? Are you all right?"

Bekker's lips twitched into a thin, humorless smile as he heard the textbook-perfect English. He slammed the phone down hard.

The captain looked around. "All right, the town's waking up." He shouted, "*Roost!*" just as the sergeant trotted up with two other men, a half-eaten piece of chicken in one hand.

"Last room is a kitchen. The floor's clear. No casualties," he reported.

Bekker nodded. "Good. Now take your squad and start Phase Two. Search the rooms, collect all the documents you find. And get Nkume up here. Let's move." He turned to de Vries. "The building's secure. Send 'Rooikat.' "

As his soldiers started tearing the office apart, Bekker heard the rattle of machine-gun fire off in the distance. From the north, he judged.

Der Merwe's second section must be earning its pay. Their job was to keep the local garrison busy and out of the fight. They were supposed to shoot early and often, pinning the Zimbabwean police in their headquarters and hopefully holding casualties on both sides to a minimum.

Nkume appeared at the top of the stairs, looking tense and reluctant.

Bekker put on a friendly smile and motioned him into the room. "Come on, Nkume, we're almost done. Show us your hidey-hole and we'll be out of here."

The black nodded slowly and went over to the right-hand door, leading to one of the rooms Bekker's men had cleared. He stepped in and then backed out, tears in his eyes.

Bekker moved to the doorway and looked in at a large apartment, complete with its own bathroom. A middle-aged black man with gray peppering his close-cropped black hair lay half in, half out of bed, his chest torn open by rifle fire. The captain stared hard at Nkume and jerked a thumb at the corpse. "All right, who's he?"

"Martin Cosate. The cell leader here. He was like a father to . . ." Nkume choked up.

Bekker snorted contemptuously and shoved Nkume into the room with the barrel of his assault rifle. "Don't worry about the stiff, kaffir. He's just another dead communist. If you don't want to join him, show us the safe."

For just a second, the informer looked ready to resist. Bekker's finger tightened on the trigger. Then Nkume nodded sullenly and walked over to a wooden chest in one corner of the room. He pushed it to one side, knelt, and ran his hands over the floor. After a moment, he pressed down hard on one of the floorboards and it pivoted up, revealing a small steel safe with a combination lock.

"Open it, Nkume. And be quick about it!" Bekker was conscious that time was passing fast, too fast.

The black began turning the safe's dial, slowly, carefully.

Scattered shots could still be heard from the north side of town. A sudden sharp explosion rolled in from the south, and Bekker swung toward his radioman for a report.

The corporal held up one hand, listening. "Third section reports a police vehicle tried to enter town. They destroyed it with a Milan, but a few survivors are still firing."

That meant Zimbabwean casualties. Bekker shrugged mentally. He was only supposed to try to minimize collateral damage. Nobody at headquarters expected miracles. Besides, a few of their own people killed might teach Zimbabwe's ruling clique to be more careful about allowing ANC operations inside their borders.

Nkume finished dialing the combination and turned the safe's locking handle. Bekker's soldiers pulled him roughly away from the hole before he could finish opening the door.

"Get him outside," Bekker snarled. He looked for the leader of his attached intelligence team and saw him standing nearby. "It's all yours now, Schoemann. Take your pictures quickly."

Schoemann's men, one with a special camera, knelt down next to the hole and carefully removed inch-high stacks of paper from the safe. Bekker watched for a moment as they took each page, photographed it, and laid it in the proper order in a pile to one side.

He felt a warm glow of satisfaction at the sight. This was the prize, the real payoff for a month of hard training and intense preparation. The information contained in this one small safe—ANC operations plans, equipment lists, personnel rosters, and more—would be a gold mine for South Africa's intelligence services. And with luck, the ANC wouldn't even know that these once-secret files had been found and copied.

More firing sounded outside and shook Bekker out of his reverie. Der Merwe and Heitman must be running into more resistance than they'd anticipated. Schoemann, on the other hand, clearly had everything under control, so he sprinted down the stairs and out into the clear night air. Reebeck, Roost, and the rest of his troops were there waiting for him, listening to the fighting still raging at either end of town. Every man knew that the clock had been running since they first entered Gawamba, and from the sound of the firing to the north and south, it was running out.

Bekker stopped near Reebeck. "Lieutenant, take your team and cover the intelligence people. Send word as soon as they're finished. I'm taking de Vries and going north."

Reebeck nodded and wheeled to his appointed task.

STRIKE FORCE SECOND SECTION, NORTH END OF GAWAMBA, ZIMBABWE

Bekker and five men double-timed north through the streets toward the police station, equipment clattering and boots thumping heavily onto the dirt. There wasn't time to make a cautious, painstaking advance now. Instead, they'd simply have to risk an ambush laid by any ANC sympathizers still at large in the town.

The South African captain didn't believe there was much chance of that. He'd seen only a few frightened faces in the windows—faces that quickly ducked out of sight at his glance. The townspeople wisely didn't seem to want any quarrel with the heavily armed soldiers running down their streets.

He pulled up short at a corner and peered around it. Several soldiers of his second section were visible down the road, in cover and firing at the yellow brick police station not far away. One man lay sprawled and unmoving, while another sat white faced, trying to bandage a wound in his own side. The rest were locked in a full-scale firefight that wasn't part of the plan.

Bekker pulled his head back and turned to the men with him. "Set up an ambush two blocks down the main street." He looked at his watch. "You've got three minutes. Go!"

He belly-crawled forward to the nearest second-section position—two men crouched behind a low rock wall. "Where's der Merwe?" he asked.

Bullets ricocheted off the front of the wall and tumbled overhead at high velocity, buzzing like angry bees.

One of the paratroopers pointed to the far side of the police station. "He headed over there a few minutes ago, *Kaptein*."

Bekker risked a glance in that direction and sat back. "Right. Stand by for new orders."

The trooper's helmet bobbed and Bekker crawled back out of the line of fire. Then he stood and ran to the right, past a row of tiny, one-room shops still shut for the night. Corporal de Vries followed. Once past the police station, he turned toward the sound of the firing, moving forward in short rushes from doorway to doorway.

At last, he was rewarded by the sight of Lieutenant der Merwe, prone and firing around a corner at one of the police station's barricaded windows. Bekker waved him back into cover and went to meet him.

The lieutenant, his least-experienced officer, was breathing hard, but didn't look overly excited. "There are at least twenty men over there and they've got automatic weapons. We've got them pinned, but right now we're just sniping at each other."

"And that's what we don't need." Bekker scowled as the firing around them rose to a new crescendo. "We've got to get them out in the open and finish them before the Pumas come in."

He put his mouth close to der Merwe's ear to make sure he could be heard over the fighting. "We've laid an ambush down the street toward Kudu. Pull your people out in that direction and we'll give these kaffirs a nasty surprise."

The lieutenant grinned and sprinted back to the rest of his men, already yelling new orders.

Bekker, with two of der Merwe's men in tow, dashed down a side street and over toward the ambush position. Sergeant Roost and his radioman met him there.

"Schoemann's finished, *Kaptein*. Everything's back in the safe just the way it was. And the Pumas are on the way."

"Excellent. Now, all we've got to do is scrape these damned Zimbabwean police off our backs. They don't seem willing to take no for an answer."

Shrill whistles blew behind them, signaling the second section's withdrawal. Bekker grabbed Roost's arm and swung him halfway round. "Take these two men and provide security one block back. Corporal de Vries will stay with me."

He moved forward and risked a quick look down the main street. Second section's paratroops had thrown smoke grenades and were shouting, "Pull back! Withdraw!" loud enough to be heard in Pretoria.

Bekker checked his rifle and slapped in a fresh magazine, then took a fragmentation grenade off his battle dress. He flattened himself against the wall of one of the houses and saw his troops run by in apparent headlong retreat. They were still dropping smoke grenades behind them, filling the street with a white, swirling mist.

Bekker waited, the seconds passing slowly, his reflexes desperate to do something to burn off the adrenaline in his bloodstream. Deliberately slowing his breathing, he held his position for another moment, and then another.

He heard shouting and running feet. Then the shouting resolved itself into orders in Shona, the chief tribal language used in Zimbabwe. He saw men appear out of the smoke and run past his alley. They were blacks, armed with assault rifles and dressed in combat fatigues. More soldiers than police, Bekker thought.

They streamed by, running full tilt right into the middle of his killing zone. Now!

"Fire! Shoot the bastards!" Bekker screamed. He pulled the pin off his grenade and tossed it into the smoke, back up the street. The South Africans hidden in buildings and alleys on either side of the street opened up at the same moment—spraying hundreds of rounds into the startled Zimbabweans.

Half hidden by the smoke, the Zimbabwean troops screamed and jerked as the bullets hit them. Most were cut down in seconds. Those who survived the first lethal fusillade seemed dazed, confused by the slaughter all around them.

Bekker's grenade went off, triggering more screams. He raised his assault rifle and started firing short, aimed bursts. Each time he squeezed the trigger, a black soldier fell, some in a spray of blood and some just tossed into the dust. His radioman was also firing and he could hear Roost shouting in triumph as well. Trust the sergeant to get into it.

Bekker let them all shoot for another five seconds before reaching for the command whistle hung round his neck. Its shrill blast cut through the firing—calling his men to order. There wasn't any movement among the heaped bodies on the street. In the sudden silence, he could hear the Pumas coming in, engines roaring at full throttle.

Their rides home were arriving.

STRIKE FORCE RENDEZVOUS POINT, OUTSIDE GAWAMBA, ZIMBABWE

Hands on his hips, Bekker watched his force prepare for departure.

Rotors turning, three transport helicopters sat in a small cornfield just outside of small-arms range of the town, while a Puma gunship orbited in lazy spirals overhead. Paratroops were streaming into the area from three directions. The whine of high-pitched engines, the dust blown by still-turning blades, and the milling troopers waiting to load created what appeared to be complete chaos. Bekker's eye noticed, though, that the wounded were being loaded quickly and gently, and that his first section, according to plan, was posted for area security.

Corporal de Vries was still at his side and reached out to grab his shoulder. The radioman had to shout to be heard. "The gunship reports ten-plus troops two streets over!"

Reflexively, Bekker glanced up at the Puma overhead. It had stopped circling and was moving forward, nose pointed at the reported position of the enemy. Time to go.

He started moving toward his assigned helicopter, walking calmly to set an example for his troops. The wounded were all loaded and the rest of the men were hastily filing aboard.

He stopped near the open helo door and turned to his radioman. "Tell first section to start pulling out." His order was punctuated by the sounds of heavy firing, and he looked up to see smoke streaming back from the gunship's thirty-millimeter cannon.

Bekker heard Reebeck's voice shouting, "Smoke!"

Seconds later, every man in the first section threw smoke grenades outward, surrounding the landing zone with a few minutes' worth of precious cover. As the separate white clouds of smoke billowed up and blended together, cutting visibility to a few yards, half of Reebeck's men sprinted from their positions to a waiting helo. The gunship's cannon roared again, urging even greater speed.

All the other South African troops were aboard now, except

for Bekker, who stood calmly next to his helicopter and watched.

A minute later, Reebeck and the rest of his men broke away from the perimeter and raced for their helicopter.

As they clambered aboard, Bekker heard a sharp popping noise over the Pumas' howling engines and the wind screaming off their faster-turning rotor blades. Rifle fire. He realized that the Zimbabweans were shooting blindly into the smoke, with a fair chance of hitting something as large as a helicopter. He forced himself to stand motionless.

Reebeck stood next to him, mentally ticking off names as his troops boarded. As the last man scrambled in, Reebeck looked over at Bekker and pumped his fist. The two officers swung aboard simultaneously and hung on as the Puma lifted ponderously out of the landing zone.

As they lifted clear of the smoke, Bekker could see the gunship pulling up as well, gaining altitude and distance from the small-arms fire on the ground. Bodies littered the three blocks between the main street and the edge of town.

The Pumas gained more altitude and he saw dust rising on the road off to the north. He took out his field glasses. A line of black specks were moving south at high speed. A Zimbabwean relief force, headed straight for the town. He grinned. They were too late. Too late by ten minutes, at least. And if you'd made it, you'd have died, too, he thought.

As if to emphasize that thought, a pair of arrowheads flashed close overhead. Bekker tensed and then relaxed as he recognized the Air Force Mirage fighters sent to provide air support if he had needed it. He also knew that at high altitude, other Mirages were making sure that the Zimbabwean Air Force left his returning helicopters unmolested.

The Pumas continued to climb, powering their way up to six thousand feet. There was no further need for stealth, and even that low altitude gave a much smoother ride than they'd had on the way in. The paratroopers were unloading and checking their weapons, dressing minor wounds, and already starting to make up lies about their parts in what had been a very successful raid.

Bekker safed his own rifle, then relaxed a little. He made sure his seat belt was secure, then lit a cigarette. Drawing the smoke deep into his lungs, he went through every step of the action—looking for mistakes or things he could have done better. It was a familiar after-battle ritual, one that cleared his mind and calmed his nerves.

Several minutes later, he finished his cigarette and tossed the butt out the open door. Some of his men were still talking quietly, but many had closed their eyes and were fast asleep. Postbattle exhaustion and a long ride were having their effect.

Nkume seemed to be the only person full of energy. He was visibly relieved at having come through the raid unscathed. And he had a much brighter future ahead. South African intelligence had promised him much for opening the ANC's secret safe. Not only would he be spared a prison term or death, he'd also be given an airline ticket to England, a forged British passport, and a large cash payment to start a new life.

Bekker saw Nkume smiling and waved to him. Nkume waved back, all his earlier fears forgotten in his exhilaration. The South African captain patted the empty seat by his side and waved the black over.

Bent low beneath the cabin ceiling, Nkume grabbed a metal frame to steady himself against the helicopter's motion and made his way across to Bekker. He leaned over the captain, saying something that Bekker couldn't make out over the engine noise. The South African nodded anyway and reached out to put his left hand on Nkume's shoulder.

With his right hand, he reached across his chest to the bayonet knife on his web gear. In one fast motion he pulled it out of its sheath and jammed it into Nkume's chest, just below the sternum.

The black's face twisted in surprise and pain. He let go of the ceiling and grabbed at his chest, nearly doubled over by the fire in his heart. Bekker could see him trying to scream, to say something, to make some sound.

Bekker pulled his knife free and yanked the wounded man toward the open door. Nkume realized what was happening, but was in too much pain to resist. Too late, one hand feebly grabbed at the doorframe, but his body was already outside the Puma and falling. The empty, unsettled land below would swallow Nkume's corpse.

Bekker didn't even watch him fall. He cleaned off his knife and resheathed it, then looked around the cabin. The few men who were awake were looking at him with surprise, but when he met their eyes, they looked away, shrugging. If the commander wanted to kill the informer, he probably had a good reason.

Bekker had already been given the only reason he needed. Orders were orders. Besides, he agreed with them. Anyone who turned his coat once could do it again, and this operation was too sensitive to risk compromising. And Nkume's crimes were too grievous to forgive. South Africa's security forces might use such a man, but they would be sure to use him up.

His last duty performed, Rolf Bekker closed his eyes and slept.

grabbed at the doorframe, but his body was already outside, in the flames and falling. The empty, unwatched land below would swallow Nkune Nkongolo.

Bekker didn't even watch him fall. He leaned out of the hatch and motioned to [illegible] looked around the cabin. The few men who were awake were looking at him with surprise, but when he met their eyes, they looked away. If the commander wanted to kill the informer, he probably had a good reason.

Bekker had already been given the only reason he needed. Orders were orders. Besides, he agreed with them. Anyone who turned his coat once could do it again. And this operation was too important to risk compromising. And if any [illegible] men [illegible] to [illegible] south where security [illegible] such a [illegible], but [illegible] would be safe [illegible].

His task duly performed, Rolf Bekker closed his eyes and slept.

CHAPTER 1

Glimmering

MAY 23—ANC OPERATIONS CENTER, GAWAMBA, ZIMBABWE

A light, fitful breeze brought the smell of death to Col. Sese Luthuli's nostrils.

He took a careful breath and held it for a moment, willing himself to ignore the thick, rancid aroma of rotting meat. Luthuli had seen and smelled too many corpses in his twenty-five years with the African National Congress to let a few more bother his stomach. The sound of strangled coughing behind him reminded the colonel that most of his bodyguards weren't so experienced. He frowned. That would have to change. To liberate South Africa, Umkhonto we Sizwe, the ANC's military wing, needed hardened combat veterans, not green-as-grass boys like these. Or like the fools who'd let themselves be butchered here at Gawamba.

Luthuli eyed the orderly row of dead men before him angrily. Twelve bullet-riddled bodies covered by a dirty, blood-stained sheet. Twelve more trophies for the Afrikaners to crow over.

"Colonel?"

Luthuli turned to face his chief of intelligence, a young man whose ice-cold eyes were magnified by thick, wire-rimmed spectacles.

"We've finished going through the wreckage."

"And?" Luthuli kept his voice even, concealing his anxiety and impatience.

"The document cache is intact. I've been able to account for everything Cosate and his staff were working on. Including the staging plans for Broken Covenant."

The colonel felt slightly better at that. He'd been fearful that Broken Covenant, the most ambitious operation ever conceived by the ANC, had been blown by the South African raid. Still, he resisted the temptation to relax completely. "Any signs of tampering?"

"None." The chief of intelligence took off his glasses and started polishing them on his sleeve. "Everything else upstairs has been ransacked—desks emptied, closets and cupboards pulled apart, the usual trademarks of the Afrikaner bastards. But they didn't find the safe."

"You're sure?" Luthuli asked.

The younger man shrugged. "One can never be absolutely certain in these cases, Colonel. But I've talked to survivors from the garrison. Things were pretty hot and heavy around here during the firefight. I doubt the Afrikaners had time to thoroughly search the center before they pulled out. If they came looking for documents, I think they emptied the desks and called it a success." He looked smug.

Luthuli's temper flared. He swung round and stabbed a single, lean finger at the row of corpses. "It was a success, Major! They've put rather a serious dent in our Southern Operations staff, wouldn't you say?"

The smug look vanished from the other man's face, wiped away by Luthuli's evident anger. He stammered out a reply. "Yes, Colonel. That's true. I didn't mean to imply—"

Luthuli cut him off with an abrupt gesture. "Never mind. It's unimportant now."

He stared south, toward the far-off border of South Africa, invisible beyond the horizon. Gawamba's vulnerability had already been all too convincingly demonstrated. They'd been lucky once. They might not be lucky a second time if the Afrikaners came back. He shook his head wearily at the thought. No profit could be gained by a continued ANC presence in the town. It was time to leave.

He turned to his intelligence chief. "What is important, Major, is to get every last scrap of paper out of this death trap and back to Lusaka where we can assure its safety. I'll expect you to be ready to move in an hour. Is that clear?"

The younger man nodded, sketched a quick salute, and hurried into the fire-blackened building to begin work.

Luthuli's eyes followed him for an instant and then slid back to the cloth-covered corpses lining the street. The spiritless husk of Martin Cosate lay somewhere under that blood-spattered sheet. The colonel felt his hands clench into fists. Cosate had been a friend and comrade for more years than Luthuli wanted to remember.

"You will be avenged, Martin," he whispered, scarcely aware that he was speaking aloud. An apt phrase crept into his mind, though he couldn't remember whether it came from those long-ago days at the mission school or from his university training in Moscow. "They whom you slay in death shall be more than those you slew in life."

Luthuli forced a grim smile at that. It was literally true. Cosate's planning for Broken Covenant had been flawless. And if the operation worked, his dead friend would be avenged a thousand times over.

The colonel marched back to his camouflaged Land Rover, surrounded by bodyguards eager to be away from Gawamba's dead. The long drive back to Lusaka and vengeance lay ahead.

MAY 25—OUTSIDE THE HOUSES OF PARLIAMENT, CAPE TOWN

Ian Sherfield stood in the sunlight against a backdrop calculated to impress viewers—the Republic of South Africa's Houses of Parliament, complete with tall, graceful columns, an iron rail fence, and a row of ancient oak shade trees lining

Government Avenue. A light breeze ruffled his fair hair, but he kept his face and blue-gray eyes fixed directly on the TV Minicam ahead.

To some of the network executives who'd first hired him as a correspondent, that face and those eyes were his fortune. In their narrow worldview, his firm jaw, friendly, easygoing smile, and frank, expressive eyes made him telegenic without being too handsome. They'd regarded the fact that his looks were backed up by an analytical brain and a first-rate writing talent as welcome icing on the cake.

"South Africa's most recent attack on those it calls terrorists comes at a bad time for the Haymans government. Bogged down in a growing economic and political crisis, this country's white leaders have pinned their hopes on direct talks with the ANC—the main black opposition group. So far, more than a year of fitful, stop-and-start negotiations haven't produced much: the ANC's return to open political organizing; a temporary suspension of its guerrilla war; and an agreement by both sides to keep talking about more substantive reform.

"But even those small victories have been jeopardized by last week's commando raid deep inside neighboring Zimbabwe. With more than thirty ANC guerrillas, Zimbabwean soldiers, and policemen dead, it's hard to see how President Haymans and his advisors can expect further progress from talks aimed at achieving peace and political reform. From talks that moderates here had hoped would help end the continuing unrest in South Africa's black townships.

"Now the government's own security forces have helped bury even that faint hope, and they've buried it right beside the men killed three days ago in Zimbabwe.

"This is Ian Sherfield, reporting from Cape Town, South Africa."

Ian stopped talking and waited for the red Minicam operating light to wink off. When it did, he smiled in relief and carefully stepped down off the camera carrying case he'd been standing on—wondering for the thousandth time why the best camera angles always seemed to be two feet higher than his six-foot-tall body.

"Good take, Ian." Sam Knowles, Sherfield's cameraman, soundman, and technical crew all rolled up into one short, compact body, pulled his eyes away from the Minicam playback monitor and smiled. "You almost sounded like you knew what the hell you were talking about."

Ian smiled back. "Why, thanks, Sam. Coming from an ignorant technoslob like you, that's pretty high praise." He tapped his watch. "How much tape did I waste?"

"Fifty-eight seconds."

Ian unclipped the mike attached to his shirt and tossed it to Knowles. "Fifty-eight seconds in Cape Town. Let's see . . ." He loosened his tie. "I'd guess that's worth about zero seconds in New York for tonight's broadcast."

Knowles sounded hurt. "Hey, c'mon. You might get something more out of it."

Ian shook his head. "Sorry, but I gotta call 'em like I see 'em." He started to shrug out of his jacket and then thought better of it. Temperatures were starting to fall a bit as southern Africa edged into winter. "The trouble is that you just shot fifty-eight seconds of analysis, not hard news. And guess who's gonna wind up on the cutting-room floor when the network boys stack us up against some gory big-rig accident footage from Baton Rouge."

Knowles knelt to pack his camera away. "Yeah. Well, then start praying for a nice juicy catastrophe somewhere close by. I promised Momma I'd win a Pulitzer Prize before I turned forty. At this rate, I'm not ever going to make it."

Ian smiled again and turned away before Knowles could see the smile fade. The cameraman's last comment cut just a bit too close to his own secret hopes and fears to be truly funny. Television correspondents weren't eligible for Pulitzers, but there were other awards, other forms of recognition, that showed you were respected by the public and by your peers. And none of them seemed likely to come Ian Sherfield's way—at least not while he was stuck broadcasting from the Republic of South Africa.

Stuck was the right word to describe his current career, he decided. It wasn't a word that anyone would have used up until the past several months.

He'd been what people called a fast-tracker. An honors graduate from Columbia who'd done a bare one-year stint with a local paper before moving on to bigger and better jobs. He'd worked as an investigative reporter for a couple more years before jumping across the great journalistic divide from print to television. Luck had been with him there, too. He'd gone to work for a Chicago-area station without getting sidetracked into "soft" stories such as summer fads, entertainment celebrities, or the latest diet craze. Instead, he'd made his name and earned a network slot with an explosive week-long series on drug smuggling through O'Hare International Airport. Once at the network, a steady stream of more hard-hitting pieces had gained the attention of the higher-ups in New York. They'd even slated him to fill an upcoming vacancy on the Capitol Hill beat in Washington, D.C.

That marked Ian Sherfield as a star. It was a short step from Capitol Hill reporting to the White House slot itself. And that, in turn, was the surest route to an anchor position or another prime-time news show. At thirty-two, success had seemed almost inevitable.

And then he'd made his mistake. Nothing big. Nothing that would have mattered much in a less ego-intensive business.

He'd been invited to appear on a PBS panel show called "Bias in the Media." One of the network's top anchormen had also been there. Ian could still remember the scene with painful clarity. The anchor, asked about evidence of bias in nightly news shows, had answered with a long-winded, pompous dissertation about his own impartiality.

That was when Ian had screwed up. Prompted by the moderator, he'd practically sunk his teeth in the anchor—citing case after case when the man's own well-known political opinions had shown up in the way stories were reported. It had been an effective performance, one that earned him a rousing ovation from the studio audience and a withering glare from the anchor.

He hadn't thought any more about it for weeks. Not until his promised promotion to Capitol Hill vanished, replaced by a sudden assignment as a foreign correspondent based in Cape Town.

That was when he realized just how badly he'd pissed off the network brass. South Africa was widely regarded as a graveyard for ambitious journalists. When the country was quiet, you didn't have anything to report. And when things heated up, the South African security services often clamped down—making it almost impossible to get any dramatic footage out of the country. Even worse, the current government seemed to be following a policy of unusual restraint. That meant no pictures of police whipping antiapartheid demonstrators or firing shotguns at black labor-union activists. The result: practically zero airtime for reporters trying to work in South Africa. And airtime, the number of minutes or seconds you occupied on America's television screens, was the scale on which TV reporters were judged.

Ian knew how far he'd slipped on that scale. Since arriving in Cape Town nearly six months ago, he'd filed dozens of stories over the satellite links to New York. And he'd shown up in America's living rooms for a grand total of precisely four minutes and twenty-three seconds. That was oblivion, TV-style.

"Hey, Sherfield! You alive in there, boyo? You ready to go?"

Ian looked up, startled out of his depressing reverie by Knowles's voice. With pieces of camera gear and sound equipment strapped to his back or dangling from both hands, his technician looked more like a pack mule than a man.

"Ready and willing, though not very able, Sam." Ian reached over and plucked a couple of carrying cases out of Knowles's overloaded hands. "Let me take those. I might need you without a hernia sometime."

The two men started walking back to their car, a dented Ford station wagon. It had been another wasted trip on another wasted day. Ian moodily kicked a piece of loose gravel out of his path, sending it skittering down the avenue past the highly polished shoes of an unsmiling, gray-jacketed policeman.

"Oh, shit," Knowles muttered under his breath.

The policeman stared coldly at the two Americans as they came closer and held out his left hand. "Papers!"

Both Ian and his cameraman awkwardly set their gear down and fished through crowded pockets for passports and work permits. Then they stood waiting as the South African idly leafed through their documents, a sneer plastered across his narrow face.

At last he looked up at them. "You are journalists?"

Ian could hear the contempt in the man's voice and felt his own temper rising. He kept his words clipped. "That's right. American journalists. Is there some kind of problem?"

The policeman glared at him for several seconds. "No, Meneer Sherfield, there is no problem. You are free to go. For the moment. But I suggest you show more respect in the future."

Ian reached for their passports and permits and saw them flutter to the ground as the South African let them fall beyond his fingers. Months of petty slights and mounting frustration came to a boil in a single instant. For a split second he saw the policeman's body as a succession of targets. First the solar plexus. Next that arrogant, perfectly shaped nose. Ian's hands curled, ready to strike. He'd demonstrate what he'd learned in two years of self-defense classes back in the States.

Then he noticed a triumphant gleam in the other man's eyes. Strange. Why'd he look so happy? Rational thought returned, overriding anger. The bastard wanted to provoke a fight. And granting him his wish would mean trouble. Big trouble.

Instead, Ian knelt without a word and picked up their scattered papers. Getting deported was not the way he wanted to leave this country.

As they unlocked the station wagon, Knowles risked a glance back over his shoulder. "That son of a bitch is still watching us."

Without looking, Ian slid behind the Fiesta's wheel. "Penis envy, probably."

His cameraman laughed softly and shut the door. "Cheer up, Ian. If the government ever lets thugs like Little Boy

Nazi there off the leash again, you'll have plenty of blood and gore to report on."

As he pulled away from the curb, Ian studied the rigid, uniformed figure still staring after them. Knowles might just be right. For some reason that didn't make him feel much better.

MAY 29—THE MINISTRY OF LAW AND ORDER, PRETORIA, SOUTH AFRICA

Karl Vorster's private office matched his personality. A scarred hardwood floor and plain white walls uncluttered by portraits or pictures enclosed a small room empty except for a desk and a single chair. The low background hum of a ventilating system marked Vorster's sole apparent concession to the modern age.

It was a concession he made unwillingly, because, like many Afrikaners, Karl Vorster preferred the past. A myth-filled past of constant sacrifice, hardship, and heroic death that colored every part of his life.

Three hundred years before, his ancestors had braved the terrible dangers of the sea to settle on Africa's southernmost point, the Cape of Good Hope—enticed from their native Holland with thousands of others by an offer of free farmland. Over the next decades, they'd conquered the local tribes while carving vast homesteads out of the arid wilderness. These cattle farmers, or Boers, saw themselves as direct spiritual descendants of the Hebrew patriarchs, leading their flocks and followers to better lands under God's good guidance.

Nearly a century and a half later, the Vorster clan joined the Great Trek outward from the Cape. They drove their cattle and their servants first into Natal and then over the Drakensberg Mountains to the high open lands of the Transvaal, determined to escape both British colonial rule and interfering abolitionist missionaries.

God granted them victory over the warlike Zulus, but He did not shelter them from the British, always just a step behind. It wasn't long before London's colonial administrators and soldiers cast their covetous eyes northward, toward the rich gold mines of the Afrikaner-ruled Transvaal.

When war broke out at the dawn of the twentieth century, Vorster's grandfather fought as a member of the local commandos—riding rings round the British troops occupying his conquered land. After leading a series of daring raids he'd finally been captured and executed. His wife, penned in a British "concentration camp," died of typhoid fever and starvation, along with twenty-six thousand other Afrikaner women and children.

Vorster's father, a dominie in the Dutch Reformed Church, never forgot or forgave the British. And when the Second World War broke out, the dominie joined the tens of thousands of Afrikaners who'd both prayed openly and acted secretly for a Nazi victory. Disappointed by Germany's defeat, he'd gloried in the 1948 election victory that brought the Afrikaner-dominated National Party to power and made apartheid the law of the land.

The dominie gave his only son three imperishable inheritances: an abiding contempt for the English and other Uitlanders, or foreigners; a firm conviction that God ordained the separation of the races; and an unyielding commitment to the preservation of Afrikaner power and purity.

Those were beliefs Karl Vorster had never abandoned in his own rise to power and position. And now he stood high within the ranks of South Africa's ruling elite.

The minister of law and order closed the file folder in front of him, nodded slowly in satisfaction, and let the trace of a smile appear on his harsh, square-jawed face. "Good work, Muller. This little raid you dreamed up has put the fear of God into kaffirs across the continent. And it couldn't have come at a better time for us."

"Thank you, Minister." Erik Muller relaxed slightly, though he kept his lean, wasp-waisted frame at attention. Vorster insisted that his subordinates show what he considered proper deference—something Muller never forgot. "I had feared that the President might be somewhat unhappy with our actions."

Vorster snorted. "Happy or unhappy, it doesn't matter. Haymans doesn't have the votes to touch me. Not in the cabinet and not among the Broeders. What does matter is that we've scotched this foolish idea of talks with a bunch of lying blacks. That's what counts." He thumped his desk for emphasis.

"Yes, Minister." Muller's right foot brushed against the briefcase he'd brought into Vorster's inner office. Sudden excitement at the thought of what it contained made him sound breathless. "And of course we also obtained a fascinating piece of intelligence from the Gawamba safe house."

Vorster looked more carefully at his director of military intelligence. The Directorate of Military Intelligence, the DMI, was responsible for strategic intelligence-gathering—including data on the black guerrilla movements warring on South Africa. A cabinet reshuffle had long since brought many of its day-to-day operations under Vorster's authority, and in that time he'd come to trust Erik Muller's calm, cold professionalism. But now the expression on the man's face reminded him of a cat come face-to-face with an extralarge saucer of cream. "Go on."

"You've seen the list of documents Bekker's team copied?"

Vorster nodded. When he'd read the DMI report, he'd simply skimmed the page-long compilation of ANC personnel rosters, equipment lists, code words, and the like. Nothing on it had struck him as being especially interesting or significant.

Muller laid his briefcase on the desk and unlocked it. "Not everything they found went on that list, Minister. I kept a particular group of documents separate."

He handed Vorster a sheaf of papers. "These refer to an upcoming special ANC operation. Something they've called Broken Covenant."

He stood silently as Vorster thumbed through the papers, watching with interest as the older man's face darkened with rage.

"God in heaven, Muller! These damned blacks are growing

too bold by far." Vorster's calloused hands tightened, crumpling the documents he still held. He stared at his subordinate. "Could such a monstrous thing really be done?"

Muller nodded slowly. "I believe so, Minister. Especially without extraordinary security precautions on our part. It's actually quite a workable plan." He sounded almost admiring.

Vorster scowled. "And what's being done to kill this thing in its cradle?" He pointed to the papers in front of him.

"Nothing . . . as yet, Minister."

Vorster's scowl grew deeper. "Explain yourself, Meneer Muller. Tell me why you've ignored such a serious threat to this government!"

Muller's pale blue eyes stayed fixed on his superior. "I've referred this matter to you, Minister, because it occurred to me that it might serve a number of political purposes. I thought you might want to personally inform the President of this plan's existence. After all, nothing could more clearly demonstrate the foolishness of trying to negotiate with our enemies."

Slowly, almost imperceptibly, Vorster's scowl faded into another thin-lipped smile. "I see. Yes, I do see."

The younger man was absolutely right. A majority of his cabinet colleagues seemed blindly determined to quiet the current round of racial unrest with words. Words! What idiocy! Vorster knew that blacks respected only one thing—power. The power of the whip and the gun. That was the only real way for true Afrikaners to maintain their *baasskap*, their mastery, over the nonwhite races of South Africa. How else could 4.5 million whites avoid being submerged by the 24 million others they ruled? Too many in Pretoria and Cape Town had forgotten those numbers in this hateful rush toward "moderation."

As Muller said, it was time to remind them.

Vorster eyed his subordinate. The man's instincts were good, but his arrogance was an irritation. The Scriptures were clear. Sinful pride opened a doorway for Satan's whispers. Perhaps Muller needed a small taste of the lash himself. Not much. Just enough to keep his mind focused on his true master.

With short, powerful strokes he began smoothing the documents he'd crushed. "Very clever, Muller. Not too clever for your own good, I hope?"

Muller stiffened. "No, Minister. But I am loyal . . . loyal to you and to our cause!"

Vorster's smile widened, though it never reached his eyes. "Of course you are. I've never doubted it." He folded the captured plans for Broken Covenant and slid them into a drawer. "Haymans has called a special cabinet meeting in Cape Town to discuss our current foreign policy. Maybe I'll use this little present you've brought to me to set the right tone for the discussion tomorrow.

"In the meantime, Muller, I want this matter held strictly between the two of us. Understood?"

Muller nodded. "You have the only printed copy of the material, Minister. And the negatives are locked in my safe."

"Has anyone else seen this?"

"Just the technician who developed the film. I've already sworn him to secrecy." Muller arched a single finely sculpted eyebrow. "In any event, Minister, I'm certain he can be trusted. He is one of our 'friends.'"

Vorster knew exactly what Muller meant by "friends." He meant the Afrikaner Weerstandbeweging, the Afrikaner Resistance Movement. The AWB existed to assure South Africa's continued domination by an all-white and "pure" Afrikaner power structure. Its publicly known leaders organized mass political rallies of gun-toting fanatics and maintained a brownshirt paramilitary group known as the Brandwag, or Sentry. They preached a gospel combining both militant nationalism and virulent hatred for those they saw as dangerous "aliens" in South Africa—blacks, Indians, mixed-race coloreds, Jews, and even English-descended whites. And though the ruling National Party dismissed the AWB as a lunatic fringe group, its membership continued to climb steadily. In fact, every gesture made by the National Party toward political and racial moderation boosted the AWB's strength.

Few, if any, knew that the AWB maintained another, more ominous organization—an organization whose members were scattered secretly throughout South Africa's political and military elite. None attended the AWB's rallies or appeared on its voter lists, but all were committed to its vision of a divinely inspired, white-ruled state. Most remained ostensible members of the National Party and even the Broederbond—itself a vast, intensely secretive organization of the Afrikaner power structure.

So the world looked at South Africa and saw it ruled by the National Party. In turn, those inside South Africa looked at the National Party and saw it guided by the shadowy hand of the Broederbond. And hidden deep within the Broederbond lay a hard core of men loyal only to the AWB and to Karl Vorster—their true leader.

After Muller left, Vorster sat silently, contemplating the opportunity given him by God and Capt. Rolf Bekker.

MAY 30—CABINET ROOM, THE HOUSES OF PARLIAMENT, CAPE TOWN, SOUTH AFRICA

Frederick Haymans, state president and prime minister of the Republic of South Africa, stared angrily across the council table at his minister of law and order.

Vorster hadn't been his choice for the post. He'd been forced on Haymans by the National Party's conservative wing, a group anxious to make sure that security policy remained in what it considered more trustworthy hands. Since then, he'd proved a constant thorn in the President's side—first by quarreling with established policies and now by outright sabotage of those same policies.

"This little Zimbabwean adventure of yours has cost us damned dearly, Vorster! I find it hard to believe that even you could act so stupidly."

Heads nodded in agreement around the table. Few of Vorster's colleagues liked or trusted him. And none saw any advantage in contradicting their president and party leader.

Vorster purpled. "That's nonsense and you know it! We haven't lost anything of real value. In fact, we captured—"

"Nothing of value?" Haymans cut him off. "Months of painstaking negotiations are about to go down the drain and you still say that! We need these talks with the ANC and the other black groups. And we need continued good relations with our neighbors."

"More nonsense!" Vorster's fist crashed onto the table. "These talks you are so fond of citing have produced nothing but hot air and trouble. Why, the ANC's terrorists even flaunt their weapons, jeering openly at our police. I tell you, we should never have allowed that collection of half-witted, bare-assed, communist thugs out of prison!

"And as for Zimbabwe and the others . . . hah!" He dismissed the rest of Haymans's argument with a contemptuous wave of his hand. "The so-called frontline states have nothing we want and nothing we need. If we show continued strength, they will come begging to us—just as they always have!"

Silence greeted his tirade, a silence broken by the foreign minister. "It's quite true that the negotiations themselves have produced little of concrete value—"

"So, you admit I'm right!" Vorster snapped.

"No." The foreign minister's irritation showed plainly on an urbane face normally able to hide strong emotion. "These talks with the ANC's and other black leaders have tremendous symbolic value—both for blacks here and for the financial superpowers abroad. They demonstrate our intent to continue making needed reforms. And to be blunt, gentlemen, we must show further progress soon if we're to keep our economy afloat."

Others in the Cabinet Room muttered their agreement. South Africa's inflation rate, unemployment rolls, and budget deficit were all rising at an alarming rate. Anyone with open eyes could see the prospect of impending economic collapse. The underlying and interwoven causes of this imminent disaster were equally clear.

Fed up with continued economic exploitation and white political domination, the nation's black-led labor unions had initiated a rolling series of crippling and costly strikes. At the same time, continuing conflicts with its neighbors forced South Africa to keep a large number of its reservist Citizen Force troops on active duty—draining both the civilian economy and the government's treasury. Even worse, the world's banks and moneylenders, wary of entanglement with an unstable, oppressive regime, were increasingly unwilling to pour needed capital into the Republic of South Africa.

Faced with this situation on taking office, Haymans and his colleagues had implemented a modest series of reforms. They'd dismantled many of the last vestiges of "petty" apartheid in cities across South Africa—policies that had banned interracial marriages, restricted black movement, and vigorously maintained "whites only" beaches, restaurants, buses, and parks. They'd moved to improve relations with neighboring states. They'd even freed captive ANC leaders and unbanned organizations they'd once labeled "terrorist." And all these reforms had been capped by talks aimed at finding some acceptable form of political power-sharing with the country's black majority.

Haymans's reforms had shown signs of paying off. Some labor unions had come back to the bargaining table. Hostile press coverage had faded away. Overseas investors had seemed more willing to provide affordable capital for major construction and development projects. And leaders from other countries across Africa had readily agreed to meet South Africa's new president.

Now everything they'd accomplished seemed at risk, thanks largely to Vorster's bloodthirsty clumsiness.

As the others argued, Haymans shook his head wearily. He had to find a way to repair the damage done by the raid on Gawamba. He had to make concessions that would salvage his negotiations with the country's black leaders. Concessions that would dominate the world's newspapers and television broadcasts. Concessions that could provide a cloak of respectability for those willing to meet South Africa halfway.

He looked up and met the foreign minister's steady gaze. They'd already discussed what must be done. They would have to accept publicly the inevitability of some form of "one man, one vote'' government for South Africa. They would also have to accept the ANC's demands for a thorough overhaul of the security services and an impartial investigation of past police activities and practices. Neither man especially liked either prospect, but neither could think of any reasonable alternatives.

''Gentlemen!'' Haymans interrupted a fierce exchange between two men who were ordinarily close friends. Quiet settled over the crowded Cabinet Room. He noticed Vorster's rough-hewn face tighten into an expressionless mask.

''This bickering won't get us anywhere. We haven't time for it.'' He paused. ''One thing is very clear—clear to me at least. And that is the need for dramatic action if we're to make further progress.''

His allies nodded their agreement. Those few who'd sided with Vorster sat motionless with folded arms and dour looks.

Haymans pressed on. ''Therefore I propose that we publicly announce our willingness to accept two of the African National Congress's latest proposals. Specifically, those concerning eventual majority rule and immediate restrictions on the security services.'' He stared Vorster right in the eye as he went on. ''In addition, I intend to honor their request for a new and more open-minded inquiry into alleged police brutality.''

Shocked murmuring broke out around the table, quiet noises of astonishment suddenly drowned out by Vorster's thundering, outraged voice. ''Treason! What you propose is treason, Haymans!''

Other cabinet ministers joined the fray, most shouting Vorster down.

''Silence!'' Haymans rose out of his chair. ''I will have order in this meeting!''

As the shouting died away, he sat back. ''That's better. Remember, we are leaders—not some group of hooligan schoolboys.''

''All the more reason why we should defeat these lunatic ideas of yours, Haymans.'' Vorster's powerful hands closed around the edge of the conference table as he fought for self-control. ''The ANC is nothing more than a communist front, a cadre of self-proclaimed terrorists and murderers. We should kill them, not kneel in surrender to them!"

Haymans ignored his red-faced minister of law and order, focusing his rhetoric instead on the other men crowded around the table. "I do not suggest that we surrender unconditionally to these people, gentlemen. That would be lunacy."

Vorster started to speak, but Haymans's calmer, more measured tones rode over his angry words. "But we must be seen to be reasonable, my friends. The Gawamba disaster has cost us dearly. We must try everything in our power to retrieve the situation. If these talks fail, the world must blame the ANC's intransigence—not ours. On the other hand, continued discussions will bring obvious benefits."

He ticked them off one at a time. "Reduced tensions both externally and internally. More overseas credit. Lower military expenditures. And the hope that we can move the ANC away from its ridiculous insistence on a strict system of majority rule."

Most of the others around the table again nodded their agreement, though many with obvious reluctance.

"I don't see this proposal as a panacea for all our troubles, gentlemen." Haymans shook his head slowly. "Far from it. But I do believe that it is a necessary political move at this point in our history. We can no longer survive by the simpleminded use of military power. Instead, we must continue the search for a compromise that protects both our people and the peace."

He noticed Vorster's face change as he spoke. The look of barely suppressed rage vanished, replaced by a cold, calculating stare.

"Will you allow us to fully debate this proposal?" Vorster's tone was surprisingly formal—almost as if he no longer cared whether he won or lost.

"Time is too short, Minister." Haymans matched Vorster's formality. "We must act soon if we are to save these vital negotiations, and I believe we've already fully explored all the relevant issues."

"I see."

Haymans could scarcely hide his astonishment. Vorster

giving up, almost without a fight? It seemed so out of character. Still, the President had learned long ago never to waste opportunities given him by opponents. He leaned forward. "Then, gentlemen, we can bring this matter to a vote. Naturally, I expect your support for my proposal."

Haymans watched the quick show of hands calmly, confident of the final tally. With the exception of Karl Vorster and two or three others, all those around the table owed their current positions and power to Haymans and his National Party faction. All were wise enough to avoid unnecessary political suicide.

Haymans smiled. "Excellent, my friends. We'll make the announcement tomorrow, after we have had time to contact the ANC and the other black groups." He avoided Vorster's unwavering gaze. "If there's nothing further to discuss, we'll adjourn this meeting."

No one spoke.

Ten minutes later, Karl Vorster strode out the front doors of the Parliament building and climbed into a waiting black limousine. His unopened briefcase still held the captured ANC operations plan called Broken Covenant.

MAY 30—IN THE HEX RIVER MOUNTAINS, SOUTH AFRICA

Riaan Oost's three-room cottage lay deep amid the sharp-edged mountains of the Hex River range. Forty acres' worth of grapevines climbed the steep hillsides above his cottage—vines that Oost and his wife tended for their absentee landlord. Six years of hard, unremitting labor had brought the vines to the point at which they would soon produce some of the world's finest wine grapes.

But Riaan Oost's need to work ceased at nightfall, ending as shadows thrown by the Hex River Mountains erased all light in the narrow valley.

Now he sat quietly in the front room of his small home, reading by the dim light thrown by a single electric lamp. When the phone rang, it caught him by surprise. He cast his book aside and answered on the third shrill ring, "Oost here. Who's calling?"

"Oost, d'ye say? I'm sorry. I'm trying to reach Piet Uys. Isn't this oh five three one, one nine three six five?" The caller's crisp, businesslike voice sent chills up Oost's spine.

He spoke the words he'd memorized months before. "No, it isn't. This is oh five three one, one nine three six eight. You must have the wrong number."

The telephone line clicked and then buzzed as the caller hung up.

Oost followed suit and turned to face his wife. She stared worriedly up at him from her needlework. "Who was it, Riaan? What's wrong?"

"Nothing's wrong." He swallowed, feeling the first surge of excitement pounding through his veins. It had been a long wait. "It was them, Marta. They've put things in gear."

She nodded slowly, knowing that the moment she'd both prayed for and dreaded had come at last. "You'll be needing help, then?"

He shook his head. "No. I'll do all the moving myself. Less chance of trouble that way. You stay here and tell anyone who calls that I've gone to bed . . . that I'm feeling a bit under the weather. Can you do that for me?" He was already pulling on his jacket.

"Of course, darling." She clasped her hands together. "But you will be very, very careful, won't you?"

Riaan Oost paused by the door, a sardonic smile on his face. "Don't worry, Marta. If anybody stops me, I'm just the simple colored boy running errands for his master. They'll never think to look closely at what I'm carrying." He blew her a kiss and went outside toward the tool shed attached to his cottage.

The ANC had recruited Riaan Oost more than ten years before. At the time, he'd been a student studying agronomy at the University of Cape Town. He'd been unusual even then—one of the few hundred mixed-race youths permitted an education beside their white superiors. He'd also displayed a quiet, unwavering determination to learn, a determination that masked his fierce resentment of apartheid and the whole Afrikaner-dominated system.

The ANC cell leader who'd spotted Oost had insisted that he spurn any contact with the student-run antiapartheid movement. And he'd obeyed, heeding the cell leader's promise of a larger, more important role in later years.

Untainted by a public connection with dissidents and unsuspected by the security forces, Oost graduated with distinction. He'd married and moved to the western Cape, trapped in the only job open to a colored man of his talents and education—tenant farmer for a loudmouthed, boorish Afrikaner.

Oost smiled grimly to himself as he unlocked the shed door. Yes, it had been a long, painful wait. But now the waiting was almost over.

He pulled a rack of tools away from the shed's back wall and knelt to examine the crates and boxes he'd uncovered. All of them seemed intact. Just as they had on delivery six months before.

With a muffled groan, he heaved the first crate into his arms and staggered outside toward his battered old pickup. Grenade launchers, automatic rifles, and explosives weighed more than wooden vine stakes and baskets of fresh-picked grapes.

Half an hour later, Riaan Oost backed his overloaded truck carefully out onto the dirt track winding down his valley. He saw his wife standing sadly at the window, waved, and drove off into the surrounding darkness.

Broken Covenant's first phase was under way.

CHAPTER 2

Staging

JUNE 1—THE HOUSES OF PARLIAMENT, CAPE TOWN, SOUTH AFRICA

When the last camera light winked out, the temperature in the packed briefing room began falling—dropping slowly from an almost unbearable level of heat and humidity normally found only in Turkish steam baths. Around the room, reporters from across the globe swapped rumors, gossip, and friendly insults, fighting to be heard above a hivelike buzz of frenzied conversation. It was the usual end to a very unusual South African government press conference.

Ian Sherfield smiled in satisfaction as he closed his notebook and watched Knowles pack away their gear. He'd finally been given a story bound to play on the air back in the States. Haymans's willingness to accept the possibility of majority rule and an in-depth, independent investigation of the security services was news all right, big news—no matter how genuine the offer was, or whether anything of substance ever came of it.

Knowing the Afrikaner mentality, Ian doubted that anything really would. Even the most moderate National Party member could never contemplate surrendering all vestiges of white domination over South Africa. And even the most reasonable ANC leader would never settle for anything less. It was a ready-made formula for failure. A failure that would generate more violence and more corpses strewn across the country's streets.

The thought erased his smile.

South Africa's story had all the elements of a grand tragedy—missed opportunities, misunderstandings, hatred, arrogance, greed, and fear. The worst part was that it seemed a never-ending tragedy, a problem completely beyond human solution.

Ian sighed, reminding himself that whatever happened would make news for him to report. He'd learned early on not to get too involved in the events he covered. It was the first lesson drummed into every would-be journalist's skull. Staying detached was the only way to stay objective and sane. Once your personal opinions and attitudes started governing the way you reported a story, you were well on the way to becoming just an unpaid propagandist for one side or the other.

Knowles tapped his shoulder. "Hadn't you better get going? I thought you had lunch plans today."

Yikes. Ian glanced at his watch. Somewhere in the middle of Haymans's press conference he'd completely lost track of the time. "I did . . . I mean, I do."

But now he and Knowles had too much work to finish before their daily transmission window opened on the network communications satellite. He'd have to call Emily and cancel. And she wouldn't be very happy about that. They'd been planning this afternoon's excursion for more than a week. Well, she'd understand, wouldn't she? After all, this was the biggest story to come his way since he'd gotten to Cape Town. Knowles wouldn't really need his help until later, but it still seemed wrong to simply vanish on one of South Africa's rare "hot" news days. Damn. Talk about getting caught in a cross fire between your profession and your personal life. Emily van der Heijden was the one good thing that had happened to him in South Africa.

Knowles saw the look on his face and laughed. "Look, boyo. You cut along to lunch. And by the time you've finished stuffing your face, I'll have the whole tape edited, prepped, and ready to go."

"Thanks, Sam. I owe you one." Ian paused, calculating how much time he'd need. "Listen, the window opens at six, right? Well, I probably won't be back until four or so to do the voice-over, wrap-up, and sign-off. Is that still okay by you?"

Knowles's right eyebrow rose. "Oh . . . it's one of those kind of lunch dates."

Ian was surprised to find himself embarrassed. If any other woman but Emily were involved, he'd simply have grinned and let Knowles's lurid imagination run wild. Hell, if he were still back in the States, Knowles wouldn't have been that far off base. But something about Emily was different. Something about her summoned up all the old-fashioned protective instincts so scorned by ardent feminists.

Ian shook his head irritably. "Sorry to disappoint you, Sam. We don't have anything really sordid on tap for today. Just lunch and a quick jaunt up the Table Mountain cableway for the view."

"Sounds great." Knowles must have heard the bite in his voice because he changed the subject fast. "You still want me to keep that slow pan across the cabinet while Haymans's making his statement?"

"Yeah." Ian nodded toward the dais behind the speaker's podium. Technicians were still swarming around the podium itself, jostling each other as they unclipped microphones and coiled lengths of tangled wiring. "I want that shot in because one of his cabinet ministers was missing. Somebody important, too. Somebody who obviously isn't much interested in showing a united front on this talks thing."

Knowles smiled broadly. "Let me guess. That well-known friend of the international press and all-around humanitarian, the minister of law and order. Am I right?"

"You get an A for today, Sam." Ian matched his smile. "Can you dig up some good, juicy file footage of Vorster for me? Something suitably ominous. You know, shots of him glowering in the back of a long black limousine. Or surrounded by armed security troops. That kind of stuff."

He waited while Knowles jotted down a quick note and went on, "Then we can weave those pictures in at the wrap-up—"

Knowles finished the sentence for him. "Thus leaving our viewers with the unpleasant, but real, impression that these talks aren't necessarily going to lead straight to the promised land of peace."

"Right again." Ian clapped his cameraman on the shoulder. "Keep this up and I'll think you're after my job."

Knowles made a face. "No thanks. You're the on-air 'talent.' I prefer being an unknown gofer. You can keep all the headaches of dealing with the network brass for yourself. All I ask is the chance to shoot some interesting film without too much interference."

Ian shrugged and turned to leave. "You may get your wish. I've got a feeling that this country's finally coming out of hibernation."

KEPPEL HOUSE, CAPE TOWN

Every table in the small dining room was occupied—each lit by a single, flickering candle. Voices rose and fell around the darkened room, the harsh, clipped accents of Afrikaans mingling with half a dozen variants of English. White-coated, dark-skinned waiters bustled through the crowd, hands full of trays loaded down with steaming platters of fresh seafood or beef. Mouth-watering aromas rose from every platter, making it easy to understand why Keppel House never lacked customers.

But Ian Sherfield had scarcely tasted the food he'd eaten or the wine he'd sipped. He didn't even notice the other diners filling the room. Instead, his eyes were firmly fixed on the woman seated directly across the table. He was sure that he'd never seen anyone so beautiful.

Emily van der Heijden looked up from her wineglass and smiled at him—a smile that stretched all the way from her wide, generous mouth to her bright blue eyes. She set her glass down and delicately brushed a strand of shoulder-length, sun-brightened auburn hair back from her face.

"You are staring again, Ian. Are my table manners really so horrible?" Her eyes twinkled mischievously, taking the sting out of her words.

He laughed. "You know they're perfect. You ought to emigrate to the UK. I bet you'd have no trouble finding a teaching job at some private school for wealthy young ladies."

"How ghastly!" Emily wrinkled her nose in mock disgust. It was just barely too long for her face, adding the touch of imperfection needed to make her beauty human. "How could I think of abandoning my fine career here in order to teach spoiled young English girls which fork to use?"

Ian sensed the faint trace of bitterness in her voice and mentally kicked himself. He should have known better than to let the conversation wander anywhere near the working world. It wasn't something she enjoyed talking or thinking about.

Emily was rare among Afrikaner women. Born into an old-line, established Transvaal family, she should have grown up ready to take her place as a dutiful, compliant housewife. That hadn't happened. Even as a little girl, Emily had known that she would rather write than cook, and that she preferred politics to sewing. Her police official father, widowed at an early age, had found it impossible to instill more "womanly" interests.

So, instead of marrying as her father wished, she'd stayed in school and earned a journalism degree. And four years of life on the University of Witwatersrand's freethinking campus had pulled her even further away from her father's hard-core pro-apartheid views. Politics became something else for them to fight about.

Degree in hand, she'd gone looking for a job. But once outside the sheltered confines of the academic world, she'd learned the hard way that most South African employers still felt women should work only at home or in the typing pool.

Unable to find a newspaper that would hire her and unwilling to admit defeat to her father, she'd been forced to sign on with one of Cape Town's English-speaking law firms—as a secretary. The job paid her rent and gave her a chance to practice her English, and she hated every minute of it.

Emily saw Ian's face fall and reached out, gently stroking his hand. "You mustn't mind my moods, Ian. I warned you about them, didn't I? They are my curse."

She smiled again. "There! You see! I am happy again. As I always am when you are near."

Ian fought to hide a smile of his own. Somehow Emily could get away with romantic clichés that would have made any other woman he'd ever known burst out laughing.

"I thought for sure that you would not come today when I heard the news of the President's press conference. How could you stand to leave such an exciting story as this?" Emily's eyes were alight with excitement. She tended to look at his career with an odd mix of idealistic innocence and muted envy.

"Easily. I wouldn't dream of abandoning lunch with a beautiful, intoxicating woman like yourself."

She slapped his hand lightly. "What nonsense! You are such a liar.

"Really, Ian, don't you think the news is wonderful? Haymans and the others may finally be coming to their senses. Surely even the *verkramptes* can see the need for reform?" Emily used the Afrikaans word meaning "reactionaries."

Ian shrugged. "Maybe. I'll believe the millennium's arrived when I see people like that guy Vorster or those AWB fanatics shedding real tears over Steve Biko's grave. Until then it's all just PR."

Emily nodded somberly. "I suppose you are right. Words must be backed by deeds to become real." She shook her head impatiently. "And meanwhile what are we doing? Sitting here wasting a beautiful day with all this talk of politicians. Surely that is foolishness!"

Ian smiled at her, turned, and signaled for the check.

Emily's tiny, two-room flat occupied half the top floor of a whitewashed brick building just around the corner. In the year she'd lived there, she'd already made the flat distinctively her own. Bright wildflowers in scattered vases matched framed prints showing the rolling, open grasslands near her ancestral home in the northern Transvaal. An inexpensive personal computer occupied one corner of a handcrafted teak desk made for her great-grandfather more than a century before.

Ian sat restlessly on a small sofa, waiting as Emily rummaged through her closets looking for a coat to wear. He checked his watch and wondered again if this trip up the cableway was such a good idea. He was due back in the studio by four, and time was running out fast.

He resisted the temptation to get up and pace. Sam Knowles was going to be plenty pissed off if he missed his self-appointed deadline. . . .

"Could you come here for a moment? I want your opinion on how I look in this." Emily's clear, happy voice broke in on his thoughts.

Ian swallowed a mild curse and rose awkwardly to his feet. God, they were already running late. Was she going to put on a fashion show before going out in public?

He walked to the open bedroom doorway and stopped dead.

Emily hadn't been putting a coat on—she'd been taking clothes off. She stood near the bed, clad only in a delicate lace bra and panties. Slowly, provocatively, she swiveled to face him, her arms held out. "Well, what do you think?"

Ian felt a slow, lazy grin spread across his face as he stepped forward and took her in his arms. Her soft, full breasts pressed against his chest. "I think that we aren't going to make it to the mountain today."

She stood on tiptoe and kissed him. "Oh, good. I hoped you would say that."

He sank back, pulling her gently onto the bed. "You know," he said teasingly, "for a good Afrikaner girl, you're becoming incredibly forward. I must be corrupting you."

Emily shook her head slightly and Ian felt his skin tingle as her hair brushed against his face. "That isn't true, my darling. I am what I have really always been. Here in Cape Town I can be free, more my true self."

He heard the small sadness in her words as she continued, "It is only when I am at home that I must act as nothing more than my father's daughter."

Ian rolled over, carrying her with him, still locked in his arms. He looked down into her shining, deep blue eyes. "Then I'm very glad that you're here with me instead."

She arched her back and kissed him again, more fiercely this time. Neither felt any further need to speak.

JUNE 3—NYANGA BLACK TOWNSHIP, NEAR CAPE TOWN, SOUTH AFRICA

Andrew Sebe stood quietly in line among his restless, uneasy neighbors, waiting for his turn to pass through the roadblock ahead. He felt his legs starting to tremble and fought for control. He couldn't afford to show fear. Policemen could smell fear.

The line inched forward as a few more people were waved past the pair of open-topped Hippo armored personnel carriers blocking the road. Squads of policemen lounged to either side of the Hippos, eyes watchful beneath peaked caps. Some carried tear gas guns, others fondled long-handled whips, and several cradled shotguns. Helmeted crewmen stood ready behind water cannon mounted on the wheeled APCs.

Hundreds of men and women, a few in wrinkled suits or dresses, others in faded and stained coveralls, jammed the narrow streets running between Nyanga Township's ramshackle houses. All had missed their morning buses to Cape Town while policemen at the roadblock painstakingly checked identity cards and work permits. Now they were late for work and many would find their meager pay docked by inconvenienced and irate employers. But they were all careful to conceal their anger. No matter which way the winds of reform blew in Pretoria and Cape Town, the police still dealt harshly with suspected troublemakers.

The line inched forward again.

"You! Come here." One of the officers checking papers waved Andrew Sebe over.

Heart thudding, Sebe shuffled forward and handed the man his well-thumbed passbook and the forged work authorization he'd kept hidden for just this occasion.

He heard pages turning as the policeman flicked through his documents.

"You're going to the du Plessis winery? Up in the Hex Rivierberge?"

"Yes, *baas*." Sebe kept his eyes fixed on the ground and forced himself to speak in the respectful, almost worshipful tone he'd always despised.

"It's past the harvest season. Why do they want you?"

Despite the cold early-morning air, Sebe felt sweat starting to soak his shirt. Oh, God. Could they know what he really was? He risked a quick glance at his interrogator and began to relax. The man didn't seem suspicious, just curious. "I don't know for sure, *baas*. The Labour Exchange people just said they wanted a digger, that's all."

The policeman nodded abruptly and tossed his papers back. "Right. Then you'd better get on your way, hadn't you?"

Sebe folded his documents carefully and walked on, his mumbled thanks unheard as a South African Airways jumbo jet thundered low overhead on final approach to the airport barely a mile away.

The policeman watched through narrowed eyes as the young black man he'd questioned joined the other workers waiting at the bus stop. He left the roadblock and leaned in through the window of his unmarked car, reaching for the cellular phone hooked to its dashboard. With his eyes still fixed on Sebe, he dialed the special number he'd been given at a briefing the night before.

It was answered on the first ring. "Yes?"

Something about the soft, urbane voice on the other end made the policeman uneasy. These cloak-and-dagger boys managed to make even the simplest words sound menacing. He raced through his report, eager to get off the line. "This is Kriel from the Cape Town office. We've spotted one of those people on your list. Andrew Sebe, number fifteen. He's just gone through our roadblock."

"Did you give him any trouble?"

"No, Director. Your instructions were quite clear."

"Good. Keep it that way. We'll deal with this man ourselves, understood?"

"Yes, sir."

In Pretoria, one thousand miles to the north and east, Erik Muller hung up and sat slowly back in his chair, an ugly, thin-lipped smile on his handsome face. The first ANC operatives earmarked for Broken Covenant were on the move.

JUNE 8—UMKHONTO WE SIZWE HEADQUARTERS, LUSAKA, ZAMBIA

Col. Sese Luthuli stared out his office window, looking down at the busy streets of Lusaka. Minibuses, taxis, and bicycles competed for road space with thousands of milling pedestrians—street vendors, midday shoppers, and petty bureaucrats sauntering slowly back to work. All gave a wide berth to the patrols of camouflage-clad soldiers stationed along the length of Independence Avenue, center of Zambia's government offices and foreign embassies.

Umkhonto we Sizwe's central headquarters also occupied one of the weathered concrete buildings lining Independence Avenue. Strong detachments of Zambian troops and armed ANC guerrillas guarded all entrances to the building, determined to prevent any repetition of the Gawamba fiasco.

Luthuli scowled at the view. Though more than six hundred miles from South Africa's nearest border, Zambia was the closest black African nation willing to openly house the ANC's ten-thousand-man-strong guerrilla force. Despite the ANC's reappearance as a legal force inside South Africa and the temporary cease-fire, the other frontline states were still too cowed by Pretoria's paratroops, artillery, and Mirage jet fighters to offer meaningful help. And without their aid, every ANC operation aimed at South Africa faced crippling logistical obstacles.

He heard a throat being cleared behind his back. His guest must be growing impatient.

"You know why I'm here, Comrade Luthuli, don't you?"

Luthuli turned away from the window to face the squat, balding white man seated on the other side of his desk. Taffy Collins, a fellow Party member and one of the ANC's chief military strategists, had been his mentor for years. Whoever had picked him as the bearer of bad tidings had made a brilliant tactical move.

Luthuli pulled his chair back and sat down. "We've known each other too long to play guessing games, Taffy. Say what you've been ordered to say."

"All right." Collins nodded abruptly. "The Executive Council has decided to accept Haymans's offers at face value. The negotiations will continue."

Luthuli gritted his teeth. "Have our leaders gone mad? These so-called talks are nothing more than a sham, a facade to hide Pretoria's crimes."

Collins held up a single plump hand. "I agree, Sese. And so do many of the Council members."

"Then why agree to this . . ."

"Idiocy?" Collins smiled thinly. "Because we have no other realistic choice. For once those fat Boer bastards have behaved very cleverly indeed. If we spurn this renewed overture, many around the world will blame us for the continuing violence.

"Just as important, our 'steadfast' hosts here in Lusaka have made it clear that they want these peace talks to go ahead. If we disappoint them, they'll disappoint us—by blocking arms shipments, food, medicine, and all the other supplies we desperately need."

"I see," Luthuli said flatly. "So we're being blackmailed into throwing away our years of armed struggle. The Boers can continue to kill us while whispering sweet nothings to our negotiators.''

''Not a bit of it, comrade.'' Collins spread his hands wide. ''What do you really think will come of all this jabbering over a fancy round table?''

Collins laughed harshly, answering his own question. ''Nothing! The hard-line Afrikaners will never willingly agree to meet our fundamental demands: open voting, redistribution of South Africa's wealth, and guarantees that the people will own all the means of production.''

Collins leaned forward and tapped Luthuli's desk with a finger. ''Mark my words, Sese. In three months' time these ridiculous talks won't even be a bad memory. The weak-kneed cowards in our own ranks will be discredited, and we can get back to the business of bringing Pretoria to its knees.''

Luthuli sat rigid for a moment, thinking over what Collins had said. The man was right, as always, but . . . ''What about Broken Covenant?''

''You've set it in motion, am I right?''

Luthuli nodded. ''A week ago. The orders are being passed south through our courier chain right now.''

Collins shook his head. ''Then you'll have to abort. Pull our people back into cover while you still can.''

''It will be difficult. Some have already left for the rendezvous point.''

''Sese, I don't care how difficult it is. Broken Covenant must be called off.'' The ANC strategist sounded faintly exasperated now. ''At a time when the Afrikaners seem outwardly reasonable, carrying out such an operation would be a diplomatic disaster we can't afford! Do you understand that?''

Luthuli nodded sharply, angry at being talked to as if he were a wayward child.

''Good.'' Collins softened his tone. ''So we'll sit quietly for now. And in six months, you'll get another chance to make those slave-owning bastards pay, right?''

''As you say.'' Luthuli felt his anger draining away as he reached for the phone. Cosate's revenge would be postponed, not abandoned.

JUNE 10—GAZANKULU PRIMARY SCHOOL, SOWETO TOWNSHIP, SOUTH AFRICA

Nearly fifty small children crammed the classroom. A few sat in rickety wooden desks, but most squatted on the cracked linoleum floor or jostled for space against the school's cement-block walls. Despite the crowding, they listened quietly to their teacher as he ran through the alphabet again. Most of the children knew that they were getting the only education they'd ever be allowed by government policy and economic necessity. And they were determined to learn as much as possible before venturing out into the streets in a futile search for work.

Nthato Mbeki turned from the blackboard and wiped his hands on a rag. He avoided the eager eyes of his students. They wanted far more than he could give them in this tumbledown wreck of a school. He didn't have the resources to teach them even the most basic skills—reading, writing, and a little arithmetic—let alone anything more complicated. And that was exactly what South Africa's rulers desired. From Pretoria's perspective, continued white rule depended largely on keeping the nation's black majority unskilled, ignorant, and properly servile.

Mbeki's hands tightened around the chalk-smeared rag, crushing out a fine white powder before he dropped it onto his desk. He swallowed hard, trying not to let the children see his anger. It would only frighten them.

His hatred of apartheid and its creators grew fiercer with every passing day. Only his secret work as an ANC courier let him fight the monstrous injustices he saw all around. Lately even that had begun to seem too passive. After all, what was he really to the ANC? Nothing more than a link in a long, thin chain, a single neuron in a network stretching back to Lusaka. No one of consequence. He thought again of asking his controller for permission to play a more active part in the struggle.

Mbeki's Japanese wristwatch beeped, signaling the end of another school day. He looked at the sea of eager, innocent faces around him and nodded. "Class dismissed. But don't forget to review your primers before tomorrow. I shall expect you to have completed pages four through six for our next lesson."

He sat down at his desk as the children filed out, all quiet broken by their high-pitched, excited voices.

"Dr. Mbeki?"

He glanced up at the school secretary, glad to have his increasingly bleak thoughts interrupted. "Yes?"

"You have a phone call, Doctor. From your aunt."

Mbeki felt his depression lifting. He had work to do.

DIRECTORATE OF MILITARY INTELLIGENCE, PRETORIA

Erik Muller stared at the watercolor landscape on his office wall without seeing it, his mind fixed on the surveillance van parked near Soweto's Gazankulu Primary School. He gently stroked his chin, frowning as his fingers rasped across whiskers that had grown since his morning shave. "Repeat the message Mbeki just received."

Field Agent Paul Reynders had been locked away inside the windowless, almost airless van for nearly eight hours. Eight hours spent in what was essentially an unheated metal box jammed full of sophisticated electronic gear—voice-activated recorders hooked into phone taps and bugs, and video monitors connected to hidden cameras trained on the school and its surroundings. His fatigue could plainly be heard in the leaden, listless voice that poured out of the speakerphone. "They told him that his aunt in Ciskei was sick, but that it was only a minor cold."

Muller ran a finger down the list of code phrases captured at Gawamba. Ah, there. His finger stopped moving and he swore under his breath. Damn it. The ANC was aborting its operation! Why?

His mind raced through a series of possibilities, evaluating and then dismissing them at lightning speed. Had the guerrillas at last realized that their Gawamba document cache had been compromised? Unlikely. They'd never have gone this far with Broken Covenant if they'd had the slightest reason to suspect that. Had his surveillance teams been spotted? Again doubtful. None of the men they'd been tracking had shown any signs of realizing that they'd been tagged.

Muller shook his head angrily. It had to be those damned upcoming talks. With the world hoping for progress toward a peaceful solution in South Africa, the ANC's politicians must be just as gutless as Haymans and his cronies. They were trying to muzzle Umkhonto's boldest stroke ever, probably fearing that even its success would backfire on them. They were right of course. Clever swine.

He almost smiled, thinking of how his ANC counterpart must have taken the news of Broken Covenant's postponement. Sese Luthuli couldn't be very happy with his own masters at this moment.

Muller raised his eyes from the captured code list to the grainy, black-and-white photo tacked up beside his favorite watercolor. Taken secretly by one of South Africa's deep-cover agents, it showed Luthuli striding arrogantly down a Lusaka street, surrounded by his ever-present bodyguards. Muller kept it pinned in constant view in the belief that seeing his enemy's face helped him anticipate his enemy's moves.

Besides, Luthuli was quite a handsome man, for a black. High cheekbones. A proud, almost aquiline nose. Fierce, predatory eyes. A worthy adversary.

Muller forced such thoughts out of his mind. He had more urgent business at hand. He could hear Reynders breathing heavily over the phone, waiting patiently for further instructions.

What could be done? If he did nothing, it would be six more months before the ANC could even hope to launch Broken Covenant again. And who could see that far into the future? Six months was an eternity in the present political climate. In six months, Karl Vorster might no longer be minister of law and order. The negotiations might still be under way. News of the documents captured at Gawamba might leak, despite all his precautions. Anything could happen.

Muller shook his head. He didn't have any real choice. If the ANC operation was aborted now, the golden opportunity it represented to the AWB, to Vorster, and to Muller himself, would vanish. That could not be allowed. He cleared his throat. "Has this man Mbeki passed his message on?"

"No, sir." Reynders sounded confident. "His contact works evenings. He probably won't even try to place a call until later tonight."

"Excellent." Muller didn't bother hiding his relief. He still had time to break the ANC communications chain. "Listen carefully, Paul. I want you to cut off all phone service to Mbeki's immediate neighborhood. By five tonight, I want every telephone for six blocks around his house as dead as Joseph Stalin. Is that clear?"

Reynders answered immediately, "Yes, Director."

"Good. And have two of your best Soweto 'pets' call me within the hour. I have something I want taken care of."

BILA STREET, SOWETO TOWNSHIP

Nthato Mbeki pressed the receiver to his ear for what seemed the hundredth time. Nothing. He couldn't hear a sound. Not even the normal, buzzing dial tone.

He slammed the phone down in frustration. The message he'd been given had to get through tonight. He couldn't afford to wait any longer. He'd have to make the call from somewhere else. Maybe the school or one of the other teachers had a working line.

Mbeki pulled on a jacket for protection against the cold night air and stepped out his front door. With the sun down, Soweto lay wrapped in darkness. Only a few feeble streetlamps lit the pitch-black sky, and even those were cloaked by smoke from the coal fires used to heat Soweto's homes.

He pulled his collar closer and started walking toward the primary school, picking his way carefully through piles of trash left lying in the street.

A hundred yards down the road, two young black men sat

impatiently in a small, battered Fiat. They'd been waiting for more than an hour, fidgeting in the growing cold.

The two men were "pets," a term used by South Africa's security services to describe the petty thieves, collaborators, and outright thugs used for dirty work inside the all-black townships. They were convenient, obedient, and best of all, virtually untraceable. Crimes they committed could easily be blamed on the violent gangs who already roamed township streets.

The driver turned to his younger, shorter companion. "Well? Is that the bastard?"

The other man slowly lowered the starlight scope he'd been using to scan Mbeki's house. "That's the schoolteacher. No doubt about it."

"About time." The driver started the car and pulled smoothly away from the curb. His foot shoved down hard on the accelerator. Within seconds, the Fiat was moving at sixty miles an hour, racing down the darkened street without headlights.

Mbeki didn't even have time to turn before the car slammed into him and crushed his skull beneath its spinning tires. By the time his neighbors poured out of their houses, Dr. Nthato Mbeki, one of Soweto's most promising teachers, lay sprawled on Bila Street's dirt surface, bloody and unmoving.

Without any eyewitnesses to question, Soweto's harried police force could only list his death as another unsolved hit-and-run accident.

The signal to abort Broken Covenant died with him.

CHAPTER 3

Broken Covenant

JUNE 14—NEAR PRETORIA, SOUTH AFRICA

Karl Vorster's modest country home lay at the center of a sprawling estate containing cattle pens, grazing lands, and furrowed, already-harvested wheat fields. His field hands and servants lived in rows of tiny bungalows and larger, concrete-block barracks dotting a hillside below the main house. The house itself was small and plain, with thick plaster walls and narrow windows that kept it cool in the summer and warm in the winter.

Twenty men crowded Vorster's study. Most were dressed casually, though a few who'd come straight from their offices wore dark-colored suits and ties. Two were in military uniform. A few held drinks, but none showed any signs that they'd taken more than an occasional, cautious sip. All twenty stood quietly waiting, their serious, sober faces turned toward their leader.

Despite the soft country-western music playing in the background and the smells wafting in from a barbecue pit just outside, no one there could possibly have mistaken the gathering for any kind of social event. An air of grim purpose filled the room, emanating from the tall, flint-eyed man standing near the fireplace.

Vorster studied the men clustered around him with some satisfaction. Each man was a member of his secret inner circle. Each man could claim a "pure" and unblemished Afrikaner heritage. Each shared his determination to save South Africa from falling into a nightmare era of black rule and endless tribal warfare. And each held an important post in the Republic's government.

Vorster held his silence for a moment longer, watching as the tension built. It served his purpose to have these men on edge. Their own inner alarm would lend extra importance to his words. Then he glanced at Muller, who stood rigidly waiting for his signal. The younger man nodded back and pulled the study door shut with an audible click. They were ready to begin.

"I'll come straight to the point, my friends." Vorster kept his words clipped, signaling both his anger and his determination. "Our beloved land stands on the very brink of disaster."

Heads bobbed around the room in agreement.

"Haymans and his pack of traitorous curs have shown themselves ready to sell out to the communists, to the blacks, and to the Uitlanders. We have all seen their rush to surrender. No one can deny it. No one can doubt that the talks they propose with the ANC would be the first step toward oblivion for our people."

More heads nodded, Muller's among them—though he hid a cynical smile as he heard Vorster's rhetoric ride roughshod over reality. He doubted that Haymans had ever seriously contemplated the complete abdication of all white authority. Still, the exaggeration had its uses. Even the faint chance of a total surrender had already roused a fire storm of anger and hatred among South Africa's militant right—a fire storm that Vorster would use to cleanse the Republic when the time came. And Muller knew that time was coming soon. Very soon. He turned his attention back to his leader's impassioned diatribe.

"We must be ready to save our people when they cry out for our aid. As they will! True Afrikaners will not long be deceived by the web of false promises of peace Haymans and his cronies are spinning. Soon the bestial nature of our enemies shall stand revealed in the clear light of day." Vorster clenched his right fist and raised it high, toward the ceiling. "God will not allow his chosen people to fall into the Devil's clutches. He will save us. And He will punish all who sin against the Afrikaner way—against God's way!"

For a split second Muller was lost in the illusion that he'd somehow stumbled into a church meeting. It was an impression reinforced by the muttered "Amen" 's that swept through the room.

Vorster's next words shattered the illusion. "Therefore, gentlemen, we must be prepared for immediate action. When the people turn to us for salvation, we must move quickly to seize all reins of power—the ministries, the military, and the information services alike. You will be our vanguard in this effort. Do you understand me?"

One of the men still wearing a suit and tie stepped forward a pace. Muller recognized the sober, jowly face of the Transvaal's Security Branch chief, Marius van der Heijden. "Not quite, Minister. Are we to plan for direct action against Haymans's faction?"

"A good question, Marius." Vorster slowly shook his head and lifted his eyes to meet those of the others around the room. "I am not planning a coup d'état. I propose no treason against the State."

He looked steadily at Muller. "No, that is not what I foresee."

Muller felt a chill run down his spine. Was the minister going to blow the Broken Covenant secret? Even one of these trusted few could inadvertently reveal the knowledge he held to the wrong people. And such a leak would prove disastrous. He opened his mouth to interrupt.

But Vorster spoke first, calming his fears. "I believe that our enemies themselves will give us the opportunity we seek. The timing will be their own. That is why you must be ready to move quickly. When God's day of reckoning comes, only those who act swiftly will emerge victorious. So be prepared. That is all I ask of you now.''

Again, the men filling the room nodded their agreement, though few bothered to hide their puzzlement. No matter, Muller thought, they'd been given all the advance warning they should need. And if the ANC's plan worked, South Africa would soon find it had new masters.

Satisfied, Vorster allowed himself to relax, momentarily concealing his naked ambition beneath a mask of benign good fellowship. ''But come now, my friends. No more business tonight, eh?''

He sniffed the air appreciatively. ''It seems that my 'boys' have done a good job with the beef tonight. And a fine thing, too. After all, this politicking is hard work, and we must keep up our strength, right?''

Appreciative chuckles greeted his attempt at humor, and the other men began drifting toward the door—ready for the barbecue that provided a cover for the evening's meeting.

As Muller started to follow, he felt a strong hand close on his sleeve. It was Vorster.

The minister tugged him back toward the fireplace, away from the others. ''Well, how goes it? Are those black bastards still on schedule? Has there been any reaction to Haymans's offer of talks?''

Muller stared impassively at him, carefully weighing the pros and cons of telling Vorster about the ANC's failed attempt to abort Broken Covenant. Until now, the minister's role in this conspiracy had been largely passive—more a matter of withholding information from others in the government than of acting on it. If he retroactively approved Muller's secret efforts to push the ANC attack forward, Vorster would be playing a more active part in betraying his erstwhile colleagues. But would he go that far?

''What is it? Has something gone wrong?'' The grip on Muller's wrist tightened.

He made no effort to pull away. Vorster sounded disappointed, not panicked. Excellent. Muller made a snap judgment. The older man's craving for power must be overcoming the inhibitions normally imposed by custom and loyalty.

He must really believe that only he could stop Haymans's sellout.

"Everything is moving forward as planned, Minister." Muller leaned forward, closer to his leader's rugged face. "Though I have been forced to take certain measures. . . ."

"What measures?" Vorster kept his voice low, but his words had a steel-hard edge to them.

Without hesitating further, Muller told him everything. Vorster stayed silent as he spoke, save for an appreciative grunt when the younger man described Mbeki's fatal "accident."

He released Muller's wrist. "You've done well."

Muller felt a wave of relief. The minister was fully committed.

Vorster clasped his hands behind his back and stared into the fire. "Some of the things we are called upon to do would be distasteful, even reprehensible, in ordinary times. But these are not ordinary times."

He sighed and laid a hand on Muller's shoulder. "We are the servants of the Lord, Erik. And the Lord's work is a heavy burden." He straightened. "But we should rejoice in that burden. It is an honor given to few men in any age."

With difficulty, Muller hid his distaste. Why bring God into it? Power was justification enough for any deed. He forced a murmur of assent to satisfy Vorster's sensibilities.

The two men turned away from the fire, two very different men driven toward the same means and the same end—absolute control over the Republic of South Africa.

JUNE 18—IN THE HEX RIVER MOUNTAINS

Riaan Oost was aware first of the silence. An eerie, all-encompassing silence spreading outward from the jagged, broken cliff face. No shrill animal cries or lyrical, lilting bird songs broke the odd stillness, and even the insects' endless buzzing, whirring, and clicking seemed muffled and far away. The dust spun up by his pickup hung in the air, a hazy, golden cloud drifting north along the rutted trail.

He slid out from behind the truck's steering wheel, careful to keep his hands in plain view. There were hidden watchers all around, armed men who feared treachery more than anything else. Oost moved slowly along the side of his pickup. His survival depended on his own caution and their continued trust. It had been that way ever since the guerrillas assigned to Broken Covenant had begun arriving at his cottage.

He leaned into the back of the truck and hoisted a large wooden crate onto his shoulder. Beer and soda bottles clinked together, cushioned by loaves of his wife's fresh-baked bread, packages of dried meat, and rounds of cheese. Supplies to keep men alive so they could kill other men.

Sweating under his load, Oost scrambled upslope toward the cliff face. Broken shards of rock and soft, loose soil made it hard going, but no one came out of hiding to help him.

The cave entrances were almost completely invisible in the fading afternoon light, covered by fast-growing brush and lengthening shadows. Oost paused about ten feet away from the largest opening and stood waiting, panting and trying to catch his breath. The instructions he'd been given were clear. The men inside the caves would initiate all contact. Any departure from normal procedure would be taken as a sign that he'd fallen into the hands of South Africa's security forces. And that would mean death.

The bush in front of him rustled and then parted as a tall, gaunt black man cradling an AK-47 stepped out into the open. Oost's eyes focused on the automatic rifle's enormous muzzle as it swung slowly toward him.

"You are late, comrade." The words were spoken in a soft, dry, almost academic tone, but Oost found them more frightening than an angry shout.

He stammered out a reply. "I'm sorry, Comrade Kotane. The Boer who owns my vineyards made an unexpected visit this morning. I couldn't leave earlier without arousing suspicion."

The other man stared hard at him for what seemed an eternity and then nodded his acceptance of Oost's excuse. He lowered the AK-47. "Is there any news?"

Oost felt the excitement he'd suppressed earlier bubbling

up again. "Yes! They've announced it on the radio. Parliament will definitely adjourn on the twenty-seventh as planned!"

A humorless smile surfaced and then vanished on the thin man's face. "So we are in business. Good. We've been waiting too long already. Are there any signs of increased police or Army activity?"

"Nothing out of the ordinary. Just the standard patrols." Oost pulled a sheaf of paper out of his pocket. "Marta and I have put together this list of their schedules and routes. You shouldn't have any trouble avoiding them when the time comes."

The other man took the papers, slung his rifle over one shoulder, and bent down to pick up the crate filled with food. Then he turned and looked back at Oost. "You've done well so far, Riaan. Keep it up and one day your grandchildren will hail your memory as a hero of the liberation."

Oost said nothing as the man pushed back through the tangle of brush and vanished. Then he turned and stumbled back down the slope, eager to get back to his wife. A hero of the liberation. The praise would please her as it had him.

Broken Covenant had ten days left to run.

JUNE 25—UMKHONTO WE SIZWE HEADQUARTERS, LUSAKA, ZAMBIA

Col. Sese Luthuli was a deeply worried man.

Long silences from his agents inside South Africa weren't unusual. Even the most urgent messages had to travel circuitously—through intricate networks of cutouts, drop points, and infrequently used special couriers. The ANC's networks were deliberately designed that way to make life hard for South Africa's internal security apparatus. Convoluted, multilink message chains meant fewer suspicious long-distance calls for the police to trace.

Luthuli had always considered the necessary time lag a price well worth paying. Now he wasn't so sure.

He halfheartedly scanned the newspaper clipping on his

desk again, already knowing that it didn't contain the information he needed. Only the *Sowetan* had considered Dr. Nthato Mbeki's death newsworthy, and then only as another example of the township's urgent need for stricter traffic control and better street lighting. Even worse, the article hadn't appeared until four days after Mbeki died. More days had gone by as copies of the paper made their way out of South Africa to Zambia. And still more time had passed before Umkhonto's Intelligence Section cross-referenced Mbeki's name with its list of active agents.

" 'Tragic Road Accident Takes Teacher's Life,' " Luthuli muttered, reading the headline aloud. Had it been a genuine accident? Probably. *The Sowetan* said so, and its editors were usually quick to point the finger at suspected government dirty work.

More important was a question the article didn't answer. When exactly had Mbeki been killed? Had he passed the abort signal on down the line or not? So far, all efforts to check with the schoolteacher's contact had proved fruitless. Shortly after Mbeki's death, the man, a team leader for a highway construction firm, had been sent south into the Natal on an unexpected job. He was still gone, out of touch and effectively as far away as if he'd been sent to the moon.

Luthuli felt cold. What if Mbeki hadn't passed the abort signal on? What if Broken Covenant was still operational?

He stabbed the intercom button on his desk. "Tell Major Xuma that I want to see him here right away."

Xuma, his chief of intelligence, arrived five minutes later.

Luthuli tapped the neatly cut newspaper article with a single finger. "You've seen this?"

The major nodded, his eyes expressionless behind thick, wire-frame glasses.

"Then you realize the disaster we could be facing?"

Again Xuma simply nodded, knowing that his superior's explosive temper could be triggered by too many meaningless words.

Luthuli's lips thinned in anger. "Well, then, what can we do about it?"

The intelligence chief swore silently to himself. He'd always loathed being placed in impossible positions. And this was certainly one of the worst he'd ever been in. There simply wasn't any right way to answer the colonel's question.

He folded his hands in his lap, unaware that the gesture made him look as though he were praying. "I'm very much afraid, Colonel, that there isn't anything we can do—not at this stage."

Luthuli's voice was cold and precise. "You had better explain what you mean by that, Major. I'm not accustomed to my officers openly admitting complete incompetence."

Xuma hurriedly shook his head. "That's not what I'm saying, sir.

"*If*"—he stressed the word, emphasizing his uncertainty—"if our abort signal didn't get through, there just isn't time now to send another. Not with the contact routines laid out in the Broken Covenant plan."

Luthuli knew the younger man was right, though he hated to admit it. Martin Cosate had been more interested in making sure that his master stroke succeeded than in making sure it could be called off. And Cosate had been especially concerned by the need for secure communications with his chosen strike group. As a result, the fifteen guerrillas who might now be assembled deep in the mountains would respond only to messages sent by specific and tortuously long routes. Any attempts at direct contact from Lusaka would undoubtedly fall on willfully deaf ears.

"Colonel?" The intelligence chief's cultured voice interrupted Luthuli's increasingly bleak thoughts. He looked up. "Personally, sir, I believe it more likely that Mbeki passed our message on before his death. Our records show that he was a dedicated man. I don't think he would have left his home that night without first completing his mission."

Luthuli nodded slowly. Xuma's reading of the situation was optimistic, but not outrageously so. The odds favored the major's belief that Broken Covenant had been aborted—as ordered. He sat up straighter. "I hope you're right. But ask for confirmation anyway. And I want an answer back by the twenty-eighth."

Xuma eyed his superior carefully. Luthuli must know that

what he wanted done was impossible. That meant the colonel was already thinking about covering his tracks should something go wildly, incalculably wrong in South Africa's Hex River Mountains over the next several days. If the abort signal hadn't gone through, the colonel could truthfully say he'd given his chief of intelligence a direct order to send another message. The blame for any disaster would fall squarely on Xuma's shoulders.

So be it.

The major saluted sharply, spun round, and left Luthuli's office at a fast walk. The colonel was a clever bastard, but two could play the blame-shifting game. Xuma had never especially liked the captain in charge of Umkhonto's clandestine-communications section anyway. The man would make an excellent scapegoat.

Besides, he told himself, the odds really were against anything going seriously wrong. Even if Mbeki hadn't passed the signal on, South Africa's security forces were still incredibly efficient and deadly. The men assigned to Broken Covenant weren't likely to get within twenty kilometers of their target before being caught and killed.

He was wrong.

JUNE 27—CAPE TOWN CENTRAL RAILWAY STATION

The seventeen-car Blue Train sat motionless at a special platform, surrounded by a cordon of fully armed paratroops and watchful plainclothes policemen. Within the security cordon, white-coated waiters, immaculately uniformed porters, and grease-stained railway workers scurried from task to task—each engrossed in readying the train for its most important trip of the year.

One hundred yards away, Sam Knowles squinted through the lens of his Minicam, panning slowly from the electric locomotive in front to the baggage car in back. He pursed his lips.

Ian Sherfield saw the worried look on his cameraman's face. "Something wrong?"

Knowles shook his head. "Nothing I can't fix on the Monster."

The Monster was Knowles's nickname for their in-studio computerized videotape editing machine. It worked by digitizing the images contained on any videotape fed into it. With every blade of grass, face, or brick on the tape reduced to a series of numbers stored in the system's memory banks, a skilled technician could literally alter the way things looked to a viewer simply by changing the numbers. These high-tech imaging systems were ordinarily used for routine editing or to enhance existing pictures by eliminating blurring or distortion. But they could also be used to twist a recorded event beyond recognition. People who weren't there when a scene was taped could be inserted after the fact. And people who had been there could be neatly removed, erased without a trace. Buildings, mountains, and trees could all be transformed and shifted about at the touch of a single set of computer keys.

Put simply, computer-imaging systems made the old truism that a picture was worth a thousand words as dead as the dinosaurs. Now only the honesty of each individual cameraman, reporter, and technician guaranteed that what people saw on their TV screens bore any resemblance to the truth.

Knowles lowered his camera. "I'm getting the damnedest kind of yellowish glare off those sleeping-car windows."

Ian tapped the South African Railways tourist brochure he held in his right hand. "According to this, that's the gleam of pure gold you're getting, Sam. Pure, unadulterated gold."

"I hope you're pulling my leg."

Ian shook his head. "Not at all. Every one of those windows has a thin layer of gold tacked on to reduce heat and glare inside the train."

"Jesus Christ." Knowles didn't bother hiding his half-envious contempt. "Is there anything they haven't thrown into that track-traveling luxury liner?"

Ian ran a finger through the list of amenities that were standard items on South Africa's Blue Train. Air-conditioned cars. Elegant private baths and showers. Five-star gourmet meals. Ultramodern air springs and extra insulation to ensure a quiet, smooth ride. Even free champagne before every departure. He smiled cynically. Whoever wrote the brochure must have been running out of superlatives near the end.

He folded the brochure and stuffed it into his jacket's inside pocket. "Cheer up, Sam. It gives us a good hook for tomorrow's otherwise boring story."

"Such as?"

Ian thought quickly. "Okay, how's this for a lead-in? 'With Parliament out of session, South Africa's president and his top cabinet leaders left Cape Town today aboard the famous Blue Train—taking their traditional ride back to Pretoria in comfort through a country still filled with millions of impoverished and disenfranchised blacks.' "

Knowles grinned. "Not bad. Probably a little too rabble-rousing to suit New York, but not bad at all."

"It doesn't really fit the facts, though, so I can't use it. I've got to admit that Haymans and his people seem genuinely willing to change the way things work in this country."

"Maybe so." Knowles sounded unconvinced. "You gonna let a little thing like that stand in the way of a good intro line?"

"I know guys who wouldn't." Ian smiled ruefully. "But I probably couldn't look at myself in the mirror if I started pulling stuff like that."

Ian heard the sanctimonious tone he'd just used and secretly wondered just how well his scruples would stand up to another few months of virtual exile in South Africa. Damn it! He needed a big story to break back onto the charts in the States. And he needed it soon.

Knowles slung the Minicam carrying case over his shoulder and checked his watch. "Well, you'd better sleep on it and get good and creative. 'Cause you've only got until eleven o'clock tomorrow morning to come up with an opening spiel."

The little cameraman easily dodged Ian's mock, slow-motion punch and headed for the station exit.

Behind them, the paratroop major commanding the Blue Train's security force shook his head in disgust. Americans. You could spot them half a mile away. They were so ridiculously frivolous. He turned and barked an order at the nearest soldiers. They snapped to rigid attention.

The major took his job seriously. He and his men were sworn to defend South Africa's top officials with their very lives. But few of them ever truly expected it to be necessary.

THE MINISTRY OF LAW AND ORDER, PRETORIA

From where he stood, Erik Muller could only hear Vorster's part of the phone conversation. He didn't need to hear more.

"No, Mr. President, I won't be taking the train with you and the others tomorrow. I'm afraid I simply have too much work to do here." Vorster's fingers drummed slowly on his desk, unconsciously mimicking the rhythm of a funeral march.

"What's that, Mr. President? It's a great pity? Oh, yes. Very definitely." Vorster's thick, graying eyebrows rose sardonically. "Yes, I've always enjoyed the food immensely. And the magnificent views as well. Especially those in the mountains."

Muller fought the urge to laugh. Instead he watched Vorster pick up a pencil and draw a quick, decisive circle on the Cape Province map spread across his desk. The circle outlined a stretch of railroad track deep inside the Hex River Mountains.

"No, Mr. President. I'm sorry, but I really can't afford to go this time. Perhaps in January when Parliament comes back into session. . . . Thank you, Frederick. That's most kind of you. And give my best wishes to your wife. . . . Yes. I'll see you soon. . . . Yes. God be with you, too." Vorster hung up.

He scowled across the desk at Muller. "That damned buffoon. Can you believe it? Haymans still has the gall to try his smooth false phrases on me. He thinks he can win my friendship even now. With the stink of his treachery all around!"

Muller shrugged. Events would soon make Haymans's words and actions irrelevant. Why worry about them?

Vorster tapped the map with his pencil. "Are your people ready?"

"Yes, Minister."

"And the terrorists?" Vorster's pencil came down again, making another black mark in the middle of his hand-drawn circle.

"They seem prepared." Muller leaned closer. "I must admit that I dislike trusting their competence in these matters, Minister. The blacks have always been sloppy. Perhaps our own people could—"

"No." Vorster waved him into silence. "It's too risky. Someone would talk or get cold feet."

Muller nodded. The minister was probably right. He straightened. "Then we can only wait and watch matters unfold."

"True."

Vorster rose from behind his desk and leaned over the map, his eyes scanning the railway route from Cape Town to Pretoria for the hundredth time. Apparently satisfied by what he saw, he carefully folded the map and slid it into a drawer.

When he looked up, the grim, determined expression on his face seemed carved in stone. "God's will be done, Muller. God's will be done."

Privately Muller hoped that God's appointed agents could shoot straight.

JUNE 28—NEAR OSPLAAS, IN THE HEX RIVER MOUNTAINS

The sun stood directly overhead in a blue, cloudless sky, bathing the narrow valley in a clear, pitiless light. Isolated patches of brush and olive-green scrub trees dotted the rugged slopes falling away from the razor-backed ridges on either side. Everything was quiet. Nothing cast a shadow and nothing moved. The valley seemed lifeless, abandoned.

But there were men there—waiting.

Andrew Sebe crouched low amid a tangle of dry brush and scattered, broken rock. He licked his bone-dry lips and tried to ignore his trembling hands. They were trembling in anticipation he told himself, not in fear. He and his comrades were nearing the climax of long days and nights of planning, preparation, and reconnaissance.

Sebe gripped the rocket-propelled grenade launcher he held tighter, careful to keep his fingers away from the trigger. He wanted to model himself after the tall, stick-thin man squatting motionless next to him. Kotane always exuded an air of absolute confidence. The guerrilla leader seemed able to suppress every emotion save a fierce determination to succeed, no matter what the cost. If only he could be as brave.

David Kotane glanced briefly at the young man beside him, noting the beads of sweat rolling slowly down his forehead. Then he looked away, searching the slopes for signs that would give his team's other positions away to wary Afrikaner eyes. There weren't any. Good. His men were following orders perfectly so far, staying well hidden among the clumps of tall grass, dead brush, and low, stunted trees.

Kotane transferred his gaze to their target—the railroad tracks barely one hundred meters away. Viewed from above, the railway looked very much like a long, whip-thin, black snake as it wound to and fro high above the valley floor. Power lines paralleled the railroad, hanging motionless in the still, calm air.

Five minutes to go. Kotane idly caressed the small white box in his hand. Two red lights glowed faintly above two metal switches.

A faint clattering sound growing slowly louder reached his ears. Rotors. Kotane looked west, his eyes flicking back and forth across the horizon. There! He spotted the camouflaged Puma helicopter weaving back and forth above the railroad tracks—flying steadily east.

Kotane motioned Sebe to the ground and flattened himself as the helicopter came nearer. The Afrikaners were making a routine last-minute aerial sweep down the rail line. No surprise there. They weren't taking any chances—not when a train filled with the white government's top officials was on its way down the tracks.

Whup-whup-whup-whup. The Puma was closer now, much closer—skimming low above the power lines. Kotane shut his eyes tight as it roared directly overhead, trailing a choking, rotor-blown hail of dead grass and dust. He stayed still, listening intently as the helicopter's engine noise faded.

Going. Going. Gone. He spat out a mouthful of weeds and dirt and risked opening a single eye. The Puma's rotor blades flashed silver in the sunlight as it rounded a bend and vanished.

Kotane sat up, elated. They'd done it! They'd evaded the last Afrikaner security patrol. Nothing could stop them now. He tapped Sebe on the shoulder. "Get ready, Andrew. And remember, make your shots count. Just like we practiced, right?"

The younger man nodded and rose to his knees, cradling the grenade launcher in both arms.

Kotane risked a quick glance at his watch and turned to stare down the track. Any moment now . . .

The Blue Train came into view from down the valley, gliding almost noiselessly along the track at thirty miles an hour. Orange-, white-, and blue-striped South African flags fluttered from the front fender of the electric locomotive. The rest of the train—twelve gold-windowed sleeping cars, a saloon car, a dining car and kitchen, generator wagon, and baggage car—stretched in a long, undulating chain behind the engine.

Kotane felt his pulse starting to race as he flicked the first switch on the little white box in his hand. One of the lights flashed green. The box was transmitting.

His world narrowed to a single point on the tracks. Ten seconds. Five. Four. Three . . .

The front of the Blue Train's engine flashed into view at the edge of his peripheral vision. Now!

Kotane flicked the second switch.

One hundred kilos of plastic explosive layered along the railroad tracks detonated directly under the engine—tipping it off the tracks in a ragged, billowing cloud of orange-red flame and coal-black smoke. Pieces of torn and twisted rail spun end over end high through the air before crashing back to earth.

Shocked by the power of the explosion he'd unleashed, Kotane sat unmoving as the blast-mangled locomotive slammed into the ground at an angle and cartwheeled downhill, smashing every tree and rock in its path.

The rest of the Blue Train went with it—blown and pulled off the track in a deadly, grinding tangle of torn metal, shattered glass, and flying debris. Car after car went rolling, tumbling, and sliding down toward the valley floor.

A rising curtain of dust cloaked the wreckage as Kotane's hearing returned.

He scrambled to his feet and ran toward the railroad tracks with Sebe close behind. The younger man still held his unfired RPG-7. Thirteen more ANC guerrillas rose from their own hiding places and followed them, seven armed with AK-47s, two more carrying grenade launchers, and four men lugging a pair of bipod-mounted light machine guns.

Kotane skidded to a stop just short of the tracks and stared down at a scene that might have leaped out of hell itself. The Blue Train's cars were heaped one on top of the other—some ripped wide open and others crushed almost beyond recognition. Bodies and pieces of bodies were strewn across the hillside, intermingled with smashed suitcases, bloodstained tablecloths and bedding, and fragments of fine china. Greasy black smoke eddied from half a dozen small fires scattered throughout the wreckage.

It seemed impossible that anyone could still be alive down there.

Kotane's eyes narrowed. Better to make sure of that while they still had the chance. The Afrikaner security forces would soon be on their way here. He turned to the men bunched around him and yelled, "Don't just stand there! Fire! Use your damned weapons!"

Sebe was the first to react. His rocket-propelled grenade ripped a new hole in one of the mangled sleeping cars and exploded in a brief shower of flame. Then the other guerrillas opened up, flaying the ruined train with a hail of bullets and fragmentation grenades.

David Kotane watched in morbid satisfaction as his men systematically walked their fire down the length of what had once been South Africa's Blue Train.

There were no survivors.

CHAPTER 4

Dead Reckoning

JUNE 28—DIRECTORATE OF MILITARY INTELLIGENCE, PRETORIA

REACTION FORCE BRAVO TWO
OPCOM 3/87: 1622 HRS

> Message begins: TO DMI-1. RECCE TEAM REPORTS TRACKING ENEMY FORCE NUMBERING 10–20 MEN MOVING NNE ON FOOT. PER SPECIAL ORDERS, NO DIRECT CONTACT INITIATED. PURSUIT UNITS STANDING BY. AMBUSH SITE NOW SECURE. TRAIN DESTROYED, REPEAT, DESTROYED. LIST OF IDENTIFIED DEAD FOLLOWS. Message ends.

Erik Muller laid the message form aside and quickly skimmed through the list of those known to be dead. He was careful to keep the expression of shocked dismay on his face as he read. It was vital that even his most trusted subordinates believe the news of this brutal guerrilla attack came as a complete surprise to him.

In truth, it wasn't terribly difficult for Muller to look surprised. Broken Covenant had produced results far beyond his wildest expectations. The President, the ministers of defense, foreign affairs, transport, energy, and education, and dozens of other high-ranking officials were all confirmed dead, apparent victims of a vicious and unprovoked ANC ambush. It was perfect. Absolutely perfect. Once the last few loose ends had been tidied up, Vorster's path to power would be clear.

His phone rang. He picked it up in midring. "Yes?"

"Communications Section, sir. I have a radio voice transmission from Bravo Two Alpha. Shall I patch him through to your line?"

"Of course." Muller's fingers tightened around the phone. Had something gone wrong?

Static hissed and whined in the background. "Bravo Two Alpha to Delta Mike India One. Over."

Muller grimaced. Military jargon held little appeal for him. It lacked all elegance. "Go ahead, Captain Bekker. Make your report."

"Roger, One." Bekker's voice was flat, all trace of emotion erased by years of rigorous training and combat experience. "The terrorists have gone to ground in a small copse of trees approximately seven kilometers north of the railroad."

Muller glanced quickly at the map. It showed a tangle of steep, rugged ridges, boulder fields, ravines, and isolated thickets. Nightmarish terrain for men moving on foot. It was amazing that the ANC's guerrillas had gotten as far as they had. "What's your evaluation? Do they know your men are following?"

Bekker didn't hesitate. "Probably. They've certainly heard or seen our helicopters by now."

Muller didn't bother to hide his irritation. "Then why have they stopped?"

"They're waiting for nightfall, Director." The captain spaced his words out, almost as if he were talking to a small child. It was clear that he didn't like having to report to a civilian—even to a civilian so high up in the ranks of the security forces. "Once the sun sets, they'll scatter—each man trying to make his own way out."

"Could any succeed?"

"One or two might make it. The ground here is so broken that even our night-vision gear will have trouble spotting them."

Muller stiffened. He couldn't afford to let any of the ANC assault team escape. Close questioning by their superiors might raise too many inconvenient questions. "I see. Then what's your recommendation, Captain?"

For the first time, a hint of barely suppressed excitement crept into Bekker's voice. "We should attack them now, before it grows dark. I can have my troops in position within half an hour."

Muller nodded to himself. These soldiers might be boorish, but at least they were usually efficient. "Permission granted. You may use whatever methods you think best."

He lowered his voice a notch. "I have only one condition, Captain Bekker."

"Yes, sir?"

"I want them all dead."

That wasn't quite accurate. The kill order actually emanated from Vorster. Muller would have preferred keeping several of the terrorists alive for show trials. The minister, though, wanted to demonstrate South Africa's willingness to utterly crush its enemies. But would the soldiers go along with such a scheme?

Muller cleared his throat. "Do you understand me, Captain?"

Static hissed over the line for several seconds before Bekker answered, "Quite clearly, Director. You don't want any prisoners."

"That's correct." Muller paused and then asked, "Does that present a problem for you?"

Bekker sounded almost uninterested. "On the contrary. It simplifies matters enormously."

Marvelous. "Good luck, then, Captain."

"It's not a question of luck, sir," Bekker corrected him. "It's more a question of ballistics and kill radii."

Muller hung up, stung by the army officer's unconcealed sarcasm. For a brief moment, he considered arranging a much-needed lesson in humility for the man—something that would teach him to show more respect for his superiors. Then he shook the thought away. Bekker's talent as a competent and calculating killer made him too valuable a tool to waste. Personal vengeance was a useless luxury when playing for such high stakes.

Muller's eyes narrowed. There would be time enough later to settle scores with those who'd wronged him. All of them. Every last one of those on a long, unwritten list kept carefully in memory from his boyhood on.

He smiled, drawing a strange kind of comfort from imagining the suffering he would someday inflict.

IN THE HEX RIVER MOUNTAINS

David Kotane wriggled backward on his belly, hugging the ground until he could be sure he was well hidden among the shadows and tall grass. Safe for the moment from prying eyes and telescopic sights, he rose and gently brushed the dirt off his clothes before squatting again with his back to a gnarled, termite-gnawed tree trunk.

He looked slowly around the small, almost overgrown clearing, studying each of the men crouching around him in a semicircle. Worn, anxious faces stared back, waiting for him to speak.

"They're all around us." The guerrilla leader kept his tone matter-of-fact, concealing his own fears.

"You're sure, comrade?"

Kotane looked squarely at his second-in-command, a gray-haired survivor of several clandestine operations, and nodded. "Quite sure. The Afrikaner bastards are being very careful, but I spotted signs of movement in every direction."

"What do we do now?" Andrew Sebe, the youngest of the group, was scared to death and it showed.

"We wait for darkness," Kotane said calmly. "There'll be no moon till late, so it'll be pitch-black out there. We'll be able to slip away right under their noses."

Sebe and several other younger, less experienced men looked relieved. The older guerrillas exchanged more knowing glances. They were well aware that the odds against surviving the next several hours were astronomical.

"In the meantime we'll take up firing positions here, here, and there." Kotane sketched the outline of an all-around defense in the dirt. "If the soldiers try to come for us before dark, we'll gut them."

Heads nodded around the circle. They had enough firepower to inflict serious losses on any attackers trying to cross the open ground surrounding their little tangle of trees. They couldn't defeat the government troops pursuing them, but they could make sure the South Africans paid a high price in dead and wounded. And in its own way that would be a kind of victory for the guerrilla team.

Unfortunately, it was a victory the South Africans had no intention of giving them.

COMMAND GROUP, REACTION FORCE BRAVO TWO

Capt. Rolf Bekker focused his binoculars on the small copse of trees four hundred meters away. Nothing. No signs of movement at all. The guerrillas weren't showing any evidence of panic—despite being surrounded by a reinforced company of battle-hardened paratroops.

He nodded slowly to himself, a thin, wry smile on his lips. Whoever commanded those ANC terrorists was good. Damned good. Of course, the attack on the Blue Train had already shown that. He'd only had to take a quick look at the torn-up tracks, smashed locomotive, and body-strewn hillside to know at once that he was up against a real professional.

Bekker's smile disappeared. It would be a pleasure to kill such a man.

He lowered his binoculars and held out his hand. Corporal de Vries, crouched nearby, snapped the microphone into his hand.

Bekker held it to his lips and thumbed the transmit button. "Bravo Two Alpha to Bravo Two Foxtrot. Are you in place? Over."

"Foxtrot here, Alpha." The lieutenant commanding a section of four 81mm mortars attached to Bekker's company answered promptly. "Deployed and ready to fire. Over."

Bekker turned and glanced down the steep slope behind him. The four mortar teams were clearly visible at the foot of the hill, clustered around their weapons as though praying.

"Give me a spotting round, Foxtrot." Bekker turned back while talking and lifted his binoculars again.

"On the way."

A dull noise like a muffled cough confirmed the lieutenant's words. Almost instantly, Bekker saw a burst of purplish smoke appear on the rolling grassland close to the copse of trees. He mentally calculated distances and angles.

"Give me another spotting round, Foxtrot. Down fifty and right thirty."

"Roger, Alpha." Five seconds passed. "On the way."

This time the smoke round landed squarely in the middle of the tiny group of trees. Hazy, purple tendrils rose from the impact point and drifted slowly north in the wind.

Say good-bye, you black bastards, Bekker thought as he clicked the mike button. "On target, Foxtrot! Fire for effect!"

Behind him, the four mortars coughed in unison, flinging round after round of HE high into the air. Four. Eight. Twelve. The crews worked rapidly, almost as though they were well-oiled machines—efficiently sending death winging on its way to a target they couldn't even see.

Bekker watched in fascination as the mortar salvos slammed into the ANC-held clump of trees. Bright, orange-red explosions rippled through the foliage, tearing, shredding, and maiming every living thing they enclosed. Other bombs burst in the air overhead, spraying a killing rain of white-hot shrapnel downward.

Within seconds, the smoke and dust thrown skyward by the bombardment obscured his view. The only things still visible within the billowing black, gray, and brown cloud were split-second flashes as more mortar bombs found their target.

Bekker let the mortars go on firing far longer than was necessary. Forty rounds of high explosive reduced the small copse of trees to a smoking wasteland of torn vegetation and mangled flesh.

THE OOST COTTAGE, IN THE HEX RIVER MOUNTAINS

Riaan Oost could hear the explosions echoing in the distance as he tossed a single suitcase into the back of his pickup truck. The sounds confirmed what logic had already told him. Kotane and his men wouldn't be returning. It was past time to leave.

Long past time, in fact. The ANC's Cape Town safe house was a three-hour drive away under normal conditions. And conditions were unlikely to be normal. Oost roughly wiped the sweat from his palms onto his jeans and turned toward the front door of his cottage. "Marta! Come on! We've got to go!"

His wife appeared in the doorway, staggering under the weight of a box piled high with photo albums and other mementos of their married life. Oost swore under his breath. She had no business bringing those. Things such as those were sure to arouse suspicion if they were stopped at a security checkpoint before reaching Cape Town.

He stepped in front of her, blocking her path to the truck.

She looked up guiltily. "I know, Riaan, I know. But I couldn't bear to leave them behind." She sniffed, fighting back tears.

Oost felt his anger fade in the face of her sadness. "I am sorry." His voice was gentle. "But you've got to leave them here. It's too risky."

He reached out and took the box out of her unresisting hands.

In silence, she watched him carry her small treasures back into the cottage.

Neither could bear to look back as they drove away from the vineyard they'd labored in for six years.

Oost was careful to drive slowly and precisely down the winding, dirt road, anxious to avoid any obvious sign of panic. With luck, they'd be on the main highway and hidden among other travelers before the security forces noted their absence.

He glanced off to the side at a marker post as they came round a sharp bend in the road. Only two more kilometers to the highway and comparative safety! He felt himself begin to relax.

"Riaan!"

Startled by his wife's cry, Oost looked up and slammed on his brakes.

The pickup slid to a stop just yards from two camouflaged armored cars and a row of armed troops blocking the road. My God, he thought wildly, the Afrikaners are already here.

Beside him, Marta moaned in fear.

One of the soldiers, an officer, motioned them forward. Oost swallowed convulsively and pulled the pickup closer to the roadblock. It must be routine. Please let it be nothing more than a routine checkpoint, he prayed.

The officer signaled him to stop when they were within twenty feet of the armored cars. Two machine guns swung to cover them, aimed straight at the truck's windshield. Oost glanced quickly to either side. The soldiers surrounding them had their rifles unslung and ready for action. He felt sick. The government knows, he thought. They have to know. But how? Could one of Kotane's men already have broken under interrogation? It seemed possible.

The sound of a car door slamming shut roused him. For the first time he noticed the long, black limousine parked just beyond the armored cars. It was the kind of car favored by high-ranking security officers. Its occupant, a tall, fair-haired white man in a dark suit and plain tie, strode arrogantly past the soldiers and stopped, his hands on his hips, a few feet away from the pickup truck.

Oost looked at the man's eyes and shivered. They were a dead man's eyes, lifeless and uncaring.

"Going somewhere, Meneer Oost?" The security agent's dry, emotionless voice matched his eyes. "A curious time to take a trip, isn't it?"

Oost could hear Marta sobbing softly beside him, but he lacked the strength to comfort her. Prison, interrogation, torture, trial, and execution. The road ahead held nothing good.

"Get out of the car, please. Both of you." Still that same dry, sterile voice. "Now."

Oost exchanged a single, hopeless glance with his wife and obeyed. Still crying, she followed suit. The hard-faced man motioned them toward the waiting limousine.

The soldiers parted to let them pass, watching wordlessly as Oost and Marta stumbled along in shock with the security officer close behind.

The man didn't speak again until they were near the long, black car. "It's a pity you're both trying to escape from my custody, *meneer*. But your actions give me no choice."

Oost heard cloth rustling and the sound of something rubbing against leather. For an instant he stopped, completely confused. What did the man mean? Then, in the split second he had left to understand, he felt oddly grateful.

The men waiting at the roadblock started as two pistol shots cracked in the still air, echoing off the rocky hills to either side of the road. Birds, frightened by the sudden noise, fled their perches and took to the air, a lazy, swirling, circling cloud—black specks against a deep blue sky.

His job done, Muller's agent slid behind the wheel of his car, started it, and drove off in satisfied silence.

EMILY VAN DER HEIJDEN'S FLAT, CAPE TOWN

South Africa's state-owned television cameras showed only what the government wanted them to show. And right now they showed a grim-faced Karl Vorster standing rigidly at a podium—backed by an enormous blue-, white-, and orange-striped national flag.

"My fellow countrymen, I stand before you on a day of sorrow for all South Africans." Vorster's harsh voice emphasized the guttural accents of Afrikaans as he spoke, pausing with evident reluctance for the simultaneous translation into English.

"I come with dreadful news—news of a bloody act of terrorism so horrible that it is without parallel in our history. I must tell you that the reports you've undoubtedly been hearing all this evening have been verified. At approximately one o'clock this afternoon, a band of black ANC communists murderously attacked the Blue Train as it passed through the Hex River Mountains."

Vorster's rough-edged, gravelly voice dropped another notch. "I have now been informed that the train was completely destroyed. There were no survivors. The President of our beloved Republic is dead."

Ian Sherfield felt Emily's grip on his hand tighten. He glanced at her. She wasn't making any effort to hide the tears welling in her eyes. No surprise there. She'd hoped that Haymans would be the leader who could orchestrate a peaceful reconciliation of South Africa's contending races. He looked back at the stern visage dominating the television screen. There wasn't much chance that Vorster would continue Haymans's negotiating efforts. Much chance? Hell, he thought, no chance. Even Gandhi would have been reluctant to trust the good will or good faith of the ANC after this attack on the Blue Train.

Ian wondered about that. What could the ANC have thought it would gain? How could they have been so stupid?

"As the government's senior surviving minister, I have assumed the office and duties of the presidency. I have done so in accordance with the Constitution—compelled by my love of God and this country, and not by any misplaced sense of personal ambition. I shall govern as president only until such time as the present emergency has passed."

Right. Ian shook his head, not believing a word. Methinks thou dost protest too much, Vorster old son.

"Accordingly, my first action as president has been to declare an unlimited state of emergency extending to all provinces of the Republic." Vorster's hands curled around the edge of his podium. "I intend to root out this terrorist conspiracy in our country once and for all. Those responsible for the deaths of so many innocents will not escape our just vengeance."

As South Africa's new and unelected president continued speaking, Ian felt Emily shiver and understood. Vorster's grim words spelled the end of every step toward moderation her nation had taken over the past decade. The newly declared state of emergency imposed dusk-to-dawn curfews on all black townships; allowed the security forces to shoot anyone violating those curfews; restored the hated pass laws restricting nonwhite movement and travel, and reimposed strict government controls on the press and other media.

Ian knew that, under normal circumstances, that last bit of news would have really pissed him off. But circumstances were far from normal. There didn't seem to be much that Vorster's new government could do to him as a reporter that his own network hadn't already done.

When reports of the Blue Train attack first started to spread, he and Knowles had filmed a quick segment and shipped it off to New York on a rush satellite feed. Flushed with triumph, they'd notified the network of their plans to fly immediately to Pretoria so they could cover the government's reaction to the ANC attack.

But they hadn't even had time to crack open a bottle of champagne in celebration before New York's top brass quashed their plans. He and his cameraman weren't needed in Pretoria, Ian had been told. The network's top anchor and his personal news team were already en route to cover the developing story firsthand. Instead, he and Knowles were supposed to "stand by" in Cape Town, ready to provide "local color" stories, should any be needed. The fact that on-site anchoring had become network-news standard procedure since the Berlin Wall came tumbling down did nothing to cushion the blow. Just because New York's story-hogging had a historical precedent did nothing to make it any more palatable.

Ian gritted his teeth. Here they were in the middle of the biggest South African news event in recent memory, and he'd been shunted off to the sidelines without so much as a thank-you. Christ, talk about a career on the skids! He'd slipped off into a black hole without even realizing it.

"Oh, my God . . ." Emily's horrified whisper brought him back to the present.

Vorster was still on-screen, rattling off a list of those he'd named to a "temporary" Government of National Salvation. Cronje, de Wet, Hertzog, Klopper, Malherbe, Maritz, Pienaar, Smit, and van der Heijden. Ian ran through the list in his mind. Some were names he didn't recognize, but those he did recognize belonged to notorious diehards. All were Afrikaners. Clearly, Vorster didn't intend to give the English-descended South Africans and other Uitlanders any share in government. Wait a minute . . . van der Heijden?

He looked sharply at Emily.

Stricken, she stared sightlessly into the screen and then, slowly, turned her eyes toward him. She nodded. "My father, yes."

Ian pursed his lips in a soundless whistle. He'd known that Emily's father was some kind of government bureaucrat. But he'd always imagined someone more suited to handling crop insurance or international trade figures—not the kind of man who'd apparently just taken the number two spot in South Africa's security forces.

For an instant, just an instant, he found himself thinking of Emily not as a beautiful and intelligent woman who loved him, but as a possible information source—as a conduit leading straight into the heart of South Africa's new government. Then he saw the sadness in her eyes and realized that was just what she feared. She was afraid of what her father's newfound power would do to what they had together.

Wordlessly, Ian reached out and took her in his arms, holding her closely against his chest. One hand stroked her hair and the back of her neck. But he found his eyes straying back to the tall, grim-faced man still filling the airwaves with words and phrases that promised vengeance and rekindled racial hatred.

JUNE 30—STATE SECURITY COUNCIL CHAMBER, PRETORIA, SOUTH AFRICA

Pretoria, South Africa's administrative capital, lay at peace beneath a cloudless blue sky. Though several newly built steel-and-glass office buildings dotted its skyline, Pretoria still seemed more a quiet, nineteenth-century university town than the prosperous, bustling governmental center of a twentieth-century state. Rows of jacaranda trees shading wide streets and an array of formal, flower-filled gardens helped maintain the illusion.

On a low hill overlooking the central city, the Union Buildings—two sprawling, three-story structures connected by a semicircular colonnade—sat surrounded by their own carefully manicured gardens. Thousands of bureaucrats, some petty, others powerful, occupied the two mirror-image buildings. From their offices emerged the constant stream of directives, reports, regulations, and queries required to govern the sovereign Republic of South Africa.

On the surface, nothing much had changed. The various ministries and departments functioned according to time-tested procedures—still carrying out the moderate policies of men whose bodies lay hundreds of miles away in a temporary morgue alongside the Cape Town railway. But all who worked in the Union Buildings knew those policies were as dead as the men who'd formulated them.

South Africa now had a more ruthless set of masters.

To defeat any attempts at electronic eavesdropping, the members of the new State Security Council met in a small, windowless room buried deep inside the Union Buildings complex. The fifteen men now in charge of their country's foreign policy apparatus, military services, and security forces sat quietly around a large rectangular table. All of them owed their appointments to one man, Karl Vorster, and all were acutely aware that their futures depended on continued obedience to his will.

Now they waited for an indication of just what that will might be.

Vorster studied the map laid out by his deputy minister of law and order. Red circles outlined South Africa's most troublesome black townships. Other colors designated varying degrees of past resistance to Pretoria's policies. The circles dotting the map were surrounded by abstract symbols—symbols that stood for the sixty thousand active-duty and reserve police officers awaiting his orders.

He nodded vigorously. "*Magtig,* Marius. This plan is just what we need. Show the kaffirs who's boss right from the start and save a lot of trouble later, eh?"

Marius van der Heijden flushed with pleasure at Vorster's praise. "Yes, Mr. President. A thorough sweep through the townships should flush out the worst rabble-rousers and malcontents. Once they're in the camps, we'll have a much easier time keeping order."

Vorster abandoned his contemplation of the map and looked up at the other members of his Security Council. "Any comments?"

One by one, they shook their heads.

Every member of Vorster's handpicked government saw the immediate security problem they faced. Years of misguided pampering by the dead Haymans and his liberal cronies had allowed the blacks to build up a network of their own leaders and organizations. Organizations around which violent opposition to a strengthened apartheid system could coalesce. And that was intolerable. The black antiapartheid movements would have to be crushed and crushed quickly.

What van der Heijden proposed was simple, straightforward, and bloody. Teams of armed police troops backed by armored cars would descend on the most radical townships en masse—searching house to house for known agitators. Anyone resisting arrest would be shot. Anyone obstructing the police in the lawful performance of their duties would be shot. And anyone who tried to flee the closing police net would be shot. Those who escaped death would find themselves penned up in isolated labor camps, unable to spread their gospel of poisonous dissent.

Vorster bent down and signed the top page of the thick sheaf of arrest orders with a quick flourish. "Your plan is approved, Marius. I expect immediate action."

"At once, Mr. President."

From his seat next to Vorster, Erik Muller watched with ill-disguised contempt as the beefy, barrel-chested man hurriedly gathered his papers and maps and rushed from the room. Van der Heijden really wasn't anything more than a typical, blockheaded provincial policeman. The man's so-called plan relied entirely on the application of brute force and overwhelming firepower to gut any internal resistance to the new regime. And where was the subtlety or gamesmanship in that?

He would have preferred a more surgical approach involving carefully selected arrests, assassinations, and intimidation. Muller shrugged mentally. Van der Heijden's Operation Cleansing Fire appealed to the new president's bias for direct action. Besides, the Transvaaler was just the kind of bluff, hearty *kerel*, or good fellow, that Vorster liked. So be it. Let the new deputy minister win this opening round. Muller would pour his energies into maintaining his authority over foreign intelligence-gathering and special operations.

Those were the next items on the State Security Council's agenda. Muller grew conscious of Vorster's scrutiny.

"Director Muller is here to bring us up-to-date on activities designed to punish the nearest kaffir-ruled states for aiding our enemies. Isn't that right, Erik?"

"Yes, Minis . . . Mr. President." Muller caught himself in time. Although he'd occupied the chief executive's office for just two days, Vorster had already shown himself a stickler for titles. Muller beckoned a waiting aide over and watched through slitted eyes as the man unrolled a large-scale map of southern Africa.

Then he rose and leaned over the map. One finger traced the jagged outline of Mozambique. "I trust you're all familiar with our covert support for Renamo?"

Heads nodded. Limited involvement in guerrilla operations against Mozambique's Marxist government had been a staple of South Africa's foreign policy for more than a decade. Under growing international pressure, the Haymans government had tried to untangle itself gradually from Renamo—with only minor success. Too many lower-echelon officers and bureaucrats, including most of the men now sitting on the Security Council, had been unwilling to end a campaign that was so successfully destroying Mozambique's economy. They'd kept supplies and intelligence reports flowing to the guerrillas despite Pretoria's orders to the contrary.

"Well, I'm pleased to report that the President"—Muller inclined his head in Vorster's direction—"has authorized an expanded assistance program for Renamo. As part of this program, we'll be meeting a much higher percentage of their requests for heavier weaponry, more sophisticated mines, and additional explosives."

Muller paused, watching interest in his words grow on the faces around the table. "Naturally, in return we'll expect a stepped-up pattern of attacks. Especially on the railroads connecting Zimbabwe with the port at Maputo and the oil terminal at Beira."

Pleased smiles sprouted throughout the small, crowded room. By cutting those rail lines, Renamo's guerrillas would once again destroy the only independent transportation links between the black states of southern Africa and the rest of the world. All their other railroads led through South Africa. Pretoria's economic stranglehold on its neighbors would be dramatically strengthened at a relatively small cost in arms and ammunition. Best of all, those doing the fighting and dying would all be black. No white blood need be shed.

One man, Fredrik Pienaar, the new minister of information, coughed lightly, seeking recognition. "What about the American, British, and French military advisors in Mozambique? Can they interfere with our plans?"

Vorster scowled. "To hell with them. They're nothing."

"The President is quite right, Minister," Muller said with a cautious glance at Pienaar. The tiny, wasp-waisted man now controlled the government's vast propaganda machine. And as a result, he could be either a powerful friend or a dangerous foe. To a considerable degree, the official "truth" in South Africa would be shaped by the press releases and radio and TV broadcasts Pienaar approved.

Muller tapped the map lightly as he went on. "The Western soldiers in Mozambique are there strictly as training cadres. Their own governments have forbidden them any combat role. Once Renamo's expanded operations get going, these cadres will have little effect on our plans. The white-ruled countries may be outwardly sympathetic to these black socialist states, but they are really providing only token aid. They no more want them to prosper than we do." His finger traced an arc along South Africa's northern border.

Muller wasn't so sure of that. The so-called democracies were often unpredictable. He consoled himself with the thought that his first analysis was undoubtedly correct. Surely no sane European or American politician would seriously want to assist a country such as Mozambique.

He sank back into his chair at Vorster's signal. His part in this afternoon's orchestrated chorus of approval for long-planned actions was over.

Vorster stood, towering above the members of his inner circle. "One major threat to our fatherland remains unchecked."

His hand hovered over the map and then slammed down with enough force to startle the older men around the table. "Here! The communists who now rule in South-West Africa. In what they call 'Namibia.' " He pronounced the native word contemptuously.

His subordinates muttered their agreement. South Africa had governed the former German colony of South-West Africa for seventy years. During that time, the diamonds, uranium, tungsten, copper, and gold produced by Namibia's rich mines had poured into the hands of South Africa's largest industrial conglomerates. Just as important, the colony's vast, arid wastelands had proved an invaluable buffer zone against guerrilla attacks on South Africa itself. A ragtag, native Namibian guerrilla movement, Swapo, had caused casualties and destroyed property, but it had never seriously threatened Pretoria's hold on its treasure trove.

But all Namibia's benefits had been thrown away when the National Party's ruling faction agreed to cede the region to a black, Swapo-dominated government. To Vorster and his compatriots, South Africa's subsequent UN-supervised withdrawal had been the clearest signal yet that Haymans's "moderates" planned a complete surrender of all white privilege and power.

Every man now sitting on the State Security Council believed that the negotiated surrender of Namibia was a stain on South Africa's honor. A stain that would have to be erased.

Vorster saw their frowns and nodded. "That's right, gentlemen. So long as communists have free rein on our western border, so long will our people be threatened."

His scowl grew deeper. "We know that these Swapo bastards give shelter to our terrorist enemies!

"We know that the mines dug with our labor, our money, and our expertise now pay for the weapons used to murder men, women, and children across this land!

"We know that these black animals openly boast of their 'victory' over us—a 'victory' given them by treachery within our own government."

Muller watched with interest as Vorster's normally florid face grew even redder. He had to admit that the man's rhetoric was effective. The President could whip men into a hate-filled frenzy even faster than the old Bible-thumping dominie at Muller's boyhood church. The security chief quickly shied away from the comparison. It awakened too many long-buried memories of mixed pleasure and shame.

A tiny fleck of spittle from Vorster's mouth landed by Muller's right hand, and he stared at it in sick fascination as his leader's tirade reached its climax.

"It shall not be so. We will not allow these enemies of our blood to laugh at us, to mock us, to freely plot our downfall! They will be punished!"

Clenched fists thumped the table in a wild, drumming rhythm as he finished speaking.

Vorster, smiling now, let his followers show their approval for a moment, then held up a hand for silence. His rage seemed to have vanished, replaced by a cold, calculating expression.

"Accordingly, I ask the ministers of defense and foreign affairs, and the director of miliary intelligence, to confer with me on specific means aimed at ridding us of this abomination, this 'Namibia.' "

Vorster stared directly into the eyes of each of the three men he'd named. "I shall impose only three conditions on our deliberations. The actions we contemplate must be swift, they must be certain, and they must be final."

Muller looked back at his leader and felt a cool shiver of delight run down his spine. He and his counterparts were being given a free hand to decide the fate of one and a half million people. It was the closest thing imaginable to being a god.

Something stirred in his loins and Muller shifted uncomfortably, wondering again at the way he always found thoughts of power and death so sexually arousing. He shook his head irritably. One thing was certain. It was a mystery that would cost the Namibian people dearly.

And that was a pleasant thought.

CHAPTER 5

Crackdown

JULY 15—PURSUIT FORCE LION, ON THE NAMIBIAN FRONTIER

One thousand feet above the arid, rolling Namibian veld, a tiny, single-engined Cessna 185 orbited—circling round and round through a crystalline blue sky. Its shadow, cast by the rising winter sun, rippled over low, barren hills and sheer-walled gullies strewn with bare-limbed trees and brown, thorn-crowned brush.

Strapped into an observer's seat in the plane's cramped cockpit, Commandant Henrik Kruger squinted through his binoculars into the early-morning glare. The movement emphasized the wrinkles spreading through the skin around his steel-gray eyes—crow's-feet worn into his otherwise boyish-looking face by years of exposure to the sun and wind. They were the marks left by nearly two decades of dedicated military service to his country.

With one hand, he reached back and rubbed a neck grown sore from too many minutes of hunching down to see out the Cessna's windows. At an inch over six feet, Kruger was just tall enough to find riding inside most South African military vehicles and aircraft uncomfortable. He preferred being out in the open air.

Nothing. Still nothing. He pursed his lips. The rugged terrain below made it difficult to spot the fleeing men and vehicles he sought, but the traces of their passage across the veld couldn't be so easily concealed. It was only a matter of keeping one's eyes open.

There. He spotted a narrow break in the normal pattern of yellowing, sun-dried grass, brown earth, and slate-gray rock. It was precisely the sort of thing he'd been searching for since it became possible to distinguish more than blacker ground against a black sky.

Kruger felt adrenaline surge through his veins and forced his excitement back. What he saw might easily be nothing more than a trail left by one of southeastern Namibia's many grazing cattle herds. He needed a closer look to be sure.

Without lowering his binoculars, he reached over the seat and tapped the Cessna pilot's left shoulder, signaling a turn in that direction. The pilot, a young South African Air Force lieutenant, nodded once and pulled the small plane into a shallow dive to the left—simultaneously throttling back to give his passenger a better view of whatever it was that he'd seen on the ground.

The marks Kruger had spotted grew larger and clearer as the Cessna raced toward them at one hundred knots. His excitement returned. They were tire tracks all right; deep, furrowed ruts torn out of the ground by two or three heavily laden Land Rovers moving cross-country. Without being told, the pilot relaxed his turn, leveling out at five hundred feet to follow the tracks westward into Namibia.

Kruger lowered his binoculars and unfolded the map on his lap with one hand while pressing the transmit button on his radio mike with the other. "Papa Foxtrot One to Papa Foxtrot Two. Over."

"Go ahead, Papa Foxtrot One." His second-in-command, Maj. Richard Forbes, sounded tired. Nothing surprising in that. Forbes and his men had already been up more than half the night searching for a band of ANC guerrillas who'd tried to cross the long, open border sector guarded by Kruger's 20th Cape Rifles.

The *kommandant* grimaced. *Guarded* was probably too strong a word. The frontier between South Africa and newly independent Namibia stretched over more than six hundred kilometers of desert and arid veld. That meant that each of the eight infantry battalions stationed at various points along the border had to watch over sectors seventy-five or more kilometers long. It was almost an impossible task—even with constant patrolling, daylight aerial surveillance, and electronic sensors planted along likely infiltration routes.

Kruger frowned, remembering the frantic events of the past few hours. A midnight clash between the guerrillas and one of his battalion's armored car patrols had turned into a brisk, bloody firefight that had left one of his men dead and two more badly wounded. To make matters worse, the guerrillas had broken contact in all the confusion, disappearing into the hills without leaving any of their own dead and wounded behind.

When a preliminary sweep confirmed that they'd turned back toward Namibia, Forbes had taken a mechanized infantry company out in pursuit—trying to stay close to the fleeing ANC infiltrators until daylight made aerial reconnaissance possible. They'd succeeded, and now it was up to Kruger to vector his men in for the kill.

He thumbed the transmit button again. "Two, this is One. Tracks heading west approximately five klicks south of your position."

Forbes came back on immediately, sounding much less tired than he had seconds before. "Roger that, One. We're moving. Deployment plan is India Three. Crossing November Bravo now. Out."

Kruger acknowledged and glanced down at his map again. The code phrase "India Three" meant that the fourteen Ratel 20 armored personnel carriers under Forbes's direct command would move parallel to the trail left by the guerrillas—avoiding any booby traps or mines they might have planted to catch foolhardy pursuers charging straight in after them. Then, once

Kruger had pinpointed the retreating ANC force, Forbes would change course, driving hard to put his infantry, machine-gun teams, and mortars out in front. With reasonable luck, the South African column would be able to smash the guerrillas in split-second ambush.

Kruger shook his head. It should work, and work at a minimal cost in casualties. But there were complications. International complications. "November Bravo" was the radio shorthand for the Namibian border. His men were now on what was ostensibly foreign soil. If they were spotted by UN or Swapo patrols before they'd had a chance to deal with the ANC guerrillas, there'd be hell to pay. The international press would surely have a field day reporting another South African "invasion" of a neighboring country.

He frowned. Although the Republic clearly couldn't afford to allow its enemies sanctuary so close to its borders, the new government's strident rhetoric wasn't making it very easy to justify these "hot pursuit" operations. It was necessary to teach the guerrillas and their supporters some hard lessons, but it seemed senseless to spill so much hot air about it. The old American adage that one should speak softly, but carry a big stick, seemed the wiser path.

"Dust on the horizon, *Kommandant*. Over there at three o'clock."

The pilot's words brought Kruger back to the present. He was a soldier with a battle to run. Politics could wait. He craned his head forward, trying to get a better view through the Cessna's Plexiglas windows.

The light plane bucked slightly in a sudden updraft and then straightened as the lieutenant regained control. As it leveled off, Kruger saw the hazy, yellowish cloud the other man had reported. Six or seven separate dust plumes streaked the air on the horizon, tossed skyward by vehicles moving cross-country at high speed.

He shook his head, puzzled. There were too many plumes. Was the ANC force larger than reported? Or had it been reinforced? Another, even worse possibility tugged at his mind. He leaned forward against the straps holding him to the seat. "Let's get closer."

The lieutenant nodded and pulled his aircraft into a gentle turn to the right. Kruger raised his binoculars again.

The specks beneath the spreading dust cloud grew rapidly larger, resolving suddenly into six large, canvas-sided trucks rolling south—led by a dazzling white jeep flying a huge blue and white United Nations flag. The same flag flew from each of the trucks.

Kruger swore under his breath. Damn and double damn. The UN peacekeepers responsible for this section of the border hadn't been alert enough to stop the ANC's attempted infiltration. But by God, they were quick enough off the mark to stop anyone chasing after the guerrillas. The UN truck convoy's course would place it squarely between Forbes's company and their quarry. His hands tightened around the binoculars.

The Cessna's radio crackled into life. "This is Captain Roald Pedersen of the United Nations Monitoring Group calling the unidentified aircraft overhead. Are you receiving my transmission? Over." The UN officer's accented English marked him as a Norwegian.

Kruger let the binoculars fall around his neck and thumbed his own mike. "Receiving you loud and clear, Captain."

"Identify yourself, please." Pedersen's politeness didn't disguise the tension in his voice.

For an instant, Kruger stared at the speeding trucks below, tempted to tell his pilot to just turn and fly away. Then he shrugged. He wouldn't gain anything by being intransigent. Observers in the truck column must have jotted down the Cessna's identification numbers by now. No one would believe this was a simple civilian joyflight gone astray. Besides, perhaps he could reason with this Norwegian peacekeeper. "This is Kommandant Henrik Kruger of the South African Defense Force."

Pedersen's next words dashed that hope. "You're violating Namibian airspace, *Kommandant*. And I'm ordering you to leave immediately."

Order? The bastard. Kruger fought his temper and spoke calmly. "I urge you to reconsider your 'suggestion,' Captain. I'm currently pursuing a terrorist force that crossed into our territory and killed one of my men. Surely we have the right to defend ourselves?'' He released the transmit button.

''I'm sorry, *Kommandant.*'' Better. The Norwegian sounded genuinely apologetic. ''But you haven't got jurisdiction on this side of the line any longer. I must insist that you turn back immediately or I will be forced to take stronger measures.''

Kruger pondered that. What stronger measures? The UN troops weren't likely to start shooting—at least not without being shot at first. But what could he do if they continued interposing themselves between his oncoming soldiers and the still-fleeing guerrillas? Blast them out of the way? Not likely. Not if he wanted to avoid a major international incident and the resulting damage to his country's reputation and his own career.

He glanced at the map still open on his lap. Forbes and his APCs would be visible to the UN convoy in minutes—dramatically raising the stakes in any prolonged confrontation. What now seemed a simple border violation by a single aircraft would suddenly become a full-scale raid by South African armored vehicles and infantry.

He swore under his breath. There weren't any good choices. He thumbed the mike's transmit button hard enough to hurt. ''Papa Foxtrot One to Papa Foxtrot Two. Over.''

Forbes's clipped accents spilled over the airwaves. ''This is Two, One.''

''Break off pursuit. I say again. Break off pursuit. Return to base.'' The words left a foul taste in Kruger's mouth. Being defeated by an armed enemy would have been bad enough. But being driven off by interfering ''peacekeepers'' was even more irritating.

He didn't doubt that the Norwegian captain and his men would try their best to catch the fleeing guerrillas. The UN troops were honorable in their own way. But they lacked the combat experience and fieldcraft to do a thorough job. The ANC's terrorists would escape to live and murder another day. It was a depressing thought to carry back empty-handed to the dusty airstrip beside the 20th's bunker-ringed camp.

JULY 18—NYANGA BLACK TOWNSHIP, NEAR CAPE TOWN, SOUTH AFRICA

Shots and screams echoed over the roar of armored-car engines and crackling police bullhorns.

"Goddamn it!" Ian Sherfield kicked wildly at the dirt, trying to vent some of his anger and frustration. It didn't help.

By rights, this should have been one of the best newsgathering days of his tour in South Africa. Hints dropped by a sympathetic officer and a long, wearying listening watch to a moderately illegal police scanner had paid off. He and Sam Knowles had come on the scene just after the government's paramilitary security units moved into the crowded huts and alleys of the Nyanga Township. But it was going to be a wasted effort unless they could get some good footage of the brutal police sweep going on just two or three hundred yards away.

And that was just what they weren't to be allowed to get. A solid phalanx of blue-and-gray-uniformed riot troopers, wheeled armored cars, and growling German-shepherd attack dogs blocked the motorway off-ramp leading to Nyanga—holding the gathering mass of foreign correspondents at bay as if they were wild animals.

Ian and Knowles could hear the shooting and see oily, black columns of smoke rising from burning homes, but they couldn't see anything from where the police had stopped them.

Vorster's security services weren't taking any chances that foreign cameras could videotape their goon squads on the rampage. No videotape meant no story—at least not on the television news broadcasts that brought the world to living rooms across America and Europe. The network anchors in New York, London, and Paris wouldn't waste much airtime reporting a story without exciting visuals.

"Well, well, well. Whatta ya know. . . . There is another way in to that dump."

Ian stopped in midkick and spun around to face his cameraman.

Knowles was leaning against the hood of their station wagon, scanning a coffee-stained and torn street map of the areas around Cape Town.

Ian joined him. "What have you got, Sam?"

Knowles's stubby finger traced a winding, circuitous route on the barely legible map. "See this? These bastards have all the major roads blocked, and probably all of the minor ones, too. But I'll bet they don't have enough men to cover every nook and crank in this rabbit warren."

Ian looked at the area Knowles was pointing to. The Philippi Industrial Park. A maze of aluminum-sided warehouses, factories, and storage sheds.

Ian shook his head regretfully. "Wouldn't work, I'm afraid." He traced the shaded border between the township and the industrial area. "There's a barbed-wire-topped chain link fence running all along this area."

Knowles grinned and reached in through the car window onto the passenger seat. He lifted a towel-wrapped bundle and briefly exposed a pair of wire cutters. "Fences, old son, are meant to be cut. . . ."

Ian thought he'd never seen his stocky sidekick look so much like the fabled Cheshire Cat. He matched Knowles's broad smile with one of his own and opened the car door.

Twenty minutes later, the two men crouched behind a rusting row of trash bins—less than fifteen feet from the chain link fence separating Nyanga Township's ramshackle huts from the industrial park's machine shops and warehouses. Tendrils of smoke and faint shouts, shots and screams, drifted faintly downwind from the north—clear proof that South Africa's riot troops were still engaged in what they euphemistically called "the suppression of minor disturbances." Ian planned to call their bloody work something very different. But first he and Knowles had to get inside the township, get their videotape, and get out. And that might not be so easy.

He risked a quick glance toward the nearest police post, two hundred yards down the fence. The ten shotgun-armed policemen manning the sandbagged post were alert, but they were looking the wrong way. They were there to stop people from escaping—not to stop journalists from breaking in.

Ian pulled his head back around the corner and carefully unwrapped the wire cutters. Knowles knelt beside him, video camera and sound gear slung from his back.

"Everything cool?" The little man sounded breathless. Not scared, Ian decided, just excited.

He nodded. "We're clear."

"Well, let's do it, then."

With their hearts pounding and equipment rattling, the two men raced to the fence and dropped flat—waiting for the angry shouts that would signal that they'd been seen. None came.

Ian rolled onto his side and slipped the wire cutter's sharp-edged jaws over a rusting metal strand near the bottom of the fence. They slipped off at his first attempt to snip through the strand. And then a second time as he tried again. Christ. His fingers felt three times their normal size. As if they'd been pumped full of novocaine.

Knowles moved restlessly beside him, but didn't say anything.

Ian wiped both hands on his pants and tried a third time, applying steady pressure to the wire cutter's twin handles. C'mon, cut, you bastard. This time the fence strand snapped apart with a low twang. Finally.

He kept working—slicing upward through the fence in a series of steady, repetitive motions. Slip the cutter's jaws over a chain link. Don't think about the police standing guard not far away. Just squeeze. Squeeze hard. Move on to the next strand and do it all again.

He finished almost without realizing it.

"That's good enough," Knowles whispered, taking the wire cutters out of his hand.

Ian came back to his surroundings and studied the ragged hole he'd torn in the fence. His cameraman was right. The opening was just big enough for them to wriggle through and just small enough so that it might not be too noticeable from a distance.

He sneaked another quick glance toward the police post.

The South African riot troops were still looking the wrong way. It was time to move, before one of them grew wary or bored and decided to scan the rest of the local scenery.

Ian rolled onto his back and pulled himself through the gap. Knowles wriggled through the fence after first passing the camera through the narrow opening.

They were inside.

Without stopping, Ian rose to his feet and raced forward into a narrow alley between two of Nyanga's small, aluminum-sided houses. Knowles followed, unslinging his camera as he ran.

Both men paused to get their bearings and then moved on—walking toward the noise of the riot spreading fast through the township. As they felt their way gingerly ahead, stepping wide over trash littering the alley, Ian took a deep breath, trying to suck air into his heaving lungs. It was a mistake. Piles of rotting, uncollected garbage, the sewage backing up from inadequate sanitation systems, and now, stray wisps of tear gas, all came together to create a single, gut-wrenching odor. He clenched his teeth, fighting down a wave of nausea.

The alley they were in ran straight north between rows of dilapidated, windowless homes, paralleling one of Nyanga's unpaved main streets. Nothing moved, except for a few scrawny rats that scampered quickly out of their path.

After a few minutes of hard walking, Knowles stopped short of what looked like a major cross street. He looked up at Ian. "Where to now, kimosabe?"

Ian cocked his head, listening to the continuing sounds of chaos. They seemed louder ahead and to the left. He stepped out of the alley and turned in that direction.

Almost immediately they started seeing people streaming south, fleeing what now sounded more like a pitched street battle than a routine, if brutal, door-to-door police sweep. Most were women and children—some carrying hastily snatched bundles of their household belongings, while others, weeping, ran empty-handed.

Ian saw Knowles raise his camera and start panning from side to side. He moved forward again, with the short, stocky cameraman tagging along by his side. The pictures of panic-stricken flight would be dramatic, but they had to get closer to the action. People back home needed to see just what Nyanga's inhabitants were running away from.

The two Americans pushed their way north up one of the refugee-choked streets, dodging frightened men, women, and children carrying what they could of their furnishings away from the fighting. The mixed smells of smoke and tear gas grew stronger, and Ian could see orange and red flames leaping from rooftops farther down the street.

There were more men in the crowd hurrying past. Many had been shot or badly beaten and were being half-carried, half-dragged away by their friends or relatives. Ian had a dizzying impression of a whirl of torn, bloodstained shirts, fearful eyes, and angry, shaking fists, some aimed in his direction.

Their undisguised hatred shocked him until he remembered his white skin. For all Nyanga's inhabitants could know, he and Knowles might be members of the state security services—taking pictures for later use both in criminal prosecutions and covert retaliation. Ian felt sweat trickling down his back and beading on his forehead. The fact that they could be in as much danger from the township's people as they were from the police hadn't really sunk in before. It wasn't a reassuring thought.

Ian slipped a hand into his pants pocket, unconsciously fingering his plastic-cased press card as if it were some kind of religious talisman. But he knew it would be a singularly ineffective protection if the township's angry young men turned on anyone trapped in the wrong-colored skin.

Knowles's hand touched his arm and he started, instantly ashamed that he'd shown his nervousness so openly.

The cameraman pointed farther up the street. "I think that's where we want to be. Whatever bastards are driving these people back are going to have to come through that."

Ian's eyes followed his friend's pointing finger and he nodded. Knowles was right, as usual. The locals had built a barricade of flaming truck and car tires, old furniture, and boxes of canned foods dragged from a nearby grocery. Greasy black smoke from the burning tires hung over the whole street, cutting off the sun and throwing everything into a kind of gray, gloomy half-light.

The two men jogged closer to the barricade, looking for a sheltered vantage point.

They could see the barricade's defenders clearly now. Young men. Teenagers. Even a few boys who couldn't have been more than ten or eleven years old. None of them were running, and all clutched a rock, chair leg, or tire iron. Any kind of improvised weapon that would give them a chance to hit back at those responsible for this unwarranted attack on their homes and families.

"Here!" Ian pulled Knowles down beside a rust-eaten car stripped of its tires, doors, and engine. They were within twenty yards of the barricade.

Knowles knelt upright and propped his camera up on the edge of the car's crumpled hood. Ian crouched beside him, feeling calmer now that they were in cover.

An eerie stillness settled over the street. Smoke from the burning tires and houses made it impossible to see far beyond the barricade. But no shapes moved in the oily mist, and fewer shots and screams could be heard. For an instant Ian wondered if the police raid was over, either called off or beaten back. Had Nyanga's people put up enough resistance to discourage South Africa's hardened riot troops?

A roaring, thundering, grinding crash jarred him back to reality, and he stared in shock as an enormous Hippo armored personnel carrier smashed into the barricade at high speed, sending tires, furniture, and boxes flying apart in what seemed slow motion. Rocks clanged harmlessly off the APC's metal hide as it lumbered on down the street—leaving a trail of crushed, still-burning debris behind itself.

Riot police appeared suddenly out of the smoke, charging through the gap left them by the Hippo. Gas masks with clear plastic visors and bulbous filters gave them a strangely alien appearance. One went down in a tangle of equipment, hit hard in the head by a thrown rock. The black teenager who'd thrown it cried out in triumph and knelt to pick up another. Both he and his joy were short-lived.

Ian winced as a point-blank shotgun blast ripped the young rock-thrower into a ragged, bleeding mess. He swallowed hard against the bitter taste in his mouth.

The police seemed to take that first shot as a signal, and they began firing wildly, indiscriminately—spraying shotgun blasts into the street and houses around the barricade. Splinters whined through the air, blown off buildings by hundreds of pellets concentrated into narrow, killing arcs. Ian felt something whipcrack past his head and ducked. Jesus. He'd never been shot at before.

He poked his head back above the car, noticing that Knowles had never stopped filming. My God, nothing seemed to faze the man.

The street looked like a slaughterhouse. Patches of its hard-packed dirt surface were stained, soaked in blood. There were bodies all around—some lying motionless, others thrashing or twitching uncontrollably in agony. A few of Nyanga's young men still stood their ground, flailing desperately away at the policemen pouring through their shattered barricade. But most were running. Riot troops chased after them, firing from the hip or swinging whips and truncheons in vicious, bone-crunching blows.

Ian jogged Knowles's elbow and jerked his head toward one of the tiny alleys opening onto the street. They had all the videotape they needed to make a damned good story out of this bloodbath. No useful purpose would be served by hanging around until the police spotted them. It was time to get out.

Knowles slung the camera over his back and followed Ian into the alley. They ran hard, jumping piles of untended garbage and forcing their way through patches where weeds had grown waist high. Behind them, the police gunfire rose to a higher-pitched, rattling crescendo, spreading rapidly to all sides. At the sound of it, both men ran faster still, trying to escape what seemed like a quickly closing net.

Ian's lungs felt as though they were on fire, and every breath burned going down. His legs seemed to weigh a ton apiece. Knowles wasn't in much better shape as he stumbled panting along behind. But he kept running, following any street or winding alley that led south—toward the chain link fence, their car, and safety.

Their luck ran out less than a hundred yards from the fence.

Four burly men dressed in brown, military-style shirts and trousers stepped into the alley ahead of them, shotguns and clubs at the ready. Their faces were hard, expressionless.

Ian skidded to a stop in front of them, his heart pounding. Knowles stumbled into him and backed up a step, breathing noisily through his mouth.

Ian raised both hands, empty palms forward, and stepped closer to the waiting men. It seemed strange that they weren't wearing the standard gray trousers and blue-gray jackets of the regular police. Just who were these guys anyway?

"My colleague here and I are journalists. Please step aside and let us pass." Nothing. Ian tried again, this time in halting Afrikaans.

The largest, an ugly, red-faced man with a flattened, oft-broken nose, sneered, "Kaffir-loving, rooinek bastards."

Ian recognized the contemptuous slang term for Englishmen and felt his hopes of skating out of this situation sink. He shook his head. "No, we're Americans. Look, we're just here doing our job."

It sounded pretty feeble even to his ears. The four brownshirts moved closer.

More feet pounded down the alley behind them.

"Don't look now, but I think we're surrounded," Knowles muttered.

The largest Afrikaner held out a large, calloused hand. "Give us the *verdomde* camera, man, and maybe we let you go with your teeth still in your mouth. A *blery* good deal, *ja?*"

His friends snickered.

Great. Just great. Ian eyed the big man narrowly. A bare-knuckled barroom brawler. Nothing fancy, there. He didn't doubt that he could take the bastard. Unfortunately, that still left at least three in front, and God only knew how many behind.

But the tape in that camera represented the biggest story to come his way since he'd landed in South Africa. He couldn't just meekly hand it over. Not without putting up some kind of resistance, even if it was only verbal. He shook his head slowly. "Look, guys. I'd like to oblige, but the camera doesn't belong to me. It's company property. Besides your own government has given us permission to cover the news here. So if you try to stop us, you're breaking your own laws."

He paused, hoping they'd take the bait and start arguing with him. Every passing minute increased the chance that someone in the regular police chain of command would show up—taking these plug-ugly paramilitary bastards out of the picture, no matter who they worked for.

They didn't fall for it. Ian saw the big man nod to someone behind him and heard Knowles cry out in pain and anger an instant later. He whirled round.

Two more brownshirt thugs stood there smirking. One shook the videocamera in his face in mock triumph while the other held Knowles's arms behind his back. Ian noticed blood trickling from a cut on his cameraman's lower lip.

That was too goddamned much. He took a step forward toward them, his teeth clenched and jaw rigid with anger.

Knowles spat out a tiny glob of blood and said quickly, "Don't, Ian. That's just what they want."

Ian shook his head, not caring anymore. One or two of these morons was going to regret pissing him off. He started to lift his hands—

Something flickered at the corner of his eye. A club? He ducked, knowing already that he'd seen it too late.

The big Afrikaner's shotgun butt smashed into the side of his skull, sending a surging, tearing, burning wave of pain through Ian's head. The alley whirled round in his dazed vision and he felt himself sliding to his knees. God, it hurt. He'd never been in so much pain before. The sunlight that had seemed so dim seconds before now seemed intolerably, horribly dazzling.

He heard Knowles shouting something he couldn't make out through the roaring in his ears. He looked up and saw a heavy leather boot arcing toward his face.

This time, mercifully, the lights went out and stayed out.

JULY 19—POLITICAL DETENTION LEVEL, CAPE TOWN MAGISTRATES' COURT

No shadows softened the cellblock's steel-barred doors, long empty corridors, and row after row of small square holding pens. There were no shadows because the harsh, overhead fluorescent lights were never turned off. They stayed on, robbing prisoners and guards alike of any sense of passing time.

As Ian lay faceup on a concrete slab that passed for a bed, he noticed that the cracked white ceiling tiles of his cell had finally stopped spinning around and around. And his head, though it still hurt, no longer felt swollen up like a pain-filled helium balloon. He almost smiled at the strange-sounding simile. Maybe he'd taken more punishment than he remembered.

Just the ability to think straight at all was a major improvement, he decided. In the hours since he'd struggled back to some semblance of consciousness, stray bits and pieces of rational thought had tumbled through his mind, coming and going among a host of jumbled memories, dreams, and half-forgotten songs. But now he could start putting all the pieces back together, forming them into some sensible picture of what had gone on since they'd tossed him into this cramped, dingily antiseptic cage.

For instance, he remembered seeing Sam Knowles being locked into a similar cell just down the hall. And this time, Ian did smile, remembering the steady stream of swear words and obscene, elaborate insults pouring out of his cameraman's mouth. Knowles at least, though bloody, had very definitely been unbowed.

That was a comforting image to hold on to in the midst of a series of much more depressing visions of his likely future. Ian had no illusions left about his network's compassion or generosity. A reporter who got himself beaten up and deported while getting an exciting story would be embraced with open arms. But a reporter who got tossed out without anything to show for it, save a few bruises, was a has-been heading straight for the television trash heap.

Ian groaned softly. Being kicked out of South Africa without the chance to see Emily again was bad enough. The thought of being sent to read the weather in somewhere called Lower Podunkia made his almost certain deportation even worse.

"Hey, you! *Amerikaan!* On your feet. The new *kommandant* wants to see you."

Ian turned his head. A warder stood just outside his cell door. Keys dangled from the man's plump hand.

Head pounding again, Ian slowly sat up and levered himself off the concrete slab. The cell door slammed open.

"Come on, man. Don't keep the *kommandant* waiting. You're in enough *blery* trouble as it is." The warder motioned him out into the corridor where Knowles and three other guards stood waiting.

Fifteen minutes later, the two men found themselves standing in front of the detention-center commandant's enormous, highly polished desk. Two bearlike guards stood to either side. Ian wondered whether they really expected Sam and him to try to jump their chief, or whether they were simply posted as part of a general pattern of intimidation. More the latter than the former, he suspected.

At first glance, the new commandant himself looked more like someone's kindly, mild-mannered junior clerk than a secret policeman. But that pleasant resemblance dissolved on closer examination. The man's pale blue, almost reptilian eyes rarely blinked behind thick, wire-rimmed glasses. And his puffy, thin-lipped face seemed permanently set in a sour scowl. He wore a plain uniform devoid of any badge of rank or other ornamentation—except for a single red, white, and black pin fastened to his tunic. The Afrikaner's fingers drummed rhythmically while he leafed through the single document blotting the surface of his desk.

Ian focused his still-blurry vision, trying to make out the insignia embossed on the man's lapel pin. For a second, it wavered in and out of focus. Then he recognized the symbol—the three-armed swastika of the Afrikaner Resistance Movement, the AWB. Jesus Christ. He struggled to keep the shock he felt off his face. The AWB's fanatics were supposed to be nothing more than a lunatic fringe group—a group despised as much by the ruling National Party as by anyone else in South Africa. So what the hell was a high-ranking official doing wearing their insignia? Not only wearing it, but wearing it proudly, he thought, studying the commandant's arrogant profile.

Things began falling frighteningly into place. The brownshirts who'd beaten them up were undoubtedly members of the AWB's Brandwag, or Sentry—a heavily armed paramilitary organization. The AWB's leaders had sworn to use their private army of storm troopers against those they labeled communists and black troublemakers. Now they seemed to be actually putting their threats into violent practice. And doing so with the active approval of those in the new government.

Ian shivered involuntarily at the thought of the AWB's ignorant, torch-carrying hatemongers running wild through South Africa's townships and city streets. What kind of madman would give such thugs free rein? He lifted his eyes from the commandant's tunic and saw the harsh, unsmiling visage of Karl Vorster staring back at him from the wall.

My God, he realized, they've already taken the time to manufacture idealized portraits of the new president. And for the first time, he began to consider the possibility that Vorster was something much worse than a somewhat simpleminded political hard-liner.

"My, my, Meneer Sherfield, what a shocking list of crimes. Violating a police line, brawling with appointed representatives of the government, breaking the Emergency Decree's restrictions on press coverage . . . what am I going to do with you?" The commandant's dry, sneering voice brought Ian back to the more basic consideration of his own personal fate.

Oh, oh. Decision time. Should he play it safe and act suitably meek and apologetic in the hope that they'd let him stay in South Africa? Or show the sons of bitches that they couldn't scare him and probably get strapped into the first plane heading overseas? He found the decision surprisingly easy to make. Somehow he found the thought of kowtowing to the prim little neo-Nazi in front of him too sickening to contemplate seriously. He mentally kissed both Emily and his career good-bye.

Ian leaned closer to the desk. "I'll tell you what you can do, you . . ." He closed his mouth on the term he'd been about to use. Even as angry as he was, it didn't seem very wise to call the prison commandant a son of a bitch to his face.

He swayed upright. "All right. Here's the deal. First, you let us out of your damned jail. Then you arrest those bastards who attacked us."

Ian took a shallow breath, calmer now. "And after that's done, we'll talk about how you can pay us back for the damage to our stuff and for this." His fingers gently brushed the painful swelling behind his left ear.

Finished, he stood waiting for the expected explosion and immediate order for his expulsion.

It didn't come.

Instead, the commandant simply smiled coldly. "I shall not debate the matter with you, Meneer Sherfield. I reserve that for those I consider equals. And you are most emphatically not my equal." His hands idly caressed the polished surface of his desk.

He stared straight into Ian's eyes. "You are a guest in this country, *meneer*. You exist at my sufferance. I suggest you remember that in the future."

Ian held his breath, surprised into silence. Were they going to let him stay?

The commandant's thin, cold smile vanished. "You have much to learn about the role you can play in South Africa, Meneer Sherfield. We Afrikaners are not the kind of weak-willed, decadent, impoverished tribesmen with whom you so-called journalists can play god. We do not care in the least what you and your prating colleagues think of us or our policies."

A fanatical gleam appeared in the man's pale, unwinking

eyes. "The true God alone shall judge our actions to save our *volk*."

"If that's the case, why not just kick us out and have done with it?" Ian heard Knowles choke back a muttered warning to shut up.

The Afrikaner steepled his hands. "I assure you most solemnly, *meneer*, if it were up to me alone, I would gladly send you back to your own godless land by the next available transport.

"But"—the hands separated and spread into the semblance of an uncaring shrug—"it seems that there are those in higher places who have some small interest in you and your friend. So I shall be merciful this once. You're free to go. Immediately." The commandant jerked his head toward the office door and lowered his eyes to the open file on his desk, apparently dismissing the whole matter from his mind.

Scarcely able to believe his good fortune, Ian was halfway to the door before he remembered their damaged gear. The green-eyeshade boys in New York were bound to squawk unless he and Knowles made every effort to find another way to pay for the needed repairs and replacements. It was the same old story. If the network bosses liked you, you could even get away with writing off a trip to the south of France as a research expense. But woe betide anyone else who turned in an expense account showing anything more pricey than lunches at the local equivalent of McDonald's.

With that in mind, he decided to press his luck a little further. He spun round sharply—stepping briskly aside as one of the guards treading close on his heels nearly blundered into him. "Not so fast, Commandant. What about our camera and sound equipment? Who's going to pick up the tab for the stuff your goon squad smashed?"

The Afrikaner's head came up as fast as a striking snake's. Despite the man's earlier contemptuous words, Ian was shocked by the undisguised hatred apparent on his face. "Get out of my office at once! And be thankful that only your *verdomde* equipment was broken. It can be repaired. Skulls and ribs are not so easily mended!"

The expression of open anger faded from the commandant's face, replaced by a calmer, colder, infinitely more chilling look of calculated malice. "Do not cross my path again, Meneer Sherfield. It would not be the action of a wise or healthy man. I trust I make myself clear?"

He glanced at the guards still standing to either side. "Now take these Uitlanders out of my sight before I change my mind and have them locked up again."

The Afrikaner's pale, hate-filled eyes followed them all the way out the door.

Neither man spoke until they were near the main gate leading out of the Magistrates' Court complex. Then, at last, Sam Knowles broke the tension-filled silence. "Jesus Christ, Ian. Remind me to loan you my copy of *How to Win Friends and Influence People* before you get us both killed."

Ian laughed softly, a somewhat forced, embarrassed laugh. "Sorry, Sam. I've learned not to eat with my hands in fancy restaurants, but I guess nobody ever taught me how to keep my big mouth shut around junior-grade gestapo wannabees like that S.O.B. back there."

"Yeah." Knowles thumped him lightly on the shoulder. "Well, the next time we're looking down someone's gun barrel, try to remember that discretion is always the best part of valor. Will you do that for me, huh?"

Ian nodded.

"Good." The little cameraman shifted gears abruptly. "Now just who the hell in Pretoria do you suppose likes you enough to spring us from the pokey?"

Ian didn't answer him until they had passed a pair of armed sentries and stood blinking in the brilliant winter-afternoon sunshine. A taxicab sat parked along the curb.

"I don't know anyone that high up in Vorster's good graces, but I know someone who does," Ian said.

The taxi's rear door opened and a beautiful, auburn-haired woman got out. Knowles pursed his lips in a silent, appreciative whistle. "I see. I do believe I begin to see."

Through suddenly narrowed eyes, the short, stocky cameraman watched his friend and partner take the steps two at a time down to meet Emily van der Heijden.

JULY 20—D. F. MALAN INTERNATIONAL AIRPORT, NEAR CAPE TOWN

The announcement buzzed and crackled through the overhead loudspeakers in the same dry, garbled, and disinterested voice used in airports all the world over.

"South Africa Airways Flight one forty-eight to Johannesburg is now ready for boarding. All passengers with confirmed seating are requested to come to the Jetway at this time."

Ian felt his pulse race as Emily kissed him hard one last time and pulled away.

He started to reach for her and stopped as she shook her head sadly. "I must leave." She blinked away sudden tears. "I'm afraid there's no more time."

Ian fumbled for the handkerchief in his jacket pocket and then gave it up as he saw Emily sling the traveling case over her shoulder. "Look, if you don't want to go, then don't. Stay here with me."

Another headshake, slightly more vehement. "I cannot, no matter how much I would wish it. My father is a hard man, Ian. To him, a bargain is a bargain—no matter how forced it might be. So if I do not return home as I promised, he'll have you rearrested and sent back to America. And I cannot let that happen."

Ian looked down at the scuffed tile floor. What was happening to her was largely his fault. She'd learned of his arrest when he hadn't shown up for a dinner date the day of the riot. Nearly out of her mind with worry, she'd done what she would ordinarily have regarded as unthinkable. She'd phoned her father, asking for his help.

As the new government's deputy minister of law and order, Marius van der Heijden had the clout needed to spring an unruly pair of American journalists. The man was also a scheming, blackmailing bastard, Ian thought angrily. His price for their release had been Emily's surrender of her hard-won independence—the independence she'd won only after years of stormy argument and outright shouting matches. In her father's words, she was to be "obedient."

Emily softly touched his arm. "You understand?"

He swore in frustration. "Jesus Christ, this isn't the Middle Ages! What's he expect you to do for him . . . cook, clean, and keep house like every other good little Afrikaner girl?"

The ghost of a smile appeared on Emily's face. "No, he knows me better than that. He just wants to keep me away from you and your 'immoral' influence."

The faint smile disappeared. "Though of course he will expect me to help him around the house. To serve as hostess for parties and *braais*." She used the Afrikaans word for barbecues.

Ian picked up her other bag, and together they walked toward the passenger line forming at the gate.

Emily kept talking, as if she hoped to bury her sadness under a flow of everyday conversation. "You see, my father's new position compels him to be more social. And it is important, I suppose, that he be able to show the kind of home his colleagues would regard as 'normal.' "

Ian nodded, but couldn't think of anything to say. He knew how much Emily valued her freedom and how much she loathed her father's extremist political positions. Now she was willingly going back to everything she had once escaped.

And all for him.

Her sacrifice made his own troubles seem small in comparison.

"Boarding pass, please." He looked up. They were already at the gate. A young, uniformed flight attendant had her hand out for Emily's ticket.

"Look, can I write or call you?" The desperation in his voice was audible.

Emily's voice dropped to a bare, husky whisper he had to strain to hear clearly. "No . . . that would be the worst thing. My father must believe I have broken entirely with you."

"But . . ."

She gently laid a finger across his lips, stilling his protest. "I know, Ian. It is terrible. But believe this. I will contact you as soon as I can. As soon as I can find a way to do so without my father's knowledge."

Her hand dropped away from his face.

The flight attendant coughed lightly. “Please, I must have your boarding pass.”

Silently, Emily handed over her ticket and stepped onto the carpeted ramp leading to the waiting plane. Then she turned.

“Remember that I love you, Ian Sherfield.”

She disappeared around a bend in the ramp before he could say anything past the sudden lump in his throat.

Ian stood watching until he saw her plane lift off the runway and turn east, sunlight winking painfully off its silvery wings.

CHAPTER 6

Early Warning

JULY 22—SWARTKOP MILITARY AIRFIELD, NEAR PRETORIA

The single-engined Kudu light utility aircraft rolled to a gentle, shuddering stop near the end of the oil-stained concrete taxiway. Even before the propeller had stopped spinning, ground crewmen were on their way, moving to tie down the Kudu's wings against sudden gusts of wind.

Commandant Henrik Kruger clambered awkwardly out of the plane's cramped cockpit, stretched, and then leaned in to shake the pilot's hand. "Thanks, Pieter. A good fast flight, that. I may even have an appetite for lunch."

He checked his watch. He had nearly an hour left before his scheduled meeting with the chief of staff for operations. "Look, I should be back from the Ministry in three or four hours. Can you stand by to run me back to Upington then?"

The plane's pilot, an Air Force captain, grinned back. "No sweat, *Kommandant*. Take your time. They've got a *blery* good officers' mess here. Once I get some food in my belly and put some petrol in the tanks, I'll be ready to go whenever you say the word."

"*Magtig!*" Kruger pulled his worn, leather briefcase out from under the seat and stepped back, touching his cap to make sure it was still on straight over his short-cropped, brown hair. Satisfied, he picked his way around the outstretched landing gear. A few meters away, a soldier waiting by a flag-decked car stiffened to attention. His transport to the Ministry of Defense, no doubt.

"Hey, *Kommandant!*"

He glanced over his shoulder at the cockpit's open side window.

The Kudu's pilot flashed a thumbs-up signal. "Give them hell, sir!"

Kruger stifled a smile, nodded briskly instead, and moved on toward the waiting staff car. As he'd suspected, the whole base must know why he'd been summoned to Pretoria at such short notice. Secrets were almost impossible to keep in close-knit, active-duty combat units such as his 20th Rifles.

It certainly hadn't taken long for his latest situation report to generate results. Though that certainly wasn't particularly surprising. Battalion commanders—even highly decorated battalion commanders—didn't often send such scathing indictments of current policy to the Defense Staff Council, but Kruger had grown weary of asking his men to do the impossible. Too many of the Permanent Force's best battalions were being used to suppress disorder in the black townships instead of being stationed on the border where they were so desperately needed.

And *desperate* wasn't too strong a word, he thought grimly. Given the current military and political situation, the frontier with Namibia simply could not be adequately defended. There were too few troops trying to cover too much territory.

Some staff officers at the Ministry of Defense had done their best to help out. They'd made sure that units such as the 20th had first call on replacements and the latest weapons and hardware.

More important, requisitions for food, fuel, and ammo

were processed with almost unmilitary speed and efficiency. In the final analysis, though, those were simply half-measures—interim steps that relieved some of the day-to-day burden on Kruger and his fellow commanders without in any way solving the strategic dilemma they faced. Pretoria must either provide more men and equipment to guard the border or find other ways to end the ANC's renewed guerrilla campaign.

Kruger shook his head, aware that the new men in charge weren't likely to make the right decisions. Like a sizable number of South African Defense Force officers, he'd privately applauded the Haymans government's moves toward some reasonable accommodation with the nation's black majority. The key word was *reasonable*. No one he knew supported the absurd notion of an eventual one-man, one-vote system for South Africa. The failing array of dictatorships scattered across black Africa showed the dangers of such a course. But few officers could hide from the knowledge that continued white efforts to hold all political power inevitably meant an ongoing and probably endless guerrilla war—a war marked by minor, strategically meaningless victories and a steady stream of maimed or dead men.

Kruger shook his head again, mentally cursing both Karl Vorster's callous determination to win this unwinnable war and the ANC bastards who'd put the new president in place by murdering Frederick Haymans.

"The Ministry, sir?" The corporal waiting by his car saluted and held the rear door open for him.

"Yes." Kruger returned the man's salute and climbed into the staff car.

He sat up straight against the seat as they pulled away from the plane and turned onto an asphalt-paved access road. Half his mind busied itself by reviewing the arguments he intended to make to the chief of staff. One corner of his mouth flickered upward briefly in a wry smile. He was probably being too optimistic. He wasn't likely to have the chance to get a single word in edgewise over the tongue-lashing he fully expected to receive.

Headquarters staffs, even in an army as flexible and informal as the SADF, always had their own rigid notions about such things as the chain of command and proper channels.

Something strange about the passing scenery tugged Kruger's attention away from his upcoming ordeal. He looked more carefully out the windows to either side. They were paralleling Swartkop's main runway and flight line. Both looked nearly deserted. And that was odd. Very odd.

The airfield was ordinarily a hive of frenzied activity. With two squadrons of transport aircraft based here, Swartkop often seemed a practical demonstration of perpetual motion as small, single-engined Kudus and larger C-47s landed, refueled, and took off again—ferrying men and equipment to the SADF's far-flung military districts.

But not today. The Kudu that had carried him here sat all by itself, parked in isolation on a vast, empty expanse of concrete. There were no planes on the taxiway taking off or landing. Kruger stroked his freshly shaved chin. Where were all the aircraft?

The staff car turned onto a wider road running past Swartkop's huge, aluminum-sided hangars and repair shops. And there they were. Row after row of camouflaged transport planes either parked in the hangars or on the flight line close by. Tiny figures in grease-stained, orange coveralls swarmed over each aircraft, opening a panel here or tightening something down there. Repair and maintenance crews, all working at top speed.

Kruger stared out the window as they drove past, taken completely by surprise. Even under normal operating conditions, perhaps one in five of a squadron's aircraft could be expected to need routine maintenance at any given time. But nothing about the frantic bustle around the forty or so parked planes struck Kruger as being routine. Had there been some unprecedented and completely unannounced act of ANC sabotage? It seemed unlikely. Even the Vorster government's stringent new censorship laws couldn't have prevented word of such a disaster from leaking out.

He sat up even straighter as a more plausible, but equally disturbing explanation presented itself. The Air Force must be preparing its planes for a prolonged surge in flight operations—round-the-clock sorties that would make it impossible to provide normal maintenance.

Kruger's mouth tightened. These were cargo aircraft and troop carriers, so whatever Pretoria had planned involved the Army. Were they finally going to reinforce the Namibian border? Maybe. He hoped so. It would certainly save him a lot of grief in his meeting with the chief of staff. He could take a scolding more easily if he knew in advance that the hierarchy agreed with his diagnosis of the situation.

The car rounded another corner, cutting off his view of the parked planes, and Kruger faced forward again. His eyes continued to sweep the surrounding terrain—automatically noting the six Cactus missile launchers of the base's SAM battery off to one side and the swarm of harried-looking Air Force officers emerging from Swartkop's Administration Center on the other. But the logical part of his mind remained fully engaged, raising and as quickly dismissing new explanations for all the activity he saw.

His first hope that the planes were slated to carry reinforcements to the Namibian frontier seemed farfetched when viewed dispassionately. No one would send large numbers of troops and equipment by air when road convoys or rail transport could serve the same end more efficiently. No, he thought grimly, these planes were being prepared for the kind of high-stakes operation where speed mattered more than cost. A major airborne assault somewhere outside South Africa's borders, for example. But where? Zimbabwe again? Or Mozambique? He'd heard that support for the Renamo guerrillas had been upped once more. Were these planes intended for one of their murderous operations?

Kruger's frown tightened further still into a thin-lipped scowl. If whatever Pretoria had in mind wouldn't help take the pressure off his men, the ears of the SADF's chief of operations were going to burn with swear words the man probably hadn't heard since his own days in the bush. And, Kruger vowed silently, to hell with his career. The lives of his soldiers were more important than his own chances of ever wearing a colonel's insignia.

Wrapped in increasingly bleak thoughts about his likely

personal and professional future, he scarcely noticed as the staff car passed through Swartkop's heavily guarded main gate and sped toward Pretoria.

SADF HEADQUARTERS, THE MINISTRY OF DEFENSE, PRETORIA

The lieutenant commanding the Defense Ministry guard post looked from Kruger's ID card to his face and back down again. Apparently satisfied by what he saw, the young officer's pen made a tick mark on a surprisingly crowded list of approved visitors.

Then he handed the ID card back and nodded at the burly noncom waiting patiently off to one side of the wood-paneled guard room. "Thank you, *Kommandant*. Sergeant Meinart there will show you to the briefing."

Kruger pocketed his card with an abrupt nod and followed the sergeant out into the Ministry's busy main hallway. The noncom walked right by a bank of elevators leading to the building's upper floors and continued straight on down the hall toward the massive double doors of the Main Staff Auditorium.

Kruger kept pace easily, exchanging salutes with passing senior officers without much conscious thought. He had more interesting things than simple military courtesies to occupy his mind. It was becoming increasingly clear that he hadn't been summoned to Pretoria for a personal harangue by the higher brass.

He shook his head slightly, irritated with himself for ever holding such a simpleminded, egotistical belief. Only an idiot could miss the signs of intense activity all around. First the frantic maintenance work at Swartkop, and now this unannounced briefing being held in the Ministry's largest meeting room. Something big was in the wind. Something very big.

His first glance around the crowded staff auditorium confirmed that impression.

More than a hundred field-grade officers packed the room—some swapping news and professional gossip in the aisles, others sitting quietly among the rows of theater-style folding chairs. Steel-blue Air Force and dark blue Navy uniforms mingled with the sober brown jackets and ties of the Army. A sea of red-and-blue berets down front signaled the presence of representatives from each of the three Permanent Force parachute battalions.

Kruger didn't bother concealing his astonishment. He hadn't seen this many of his fellow unit commanders together in one place for years. He scanned the room again, counting stars. My God, the auditorium held at least two-thirds of the Army's Permanent and Citizen Force battalion commanders, six brigadiers, and the two complete division-level staffs.

He stiffened. No one in his right mind would assemble the kind of force these men represented for anything less than a massive, combined-arms operation. He grew even more uneasy at that thought. What was Vorster planning? Some sort of massive exercise? A real military operation?

Kruger's uneasiness about the government's intentions had nothing to do with any kind of misplaced pacifism. He loathed the ANC's sneak attacks and terrorist bombings as much as any other serving South African officer. Twenty years of cross-border warfare had taught him that the guerrillas were his enemies. And as enemies, they were legitimate targets for South Africa's military forces—no matter where they sought sanctuary. But quick, in-and-out commando raids were one thing. This implied something much bigger.

Military operations were always expensive. They consumed both lives and money at a breakneck pace. And the Republic's economy was already under tremendous strain. Unemployment among the blacks, inflation, and interest rates were all rising. He'd seen the evidence on infrequent visits to his hometown in the northern Transvaal. In emptier shelves in the little country stores. In the growing numbers of able-bodied black men slouching aimlessly by the roadsides or fields. In sky-high petrol prices that increasingly kept people at home unless travel was absolutely necessary.

Kruger shook his head. This wasn't the right time for seeking high-priced military glory. He only hoped somebody on the Defense Staff Council had the balls to explain that to the new cabinet.

"Hey, Henrik, man! What're you doing here, you *blery* footslogger? I thought this meeting was for officers and gentlemen only."

Kruger wheeled round, a grin spreading across his face despite his inner worries. Though he hadn't seen Deneys Coetzee in person for more than two years, no one who'd met him could ever forget the cocky little man's rough, gravelly voice and bluff, open face. Fifteen years before, they'd served together in Namibia as green-as-grass junior officers. Months of hard campaigning in the desolate, arid Namibian bush had left both a complete trust in each other's professional competence and a lasting friendship.

Kruger whistled out loud at the three stars and pentagon on Coetzee's shoulder tabs. "They made *you* a brigadier? Now I know the world is a crazy place."

Coetzee waggled a finger in his face. "*Ag*, man. You ought to show more *blery* respect for a superior officer. Besides, I'm not just a brigadier, you know. I'm on the Ministry staff now."

Kruger mimicked a slight bow. "So you've finally escaped from the field, eh?"

"That's right." Coetzee made a show of brushing invisible dust off his immaculately tailored jacket. "No more mud, flies, or snakes for me, man. I'm a happy desk warrior for the foreseeable future and glad of it."

Kruger took a closer look at his friend. Coetzee hated paperwork and red tape more than anything in the world, so he must be lying. But staff assignments were the price one paid for professional advancement. Nobody who wanted to make general someday could avoid them forever. And like Coetzee, Kruger knew he'd have to give up his own field command for a staff slot in the next couple of years. It wasn't something to look forward to, but it was inevitable.

"Attention!" The shouted command silenced all conversation in the crowded auditorium and brought every officer in the room to his feet.

The tall, lanky, white-haired figure of Gen. Adriaan de Wet, the SADF's commander, strode onto the stage. Kruger grimaced. He'd served two tours under de Wet—the first as a company commander in a brigade commanded by the older man, and the second as a deputy operations officer at the divisional level. Neither assignment had taught him much respect for de Wet's abilities as a combat commander or administrator. Army gossip said the general held on to his post by kissing up to whichever political faction held power at the moment—and Kruger believed the gossip.

De Wet crossed to a podium and stood silently for a moment, eyeing the assembled commanders and their staffs standing at attention. Then he waved them down. "At ease, gentlemen. Find a seat if you haven't already. We have much to do here today."

Kruger and Coetzee settled themselves in two seats near the back.

At an impatient nod from de Wet, teams of junior officers began moving up and down the auditorium's aisles, handing out red-tagged black binders. Astonished gasps and muttered exclamations followed them through the room.

Kruger took one of the binders from a pile given him by a somber-faced lieutenant and passed the rest on down the row. He scanned the first page and felt the blood draining from his face.

OPERATION NIMROD—MOST SECRET

SADF Order of Battle for Nimrod

44th Parachute Brigade
—Brigade HQ
—2nd Parachute Battalion
—3rd Parachute Battalion
—4th Parachute Battalion

8th Armored Division
—Division HQ
—81st Armored Brigade

—82nd Mechanized Brigade
—83rd Motorized Infantry Brigade
—84th Field Artillery Regiment

Elements of the 7th Infantry Division
—Division HQ
—71st Motorized Infantry Brigade
—72nd Motorized Infantry Brigade

Elements of the Air Force Transport Command
—No. 44 Squadron (C-47s)
—No. 28 Squadron (C-130s and C-160s)
—No. 18 Squadron (SA.330 Super Puma helicopters)
—No. 30 Squadron (SA.330 Super Pumas)

Elements of the Air Force Strike Command
—No. 2 Squadron (Mirage IIICZs)
—No. 7 Squadron (MB 326 Impalas)
—No. 4 Squadron (MB 326 Impalas)

Objectives for Nimrod

1) Reoccupation of the South-West Africa Territory (aka Namibia) as far north as the line running from Grootfontein through Kamanjab.

2) Restoration of complete military, political, and economic control over the reoccupied zones of the SWA.

3) Destruction of Swapo's armed forces and political structure.

4) Destruction of all ANC base camps and command centres inside the SWA.

General Concept of Operations

Nimrod is designed around a series of swift, powerful thrusts into Namibia by powerful mechanized, motorized, and airborne elements of the SADF. These attacks will be aimed at key communications hubs and other geographic points of operational value.

By bringing overwhelming force to bear against Swapo's poorly trained and ill-prepared troops, the units participating in Nimrod will be able to seize their initial objectives rapidly and at minimal cost. Once these have been achieved, the assault forces will regroup and redeploy for advances against their secondary targets.

Throughout the operation, force sizes must be carefully balanced against our limited ability to move supplies over Namibia's sparse road and rail network. Nevertheless, it is believed that the use of larger, more powerful units will give the speed so vital to the success of this campaign.

On D-1, advance elements of the 82nd Mechanized Brigade . . .

Kruger stopped reading. My God, he thought, this is madness. Absolute madness. But he couldn't ignore the excitement bubbling up within his dismay. No professional soldier could have remained unmoved. The briefing binder he held in his hand described the single largest South African military operation planned since the end of World War II. More men, more vehicles, and more firepower than he had ever imagined would be assembled for a single purpose. In a way it was bloody ironic. For months he'd been complaining about the ANC sanctuaries inside Namibia. But he'd certainly never dreamed anyone would seriously propose trying to solve the guerrilla threat with a full-scale conventional invasion.

Drums and bugles echoed in the innermost recesses of his mind—accompanying visions of long columns of tanks and APCs rolling forward through dust and smoke. He looked up from the operations plan. The faces of the officers around him showed the same odd mix of disbelief and pride.

Kruger shook his head. Real war was never glorious. Bugles could never be heard over the screams of the wounded or the roar of the guns. And yet . . .

He felt Coetzee touch his arm. "Well, Henrik? What do you think of our leader's little scheme, eh?"

Kruger looked at his friend. "Tell me true, Deneys . . . has the President lost his reason? We'll have to mobilize a large part of the Citizen Force to assemble all the units for this thing. What's going to happen to the factories and mines while half the skilled laborers and middle managers are off being soldiers? What idiot has convinced him that we can carry this out without paying a horrible price?"

"*Hsst!* Lower your voice, Henrik." Coetzee somehow looked suddenly older. He glanced quickly to either side, making sure that no other officers were in earshot. "Do you remember Duncan Grant, Andries van Rensburg, or Jan Kriel?"

Kruger nodded slowly, taken aback by Coetzee's sudden fear. He knew all three of them well. An image of big, black-bearded van Rensburg leading his men in a madcap charge against a Cuban machine-gun position inside Angola popped into his mind. Now there was a soldier with guts. And the other two were equally brave and equally competent officers.

Kruger scanned the auditorium again, checking faces more carefully. "I'm surprised they're not here today."

Coetzee looked grim. "They're gone, Henrik. Forced out of the Army. Along with several others."

"Good God!"

Heads turned to look in their direction and Kruger spoke more softly. "What the hell for? Those three were some of the best men we had. And with this craziness coming up" —he shook the black binder outlining Operation Nimrod— "we're going to need every experienced combat leader we can find."

"True." Coetzee's voice was flat, apparently drained of all feeling. Only the closest of his friends could possibly have recognized the contempt dripping from every word. "But it seems that Grant, van Rensburg, and Kriel each made the mistake of voicing their concerns about this plan concocted by the President and General de Wet."

"So?" Kruger was puzzled. The SADF's officer corps

prided itself on its professionalism and honesty. It had never been known as a haven for bootlickers—despite the occasional fool such as de Wet.

Now it was Coetzee's turn to look surprised. "My God, Henrik. You have been out in the field for too long a time, man. Things have changed since Haymans's death . . . and not for the better, either. Anybody who doesn't click his heels and mouth the right slogans gets labeled a 'defeatist malcontent' and shoved into early retirement.

"So if you want to keep your battalion, you'd best keep your head down, your mouth shut, soldier on, and hope the voters throw this gang out soon. After all, we still have our duty, right? They can't take that away from you unless you let them. *Klaar?*"

Kruger nodded, not sure that he could easily follow Coetzee's well-intended advice. Keeping quiet had never been one of his strong points. How long could an honorable man serve a government that treated brave men such as van Rensburg and the others so shabbily? Or carry out national security policies so unlikely to serve the long-term interests of the nation?

General de Wet's precise, perfectly modulated voice broke into his internal debate. "I hope all of you have taken the time to page through this operations order."

Heads nodded around the crowded auditorium.

"Good. Then we can move on to the details." De Wet flipped to the next page of his prepared text and looked up at his assembled officers. "I shall not bother to bore you with the higher strategy behind this decision. I believe that Nimrod's basic outline is as clear as it is bold."

The general smiled thinly. "Indeed, gentlemen, we are fortunate to serve a president and cabinet so versed in military matters and so dedicated to the survival of our nation."

Kruger noticed with some interest that fewer heads nodded this time. Evidently, some of the other officers hadn't been swept up by the prevailing determination to "get along by going along"—no matter what the cost and no matter how idiotic the policy. Perhaps there was some hope left for the Army.

Despite his doubts, Kruger paid close attention as de Wet began outlining specific assignments, objectives, and timetables. Coetzee was right. Whatever he might think of the direction being taken by Vorster's government, he was still a soldier with a sworn duty to obey legitimate orders issued by South Africa's legitimate rulers. There would be time enough later to debate the rights or wrongs of this Operation Nimrod. For the next several weeks he and his fellow commanders would have their hands full just trying to make sure their men were ready for battle.

He only hoped that Pretoria's shortsighted desire for vengeance against little Namibia wouldn't cost too many of them their lives.

JULY 30—IN THE NORTHERN TRANSVAAL, NEAR PIETERSBURG

The stars were out in force—shining cold and sharp through the high veld's dry, thin air.

Torches guttered from metal stands scattered around the brick-lined patio, creating a curiously medieval atmosphere. Acrid tobacco smoke rose from half a dozen burning cigarettes and mingled with the aroma of slowly roasting meat. Small groups of casually dressed middle-aged men clustered around the central barbecue pit. Their low, guttural voices and occasional hard-edged laughter carried far through the still, silent night.

Emily van der Heijden frowned as she leaned over the tiled kitchen countertop, filling glasses with soft drinks and lemon-flavored mineral water. Even as a child, she'd thought her father's friends were a rather dull, coarse, and unthinking bunch. Nothing in the snatches of conversation she heard drifting up from the patio changed that impression.

She'd already heard enough to make her ill. These men, most of them now high-ranking government officials, seemed callous almost beyond belief. Contemptible words such as *kaffir* rolled too easily off their tongues as they casually discussed the desirability of "shooting a few thousand more of the most troublesome black-assed bastards to cow the rest." All had nodded sagely at the idea. One had even gone so far as to claim that "there's nothing the black man respects more than a firm hand and a touch of the whip."

Emily paled with anger and slammed the glass she'd just filled down hard on a circular serving tray. Liquid slopped over the edge and stained her sleeve and white, full-length apron.

"Here now, *mevrou*. You'd better calm down and wipe that ugly sneer off your face before you embarrass your poor father. You wouldn't want to do that, would you?" Malice edged every word.

Angrier still, Emily turned her head to look at the dour old woman standing beside her at the counter. Tall and stick-thin beneath her shapeless black dress, Beatrix Viljoen had been her father's devoted housekeeper for as long as Emily could remember. And the two women had been enemies for every hour of every day of that time.

Emily despised the domineering older woman's ceaseless efforts to make her into a "proper" Afrikaner woman—a woman concerned only with the wishes of her husband, the health of her children, and the written, inflexible word of God. In turn, the housekeeper resented Emily's ability to go her own way, unbound by convention or propriety.

Their dealings over the years had been a series of cold, calculating, and venomous confrontations—exchanges wholly unmarked by any warmth or friendly feeling. As her widowed father's only child, Emily had generally come out ahead in these skirmishes.

All that had changed since her frantic phone call to get Ian out of jail and her enforced return home. Marius van der Heijden had been bitterly angry about his daughter's "sinful" liaison with the American reporter—someone he referred to only as "that godless and immoral Uitlander." Emily still wasn't sure which angered him more: her involvement with Ian, or the possibility that it could be used against him by one of his political rivals. It scarcely mattered. The hard fact was that his anger had put Beatrix Viljoen in the catbird seat.

It wasn't something the housekeeper ever let her forget.

"Well, *mevrou?* Am I not right?"

Emily saw the eager look in the other woman's eyes and bit down the ill-tempered reply she'd been about to make. Quarreling with Beatrix wouldn't help her escape this trap she'd put herself in to save Ian. Instead, she quietly picked up her loaded tray, turned, and walked out onto the dim, torchlit patio.

Silently fuming, she orbited through the separate groups of men—stopping only to allow them to pluck drinks off the tray she held in both hands. As always, their ability to ignore her was infuriating. Oh, they were courteous enough in a ponderous, patronizing way. But none of them bothered to hide their view of her as nothing more than a woman—as a member of the sex ordained by God for marriage, child-rearing, housework, and nothing more.

She stopped circling and stood beneath the fragrant, sweeping branches of an acacia tree planted long ago by her grandfather. Her tray held more empty than full glasses, but she was reluctant to leave the patio's relative quiet. Going back to the kitchen meant enduring another verbal slashing from Beaxtrix's knife-sharp tongue.

Emily took a deep breath of the fresh, cool night air, seeking refuge in the peaceful vista spreading outward from the torchlit patio. It was the one part of the Transvaal that she had missed in Cape Town. Her father's farmhouse sat on the brow of a low hill overlooking a shallow, open valley. Gentle, grassy slopes rolled down to a meandering, tree-lined stream—brimming during the summer rains, but dry now. Happier memories of her carefree childhood rose in Emily's mind, washing away some of the frustrations and tension of the present.

"I tell you, man, the leader is a genius. Practically a prophet touched by God himself."

"You speak true, Piet."

Emily stiffened. The voices were coming from the other side of the tree. Damn them! Was there nowhere she could go to find a moment's peace? She stayed still, hidden from view by the acacia's low, overhanging branches—hoping the two men, whoever they were, would wander off as quickly as they'd apparently come.

Cigarette smoke curled around the tree. "You remember the *braai* at his home last month? Two weeks before those kaffir swine killed Haymans and his own pack of traitors?"

The other man laughed. "Of course, I do. I tell you, Piet, at first I thought the leader had been smoking some of his field hands' dagga. Telling us to be ready for great change, for our days of power, and all that. But now I see that he was inspired, given the gift of foretelling like our own modern-day Solomon."

Emily's stomach churned. Karl Vorster . . . a prophet? The very thought seemed blasphemous. But could there be a horrifying truth behind the two men's sanctimonious ranting? Just as the symptoms of a deadly illness could be cloaked by those of another, less serious disease? Until now, she'd viewed Vorster's rise to power as simply the grotesque side effect of the ANC's trigger-happy attack on the Blue Train. But perhaps that was too simple a view. Had Vorster known of the ambush in advance?

My God, Emily thought, dazed. If that was true . . . the events of the past several weeks flickered through her mind—each taking on a newer, more sinister significance. The swift retribution for the train attack. Vorster's meteoric assumption of power. The immediate proclamation of various emergency decrees and punitive measures against South Africa's blacks—measures that could only have been drafted days or weeks before news of the Blue Train ambush reached Pretoria. It all fit. She tasted something salty in her mouth and realized suddenly that she'd bitten her own lip without being aware of it.

The first man spoke again, quieter this time so that Emily had to strain to make out his words. "Only one thing troubles me, Hennie. I cannot bring myself to trust all of those our leader allows around himself. Especially . . ."

"That pretty boy Muller?" the other finished for him.

"*Ja*. That one will be trouble for us all, you mark my words, Hennie."

Light flared around the tree trunk for a split second as the other man struck a match and touched it to a new cigarette. "Also true, Piet. And van der Heijden agrees with us. But what can we do about it? So long as Muller does the dirty work, he'll have the leader's ear and confidence. After all, no man throws away an ax that's still sharp."

"Then we must sharpen our own axes, my friend. And I know just the neck I'd like to use them on. . . ."

Their voices faded as the two men sidled away from the tree, returning to the larger group standing around the open-air barbecue pit.

After they'd gone, Emily stayed motionless for several minutes, lost in thought. Muller . . . the name was familiar. She'd heard it pronounced contemptuously by her father. And also by Ian. But who was this Muller? Clearly some kind of official in Vorster's old Ministry of Law and Order. An official disliked by his peers and apparently heavily involved in Vorster's "dirty work." Just the kind of man who would know whether or not Vorster had had advance warning of the ANC's plans to attack the Blue Train.

Her hands closed tighter around the tray. She had to find some way to get word of what she suspected to Ian. He would know how to turn the fragments she'd gathered into a coherent, supportable news report. Her heart pounded with excitement. Why, this could turn out to be the big break Ian had been searching for so desperately. If it could be proved, such a story was bound to create the biggest news flash in South Africa's recent history.

Her excitement grew as she realized that it could have even more far-reaching consequences—political consequences. Few things were more abhorrent to Afrikaners than treachery. So how would her fellow countrymen react to the discovery that their new president was nothing more than a blackhearted backstabber?

Emily scarcely noticed when Beatrix Viljoen tracked her down under the acacia tree and dragged her back to the kitchen.

CHAPTER 7

Capital Moves

AUGUST 3—STATE SECURITY COUNCIL CHAMBER, PRETORIA

Maps and charts covered the walls of the small, windowless meeting room. Each showed a separate piece of the elaborate preparations for Operation Nimrod—South Africa's planned reconquest of Namibia. And each had played a part in the defense minister's final briefing for Vorster and the members of his State Security Council.

For two hours, the men seated around the large rectangular table had been bombarded with facts, figures, and freely flowing military terms. Phase lines. Airlift requirements and resupply capabilities. Mobilization tables. Free-fire zones. All had been woven into a single seamless portrait of impending and inevitable victory.

As Constand Heitman, the minister of defense, took his seat, Karl Vorster's eyes flickered back and forth, scanning the faces of his subordinates. This was the first time most of them had heard the details of his plans for Namibia. He expected their reactions to be instructive.

He nodded his thanks to Heitman and turned to face the rest of the Council. ''Well, gentlemen? Are there any further questions?''

One of those seated at the far end of the table started to lean forward to speak and then stopped.

''Come, Helmoed, what troubles you? Have you seen some flaw in our proposal?'' Vorster's voice was deceptively calm.

The man, Helmoed Malherbe, the minister of industries and commerce, swallowed hard. No one was ever eager to appear to oppose any of the State President's cherished plans. A month in power had already shown Vorster's unwillingness to tolerate those who disagreed with him.

Malherbe cleared his throat. ''Not a flaw, Mr. President. Nothing like that. It is just a small concern.''

''Out with it then, man.'' Vorster's polite facade cracked slightly.

Malherbe bobbed his head submissively, obviously rattled. ''Yes, Mr. President. It's the scale of Citizen Force mobilization this operation requires. If Nimrod takes longer than planned, the prolonged absence of these men from our factories could have a serious impact on our economy.''

Vorster snorted. ''Is that all? Very well, Malherbe. Your concern is noted.''

He looked at the others around the table. ''So, gentlemen. You have heard the industries minister? If the kaffirs can hold back our tanks with their rifles for a month or two, we may have to ask our people to tighten their belts a little. Terrible, eh?''

Chuckles greeted his heavy-handed attempt at humor. Malherbe sat red-faced, shamed into silence.

Satisfied, Vorster turned to Erik Muller, sitting quietly by his side. ''What of the other black states—Mozambique, Zimbabwe, and the rest? Can they interfere with Nimrod's smooth completion?''

Muller shook his head decisively. ''No, Mr. President. Our covert operations have them all off-balance. They're too deeply embroiled in their own internal troubles to give us much trouble.''

Marius Van der Heijden snorted contemptuously, but said nothing.

Muller frowned. Van der Heijden was the leader of those on the cabinet who despised him, and the man's enmity was coming more and more to the surface. What had once been a simple rivalry for power and position was fast taking on all the signs of a blood feud. It was a feud Vorster had done little to discourage. Instead, the President seemed perfectly content to watch their infighting as if it were some kind of sporting event staged solely for his amusement.

And why not? Muller thought. Our sparring doesn't threaten his hold on power, and it prevents either of us from gaining too much control over the security services. His respect for Vorster's shrewdness climbed another notch—as did his carefully concealed dislike for the older man.

Vorster turned to the foreign minister, a gaunt, sallow man. Rumor said he was fighting some form of deadly cancer. It was a fight he seemed to be losing. "And what of the world's other nations, Jaap? Have we anything to fear from them?"

The foreign minister shook his head. "Nothing more than words, Mr. President. The Western powers have already done their worst. Their sanctions can scarcely be made stricter. And the Russians haven't the resources left to threaten us. They're too busy watching their empire crumble to be concerned with what happens ten thousand kilometers from Moscow."

Vorster nodded approvingly. "True. Very true."

He looked around the table again. "Very well, gentlemen. Any last comments?"

The silence dragged on for several seconds.

At last, one of the junior cabinet ministers raised a reluctant hand. "One thing still troubles me, sir."

"Go on." Vorster's temper seemed more in check than it had earlier.

"The Western intelligence services and spy satellites are bound to spot signs of our mobilization for Nimrod. Since it's essential that we obtain tactical and strategic surprise for this campaign, shouldn't we have some kind of cover story to explain our troop movements?"

Vorster smiled grimly. "A very good point, young Ritter. And one that has already been taken into consideration."

He nodded toward Fredrik Pienaar, the minister of information. "Fredrik and I have already begun to lay the groundwork. Tomorrow, I shall speak to our most loyal supporters from the Transvaal. And when the interfering democracies hear what I have to say, they'll be quite convinced that our soldiers are going to be used only for cracking kaffir heads inside this country. Little 'Namibia' will be the furthest thing from their minds."

The men around the conference table nodded in understanding and agreement.

"Good. That's settled, then." Vorster turned to the minister of defense. "Very well, Constand. Notify all commands. Operation Nimrod proceeds as planned."

South Africa was on its way to war.

AUGUST 4—ABC'S "NIGHTLINE"

The reporter stood at the corner of C and Twenty-third streets in downtown Washington, D.C. The gray government building behind her provided a neutral background for her carefully coiffed hair and green summer dress. More importantly, the sign saying STATE DEPARTMENT told her viewers where she was and that great events were afoot. Bright white TV lights lit the sky.

"If congressional Democrats can agree on anything these days, it's that the administration's response to recent developments in South Africa has been halting, confused, and wholly inadequate. And as Pretoria's violent crackdown on dissent continues, congressional demands for further economic sanctions seem likely to intensify. All this at a time when administration officials are already working late into the night—trying desperately to restructure a South Africa policy thrown badly out of whack."

The camera pulled back slightly, showing a lit row of windows at the top of the State Department.

"And something else seems certain. South African state

president Karl Vorster's latest public harangue will do absolutely nothing to douse the sanctions furor building up on Capitol Hill. If anything, his rhetoric appears calculated to send apartheid opponents around the world into fits."

She disappeared from the screen, replaced by footage showing Vorster standing on a flag-draped dais. The bloodred, three-armed-swastika banners of the Afrikaner Weerstandbeweging mingled with South African blue-, white-, and orange-striped national flags.

Vorster's clipped accent made his words seem even harsher. "We have given the blacks of our country every chance to participate in a peaceful exchange of ideas. Every chance to work toward a sharing of power and increased prosperity, for them and for all South Africans."

He paused dramatically. "But they have shown themselves to be unworthy! Their answer to reform is murder! They reply to reason with violence! They are incapable of peaceful conduct, much less of participating in the government. They have had their chance, and they will not have another. Never again! That I promise you, never again."

A roar of approval surged through the hall and the camera panned around, showing a sea of arm-waving, cheering white faces.

As the thunderous applause faded, the camera cut back to the reporter standing on the State Department steps.

"Vorster's speech, one of his first since taking over as president, came at the close of a day-long visit to the rural Transvaal, his home territory and a stronghold of ultraconservative white opinion. And nobody who heard him speak can have any doubt that he's giving South Africa's diehards just what they've always wanted. Tough words and tougher action.

"This is Madeline Sinclair, for 'Nightline.' "

The camera cut away to show the program's New York–based anchorman. "Thank you, Madeline. Following this break, we'll be back with Mr. Adrian Roos, of the South African Ministry of Law and Order, Mr. Ephriam Nkwe, of the now-banned African National Congress, and Senator Steven Travers of the Senate Foreign Relations Committee."

The anchorman's sober, serious image vanished, replaced by a thirty-second spot singing the praises of a Caribbean cruise line.

AUGUST 5—THE RUSSELL SENATE OFFICE BUILDING, WASHINGTON, D.C.

Sen. Steven Travers's innermost congressional office was decorated with a mixture of autographed photos, the Nevada state flag, and a stuffed lynx nicknamed Hubert by his aides. "Hubert" disappeared whenever any of the most prominent animal-rights lobbyists paid a visit. But the lynx always reappeared to reassure home-state visitors that Travers—no matter how liberal he might be in foreign affairs—was still the plain, gun-toting cowboy his campaign commercials always showed.

The photos crowding the office's rich, wood-paneled walls included shots of the senator with his wife and family, with two presidents (both Democrats), and with several Hollywood stars—all famous for the various liberal causes they supported. A recent addition was a picture of himself in the Capitol rotunda, shaking hands with ANC leader Nelson Mandela.

The pictures all showed a tall, slim man with sandy hair slowly going gray and a handsome, angular face. He looked good in a suit—a fact that hadn't endeared him to other, less telegenic senators back when cameras first started recording every minute of the Senate's floor debates for posterity. Right now the suit hung on a hanger in his office closet, and Travers lounged comfortably behind his desk wearing jeans, a Lacoste shirt, and loafers.

His small, normally neat office seemed crowded with two legislative aides, two staff lawyers, and a close friend. Coffee cups and boxes of doughnuts littering the floor and desk made it clear that they had either started very early or worked very late.

"Hey, guys, time's awasting. I've got a committee meeting

in three hours," said Travers, looking at his watch, "with a CBS interview thirty minutes before that."

He started to yawn and then closed his mouth on it. "Not that the 'Nightline' spot didn't come out pretty good, but I can't keep spouting the same stuff over and over. Things are going wrong too fast over there."

Travers reached forward and pulled a red-tagged manila folder out of the pile on his desk. "I mean, look at this!" He flipped the folder open and tapped the first sheet. "The CIA says that bastard Vorster's even mobilizing more troops to go after the black townships. People are gonna look to me to provide the Senate's response, and I can't just go on repeating the same old tired calls for more sanctions. I need something new—something that'll grab some headlines and grab Pretoria by the throat."

Travers had championed the antiapartheid cause in the Senate ever since his election two terms ago. It had been a happy marriage of personal belief with a popular cause. And now he was one of the senators first on the media's list for official reaction whenever South Africa hit the news.

"Steve's right. This is his chance to take the lead on this issue in the public mind. The rest of these fuds up here on the Hill will just thunder and blast without really saying anything. The media wants an American answer to this South African problem. And whoever gives 'em one is gonna be their fair-haired boy for quite a while." George Perlman was Travers's political advisor and reality check. He'd spent most of the night watching the brainstorming, the arguments—only speaking when the discussion wandered or when he felt a fresh viewpoint was needed.

Perlman was a short, balding man dressed in slacks and a pullover sweater. As a seasoned old campaigner, he was ensconced in the most comfortable chair in the office. He was fifteen years older, but despite their age difference, he and the senator had become friends years ago. It was a friendship cemented by the fact that Perlman had masterminded Travers's successful reelection campaign.

Perlman continued, "Plus, with the White House moving

so slowly on this thing, we can slam the President effectively and pick up some points from the party faithful. And now's a real good time to do that. We could sure use some first-rate recruiting PR to bring in the volunteers and the big-buck contributors."

The men crowded into Travers's office nodded. As always, Perlman's political instincts were right on target. The next presidential election might be more than three years away, but three years was the blink of an eye when you were contemplating setting up a national campaign organization. And even though the senator hadn't yet made up his mind to push for the nomination, he always believed in keeping his options open.

"True." Travers's eyes flickered toward a calendar. Twenty-nine months to the first primaries. "But I'm still hanging out there without anything new to say."

He looked back toward one of his legislative aides. "Got any more ideas, Ken?"

Ken Blackman was the senior of Travers's two Foreign Relations Committee staffers. A liberal firebrand since his student days at Brown University, he helped draft the legislation that kept the senator's name in good standing with the right D.C.-based lobbying groups. He was ambitious, and nobody could doubt that he had hitched his wagon firmly to Travers's rising star.

Short and thin, he paced in the small space available, almost turning in place with every third step. "I think we should stick with a serious call for deeper, more meaningful sanctions. Not just petty stuff like Krugerrands, but everything that makes South Africa's economy tick over. We could back that up with strong pressure on other countries to cut their own trade with Pretoria even further."

David Lewin, Travers's other aide and Blackman's biggest in-house critic, shook his head. "Wouldn't do any good. There isn't that much left to cut. Our trade with South Africa is already so low that they won't miss the rest." He held a list of Commerce Department import-export figures out in front of him like a shield.

"It would still be symbolic. It would show them we don't like what they're doing," Blackman argued. His nervous pacing accelerated.

Travers wagged a finger at him. "C'mon, Ken. You know what an Afrikaner thinks of outside opinion. Calling a Boer pigheaded is a compliment over there."

Lewin nodded. "Besides, nobody can agree on whether the sanctions we already have in place have any effect—positive, negative, or none at all. I've seen persuasive arguments for all three cases. And the South Africans aren't talking."

"They were quick enough to ask us to lift them after they let Mandela out of prison!" Blackman's face was red. Sanctions were the antiapartheid's equivalent of the Ten Commandments. Questioning their effectiveness was like asking the pope if he really believed in God.

"Yeah. But they still didn't make any new reforms when we refused." Lewin moderated his tone, becoming more conciliatory. The senator was pretty clearly coming down on his side of this argument, so it didn't make a lot of sense to piss Blackman off any further. After all, they still had to share an office with each other. "There are too many stronger political forces, local forces, in South Africa for simple economic sanctions to have much effect."

He shrugged. "And even if the old Pretoria government could have been influenced by sanctions, how about a hardliner like Vorster? Hell, all we'd probably be doing is giving him new ammunition on the domestic front. Some real 'circle the wagons, boys, the Uitlanders are coming' stuff. The diehard Afrikaners lap that up like candy."

Despite seeing Travers nodding, Blackman tried again. "Look, I'm not saying a tougher sanctions bill will bring a guy like Vorster to his knees, begging for our forgiveness. But it's a step our friends on this issue will expect us to take. And if TransAfrica and the rest see us backing off something this bread-and-butter, they're going to start yelling that we've sold out to the 'do nothing' crowd over at the White House."

A sudden silence showed that he'd hit the mark with that. Political pressure groups had an avid addiction to name-calling. They also had notoriously short memories and a tendency to see betrayal in any act of moderation. And with a possible run for the presidency coming up, Travers couldn't afford to get caught in a mudslinging match with his own allies.

Perlman caught the senator's eye and motioned gently toward the corner where Blackman waited, dancing back and forth from foot to foot.

"Good call, Ken," Travers agreed. "We'll work up some more stringent export-import restrictions. Just so long as we all realize they won't go anywhere and wouldn't do much good even if we could get 'em past a presidential veto."

Blackman nodded, satisfied to have won even a token victory. He started scribbling notes on a yellow legal pad. Lewin looked amused.

One of the lawyers piped up, "Can we put pressure on other countries to do more? How about on the British? They're South Africa's largest trading partner."

Travers shook his head regretfully. "Not a chance. The Brits have cut back some, but any more sanctions aimed at Pretoria are going to have to be their own idea. The EEC's been all over them for years, and they've never been able to influence London. Besides, the UK's backed us too many times in some real tight spots. You don't twist your best friend's arm. I'd get killed in the full committee if I tried to push a bill like that."

Blackman looked up from his legal pad, his pen tapping rhythmically against his lower front teeth. "How about direct financial support for the ANC or some of the other black opposition groups?"

The other lawyer, a recent Harvard graduate named Harrison Alvarez, laughed cynically. "Jesus, the Republicans would love that."

He mimicked the hushed, breathless tones so common in campaign hit pieces: "Did you know that Senator Travers supports U.S. taxpayer funding for a terrorist movement with socialist aims?"

Alvarez gestured toward a stack of press clippings on Travers's desk. "I mean, Ken, get real. The ANC just killed half the South African government, for Christ's sake!"

"They deny responsibility," Blackman retorted.

"You better believe it, after all the heat they've taken lately." Travers shook his head slowly. "Let's face facts. The ANC is the prime suspect in the attack on Haymans's train. Now, I wouldn't put it past a thug like Vorster to manufacture black guerrilla bodies on demand, but why should he need to?"

He shrugged his shoulders, as if admitting that his own question was unanswerable. "Besides, even if the ANC's not responsible for the train massacre, the Republicans would still beat us over the head with it. We have to hold the high ground on this issue—call for popular actions while the administration refuses to move. Feeding money to guys with AK-47s isn't going to cut it."

The others muttered their agreement.

Blackman started pacing again. "Okay, if we can't affect the South Africans themselves, how about doing something to ease their stranglehold on their next-door neighbors?"

"Like what?" Travers sounded tentative.

Blackman persisted. "A large-scale aid program for all the countries bordering South Africa. Economic assistance, maybe even military help."

Lewin stepped in, eager to score a few more points at his rival's expense. "We'd still be giving aid to Marxist governments. The Republicans—"

"In this day and age being a Marxist isn't a crime. It's just stupid," Perlman cut in. He looked thoughtful. "It's a good dynamic. All of those countries are dirt-poor. Even if their governments are corrupt or Marxist or both, we can still show real need."

He grinned at Travers. "Yeah, Steve, I can see your speeches now. The Republicans, using 'petty politics' to decide whether or not kids get the food they need. We could do a lot with that."

Blackman looked faintly disgusted. The senator's friend and longtime advisor always saw everything through a tightly focused political lens. Sometimes it seemed that simple right and wrong escaped his notice.

And Blackman was sure that expanded aid to the frontline

states was right. South Africa had kept its neighbors weak and poor for far too long—locked into total dependence on the white regime's industries, transportation system, and power supply. U.S. assistance that reduced that state of helplessness would be the surest way to strike at the Vorster government.

Alvarez looked less certain. "And how much of any money we send over there is really going to get past these corrupt governments?"

"Who cares?" Travers shrugged. "Once we've passed the dollars on to them, it's out of our hands. We can find some villages where they're unloading bags of food, or building roads. We'll make a trip there, take some dramatic pictures. Should be good for a few TV spots." He winked at Perlman.

Blackman ignored the crasser political implications. They were a necessary part of working in Washington. "I'd suggest going to Mozambique. They've been trying to build that railroad through to Zimbabwe for years, but South Africa's pet guerrilla force, Renamo, keeps blowing it up. If we could help Mozambique finish that rail line . . ."

Travers rubbed his chin thoughtfully. "Yeah. I like it." He sat back in his chair and gazed up at the ceiling. "You know the more I think about this the more I like it." He rocked forward. "Here's what I see. We put together a good-sized package of civilian and military aid for the frontline states, focusing on areas hit by South African–backed insurgencies. Say a five or six hundred million dollars' worth. Enough to really sting Pretoria. I think I can get something like that through the committee without too much trouble."

Lewin frowned. "The Appropriations Committee's going to be the big stumbling block. Where do we get the money?"

Travers grinned. "Simple. We reprogram the bucks out of the defense budget. Hell, the administration's already done that for Nicaragua and Panama. They've set the precedent. We'll just follow their lead."

There were broad smiles around the room. It was perfect. Nobody could accuse them of being fiscally irresponsible or boosting the budget deficit. And besides, the defense budget was fair game these days. Everybody wanted a piece of that pie, and calls for still another slice wouldn't raise too many eyebrows around Washington.

Travers paused, considering. "One thing more. What can South Africa do to retaliate, if we put a major aid program in place?"

"Against us? Nothing." Blackman's response was fast, almost automatic. There was silence for a moment as the rest considered the possibilities.

"Ken's right," Perlman said. "As few dealings as we have with South Africa, they wouldn't hurt us by cutting trade from their end."

"What about strategic minerals?" Alvarez asked. "The chromium, titanium, and the rest? They could chop sales of those. DoD and Commerce could come down hard about the national security risks from that."

"And cut their own throats? Not a chance, Harry. They need that foreign credit for the stuff they do buy abroad, especially oil. That's about the only resource South Africa's not loaded with." Travers sighed. "The world's treasure house, run by a bunch of political cavemen—"

Blackman broke in. "The senator's right. Vorster and his people can't do squat about an aid bill. Oh, they'll probably step up their covert activities in the region. More raids, more propaganda—all of which will cost them money and more goodwill. If they keep at it, and if the frontline states ever get their act together, South Africa's gonna be bordered by some powerful enemies."

Travers decided they had a consensus. "All right, let's do it. I want you two to start drafting the specifics." He pointed to Blackman and Lewin and then glanced at his watch. "I need an outline in an hour. In the meantime, I'm going to make some phone calls. George?" He looked over at his advisor.

"I like it. Whether this bill passes or not, it's a political win for us. I'll do some calling as well. I'll take care of the media and the national committee. I think most of the party will like the idea. We'll give it a big push." Perlman chuckled. "Another test of strength with the 'no-vision' administration."

They all smiled.

AUGUST 6—NATIONAL SECURITY COUNCIL MEETING, THE WHITE HOUSE

When the Vice President entered the room, all conversation ceased, both by custom and by design. NSC meetings were supposed to start on time and their participants didn't like wasting precious minutes exchanging meaningless pleasantries. Those were reserved for Washington's favorite indoor sport—the high-powered, late-evening cocktail party. Working hours were for work.

Vice President James Malcolm Forrester shared that same driving dedication to the job. He strode briskly to the chair at the head of the table and sat down. Civil nods greeted him.

After a somewhat rocky start, Forrester had come to be regarded by his administration colleagues as a solid team player and a first-rate organizer. He paid a lot of attention to his duties as the NSC's chairman, which was appropriate, since it was his most important role. Attending foreign funerals and delivering speeches to an often endless round of political fund-raisers couldn't compare with helping to decide serious questions of national security.

The NSC reported directly to the President, recommending courses of action to him on any matters relating to war and peace. Its permanent members included the secretaries of state and defense, the national security advisor, and the director of the CIA. Other agency and department heads were asked to sit in or provide information as needed. In a very real sense, the NSC represented a focal point for every major intelligence, military, and diplomatic resource possessed by the United States. In a crisis, its frantic, fast-paced deliberations could result in the dispatch of urgent communiqués, spy planes, carrier battle groups, or even divisions of ground troops to any point on the globe.

But no imminent doom appeared to menace the United States or its allies, so the atmosphere was relaxed. This meeting was routine.

So routine in fact that several of the NSC's permanent members hadn't bothered to attend. Instead, they'd sent a mixed bag of deputies to fill the seats around the meeting room's large central table. Each was accompanied by an assistant ready to handle all the necessary briefing and background materials, and several stenographers waited to record every remark.

Typed agendas rested in front of each person, and clear crystal pitchers of iced coffee and lemonade occupied the middle of the table. They would be empty by the time the meeting adjourned. Even this far below ground, the White House air-conditioning system couldn't completely cool Washington's sweltering late-summer air.

The subbasement meeting room had an oddly colonial appearance, with wooden wainscoting and elaborate molding on its low ceiling. The multimedia projection screen hung on one wall would have jarred an architect's sensibilities, but this was a working space—not a tourist showcase. There would never be any photo opportunities here. The only decorations on its walls were maps of the world, the USA, and the Soviet Union.

The Vice President flipped to the first page of his agenda and watched as the others followed suit.

Forrester was not a tall man, something that was rarely noticed because he always seemed to be in motion. Trotting down airplane ramps in foreign countries. Striding into flag-draped banquet halls. Or racing through a rapid-fire round of golf at the Congressional country club. He often joked that he was actually six foot eight, but had put the extra inches in escrow to avoid appearing taller than the President. It was a joke that reflected the all too bitter truth that the vice presidency was an office with too much ceremony and too little responsibility, but right now he had real work to do.

He tapped the table gently, calling the meeting to order. "All right. Let's get down to it."

He tossed the printed agenda back onto the table. "Unfortunately, the first item before us didn't come up in time to make it onto the documents sent to you for review last night. South Africa popped up at my breakfast with the President this morning. He's asked us to discuss a response to Pretoria's latest actions—including this new troop call-up the wire services are reporting."

Some of the men sitting around the table looked momentarily blank. South Africa was a long way outside the boundaries of their ordinary day-to-day concerns. For most of their professional lives, the continuing U.S.-Soviet military and political tug-of-war had been the central reality. Some of them still found it difficult to adjust to a world where conflicts didn't necessarily slide neatly into the usual East versus West pigeonhole.

Besides, data on Africa's internal affairs rarely made it through the screening process managed by each cabinet department's and intelligence agency's junior staffers. All too often it wound up occupying waste space on rarely punched-up computer disks or gathering dust in rusting file drawers.

Forrester hid a wry grin. For once, he had an advantage over most of the experts around this table. As a senator, he'd served on the Foreign Relations Committee and had spent a lot of time fencing with antiapartheid zealots on the Senate floor.

He looked toward the end of the table, toward a dapper, bookish-looking little man whose narrow face bore a somewhat incongruous full beard and neatly trimmed mustache. "Look, Ed, why don't you give us a quick rundown on our recent 'relations' with South Africa's new government." He didn't bother to hide the irony in his voice.

"Certainly, Mr. Vice President." Edward Hurley, the assistant secretary of state for African affairs, nodded politely. His presence at the meeting was the result of a hurried, early-morning call by Forrester to the State Department.

Hurley studied the faces around the table. "Essentially, our relations with the new government headed by President Vorster can best be summed up as 'cold and barely correct.' "

He paused, took off his tortoiseshell glasses, and started cleaning the lenses with a rumpled handkerchief. "We had another indication of just what that means last week when our ambassador, Bill Kirk, visited Vorster for the first time since the Blue Train massacre. Bill had instructions from the secretary to find out just how far Pretoria plans to go in reintroducing strict apartheid."

Hurley smiled thinly and put his glasses back on. "Unfortunately, Ambassador Kirk never had the chance to ask. Instead, he was forced to sit through a half-hour-long lecture by Vorster on *our* foreign policy failures in the region. Shortly after that, Pretoria notified us that they were unilaterally reducing the number of our embassy staff personnel. And Vorster's flatly refused all further attempts to meet with him. We've been shunted down to below the ministerial level."

Muttered disbelief rolled around the table. What the hell was South Africa's new leader playing at? Political disagreements between Washington and Pretoria were common enough, but why the flagrant and apparently calculated discourtesy?

The Vice President watched his colleagues closely, wondering how they'd react to the full version of Vorster's snub. Just reading Kirk's telexed summary of the meeting had raised his own blood pressure.

Apparently Kirk hadn't even been given the opportunity to say hello. Instead, Vorster had launched straight into a scathing diatribe full of contempt for what the South African called "America's shameful and treacherous conduct." The man had gone on to accuse the U.S. of meddling in Pretoria's internal affairs—of inciting "innocent blacks" to violence and disorder. Forrester assumed that was a reference to several recent State Department statements deploring the white regime's police crackdown on the black townships. Hardly justification for what amounted to a full-fledged kick in the teeth.

He eyed the ponderous, white-haired man sitting to his immediate right. Forrester had long suspected that Christopher Nicholson, former federal judge and current director of the CIA, spent almost as much time developing sources inside the White House as he did administering the Agency's far-flung overseas intelligence-gathering. His presence at what had been expected to be a routine NSC meeting confirmed that suspicion.

The Vice President decided to see just how thoroughly Nicholson had prepared. "Got any bio on this clown Vorster, Chris?"

Forrester was a firm believer in knowing as much as possible about the world leaders he might have to deal with. Despite the reams of bloodless statistical analysis by legions of social scientists, economists, and other "experts," world politics still all too often seemed to boil down to a question of personalities.

To his credit, the CIA chief avoided looking smug. "Fortunately I do, Mr. Vice President. We've also run through the archives and come up with some photos of the gentleman in question."

Nicholson's aide flipped through a thick sheaf of papers and handed several heavily underlined sheets to his boss. The CIA director took them and nodded politely toward a junior staffer standing near the door. "Anytime, Charlie."

The lights dimmed slowly and a slide projector whirred—throwing a grainy, black-and-white photo onto the wall screen. The photo showed a much thinner, much younger Karl Vorster.

"Karl Adriaan Vorster. Born 1928 in the northern Transvaal. Law degree from Witwatersrand University in 1950. Sociology degree from Stellenbosch University in 1956. Became a member of the Broederbond sometime in the early fifties, probably in 1953 . . ."

Forrester nodded to himself as Nicholson droned on, running through Vorster's steady, if unspectacular, rise to power within the ruling National Party. As a young lawyer, the South African must have been in on the very beginnings of Pretoria's efforts to codify racial segregation and white domination—its policies of strict apartheid. His membership in the Broederbond, South Africa's secretive ruling elite, made that a certainty.

The slide projector clicked to another photo, this one showing Vorster climbing out of the back of an official car. "Right after he got his doctorate, he joined the government. Since then, he's held a succession of increasingly senior posts in both the Bureau of State Security and Ministry of Law and Order."

Nicholson turned to face the Vice President. "Essentially, sir, this man Vorster has been working to keep the black population in its place for over forty years."

Another photo. This time showing an older, more jowly Vorster standing beside a gaunt, balding man in a plain black cassock. "He's also very religious, belongs to the Dutch Reformed Church, which is the mainstream religious denomination in South Africa. Sprinkles biblical references throughout virtually every speech or even conversation. Naturally, he's an active member of a group opposing racial reform within the church."

Naturally. Forrester frowned. "What about the past few years? What's he been up to?"

The CIA chief flipped to the back page of his notes, then raised his eyebrows. "He's been very active lately. He's made a lot of statements and given a lot of speeches against reforming the apartheid system. While the rest of the National Party has slowly changed, he hasn't budged an inch."

Nicholson's pudgy forefinger settled on a paragraph near the bottom of the page, and his lips pursed into a soundless whistle. "In fact, back in 1986, when they abolished the law against interracial marriages, he said, quote, The mixing of the white and lower races can only result in a reversal of the evolutionary process. Unquote."

Nervous laughter rose from the rest of the group. The idea that anyone in this day and age, especially a head of state, could actually hold such a grotesque belief seemed impossible to accept. Nicholson's black assistant grimaced.

Forrester shook his head. "If he's been so out of step with his own party, how's he managed to stay in government so long? And why would he want to?"

Hurley answered him. "The Haymans government probably kept him on as a sop to their own conservative wing. They'd been taking a lot of flak from the Herstige National Party and the rest of the right-wing splinter groups. I'd guess the thought was that Vorster's continued presence in the cabinet might help dissuade more conservatives from jumping ship to the opposition."

Forrester nodded. He wasn't a stranger to that kind of reasoning.

"As for why he stayed on?" Hurley shrugged. "Probably figured he could get farther in the National Party, even if he agreed more with the radical right."

"Exactly," Nicholson agreed. The CIA director tapped another page of notes. "But sources say he's also met with leaders of the AWB—the neo-Nazi Afrikaner Resistance Movement—and the Oranjewerkers, a far-right group that wants the Orange Free State and the Transvaal to secede from the RSA so they can form their own 'pure' white societies. Rumor has it that Vorster's even a covert member of some of these groups."

"Probably more than that." Hurley was cleaning his glasses again. "AWB flags and pins are showing up all throughout the South African government."

"Swell. Just swell." Forrester nodded to the staffer near the lights. They came back on, revealing a tableful of worried-looking men and women. "So we've got an incipient Nazi in power over there. And if that quote is typical, one who appears to be only loosely connected to reality. And now he's decided to pick some kind of diplomatic fight with us. Over what we don't know."

Hurley resettled his glasses on his nose. "Getting into a verbal shoving match with us isn't as crazy as it sounds. It'll play well with his hard-core supporters. Gives him another scapegoat to blame for any foreign policy or economic problems."

Nicholson nodded. "It's standard Afrikaner practice. Blame the communists. Blame the blacks. Blame backstabbing by Washington or London. Blame anybody but themselves."

"So how do we respond?" Forrester's question was partly rhetorical. He already knew all the standard answers. They could recommend recalling the U.S. ambassador for consultations or suggest reducing Pretoria's diplomatic staff in a tit-for-tat exchange. But that wasn't enough. The man in the Oval Office would want more.

Forrester rubbed his chin. "Do we have any official visits scheduled in the next few months?" Canceling an already slated trip was one way to slap another government in the face for perceived wrongs. It wasn't the most direct way to retaliate, but at least it usually didn't add to the budget deficit or cost additional taxpayer dollars.

One of Hurley's aides shook his head after consulting a briefing book. "I'm afraid not, Mr. Vice President. No official contacts. Several requests for low-level visits. We've been denying those as per standard policy."

Hurley leaned forward. "What about supporting deeper sanctions? Congress is starting to make noises in that direction."

Forrester held up a hand. "That's a 'no go' from word one, Ed. The President's firm on that. Further economic sanctions wouldn't work. They'd only hurt some of the people we're trying to help. He's convinced we should put our efforts elsewhere. There's got to be some other leverage we can use against South Africa."

Hurley looked doubtful. "I can't see anything, at least not right off the bat. We don't have any close allies in the region—no strong ties to any other country, in fact. Certainly nobody the Afrikaners would listen to. There aren't any large communities of U.S. citizens down there, and our corporations have slowly been divesting themselves—more from their own concern over Pretoria's instability than from any political pressure here at home."

The little man shrugged. "So on a day-to-day basis, the South Africans have little to do with us, and we have little to do with them. I just don't see what the new pressure points are."

An assistant secretary from the Commerce Department spoke up. Forrester couldn't even remember the man's name. "What about this idea that Senator Travers pushed last night on TV? What about funneling additional aid to the frontline states?"

"Pure grandstanding!" Nicholson snorted. The CIA director and Travers had locked horns on foreign policy more than once in the past. "I've seen the dossiers of most of the leaders of those countries. My God, I doubt if more than one cent on the dollar would ever make it past their Swiss bank accounts."

Forrester held his tongue. He shared Nicholson's assessment of the practical value of Travers's proposed foreign aid package. But he'd learned long ago not to underestimate the Nevada senator's ability to read the domestic political scene. And he knew the President had learned the same lesson. Travers's proposal was being given serious consideration by the nation's chief executive. It was grotesque, but given the way Washington sometimes worked, three or four hundred million wasted dollars might be viewed as a cheap price for blunting a political rival's initiative.

The Vice President mentally shrugged. So be it. That was a call the President would have to make. He turned back to the debate still raging around the conference table.

Obviously impatient with all the hemming and hawing around the table, a lean-faced man wearing the stars and uniform of a U.S. Army lieutenant general sat forward.

"Yes, General?"

Gen. Roland Atkinson, the Joint Chiefs' representative, pointed a long, bony finger straight at Hurley. "Look, Ed, what's your best guess about where that damned place is heading? I mean . . . hell, is this Vorster character going to be around long enough for us to really worry about?"

Forrester nodded to himself. The general had a good point.

Hurley looked somber. "I'm afraid things are going to get a lot worse. South Africa was just starting to build up some goodwill abroad as reforms were made. This reversal is going to cost them. Remember what happened when China changed horses?"

Heads nodded gingerly. Tiananmen Square was still a sore point for the administration.

"Unfortunately, we don't know just what Vorster has planned. He's certainly surprised us with this complete reversal of previous government policy." Hurley shook his head. "It's hard to predict the effects when you don't even know what the causes will be."

Forrester tried to pin him down. "C'mon, Ed. We've seen what Vorster is like. We've seen those police sweeps. And now they're bringing the Army into it. I think his ultimate aims are pretty clear. He seems damned determined to bring back the 'good old days' of total apartheid. Assume that's what he's after . . . what happens then?"

Nicholson spoke up. The CIA director looked faintly ill. "Massive instability, Mr. Vice President. Despite Pretoria's ban and bloody crackdown, our intelligence sources confirm that the ANC and other opposition groups are rapidly growing in strength and organization. Their guerrilla organization is rebuilt and is now attracting a lot of new recruits. Vorster's pushed a lot of more moderate blacks into the arms of anybody with guns and the guts to use them."

He stopped talking and turned toward Hurley.

The assistant secretary of state was quiet for a moment longer, obviously evaluating his response. "Director Nicholson is right. We can expect to see many more deaths, mostly black, as the violence mounts." He took a deep breath. "Then, at some point, a general revolt. The black population decides they've got nothing to lose and just starts a civil war. Forget a 'people power' revolt like the Philippines. This would be very bloody. And there's no guarantee the blacks could win. The whites have tremendous advantages—both organizationally and militarily."

Forrester nodded somberly. He'd seen the reports on South Africa's Defense Force. At full mobilization, it could put three hundred thousand men in the field—well-trained troops equipped with thousands of armored cars, highly sophisticated field artillery, close-support aircraft, and grim determination.

Hurley sighed. "This wouldn't be an organized revolution like Romania, with a single, powerful resistance group. The ANC, the Zulu Inkatha party, and the Pan-Africanist Congress would all be fighting each other as well as the whites.

We'd probably end up with something like Beirut, but spread all over the southern tip of Africa—not just confined to a single city."

The Commerce Department representative looked appalled. "Jesus, if that happens, gold prices would go through the roof. That would crucify the value of the dollar." He stared down at the table. "Our balance of payments is bad enough now. It could get really bad."

The others around the table knew exactly what he meant. Higher unemployment, higher inflation, higher interest rates, and the very real risk of a global trade war that could spark a new Great Depression.

Forrester glanced at Nicholson. "What about strategic minerals?"

The CIA director arched an eyebrow. "Spot shortages, of course. Maybe something worse, depending on how the other suppliers like the Soviet Union react."

Forrester asked Hurley, "One final question. How long before the lid comes off?"

Ed Hurley looked worried, a little like a caged animal. "There are so many unknowns, sir. I wouldn't even begin . . ."

The Vice President spoke reassuringly. "C'mon, Ed, nobody's going to write it down. Can you at least put limits on it?"

"It might be years, sir. The black population of South Africa existed for years under apartheid without revolting. They will need some intolerable situation to push them over the edge. With a loose cannon like Vorster, that might happen tomorrow. Other than those general thoughts, I really can't say."

Forrester shook his head wearily and looked around the table. "All right. We're all agreed that open civil war in South Africa would be a disaster for the United States and for all our major allies. It would drive up prices of strategic minerals and other critical items. The cost of everything using them would go up—and that's about everything that's made in this country. Aside from those costs, the price of gold rising sharply could trigger panics and buying sprees. A civil war in South Africa could bring on a massive depression here in the U.S., maybe worldwide.

"It's a long-term threat, but with Vorster in charge, it's a very probable outcome. Now the question is, just what do we recommend to the President?"

"Increase our stockpiles of strategic minerals." General Atkinson seemed certain. "Hell, we can't do much to influence what goes on inside that crazy country. I'd say we'd better start preparing for the worst."

Forrester nodded his agreement. "We'll need a list of those minerals unique to South Africa."

Hurley shook his head. "I'm sorry, Mr. Vice President, but we'll need to put any major commodity South Africa produces on that list. If things fall apart over there, prices on all of them will skyrocket."

That made sense. Anything that closed down South Africa's mines would send panic buyers around the world scurrying for whatever resources were left.

Forrester scribbled a quick note to himself and then glanced down the table at General Atkinson. "All right, General. If the balloon does go up in Pretoria, do we have any military plans for that area? What if the President volunteers to move UN peacekeeping forces into the region? Can we lift them?"

Atkinson seemed at a loss. "Sir, I don't think we have any plans for operations down there. It's a long way from home."

"It's a long way from anywhere," Forrester agreed. "But let's start looking at the possibilities. How many troops could we pick up from some third country and move to South Africa without affecting our other strategic commitments? What if we have to evacuate our embassy or all the foreign nationals down there? How about sending a hospital ship with a naval escort?"

He saw the surprised looks on several of the faces around the table. "Look, gentlemen. This is all extremely speculative. But I am suggesting that we start exploring our options—all our options."

He scowled. "I, for one, am sick and tired of being blindsided by world events. So if things go from bad to worse in Pretoria, I want the data we'd need to make smart decisions on hand. Not sitting in some goddamned filing cabinet, five years out of date. Clear?"

Heads nodded meekly. Good. Maybe it paid to throw a mini–temper tantrum every once in a while.

Forrester turned to General Atkinson. "Okay, Roland. Have your planners put something together and keep it in your back pocket. If things turn ugly, we need to be seen making some positive moves down there."

Atkinson made a note to himself.

"One thing more, ladies and gentlemen." Forrester looked sternly at the other men and women seated around the table. "The fact that I've asked the general to draw up plans for hypothetical contingencies"—he stressed the word—"*hypothetical* contingencies in South Africa is something that doesn't leave this room. No press leaks. No heads-up warnings for your favorite congressmen or senators. Nothing. We don't need a public firestorm over what may turn out to be nothing more than a nasty internal dispute."

Both Nicholson and Hurley looked relieved.

The CIA director leaned forward.

"Yes, Chris?"

"Just one thing more, Mr. Vice President. I've got my people working on a continuing assessment of Vorster's government: biographies, possible courses of actions, and so on. Something to give our analysts more hard data to sink their teeth into." Nicholson frowned. "But with half the old leadership wiped out, and with things changing so fast, it's taking longer to produce the material than I'd like. I'd appreciate any help the other agencies and departments could give my people."

Forrester looked meaningfully at Hurley. "I'm sure that any of the other intelligence agencies with South Africa files will be more than happy to cooperate. Right, Ed?"

Hurley nodded ruefully, acknowledging the Vice President's unspoken criticism. From time to time, the State Department's Bureau of Intelligence and Research exhibited an unfortunate tendency to regard the CIA and the other intelligence agencies as overpaid and not overly bright errand boys. As a result, real interdepartmental cooperation often seemed more difficult to obtain than a ratifiable U.S.-Soviet strategic arms control treaty.

Satisfied that his message had gotten across and conscious of his next scheduled meeting, Forrester tapped the table. "All right, let's sum things up. As I see it, we recommend going tit for tat on the diplomatic front as a first step. Any objections to that?"

He looked slowly around the table. One by one, those present shook their heads. Staff reductions and strong notes were the small change in any diplomatic confrontation.

"Okay. I'll pass that on to the President this afternoon." Forrester shuffled his notepaper into a neat pile. "In the meantime, we'll put our staffs to work on more substantive responses. Up to and including expanded strategic minerals stockpiling and some low-key contingency plans for moving a UN peacekeeping force into the region should all hell break loose. And we'll recommend a heightened intelligence-gathering effort for the area. More satellite passes and more SIGINT work. That sort of stuff. Maybe we can get a better read on just what this Vorster character has in mind. Comments?"

More silence from around the table. Forrester's summary of their recommendations was on target. Left unspoken was the feeling that they'd once again labored mightily to produce more of what Washington was famous for: empty hot air.

As the NSC meeting broke up, Hurley leaned close to Forrester. "Patience isn't Vorster's strong suit, Mr. Vice President. I don't think we'll have to wait long to see what he's up to."

AUGUST 10—JAN SMUTS INTERNATIONAL AIRPORT, JOHANNESBURG, SOUTH AFRICA

The Jan Smuts International terminal building looked much like any other terminal in any other major airport anywhere in the world. Indecipherable boarding announcements and courtesy phone pages crackled over the public address system.

Cafeterias, bars, and small newspaper and book kiosks did a booming business as hungry, nervous, or bored travelers tried to pass the time before their flights. And television monitors showing arrivals and departures glowed from gleaming overhead metal stands.

But there were differences. Ominous differences. Most of those now waiting for incoming flights were men. Young men in their twenties and early thirties. Young men in military uniform—Citizen Force reservists summoned from their schools and jobs by Pretoria's recent Emergency Decree. Some looked as though their uniforms had shrunk or their stomachs had grown, but most were lean and fit—kept in shape by up to one full month of required military service in each calendar year.

Two American journalists in civilian clothes looked very much out of place in the sea of khaki-colored uniforms.

Ian Sherfield took his traveling case and identity papers from an unsmiling internal-security trooper and turned to help Sam Knowles. The little cameraman looked even more like a pack animal than usual. Pieces of video gear and sound equipment were slung across his sturdy back and shoulders and piled high on a squeaking, dented luggage cart.

"Behold the miracle of modern miniaturization." Knowles sounded disgusted. "Now instead of just being buried under the weight of a single camera, I can rupture myself carrying the camera plus the rest of this shit."

They started down the terminal, half-pushing and half-dragging the overloaded luggage cart.

"Just whose bright idea was this move anyway?" Knowles huffed as he awkwardly maneuvered around a clump of curious South African soldiers.

Ian grinned but didn't answer. The cameraman knew full well that he'd been badgering the New York brass for this change of location for nearly a month. With Parliament out of session and Vorster running the government practically single-handed, Cape Town was nothing but a pleasant backwater. Johannesburg, less than thirty miles from Pretoria, made a much more sensible base of operations. And since the network already leased a studio and satellite relay station in the city, New York's bean-counting accountants hadn't been able to complain about added costs. At least not much.

Besides, being in Johannesburg put him that much closer to Emily.

They emerged into weak, late-afternoon sunlight and the loud, echoing roar of traffic. Chartered buses and trucks carrying more uniformed reservists jammed nearly every foot of curb space outside the terminal building. A sharp, unpleasant tang of mingled auto exhaust and unburnt jet fuel permeated the air. Ian fought the urge to cough, suddenly remembering that, at five thousand feet above sea level, Johannesburg sometimes had nearly as many air pollution problems as Denver did, back in the States.

Knowles nudged him with one camera-laden shoulder, indicating a young, stick-thin black man dressed in a drab black suit, white shirt, and narrow black tie. He held aloft a hand-lettered sign with their names. Or at least a close approximation of their names. Sherfield's was misspelled.

"We're Sherfield and Knowles. What's up?" Ian had to yell to be heard over the sound of traffic.

The young black man gestured nervously over his shoulder toward a parked Ford Escort. "I am Matthew Sibena, *meneer*. I am to be your driver while you are here in Johannesburg. Meneer Thompson sent me to pick you up."

Ian nodded his understanding, surprised that Larry Thompson, the network's penny-pinching Jo'burg station chief, had gone to all this trouble. "Well, that's nice of him. But I'm sure that we'll be able to manage things ourselves. How about just dropping us off at the nearest car-hire firm on your way into the city?"

Sibena looked even more worried. "Oh, no, *meneer*. That is impossible. It is a new security regulation, you see. All foreign newsmen must now have a South African driver. That is why Meneer Thompson has hired me."

Ian swore under his breath. Vorster's government seemed to be doing everything it could to make the job of reporting events in South Africa even more difficult and more expensive. So now he and Knowles would have to work with this kid tagging along behind them. Ter-bloody-rific.

Then he shrugged and moved toward the parked car. They'd just have to see how things worked out. "Okay, you're our official driver. So let's drive."

The young black man looked greatly relieved.

Ian stopped in midstride and turned toward him. "One thing, Matt. Call me Ian. And that pack mule over there is Sam Knowles. Save the *meneer* crap for Afrikaners."

Sibena looked shocked at the idea of calling a white man by his first name. Then he nodded hastily, smiled shyly, and hurried forward to help Knowles pile his gear into the Escort's small trunk and its scarcely larger backseat.

While he worked, trying to squeeze bulky equipment packs into every available nook and cranny, Ian and Knowles exchanged a lingering, speculative glance. Matthew Sibena undoubtedly worked for the network. The only question was, just how many other employers did he have?

AUGUST 13—ALONG THE N1 MOTOR ROUTE, SOUTH OF JOHANNESBURG

Truck after truck roared past down the broad, multilane highway, mammoth diesel engines growling loud in the still night air. Some carried troops wedged tightly onto uncomfortable wood-plank benches. Others were piled high with crates of food, water, and ammunition. A few trucks towed 155mm and 25-pound howitzers wrapped in concealing canvas. Full-bellied petrol tankers brought up the rear, gears grinding as their drivers tried to keep up.

The convoy, one of many on the road that night, stretched for more than six kilometers, moving steadily south at forty kilometers an hour—heading toward the road junction where it would turn northwest off the main highway. Northwest toward Namibia.

Northwest toward war.

CHAPTER 8

The Diamond War

AUGUST 18—20TH CAPE RIFLES' FORWARD ASSEMBLY AREA, NEAR THE NAMIBIAN BORDER

Very little of the light provided by the small, battery-powered lamp leaked out through the edges of the command tent's tightly closed flap. But even those thin slivers of light seemed bright against the ink-black night sky outside. With the moon already down and dawn still an hour away, the battalion's ranked APCs and armored cars were almost invisible—dark rectangles against darker boulders and tangled patches of thorn bushes, tall grass, and thistles. Their squat, camouflaged shapes blended easily with the rough, rocky scrubland marking this southern edge of the Kalahari Desert.

An eerie silence hung over the rows of parked vehicles. No radios crackled or hissed. Voices were hushed, and orders normally bellowed were now given in swift, harsh whispers. Only the occasional crunch of boots on loose rock marked the passage of sentries patrolling ceaselessly around the battalion's perimeter. The men of the 20th Cape Rifles were on a war footing.

Inside the command tent, Commandant Henrik Kruger looked round the circle of grimly determined faces caught in the lamp's pale, unwavering light. He knew that many of the battalion's officers shared his unspoken misgivings about this operation's political wisdom. If anything, those misgivings had grown stronger since General de Wet's preliminary briefing nearly a month before.

But none of them, himself included, would disobey orders. Once soldiers started picking and choosing which commands they would obey and which they would ignore, you had anarchy or worse. Black Africa's assortment of fragile, coup-ridden, and corrupt governments showed that all too clearly.

South Africa was different. A civilized nation. A nation of law. Or so he hoped.

Kruger shook himself and looked down at the heavily annotated map before him. His company commanders followed suit.

He tapped the thick black line showing their planned axis of advance. "Speed! That's the whole key to this op, gentlemen. If we move fast from the start, we win fast and easy. The Swapo bastards won't know what hit them. But if we move slow at first, we'll get bogged down and move even slower later. And that's something we can't afford."

The other men nodded their understanding. Intelligence reports portrayed the new Namibian Army as inexperienced and underequipped. Its officers and men were still trying to cope with the difficult transition from being an often-hunted, often-harried guerrilla army to being a conventional defense force. South Africa's powerful airborne, armored, and motorized forces should have little trouble crushing them.

Conquering Namibia itself was entirely another matter.

The country stretched more than one thousand kilometers from south to north—most of it an unpopulated, arid wasteland. Windhoek, its capital city, the diamond and uranium mines, and everything else of any value lay far to the west and north, spread across hundreds of thousands of square kilometers of rugged, inhospitable terrain.

Just supplying food, fuel, ammo, and water to the brigades and battalions slated for this invasion would absorb almost all of South Africa's military air transport and a good deal of its ground transport. Every extra day they took to achieve their objectives would increase the strain on the Republic's economy. A quick war meant fewer casualties, lower costs, and less international outrage. A quick war was vital.

Kruger slid the map aside with an abrupt, impatient gesture. "Our march order reflects this need for a rapid advance."

He turned to the short, dark-haired major commanding the battalion's attached reconnaissance squadron. "Your boys will lead off, Daan. You'll be moving about six to seven klicks ahead of the main column—probing for strong points and smashing anyone else trying to resist. Clear?"

Maj. Daan Visser nodded vigorously. His fast, powerfully gunned Rookiat and Eland armored fighting vehicles were perfectly suited to the job they were being given. They had the speed and firepower needed to blast open a hole in whatever hasty defenses the Namibians managed to assemble.

The mission was probably Visser's idea of heaven, Kruger reflected. The major had always prided himself on being the perfect hell-for-leather, death-or-glory cavalryman. It was an attitude reflected in everything he did, said, and even wore—right down to the bright orange scarf tucked into his camouflaged battle dress, in place of the regulation necktie, and the black beret rakishly perched above his right eye.

Kruger admired the man's proven bravery. He just hoped Visser had the common sense to go with his guts.

"And the rest of the battalion, *Kommandant?*" Major Forbes, his executive officer, prompted.

Kruger noted the XO's careful use of Afrikaans and bit back a frustrated sigh. It was evidence of the one continuing weakness in his battalion and in the South African Army as a whole—the deep and abiding mistrust between those of Afrikaner heritage and those of English descent.

Forbes was a good example of the price paid for that mistrust. He was a first-class soldier and a fine officer, but some of the battalion's Afrikaner diehards were still unwilling to accept him as an equal. Despite the fact that his family had lived in Cape Town for nearly a century, they labeled him as nothing more than an interfering, toffee-nosed rooinek and outsider. Forbes, aware of their feelings, had tried everything he could think of to blend in with the Cape Rifles' Afrikaner majority—even to the extent of speaking accentless Afrikaans every chance he got. All to no avail.

Kruger came back to the present. He had more immediate problems to confront. Besides, once the shooting started, the first man who showed disrespect for the XO or who disobeyed one of his orders would swiftly discover that Henrik Kruger valued competence far more than a common ancestry.

"The infantry will follow Major Visser's squadron. Companies A, B, and then C." A scarred finger stabbed the portable, folding table three times, emphasizing each unit's position in the main column. "You'll move in road march formation, but I want flank guards out and alert."

He smiled thinly. "Ratel APCs are expensive, gentlemen. Lose one to a lucky shot from some Swapo RPG and I'll see that it's docked from your pay."

Nervous laughter showed that his warning had hit close to home. Ratels offered good protection against bullets and shell fragments, but rocket-propelled grenades could turn them into flaming death traps. The only way to deal with an enemy soldier carrying an RPG was to see him and kill him before he could fire.

Kruger turned to the tall, burly, towheaded officer on his right. "D Company will bring up the rear. No offense, Hennie, but I hope we won't have too much work for your boys on this jaunt."

Hennie Mulder, the captain commanding his heavy weapons company, nodded soberly. His truck-carried 81mm mortars and Vickers heavy machine guns represented a large part of the battalion's firepower, but they were also relatively immobile and required time to deploy. The battalion would only need D Company's weapons teams if it met strong resistance—and that, in turn, would mean Nimrod was going badly.

"*Kommandant?*"

Kruger looked toward the hesitant voice. Robey Riekert,

his youngest and least experienced company commander, had a hand half-raised. "Yes, Robey?"

"What about artillery support, sir? Do we have any guns on call?"

Kruger shook his head. "Not deployed. With luck, we'll be pushing ahead too fast. But there'll be two batteries of SP guns attached to the column behind us. So if we run into any real opposition, we'll be able to give the Swapos a few one fifty-five millimeter shells for their pains."

More laughter, this time less forced.

A sudden howling, thrumming roar drowned their laughter, grew louder still, and then faded as fast as it had come. Startled, several officers cast frightened glances up toward the tent's low canvas ceiling and then looked sheepish as they made sense of the noise. The battalion had just been overflown by several large aircraft. Aircraft flying westward into Namibia.

Kruger checked his watch. Nimrod was on schedule. He stood straighter. "Very well, gentlemen. That's our cue. You may put your companies on the road. Good luck to you all."

The tent flap bellied open briefly and sagged back as his officers ran toward their waiting commands.

A COMPANY, 2ND BATTALION, 44TH PARACHUTE BRIGADE, OVER NAMIBIA

The ride was much rougher this time, even though they weren't flying as low as they had been on the Gawamba raid. There was a reason for that. Air Force manuals said that the big C-160 Transall troop carriers exhibited "poor gust response," which was an aerodynamic way of saying that turbulence at low altitude made the plane bump and shudder like a truck on a rutted road.

Capt. Rolf Bekker found himself yawning uncontrollably —a yawn that nearly made him bite through his tongue as the Transall bucked upward, caught in yet another air current rising off Namibia's rugged hills. He forced his mouth shut and frowned. They'd already suffered through two hours of this jarring ride since taking off from the staging airfield near Bloemfontein. How much farther did they have to go, for Christ's sake?

He shook his head wearily. Fatigue must be muzzling his ability to think. He knew precisely how much longer they had to fly before reaching the target. And he knew exactly how long it had been since he'd had a decent hour's sleep.

Bekker was enough of a soldier not to complain about the hour set for their drop, but a dawn landing meant a midnight assembly for a four A.M. takeoff. The hectic preparations had been structured to allow him six hours sleep, but last-minute crises and changes had robbed him of all but a brief nap. There was certainly no way he could sleep on this plane, not with its washboard ride on a hard metal seat.

So, Bekker thought, I will start the biggest military operation in my career tired and short on sleep. When he was tired, he got irritable—not entirely a bad thing.

He only wished he had a better view of the ground below. Bekker preferred going into combat in helicopters—at least their open doors usually gave the troops a chance to get oriented before touchdown. Now, though, he had just a single window to look out of, a window about as clear as the bottom of a beer bottle. He and his men would have to jump trusting that the Transall's pilot could see the drop zone, and trusting in his ability to put them in it.

Bekker wriggled around, straining against the seat straps to look out the window. Nothing but dark sky, paling faintly to gray behind them. He couldn't even see the rest of the battalion, spread out in five other aircraft.

There were supposed to be other planes in the air as well—Impala II ground attack aircraft to provide close air support, and Mirage jet fighters supplying top cover. None were visible through the dirt-streaked window. Nothing but the huge spinning blades of the Transall's portside turboprop.

Bekker pulled his eyes away from the empty window and scanned the rows of fold-down metal seats lining either side of the plane's crowded troop compartment. Just over eighty men sat silently, slept, talked, or read as they waited to risk their lives. He and his troops were dressed in heavy coveralls and padded helmets—gear designed to help absorb some of the shock generated by slamming into the ground at up to twenty-five kilometers an hour. Parachutes increased the bulk of their weapons and packs. They only carried one chute each. At this altitude, there wouldn't be time for a reserve chute if the first one failed.

The eighty men in this plane represented just half his company. The rest, led by his senior lieutenant, were on another cargo plane—nearby, he hoped. They'd better be. He'd need every available man to accomplish his mission.

He sighed. At least with a low-altitude drop and static lines, all the troops jumping from this Transall should come down close together. And the Namibians would be totally surprised.

A bell sounded and a red light over the door came on. The jumpmaster waiting near the door straightened. Holding up his right hand with the fingers extended, he shouted, "Five minutes!"

At last. Bekker hit the strap release and rose from his seat. "Stand and hook up!"

His men hurried to comply, hurriedly slinging the weapons they'd been checking or stuffing books into already bulging pockets. As they stood, the floor of the plane tilted back sharply as it pulled into a steep climb from a "cruising" altitude of one hundred fifty meters up to three hundred—the minimum safe altitude for a static line drop. The engine noise changed, too, building from a loud, humming drone to a teeth-rattling bass roar as the loaded plane clawed for altitude.

Bekker was sitting in the front of the cargo compartment, near the nose. As his men hooked up, he walked rearward, looking over the two files of paratroopers, one standing on each side of the plane. He inspected each static line to make sure it was properly routed, then swept his eyes over the rest of their equipment—personal weapons, grenades, radios—all the material they'd need to survive once on the ground and in contact with the enemy.

From time to time he stopped to clap a shoulder or to

exchange a quick joke, but mostly he moved aft in silence. These men were all combat veterans, and they were as ready as he could make them. With little time to spare, he came to the head of the lines of waiting men. He turned and stood facing the closed portside door. On the opposite side of the cabin, Sergeant Roost took his position by the starboard door.

Bekker hooked his own static line onto the rail and watched closely as his radioman, Corporal de Vries, checked it and his other equipment. The shorter man mouthed an "Okay" and gave him the thumbs-up.

The final seconds seemed to take hours.

As the Transall leveled out, its engine noise dropped from a roar, down past the previous drone to a steady low hum. Bekker knew the pilot was throttling down to minimum speed, trying to reduce the rush of air past the aircraft. At the same time, the jumpmaster prepared the two side doors, one after the other.

Swinging inside and back, the opening door let in bone-chilling cold air and the roar of laboring engines. Bekker had to steady himself against the buffeting as the air roared in.

The jumpmaster nodded, and the captain swung forward to stand in the opening, hands gripping the door's edge on either side.

Bekker looked out and down on a brown and hilly landscape. One dry riverbed to the south was marked by a dotted pale-green line of stunted trees and brush. Rocky hills rose farther to the southeast, with a single road paralleling them to one side, leading straight to their target, Keetmanshoop.

The town of Keetmanshoop had no industry. There weren't any diamond or uranium mines nearby, and only enough farms to feed the local population of some fifteen thousand souls. But Keetmanshoop was worth its weight in gold to the South African invasion force.

From his perch, Bekker could see the town laid out in a precise, right-angled grid below him. Columns of smoke from burning buildings showed where Air Force Impalas had bombed and strafed identified Namibian army barracks and command centers just moments before. He could also see what did make Keetmanshoop so valuable—the metaled two-lane roads leading to it like a spiderweb, and the rail lines arcing out to the east, north, and south. And most important of all, the airport.

Just a single two-thousand-foot strip, it was the logistical anchor on which Operation Nimrod rested. Without that small runway, South Africa wouldn't be able to move men and supplies into Namibia quickly enough to sustain its offensive. With it, they could just squeak by.

One small burden disappeared as he scanned the runway. The field seemed undamaged, and there weren't any Namibian military aircraft parked on the tarmac. Even better, he couldn't see any fire rising from the two or three sandbagged antiaircraft positions clustered around the airport's small red-brick terminal.

The bell rang again, and the light over the cargo door flashed from red to green. The Jumpmaster slapped his shoulder. Now!

First in line, without thinking or feeling, Bekker simply stepped out the open door and into space. A blast of cold air punched into his lungs. He dropped earthward in a split second of gut-wrenching free-fall before he felt the static line tug.

The parachute streamered out of its pack and snapped open—slamming him painfully against his harness in sudden deceleration. He glanced up and saw the billowing, sand-colored canopy that meant he could add another successful jump to his logbook. Now high overhead, the huge Transall lumbered on, still spewing out men and weapons canisters. Other transports followed, each laying its own drifting trail of slowly falling parachutes.

Bekker looked down and felt adrenaline surging through his veins. Fifty meters. Thirty. Twenty. This was what he lived for—being in the front of the assault wave, leading the attack.

The ground rushed up to meet him, and he bent his legs and rolled as he hit.

CUBAN EMBASSY, RUA KARL MARX, LUANDA, ANGOLA

The sun, rising in a cloudless early-morning sky, bathed Luanda's government ministries, shops, and dense-packed shanties in a pitilessly clear light—revealing layers of dirt and spray-painted political slogans coating once-whitewashed walls. The capital city of the People's Republic of Angola had grown shabbier with each passing year of bloody civil war and Marxist central planning.

Luanda's government offices were still shut, their outer doors padlocked and windows dark. The bureaucratic workday never began till long after sunup.

Angola's socialist ally and military protector evidently had a somewhat different attitude toward time. Lights were already winking on all across the fortified Cuban embassy compound on Rua Karl Marx—Karl Marx Street.

Gen. Antonio Vega was still dressing when Corporal Gomez knocked on the door and without waiting burst into the room. "Comrade General, our embassy in Windhoek is on the phone. They're saying that someone just attacked the city with aircraft! The—"

Vega, a tall, slender man with a stern, narrow face and gray-streaked black hair, stood facing a small mirror propped up on his nightstand. At the moment, he was only half-clothed, one bare shoulder showing the delicate tracery of scar tissue left by fragments from an exploding mortar round. It was a scar he'd earned more than thirty years before while leading one of Fidel Castro's guerrilla units against the old Batista government.

Visibly annoyed at being interrupted, Vega snorted. "What? Ridiculous. Those idiots must be seeing things." He continued pulling on his uniform shirt, though with slightly more speed than usual. "It would be straining their military expertise to recognize an air raid, even if one did occur."

Gomez blushed. Vega had a razor-sharp tongue—a tongue that matched his wits. It was said that even Castro felt the edge of the general's icy sarcasm from time to time. The corporal doubted that. Senior military men who angered Fidel Castro once never lived long enough to anger him a second time.

Gomez, waiting with noticeable impatience near the door, did not agree or disagree, but instead volunteered, "The ambassador was on the phone to Windhoek when I was sent to find you, sir."

Vega finished buttoning his shirt and grabbed his uniform coat. He strode quickly out the door, not bothering to close it or order Gomez to follow. The corporal did both without being told and raced after him down the carpeted hall toward the embassy's Command Center.

Cuba's ambassador to Angola, Carlos Luiz Tejeda, stood surrounded by a small crowd of wildly gesticulating aides and officers. He had one ear pressed hard against a red telephone, trying to listen amid the increasingly frantic din.

Vega slowed to a walk.

The noise level dropped abruptly as all of the officers and most of the political aides in the Command Center stopped talking and moved to the sides of the room. The general's contempt for unnecessary chatter was well-known.

Tejeda saw Vega and nodded gravely, but continued talking on the phone. A chair materialized near the general and he sat down.

Tejeda ended his phone conversation by asking for hourly updates and hung up. He stood silent for a moment. Then he took off his gold-rimmed glasses before wearily rubbing one hand over his face.

Vega realized with some surprise that Tejeda was unshaven and dressed only in slacks and a half-buttoned dress shirt. In all the years they'd worked together, he'd never seen the man so unkempt. The ambassador was ordinarily something of a dandy. Things must be serious.

Tejeda's next words confirmed that. "General, I have grave news. We now have confirmation that South African forces have invaded Namibian territory."

Vega sat quietly as the ambassador outlined the situation —at least as far as it could be determined from the first sketchy reports. An air raid on Windhoek. Airborne landings in Keetmanshoop. And unconfirmed sightings of South African armored columns pouring across Namibia's southern border.

"Widespread attacks," Vega commented. "This isn't just a simple cross-border raid, Comrade Ambassador."

Tejeda put his glasses back on. "Agreed. I've already put a call through to Havana. I expect to hear from the foreign minister himself in half an hour or so."

Surprised, Vega checked his watch. It was past midnight in Cuba, an ungodly hour even in a godless country. The foreign policy apparatus wasn't usually so quick off the mark.

Tejeda nodded. "Yes, Havana is greatly concerned. That is why I shall need to give the minister your assessment of the current military situation in Namibia. And he will also expect our joint recommendations for reaction to this South African aggression."

"Our what?" Vega was nonplussed. "On the basis of fragmentary phone reports?" His voice was testy, almost angry.

"General, please." Tejeda tried to soothe him. "You are the senior Cuban officer in Africa and we need your expertise. I have little experience in military matters. Certainly there must be broad conclusions you can draw, measures you can recommend to safeguard our interest."

Vega knew he was being soothed. Tejeda had served as an officer in the Cuban Army, and even if he had never seen combat, he had to understand what this meant. Still, he didn't mind being soothed, and the foreign minister, and ultimately Castro himself, would not be put off. He stood and walked over to the map of the area on the wall.

As chief of his country's military mission to the Luanda government, Vega commanded the Cuban infantry, armor, and air defense units left in Angola. It was an army that had been shrinking steadily for the past several years. Since the signing of the Brazzaville Accords, which promised South African withdrawal from Namibia in return for Cuban withdrawal from Angola, his command had fallen steadily from a high of fifty thousand troops down to its present level of barely ten thousand men.

It was a reduction in strength he felt sure Havana already regretted.

Vega had held his command for four years, fighting Unita—the guerrilla movement opposing Luanda's Marxist government—and occasionally Unita's South African backers. He knew the area, and he knew his friends and his enemies. And all sides in the conflict recognized him as a brilliant tactician and a courageous combat soldier.

He pondered the map for a moment, conscious of the eyes fixed on his uniformed back. He tapped a road junction circled in red near the bottom. "Keetmanshoop may be the first step in South Africa's invasion, but it cannot be the last."

His finger traced the road northward and stopped. "There. That is where they must go to succeed. Windhoek. Namibia's capital and economic center."

Vega moved his hand west, to the Namibian coast. "No competent general would launch a single-pronged attack on such an important objective. There must be a second enemy column moving inland from the enclave at Walvis Bay.

"Two columns. Both converging on Windhoek to trap and crush the Namibians like this!" He clapped his hands together, startling several of the junior officers in the room.

Others nodded slowly. Vega's logic was impeccable. With Windhoek in hand and Namibia's new army smashed or scattered, South Africa would once again control three-quarters of its former colony's mineral wealth and transportation net.

Tejeda looked up from a pad of hastily scribbled notes. "Did we have any intelligence about South African movements? Was there any warning at all?"

Vega saw every piece of information the DCI, the Cuban intelligence service, collected in Africa. He shook his head. "Nothing that made a pattern or indicated an operation this massive. But naturally, we'll go back and reevaluate the data to see if any of it falls into place now." He nodded to one of the officers, who stiffened to attention and then hurriedly left the room.

Tejeda looked even more worried. "Can the South Africans win?"

"Certainly, if Pretoria commits enough troops. Troop strength is the key. Namibia may be weak, but it's still a huge area—seven times larger than all Cuba." Vega paused, calculating. "Vorster and his madmen would have to commit virtually all of their regular forces. That would leave them weak everywhere else." There was a speculative tone to his last sentence.

"So what can we do to counter this aggression, General?" Tejeda asked.

"Right away?" Vega clasped his hands behind his back, staring at the troop dispositions shown on the map. "Freeze the withdrawal. No more units should be removed until we know what Unita will do. I'm sure that the South Africans will use their stooges to try to distract us."

He spun round from the map, looking for his chief of operations. "Colonel Oliva, you will put all our units on immediate alert. Tell them to expect increased Unita attacks. And pass the warning on to the Angolans as well."

Oliva headed for a phone.

Tejeda stepped closer to Vega. "I'm sure Havana will agree to stopping the withdrawal. We've certainly halted it in the past for less."

Vega nodded, agreeing, and walked back over to a chair. He sat down heavily. "Another year and I could have been home. The damned Boers just can't leave anyone alone. And the Americans. They're behind this, too." He grimaced. "As long as the capitalists have an outpost in Africa, there will be no peace in this region."

Tejeda looked concerned. Vega rarely showed fatigue or strong emotion. "Do you have any other recommendations, General?"

"Not at the moment, Comrade Ambassador." Vega suddenly sounded tired, as if the thought of further service in this cursed country had drained him of energy. "I may have other ideas when we get more information."

Tejeda's secretary entered the Command Center. "Sir, Minister Fierro is calling."

Vega left as the ambassador picked up the phone. He had a lot of thinking to do.

CNN HEADLINE NEWS

CNN's Atlanta-based anchorman managed to convey an impression of dispassionate concern with little deliberate effort. "Our top story this hour, South Africa's invasion of Namibia."

The screen split, showing a stylized map of Namibia in the upper right-hand corner, just over the anchor's shoulder. "Roughly eight hours ago, at dawn local time, South African warplanes, paratroops, and tanks struck deep into the newly independent nation of Namibia. Heavy fighting is reported, and there are also unconfirmed reports that UN peacekeeping troops along the Namibian border have been disarmed and penned in their compounds by units of South Africa's invasion force."

The newsman's dapper image disappeared, replaced by soundless file footage of one of Vorster's angry, arm-waving speeches. "The invasion took most experts by surprise—despite Pretoria's recent claims that black guerrillas have been using the former colony as a staging area for attacks inside South Africa."

Vorster's image disappeared, replaced by that of a grave-faced man the anchor identified as a spokesman for the Namibian government. "This attack is clearly aimed at re-establishing Pretoria's domination over our country. Namibia will not surrender. We will not yield. Instead, we call on the United Nations Security Council for immediate assistance in repelling this aggression."

The anchorman reappeared, flanked this time by a picture of the White House. "In Washington, the State Department has issued a short statement condemning South Africa's military action. The White House is expected to issue its own statement later in the day.

"In related news, violent incidents inside South Africa have been rising steadily in the wake of President Vorster's new security measures. . . ."

CUBAN EMBASSY, LUANDA, ANGOLA

Night had come almost unnoticed to Luanda.

A single hooded lamp cast shadows on the wall as Gen. Antonio Vega sat eating alone in his office, reviewing the latest sketchy intelligence coming out of Windhoek. No clear picture had yet emerged, but one thing was obvious. Namibia's young army was losing and losing fast. And in a war still less than a day old.

He looked up in intense irritation when Corporal Gomez stuck his head through the door to let him know that the ambassador wanted to see him. Again.

Vega swore briskly, swept the sheaf of intelligence reports into a neat pile, and strode out the door with Gomez in tow.

Tejeda's office faced an arc-lit inner courtyard—a safe haven should any of the many Angolans who loathed their country's nominal protectors decide to turn sniper. The ambassador was now fully and formally dressed, but he looked much worse, plainly a man deprived of needed sleep and having had a very full day.

Tejeda glanced up from the message flimsy he'd been studying carefully. "We have new orders, General." His tone was portentous, almost comical, but Vega knew he was serious. The ambassador never joked about orders from Havana. It wasn't healthy.

Vega took the message from him. It wasn't long. The important ones never were.

"Cuba has pledged its internationalist support of the Namibian people against South Africa's imperialist aggression. Under an agreement reached this afternoon with the Swapo government, this will include the deployment of military units in combat operations against Pretoria's racist invaders."

Tejeda nodded. "Radio Havana will broadcast that"—he looked at his watch—"in about half an hour. I have direct orders for you as well. Orders from the Defense Ministry."

Another telex message. Longer this time.

"Gen. Antonio Vega's area of responsibility is expanded to include Namibia. Use existing forces and reinforcements (see attached) to assist the Swapo government in defeating South Africa's invasion force."

A list of units and estimated arrival times followed. Vega felt lightheaded. Fighters, armor, the best infantry units—Fidel was evidently prepared to send the cream of the Cuban armed forces into combat against South Africa!

But there were problems. He looked up, meeting Tejeda's watchful gaze. "Comrade Ambassador, have the Russians agreed to support this?" Vega had to force the question out through clenched teeth. Just asking it seemed to reinforce Cuba's dependence on an increasingly untrustworthy patron.

The Cuban Army's presence in Angola was possible only because Soviet cargo planes and ships kept it in supply and up to strength. Cuba itself had only a few ships and a scattering of light transport aircraft. Not enough to support a sizable force outside the island's own shores. So none of Castro's extravagant promises to the Namibian government could be met without extensive Soviet backing. Vega had few illusions left about Moscow's continued devotion to its socialist brothers overseas.

Tejeda smiled thinly. He shared the general's disdain for the USSR's fair-weather communists. "Surprising though it may seem, Comrade General, Moscow's response to our requests have been very positive. Defense Minister Petrov himself telephoned Fidel to say that four merchant ships and twenty Ilyushin cargo aircraft will be transferred to our control. Also, advanced MiGs are being flown from Russia for use by our pilots. They're scheduled to arrive within twenty-four hours."

Incredible. It was a generous offer, especially the fighter flights. Cuba's own MiGs didn't have the range to fly clear across the Atlantic, and just crating them for seaborne passage would have added a week to the time needed to get them into combat over Namibia.

A generous offer, indeed. And that was strange.

Of late, the Soviet Union's support for Castro's African policies had been lukewarm at best. As it foundered in a sea of internal political and economic troubles, the Kremlin had even begun grumbling about the above-market prices it paid for Cuba's sugar crop. Prices that kept Cuba's own failing economy afloat.

So what was the catch? "Just what does Moscow expect in return?"

"Nothing, at least for now." Tejeda shrugged. "Apparently they see certain benefits in helping us help the Namibians. As the Americans would say, opposing South Africa is now good PR."

"They can afford it. But can we?" Vega countered. Angola paid Cuba in hard cash for every Cuban soldier inside its borders. That money, most of it ironically coming from an American-owned oil refinery, would have been missed after the slated withdrawal from Angola. Cuba was a poor country.

For years, the Americans, the IMF, and everyone outside the shrinking communist world had been trying to starve Cuba's economy into ruin, with marked success. The nation desperately needed foreign exchange. Given that, Vega wasn't sure his country could bear the cost of a full-fledged war.

Tejeda frowned. Vega's question wasn't just defeatist, it could even be interpreted as a criticism of Havana's decisions. And that wasn't like the general at all. "Surely that isn't your concern, Comrade General. The Foreign Ministry assures me that they are already negotiating the needed agreements with Windhoek. Finances will not be a problem."

"Fine," Vega said, "you broker the deal for Namibian diamonds. Just don't tell me the money's run out once I've committed my forces."

Tejeda turned bright red. "General, please. Fidel has already pledged Cuba's support for Namibian independence. A pledge that we will carry out even if we have to impoverish ourselves."

Vega looked skeptical. Fidel Castro was a committed revolutionary, but not a madman. Cuba already stood on the brink of poverty. Revolutionary fervor wasn't an adequate substitute for a steady and expensive stream of munitions, food, and fuel.

The ambassador hurried on. "Besides, there are important geopolitical considerations at stake here. Considerations that cannot be ignored. We have always tried to lead third-world opinion. Fighting, actually risking Cuban lives to save one of those third-world states, will help our image abroad. The next time a Western nation looks at us, they will have to see us as we really are. The Washington-controlled embargo will weaken, at least. It may even break."

He smiled. "Don't worry, Comrade. We have much to gain by winning in Namibia. You will have every resource you need."

Vega nodded, somewhat reassured. Havana wasn't ignoring the real world. Good.

The treaty-mandated withdrawal from Angola had seemed likely to end Castro's influence on the continent. One more communist retrenchment in an era already filled with surrender. Leaving Luanda would also have meant abandoning a valuable source of hard currency for Cuba's hard-pressed economy.

His own reasons for intervening in Namibia were less complicated. Vega wanted to hurt South Africa, to wreck its plans. He and his troops had fought Pretoria's expeditionary forces and Angola-based Unita stooges for years. Each encounter had carried its own grisly price tag in dead and wounded comrades, and none had been decisive. The war in Angola had been a series of pointless battles with no final objective.

Worn-out by years of fruitless skirmishing, Vega had been ready to return home—home to bask in Cuba's warm Caribbean sun. South Africa's invasion of Namibia offered him a chance for a decisive, stand-up fight.

He was ready. Cuba had been fighting in Angola since 1975, so he had a pool of experienced officers, combat veterans who knew how to fight and who knew the conditions in southern Africa.

Vega also knew the risks the South Africans were taking in their drive to seize Namibia quickly. Risks Pretoria's commanders were willing to take because they didn't expect to meet competent military opposition. Risks he intended to make them regret.

UMKHONTO WE SIZWE HEADQUARTERS, LUSAKA, ZAMBIA

Col. Sese Luthuli fielded yet another frantic phone call. A panicked voice in the receiver said, "This is Jonas." At least he had enough sense to use his code name, Luthuli thought. "I've gotten reports from all of my cells. The South Africans are moving in numbers, Colonel! The Gajab River camp has been overrun!"

Luthuli fought the urge to lash out at this man. He knew "Jonas," an Ovimbundu tribesman in his thirties with a good record in the struggle. He had no sense, though, and could not be trusted in combat. This had relegated him to administrative duties, which had now probably saved his life.

The man's information was hours old. Luthuli had to give him the bad news without panicking him entirely, and quickly. Nobody knew how fast the Boers were moving.

"Jonas, listen. Find everyone you can and get out of Namibia any way you can. South Africa's armies are on the move, and we have to abandon all our camps."

"But comrade, without them our organization will fall apart! Our supplies, our communications—"

"Will have to be rebuilt," Luthuli interrupted. "We must save what we can and start over. Headquarters does not think the South Africans will go beyond Namibia's borders. If you can make it to Angola, or Botswana, you should be safe."

"But we will lose so much! Shouldn't we strike at the enemy?"

Inwardly, Luthuli smiled. So there was a little fire in him after all. "We are, comrade, but that is not your task. You must organize the evacuation, and quickly. We must live to fight on. I must go now. Good luck."

As he hung up, the colonel heard the voice protesting, asking for instructions. He shrugged. How much direction did a man need to run?

He hoped there would be friendly faces for his men in Botswana and Angola. Ever since Broken Covenant, foreign support for the ANC had dried up. Money from America and Europe, even weapons from socialist supporters, had stopped completely. The Namibian training camps had become mere holding pens as they searched for resources. You can indoctrinate a man with words, but they needed more than that to fight the South Africans.

Luthuli felt bad about lying to him, as well. There had been no attempt to strike back at the advancing Boer armies. Umkhonto we Sizwe was a political army, a resistance group. The typical guerrilla cell was armed with a few pistols and rifles and usually had no more than five men. Heavy weapons, such as machine guns and rocket launchers, had limited ammunition and were saved for important targets. When his men moved, they used borrowed civilian transport, or they walked.

Scattered in small groups all over South Africa, the guerrilla cells spent more time dodging Vorster's security forces than they did planning and executing guerrilla attacks. And those attacks were always carefully scouted, with planning and practicing that normally took days. Umkhonto could no more hurt the massive South African war machine than a small child could fight with a heavyweight boxer. All of his guerrillas, scattered across the country, probably had no more combined fighting power than a battalion of South African troops.

Luthuli looked at the map in his office, at the documents on his desk. The only men he had left were the survivors of the crackdown that had followed Vorster's takeover, the result of Broken Covenant. The "reforms" under Haymans had proceeded just far enough for the ANC to move into the light, for its members to expose themselves. He had argued against it, fought tooth and nail to keep Umkhonto secret and powerful. Now it lay in shards, most of their leaders and half of their fighters rotting in prison.

Luthuli had not given up. He was a realist, though. Umkhonto's violence was always aimed at political targets, designed to influence leaders at home and world opinion abroad. Mortaring a military base, bombing a railway station, even a careful assassination, were all designed to show the willingness of the African people to struggle, to answer the Boer's violence with their own.

None of this mattered in wartime. Five people killed by a

bomb on a bus could not compare to the casualty lists coming from the front. Any attack his people made now would simply cause them to be lumped in with the other military enemies. The ANC had been overtaken by events.

Even before the Namibian invasion, Luthuli had faced rebuilding a shattered organization, lacking the money or weapons to even maintain it. He also lacked political support, since the ANC was viewed by many states as the cause of all the troubles. And even if he could rebuild his forces, they would have to be trained and equipped to fight a much more conventional war. Now he had lost the base camps.

It was time to ask for help, to appeal for more than just supplies and cash. He knew that there would be a price to pay, but if Umkhonto did not receive massive assistance soon, it would cease to exist, and the struggle would die with it.

There was only one country he could turn to for support. They had stayed true to their Marxist beginnings. Even though they weren't as rich as the Russians, the fires of revolution still burned in Havana.

He picked up the phone.

AUGUST 19—20TH CAPE RIFLES, ON MOTOR ROUTE 1, FIFTY KILOMETERS SOUTH OF KEETMANSHOOP

Smoke from the burning village eddied over the highway, adding an acrid tang to air already stained by diesel fumes and the sickly sweet smell of high explosives. Bodies and pieces of bodies were scattered haphazardly through a tangle of collapsed houses and fire-blackened huts. Some of the corpses were in Namibian uniforms but most were not. A few dazed survivors squatted beside the village well, their faces set in rigid masks of mingled horror and grief.

A futile show of resistance by Namibian police had given Maj. Daan Visser's armored fighting vehicles and scout cars the only excuse they needed. Just five minutes of machine-gun fire and several HE rounds from 76mm cannon had turned the little Namibian settlement into a charnel house. Then

Visser's men had roared off northward into the late-morning light, leaving the battalion's main column to clear up the mess and secure any prisoners.

Commandant Henrik Kruger shook his head wearily and turned away, trying to concentrate on the developing strategic situation shown on his map. Colored-pencil notations showed the last reported positions of all known South African and Namibian units.

In a nonstop drive since crossing the frontier, Kruger and his men had steamrollered their way west to Grunau. Up a winding pass climbing through the Great Karas Mountains, then north toward the paratroop-held airhead at Keetmanshoop. More than 280 kilometers in just thirty-six hours. Resistance had been light—almost nonexistent, in fact. Only a few easily crushed pockets such as the police post in this village. The column advancing from Walvis Bay reported similar progress.

Good. But not good enough. Kruger folded the map with abrupt, decisive strokes and handed it to a waiting staff officer, a baby-faced lieutenant.

They were already eight hours behind schedule—at least according to the wildly optimistic invasion timetables prepared by Pretoria. That shouldn't have come as a surprise to anyone. Moving long columns of men and equipment over vast distances was always a time-consuming business—even without meeting determined enemy resistance.

Kruger's own advance was a case in point. The trucks and APCs carrying his battalion had been on the road continuously for more than a day and a half, pushing north with only scattered five- and ten-minute rest breaks. They were starting to pay a price for that. Exhausted drivers were falling asleep at the wheel or growing increasingly irritable. The result: a rising number of minor traffic accidents and breakdowns, each exacting additional delay. Resupply halts were taking longer, too. Tired men took more time to refuel and rearm their vehicles.

Something would have to be done about that.

With the young lieutenant trailing behind, he moved around to the armored side door of his squat, metal-hulled Ratel command APC. Up and down the length of the long column, other vehicle commanders were already gunning their overworked engines to life. Blue-gray exhaust billowed into the hazy air.

His mind was made up. Once the battalion reached the paratroops at Keetmanshoop, it would have to halt for at least six hours to rest and recover. He didn't like it, but he couldn't see any other realistic alternative. Not that that would leave him with a combat-ready unit. Still, every hour of added delay gave the Namibian Army more time to pull itself together. Plus there were rumors that the Cubans had promised their assistance.

Kruger frowned. That was a disquieting possibility. He respected the Cubans. They were communists, it was true, but they made tough soldiers nonetheless.

He swung himself back inside the command vehicle's cramped interior. Moments later, the column of camouflaged APCs, trucks, and armored cars trundled north again, driving hard for Keetmanshoop and some promised sleep. The shattered village continued to burn behind them.

AUGUST 20—PANTHER FLIGHT, OVER WINDHOEK

Lt. Andreis Stegman always enjoyed flying, every second he was in the air. And why shouldn't he? He was one of the best pilots in the South African Air Force. He had to be, because he'd been assigned to fly one of the SAAF's thirty Mirage F.1CZ jet interceptors—the most advanced fighter in South Africa's inventory.

The Mirage was a beautiful plane, fast and maneuverable. Its South African–built air-to-air missiles might not be the most modern in the world, but Stegman knew he could hold his own against any likely opponent.

Stegman and his wingman, Lt. Klaus de Vert, were on fighter patrol over Windhoek. Their ability to loiter right over Namibia's capital without any sign of opposition confirmed South Africa's complete air superiority. Namibia's pathetic fleet of antiquated propeller-driven planes had been destroyed on the first day—strafed on the ground or shot out of the sky with contemptuous ease.

The two swept-wing Mirages circled slowly at eleven thousand meters, orbiting over a light scud of clouds four thousand meters below. At this altitude, there wasn't a hint of turbulence and the sky overhead was a bright pale blue. Except where drifting white patches of cloud blocked his view, Stegman could see more than three hundred kilometers of southern Africa's dusty brown surface in every direction.

It wasn't the most exciting flying, but Stegman loved it all.

He tried to concentrate on the task at hand. They were obviously supposed to attack any enemy aircraft that appeared, but their primary mission involved interdicting Windhoek's airport. Cargo aircraft trying to take off or land at the field would be sitting ducks for his and de Vert's high-performance fighters.

Stegman alternated between scanning the sky, checking his radar screen, and running his gaze over the Mirage's flight instruments in a regular pattern. The pattern had long since become second nature to him. He had over five hundred hours in fighters, and even one kill to his credit.

He smiled cruelly behind his oxygen mask, remembering the frenzied air battle. It had happened over Angola during the SADF's last major ground operation. They'd been supporting Unita, helping to repel a major Angolan and Cuban offensive against the guerrillas. Stegman, then just a junior lieutenant, had been flying as wingman to Captain de Kloof on a routine fighter sweep over the operational area.

They'd been jumped by two MiG-23 Floggers coming up from low-level with their radars off in a classic bushwhack. By rights de Kloof and he should have been dead. The Russian-built fighters were faster and equipped with radar-guided missiles. But Stegman had learned that day which is more important—a plane or its pilot.

In a vicious, swirling dogfight, de Kloof had closed the range and maneuvered into the MiGs' rear cone. From there, two quick missile launches gave Stegman and him a kill apiece. It was a good memory and a valuable lesson. There'd been rumors that Cubans were piloting Angolan aircraft, but whoever had been flying, they hadn't been able to match South African skill.

The victory had given Stegman his current status as a flight leader. And Major de Kloof was now his squadron commander.

Stegman broke his scanning pattern to check his fuel level. They were about six hundred kilometers from base, and fighters drink fuel quickly, especially in combat. The same gas could keep him aloft for an hour on patrol, but only about three minutes in combat.

Good. They'd only used up about half their patrol time and still had a healthy reserve.

Suddenly, his radar warning receiver sounded, emitting a pulsed buzzing noise. Stegman stabbed a button that silenced the alarm and glanced at the bearing strobe on the dial. It showed a narrow fan of lines off to the northwest. Each line represented the bearing to an aircraft fire-control radar whose pulses were being picked up by sensors on the Mirage's fins.

"Klaus, bandits at three two zero!"

Stegman heard de Vert's mike click twice in acknowledgment as he turned toward the incoming enemy planes. Stegman knew that his wingman was already maneuvering one hundred meters below to form line abreast with a half-mile spacing, all without any verbal order or discussion. In air combat, there wasn't time for lengthy consideration or long orders. Anything over one short sentence was long.

Every flight leader and his wingman spent long hours beforehand, working out a mutually agreeable set of air-to-air tactics and maneuvers. The Air Force recommended certain general procedures and tactics, but any realistic agreement also had to measure the skill levels and personal fighting styles of the two pilots flying together. Their agreement, hammered out over many days and sorties, described exactly what each pilot would do in dozens of situations, automatically and without exception. A pilot would risk death rather than use an undiscussed maneuver, because to do so meant risking his wingman's life instead.

Stegman's own radar screen was blank, so the enemy

planes were at least thirty kilometers out. The Mirage's French-designed Cyrano IV radar could see larger aircraft at fifty klicks, but cargo aircraft didn't carry fire-control radars. These bandits were fighters.

He checked his radar warning screen again and noted that the enemy radar pulses were gone. Interesting. Either the bandits had turned off their radars or they'd gone home.

Stegman hoped they hadn't gone home. He wanted more kills.

The South African thumbed his radio mike, switching frequencies. "Springbok, this is Panther Lead."

A fighter controller sitting eight hundred kilometers south at Upington Air Base answered promptly.

Stegman sketched the situation in a couple of terse phrases and acknowledged Upington's promise that two more fighters would be launched as backup. The promise was nice, but meaningless. They were more than fifty minutes' flight time out of Upington. He and de Vert were on their own.

He decided against closing at high speed. Fuel was too precious, and his duty was to cover Windhoek. This could be some sort of diversion, designed to pull them away from the airfield long enough for still-undetected cargo planes to land or take off.

There. Four glowing points of light appeared on his radar screen. Enemy aircraft. He squinted at the screen, trying to extract more information from the tiny blips. The bandits seemed to be flying at lower altitude, and they were moving fast. Damned fast. Even with his relatively low cruising speed, they were closing at over two thousand kilometers per hour! Then he realized the bandits must be coming in on afterburner.

"Closing to engage. Drop tanks!" Stegman shoved his own throttle forward and locked his radar onto the lead aircraft. As the Mirage's engine noise increased, he thumbed a button on the throttle—jettisoning the empty drop tanks attached to his wings. Normally the empty tanks were saved for reuse at base, but their size and weight slowed down a fighter. Going into combat with the tanks still attached would be like fighting a boxing match wearing a ball and chain.

He checked his armament switches and selected his outer portside Kukri missile—a heat-seeker optimized for dogfighting, not for long range. He'd have to get close to use it. The Mirage carried four of them, plus an internal 30mm cannon.

His radar warning receiver warbled again. The bandits had switched their radars back on. Since they'd probably detected him earlier, the radars were almost certainly on this time for one thing only—a long-range missile launch.

Time to warn de Vert. "Windmill! Evading!"

Stegman took a quick, deep breath and jammed the throttle forward all the way to afterburner. *Windmill* was the code for incoming missiles. He felt a mule kick through his seat back and heard a thundering roar behind him as raw fuel poured into the jet's exhaust and exploded. His own speed quickly increased to over twelve hundred kilometers per hour while his fuel gauge spun down almost as fast.

He swept his eyes back and forth across the sky, looking for the telltale enemy missile trails and trying hard to remember the important pieces of dozens of intelligence briefings. Angolan MiG-23s carried Soviet-made AA-7 Apex missiles. They were only fair performers, and the intel boys said that they were susceptible to a combination of chaff and a high-9 turn.

Hopefully, Stegman's own speed, plus that of the missile, would make for such a high closing rate that the missile couldn't react fast enough to a last-second turn. Add some slivers of metallized plastic that would give false radar returns and the missile should break lock every time. Or so they said.

There! He could see white smoke trails now, coming in fast from below. His finger was already resting on the chaff button, and he started pressing it at half-second intervals. At the same time, he threw the Mirage into a series of weaving turns, always starting and finishing each turn with the smoke trails at a wide angle off his nose.

He glanced over his shoulder to check de Vert and was relieved to see his wingman spewing chaff and corkscrewing all over the sky.

High g forces on each turn pressed him down into his seat,

forcing him to fight to hold the incoming missiles in view. He could see four trails now. Two aimed at him.

Stegman yanked the Mirage into another turn, even tighter than his first series. Come on! Miss, damn you. One missile failed to follow him and flashed past—heading nowhere.

But the second smoke trail visibly bent and curved in around toward his plane. Shit. Only seconds left. He pressed the chaff button again and turned again, pulling six or seven g's, almost hearing the wings creak with the stress. He lost the missile and in that moment thought he was dead.

A rattling explosion behind him. But no accompanying shock wave, fire, or blinking red warning lights. Thank God! The missile must have been decoyed away at the last moment. Stegman breathed out and leveled off, glancing to either side for de Vert's plane. Nothing above or to port.

Then he saw it. A ball of orange-red flame tumbling end over end out of control toward the ground. De Vert hadn't been lucky. And now he was dead.

Stegman didn't waste time in grief. That could come later. Right now he'd have trouble just saving his own life.

He started looking for the enemy, tracing back along the wispy, dissipating smoke trails left by their missiles. The bandits should be in visual range . . . he'd covered a lot of distance during those few seconds on afterburner.

There they were. Stegman spotted the small specks—faint gray against a faint blue sky—there were his enemies, ahead and to the left. There were four of them, breaking in pairs to the left and right, crossing over each other.

He smiled thinly. That was a mistake. He wasn't going to panic just because he was outnumbered four to one. Instead, he'd even the odds by concentrating on a single aircraft. And with four planes swerving all over the sky, he'd have a much easier time finding an enemy vulnerable to attack.

Stegman pushed the nose down a little to unload the wings, then yanked the Mirage over hard, into a high-g port turn. He noticed something strange about the bandits as he turned toward them. MiG-23 Floggers were bullet-shaped, single-tailed, swing-wing fighters. In combat position, a Flogger's wings should have been tucked back against its fuselage like those of a falcon making an attack. These aircraft looked totally different. They had wide, flattish fuselages, twin tails, and clipped swept wings.

The near pair was turning away from him, probably trying to lure him into a squeeze play. Fat chance.

He stayed in his turn for a few seconds more, using his helmet sight to line up a Kukri shot. The bandit slid inside his aiming reticle and into the path of the Kukri's infrared seeker.

Tone! As soon as he heard the missile's seeker head warble, Stegman pulled the trigger on his stick and then broke hard right. A jolt signaled that the Kukri had successfully dropped off its rail and was on its way.

The two farthest fighters were swinging in on him fast, and he saw flame sprout from under the lead jet's starboard wing. Jesus. He turned toward them and barrel-rolled, spiraling across the sky to break the lock of the incoming missile, whatever it was.

A fiery streak flashed past his cockpit and vanished.

Racing toward one another at a combined speed of more than twelve hundred knots, the three adversaries zipped by in an eyeblink—giving Stegman his first clear view of his opponents. MiG-29 Fulcrums! But even more interesting were the markings. They had gray air-superiority camouflage and carried a blue-and-red roundel. Angolan aircraft were usually sand and green colored, and their insignia was black and red. What the hell was going on?

He rolled right and dove, hoping to be harder to see against the desert landscape so he could gain a few seconds to select another target. A gray-white ball of smoke and orange flame appeared off to one side, with a spreading line of smoke leading to it. His Kukri shot had hit! Scratch one MiG. One for de Vert.

Stegman kept his eyes moving, roving back and forth across the sky.

In fast-moving fighter combat, a pilot's most important asset is "situational awareness"—the ability to visualize his own plane, those of his allies, and those of his opponents in three-dimensional space, their paths and their possibilities, while using that knowledge to kill the enemy.

He knew two of the MiG-29s were curving around behind him, and he could see the third just visible to his left and rear. He snarled. Having one opponent behind you in air combat was dangerous enough, but three was big trouble. As if to confirm his evaluation, his radar warning receiver sounded again—signaling another long-range missile inbound.

Stegman yanked the stick right, rolling the aircraft so that it was inverted, then pulled up hard. The nose of the Mirage pointed straight down, toward the ground, air speed increasing dramatically as both its jet engine and gravity worked together. As the Mirage maneuvered, he released still more chaff, as a precaution.

He was trading altitude for speed, applying the old fighter dictum that "speed is life." At the same time, he rolled the Mirage, trying to locate the enemy.

He found them, first a single dot and then two more, with fuzzy white trails from the pair that seemed to go straight for a while before wandering aimlessly about the sky. The signs of radar-guided missiles that had missed—confused by his sudden dive into ground clutter. All three MiGs were about four thousand meters above him.

Stegman felt pain in his ears and yawned to equalize the pressure. He'd lost a lot of altitude, and he had to decide in a single instant how to spend his remaining energy. Fight or flee?

He wanted to go back and send the three MiGs crashing to the earth one by one. But it just wasn't on. The enemy pilots weren't making enough mistakes. They still outnumbered him. No, it was time to be discreet.

Stegman rolled his aircraft a few more degrees, so that its clear plastic canopy pointed southeast, and started to pull out of his turn. G forces pinned him to his seat, but he forced his head up against the extra weight so that he could watch the altimeter. Three thousand meters. Two thousand. Fifteen hundred. The spinning needle's progress slowed, and he leveled off at a thousand meters—flying southeast at more than a thousand kilometers per hour.

He glanced over his shoulder, watching for signs of pursuit. If the MiGs wanted to catch him now, they'd have to increase their own throttle settings, burning more fuel, and all the time moving farther from their base.

Stegman throttled back to cruise and looked at his own fuel gauges. He scowled. The *verdomde* MiGs may get another kill after all, he thought. Upington was still more than seven hundred kilometers away, and he'd burned way too much fuel in combat. He pulled back on the stick, more gently this time. He was out of danger, and it was time to climb to a higher altitude. That would stretch out his remaining fuel. With luck, his Mirage might fly on fumes long enough to reach the emergency field at Keetmanshoop.

Cursing continuously under his breath, Stegman reached for his map and started plotting a new course due south.

All in all, this hadn't been one of his better days.

FULCRUM FLIGHT, OVER WINDHOEK

Fifty kilometers back, three MiG-29 Fulcrums orbited at eleven thousand meters, wings rocking in triumph. The surviving South African Mirage had lived up to its name, quickly disappearing from combat after the initial exchange. Capt. Miguel Ferentez tried to restore order on the radio circuit.

"Quiet! Lieutenant Rivas, you are a pilot, not a gladiator! And Jorge, this is a tactical net, not a sports arena loudspeaker! Be silent!"

No one responded, and Ferentez knew that they were all chagrined over the amateurish whooping and cheering that had filled the circuit seconds earlier. The loss of one of their flightmates barely tempered their enthusiasm. They had won an important victory.

None of them had seen combat before. Even Ferentez, who had flown a tour in Angola on MiG-21s, had never engaged enemy fighters before. Still, he was professional enough to curb his elation over a successful combat. There was work to do. He checked his gauges.

Satisfied, he changed frequencies, reporting in to the controllers based at Ondjiva Air Base, six hundred kilometers north—just inside Angola. "Windhoek is clear. And we have fuel for another ten minutes' patrol." Another flight of four MiGs were minutes behind him, screening the transports, and would relieve him before he had to return to base.

Ferentez was sorry the second Mirage had escaped. Eliminating South Africa's entire air patrol in one fell swoop would have been a smashing first victory. Nevertheless, he and his fellow pilots had accomplished their mission. Lumbering Soviet transports from Luanda, with close fighter escort, were now just thirty minutes away. Transports crammed with troops, weapons, and supplies to help bolster the defense of Windhoek. They would land without interference—thanks to his Fulcrums.

Ferentez smiled slowly. Pretoria couldn't possibly ignore Cuba's challenge to its aggression. This afternoon's successful combat over Namibia's capital was sure to be only the first of many.

U.S. DEPARTMENT OF STATE, WASHINGTON, D.C.

Edward Hurley's office was lined with books. Most were about Africa, but they included every topic. He tried to keep the room neat, but there were always about five projects under way at the same time. Papers spilled off a side table and lay in heaps on the floor, like bureaucratic land mines for an unwary visitor.

The morning light illuminated his desk, also covered with papers, but of a much more immediate nature. It also shone down on Hurley's form as he bent over them, trying to build a coherent picture of what was going on in South Africa.

Hurley rubbed his eyes. Nobody he knew had gotten much sleep since the Namibian War began. He'd spent the last three nights trying to build up a decent picture of what was going on. In addition to being cranky from lack of sleep, Washington needed answers.

Thankfully, he might be able to provide some. A picture was building, although most of it was inferred from scraps and rumor. Trying to get it right, quickly, was always risky. Based on satellite photos, embassy reports, and news reports, it looked as if Vorster's government was succeeding in taking back Namibia—violently.

He smiled silently to himself. All their fears had come true. Remembering his unwilling prediction, Hurley wondered if this was the trigger that would tear South Africa apart. Still, at the moment it was just another foreign war. Find out as much as you can, then fit the pieces together. See if it will affect the U.S., and keep out of it as much as possible. It was a job he'd done many times before, and he was good at it.

Hurley looked at his watch. There was an NSC meeting in about two hours. That was enough time to have his notes typed, and for him to wash and get something to eat. He started assembling his briefing, making notes for the typist and arranging the papers in proper order.

He had almost finished when a staffer knocked on his open door. Bill Rock, a lanky Virginian, was his assistant. He had been awake almost as long as his boss and showed it. Now he handed Hurley another handful of papers. "You'd better check this out, Ed. Hot stuff."

Hurley took them, reluctantly, and looked for a place to set them on his desk. It was too late to add any more details to his brief, and . . .

Rock noticed his intention and quickly spoke up. "I mean it, boss. Some of our signals spooks are picking up a lot of Spanish radio transmissions—south of the Angolan-Namibian border. I checked at the Cuban desk, and there's been activity—a lot of it."

Sighing, Hurley started leafing through them, at first turning the pages slowly, but speeding up as he progressed, until finally he did little more than scan the heading on each page.

Half-abstractedly, he looked at Rock and said, "Get me more," as he reached for the phone. Punching a four-digit number, he listened to a ring, then an answer. "This is Assistant Secretary Hurley. I need to speak to the secretary immediately."

CHAPTER 9

Roadblock

AUGUST 23—20TH CAPE RIFLES, NEAR BERGLAND, 40 KILOMETERS SOUTH OF WINDHOEK

Motor Route 1 ran straight through the small village of Bergland and continued, climbing steadily upward deeper into the rugged Auas Mountains. Just north of Bergland, the South African construction crews who'd built the road had chosen to go through rather than over a steep boulder- and brush-strewn ridge running from east to west. Armed with dynamite and bulldozers, they'd torn open a fifty-meter-wide gap, laid down the road, and moved on—never considering the difficulties their handiwork might create for a future invader.

They'd never imagined that their own sons would be among those trying to fight their way through the choke point they'd created.

Now Bergland's narrow streets were crammed with armored cars and troop carriers. Their scarred metal sides and gun turrets looked out of place among pristine, gabled homes and shops dating from the German colonial period.

South Africa's spearhead had ground to a complete and unexpected halt.

Commandant Henrik Kruger jumped down off the Ratel before it had even stopped moving and jogged toward the small group of dust-streaked officers clustered around a Rooikat armored fighting vehicle. A map case and canteen slung from his shoulder clattered as he ran. A young lieutenant followed him.

Maj. Daan Visser saw them coming and snapped to attention, an action swiftly imitated by his subordinates. All showed signs of increasing wear and tear. Visser's bloodshot eyes were surrounded by dark rings, and sweat, oil, and grease stains further complicated the camouflage pattern on his battle dress. Five days of nonstop driving punctuated by several short, sharp, and bloody skirmishes had left their mark.

"What's the holdup here, Daan?" Kruger didn't intend to waste precious time exchanging meaningless pleasantries. His battalion was nearly a full day behind schedule, and the fact that the schedule was ludicrous did nothing to soften the complaints coming forward from Pretoria.

"My boys and I ran into some real bastards just beyond that ridge." The major gestured to the north, his words clipped by a mixture of fatigue and excitement. "Caught us coming out of the cut."

Kruger raised his glasses to study the spot. The paved two-lane road crossed an east-west ridge there, and its builders had cut a path through the higher ground. The result was a narrow passage barely wide enough for two vehicles to pass. The *kommandant* was certain that every antitank weapon the enemy possessed was pointed at the other end of that lethal channel. As he examined it, searching for other passes, the major continued to report.

"They were zeroed in on us. We didn't have room to deploy, so we popped smoke and reversed back here to regroup."

Kruger nodded, agreeing with Visser's decision. The defile was a potential death trap for any troops or vehicles trying to force their way through against determined opposition. "Any casualties?"

Visser shook his head. "None, thank God. But it was damned close." He pointed to a thin wire draped over the Rooikat's turret and chassis. "Some kaffir swine nearly blew me to kingdom come with a fucking Sagger."

Kruger pursed his lips in a soundless whistle. The Sagger, a wire-guided antitank missile, must have passed just centimeters over the Rooikat's turret—leaving a length of its control wire as testimony of the near miss. And Namibian missile teams on the other side of the ridge could mean only one thing: they planned to stop his battalion's advance right here and right now.

Very well. If the Namibians wanted to risk a stand-up slugging match, he'd oblige them. The more Swapo troops they killed now, the fewer they'd have to contend with later.

Kruger stared up the steep slope leading to the ridge crest. "Can you get your vehicles over that?"

Visser nodded. "No problem, sir. But I'll need infantry and artillery support to deal with those *blery* missile teams."

"You'll have it." Kruger snapped open his map case, looking for a chart showing the terrain beyond the ridge. It wasn't the best place he'd ever seen for a battle. Pockets of dense brush and small trees, ravines, boulder fields, and rugged hills all offered good cover and concealment for a defending force. He didn't relish making a frontal assault against people holding ground like that, but there wasn't any realistic alternative—not in the time available. Taking the only other southern route onto the Windhoek plateau would involve backtracking nearly sixty kilometers and then making another approach march over more than three hundred kilometers of mountainous, unpaved road.

Kruger shook his head wearily. He was out of bloodless options. The battalion would simply have to grind its way through the Namibian-held valley beyond Bergland—trusting in superior training, morale, and firepower to produce a victory.

He turned to the young lieutenant at his side. "Radio all company commanders to meet me here in fifteen minutes."

Operation Nimrod was about to escalate.

FORWARD HEADQUARTERS, 8TH MOTOR RIFLE BATTALION, CUBAN EXPEDITIONARY FORCE, NORTH OF BERGLAND

Senior Capt. Victor Mares crouched beneath the tan-and-brown camouflage netting rigged to cover his wheeled BTR-60 APC. He shook his head slowly from side to side, not wanting to believe what he'd just heard through his earphones. He clicked the transmit button on his radio mike. "Repeat that please, Comrade Colonel."

The bland, cultured voice of his battalion commander took on a harder edge. "You heard me quite well the first time, Captain. You are to hold your current position. No withdrawal is authorized. I repeat, no withdrawal is authorized. Our socialist brothers are depending on us. Remember that. Out."

The transmission ended in a burst of static.

Mares pulled the earphones off and handed them back to his radioman. Had his colonel gone mad? Did the idiot really expect two companies of infantry, a few antitank missile teams, and a small section of 73mm recoilless antitank guns to hold off the entire oncoming South African column? It was insane.

The lean, clean-shaven Cuban officer ducked under the camouflage netting and moved forward to the edge of the small clump of trees occupied by his command group. Helmeted infantrymen squatting behind rocks or trees glanced nervously in his direction. Most carried AKM assault rifles, but a small number carried RPK light machine guns or clutched RPG-7s.

Fifteen other BTR-60s and infantry squads were scattered in a thin line about three hundred meters closer to the South African–held ridge—concealed where possible in brush, behind boulders, or in shallow ravines. The foot soldiers hadn't even had time to dig in. Everywhere weak, nowhere strong, the captain thought in disgust.

Mares and his men had been rushed south from Windhoek in time to block the highway above Bergland, but not fast enough to seize the ridge just north of the village. In his judgment, that made the position completely untenable. The ridge blocked his companies' lines of sight and lines of fire —allowing the South Africans to mass their forces in safety and secrecy. They could attack his overextended line at any point without warning.

And now his politically correct, but combat-wary commander had refused permission to retreat to more defensible positions closer to Windhoek. All apparently to impress the Namibians with Cuban courage and determination.

Wonderful. He and his troops were going to be sacrificed to make a political point. Madness, indeed.

"Captain!" A call from farther down the line. With one hand on his helmet to keep it from flying off, Mares dashed over to where one of his junior lieutenants crouched—scanning the ridge through a pair of binoculars.

"I see movement up there, Captain. Men on foot, in those rocks." The lieutenant pointed.

Mares lifted his own binoculars. Uniformed figures, antlike despite the magnification, came into focus. South African infantry or forward observers deploying into cover. He slapped the lieutenant on the shoulder. "Good eyes, Miguel. Keep looking."

The young officer smiled shyly.

Mares rose and raced back to his command vehicle, breathing hard. The South Africans might have all the advantages in this fight, but he still had a few surprises up his sleeve. A few high-explosive surprises.

The Cuban captain slid to a stop beside the camouflaged BTR-60 and grabbed the radio mike. "Headquarters, I have a fire mission! HE! Grid coordinates three five four eight nine nine two five!"

B COMPANY, 20TH CAPE RIFLES

High on the ridge overlooking the road to Windhoek, Capt. Robey Riekert squatted behind a large rock, watching as his lead platoon filtered through the boulder field looking for good observation points and clear fields of fire. His senior sergeant and a radioman crouched nearby.

Engine noises wafted up from behind the ridge where two troops of Major Visser's armored cars, eight vehicles in all, were toiling slowly up the steep slope. Ratel APCs carrying B Company's two remaining infantry platoons were supposed to be following the recon unit.

Satisfied that his troops were settling in, Riekert turned his attention to the desolate, tangled landscape to the north. Ugly country to fight a war in, he thought. "See anything?"

The sergeant shook his head. "Not a damn thing."

Riekert focused his binoculars on the nearest thickets of brush, panning slowly from left to right. "Maybe they've gone, eh? Pulled back closer to the city." He winced as he heard the hopeful note in his voice. He didn't really want to fight in a pitched battle. He'd seen the statistics too many times. Junior officers died fast in close contact with the enemy. And Robey Riekert wanted to live.

"I doubt it, Captain." The sergeant jerked a thumb northward. "No birds, see? You take my word for it. Those bastards are still out there."

"Perhaps, but . . ." Riekert froze. There. Outlined vaguely against dead, brown brush and tall, yellowing grass. A squat, long-hulled shape.

Oh, my God. The enemy had armor, too. He whirled to his radio operator. "Get me the colonel. Now!"

A high-pitched, whirring scream drowned him out, arcing down out of the sky. *Whammm!* The ground one hundred meters below Riekert's position suddenly erupted in smoke and flame—ripped open by an exploding shell.

The young South African officer sat stupefied for an instant. He'd never been under artillery fire before.

Whammm! Another explosion, closer this time. Rock fragments and dirt pattered down all around.

Riekert snapped out of his momentary paralysis. "Cover! Take cover! Incoming!"

The whole world seemed to explode as more and more shells rained in—shattering boulders and maiming men, blanketing the ridge in a boiling cloud of smoke and fire.

Capt. Robey Riekert, SADF, never heard the Cuban 122mm shell that landed just a meter away. And only a single blood-soaked epaulet survived to identify him for burial.

FORWARD COMMAND POST, 20TH CAPE RIFLES

"Damn it!" Henrik Kruger pounded his fist against the metal skin of his Ratel as he watched the barrage pound his forward infantry positions. "Sagger missiles, armor, and now artillery! Goddamn that stupid, bootlicking bastard de Wet! What the hell has he gotten us into?"

His staff looked carefully away, unwilling to comment on his tactless, though accurate, assessment of the SADF's commanding general.

Kruger forced himself to calm down. Rage against his idiotic superiors could wait until later. For the moment, he had a battle to conduct and a battalion to lead.

Unfortunately, his choices were strictly limited. Tactical doctrine said to suppress enemy artillery with counterbattery fire. But tactical doctrine didn't mean squat when the nearest artillery support was still six hours away by road. And the battalion's heavy mortars didn't have the range to reach the enemy firing positions.

That left him with just two options: either retreat back behind the ridge, pinned in place until friendly guns could get into position; or charge into close contact with the enemy troops, making it impossible for them to use their artillery superiority for fear of hitting their own men.

Time. Everything always came down to a question of time. The longer he waited, the longer the Namibians had to bring up reserves and fortify their positions.

Kruger thumbed the transmit switch on his mike. "Delta

Charlie Four. Delta Charlie Four, this is Tango Oscar One. Over.''

Hennie Mulder's bass baritone crackled over the radio. ''Go ahead, One.''

''Are you in position?''

Mulder's reply rumbled back. ''Sited and ready to shoot.''

Kruger nodded to himself. Good. D Company's 81mm mortars were his only available indirect fire weapons. And Mulder's heavy weapons crews were about to earn their combat pay for the first time in this campaign.

8TH MOTOR RIFLE BATTALION, CUBAN EXPEDITIONARY FORCE

Karrumph. Karrumph. Karrumph. The first South African mortar rounds landed fifty meters in front of the thin Cuban skirmish line. Gray-white smoke spewed skyward from each impact point. More rounds followed, each salvo closer still to the soldiers and vehicles scattered across the valley. In seconds, a gray haze drifted over the line, billowing high into the air and growing steadily thicker as more and more shells slammed into the ground.

Senior Capt. Victor Mares stood close to the open side hatch of his parked BTR-60 and stared south, straining to see through the South African smoke screen. Nothing. Nothing but the dull, dark mass of the ridge itself. Damn it.

His hand tightened around the radio handset. The smoke made his Sagger teams useless. The wire-guided missile had to fly at least three hundred meters before its operator could control it. Visibility was already down to one hundred meters or less.

He clicked the handset's transmit button. ''All units, report in sequence!''

Negative sighting reports crackled over his headphones, rolling in from the platoon commanders stationed left to right along his line. Nobody could see through the smoke or hear anything over the deafening noise of the mortar barrage.

Crack!

Mares jumped. That wasn't a mortar round exploding. It was the sound made by a high-velocity cannon.

Whaamm! A BTR near the middle of his line blew up in a sudden, orange-red fireball, blindingly bright even through the obscuring smoke screen. Greasy black smoke from burning diesel fuel boiled into the air.

"Here they come!" Panicked shouts poured through his headphones as South African Rooikat and Eland armored cars surged out of the smoke at high speed with all guns blazing. Three more BTRs exploded, gutted by 76 and 90mm cannon shells that tore through thin armor intended only to stop fragments. Machine-gun fire raked the nearby thickets and boulder fields—slicing through brush, ricocheting off rocks, and puncturing flesh. Cuban soldiers screamed and toppled over, some still twitching, others already dead.

Helmeted South African infantrymen were visible now, advancing in short rushes, firing assault rifles and light machine guns from the hip. Squat, boxy shapes trundled out of the concealing smoke behind them—armored personel carriers armed with machine guns and 20mm semiautomatic cannon.

Mares stood motionless, shocked by the ferocity of the South African assault. His troops were being cut to pieces right before his eyes.

A BTR roared past him, sand spraying from under spinning tires. Hatches left open by its disembarked and abandoned infantry squad clanged to and fro. Other vehicles followed, fleeing the carnage spreading up and down the Cuban front line.

The 8th Motor Rifle Battalion was collapsing.

FORWARD HEADQUARTERS, 20TH CAPE RIFLES

Henrik Kruger's Ratel command vehicle lurched abruptly as its front wheels bounced over a rock the driver hadn't seen. He braced himself against the open turret hatch and kept scanning the steep, brush-choked slope stretching before him.

Three Ratels were moving a hundred meters out in front

—spread wide in a wedge formation. More APCs were farther ahead, already down on the valley floor and vanishing into the smoky haze. Incandescent, split-second flashes from inside the smoke screen showed where vehicles were firing. Flickering, molten-orange glows marked the smoldering funeral pyres of their victims.

A blurred, static-distorted voice crackled over the radio.

Kruger took one hand off the hatch coaming to press his headset closer. The constant din created by barking tank cannon, chattering machine guns, mortars, and screaming men made it difficult to hear—let alone think. "Say again, Echo Four."

"The bastards are running, Tango Oscar One! Repeat, we have them running!" Maj. Daan Visser's wild exhilaration came clearly over the airwaves. "Am pursuing at full speed!"

What? Kruger suddenly felt cold. At full speed, Visser's armored vehicles would soon outpace the rest of the battalion. And that meant his infantry companies wouldn't have the armored support they needed. It would also leave the Rooikats and Elands moving blind through enemy-held territory.

He squeezed the transmit switch on his mike. "Negative, Echo Four. Wait for the infantry. Do not, repeat, do not pursue on your own!" He released the switch, listening for a reply.

He never got one.

ROOIKAT 101, ATTACHED RECON SQUADRON, 20TH CAPE RIFLES

Diesel engine roaring, the eight-wheeled Rooikat AFV bounced up and over the lip of a narrow gulley at high speed. Small trees and thorn bushes lining the gulley were either knocked aside or flattened and crushed by its big radial tires.

Maj. Daan Visser stood high in the Rooikat's open commander's cupola. Dark, tinted goggles and a fluttering orange scarf protected his eyes and his mouth from the sand and acrid smoke. The long barrel of a cupola-mounted machine gun bounced and rolled beside him.

For the moment, Visser and his crew were effectively alone on the battlefield. Swirling smoke and dust had so cut visibility that the seven other Rooikats and Elands of his two troops were out of sight and out of command. And they'd left the supporting infantry far behind. From the sounds echoing through the haze, the footsloggers were still busy mopping up scattered resistance.

Visser grinned beneath his scarf. Let Kruger's poor, cautious sods worry about routing out every last sniper. He and his lads would show them the right way to win this war. Smash a hole in the Swapo lines, pour through, and then run the survivors into the ground. That was the road to victory. And to glory.

Forty meters ahead, a fleeing BTR-60 blundered out of the smoke into the Rooikat's path. "Gunner, target at one o'clock!"

The AFV's overlarge turret whined, spinning thirty degrees to the right. "Acquired!" The gunner's voice reflected Visser's own exultation. Nothing was easier than shooting at people unable or unwilling to shoot back.

"Fire!" The turret lurched backward as its main gun fired, easily absorbing the sudden shock. A 76mm armor-piercing shell ripped the enemy APC open from end to end in a spray of white-hot fragments and fuel.

Seconds later, the Rooikat raced by the BTR's shattered, blazing hulk, passing so close that Visser could feel the heat of the flames on his face. Another kill. Another trophy.

Something moved in a dense patch of brush off to his left. He spun round in the open cupola, eyes searching for the enemy vehicle that would be his Rooikat's next victim.

It wasn't a vehicle. Just a lone infantryman who'd risen from the tangle of thorns and tall grass in a single, fluid motion—with an RPG-7 at the ready. Time seemed to slow.

Visser noticed something odd. The man was light skinned, not a black. The grenade-tipped muzzle of the RPG swung left, tracking the still-moving Rooikat.

Oh, my God. Visser clawed frantically for the machine gun mounted next to him, ice-cold fear surging upward to replace elation. If he could just swing the MG around in time, he'd cut the swine in half. . . .

The foot soldier fired his RPG at point-blank range. Trailing flame, the 85mm rocket-propelled antitank grenade flew straight into the side of the Rooikat's lightly armored turret and exploded.

In a strange sense, Maj. Daan Visser was lucky to the end. The blast killed him instantly. His three crewmen weren't so fortunate. They burned to death in the fire that swept through the Rooikat's mangled turret and hull.

20TH CAPE RIFLES

Commandant Kruger looked out across a valley unloved by nature and now ravaged by man.

Burning vehicles spewing smoke dotted the battlefield—some alone, others in small clusters. Bodies littered the ground near each wrecked vehicle. Brush fires set by mortar rounds and exploding fuel tanks crackled merrily, punctuated by short, sharp popping sounds as the fires swept over dead or wounded men carrying ammunition.

Medical teams roamed the valley, searching for men who could still be saved. Overcrowded ambulances were already wending their way south from the battalion aid station—transporting serious cases to the evac hospital set up in Rehoboth. Some were bound to die on the sixty-kilometer trip.

Technicians and mammoth tank recovery vehicles clustered around some of the wrecks—preparing to drag away any that could be repaired. Still more quartermaster corps units crisscrossed the battlefield, collecting the individual weapons—rifles, machine guns, and RPGs—dropped by both sides.

Other men stumbled or were prodded toward the rear with their arms raised high in surrender. Small groups of prisoners being driven south at bayonet point. Cuban prisoners.

Kruger frowned. The presence of Cuban motor rifle units explained the stiff resistance his men had faced, but it raised another even more troubling issue. South Africa's intelligence services had claimed that a shortage of strategic transport would make it impossible for Cuba to interfere with Operation Nimrod. It didn't take a genius to see that they'd been dead wrong.

The question was, how many Cubans were already in Namibia and how fast were they arriving?

Footsteps crunched on the sand behind him. He turned slowly and saw the short, stocky, grim-faced officer who'd replaced Visser. "Well, Captain?"

The other man swallowed hard, obviously still reluctant to believe what he had to report. "Scarcely half the squadron is ready for action. Two Rooikats and an Eland are total write-offs. Two more need major repair."

Kruger nodded. The casualty figures tallied precisely with his own preliminary estimate. Visser's idiotic cavalry charge had done serious damage to the enemy, but it had also wrecked his own force. And when added to the serious losses suffered by B Company, that spelled big trouble for the 20th Cape Rifles.

They'd driven the Cuban force back several kilometers, but the victory had been bought at too high a price. The battalion's attached armored units needed time for rest and repair. His infantry companies were thoroughly disorganized and urgently needed replacements for those who'd been killed or wounded. And worst of all, Hennie Mulder's heavy mortars were almost out of smoke rounds and were low on everything else, including HE.

Kruger swiveled north, his eyes narrowed—studying the thin asphalt strip of Motor Route 1 as it wound its way higher and higher into the rugged Auas Mountains. Every instinct and every ounce of experience told him that the days of lightning-swift advances and easy glory were over. One afternoon's fiery engagement had blunted the SADF's headlong plunge into Namibia.

Resolute and well-equipped defenders could hold that mountain pass with relative ease—parrying attacks launched on what would become an increasingly narrow front. The war would become a war of attrition—a war in which soldiers sold their lives for a few square kilometers of relatively worthless ground.

One thing was clear. If South Africa wanted Windhoek, it was going to have to pay a high price. A price Henrik Kruger wasn't sure his country could afford.

8TH MOTOR RIFLE BATTALION

High on a boulder-strewn hill six kilometers closer to Windhoek, Senior Capt. Victor Mares sat slumped against the side of his BTR-60, surrounded by the remnants of his command group. A rust-brown bloodstain spread across his battle dress served as a reminder of his dead radioman—cut down by South African MG fire during the last frantic rush to board the APC and escape.

What was left of his two companies—five battle-scarred BTRs and a handful of ragged infantry—held temporary firing positions covering the road. The Cuban captain doubted whether they'd last more than five minutes against a renewed South African attack. The 8th Motor Rifle Battalion had been decimated.

Oddly enough, though, the South Africans seemed in no hurry to press their advantage. Maybe they'd taken more damage than he'd realized. Maybe they were overconfident. Maybe they were retreating to try another route through the mountains. Mares was just too damned tired to care. Sleep crept up, filtering in through a nervous system already drained by the excitement and sheer terror of battle.

"Captain!"

Mares sat bolt upright and stared at the young lieutenant scrambling frantically up the hill toward him.

"Captain! They're here! They're here!"

Hell. He jumped to his feet, despair replacing fatigue. In minutes, he and his men would be dead or dying. And the damned South Africans would be racing past them to capture Windhoek.

Then Mares realized that the lieutenant was pointing north—not south. North toward a long column of wheeled APCs and trucks towing antitank guns. A Cuban flag fluttered from the lead GAZ-69 jeep's long, thin radio antenna.

His battalion's sacrifice had not been in vain. The road to Namibia's capital was closed.

AUGUST 24—WINDHOEK AIRPORT, NAMIBIA

Huge, multiengined jet transports orbited slowly low over Windhoek's single airstrip, waiting for their turn to land on an already crowded runway. Those already on the ground taxied toward waiting work crews and fuel trucks.

Of all the hundreds of men at the airport, only four wore civilian clothing.

Several Cuban soldiers and two officers escorted the French free-lance reporter and his camera crew—shepherding them through apparent chaos while they looked for just the right spot to shoot the promised interview.

Time and again they stopped, only to walk on when the soundman shook his head—driven on by a maddening combination of wind and roaring jet engines that made recording human voices impossible.

At last, they found a sheltered spot with a fine view of the flight line. The Frenchman stepped out in front of the camera. He was a tall, rangy man, and years of outdoor assignments in world trouble spots and war zones had given him a windburned and disheveled look that makeup could not conceal. One of the two Cuban officers followed him and stood at his side.

"Very well. Let's try to do this in a single take, okay?"

His crew and the Cubans nodded, all hoping to get in out of the wind and noise. The cameraman lifted his Minicam onto his shoulder and punched a switch. "Recording."

"This is Windhoek Airport. Normally a small field serving the rustic capital of the world's newest nation, it is now the center of a fierce military struggle. With South African military units about fifty kilometers away from the city, Cuban and Angolan reinforcements are being airlifted in at a breakneck pace. While the exact numbers are a closely guarded secret, each of the big Il-76 transports you see landing behind me can carry more than one hundred fifty troops or two armored fighting vehicles." The reporter paused, waiting as a jet screamed past on final approach. "And planes have been landing like this for the past two days.

"With me is Colonel Xavier Farrales of the Cuban Army." The colonel was a short, dark-skinned man in dress uniform. Although the winter season moderated the heat somewhat, the colonel was clearly uncomfortable. He had his orders, though, and knew exactly what he had to say. He smiled warmly and nodded at the camera.

The Frenchman turned toward him, mike in hand. "Colonel, Western intelligence sources have claimed that these big Ilyushin transports aren't part of Cuba's regular Air Force. And there've been other, as yet unconfirmed, reports of advanced surface-to-air missiles and other hardware being used here that aren't normally in your country's inventory. Certainly all this must be a tremendous financial drain on your country. How much financial and logistic support has the Soviet Union promised to provide? And does Moscow plan to commit its own ground troops?"

The colonel's English was accented but clear. He had been carefully chosen for this task. Smiling, he said, "Certainly Cuba is a small country. We have little to spend but our soldiers' blood, and much of this would be impossible without fraternal assistance. We are receiving help from many of our socialist allies. Naturally, I cannot speak for the depth of any one country's support. Any participation in this struggle for freedom is honorable, no matter how large or how small."

The Cuban officer's smile grew slightly less sincere. "We would even welcome assistance from the West's so-called democracies. South Africa's aggression is a matter that should cross all ideological boundaries."

The reporter hid a grimace. Political doublespeak made poor television. He persisted. "But what are your country's long-range intentions in Namibia? What do you hope to gain from your involvement in this war?"

Farrales puffed up his beribboned chest. "Cuba's only goal is to drive the South Africans from Namibia and to secure its sovereignty for the future. All our efforts, both diplomatic and military, are designed to achieve this result. That is why our forces are converging here, at Windhoek, to repel the completely unjustified attack made by Pretoria's racist forces. Cuba is only fulfilling her internationalist duty."

The Frenchman nodded. He could recognize a closing statement when he heard one. Fine. They wouldn't get much useful play out of the colonel's pompous rhetoric, but at least they'd be able to sell some good, dramatic pictures of Cuba's massive airlift. He stepped back and made a cutting motion across his throat, signaling his cameraman to stop shooting. "Thank you, Colonel. You've been most helpful."

Farrales took the Frenchman's offered hand, shook it, and walked away—glad to have escaped so easily. Western journalists were usually irritatingly cynical and uncooperative. In any event, the reporter and his crew would be on an airplane bound for Luanda inside the hour. From there, their story would be edited and transmitted around the world—pouring visual evidence of Cuba's power and resolve into the homes of tens of millions.

Gen. Antonio Vega's temporary headquarters occupied one wing of the small airport terminal, and Farrales made haste to report. After being passed through by the general's aide and radio operator, the colonel knocked twice on a wooden door and entered without waiting.

Vega sat at a camp desk, surrounded by maps, books, and pieces of paper. His uniform coat hung from a hook with his tie draped over it. Wearing a rarely seen pair of glasses, he worked steadily, punching in numbers on a German–manufactured pocket calculator.

Farrales saluted.

"Report, Colonel." Vega's tone was impatient, and he did not look up from his work. "Were you successful?"

"Yes, Comrade General. I included the information we wanted to make known and rubbed their noses in the West's cowardice as well."

Vega glanced at him, smiling now. "Good. Very good." He turned back to his work, still speaking. "Since this interview went so well, Colonel Farrales, see how many others you can set up. As long as the Western media is singing our song, let's help them sing it. It's nice to have them on our side for a change."

Vega finished his calculations and made a series of rapid notations on one of the maps. Then he stood up, stretched, and started to clear the camp desk. "Now, get my aide in here. I want to be on the next plane to Karibib."

Forty minutes later, the Frenchman and his film crew boarded an Angolan TAAG airlines An-26, a Russian-built transport aircraft that was also used as a civil airliner. No amount of bright paint could hide its military origins. The rear loading ramp was a dead giveaway, as were the seats that folded up against the cabin sides.

As the An-26 took off and climbed high above the barren Namibian landscape, its pilot turned a little farther to the east than normal. This ensured that the plane passed well out of sight of the small town of Karibib—140 kilometers northwest of Windhoek, as the transport flies. It was 180 kilometers by what passed for a road.

Gen. Antonio Vega's plane, a Cuban Air Force An-26 in a drab sand-and-green paint scheme, followed ten minutes behind—closely escorted by two MiG-29s. But instead of continuing north toward Luanda, the large twin turboprop slid west—on course for Karibib.

KARIBIB AIRHEAD, NAMIBIA

Twenty minutes out of Windhoek, Vega's An-26 orbited, circling low over Karibib's single, unpaved runway. The traffic pattern over the small airstrip was jammed with military aircraft of all sizes and types.

For once, Vega had refused the privileges associated with his rank, content to wait his turn in the landing pattern. Nothing could be allowed to interfere with this operation—especially not meaningless and time-wasting ceremony.

As the plane circled, he watched the frantic loading and unloading process going on below him. Huge Il-76, smaller

Antonov aircraft like his own, and even Ilyushin airliners from Air Cuba, all had to land, unload, and fuel simultaneously, then turn round for an immediate takeoff. Karibib's airfield only had room for three aircraft on the field at once.

Fighters circled higher, constantly on watch for snooping South African reconnaissance planes.

In the distance, Vega saw a small tent city and rows of parked vehicles. There should have been more of them. But at this range from their bases, even the USSR's big Il-76s could only carry two armored personnel carriers. As a result, it had taken more than thirty sorties over the past three days just to ferry in the equipment for a reinforced motorized rifle battalion.

Vega frowned. So small a force for such an important mission. He would have preferred sending a regiment-sized tactical group, but time was short and the opportunity he saw was bound to be fleeting. With calculation and a little luck, the gamble he planned to take would pay off. And in a pinch, he could skip the calculation.

"Antonov One One, you are cleared to land." The controller's voice sounded bone tired, reflecting nearly seventy-two hours of nonstop flight operations directed from a small trailer parked off to one side of Karibib's dirt runway.

"Acknowledged, Control. On final, now."

Vega slid forward against his seat belt as the transport dropped steeply and all but dove for the strip. He felt his stomach churn and swallowed hard, fighting to keep a placid appearance. Senior commanders in the Cuban Army did not get airsick in front of their subordinates. He knew what was happening; it was only his stomach that hadn't been informed.

The pilot's combat landing was rough, but acceptable, and as soon as they had taxied to what passed for a tarmac, ground crewmen chocked the wheels and started to refuel the Antonov's tanks from fuel bladders and a portable pump.

The plane's rear ramp whined open before its propellers had even stopped spinning.

Col. Carlos Pellervo was waiting, breathless, with the rest of the battalion staff as Vega's command group left the plane. He braced and saluted as the general approached.

Vega returned the salute, and both men dropped their hands. Pellervo remained at rigid attention.

Still feeling queasy from the flight, Vega sourly noted the man's harried expression and partially unbuttoned tunic. Though politically well-connected, Pellervo hadn't been his first choice for this post. Unfortunately, the man's battalion had been the first unit that could be spared from the buildup around Windhoek.

Vega frowned. He wasn't a stickler for spit and polish, but there were certain standards to be maintained. "Good afternoon, Colonel." His voice grew harsher. "I assume you received word of my intention to inspect your troops? I know for a fact that a message was sent more than two hours ago. Have I interrupted a siesta or some other form of recreation?"

Pellervo blanched. "No, Comrade General!" He hurried on, practically stammering. "I was called away a short time ago to resolve a problem with our ammunition storage. It has just been corrected."

Vega looked him up and down. "Comrade Colonel, you should not let one crisis upset your plans or cause you to rush. I need officers who can remain calm in confusion, who can improvise and overcome difficulties. Is that clear?"

Pellervo nodded several times, his face pale beneath a desert-acquired tan.

Vega changed tack, satisfied that his reprimand had hit home. "Are your preparations on schedule?"

"*Sí*, Comrade General, everything is going according to plan." Pellervo waved a chubby hand toward the busy airfield, obviously relieved to be out of the spotlight.

"Excellent." Vega turned away, hands clasped behind his back.

The attack slated to begin in just five hours was still risky, but he couldn't see any reasonable alternative. Soviet air transports could ferry in enough men and gear to hold Namibia's northern regions against South Africa's invasion force, but they couldn't carry large numbers of heavier weapons and armor. The tanks and heavy artillery he needed to mount a successful counteroffensive could only come by ship.

And just one port on the Namibian coast was large enough

to accommodate the Soviet-owned freighters and troop transports already at sea. Just one.

Vega stared southwest, away from Karibib's busy airport, his eyes scanning the barren Namibian desert. South Africa's high command was about to learn that two could play this game of strategic hide-and-seek and misdirection.

AUGUST 25—5TH MECHANIZED INFANTRY, SEVENTY-FIVE KILOMETERS WEST OF WINDHOEK, ON ROUTE 52

The eastern sky had brightened from pitch-black to a much lighter, pink-tinged gray—a sure sign that sunrise wasn't far off. Sunrise and the start of another day of war.

The hulls of dozens of South African armored vehicles stood out against the vast sand wastes of the Namib Desert. To the south, the rocky, rugged slopes of the Gamsberg rose twenty-three hundred meters into the cloudless sky, punching up out of the desert floor like a giant humpback whale coming up for air. Other mountains rose beyond it, all shimmering a faint rosy red in the growing light, and all leading generally east toward the Namibian capital of Windhoek.

Col. George von Brandis sat atop his Ratel command vehicle studying his map. Von Brandis, a tall, slender, balding officer, was not happy. Not with the position of his battalion. Not with his mission. And not with his orders.

He and his men had been driving steadily eastward since leaving Walvis Bay, South Africa's coastal enclave, before dawn on the eighteenth—crushing a few minor border posts and a company-sized Namibian garrison holding the Rossing uranium mine in the process. Since then, they'd met little resistance and made tremendous progress.

By rights he should have been exhilarated by the 5th Mechanized Infantry's successes, but von Brandis couldn't help looking worriedly over his left shoulder—off into the vast emptiness to the north. General de Wet and his staff were fools if they thought the Angolans and Cubans were going to leave him alone. Luanda's Marxists had too much to lose if South Africa reoccupied its former colony. They were bound to hit him soon. Even if there weren't any major enemy units to the north, there certainly weren't any South African units out there either. The flat, arid landscape stretched off to his left like an unknown world.

Von Brandis looked at his map. His supply lines also concerned him. He'd taken everything but a small security detachment with him when he left Walvis Bay. Follow-up reinforcements were slated to garrison the port, but until they arrived, the place was almost defenseless. And any enemy who captured Walvis Bay would control his battalion's only link with South Africa.

Damn it. He crumpled the map and stuffed it into a pocket of his brown battle dress. Pretoria's orders posed an unresolvable dilemma. He'd read the careful, staff-written phrases a hundred times, but being carefully crafted didn't make them any clearer.

The 5th Mechanized Infantry had been ordered to push east toward Windhoek as rapidly as possible, maintaining constant pressure on Namibia's defense forces. Von Brandis and his men were supposed to seize territory and pin the enemy units deployed around Windhoek, especially Namibia's single motorized brigade. In a sense, they were supposed to draw the enemy's eyes and firepower away from the far stronger SADF column advancing from Keetmanshoop.

No problem there. A clear, though somewhat dangerous, mission.

The trouble came in a last-minute addition tacked on when Pretoria realized its limited resources would not permit the swift reinforcement of Walvis Bay. So de Wet's staff had "solved" its problem by ordering the 5th Mechanized Infantry to be everywhere at once. Advance aggressively on Windhoek, but ensure the security of Walvis Bay. Pin most of the enemy mobile force, but take no offensive actions that might expose the base to loss.

In other words, he was supposed to move fast and hard against the Namibians, while simultaneously covering hundreds of kilometers of exposed flank and keeping his rear secure. Right.

The colonel grimaced. They didn't pay him to play safe,

or to avoid risks. The best way to keep his flanks safe was to keep moving so rapidly that the enemy never knew exactly where his flanks were.

Noises rising from the vehicles laagered all around his Ratel told him his battalion was waking up. He looked around the encampment. The 5th's camouflaged armored cars and personnel carriers were vastly outnumbered by a fleet of canvas-sided trucks, petrol tankers, and other supply vehicles bringing up the rear. A huge logistical tail was a necessary evil when fighting in Namibia's arid wastelands. Without large quantities of ammunition, fuel, food, and especially water, the battalion's fighting vehicles would be helpless.

He yawned once and then again. It had taken all night to refuel and rearm the unit's operational vehicles, and his maintenance crews were exhausted from recovering and repairing those that had broken down during the long, wearing advance. More than twenty Eland armored cars, Ratel personnel carriers, trucks, and towed artillery pieces had needed their foul-mouthed swearing, sweating attention.

Now refitted, but hardly refreshed, his men were walking about the battalion laager in the predawn gray, starting engines, checking equipment, and brewing tea against the early-morning chill. It was just bright enough to see the shadowy forms of the men and their vehicles as a blinding red bar of light edged over the hills on the eastern horizon.

Von Brandis squinted into the rising sun, looking for the enemy he planned to destroy before continuing his drive on Windhoek. The remnants of a Namibian battalion were dug in on a line of low hills, really just rises, stretching from north to south. Remnants might even be too strong a word to describe what should be left of the Swapo unit, he thought. The 5th Mechanized had already smashed one company-strength force of Namibian infantry the day before, and a second that same afternoon.

Unfortunately, the battalion's need to refuel, rearm, and repair its broken-down vehicles had prevented a full-scale exploitation of those victories. The night's respite had given the Namibians time to assemble a scratch force blocking the western route to their capital.

Von Brandis shrugged. One quick firefight should do the trick. He unfolded a battered, oil-stained map. It never hurt to reexamine an attack plan formulated late at night by lamp light.

"Morning, *Kolonel*." His driver, Johann, handed him a chipped china mug.

Sipping the strong, scalding-hot liquid, von Brandis studied the map and tried to ignore the Ratel's bumpy, hard metal decking beneath him. He also tried to forget his rumpled appearance and barnyard smell after a week in the field. Some of his troops swore that the stink of unwashed clothing, dried sweat, and cordite made the best snake repellent known to man. He didn't doubt it. No self-respecting reptile would dare come within half a klick of anyone who smelled so bad.

But despite all its drawbacks, the colonel had to admit that he enjoyed campaigning. He liked the hard, outdoor life, the rewards that came with higher rank, and the challenge of defeating his country's enemies. He studied the map as if it were a chessboard, looking for a tactical solution that would spare his men any loss and crush the Namibians completely.

Reality never quite measured up to paper expectations, but he was happy with his present plan. It should produce heavy enemy casualties with a minimal expenditure of ammunition, fuel, and friendly lives.

He was measuring distances when Major Hougaard's voice crackled over his radio headset. "All Foxtrot companies ready to go. Foxtrot Delta is already moving."

The sound of engines roaring behind him confirmed his executive officer's report.

Excellent.

Von Brandis traced the gully he'd found on the map. It paralleled Route 52 to the south, bypassing the low hills in front of them before winding north. On his orders, the battalion's dismounted scouts had spent the night checking it and quietly clearing the depression of a few sleeping guards. They now watched the Namibians from the gully's edge and awaited D Squadron's Eland armored cars.

With infantry squads riding on top, the 90mm gun–armed

Elands would flank the Namibian entrenchments and flush the Swapo bastards out of their holes. Once that had happened, von Brandis planned to hit them with an HE barrage from his battery of towed mortars and then mop them up with a Ratel-mounted infantry assault. It was a bit of overkill, he thought, for a bunch of untrained kaffirs, but twenty years of warfare in Angola and Namibia had taught him never to underestimate the fighting power of a dug-in enemy.

Also, he wanted to crush the enemy battalion—to so shatter the unit that the Namibians would have to commit fresh reserves. Anything that drew Swapo or Cuban troops away from the Auas Mountains would help revive South Africa's stalled southern attack. Von Brandis knew his force was supposed to be Nimrod's secondary effort, but there were many ways to win a war.

He scanned the brown, treeless slopes about two and a half kilometers away, just outside heavy machine-gun range. Nothing. No signs of life at all. The hills looked as barren as an arid, airless moonscape.

Von Brandis checked his watch and then his map—following D Squadron's flank attack in his mind's eye. Right now the company should be carefully picking its way along the rocky, waterless stream bed, thirteen armored cars with foot soldiers from C Company clinging to them as they bumped and swayed over uneven ground. The scouts were covering their approach, thank God.

He lowered the map again and swung his binoculars left and then right, checking the battalion's other units. They were formed, hidden by folds in the ground. A and B Company's Ratels were unbuttoned, but their troops were close by, ready to board and make the planned final assault.

It was getting lighter, and he could imagine the Namibian commander congratulating himself on successfully holding the South Africans at bay for a whole night. A man's spirits rose with the sun. The Swapo clown was probably trying to decide how he could strengthen his defense or even scrape up enough reinforcements for a limited counterattack. . . .

"Foxtrot Hotel One, this is Foxtrot Sierra One. Enemy

positions are starting to stir. We can hear Delta's engines.'' The scout captain sounded bored—a triumph of training over nerves.

Von Brandis tensed. This was the period of greatest danger. If the Elands were caught while confined by the steep gully walls, they'd be easy targets for Namibian RPGs. If that happened, he was prepared to order an immediate frontal assault to rescue the armored car squadron and its attached infantry. Though normally a dangerous course, it would probably succeed against such a weak Swapo unit—especially one already distracted by a move against its left flank.

''Hotel One, this is Sierra. Ready.'' The short transmission from the scouts meant that they were in position. He could expect to hear firing anytime.

Von Brandis heard the *crack* of a high-velocity gun, but it was somehow a deeper, fuller sound than that made by an Eland's 90mm cannon.

Whooosh! A shell screamed overhead and burst about a hundred meters to the right, dangerously near a group of A Company Ratels. The explosion threw up a cloud of dirt and rock and triggered a mass movement of men and vehicles. The sound of engines starting and hatches slamming almost covered the sound of other guns, clearly firing from somewhere ahead on the Namibian-held ridge line. The scream of incoming projectiles and thundering explosions became almost continuous.

His vehicles were all under cover, to prevent observation as much as to protect them from incoming fire. Still, the Namibians were shooting mainly to keep their heads down, and it was working.

The colonel fought the urge to take cover inside his Ratel and instead scanned the enemy ridge again. A momentary puff of gray smoke and stabbing orange flame caught his eye. He focused the binoculars. There! The shot came from a small, dark bump lumbering downhill toward his battalion's positions. Suddenly, as if his eyes now knew what to look for, he realized that there were three . . . five . . . eight, nine, ten other vehicles, all firing and moving. A tank company!

Small dots clumped behind the tanks. Infantry trotting to keep up with their armored protectors. He lowered his binoculars. My God, the Namibians were actually launching a combined arms counterattack on his battalion. It was astounding, almost unbelievable.

New noises rose above the unearthly din. While the tank shells made a low, roaring whoosh, these were high-pitched screams, followed by even bigger explosions. Heavy mortars!

Von Brandis dropped into the Ratel and slammed the hatch shut. He needed no further encouragement. Time to act. He looked at the map, trying to remember where the wind was blowing from. From the west. Good. He tapped the young Citizen Force corporal acting as his radioman on the shoulder. "Tell the mortars to drop smoke five hundred meters in front of our position. Then warn the antitank jeeps to be ready to fire when the enemy tanks come out of our smoke screen."

Aside from the Eland armored cars already committed to the flank attack, the only antitank weapons the battalion had were ancient French-designed SS.11 missiles mounted on unarmored jeeps. Von Brandis hadn't been able to identify the tanks at such range, but they were probably T-54s or T-55s. He'd fought them before—big, lumbering behemoths with 100mm guns and heavy armor. Then he remembered the Angolans and Cubans were in the act. They had T-62s, with 115mm guns and better fire-control gear.

Christ! His SS.11s were an even match for enemy T-55s, but he didn't know if their warheads could penetrate the frontal armor of a T-62. He had the unpleasant feeling he was about to find out.

Where the hell was D Squadron? He needed those big-gunned armored cars in the battle now—not pissing around down in the bottom of that bloody gully. He fiddled with his radio headset, waiting impatiently as he listened to the radio operator passing his instructions to the antitank section. The corporal stopped talking. A clear circuit! Von Brandis squeezed the transmit switch on his mike. "Foxtrot Delta One, this is Foxtrot Hotel One. What is your status, over?"

Cannon and machine-gun fire mixed with the voice in his earphones. "Hotel One, this is Delta One. Engaging enemy infantry force. Have located one battery large mortars. Am attacking now. No casualties. Hotel, we see signs of tank movement. Repeat, we see many tread marks, over."

Thanks for the warning, Von Brandis thought, but said nothing. "Delta One, detach one troop to attack the mortars, but bring the rest of your force back west soonest! We are under attack by a tank company and an unknown number of infantry."

The radio easily carried the Eland squadron commander's shock and surprise. "Roger. Will engage tanks to the west. Out!"

Nearly four minutes had passed, enough for the oncoming enemy tanks to advance a few hundred meters. Von Brandis peered through the small, thick-glassed peepholes in the APC's turret. Nothing. He couldn't see a damned thing.

Cursing the misnamed "vision blocks" under his breath, he opened the roof hatch again and used his binoculars to study the advancing enemy formation.

Mortar rounds burst in front of the charging tanks—spraying tendrils of gray-white smoke high into the air. Created by a chemical reaction in each mortar shell, the smoke was working—blown by a light northwesterly breeze toward the advancing tank company, reducing the effectiveness of their fire.

Karumph! A mortar explosion nearby reminded him that they were still in trouble, and he mentally urged D Squadron onward. The battalion needed their firepower.

The enemy tanks were still shooting as they drew nearer, starting to vanish in the South African smoke screen. Von Brandis ignored them. Moving fire from a tank, especially an old one, isn't that accurate. His own men were holding their fire, waiting until the enemy emerged from the smoke inside effective range. Then the fun would start, he thought.

More shells slammed into the desert landscape. The Namibian mortar barrage was getting close. Damned close. Too late, Von Brandis realized that the enemy gunners were randomly concentrating their fire on different parts of his spread-out position. Unable to see their targets, they were simply lobbing rounds at designated map references. Unfortunately, they'd apparently chosen the small depression occupied by his command post for their latest firing point. Even blind fire, when concentrated in a small area, could be devastating.

Whammm! He slammed the Ratel's hatch shut again as an explosion just twenty meters away shook the APC and sent fragments, not pebbles, rattling off its armor. Von Brandis dogged the hatch and spun round to follow the situation through the vehicle's vision blocks.

Twin hammer blows struck the Ratel's left side. The first mortar round seemed to slide the eighteen-ton vehicle physically sideways, then a second shell lifted it and tipped it over.

Von Brandis and the rest of his staff tumbled and twisted inside the APC's tangled interior. Loose gear fell through the air, and they fought to keep from impaling themselves on the troop compartment's myriad sharp points and corners. Worst of all, someone's assault rifle hadn't been secured in its clips.

The R4 spun through the air as the Ratel tumbled, slammed into the deck, and went off. A single, steel-jacketed round ricocheted from metal wall to metal wall, showering the interior with sparks, before burying itself deep in the assistant driver's belly. The man screamed and collapsed in on himself, his hands clutching convulsively at the gaping wound.

Von Brandis fought a personal war with the edge of the map table, a fire extinguisher handle, and his radio cord. Finally freeing himself and standing up on the canted deck, he tossed a first aid kit to his driver and reached up to unlock one of the roof hatches.

He bent down and looked before crawling out, taking his own assault rifle with him.

Everyone was still under cover against random mortar volleys and suppressive fire from the advancing enemy tank company. He scanned the forward edge of the battalion's gray, roiling smoke screen. Nothing in sight there. Right, the enemy armor should still be about a kilometer away.

The Namibian mortars had shifted targets within his battalion's position and now seemed to be bombarding an empty piece of desert. Good. That was one advantage of a dispersed deployment. A fine haze of dust and smoke obscured anything over five hundred meters away and made him cough. It was getting warmer, but the sun wouldn't burn off this acrid mist.

The disadvantage of dispersion was the difficulty of getting from place to place, especially under fire. His executive officer's command Ratel was more than a hundred and fifty meters away, behind a low rise near A Company's laager and fighting positions.

He leaned down through the open hatch. "I'm going to Major Hougaard's vehicle! Frans, come with me. The rest of you stay put!"

As soon as the radio operator crawled out and climbed to his feet, the two men sprinted off, ducking more out of instinct than reasoned thought as shells burst to either side. Mortar fragments rip through the air faster than any human can hope to react.

It was only the barest taste of an infantryman's world, but the colonel longed for the relative safety of his command vehicle. Running desperately across open, hard-packed sand under fire seemed a poor way to run a battle.

They reached the side of Hougaard's Ratel and von Brandis banged on its armored side door with the hilt of his bayonet. It opened after a nerve-racking, five-second pause, and the two men piled inside the Ratel's already crowded interior.

Von Brandis squeezed through the crush toward a round-faced, bearded man with deceptively soft-looking features.

"Colonel, what on earth . . . !" Major Jamie Hougaard exclaimed, then cut off the rest of his sentence as superfluous. It was obvious that his commander's vehicle had been hit. And the details would have to wait.

"What's the situation?" Von Brandis didn't have time to waste in idle chitchat. He'd lost a precious couple of minutes while transferring to this secondary command post.

Hougaard held his hand over one radio headphone, pressing it to his ear as he listened to a new report just coming in. "The Elands are engaging that *verdomde* mortar battery now. And that should put a stop to this *blery* barrage. They've killed a lot of infantry, too."

Von Brandis nodded. That was good news, but not his

main concern. What about the enemy tanks? They'd reach the edge of his smoke soon. Luckily, the forward observer for his own mortar battery was located in Hougaard's vehicle.

He turned to the young artillery officer and ordered, "Fire only enough smoke to maintain the screen. Mix HE in with the smoke rounds, fuzed for airburst."

The lieutenant nodded his understanding eagerly. A few mortar rounds bursting in midair, showering the ground below with sharp-edged steel fragments, should strip the attacking infantry away from their tanks.

Hougaard handed him a headset. He shrugged out of his helmet and slid the set over his ears in time to hear Hougaard's voice over the circuit. "Delta One, repeat your last, over."

The armored car squadron commander's voice was exultant. Though he was momentarily drowned out by the sound of his own big gun firing, von Brandis still understood his report. "Roger, Foxtrot Hotel Two. We are in defilade, engaging the tanks from the rear at one thousand meters. Three, no, five kills! Continuing to engage. Enemy attack breaking up."

His voice was masked again by a *boom-clang* as the Eland's 90mm gun fired and the breech ejected a spent shell casing. "Excuse me, Hotel, but we're a little busy here. Out."

Von Brandis and Hougaard grinned at each other. They were winning. No enemy force could take that kind of pounding from the rear for long.

Von Brandis turned to the young artillery officer again. "Change that last order. Cease smoke, and start a walking barrage fifteen hundred meters out with airbursts. Let's really break these bastards up!"

As the smoke cleared, von Brandis saw burning vehicles and bodies sprawled in a rough band a kilometer from his own line. There were still a few enemy tanks operational, but as they turned to engage the threat to their rear, the battalion's jeep-mounted antitank missiles had easy shots and quickly finished off the survivors. Dirty-gray puffs of smoke appeared up and down the enemy line as his mortars worked the exposed Namibian infantry over.

The enemy attack was routed. Soldiers fled in all directions, a few raised their hands in surrender, and many just stood in shock and stared at nothing.

Von Brandis smiled. He had his victory and a clear road to Windhoek.

"Colonel, message on the HF set." Each command vehicle had one high-frequency radio, and several ultrahigh-frequency sets. The UHF radios were used for short-range battlefield messages sent in the clear or using simple verbal codes. High-frequency radio was only used for long-range transmission, and messages were always encrypted.

Von Brandis picked up the handset. "This is Foxtrot Hotel One, over."

"One, this is Chessboard. Stand by for new orders."

He pursed his lips in a silent whistle. Chessboard was the call sign for Gen. Adriaan de Wet, commander of the whole bloody South African Army. Something big was in the wind.

Von Brandis recognized de Wet's voice. Not even thirteen hundred kilometers' worth of static-riddled distance could disguise those silky, urbane tones. It also couldn't disguise the fact that the SADF's commander was a very worried man. "*Kolonel*, our reconnaissance aircraft have spotted an enemy force approaching Swakopmund. They were only about a hundred kilometers northeast of the city at dawn this morning. Accordingly, I'm ordering you to turn your battalion around and intercept the enemy as soon as possible."

What? Von Brandis didn't immediately reply. He swayed on his feet, trying to make sense out of what he'd just heard.

Swakopmund was a small city just to the north of Walvis Bay—the 5th Mechanized Infantry's supply base. Every ounce of petrol, round of ammunition, and liter of water the battalion needed came through the port. And now an enemy force threatened that? My God.

Von Brandis's mouth and throat were suddenly bone-dry. "What strength do we face, General?"

"Intelligence thinks they are Cubans, in battalion strength."

Von Brandis was shocked. There would be no walkover this time.

De Wet continued, wheedling now. "You have the strongest South African force in the area, *Kolonel*. More urgent logistic demands from the other columns have made it impossible to significantly reinforce Walvis Bay. I repeat, you must return and crush this Cuban force or we will lose the port. We're flying in additional troops now, but we can't get them there fast enough to hold the city without help. Can you do it?"

There was only one acceptable answer. "Yes, sir." Still holding the mike, von Brandis leaned over Hougaard's map table, silently calculating the amount of ammunition and fuel his men had left after the morning's fierce tank battle. "One thing, General, we'll need a resupply convoy out here. I'm low on petrol."

"I'll see to it at once, Foxtrot. Good luck. Remember that we're counting on you." The transmission from Pretoria faded into static.

Von Brandis tore the radio headset off. Those bloody idiots had really done it this time. They'd left him dangling out on a damned thin limb—and almost in sight of the whole campaign's primary objective.

Now his battalion would have to make a hard, fast, vehicle-wrecking journey back west on Route 52. A journey that could only end in a desperate battle with an enemy force of at least equal strength.

He bit back a string of savage curses and started issuing the orders that would put his battalion on the road in full retreat from the Namibian capital.

CHAPTER 10

Dead End

AUGUST 26—5TH MECHANIZED INFANTRY, 150 KILOMETERS EAST OF WALVIS BAY

The blackened trucks and bodies stood out against the Namib Desert's harsh landscape. Sun-scorched sand and rock did nothing to soften or hide the shattered remains of the battalion's resupply convoy.

Dismounted scouts were already searching the area for possible survivors as von Brandis's Ratel reached the scene and stopped. The wrecks were cold and the bodies blackened by a full day's exposure to the sun.

Lieutenant Griff, the scout platoon leader, ran over as the command vehicle halted and called up to his colonel, "Nothing usable left, sir. And nobody left alive, either." Von Brandis sighed as the lieutenant continued his report. "Definitely an air attack, *Kolonel*. No shell casings or tracks except those belonging to the convoy."

Griff motioned toward the mass of charred wreckage and corpses. "We've found eleven bodies and seven burnt-out vehicles, including three fuel tankers and what must have been two ammo trucks. There are signs of one vehicle headed back west, but I can't tell how many men were in it."

Von Brandis nodded coldly, his expressionless face matching the scout officer's matter-of-fact tone. They'd both seen too many dead men in the past few days to care much about seeing several more. The wrecked convoy's cargo was a much more serious loss.

He climbed out of the Ratel's roof hatch and jumped down to the ground. Stretching, he worked out the kinks that had formed in the last six hours of travel. They'd been moving since well before dawn, rattling and rolling along Route 52's unpaved gravel surface. He smiled sardonically. No doubt this road would have been a lot easier to drive in the BMW parked outside his home in Bloemfontein.

Von Brandis paced slowly around the remains of the resupply convoy, keeping clear of burial parties now going about their work with grim efficiency. Although the desert's scavengers had already paid the dead men a first visit, nobody wanted to leave the Namib's jackals anything more to eat.

Behind him, he heard the rest of his battalion slowing to a halt. Hatches clanged open as the troops got out and talked in low tones.

At first, he wandered almost aimlessly, his body working automatically as his brain tried to plow though the confusion to devise a workable plan. The 5th Mechanized Infantry's officers and men knew how serious a setback this was, and von Brandis had to provide them with firm, decisive leadership.

They'd depended on this convoy for fuel and ammunition and food. Without it, they had barely enough fuel to reach Walvis Bay. Each of the battalion's armored car and infantry units carried almost a full load of ammunition, but ammo disappeared fast in battle. At least they had rations and water for a couple of days.

All right. The Cuban column was still reported moving

toward Walvis Bay. Von Brandis had orders to return and defend the port. The equation seemed simple and straightforward. Scouting, contact, and one hell of a fight.

He glanced at the horizon, silently calculating distances and fuel consumption rates. Right. It could be done. With effort, the 5th Mechanized could get back to the port with just enough fuel and ammo for one last battle—a battle it would simply have to win. As von Brandis turned and walked back to the parked Ratel, he was already starting to feel tentative ideas and plans forming.

His officers had anticipated his calling an orders group and were already gathered in the shade of the vehicle. The group of tired and dirty soldiers looked at him expectantly.

Von Brandis drew a deep breath and strode up confidently. He had to infuse strength and purpose into these men. "All right, gentlemen. We're inconvenienced, but we're not out of options."

He waved a hand down the length of the stalled column. "Move the logistics vehicles off the road into laager and drain their petrol tanks. Strip off everything of value as well. Spare antiaircraft machine guns, medical kits, tool kits. Everything. We don't want to make some wandering black scavenger rich, do we?"

That drew a quick, guttural laugh. Good. They still had some spirit left in them.

"And Jamie, just before we leave, broadcast a message over the HF set—in the clear. Tell Pretoria that we're critically short of fuel and will laager here until another supply convoy can reach us."

More smiles and slow, delighted nods.

Von Brandis showed his teeth. "That's right, gentlemen. Let's let the bastard Cubans think they've trapped us." He clasped both hands behind his back. "We'll show them just how wrong they were at Walvis Bay."

Half an hour later, the much-diminished battalion road column moved on, driving west in a cloud of dust.

AUGUST 27—FORWARD HEADQUARTERS, CUBAN EXPEDITIONARY FORCE, SWAKOPMUND, ON THE NAMIBIAN COAST

The Strand Hotel's restaurant windows looked out on a deceptively peaceful vista—a wide expanse of sandy beach and endless, rolling, white-capped waves. Tables crowded with late-morning diners reinforced the momentary illusion that life in the tiny seaside town was still moving slowly along its placid, everyday track. Only the fact that all of those eating were men in Cuban Army uniforms shattered the illusion.

One man sat eating alone at a table with the best view. Polished stars clustered on his shoulder boards.

Gen. Antonio Vega had taken a calculated risk in flying to Swakopmund. Two risks, actually, if one included the antiquated An-2 utility plane that had carried him on a low-level, engine-sputtering flight from Windhoek to Swakopmund. The real risk, though, was leaving the central fight, the defense of the capital, to oversee the progress of this "secondary attack."

But just as a well-balanced machine can rotate on a single pivot, the battle for Windhoek would be won or lost out here, at the coast.

Though Swakopmund was technically Namibian territory, when the war started it had been swiftly occupied and garrisoned by a company of South African Citizen Force reservists. Since then, they'd been content to hold in place and enjoy the light sea breezes while the rest of the SADF fought its way through Namibia's harsh deserts and rugged mountains. Their easy life had ended the day before when Colonel Pellervo's armored personnel carriers and T-62 tanks appeared on the horizon—driving fast for the town and the Atlantic coast.

Vega smiled sardonically. According to the reports he'd seen, the Afrikaner conscripts had fled Swakopmund without firing a shot. A sensible decision, he thought, eyeing one of the two long-gunned tanks left by Colonel Pellervo to protect the Cuban Army's hold on the former German colonial town.

After its bloodless victory, Pellervo's 21st Motor Rifle

Battalion had spent the night resting and refitting for its push south against the operation's primary objective—Walvis Bay. It was a pause Vega regretted but knew to be necessary. The two-hundred-kilometer road march from Karibib had left the battalion's officers and men short of sleep, fresh food, and water. More importantly, it had pushed many of their vehicles to the edge of mechanical breakdown. Long-distance travel was always hard on tank treads and engines.

Fortunately, ten hours of rest and frantic repair in a campsite on the south side of Swakopmund had worked miracles on the motor rifle unit's combat readiness. It had also given Pellervo a chance to secure the town fully. Under his martial law decrees, the black residents who'd welcomed the Cubans as liberators were free to go about their daily business. The surly, suspicious white descendants of Swakopmund's German colonists weren't so lucky. They'd been confined to their homes to prevent them from passing information about the Cuban battalion's movements and strength to the South Africans still holding Walvis Bay. They'd also been warned that anyone caught outside could look forward to a short trial and a speedy execution amid the sand dunes surrounding the town.

Vega and his forward headquarters staff had arrived at dawn and immediately occupied the Strand Hotel, picked because it offered the best food and accommodations available in this small resort town. He was detached enough to appreciate the irony of a Cuban general eating a meal of bratwurst and sauerkraut while fighting a war in Africa.

Finished, he rose from his early lunch. It was past time to get back to the business at hand.

The forward headquarters itself had been set up in one of the hotel's larger meeting rooms, and Vega was pleased to see it busy but quiet as he walked in. Following his standing orders, only the two sentries by the door saluted and snapped to attention, but almost everyone else nodded in his direction. Generals always had a magnetic effect on those under their command.

Acknowledging his staff's various greetings, he walked briskly over to the situation map tacked to one wall. It showed both Swakopmund and Walvis Bay, thirty kilometers to the south. A half hour's ride in a good car, but a full morning's travel for a motorized battalion deployed for combat.

The two towns sat like islands surrounded by a desert sea. Two-lane highways spanned out north, south, and east, linking them with other towns hundreds of kilometers away. The real sea, the Atlantic Ocean, lay to the west.

Pellervo's battalion had started for Walvis Bay at dawn, but was only now nearing the South African port. It wasn't a large city. In fact, it was just a small, ugly town, more famous for its fish processing plant than anything else. But Walvis Bay possessed the only deep-water harbor on the Namibian coast.

And that made Walvis Bay worth fighting for.

The port had remained in South Africa's hands when the rest of Namibia gained its independence on a simple technicality. Occupied by the British before World War I, Walvis Bay had been handed over to South Africa directly instead of being included as part of the old League of Nations mandate over the South-West Africa Territory. As a result, the 1989 UN agreement that gave the rest of the ex-German colony its freedom from Pretoria hadn't covered Walvis Bay's vital port facilities.

And that is how the West divides up its spoils, and how South Africa keeps its stranglehold on what is supposed to be a sovereign country, Vega thought, frowning.

A more cheerful thought wiped away his frown. In attacking Walvis Bay, his troops were invading South African territory, undoing some of the harm done to Namibia by the West. And capturing the port would not only deprive Pretoria of a vital naval base and supply center, it would also give Cuba and its socialist allies the facilities they needed to pour in shiploads of heavy tanks and guns, troops, and equipment. The men and material needed to crush South Africa's imperial ambitions once and for all.

Vega studied the situation map closely. Markers showed Pellervo's 21st Motor Rifle approaching the outskirts of Walvis Bay. Other markers depicted the likely defensive positions of the two companies of enemy infantry holding the port.

Vega mused again, calculating the odds. Two companies, dug in, against a reinforced battalion. The South Africans knew the area better, but his air bases were closer. The general smiled. An even match for a strategic goal.

A discreet cough drew his attention to the expectant face of one of his operations officers. "Yes?"

"Sir, Colonel Pellervo reports receiving some small-arms fire. Probably from enemy outposts. He requests artillery support."

Vega shook his head impatiently. "Tell him to press on. The South African outposts will fall back. The Twenty-first has to keep moving or the timing of our air strike will be off."

He glanced at his air officer, who saw his expression and automatically confirmed that. "The MiGs are on schedule, Comrade General. ETA in ten minutes."

Vega checked the map one more time. Good. Very good. The battle for Walvis Bay would open with one hell of an airborne bang.

5TH MECHANIZED INFANTRY HQ, OUTSIDE WALVIS BAY

Col. George von Brandis lay prone, hugging the cold, stony ground. Through binoculars, he watched the enemy's dust cloud approaching.

He hated being outside the cover offered by the port's houses, aluminum-sided canneries, and entrenchments, but there hadn't been time to get the battalion inside before first light, and he couldn't risk being caught unprepared in the open. His vehicles were down to their last few liters of fuel, and the men were exhausted.

The 5th Mechanized had spent the dark, predawn hours finding hides and defilades along the road between Swakopmund and Walvis Bay. The best defensive position lay close to the port itself where a railroad line paralleled the road—its raised embankment offering perfect cover for his infantry, jeep-mounted antitank missiles, and cannon-armed Elands.

Von Brandis adjusted the focus on his binoculars and saw squat shapes emerging from the hazy, yellow dust cloud. The Cubans couldn't be farther than five kilometers away. Come on, you bastards. Keep coming.

With so little fuel left and only its basic load of ammunition available, his battalion had only one viable option—a devastating short-range attack aimed at the Cuban flank. Hit them hard enough with a surprise attack and those Latin bastards will samba their way back to Luanda, he thought.

And the attack should damn well be a surprise. Two volunteers had stayed behind in Hougaard's abandoned command Ratel. They were continuing to transmit status reports and requests for aid. His own force had maintained radio silence while speeding westward through the night to minimize the chance of being spotted by enemy air reconnaissance.

Not even the defenders in Walvis Bay knew they were here. He had considered sending in a runner, but two kilometers of open terrain separated his nearest positions from the town. Too far. Whomever he sent would almost certainly be captured or killed.

Von Brandis grinned mirthlessly. The reservists holding Walvis Bay must be feeling a lot like the British soldiers who'd defended Rorke's Drift against the Zulus a century before—outnumbered and all alone. They will be a happy bunch when we show ourselves, he thought.

The Walvis Bay garrison didn't really need to know that the 5th Mechanized was here anyway. The tactical setup was simple. The Cubans could only advance down one road to attack the town. Von Brandis had deployed his men about eight hundred meters east of that road, ready to shoot only after the garrison opened fire. With luck, the Cubans wouldn't realize they were being shot at from more than one direction until after his Elands and antitank missiles had slammed in a few unanswered volleys. Another slight edge, von Brandis thought, and I'll need every advantage I can get.

He planned to open fire only when the Cubans were at close range, under a thousand meters. To make sure surprise was maintained, only one man in each of his companies was allowed to observe the enemy and report. The rest of his infantry stayed hidden below the railroad embankment. All vehicle engines were also off. Normally kept running to provide electrical power to the guns, the engines were shut down both to save fuel and to reduce noise. They would only be turned over at the last minute.

The Cubans were still closing, now just about three thousand meters away. They were leading with their tanks, clanking, big-gunned monsters spread out in line abreast. Wave after wave of BTR armored personnel carriers followed the tanks.

The tanks were tough customers, but the BTRs were just big wheeled boxes with light armor at most. They were vulnerable to cannon, antitank missiles, even heavy machine guns. Von Brandis sighed. There were a hell of a lot of them, though.

Smaller armored cars prowled round the flanks of the Cuban formation, accompanied by a couple of mobile antiaircraft guns, ZSU-23-4s with their radar antennas deployed and ready.

Suddenly, von Brandis heard a cross between a scream and a roar coming from the north, coming closer fast. Jets! He swiveled his binoculars up and beyond the oncoming Cuban formation.

There they were. Four winged, arrowhead shapes emerged from the dust cloud—flying straight down the road toward Walvis Bay in two pairs. As the MiGs flashed over the town's low, flat-roofed houses and warehouses, small cannisters fell from their wings and tumbled end over end toward the ground.

Afterburners roaring, the MiGs accelerated and turned right, thundering out over the ocean. Thousands of frightened birds burst into frenzied motion, blackening the sky over Walvis Bay's lagoon.

Behind the accelerating jets, the cannisters, cluster bombs, broke apart into falling clouds of tiny black dots. Walvis Bay disappeared—cloaked by smoke and dust as hundreds of bomblets went off almost at once. Tiny flashes of orange and red winked through the smoke, accompanied by a loud, crackling series of explosions that reminded von Brandis of the noise made by the firecrackers tossed at Chinese New Year's parades.

Each bomblet carried enough explosive to wreck an aircraft or a vehicle, and each blast sent dozens of high-speed fragments sleeting through the air and any walls or roofs in the way. Von Brandis hoped that Walvis Bay's defenders had dug deep trenches.

The sound of the MiGs faded.

He switched his attention back to the advancing Cuban formation, now a few hundred meters closer. The tanks were near enough for him to make out the shape of their turrets, and he could see a large bore evacuator halfway up the gun barrel. T-62s. Bloody great big, thick-armored T-62s. Wonderful.

He heard the jets again and swiveled to look over the town. The MiGs must have turned again out over the water, because this time they were coming head-on from the west—flying just above the wavetops.

The four aircraft suddenly pulled up, quickly gaining altitude, then dove. Each jet's nose disappeared in a stuttering, winking blaze of light—cannon hammering the garrison crouching in its foxholes and slit trenches. Flames and oily, black smoke rose from burning cars and buildings. Von Brandis couldn't see any tracers rising from defending antiaircraft guns. They'd either been knocked out or abandoned by frightened crews.

Again, the MiGs broke off their attack, but this time they didn't turn over the town. Instead, they flew on, straight toward him! Von Brandis shouted, "Down!" and scrambled down off the small rise he occupied, knowing already it was futile. His battalion was concealed from the road, but not from aerial observation. The Namib's barren terrain simply offered nowhere to hide.

He looked up as the jets screamed overhead a hundred meters up. The sound deafened him. He was close enough to see the red and blue Cuban insignia, the shoulder-mounted delta wings, the triangular tail, the square inlets. Cuban MiG-23 Floggers.

The MiGs flashed by and he heard a few of the machine guns in his battalion firing as they pulled away. Fine. There wasn't any point in trying to hide now, and the machine gunners might even hit something.

One of the jets pulled up, turning tighter than the rest. For a moment, von Brandis thought it had been hit, but instead the MiG-23 gracefully turned and rolled and came back over his battalion. It made no move to attack, but he heard the jet's howl as it made a single high-speed pass down the length of his defensive line.

Shit. So much for surprise.

Von Brandis scrambled back up the hill, yelling for his radioman to follow. Both men flopped belly-down at the crest. The Cuban tanks and APCs were roughly two thousand meters away—still well outside effective range.

The South African colonel shook his head in resignation. It was just too damned bad that nothing in war ever went as planned. "Tell all commanders to open fire. Aim for the APCs."

FORWARD HEADQUARTERS, CUBAN EXPEDITIONARY FORCE

The air officer spun round in shock, one hand clapped to his earphones. "Comrade General, one of our aircraft reports men and vehicles east of the road, near the railroad embankment!"

What? Vega sat bolt upright. "Find out how many!"

He jumped up from his desk for a closer look at the map. That damned railroad embankment! He should have insisted that Pellervo's recon units scout the area more thoroughly.

He was still moving when another radioman whirled in his direction. "Colonel Pellervo reports he is taking fire from the east!"

Vega took the last few steps to the map at a run. No doubt

about it. They'd been ambushed. Some South African was playing it pretty smart. But how smart? He snapped a question toward the air officer. "How large is the enemy force?"

"The pilot says he can see over a dozen vehicles."

That's it, then, Vega thought. At least a company and probably more. He slammed a clenched fist into his cupped palm. He should have known better than to believe the radio intercepts they'd picked up from out in the Namib.

No time now for recriminations. Quickly he ordered, "Have the fighters strafe the South African bastards! And then see how soon we can get another air strike out here."

The air officer nodded hurriedly and turned to his radio set. "Arrow Lead, this is Forward Control . . ."

Vega turned his attention to the fast-developing ground battle. The South African armored units behind the embankment were clearly a bigger threat than the infantry garrison cowering in what was left of Walvis Bay. They were now the primary targets. On the other hand, even antiquated antitank missiles fired from the town could wreak havoc on Pellervo's units as they turned east. The garrison would have to be neutralized.

He looked for his artillery officer and found him hovering nearby. "Signal the battery to lay smoke along the northern edge of the town."

That should blind the Afrikaner bastards. Let them waste missiles firing at empty sand while Pellervo's tanks annihilated the enemy sheltering behind the railroad embankment.

Vega motioned his operations staff closer. "All right. Let's get down to work. Tell Pellervo to deploy his tanks and infantry to the east for a dismounted attack. We'll worry about the town later."

Officers scurried toward the radios to obey.

5TH MECHANIZED INFANTRY

Von Brandis climbed into his Ratel and used the turret optics to examine the advancing enemy line. Johann, his driver, now serving as turret gunner, waited nervously. The command Ratel's small turret held only a heavy machine gun—a weapon that would irritate but not injure a T-62.

Stepping up to the highest magnification, von Brandis was gratified to see several burning BTRs topped by rising pillars of smoke. The 90mm guns on his Elands hadn't a prayer of knocking out a tank at two thousand meters, but their shells tore up the thinly armored Cuban personnel carriers like cheap tin cans. Boers have always been good shots, he thought, and we need that expertise now.

The tanks were wheeling now, the entire formation pivoting on its left flank. In less than a minute, his battalion faced a line of ten T-62s—gun barrels, turrets, and thick frontal armor all facing east. They'd stopped moving, though. Why? Then he saw infantry dismounting from some motionless BTRs, while other APCs, already empty, withdrew at high speed.

He shouted down into the Ratel's crowded interior. "Infantry attack forming. Lay mortar fire eighteen hundred meters in front of us and adjust for a walking barrage."

Staff officers acknowledged and began issuing orders to the battalion's heavy weapons company.

Von Brandis frowned. The mortar fire would help slow the oncoming infantry, but it wouldn't even scratch the paint on the T-62s.

Moving slowly, very slowly, the tanks started clanking forward, smoke pouring from the rear of each vehicle. They were making smoke by spraying diesel fuel on their engine exhausts, covering the infantry coming on behind in a gray-white blanket.

Mortar rounds began throwing up sand and smoke in front of the advancing Cuban line. He jumped down out of the turret and let the young artillery observer climb into his seat. From there, the lieutenant would be able to see well enough to adjust the barrage right on top of the enemy force.

Trying to find a place to stand, von Brandis almost tripped over someone's feet, then jammed his leg into the map table. Good God. Running a battle from inside this metal zoo was like trying to conduct a symphony on a commuter-packed subway train. Fed up, he grabbed his headset, opened one of the roof hatches, and climbed out onto the Ratel's armor-plated roof where he could see.

The mortars were now landing in the smoky haze behind the Cuban tanks. He couldn't tell if they were doing damage, but at least they were bursting in the right spot. His armored cars had ceased fire, out of easy BTR targets and not even bothering to test their lighter cannon against the T-62s' angled frontal armor until they were much closer.

The rattle of antiaircraft guns broke his attention away from the tanks. The aircraft were back! Von Brandis quickly scrambled off the Ratel's roof and dropped to a crouch behind its left side. Peering around the front of his vehicle, he saw the Flogger approach and make its attack.

From the Cuban pilot's point of view, he knew that his battalion was deployed in an ideal formation. Spread out in line along the embankment, with no cover to the top or rear, his Ratels and Eland armored cars were terribly vulnerable.

The plane came over fast, its automatic cannon blazing again—chewing up sand and rock in a straight line along the 5th Mechanized. Something blew up about three hundred meters away, but the MiG-23 didn't break off. Instead, its nose came up for a few seconds, looking for all the world like a hunting dog seeking new prey. Then the nose dipped again, firing at a new target.

This time he saw the cannon shells strike around a nearby Ratel personnel carrier. There wasn't any clear-cut impression of a line of shells walking toward the vehicle—just a flurry of fiery explosions on and around it. At least three shells struck the Ratel, and one hit a man outside, literally blowing him into pieces.

Von Brandis heard screaming, and men poured out of the Ratel's side and roof hatches in a torrent of boiling black smoke. Several were wounded, bloodied, or burnt. Damn. The vehicle was wrecked and its squad was crippled.

He heard another jet roaring in and hoped that this time the battalion's antiaircraft battery would bring it down. He glanced at the nearest gun—a twin 20mm mounting. It was manually pointed and lacked radar ranging, but at least the blasted thing was better than a vehicle-mounted machine gun. Four of them were deployed up and down his line.

Tracers arced upward into the air, passing close to the second MiG, but none hit it. Instead, the MiG destroyed an Eland armored car, fireballing its fuel tank in a spectacular orange and red explosion.

There was a new note to the sounds around him, and von Brandis realized his Elands had opened fire again. He climbed up the embankment and flattened himself along the railroad tracks—binoculars already up and focused. The Cuban tanks were less than a kilometer away. An Eland fifty meters to the right fired, and he felt a momentary exhilaration as he saw the shell strike a T-62 dead center.

But when the smoke cleared, the tank rolled on apparently unharmed. A bright smear on the bow armor showed where the 90mm armor-piercing shell had struck and been deflected.

Movement to the left caught his eye, and he saw a flickering black dot reach a tank. Smoke, fire, and sand fountained into the air. Another hit! This time, though, the Cuban T-62 shuddered to a squealing halt as all its hatches blew open in a sheet of flame. Nobody appeared in the hatch openings.

At least the antitank missiles were working, von Brandis thought. Another jet roared low overhead and he turned to see one more of his Ratels and an antiaircraft gun burning. Dead or wounded men lay sprawled close by each of them.

Damn it. They were being murdered by these bloody MiGs. Where the hell were their own planes? He felt a twinge of self-doubt. Maybe he should have risked a radio call to Pretoria instead of seeking complete surprise.

The noise of battle was increasing as the range closed and more weapons on both sides were able to fire. He watched a few more shots by the armored cars as they tried to knock out the T-62s, all ineffective against their heavy front armor. Sand sprayed around him as a stray Cuban shot slammed into the embankment. Time to go.

Von Brandis scrambled down the embankment to the waiting Ratel. Its turret was now firing, and he instinctively sheltered under its sides as another MiG screamed over.

He grabbed the dangling radio headset and put it on. Turning the earphone volume to maximum, he shouted, "Foxtrot Delta One, redeploy to the south! You need to get flank shots on the tanks! Over!"

The reply was barely audible, but D Squadron's commander spoke slowly. "Cannot move. Not enough fuel. Two vehicles empty, laying turret manually. Aiming at tank tracks, will immobilize." The *bang-clank* of a cannon's firing punctuated his words.

More MiGs raced down the length of his line, strafing everything in their path. Each pass left more of his vehicles burning or abandoned.

Crack! Crack! Crack! The Cuban T-62s were now in range. Even though they had larger guns, it was hard to hit a small, dug-in target from a moving tank, so they'd held their fire until now. The crash of big armor-piercing shells filled the air.

HEADQUARTERS, CUBAN EXPEDITIONARY FORCE

The young staff officer's high-pitched voice revealed his excitement. "Comrade General! Colonel Pellervo reports that his tanks are just five hundred meters from the enemy!"

Vega nodded gravely. Now for the kill. "All right, order our aircraft home, then shift the artillery fire as planned. Adjust, then pour a full rate of fire onto the enemy for three minutes."

He allowed himself the faintest flicker of a smile as his orders were repeated over the radio. He'd spent years imagining the best way to crush a South African battalion in combat, drawing up and rejecting plan after plan—each aimed at matching his army's strengths against the enemy's weaknesses. Now it was working. The South Africans caught behind the railroad embankment simply couldn't match his air power or artillery superiority.

5TH MECHANIZED INFANTRY

When von Brandis saw the aircraft leave, it was the first ray of hope in what had become an increasingly bleak situation. The MiGs must finally have run low on fuel or ammunition. Then he started wondering if he could get his remaining antiaircraft guns up to the embankment and redeployed before the Cuban infantry reached it. Those 20mm cannon would work well against personnel.

It was getting hard to see. Each explosion kicked up sand and dust, and the smoke of the burning vehicles only added to the murk. It clung to his skin and filled his lungs. The enemy troops were visible only as dim, moving shapes—though luckily still clear enough to aim at.

The Cuban foot soldiers were still advancing, coming on at an energy-conserving walk while their tanks had stopped and were firing their cannons and machine guns over their heads. Von Brandis could only see three T-62s on fire. Two or three more had been stopped by track hits, but that didn't keep them from shooting.

He lowered his binoculars, considering his next move. He and his men weren't out of trouble yet, but concentrated small-arms fire should be enough to stop this damned infantry attack. He didn't have to expose his surviving armored cars and APCs to the T-62s.

Von Brandis started to grin. The Cuban commander had made his first serious mistake. The man should have kept his tanks together with the infantry.

In the roar of battle around him, he didn't even hear the first few artillery shells whirring in from high overhead.

21ST MOTOR RIFLE BATTALION, CUBAN EXPEDITIONARY FORCE

The battery of towed 122mm howitzers attached to Colonel Pellervo's battalion was eight kilometers back, deployed out of sight amid a sea of sand dunes fronting the Atlantic. But the artillery observer who controlled their fire occupied the tank next to Pellervo's.

He was good and needed just four sighting rounds to get the battery on target. The first two were long, the third a little short, but the fourth landed squarely on the railroad tracks. "Fire for effect!"

Each D-30 122mm gun could fire four shells a minute, for a short period of time. There were six howitzers in the battery, so twenty-four shells a minute rained onto the exposed South African battalion—shattering infantrymen caught out in the open, spraying fragments through open vehicle hatches, and fireballing armored cars with direct hits.

The Cuban gunners kept firing for three long, murderous minutes.

5TH MECHANIZED INFANTRY

Whammm! Whammm! Whammm!

Von Brandis felt as if he'd been kicked in the stomach by a mule as the first full Cuban salvo landed—each impact jarring and rattling the ground. He flattened, face pressed down into the heaving earth, deafened by the noise.

Each explosion threw a geyser of dirt into the air, sometimes mixed with fragments of men or equipment. Vehicles were torn open or simply blown to pieces. Fragments whizzing out more than twenty meters from the point of each explosion cut down anyone not totally prone—making it impossible for his men to keep firing and stay alive.

Von Brandis knew exactly what the Cubans were doing and knew they had won. But he couldn't stop fighting. Walvis Bay was vital, and he had to keep trying to save it. He started crawling down the line, finding any officer or noncom still alive—screaming the same thing over and over. "Call the men back four kilometers. Run with whatever you've got. We'll try to regroup and slip into town."

Holding their bodies tight against the storm of explosions, most nodded their dazed understanding. A few had simply stared at him, shell-shocked beyond the ability to comprehend.

Von Brandis had been able to find two of his officers and three noncoms when the shell found him. He never felt it.

FORWARD HEADQUARTERS, CUBAN EXPEDITIONARY FORCE

Vega watched his operations officer acknowledge the incoming transmission and pull his earphones off. The man's wide, white-toothed grin signaled good news. So did the way he straightened to attention. "Comrade General, the Twenty-first Motor Rifle reports overrunning the South African line. They did not withdraw."

Vega nodded. He'd never denied that the Afrikaners were brave. "What are our losses?"

Another smile. More good news, then. "Roughly fifteen percent, Comrade General. But Colonel Pellervo believes many of his tanks can be repaired."

Vega sighed with relief. His casualties were acceptable. Especially for such a close-fought action. The 21st Motor Rifle was still combat capable.

He turned to his radio operator. "Send this message to the embassy in Windhoek: 'Defeated enemy counterattack outside Walvis Bay. Expect to take port by dusk. Send information on freighter arrival times.' "

As his staff crowded round to congratulate him on the victory, Vega allowed himself a brief, wintry smile. Then he shook his head. "I thank you, comrades. But we are not finished here. Tell Pellervo to get turned around. We've got to be in Walvis Bay by nightfall."

South Africa's army had lost a precious battalion, and Cuba would have the harbor it needed.

CHAPTER 11

Home Front

AUGUST 29—UNIVERSITY OF THE WITWATERSRAND, JOHANNESBURG

The University of the Witwatersrand looked more like a battlefield than a center of learning.

Torn posters, hand-lettered banners, and flags littered the university's once-pristine lawns and tree-lined walkways. Thinning wisps of tear gas drifted past slogan-daubed gray stone buildings, swirling in a fitful westerly breeze. Squads of shotgun-armed riot troops wearing visored gas masks stood guard at every intersection and entrance.

Other policemen accompanied white-coated medical teams picking their way carefully across an open square—sorting through the scattered bodies of unarmed student demonstrators. Those found to be only lightly wounded were yanked to their feet and hauled off toward rows of canvas-sided trucks already filled with hundreds of other detainees. The trucks were manned by brownshirted AWB "police volunteers." Those more seriously injured were piled onto stretchers and loaded onto waiting ambulances. The rest were dragged off to one side of the square—joining a steadily lengthening line of blanket-covered corpses.

None of the Security Branch troopers thought to look behind them, toward the second-story windows of a small brick apartment building just across Jan Smuts Avenue.

"Got it." Sam Knowles shut his camera off and backed away from the window.

"Great." Ian Sherfield stopped jotting rough notes for his voice-over commentary, flipped his pocket notebook shut, and joined Knowles by the back flight of stairs. They'd been tipped to the planned antiwar, anti-Vorster protest in time to find the perfect site for concealed camerawork—a vacant one-bedroom flat. A flat they'd secured with the hurried "gift" of several crumpled twenty-rand notes pressed into the sweaty palm of the building's fat landlord.

The two American newsmen had come hoping they could get some good footage of a major student demonstration. Something to show that not all of South Africa's white minority supported Vorster's brutal crackdown or his Pearl Harbor–style surprise attack on Namibia. What they hadn't expected was a full-fledged police massacre of Witwatersrand's white, mostly English-descended students.

Random shots crackled from outside, rising above the screaming sirens of ambulances rushing wounded to area hospitals.

Ian shook his head in amazement. Skin color no longer seemed the determining factor in judging police reaction. Vorster's bullyboys were going after anyone who openly protested government policy. He wondered how members of South Africa's economically powerful but politically weak English minority would react to seeing their sons and daughters gunned down by riot troops.

Not very well, he guessed, feeling the same odd mix of elation and sorrow he always felt when covering a newsworthy tragedy. He could never shake the sense that he ought to have been doing something to help—not simply standing in the background waiting, watching, and recording.

Still, that was exactly what his job entailed. Reporters who involved themselves in the events they were covering were activists—not journalists. And besides, this was the story he'd been looking for so long. If he could smuggle the horrifying footage they'd just shot out of the country . . . Of course, that was a big if.

Ian watched as Knowles deftly slid the tape cassette from his camera into an unlabeled carrying case and replaced it with another showing random Jo'burg street scenes they'd shot earlier in the day. Precaution number one, he thought. Any South African policeman who grabbed their camera this time would be hard-pressed to stay awake long enough to realize he was watching the wrong tape.

Finished, the little cameraman stood up, shaking his head. "I still don't see how we're gonna work this. I mean, sure, we can get the tape back to the studio. No problem there." He shrugged into his shoulder harness. "But how the hell do you plan to get it onto the satellite link past the censor?"

Ian moved past, heading down the stairs. "Simple. We aren't even going to try putting this out over the satellite."

Knowles clattered down the stairs right behind him. "Oh? You got some kind of steroid-pumped carrier pigeon I don't know about?"

Ian grinned and held the door to the outside open. "Nope."

"What then?"

He followed the cameraman out into a narrow, trash can–filled alley. Their tiny Ford Escort sat blocking the far end of the alley. Matthew Sibena, their young black driver, was already behind the wheel with the motor running.

"C'mon, bossman. Don't keep me hanging . . . what've you got up your sleeve?"

Ian's grin grew wider. "How about the embassy's diplomatic bag? I've got a friend in the public information section who's willing to play along. And he's got a friend back in D.C. who'll make sure our tape gets on the right plane to New York."

Knowles whistled softly. "Pretty hot shit. I knew there was a good reason you charm-school grads get paid more than a lowly tech like myself."

Ian nodded, unsuccessfully resisting the temptation to look smug. It was foolproof. Not even the South Africans would risk a major diplomatic incident by searching boxes or bags shipped under the U.S. embassy seal. Their footage would air all over the world before Vorster's censors realized what had happened.

And all hell would break loose right after that. He frowned. He and Knowles would almost certainly be expelled for violating South Africa's new press law. No great sorrow there, he thought.

Except for Emily. He'd lose her for sure.

Ian sighed. He'd probably already lost her.

She'd been gone for more than a month and he hadn't heard a single word from her—not one card, not one letter, not one phone call. Either Emily was still locked up out of touch or she'd decided to try to forget him. And if that was the case, he couldn't really blame her. Their love affair hadn't brought her anything but trouble.

Nothing but trouble. Afrikaner families revolved almost entirely around the father. The father's wishes. The father's orders. The father's beliefs. So how could he have expected Emily to withstand her own father's rage for very long?

Knowles nudged him. They'd reached the end of the alley.

Sibena popped the trunk and got out to help them load the car. He looked scared.

"Anything wrong, Matt?"

The South African shook his head rapidly. "No, *meneer*, ah, Ian. But when I heard the shooting and the sirens from there . . ." He flapped his hand toward the university and swallowed hard. "I was frightened of what the police might do if they found me here."

Ian nodded sympathetically. He couldn't blame Sibena for being afraid. In fact, he'd half-expected to find the kid gone when they came out. It couldn't have been easy sitting out in the open, just waiting for an AWB thug to wander along, whip or gun in hand.

The young black man had more than earned his meager pay over the past couple of weeks. Unfailingly and excessively polite, he'd displayed a working knowledge of every major thoroughfare and back alley in Johannesburg. Even skeptical Sam Knowles had to admit that his shortcuts had saved them several hours of transit time. But they'd never been able to gain his trust. No matter how hard they tried to reassure him, Sibena always seemed braced for a blow or curse.

Sound gear, camera, and tapes securely loaded, Knowles slid into the front beside their driver while Ian crammed himself into the Escort's cramped backseat.

The South African's hands clutched the steering wheel. "Where to now, Meneer Sherfield?"

The habits of a lifetime were hard to break.

Ian leaned forward over the seat. "Just take us back to the studio, Matt. Nice and easy. I don't want anybody in uniform taking an interest in us before we've dropped our little package off. Got it?"

Sibena nodded convulsively and cautiously pulled out into traffic, threading his way south through a steady stream of ambulances, military trucks, and wheeled APCs. Helmeted policemen riding north toward the university stared down at the little car, but nobody made any move to stop them.

Not right away.

Not until they were within five minutes' drive of the TV studio and relative safety.

Ian heard the wailing, high-pitched siren first. He swung round in the backseat and stared out through the Escort's rear window. Damn. A police car racing fast up Market Street, blue light pulsing in time with the siren.

"Oh, God." Sibena pulled off to the side and switched the engine off with shaking hands.

The squad car pulled in behind them.

Ian leaned forward again, trying to reassure the younger man. "Don't sweat it, Matt. You're with us, right? You haven't done anything wrong." He just wished his own voice sounded more in control.

Sibena gulped a quick breath and nodded.

The police car's doors popped open and three blue-jacketed officers climbed out. They stood staring at the Escort's rear bumper for a moment, then one leaned in through the car window, reaching for a radio mike.

"Checking our number plates," Knowles muttered.

Ian nodded. One of the riot troops must have gotten suspicious and reported them. Now what? Could they bluff it out? Fast-talk their way past these creeps long enough to hide the film inside the studio?

Maybe. And maybe not. He grimaced. This was getting ridiculous. Every time they got close to a big story, South Africa's security forces seemed ready and waiting to snatch it away from them.

The policeman with the mike thumbed it off and motioned in their direction. The other two moved forward, hands resting prominently on the pistols holstered at their hips. Pedestrians who'd gathered around the two parked cars, drawn by the flashing lights, scattered out of their way—curiosity suddenly quenched by a sensible desire not to get caught up in whatever was going on.

The older of the two policemen, glowering and gray haired, rapped impatiently on Ian's window.

He rolled it down, reminding himself to be polite no matter how hard the South African tried to provoke him. The tape locked in their trunk was too important to risk losing in a senseless run-in with the police. "Yes?"

"You are Sherfield?" The policeman's harsh, clipped accent marked him as an Afrikaner.

Ian nodded cautiously.

The policeman's lips twitched into a thin, unpleasant smile. "I ask that you all get out of the car. Now, please." His tone made it clear he hoped they'd refuse.

Swell. Another South African cop out for journalistic blood. Ian caught Knowles's raised, questioning eyebrow and shrugged. What realistic choice did they have?

Ian popped the door and clambered awkwardly out of the Escort's backseat. Knowles and Sibena followed suit. Sweat beaded the young South African's frightened face.

Ian folded his arms, trying to appear unconcerned. "What seems to be the problem?"

The Afrikaner's fixed smile thinned even further. "You and your 'colleagues' "—he stressed the word contemptuously—"were seen filming a minor demonstration at the

University of the Witwatersrand. That is a serious violation of our law."

Blast. Some of the riot police must have spotted them. Or somebody else had betrayed them. Maybe the landlord they'd bribed . . .

Ian shook his head. "I'm afraid your information is inaccurate, Officer. We're on our way back from shooting a few background pictures of your city. Nothing controversial or prohibited. Certainly nothing exciting."

"In that case, *meneer,* you won't mind letting us take a look at them, eh?"

Ian hid a smile of his own and did his best to look upset. "If you insist. But I'll protest this interference to the highest levels of your government." He turned to Knowles. "Please give these gentlemen the tape from your camera, Sam."

His short, stocky cameraman looked sour as he unlocked the trunk and reluctantly handed over the wrong cassette. He started to slam the trunk shut.

"Halt!"

Knowles stopped in midslam, his back suddenly rigid.

The Afrikaner shouldered him aside and bent down for a closer look at the gear piled inside the trunk. He pawed through the stacks of equipment and muttered in satisfaction as he uncovered the carrying case full of unlabeled tapes. "And what are these, Meneer Sherfield?"

Ian tried to keep his voice even. "Blank cassettes."

"I see." The policeman nodded slowly, his eyes cold. "I think we shall confiscate these as well. If they really are blank, they will be returned to you."

Damn it. Another story and hours of hard work down the drain. He tried to ignore Knowles's quiet, steady swearing and said stiffly, "I insist on a receipt for the property you've illegally seized."

"Certainly." The Afrikaner looked amused. He nodded toward his counterpart, a younger man who'd hung back from the whole scene as though reluctant to involve himself. "That fellow there will be glad to write any kind of receipt you want, won't you, Harris?" Spite dripped from every word.

Ian glanced at the younger policeman with more interest. What could he have done to warrant such hatred from his older colleague? Maybe he just had the wrong last name. Some Afrikaners never bothered to hide their long-standing, often mindless dislike for those descended from South Africa's English colonists. It was a feeling that the English usually reciprocated.

Without another word, the older man turned on his heel and strode back to the waiting squad car, holding the case of videotapes out from his body as though they were contaminated.

"Mr. Sherfield?" The younger policeman's voice was apologetic.

Ian looked steadily at him. "Yes?"

The South African held out a piece of paper. "Here is that receipt you asked for."

Ian took it and stuffed it into his shirt pocket. Great. Instead of a story that would lift the lid on Vorster's security services, he had a junior policeman's signature on a piece of meaningless official notepaper.

The policeman cleared his throat and stepped closer, lowering his voice so that his colleagues couldn't hear him. "I'm truly sorry about this, Mr. Sherfield. Not all of us are happy with the things that are happening in our country. But what can we do? We must uphold our laws—no matter how much we may regret them."

Ian restrained an impulse to feel sorry for the man. Individual apologies couldn't atone for insufferable acts. "I imagine that's exactly the same excuse used by Russian cops. And by those in Nazi Germany, for that matter."

The policeman flushed and turned away, his face almost as unhappy as Ian felt.

Doors slammed shut and the police car pulled away from the curb, accelerating smoothly into traffic. None of its occupants looked back.

Knowles stared after the squad car, anger in his eyes. "Well, fuck you, too, you bastards."

Sibena just stood silently, eyes firmly fixed on the sidewalk.

Ian shut the Escort's trunk and opened the rear door. "C'mon, guys. No sense in standing around brooding about it." He tried to tone down the anger in his own voice. "Hell, it's not like that's the first piece of film we ever lost."

Knowles glanced at him. "No, it sure isn't." He lowered his chin, looking even more stubborn than usual. "Kinda funny, though, ain't it? I mean, how the cops always seem to know right where we are and exactly what we've been up to. Almost like they've got their eyes on us all the time.

"Now just how do you suppose they're doing that?"

Ian shook his head, unsure of what the cameraman meant. He'd certainly never spotted any police patrols following them. Then he followed Knowles's steady, unblinking gaze. He was looking straight at Matthew Sibena's slumped shoulders and downcast face.

AUGUST 30—PRESIDENT'S OFFICE, THE UNION BUILDINGS, PRETORIA

Karl Vorster's spartan tastes were not yet reflected in the furnishings of the office suite reserved for South Africa's president. Since taking power he'd been too preoccupied by both external and internal crises to worry about redecorating.

And thank God for that, Erik Muller thought, sitting comfortably for once in a cushioned chair facing Vorster's plain oak desk. The dead Frederick Haymans may have been a softhearted fool, but at least he'd had some modicum of taste.

Across the desk, Vorster grunted to himself and scrawled a signature on the last memorandum in front of him. The memo's black binder identified it as an execution order.

"So, another ANC bastard gets it in the neck. Good." The suggestion of a smile appeared on Vorster's face and then vanished. "Is that everything, Erik?"

"Not quite, Mr. President. There's one more item."

"Get on with it, then." Vorster's flint-hard eyes roved to his desk clock and back to Muller. "General de Wet is briefing me on the military situation in a few minutes."

Muller clenched his teeth. South Africa's chief executive

was spending more and more of his precious time trying to micromanage the stalled Namibian campaign. And while Vorster moved meaningless pins back and forth on maps, serious political, economic, and security problems languished—unconsidered and unresolved.

Muller cleared his throat. "It's a travel-permit request from Mantizima, the Zulu chief. He's been invited to testify before the American Congress on this new sanctions bill of theirs."

"So?" Vorster's impatience showed plainly. "Why bring this matter to me? Surely that's something for the Foreign Ministry to decide."

Muller shook his head. "With respect, Mr. President, there are vital questions of state security involved—too many to entrust such a decision to the minister or his bureaucrats." He pushed the document across the desk.

Vorster picked it up and skimmed through the Zulu chief 's tersely worded request for a travel permit. "Go on."

"I believe you should reject his request, Mr. President. Beneath that toothy smile of his, Gideon Mantizima's as much a troublemaker as any other black leader. I fear that he could make even more trouble for us in Washington if you allow him out of the country." He stopped, aware that he'd probably overplayed his hand. The President seemed to be in a deliberately contrary mood.

Vorster waggled a finger at him. "That is nonsense, Muller. I know this man. This Zulu has cooperated with us in the past when all the other blacks toed the communist line. He's even opposed sanctions by the Western powers. Why, I can almost respect him. After all, he descends from a warrior tribe, not from wandering trash like the rest of the kaffirs."

He sat back in his chair, hands folded across his stomach. "No, Muller. Mantizima and his followers hate the ANC almost as much as we do. They've been rivals for decades. And we rarely interfere in the way the Zulus handle affairs within their own tribeland. The chief has no reason to make trouble for us."

Vorster rocked forward, pen in hand. "Let him visit America. His testimony will only confuse our enemies in their Congress and show the world that we have nothing to fear."

Muller watched in silence as his leader signed the travel permit. Vorster's growing tendency to see only what he wished to see disturbed him. In the past, Mantizima had publicly opposed economic sanctions on South Africa because he believed they hurt his people more than they hurt whites—not as a favor to Pretoria. And the wily Zulu chief's struggle with the ANC was a battle for future political power in a black-majority government—not the signpost of a permanent alliance with the forces of apartheid.

He took the signed permit from Vorster's outstretched hand and left quietly. Further argument would only endanger his own position.

Gideon Mantizima might continue to cooperate with Pretoria, but Muller doubted it. The Zulu chief was shrewd enough to recognize a dead end when he saw one. South Africa's director of military intelligence suspected that Vorster would regret allowing Mantizima the freedom to choose a new course.

SEPTEMBER 1—JOHANNESBURG

The doorbell buzzed, waking Ian Sherfield from a fitful, dream-ridden sleep. Another buzz, louder and longer this time. He opened his eyes reluctantly, fumbling for the bedside lamp switch. Two in the flipping morning, for God's sake. Who the hell could that be? Johannesburg, like all of South Africa's major cities, was under a midnight curfew.

Ian stumbled out of bed and struggled into a pair of jeans while hopping toward the front door. Pain flared briefly as he slammed a knee into a sofa. The tiny furnished flat he'd rented was reasonably priced and convenient, but he still hadn't lived there long enough to navigate safely in the dark.

Three short, sharp obscenities helped dispel most of the pain, but he was still hobbling when he got to the door. He yanked it open, ready to vent some well-earned anger on the idiot who'd disturbed him.

It was Emily.

Even bundled in a long winter overcoat against the chill

night air, she was beautiful. A single suitcase rested on the floor behind her. She smiled shyly, looked down at herself, and then up at him, her eyes shining. "Do I look like a ghost, maybe?"

Ian realized he was standing slack jawed, mouth open like a drooling village idiot. He hastily closed it and pulled her into his arms.

Emily responded eagerly to his kiss.

When they came up for air, she stepped back slightly, a mock-serious look on her face. "Well, Mr. Reporter, may I come in? Or shall I sleep here in your hallway?"

"Hmmm." Ian stroked his chin, as if pondering the question. "I guess I could loan you some blankets and a pillow. Might get kinda cold out here, though. My neighbors might complain, too. I guess you'll have to come inside."

Laughing, he dodged her kick and led her into the flat.

Emily wrinkled her nose at the decor, a failed mix of cheap framed posters, plastic flowers, dark-colored carpeting, and imitation Scandinavian-design furniture. Knowles had best characterized the place as a study in Twentieth Century Bad Taste. Ian wished he'd thought to wash the dishes stacked in his small sink. His bachelor habits were often embarrassing.

She wagged a finger in his face. "Clearly you are not fit to live alone, Ian Sherfield. You need a good woman to look after you."

That was too perfect an opening to pass up. He smiled. "I've tried finding one, but I guess I'm stuck with you."

She smiled back. "Yes, perhaps that is so."

Which raised an interesting question. "What about your father? Does he know you're here?"

Sorrow briefly touched her eyes as she shook her head.

"But Emily, he'll . . ."

"Sshh." She laid a soft, sweet-smelling finger across his lips. "My father has not been home for these two weeks and more. He spends all his days in Pretoria, organizing this . . . this butchery." Her words were clipped, angry, and he remembered that she'd been a student at the University of Witwatersrand. Some of her friends or teachers might have been among those he'd seen lying motionless on the pavement—gunned down by the police her father commanded.

She paused for a moment and then went on, calmer now. "Besides, I told that witch Viljoen I was returning to Cape Town to stay with some friends there. They'll cover for me if he should call."

Ian nodded, deeply moved by the risks she was running to be near him.

She shrugged out of her heavy coat and sat down on the sofa. He sat next to her.

"Anyway, Ian, I have news that would not wait any longer. Unbelievable news!" Her words tumbled out over one another, anger turned to excitement.

As she recounted the story of her father's party and the muttered conversation she'd overheard, Ian felt his own pulse speeding up. If he could prove that Vorster had advance warning of the ANC's Blue Train ambush . . . My God! He'd make headlines around the U.S. Hell, around the whole world!

But how could he get that kind of proof? South Africa's new rulers weren't going to come clean just because he asked a few pointed questions. He frowned. This guy Muller Emily had mentioned was the key. Muller. The name was somehow familiar.

Memories fell into place as long hours of study paid off. Erik Muller was some kind of cloak-and-dagger honcho. Ran South Africa's Directorate of Military Intelligence. Rumor said he handled most of the government's dirtiest jobs—surveillance, blackmail, even assassinations. Just the kind of man you'd expect to be one of Karl Vorster's favorites, Ian thought. And just the kind of man who'd know the truth about the Blue Train massacre.

So somehow he had to get a hook into this Muller character. Find some way to either force or persuade the man to come clean. That wasn't going to be easy. . . .

Reality reared its ugly head. "Damn it!" He slammed a clenched fist into his thigh.

"What's wrong?" Emily looked concerned.

"I forgot that Sam and I probably have our own spy tagging along with us wherever we go."

He filled her in on their suspicions of Matthew Sibena. "Personally, I think the kid's being forced to inform on us. Sam isn't so charitable."

"Then get rid of him. Fire him, and hire another driver."

"Who will come from the same place as Matthew." Ian shook his head. "No, I think we should hang on to him. He seems like a good kid, and I really believe he hates Vorster as much as we do."

He shrugged helplessly. "Anyway, Matt's reasons don't matter much. The fact is, if I start sniffing around Muller's tail, the bastard's going to get wind of it before I've even properly started. And then, *whoosh,* Sam and I are out of the country on the next jet leaving Jan Smuts International."

He lapsed into a depressed silence, only looking up when Emily lightly tapped his knee.

"You're forgetting something else, Ian Sherfield." Her eyes twinkled mischievously.

"Oh? And what's that?"

"Me!" She leaned closer to him, completely serious now. "I have a journalism degree, too. I know how to do research. How to interview sources. How to track down the truth. And I am a Transvaaler, just like this Erik Muller."

She took his hand. "Let me hunt this man for you while you and Sam lead these spies on a wild-goose chase. Please?"

Ian looked down at their intertwined fingers. Everything she said made perfect sense, but . . . "It could get dangerous. Muller's supposed to be a killer by trade."

Emily nodded. "True." She smiled wryly. "But remember that I am just 'a weak woman' to most of my countrymen. No self-respecting Afrikaner man could ever see me as a serious threat."

She had a point there. Ian felt his excitement returning. They might just be able to pull this off after all! He leaned forward, scrabbling on the glass-topped coffee table in front of the sofa for a piece of notepaper. "Okay, here's how we'll work this. . . . We'll need some background info first. The *Star*'s probably the best place to start . . ."

Emily reached over and gently took the piece of paper out of his hand. Her fingers slid between his again, rubbing slowly up and down in a familiar erotic rhythm. She looked up at him with warm, almost glowing eyes. "I think such planning would be best left until morning, don't you?"

Oh.

She rose and pulled him willingly toward the bedroom.

SEPTEMBER 2—PRESIDENT'S OFFICE, THE UNION BUILDINGS, PRETORIA

Karl Vorster watched the flickering image on his television closely, working himself into a towering rage. Gideon Mantizima's "Nightline" interview had been videotaped the day before by South Africa's Washington embassy and flown posthaste to Pretoria via London. From there the tape had bounced upward through the Foreign Ministry like a red-hot potato until at last it landed on Vorster's desk.

"Kaffir bastard!"

Mantizima's prerecorded image took no notice. The Zulu leader was a short, broad-shouldered man who wore his perfectly tailored Savile Row suit with natural authority. And when he spoke, his precise, well-modulated voice reflected an accent acquired during several years of advanced study at the London School of Economics. He sat comfortably in a chair, framed by a plain, pale-blue studio backdrop—apparently unflustered by the knowledge that his words and picture were being broadcast to several million television sets all across the United States. As the leader of Inkatha, one of South Africa's largest black political organizations, Mantizima was used to the exercise of power in all its forms.

The screen split, showing "Nightline" 's New York–based anchor. Polite skepticism tinged the anchor's own precise voice. "As you know, Chief Mantizima, many leaders of the ANC and other antiapartheid organizations have said that you're nothing more than an apologist for Pretoria's racial policies. Surely your continued opposition to Western economic sanctions seems likely to reinforce those charges?"

Mantizima shook his head vigorously. "Your information is out-of-date, Mr. Thorgood. It is true that I once opposed sanctions as counterproductive—as bound to hurt our own people while discouraging constructive talks on South Africa's future. But that was before this madman Vorster came to power. I had hoped that the Haymans government would someday see reason. I have no such hope for this new government dominated by thugs and murderers."

The anchorman sat forward, visibly interested. "Are you suggesting that you now support tighter economic sanctions?"

Mantizima nodded once, his jaw firm. "Yes, Mr. Thorgood. That is exactly what I am saying. And that is the message I intend to carry to both your Congress and your president. In fact, I now believe that sanctions alone will not suffice."

For once, "Nightline" 's top-rated moderator looked confused. "But what other . . ."

Mantizima's once-smiling eyes grew cold. "Direct intervention. Only the full application of all the power in the hands of the Western democracies can put an end to this man Vorster's genocidal reign of terror."

Silence filled the airwaves for what seemed an eternity. Gideon Mantizima had done what no other politician or pundit had ever been able to do. He'd left "Nightline" 's veteran anchorman speechless.

"Off! I want that *verdomde* machine off! Now!" Vorster's shout echoed around the wood-paneled walls of his office. From one corner, a pale, visibly frightened aide scurried to obey. The other men clustered around the television set shrank back into their chairs.

Mantizima's image vanished in midsentence.

Vorster rose from behind his desk, his face grim. "Treason! Treason so black that it stinks in my nostrils." His hands balled into fists. "We've treated this, this *skepsel*"—he used the Afrikaans word meaning "creature"—"almost as if he were a man for years. Allowed him to administer his own tribeland, even. And this is how we are repaid!"

He turned to face the foreign minister. "I want Mantizima's passport revoked immediately, Jaap."

The foreign minister, more skeletal than ever, sat wrapped in a heavy overcoat. He looked troubled. "Is that wise, Mr. President? Why not simply arrest him on his return?"

Vorster shook his head decisively. "No. Imprisonment or execution would only make him a martyr for Zulu hotheads." He smiled unpleasantly. "By cutting him off from his followers, from his base of power, we will make this Mantizima just another wandering black beggar without a voice. He'll wither away without troubling us further."

Jowly Marius van der Heijden looked up, an ambitious gleam in his eye. "And what of KwaZulu, Mr. President? Which black will you appoint to rule the homeland in Mantizima's place?"

The others nodded. Van der Heijden had a good question. KwaZulu consisted of patches of separate territory scattered throughout Natal Province—most on or near the road and rail lines linking the province with the rest of South Africa. And that meant Pretoria could not risk prolonged disorder in the homeland. Someone would have to fill the leadership vacuum left by Mantizima's de facto exile.

"None! As of this moment, KwaZulu's special status is ended. All administrative and police matters in the area will come under our direct supervision.

"This so-called warrior tribe will again learn to fear the lash, the gun, and our righteous anger—as they did in the days of our forefathers."

His advisors murmured their approval.

South Africa's 6 million Zulus would pay in blood for their chief's arrant treachery.

SEPTEMBER 4—NEAR RICHARDS BAY, NATAL PROVINCE, SOUTH AFRICA

The Uys family farmhouse lay sheltered in a small valley meandering southeast from the Drakensberg Mountains toward the Indian Ocean. A shallow, gravel-bottomed creek burbled gently past a large, one-story stone house, attached garage, and shearing pens. Sheep wandered the hillsides above the valley, moving with docile stupidity from one patch of tall, green grass to the next.

It seemed the very picture of peace and tranquillity. But that was an illusion.

Piet Uys held the phone in shaking, work-gnarled hands, listening to the first three unanswered rings with mounting panic.

"Richards Bay police station." The voice on the other end was dry and businesslike—almost disinterested.

Uys took a quavering breath. "This is Piet Uys of two Freeling Road. I want to report a theft in progress."

The voice grew more interested. "What kind of theft, Meneer Uys?"

"I have seen several blacks prowling around my sheep pens. They want my sheep!" Fear crept into the elderly farmer's voice. "We need the police here, as quick as you can. Please!"

"Calm down now, *meneer*. We'll have a patrol on the way up there in minutes. Just stay in your house and don't get in the way. We'll deal with those blacks for you."

"Yes, yes, I will stay inside. Hurry, please." Uys hung up and stepped back from the phone, hands held away from his sides.

"That was very good, Mr. Uys. Very good, indeed. You've been most cooperative."

The Afrikaner farmer looked up into the sardonic eyes of the tall, muscled Zulu leaning negligently against his kitchen countertop. "You will not harm us then . . . as you promised?"

The Zulu smiled wryly and shook his head. "Of course not. We do not make war on women, children, or old men. We leave that to your government." The black man stood up straight, suddenly seeming even taller. "But the police are another matter entirely. They are fair game."

He stroked the R4 assault rifle cradled in his hands. "A beautiful weapon, Mr. Uys. Another reason we owe you our thanks. It will make our task this morning much easier."

Uys's leathery, weather-worn face crumpled. He'd been

issued the rifle as a member of the neighborhood Commando—one of South Africa's paramilitary home-guard units. And commandos were supposed to kill antigovernment guerrillas, not arm them. He'd failed his nation and failed his people.

The Zulu leader watched him sob for a moment and then turned away, disgusted. He looked at the younger black man standing close to Uys's moaning, panic-stricken wife. "Watch them closely, but do not hurt them. You know when to leave?"

The younger man nodded, eyes bright and excited.

"Good. *Mayibuye Afrika!*" The older Zulu raised his new assault rifle high in a salute and strode out of the farmhouse toward the rest of his waiting men.

White South Africa was about to learn that not all Zulus had forgotten their warrior past.

NATAL POLICE PATROL, NEAR RICHARDS BAY

Blue light flashing, the police squad car turned off the highway to the left, bumping over gravel and loose dirt onto an unpaved track leading to the Uys family steading.

Four uniformed officers of the South African police crowded the car—two in back and two in front. All were middle-aged reservists called back to duty when the younger men went north to join the police and Army sweeps through black townships.

"*Ag*, man, I tell you, there's been some *blery* heavy fighting up there in the Namib. Lots of boys won't be coming home. That's what I'm hearing anyway." The driver kept his eyes on the road, but his mind was on the argument they'd been having off and on since leaving the station that morning.

One of the two men in back snorted. "And I say that's just defeatist bullshit, Manie. I read the papers, man, and I've seen nothing about heavy casualties."

"No surprise there, man! You think they're going to print everything that happens? Just so some communist spy can read it with his morning post?" The driver smiled as his sarcasm drew chuckles. He glanced over his shoulder at a beet-red face. "They're tossing big shells back and forth up there, Hugo. And I know what that's like. I was in Angola back in '75 when those *verdomde* Cubans started pouring one hundred twenty-two millimeter shells in on our poor heads like they was raindrops. I said to myself, I said, Manie . . ."

A barrage of groans drowned out the driver's thousandth recitation of his heroic wartime exploits.

The squad car bounced and rolled over ruts left by the heavy trucks that carried Piet Uys's wool to market and his unneeded sheep to the slaughterhouse.

The youngest of the four men squirmed uncomfortably in the front seat. "How much farther to this place anyway? I've got to take a piss like you wouldn't believe."

The driver laughed. "I'm not surprised, man. You must have drunk ten cups of coffee with your lunch. Don't you know all that caffeine's bad for you? It will kill you someday. Shit!"

He slammed on the brakes and fought for control as the squad car fishtailed to a bone-jarring stop amid a yellow-gray cloud of dust and thrown gravel. Rocks spanged off the cab of the large, open-topped truck blocking the road.

"Christ! Those damned blacks could have killed us with that stunt!" The driver sounded personally aggrieved at the thought that anyone would wish him harm. "Get out and see if they've left the keys in the cab, Hugo. Otherwise we have to go around."

The beefy policeman in back nodded and reached for the squad car's door handle. He never finished the movement.

Bullets shattered the front windshield and punched in through the car's thin metal sides—tearing through flesh and ricocheting off bone before tumbling off end over end into thin air. Three of the four South African policemen died instantly. The fourth lived just long enough to claw futilely for his holstered pistol before sliding slowly down the blood-soaked seat.

Thirty meters up the hillside, the Zulu leader rose from his crouch, already replacing the half-used clip in his assault rifle with practiced hands. He turned to the small group of men hiding beside him. "Take all their weapons and ammunition. And look for a portable radio set. We will need it all before we are done."

He watched in silence as they raced down the hill toward the bullet-riddled police car. The assault rifles, shotguns, and pistols carried by the dead policemen would more than double the firepower at his disposal. Better still, the news of this bold deed would spread, drawing more young men from the kraals and city streets to his side—and to the cause of his exiled chief.

He smiled. After more than a century of uneasy peace, the Zulu war regiments, the *impis,* were once again on the march.

SEPTEMBER 6—MINISTRY OF LAW AND ORDER, PRETORIA

Brig. Franz Diederichs sat at attention in front of Marius van der Heijden. A general in the Security Branch of the South African Police, Diederichs was a short, wiry man whose narrow face was dominated by a pair of cold blue eyes and a cruel, thin-lipped mouth. It was a face that reflected its owner's character and temperament.

"You understand the importance of this assignment, Franz?"

Diederichs nodded once. "Yes, Minister."

Van der Heijden ignored him. In his view, subordinates were, by definition, incapable of fully understanding anything they hadn't heard at least twice. "The President's decision to give this ministry direct control over KwaZulu reflects his personal confidence in our ability to get the job done. Nothing must shake that confidence, understood?"

Diederichs nodded again, carefully concealing his impatience. Both van der Heijden's mannerisms and his ambitions were well-known to those who worked for him.

"Good." The deputy minister of law and order laced his fingers across a prominent paunch. "Then you will also understand my insistence that this 'insurrection' "—he sniffed contemptuously, as though that were too significant a term for what was happening in Natal—"be smashed as quickly as possible."

Diederichs leaned forward. "Will I be able to call on additional police units or troops, Minister?"

Van der Heijden shook his head. "No. Manpower is too scarce at the moment. Every trained man is needed for service on the Namibian front or to help maintain order in the townships. You must work with what you have. You must use terror, Franz!" He pounded his desk once and pointed a plump finger in Diederichs's direction. "Terror must swell your ranks!" His outstretched finger swiveled and came to rest, aimed now at the portrait of Karl Vorster hung prominently on the far wall. "The President himself agrees with this precept. In his own words, *Brigadier*. In his own words! He has said that he wants one hundred dead Zulus as payment for every policeman they have so foully murdered. Ten kraals are to be wiped from the face of the earth for every white farm they dare to attack! Blood must answer for blood! And fire for fire! Show no mercy toward these traitorous blacks, Franz." Van der Heijden paused, breathing hard. "End their cowardly ambushes. Root them out. And then kill them!"

For the first time since entering the room, Diederichs allowed himself a single, short smile.

CHAPTER 12

Storm Warning

SEPTEMBER 7—CNN HEADLINE NEWS

The dramatic images from Namibia occupied center stage during CNN's hourly news recap. "In a visit designed to show the depth of Cuba's support for Namibia, Cuban president Fidel Castro today landed in Walvis Bay on a whirlwind tour of the war zone." A smiling, cigar-chomping Castro seemed perfectly at home in a sea of military uniforms. His apparent vigor contradicted persistent rumors of ill health, though the bushy, once-brown beard had gone almost completely gray.

The video image showed Castro, with Vega at his side, touring the captured South African port. Several Cuban-flagged merchant ships could be seen behind them hurriedly off-loading tanks, planes, and artillery onto Walvis Bay's long piers. Antiaircraft units and SAM batteries guarded against South African air attack.

The view shifted to show troops in fortifications outside the town, cheering wildly as Castro and his general appeared.

The footage ended with a close-up shot of a jubilant Fidel Castro pumping his clenched fist in the air in triumph.

Castro's elated image vanished and CNN's high-tech Atlanta studio reappeared. "In other news from overseas, India's foreign minister again insisted that Pakistan abandon its covert support for . . ."

FORWARD HEADQUARTERS, CUBAN EXPEDITIONARY FORCE, THE STRAND HOTEL, SWAKOPMUND, NAMIBIA

Night had fallen across the Namibian coast.

Thirty kilometers north of Walvis Bay's ship-choked anchorage, high-ranking Cuban officers again filled the Strand Hotel's formal dining room. Candlelight gleamed off polished silverware, fine crystal, and shoulder boards crowded with stars. Black waiters and busboys moved from table to table, for once plainly happy in their work. The Strand's white managers and wine stewards were not happy. They clustered near the kitchen entrance, sour faced and carefully supervised by armed guards.

Outside, the Atlantic surf boomed, sending the hissing, foam-flecked remnants of waves surging onto Swakopmund's sandy beaches. The infantry squads dug in above the high-water mark were all alert—their machine guns, mortars, and other heavy weapons manned and ready. Searchlights mounted on T-62 tanks parked hull-down among the dunes probed out to sea, stabbing through the darkness at precise, timed intervals.

Inside, the assembled officers ate, gossiped, toasted one another, and covertly eyed the two men who sat alone at the head table.

Gen. Antonio Vega toyed with his pastry dish, conscious that Cuba's president and absolute ruler ate with lip-smacking gusto beside him. He frowned slightly at the sugary and fruit-filled concoction. He'd always preferred plainer fare, soldier's fare—rice and beans, sometimes mixed with a little beef or chicken. Food that satisfied hunger without leaving one lolling about in an overfed stupor. The kind of food you could get in Cuba—at home.

His leader's tastes were quite different, and Vega knew better than to try imposing his own culinary views on Fidel Castro. Particularly not when he was about to urge that communist Cuba undertake one of the largest political, military, and strategic gambles in its short history.

Vega sipped his wine, studying the crowded dining room over the rim of his glass. It was an astonishing sight. There were probably more senior Cuban military men concentrated here in this tiny hotel on Africa's most desolate coast than there were left in all of Havana.

So many men in fact that the Strand Hotel had been hard-pressed to accommodate them all. Vega had gladly turned his quarters over to Castro, but their two staffs had engaged in a very careful assessment of relative ranks before the remaining rooms could be assigned. In the end, several of Swakopmund's wealthiest burghers had been turned out of their homes to make room for some of the junior officers.

This evening's dinner had been served in shifts, with the lowest-ranking officers and staff members eating quickly and early, so that the two principals and their higher aides could eat at a fashionable hour, before moving on to the important business at hand.

Important business, indeed, Vega thought, keeping a tight rein on his expression. Castro and his entourage must see only the outer man—calm, cool, collected, and thoroughly professional. The storm of mingled emotions—excitement, nervousness, and joy—that ebbed and flowed inside him had to stay hidden. Marxist-Leninism was a scientific faith, and its true believers were supposed to remain unswayed by sentiment, personal ambition, or petty hatreds.

"Excellent, Antonio. A fitting conclusion to a glorious day." Castro pushed his empty plate aside and absentmindedly combed his fingers through his beard, brushing away small crumbs and flakes of pastry crust.

Vega lowered the wineglass and inclined his head, acknowledging the compliment.

Castro bent his own head for a moment, puffing one of his trademark cigars alight. Then he looked up, shrewd eyes fixed on Vega's face. "You may begin the briefing, General. Medals and propaganda films have their own time and place, but now we must contemplate the next steps in this war. And as the saying goes, the wise man makes sure his shoes are tied before setting out on any journey."

Vega smiled. As always, Castro knew how to get to the heart of the matter. Vega nodded to one of his hovering staff officers, who in turn motioned to the cadre of young lieutenants stationed at the door.

Instantly, they spread through the room—shepherding the waiters and other hotel workers outside. The low buzz of conversation from the other tables died away as several more junior officers brought in a large, cloth-covered easel.

Vega's senior intelligence officer, Col. Jaume Vasquez, stepped forward and stood near the easel. Vasquez, a short, slender man with an aristocrat's high cheekbones and long, thin nose, seemed to have taken special pains with his appearance this evening. Every crease on his tailored dress uniform hung razor-sharp and his polished black shoes gleamed brightly. Only the faint sheen of nervous perspiration on his forehead marred the image of absolute perfection.

Vega sympathized with the colonel's case of nerves. Few men ever stood so close to one of history's great turning points. It still felt strange to realize that the whole course of a war and the very future of several nations would be determined here, in the rustic dining room of a small hotel off in the middle of nowhere.

The intelligence officer waited in silence until the dining room doors closed firmly—shutting out curious junior staffers and potential spies alike.

Vasquez pulled away the cloth covering his easel, revealing a map of northern and central Namibia. Red lines and arrows showed the current situation facing Cuba's Expeditionary Force. "*Señor Presidente, Señor General,* the battlefront has stabilized along an east-west line running from Walvis Bay to Windhoek to the village of Gobabis, here." He tapped the map, pointing out a small town near Namibia's border with

Botswana. "The enemy's main force remains concentrated near the passes leading to Windhoek. Radio intercepts, prisoner interrogations, and air reconnaissance all indicate the presence of at least one mechanized brigade around the town of Rehoboth."

Vasquez ran a lean, manicured finger up the highway north from Rehoboth, stopping at a tiny dot. "This represents the deepest South African penetration into the Auas Mountains. One battalion holding the village of Bergland. All available evidence indicates that the South Africans periodically rotate troops forward to this area from their staging base at Rehoboth."

Castro sat forward in his chair, his bushy eyebrows arched. "Why only a single battalion? If Windhoek truly is their main objective, why don't the South Africans apply more combat power there?"

Vega nodded to himself. A good question. Now, would the colonel falter, or could he answer to Castro's satisfaction?

The intelligence officer passed his unspoken test. "They cannot move more than a single battalion forward, *Señor Presidente*, because the road net north of Bergland isn't able to support a larger force. Cramming more troops and vehicles into a narrower frontage would only make life easier for our gunners and antitank missile teams."

Castro chuckled and waved Vasquez on.

The colonel moved his hand westward until it touched the coast. "Our position at Walvis Bay is doubly secure. The only roads come from Windhoek or across five hundred kilometers of unsettled wilderness. Any South African force trying to recapture the port must either come by sea or take one of these roads."

Vasquez shrugged, as though it made little difference. "The support of our gallant Soviet allies guarantees us control of the sea route, and we now hold unquestioned air superiority over this section of the front. As a result, no South African column can approach without being detected and bombed into oblivion."

Vega watched Castro's smile grow wider and matched it with one of his own. Bombed into oblivion. Now there was a wonderful image. He almost hoped Pretoria would be foolish enough to order such a doomed counterattack. Any venture that sucked more South African troops deeper into Namibia's near-roadless hinterland would make his job easier later on.

Vasquez turned his attention and that of his audience to the east. "Our units defending Gobabis are less secure, because the town is surrounded by a net of villages and roads, but from Gobabis all roads lead to Windhoek. And we hold Windhoek in strength." Heads nodded sagely across the room. All were agreed on the strategic value of the capital.

Vasquez turned slightly, facing Castro and Vega squarely. "To all intents and purposes, South Africa's attempt to seize Namibia in a lightning campaign has failed. True, its soldiers occupy the southern half of this country, but we control areas containing more than two-thirds of the population and most of the mineral resources. In addition, sources report that South Africa's losses have been much higher than expected."

Vega noted that Vasquez left the other half of that equation carefully unspoken. Cuba's own casualties had also been heavy.

Castro flicked cigar ash onto one of the Strand's best china plates. "So then, what can we expect the madmen in Pretoria to try next, Colonel?"

Vasquez smiled thinly. "Barring commando attacks by small parties, an attack of any size must come north along Route One, directly from Rehoboth and Bergland. Given the existing logistical and strategic situation, we can see no other serious option for the South Africans. The Afrikaners can do nothing but continue to batter away at our mountain defenses—choking the road with their corpses and with their wrecked vehicles." He stepped away from the easel, signaling the end of his formal remarks.

Vega allowed himself a moment's self-congratulation. Vasquez had done a good job. Clear, concise, and factual. And like all successful presentations, the colonel's briefing had ended on just the right theatrical note.

Castro nodded his satisfaction and sat quietly for an instant, wreathed in cigar smoke. Then he looked up. "Tell me, Colonel, how much of the enemy's force is committed to this war?"

Vasquez didn't even consult his notes. "We've identified units belonging to three brigades, *Señor Presidente*—half of South Africa's regular army. Counting reserves, more than a third of its national forces."

Castro countered, "But Pretoria hasn't fully mobilized its reserves yet. True?"

Vasquez bowed his head slightly, acknowledging the point. "Selected units are still being called up, *Señor Presidente*."

Castro turned to Vega. His words were blunt. Tact wasn't a social grace often found in absolute rulers. "So, General, you have stopped this first assault, but the Afrikaners haven't fully committed their reserves." He leaned closer, his eyes cold and hard. "I need to know, Antonio. Can you hold against a second, even larger, offensive?"

Vega had been expecting the question. It dovetailed perfectly into the proposal he hoped to make in a moment. "I can, *Presidente*. With the two brigades now in Namibia, I can stop up to two South African divisions. As you know, the defender has the advantage, three to one."

"But by the same rule, you need more than a division yourself to advance against the South Africans. And the road net south will not support an offensive of that size."

Vega was pleased. Castro's preferred nickname was *El Artillero* or "The Gunner." He had not lost his military skills. Inwardly, the general took a deep breath, thinking, now it begins. "That is true. As matters stand now, we are deadlocked, *Presidente*. We can build up above two brigades, but Pretoria can also reinforce its army—leaving both sides caught in an escalating stalemate. Such a stalemate would continue until one side or the other was exhausted."

Castro frowned and Vega frowned with him. Cuba could not win such a prolonged war of attrition. It was a poor country, without even a fraction of South Africa's resources. Vega knew that national will counted, but he was a practical man and he always calculated the odds before making a bet. And staying locked into the current military situation was the equivalent of staking one's entire life savings on an already disqualified horse. His army's capture of Walvis Bay had staved off defeat—not guaranteed victory.

Vega watched his leader's face as he considered the options, knowing that Castro was running through the same set of unpalatable choices he'd already considered and rejected.

Withdrawal was out. Too much of Cuba's international prestige was already at stake. Havana's support for little Namibia had garnered both praise from the world community and much-needed revenue from the country's diamonds, gold, and uranium.

On the other hand, they couldn't simply accept the status quo. Pretoria's armed forces would eventually exhaust Vega and his men—wearing them down, man by man.

And that seemed to leave one equally futile and even more expensive option—a desperate race to match South Africa's steady troop buildup. A race that would still inevitably end in eventual exhaustion and defeat.

Castro's disappointed scowl grew deeper. He'd come to Namibia for a celebration and instead found the likelihood of ultimate failure.

Vega nodded soberly to himself. Cuba's president had a good military background, but he clearly couldn't see a way out of their box, either. The general drew himself up straighter. It was time to take his own gamble.

He cleared his throat. "I have a plan, sir—a good plan, I believe. But it involves a certain amount of risk."

Castro looked up sharply. "Risk of loss is better than certain loss." He eyed his general closely. "Tell me of this plan of yours, Antonio."

Purposefully, Vega stood up and strode over to the easel. "*Señor Presidente,* I am convinced that we must look beyond the struggle for Windhoek, or even for Namibia. This invasion is only the latest in a series of South African aggressions on this continent. It demonstrates once and for all that Pretoria's racist government is incapable of reform."

Castro looked a little impatient. Political orations were usually left to him, but many of the staff officers clustered around the room nodded and Vega took heart from that. "Our internationalist duty brought us here to fight against capitalist aggression. As loyal socialists, we are glad to do so. But we are only engaged in fighting the symptoms of this disease—this racist blot on Africa's soil. Even a victory here in Namibia will not end Pretoria's machinations. Therefore, I propose that we take direct action against these Afrikaner imperialists."

Vega flipped the Namibian situation map over the back of the easel, revealing a map showing all of southern Africa. Red phase lines and arrows converged on Pretoria from three separate directions. He saw Castro's eyes widen in surprise. "We must occupy South Africa, destroy its corrupt, capitalistic regime, and build an African socialist state in its place!"

Vega had expected shocked gasps or muttered exclamations. Instead, his words were met by absolute silence. All eyes were riveted on the map, and Vega quickly motioned to a lieutenant, who started passing out copies of a thick document, first to Castro, then to everyone else in the room.

Cuba's president glanced down at the binder in his hands and then back up at Vega in open disbelief. "Let me see if I understand you correctly, General. You are proposing that we invade South Africa itself?"

Vega nodded, aware that many in the room must think him mad.

"And you make this proposal for expanding the war after proving that we cannot win even a more limited campaign here in Namibia?" Castro didn't bother concealing his sarcasm and Vega shivered slightly. The President's biting wit had an unfortunate tendency to slide into murderous rage.

He composed himself. "Yes."

Castro visibly fought for control over his growing anger. Vega had a reputation as a brave and intelligent soldier, not as a suicidal idiot. "Explain yourself, General."

"It is a question of who holds the initiative, *Señor Presidente*." Vega was careful to show every sign of respect. "So long as we fight only in Namibia, we are deadlocked. The war will move along the lines of a strict mathematical formula. So many troops, tanks, and guns producing so many casualties and consuming such and such a proportion of each nation's treasure. We will lose that kind of a war.''

He paused as murmurs of agreement rose from the watching officers. ''And that is precisely why we must not fight the way Pretoria expects us to fight. Cuba must seize the initiative. Cuba must carry this war into a new arena, a new phase of revolutionary combat!''

He took a step toward Castro. ''South Africa's whites are strong, *Señor Presidente,* when they fight on foreign soil. But at home they are a weak, increasingly fearful minority —kept safe only by their monopoly on the instruments of military power. South Africa's vast black and colored proletariat is polarized and anxious for liberation from the capitalists who keep it poor, undereducated, and underpaid.''

He could see Castro's anger fade away, replaced by a look of dawning comprehension. The Cuban president muttered more to himself than anyone else. ''A revolution waiting to happen . . .''

Vega nodded. ''Exactly. A revolutionary fire storm we could ignite with a sudden, unexpected counterattack into South Africa itself.'' He tapped the map contemptuously. ''With most of its professional army tied down in Namibia, a wholesale uprising would shatter Pretoria's racist state once and for all.

''We have already gathered tremendous international goodwill for our fight here in Namibia. Imagine our standing if we destroy the agent of Western imperialism in Africa—the last colonial power, still fighting to retain control of the scraps of its empire!'' Vega's eyes were shining now, and his voice was clear and strong.

He went on, hammering home every conceivable advantage. ''A socialist South Africa would have tremendous resources at its disposal, sir. The gold, diamonds, uranium, and other strategic minerals the capitalists crave. The resources the plutocrats will come begging for. And with our guidance, this new South Africa could lead the rest of Africa fully out from under Western domination. We could revitalize the socialist movement worldwide!''

Castro was smiling now, a full-mouthed, toothy, sharklike grin. Then the smile faded. ''And what of the Soviet Union, Antonio. How will we persuade them to back such an audacious venture?''

With the prospect of riches, of course, thought Vega. Over the past few years, the Soviets had shown themselves to be fair-weather communists—unworthy of the great Lenin. But that was not what Castro would want to hear. ''We must remind the Soviets of their own history, drag them kicking and screaming back to their own revolution! This will be a war of liberation, waged not just by us, but by the entire international socialist movement against the last, worst vestige of Western colonialism in Africa!''

Vega paused for breath and heard his voice replaced by the sound of clapping, first from just Fidel Castro, and then from the rest of the assembled officers—all of them applauding the Victor of Walvis Bay.

He stood motionless, smiling gravely, inwardly elated. Castro was convinced. Cuba would carry its war into South Africa's own streets, fields, and mines. Karl Vorster and his arrogant Afrikaners would reap the very whirlwind of death and destruction they themselves had sown.

SEPTEMBER 9—20TH CAPE RIFLES, NEAR BERGLAND, NAMIBIA

Fires set by the day's last artillery barrage flickered redly on distant hillsides—tiny points of light glowing against the dark mountains and darker sky. Nightfall hid the ugly debris left by war—open ground pockmarked by shell bursts, mangled wrecks that had once been fighting machines, and bare, boulder-strewn hills scarred by slit trenches and sandbag-topped bunkers.

Commandant Henrik Kruger lowered his binoculars. Nothing. No secondary explosions or any other signs that the artillery fire had had any real effect. The Cubans were too well dug in. From all appearances, this latest barrage had done nothing more than tear up a few more acres of worthless Namibian soil.

He sighed and turned away, half-walking, half-sliding down the ridge toward his command bunker. Clusters of weary, bedraggled men clambered upright from around small camp stoves as he passed by, some clutching mugs of fresh-brewed tea, others half-empty mess tins.

Kruger forced a smile onto his face as he acknowledged their soft-voiced greetings. It wouldn't do for the battalion to see its leader looking discouraged. Three weeks of hard marching, hard fighting, heavy casualties, and now this endless, wearing stalemate had ground the 20th Cape Rifles down.

They still attacked with as much courage and expertise as ever, but without the boundless self-confidence and easy assurance of certain victory that had once characterized South Africa's army. Too many of the best noncoms and junior officers were gone—dead or lying maimed in military hospitals. Those who survived were bone tired. Their rare moments of rest were disturbed by the disconcerting rumors flowing north out of South Africa. Rumors of defeats and crippling losses near Walvis Bay. Of student riots and police shootings. Of a guerrilla war spreading like wildfire through Natal Province. Of a strained economy beginning to unravel.

Kruger ground his teeth together. Goddamn those idiots Vorster, de Wet, and all their mewling lapdogs! In less than three months, they'd managed to drown the country in a sea of troubles—foreign war, civil insurrection, and economic chaos. What disaster would be next?

Scowling, he pushed through the bunker's blackout curtain into a low-roofed room dimly lit by battery-powered lamps. Several officers and NCOs filled the small space to capacity. All were working steadily—updating situation maps and logs to reflect the results of the day's fighting and reports from other parts of the widely scattered Namibian front. He paused to scan their handiwork.

"*Kommandant?*"

Kruger swung toward the voice. It belonged to Capt. Pieter Meiring, his bearded, bespectacled operations officer.

"Brigade called while you were up on the ridge, sir. The brigadier would like to see you as soon as possible." Meiring's tone was flat, drained by fatigue of any emotion.

Kruger bit back a savage oath. Blast it. It was a sixty-kilometer trip to Rehoboth. What the hell did the man want that couldn't be discussed over the radio or field phone?

He looked at his watch. Nearly eight o'clock. "Any word from Major Forbes?"

"No, *Kommandant*."

Another irritation. He'd sent his second-in-command back to Rehoboth that morning on a mission to straighten out the battalion's steadily worsening supply situation. Mortar rounds, rifle ammo, and petrol weren't coming forward fast enough or in large enough quantities. So he'd told Forbes to go back and kick a little logistical ass. Men could fight for a time without adequate sleep, but they certainly couldn't fight without bullets or fuel for their vehicles.

Kruger shook his head disgustedly. One more problem piled on his already overloaded platter. He looked up at Meiring. "All right, Pieter. Get my Ratel ready to go. I'll bring Forbes with me and try to get back as soon as I can. Plan for an orders group at . . ." He paused, estimating travel times and Brigadier Strydom's well-known penchant for long-winded shoptalk. "Set it for oh one hundred hours. That should be late enough."

Meiring sketched a salute and hurried away.

Kruger turned to check the situation map again and absentmindedly rubbed his chin. Stubble rasped under his fingers. "Andries!"

"Sir?" His orderly materialized out of the crowd.

"Bring me my razor and a bowl of hot water." He smiled. "I don't want to shock our rear-echelon warriors, do I? They shouldn't think we let a few minor problems like bullets and bombs interfere with our grooming."

It was a feeble attempt, but it worked. Laughter rumbled through the bunker. Most South African staff officers were veterans of combat in Angola and Namibia, but there were still enough spit-and-polish desk soldiers among their ranks for the old slanders to be funny.

Kruger chuckled with them, glad his men could still find something to laugh about.

82nd MECHANIZED BRIGADE HQ, REHOBOTH, NAMIBIA

Rehoboth lay nestled among hills marking the southern edge of the Auas Mountains. The town was home to a conservative, intensely religious, mixed-race group who'd fled north from Cape Town through the Namib more than two centuries before. Their plain, old-fashioned houses were a testament both to their faith and to their poverty. But the darkness and silence behind each window reflected a dusk-to-dawn curfew imposed by South Africa's army.

Outside the town, small herds of cattle and brown, black, and gray karakul sheep wandered over widely scattered grazing lands, slowly eating their way closer to slaughter or shearing. Several cows looked up from their rhythmic chewing, momentarily made curious by the sound of an engine growling past along the highway. Dim blackout headlamps briefly outlined them against the hillside and then swept away as the Ratel APC headed south toward a vast, new tent city on the outskirts of Rehoboth. The cows lowed mournfully to one another for a few seconds before stooping again to the dry grass close at hoof.

The 82nd Mechanized Brigade's tents, vehicle parks, supply dumps, and maintenance workshops sprawled over more than a hundred acres. Patrolling armored cars protected the brigade perimeter against ground attack, while a Cactus SAM battery and light flak guns offered coverage against Cuban air raids. Enough light leaked out through tent flaps or seams to show that many men were still wide-awake.

All lights were on at the large, peaked tent serving as Brigade headquarters.

Commandant Kruger clambered out his Ratel's side hatch and stood looking up into the star-filled night sky. He breathed in and out a few times, clearing the sweat-sour stench of the APC's cramped troop compartment out of his nostrils. He wasn't in any particular hurry to find out what Brigadier Strydom had up his perfectly tailored sleeve.

Kruger's respect for his immediate superior had precipitously declined over the last three weeks. Strydom had shown himself all too eager to tell Pretoria what it wanted to hear —and not what needed to be said. He'd also demonstrated a fondness for issuing meaningless and contradictory orders in the midst of battle. In the *kommandant*'s view, his brigade commander should be up at Bergland seeing the situation for himself—not sitting sixty kilometers behind the front, cloistered with his toadying staff.

The cool, crisp breeze shifted slightly, bringing with it a new smell. A sickly sweet odor that he recognized instantly. The smell of death and rotting corpses. Kruger frowned at the unpleasant aroma. There'd been no resistance here at Rehoboth, so why the smell?

He turned, looking for explanations, and found them dangling from a gallows erected beside the headquarters tent.

My God. Six bodies swung to and fro from long, creaking ropes rocked gently by the wind. None were in uniform. None were white. And two appeared to be women. Kruger swallowed hard against the bitter-tasting bile surging up from his stomach. What kind of madness was at work here?

There was only one way to find out.

He settled his helmet firmly on his head and strode briskly toward the two sentries posted at the command tent's main entrance.

One checked his ID while the other kept a flashlight centered on his face. Kruger noticed that both were careful not to glance toward the gallows.

Twenty officers and as many noncoms and enlisted men bustled to and fro inside the tent—reports and message flimsies clutched in their hands. Maps crowded with military symbols hung from canvas walls or rested on trestle taps.

Powerful radio sets crackled and hissed over the low-voiced mutter of a dozen whispered conversations. All the usual signs of a higher military headquarters busy preparing for the next day's operations.

He glanced around the tent. No sign of Maj. Richard Forbes. Where the devil was the man?

Brig. Jakobus Strydom stood shoulder to shoulder with another, much taller man looking at one of the maps. He turned as Kruger approached. "Ah, Henrik . . . it's good to see you."

"Sir." Kruger nodded and saluted, intentionally staying formal.

The shadow of a frown crossed Strydom's narrow face. He gestured toward the fleshy, red-faced man beside him. "I don't think you know Kolonel Hertzog."

"*Kolonel*." Kruger inclined his head politely.

"The *kolonel* is a special visitor from Pretoria, Henrik. One of the President's own military aides."

So. This was one of Vorster's spies. Kruger looked more carefully at the man and got another shock. Hertzog wore an AWB pin on his uniform coat.

Involuntarily, Kruger's mouth curled upward in disgust. Cold eyes stared back at him out of a puffy, double-chinned face.

"You've seen something that troubles you, Kommandant Kruger?" Hertzog's smug, arrogant voice mirrored his appearance.

Kruger addressed his words to Strydom. "The gallows outside this tent—"

"Are filled with traitors, *Kommandant*. Hostages executed in just reprisal for futile attacks on our supply columns," Hertzog interrupted him. "My idea, actually. In accordance with the wishes of our beloved President. I trust that you have no objection?"

Kruger stared openmouthed at him, scarcely able to believe what he'd just heard. Hostages? Innocent civilians rousted from their beds at gunpoint and killed simply because Namibian soldiers were shooting at supply trucks? It was worse than insane. It was criminal. He'd seen dead civilians before—men, women, and children caught by artillery or in a cross fire. You expected such things in war. But this was something quite different. Cold, deliberate, calculated butchery.

Strydom took him by the arm and turned him away from Hertzog. "Never mind about the methods used to ensure rear-area security, Henrik. They're out of your jurisdiction." The unspoken warning in the *brigadier*'s voice was plain.

Kruger closed his mouth and looked closely at his superior. A nerve twitched irregularly beneath Strydom's right cheek. My God. The man was frightened. Scared out of his wits by this bloody bullyboy, Hertzog.

"Now, as to why I summoned you here . . ." Strydom's evident unease intensified. "Your second-in-command . . ."

Kruger held up a hand. "Yes, sir. Where is Major Forbes?"

"Major Forbes is under arrest, *Kommandant*." Hertzog moved closer, a grim smile on his face. "He's on his way back to Pretoria under guard at this very moment."

"What?" Kruger's hands balled into fists. "What in God's name for?"

"For suspected treason." Hertzog's smile grew less grim and more smug. "Earlier this afternoon, I myself heard the Englishman slandering our president and the chief of staff. Naturally, I arrested him at once. One cannot allow such insults to go unpunished. I'm sure you agree." Hertzog spun round on his heel and walked away without waiting for a reply.

Kruger glared at the man's departing back, fighting the temptation to pull his pistol and pump the bastard full of 9mm slugs. He didn't doubt that Forbes had used a few choice swear words to describe his dissatisfaction with recent events, but certainly nothing that any sane man would call treasonous. And if that was how Vorster and his cronies planned to define treason, who then was safe?

Strydom moved into his line of sight. "Keep your mouth shut, Henrik, I beg of you. I cannot spare any more of my experienced officers."

He led Kruger over to a map table. Several junior officers scattered out of their path. Strydom leaned over the map, tracing the positions held by the 20th Cape Rifles with a thumbnail. "Your attack today was a success, I see."

"A success?" Kruger found it difficult to talk through clenched teeth.

"Your battalion gained ground, true?" The *brigadier* risked a glance over his shoulder. Hertzog leaned carelessly against the opposite tent wall, cold eyes carefully fixed on them.

Kruger slammed a fist onto the map, startling several nearby staff officers. "Oh, we gained ground all right, *Brigadier*. Three hundred *blery* meters of open, useless wasteland and one stinking gully! And capturing that fucking ground cost me ten killed and thirty-six wounded! At that rate, our whole *verdomde* country will be bled white before we reach Windhoek!"

Strydom grabbed him by the arm again and leaned closer, his voice low, fearful, and urgent. "Shut up, Kruger! Do you want to be arrested, too? Do you want your men commanded by someone like that?" He jerked his head in Hertzog's direction.

Kruger shook his head reluctantly. A thug and political hack in charge of his battalion? Madness.

"Now listen to me, Henrik, and listen closely. Your attack today was successful—just as your attack tomorrow will be successful. Pretoria does not want to hear about failure, about supply difficulties, or about casualties. Do you understand me?"

Kruger stood motionless for what seemed an eternity. What Strydom was suggesting violated every tenet of his training and experience as a South African officer. What had happened to his nation? How could it have fallen into the hands of such brutal incompetents? He glanced again at Hertzog's smug, gloating face and nodded slowly, feeling ashamed as he did so.

He would buckle under for the moment—but only for the moment. Only to save some of his men.

SEPTEMBER 10—THE KREMLIN, MOSCOW, R.S.F.S.R.

Outside the Kremlin's red-brick walls, the streets of Moscow were full of shoppers—shoppers standing in record-long lines for a few of the basic necessities. Bread already gone stale in warehouses. Shriveled potatoes. Rotting cabbage. Rare cuts of meat more gristle and bone than anything else. Soap that wouldn't lather, and gasoline so filled with impurities that it wrecked almost as many engines as it powered.

It was the seventh year of perestroika, the grand program of economic restructuring. It was the seventh year of continuing failure.

Within the Kremlin's walls, the Soviet State Defense Council met in a small, elegantly furnished chamber. Ten chairs surrounded a rectangular oak table topped only by notepads, pens, and a tray holding two bottles of vodka. The State's antialcohol campaign continued unabated, but serious decisions always seemed to call for something more stimulating than tea or fizzy mineral water. A German-manufactured word-processing system occupied one corner of the room, ready for use by the secretaries who would record any major decisions for later translation into action directives for specific ministries or individuals.

Only six of the ten chairs were occupied. The Soviet State Defense Council was made up of the highest-ranking members of the Politburo, itself a body of elite decision makers whose power had been only partly diluted by the USSR's newly formed Congress of People's Deputies. Any large body takes its lead from a smaller body, and from smaller and smaller groups, until finally the power is wielded by a few key individuals.

The President of the Soviet Union looked wearily around the table, his red-rimmed eyes roving from face to face. The minister of defense, plump and pudgy despite a precisely tailored suit and rows of unearned medals. Next to him, the chief of the general staff, seated stiffly in full dress uniform. Directly across the table, the cherubic, bushy-eyebrowed chairman of the KGB, who sat next to the foreign minister

—apparently on the general principle that one should always stay close to one's greatest rival. And to his immediate right, the boyish face of a comparative newcomer, the academician who now served as the President's chief economic advisor.

One face was missing, the gray, skeletal visage of the Communist Party's chief ideologist. The old man had been in the hospital for several weeks, fighting a losing battle with pneumonia. It was just as well, the President thought. If he wanted lectures on abstract political philosophy, he could always get them from his wife. The Soviet Union's national security decisions needed a firmer basis in reality. Now more than ever.

Behind him, a clock softly chimed three times, signaling the passage of as many fruitless hours since they'd begun debating Fidel Castro's astounding call for the direct invasion of South Africa. He rapped the table sharply with a pencil, interrupting a heated exchange over the KGB's failure to give them advance warning of Castro's intentions. "Comrades, please, we're not getting anywhere with this squabbling. Time is short. We should confine ourselves to the matter directly at hand."

In theory, this discussion was unnecessary. In theory, he held more personal power than any Soviet leader since Joseph Stalin. In theory, he could simply impose his will on these five men, and through them on the USSR's still potent instruments of political power—the military, the secret police, and the bureaucracy. The President laughed inwardly. As usual, theory meant little in the real world.

The members of the Defense Council couldn't topple him from power. He had that much security. But their opposition to his policies could render him an ineffective figurehead. He'd seen it happen to other Soviet leaders as illness or repeated mistakes robbed them of their authority. Orders could be misinterpreted or simply shunted to the wrong place within the USSR's vast, unresponsive bureaucracy. Directives could either be simply ignored or put into action with crippling slowness.

No, he needed a consensus from these men.

Castro's proposition had hit them hard. Accepting it would mean dramatically altering the USSR's established national security policy. No one knew that better than he did.

Under his guidance, the Soviet Union had turned inward in the late 1980s—no longer interested in costly "foreign adventures." The change hadn't come out of the goodness of his heart. It had come as part of a desperate attempt to head off total economic collapse.

By cutting its losses overseas, the USSR had been able to reduce its military spending—freeing more resources for the production of the consumer goods increasingly demanded by Soviet citizens. Those sweeping changes in foreign policy had been accompanied by equally sweeping changes at home—changes symbolized by the terms *glasnost* and *perestroika*.

But both glasnost and perestroika were foundering. Too many of the USSR's constituent republics were clamoring for full independence. And too many of perestroika's economic reforms were being smothered by the dead weight of a Soviet system unable to tolerate individual initiative and private enterprise.

The President shook his head.

So now Cuba, which had rejected and condemned his reform program, and which cost billions of rubles in military aid and price supports for its sugar crop, wanted to involve the Soviet Union in a war at the end of the world!

On the surface, it would seem easy to refuse Castro's request. And yet, there were certain possibilities . . .

The foreign minister's elegant, carefully modulated voice broke into his private train of thought. "I tell you, comrades, Castro's plan is simply too costly. I've seen the reports. Just supplying Cuba's army in Namibia is draining our hard-currency reserves and absorbing a substantial portion of our transport aircraft and ships. We cannot afford to expand our involvement in this conflict."

"I disagree, Alexei Petrovich." The head of the KGB leaned forward in his chair, his deceptively kindly face creased by a frown. "We've gained important international goodwill by helping the Namibians—goodwill we may yet be able to translate into trade and technology agreements.''

That was unlikely, the President knew. Goodwill and words of praise were cheap. Trade and technology agreements were costly. So far, the West's leaders had proven extraordinarily adept at avoiding serious commitments. And while it was pleasant to be portrayed as being on the side of freedom and human progress, kind words were no substitute for the material aid the USSR desperately needed to revitalize its deteriorating economy and its aging industrial infrastructure. No substitute at all.

The foreign minister turned sideways in his seat to face his rival. ''These agreements you speak so glowingly of will not materialize in the aftermath of an embarrassing defeat, Comrade Chairman! And that is precisely what this Cuban proposal will produce.'' He looked toward the minister of defense. ''Isn't it true, Dmitri, that South Africa's army remains the most powerful on that continent—despite being stalemated in Namibia?''

''True.'' The defense minister paused, pouring a tiny dram of vodka into a newly emptied glass. ''Military logic argues that this invasion Castro plans would be doomed before it began.''

For the first time during the debate, Marshal Kamenev, the chief of the general staff stirred.

The President glanced curiously at him. Unlike his superior, the defense minister, Kamenev had a proven combat record—both in the Great Patriotic War and in Afghanistan. ''Yes, Marshal? You have a comment?''

Kamenev nodded slowly. ''Yes, Comrade President. I agree that South Africa's armed forces appear on paper to be immeasurably superior to those of its current enemies. But appearances can be deceiving, no?''

The President was intrigued. ''Go on, Nikolai.''

''Much of Pretoria's strength is tied down within its own borders holding the blacks and other races in check. If they strip the interior of enough men to crush Castro's invasion force, South Africa's whites risk leaving their own homes defenseless. I don't believe that's a risk they'll be willing to run.'' Kamenev shrugged. ''As matters stand, I believe we see an equal correlation of forces in southern Africa—superior South African ground strength matched by weakness at home. And under those circumstances, Castro's plan could succeed.''

''But at what cost?'' the foreign minister countered. ''Do we want to provoke American intervention on South Africa's side? Do we want a direct military confrontation with the United States? Now? That could well be the result of helping Cuba escalate this war!''

''Calm yourself, Alexei Petrovich.'' The KGB's chairman smiled sardonically. ''Washington would not dare aid Pretoria's racist regime. Such an imperialist move would outrage its own people, its allies, and all the world's 'nonaligned' nations.

''And even if the Americans were foolish enough to involve themselves, Cuba's plan does not require direct action by our troops or aircraft, merely political support and logistical backing. The risk of direct contact or combat losses is minimal!''

The foreign minister's face turned a dangerous shade of red. ''Nevertheless, comrades, we have nothing to gain and much to lose!''

The embarrassed silence surrounding this outburst was broken by the sound of a throat being nervously cleared. The President looked to his right. ''You have something to add, Professor Bukarin?''

His economic advisor nodded slowly. ''Yes, Comrade President.'' He turned to the beet-red foreign minister. ''Your statement was not quite accurate, Comrade Minister. Between us, South Africa and the USSR produce substantial portions of some of the world's most important strategic minerals.''

''I've seen the trade figures,'' the foreign minister said curtly.

Bukarin nodded politely. ''My point is this, comrades. The previous South African government once asked us to join them in a world gold cartel. It was an idea with some merit.

And would not a friendlier, more accommodating South African government be eager to join a broader cartel—one controlling the world's strategic-minerals market? Surely that would be a logical development—a small price to be paid for our support?''

So it would. Much of what the young man said made perfect sense. The President stroked his chin reflectively. De facto control of South Africa's resources would give the Soviet Union a vital economic edge in its bargaining with the West. Soviet state export companies could match any price increases initiated by a new ''revolutionary government''—greatly increasing the flow of needed hard currency into Moscow's treasury. And at the same time, those higher prices would greatly retard the West's economic growth—giving the USSR a chance to close the gap. That would also prove to the world that the rumors of the Soviet state's impending demise were greatly exaggerated.

Slowly forming smiles on several of the faces around the table showed that many of his colleagues saw the same advantages. But not all. Both the foreign minister and the defense minister looked unconvinced.

The President frowned. Consensus still eluded him. Very well, perhaps he could offer them a face-saving compromise. He rapped the table briskly. ''Comrades, I think we have discussed this issue long enough. What I propose is this: we will back Cuba's preliminary military buildup while withholding final approval for the invasion itself. That can await further developments in Namibia and in South Africa itself. And we shall insist on absolute secrecy. In that way, we can keep our options open.''

He locked glances with the foreign minister. ''If nothing else, such a troop buildup might give us a stronger bargaining position in any negotiations to end the Namibian conflict. True, Alexei?''

The foreign minister bowed his head slightly, acknowledging the point.

''Good. Then this matter is settled. We'll inform President Castro that his plans can proceed—though with the conditions I've outlined. Clear?''

Heads nodded around the table, some with enthusiasm, others with evident reluctance.

Keys rattled in the corner as one of the Defense Council's secretaries typed the President's decision into the electronic record. Fidel Castro would get the ships, planes, and supplies he needed to prepare his counterstroke against Pretoria.

CHAPTER 13

Whirligig

SEPTEMBER 15—NATIONAL SECURITY COUNCIL MEETING, THE WHITE HOUSE

It was one of the fine, crisp mid-September mornings that made summer in the District of Columbia bearable. If you could somehow hang on through the sticky steam-bath days of July and August, a cool, clean breeze was bound to come along to drop the temperature and blow away the smog.

The change in the weather was invigorating, and even two floors below ground level its effects could be seen in the faces of the men and in their conversation as they waited for the Vice President to arrive.

Their upbeat attitudes masked underlying worry. Although this was a regularly scheduled NSC session, there was only one topic on the agenda—the situation in southern Africa. The unspoken sense of crisis was reflected in the names and ranks of those present. With the sole exceptions of the secretaries of state and defense, all of the NSC's principal members had come themselves—each accompanied by a small entourage of aides.

The secretary of state was in Europe, consulting directly with America's NATO allies over events in southern Africa. The secretary of defense was tied up on a more prosaic task—touring a series of West Coast military bases earmarked for closure and sale. Flying either man home in time for the meeting would only have created unwelcome media attention.

Nevertheless, the majority of the administration's brain trust sat around a crowded table in the Situation Room—assembled two floors below the green lawns and rose gardens of the White House in an effort to try to unscrew the inscrutable.

A low buzz of conversation and muttered speculation died instantly as Vice President James Malcolm Forrester strode past the Marine sentries at the door. His manner was hurried as he took his seat and pulled a thick manila folder from his leather portfolio.

"Sorry for the delay, ladies and gentlemen, but I've just received additional guidance from the President about the Namibian war and our response to it." He turned to the short, bearded man seated across the table. "Ed, why don't you bring everybody up-to-date? No sense in going ahead until we've all got the same information."

"Yes, sir." Assistant Secretary of State Edward Hurley looked collected and organized as he rose from his chair and leaned forward to turn on an overhead projector.

Forrester ignored a disappointed frown from the deputy secretary of state. Whitworth might be Hurley's immediate superior, but he didn't have the detailed knowledge necessary to handle the briefing. Besides, Forrester had long suspected that the State Department's number two man was one of those "highly placed officials" who enjoyed leaking stories that made him look bad.

An aide near the door dimmed the lights slightly.

Hurley placed his first slide on the glass. Though clearly put together at the last minute, it was also well laid out and clear—a rare quality in Washington, D.C. "This slide lists important events that have occurred since our meeting a week ago. As you can see, only three of the fourteen involve military incidents in Namibia. The rest are political events, guerrilla attacks, or serious civil disturbances.''

Jesus. Forrester scanned the chart while Hurley rattled off a quick summary of each event. At first glance, the fighting in Namibia seemed almost a sideshow compared to what was happening inside South Africa's own borders. South Africa's population was at war with itself. Between guerrilla bombings, black-on-black power struggles, and the government's ''security measures,'' hundreds of people were dying every week.

Hurley replaced the chronology with a map, labeled TOP SECRET. ''According to all available sources, this is the present disposition of Cuban and South African forces in Namibia. Essentially, the military stalemate continues. There have been no significant advances or retreats for weeks. Just a steady series of artillery bombardments and small-scale, but costly, infantry assaults.''

Forrester nodded somberly. He'd seen the South African casualty estimates produced by the Defense Intelligence Agency. Forty-five dead and more than one hundred and fifty wounded in the past week alone. That didn't sound like much of a war. Not until you remembered how small South Africa's white population really was. On a proportional basis, Pretoria's Namibian losses over the last seven days were the equivalent of more than 2,200 dead and 7,500 wounded Americans.

He stared at the unit symbols shown on the map—most clustered in the mountains south of Windhoek. South Africa's mechanized and motorized battalions were nearly immobile —forced to remain in place while an inadequate logistics system tried desperately to stockpile the fuel reserves needed for a renewed offensive.

In the meantime, both sides were continuing their troop strength buildups. Total South African strength in Namibia had climbed by nearly a brigade—an increase matched by the Cubans. Castro, unworried by any serious external threat, evidently felt able to commit an even greater share of his reserves to the region.

Hurley placed another chronology on the projector. "These are events in the region that either affect or are affected by the war in Namibia. All of the frontline states—Mozambique, Zimbabwe, and Botswana—are being forced to cope with dramatically increased guerrilla activity. Most are insurgencies we know are supported by Pretoria." He pointed to a separate heading near the bottom. "Unita has also been very active, almost certainly at South Africa's request. Unita guerrillas have been attacking Angolan rail lines and bridges, trying to slow down any Cuban reinforcements on their way south to Namibia."

Forrester scowled and made a note. Unita's de facto support for South Africa's Namibian adventure was a sore point in Washington. The anticommunist Angolan guerrilla movement happened to be supported by both the United States and South Africa—one of the few places where the foreign policies of the two countries coincided—much to Washington's chagrin.

Unita's willingness to complicate Cuba's troop movements into Namibia was understandable. The guerrillas rightly viewed Castro's troops as an occupying army. But that didn't make their aid for South Africa's invasion any more palatable or wise. Not given the current situation.

Some of the left-wingers in Congress were using the situation to scream for an immediate end to U.S. support for Unita. Forrester snorted. As if that would solve anything. Abandoned by the United States, Unita wouldn't have any choice but to do everything its sole remaining backer, South Africa, asked. Instead, the CIA had been working behind the scenes, urging Unita to stay neutral in the Namibian conflict. So far, though, all attempts at persuasion had failed. Castro's troop trains and tank flatcars were targets simply too tempting to pass up.

Hurley's fourth and final slide showed a grainy, news-agency photo of Karl Vorster at an AWB rally. Every surface was covered with banners emblazoned with the AWB's three-armed swastika. "At home, Vorster continues to integrate members of the AWB and other radical right-wing groups into South Africa's governmental structure. We don't have precise numbers, but there have clearly been a tremendous number of personnel changes at all levels—national, provincial, and local. The results are equally clear. Vorster has gained undisputed control over all levels of government. In other words, ladies and gentlemen, he has consolidated his power base and will no longer have to move so cautiously." The last sentence was heavy with irony.

The room lights came back up as Hurley switched the overhead projector off and slid back into his chair.

Forrester nodded his thanks and looked around the table. "Right. Even with Pretoria's news blackout, smuggled video makes it clear that things over there are bad. Very bad."

He frowned. "Let's not mince words, people. This is killing us politically here in the States. The American people want us to act. They feel that if this administration can't stop the violence in South Africa, it's our fault, too. Everyone with an ax to grind is getting a free ride out of this thing."

The other members of the NSC nodded sagely. Congressional leaders such as Steven Travers, press commentators, and other "I told you so" specialists were on the airwaves day in and day out—all hammering away at administration "inaction." Technically, NSC meetings didn't revolve around domestic political concerns. In practice, though, domestic politics was all too often inseparably intertwined with national security issues.

Forrester leaned forward. "That's bad enough. What's worse is that Cuba and the other communist states are getting a lot of good press out of their aid for Namibia. They're sure as hell expanding their influence in the region."

He fixed his eyes on the small cluster of dark-suited intelligence-agency representatives and uniformed military officers at the other end of the table. "Now what the President wants to know is, how much worse can we expect this situation to get? Are there any signs that the fighting in Namibia could escalate?"

"Mr. Vice President, I have some new information on that point."

Forrester looked at the speaker. Christopher Nicholson, director of the CIA, looked as smoothly self-confident as ever.

"Yes, Chris?"

Nicholson signaled a junior aide, who stepped up to the table and began handing out copies of a two-page document. "The first page is a report from our people in Israel. They report several C-130 Hercules aircraft are missing from Hatzor airfield, an Israeli Air Force transport base. And we've also heard that the Israelis are making discreet enquiries in other countries operating the C-130, looking for spare parts or even surplus aircraft. They're offering payment in gold."

Everyone in the room knew where that gold was coming from—Pretoria's central bank. South Africa and Israel had a long history of joint arms transactions and weapons research programs. Neither country especially liked the other, but both were adept at justifying their relationship on the old "the enemy of my enemy" principle.

Forrester shook his head. Trading gold for needed transport planes made sense, but it would cut dangerously into South Africa's on-hand reserves. And that was a good measure of Pretoria's growing desperation.

"But South Africa isn't the only one looking for help. Cuba's out in the arms marketplace, too." Nicholson flipped to the next page. "The data on this second page comes from signals intercepts and from satellite photos taken over Libya. Our SIGINT group in Italy has been picking up increased activity at all Libyan Air Force bases, and we're now seeing only a fraction of the transport planes normally stationed at those bases."

Nicholson rocked back in his chair, a self-satisfied smile on his face. "Naturally, that aroused our curiosity. So I ordered a satellite pass over Libya's military equipment storage areas, especially the one southwest of Tripoli. Qaddafi's always had more hardware than he has troops or pilots—hardware he keeps parked out in the desert."

The CIA director tapped the table with a single, fleshy finger. "My imagery analysts tell me there are definite indications that equipment is disappearing out of those storage areas. We are still trying to determine exactly how many tanks, APCs, and artillery pieces are missing, but it could be quite a lot."

Forrester sighed. Somehow Libya's Colonel Qaddafi always managed to poke his nose into every world hot spot. Bombing raids, attempted coups, and diplomatic isolation—nothing seemed to faze the bastard. "Could the Libyans simply be scrapping obsolete equipment?"

Nicholson shook his head, snatching away that faint possibility. "Unlikely. Qaddafi's a lunatic, but he's not a wasteful man. He's much more likely to have sold these missing weapons or to have sent them where they could cause the most trouble."

"Someplace like Namibia?"

Nicholson nodded. "Exactly. What little we've been able to confirm indicates the missing gear was all second- or third-line equipment—T-62s, BTR-60s, and the like. Precisely the kind of hardware the Cubans are using in Namibia."

Forrester felt his frown slide into a grimace. "Wonderful. So both the South Africans and Cubans are making new friends. Is anyone else getting into the act?"

Nicholson looked suddenly uncertain. It wasn't a look Forrester was used to seeing on the CIA chief's face. "I don't have anything definite . . ."

"But you have other information?"

"We've identified some other possible weapons shipments, Mr. Vice President, but the data could support several different conclusions. I'd prefer not to confuse the issue until we've been able to obtain confirmation."

Forrester stared right into Nicholson's eyes. "I'll keep the caveat in mind, Director Nicholson, but I think we should hear what you've got."

"The data is extremely sensitive, sir, and we have no way of knowing if it's related to the Namibian crisis or not." Nicholson twisted slightly in his chair. He was uncomfortable with ambiguities and liked to have everything he presented tied up in a nice, neat, typed package. He also hated to be wrong.

"Sensitivity is obviously not an issue here. Please fill us in." Although Forrester used the word *please*, his harsh tone made it clear that he wasn't asking, he was ordering.

Several of the other NSC members coughed lightly or turned away, hiding sudden grins. Nicholson's innate Ivy League arrogance often rubbed his colleagues the wrong way.

The CIA director knew when he'd made a mistake. He swiveled in his seat and took a folder bordered with red and white stripes from a silent aide. He was careful to keep the folder turned so the label on the front was hidden.

Nicholson flipped the folder open and studied it carefully for a few moments. "Our agents and monitoring stations in the Far East and northern Pacific have noted significant increases in back-channel arms purchases." He arched an eyebrow at Forrester. "Naturally, we're always trying to track who sells and who buys what, but it's a damned difficult task. Too many middlemen. Too much money. And too many foreign governments too willing to help the arms dealers keep a lid on their activities."

Forrester nodded politely and motioned him onward.

"Both the North Koreans and Chinese have been making extra shipments of tanks, artillery, and surface-to-surface missiles—apparently in response to orders placed over the past several weeks. In and of itself, that's not so unusual. Most of the weapons systems being sold are those Beijing and Pyongyang have sold in the past to regular customers like Iran."

No surprise there. Both North Korea and China were cash poor and willing to sell weapons to anyone willing to pay.

Nicholson shrugged. "Trouble is . . . we haven't been able to spot the hardware arriving at any known transshipment point." He closed the folder and looked around the group. "Now the equipment could simply still be in transit to a regular customer, or on hold in some third country until final transport can be arranged."

"But there is a chance these tanks, guns, and missiles are going to Cuba or Angola?"

"It's not impossible, Mr. Vice President," Nicholson conceded.

Charming. Castro evidently wasn't content to rely solely on Soviet-supplied weapons. And by expanding his sources of supply, the Cuban dictator was also reducing Moscow's leverage over his actions in southern Africa.

Forrester turned to the lean, square-jawed man in the next chair over. Hamilton Reid, the secretary of commerce, had the relaxed, confident air that often went with old money invested wisely. "The President's also concerned about the economic effects of this damned crisis."

"And wisely so." Reid didn't need to kowtow and didn't bother trying. "Prices for key strategic minerals like titanium, chromium, platinum, and the others are showing a steady rise. It's mostly psychological, so far. South Africa's production hasn't been affected by the fighting in Namibia. If anything, Pretoria's actually selling more than it normally would to finance these arms deals the director told us about. But the financial community's never been entirely rational."

Several of the men and women around the table laughed softly. They'd all seen the studies suggesting that random dart throws did a better job of forecasting the stock market than any other system.

The secretary of commerce acknowledged their laughter with a slight smile of his own. "We've been working closely with the other major trading nations—especially the British and the Japanese—to do what we can. We've all been leaning on our respective commodities exchanges in an effort to slow things down. High-level briefings to show there's no immediate supply problem. Temporary market closings when prices rise too fast. That sort of thing."

His smile dimmed. "All with only moderate success. Right now, the commodities exchanges are capable of handling these higher minerals prices. That may not last. There's a kind of critical mass to these situations."

Forrester nodded his understanding. In the past month alone, the Strategic Commodities Index had shot up more than 30 percent. If the prices for key strategic minerals started climbing any faster, they could trigger a wave of panic buying—a kind of feeding frenzy that might send prices soaring through the roof. Scaremongers were already touting the possibility of 300 or 400 percent price rises.

And that could spell disaster for the United States, Great Britain, and almost every other industrialized nation in the world. The minerals largely supplied by South Africa, a few of its neighbors, and the Soviet Union were vital to a wide range of industries—steel, oil refining, chemicals, and electronics to name just a few. Dramatically higher minerals prices would mean significantly higher production costs for jet engines, gasoline, computers, consumer electronics, and thousands of other products. That, in turn, could send a flood tide of higher prices, lower sales, and lost jobs surging through the economy.

Forrester frowned. Most Americans didn't realize it, but much of their nation's prosperity depended on a steady flow of reasonably priced minerals from overseas. Some of the percentages spoke for themselves—98 percent of all manganese, 92 percent of all chromium, and 91 percent of all the platinum-group metals consumed by American industry were imported. All told, the U.S. was critically dependent on foreign suppliers for twenty-two of the thirty-odd minerals government planners viewed as essential for industrial and defense needs. And America's allies weren't in much better shape. Preliminary figures showed the nation's trade deficit and inflation rate both starting to climb again.

Forrester looked up at the rest of the NSC and ran his eyes over a roomful of newly gloom-filled faces. "Right. We're in something of an economic box. But we're not alone. That's why I've asked Hamilton to have his staff prepare an analysis of South Africa's own economic picture."

Reid didn't bother with papers or projectors. "Put simply, South Africa's economy cannot survive the current situation. Pretoria is caught between an increasingly expensive foreign war and a steadily less productive domestic economy. Many of the country's white workers are now in uniform, and those few skilled black laborers who might have replaced them are either dead, in prison, or barred from filling them. Nothing short of complete peace can significantly alter the situation."

The commerce secretary looked carefully from face to face. "If conditions do not change, our analysis indicates we can expect a total South African economic collapse in less than a year. Even the harshest imaginable austerity measures can delay such a collapse by a year beyond that at most."

The chairman of the Joint Chiefs of Staff, Air Force General Walter Hickman, had been silent up to this point. As the commerce secretary paused, he broke in. "I think that assessment may be a little extreme, Mr. Vice President. I remember several predictions that Iran's economy would completely collapse in the 1980s, during its war with Iraq. None of them came true. Massive inflation and unemployment, sure. But not total chaos."

Reid showed no signs of being disturbed by Hickman's disagreement. "The difference, General, is that Iran's population wholeheartedly supported the war with Iraq. Fanaticism can feed people for quite a while." He shook his head slowly. "But South Africa is much more divided—even the white community is split over Vorster's racial policies and the Namibian war. There is no one flag that everyone can rally around."

Hurley pressed him. "What exactly do you mean by 'collapse'?"

"Reduced production from the mines and factories, followed by food and fuel shortages. At first, those shortages will only affect the poorest, most vulnerable segments of South Africa's population—the blacks, coloreds, Indians, and other nonwhite ethnic groups. But the country's whites won't be immune for long. As things get steadily worse, anyone who can leave, will—draining South Africa of the skilled people most needed to keep its economy running." Reid looked suddenly grim. "In the final stages, we could expect widespread violence and looting—with daily death tolls that would make what we've seen so far look like a picnic. And add this factor—there is no country willing to come to South Africa's aid, no source of outside assistance to stop a headlong slide into chaos."

My God. Forrester winced at the horrific images conjured

up by the commerce secretary's matter-of-fact words. Idle, abandoned factories and shops. Burning homes. Floods of refugees fleeing starving cities. Bodies littering the streets. Genocide. Race war. Unbidden, the term popped into his brain—Armageddon in South Africa.

He turned to Hickman. "General, could this goddamned war go on for this year or two the secretary's talking about?"

Hickman nodded slowly, reluctantly. "Yes, sir, easily that long. Barring internal collapse in either Cuba or South Africa, this could be another bloody stalemate. Neither side holds a clear military advantage. The communist forces are at the end of a long supply line, and Soviet-style logistics are nothing to brag about. Hell, we'd have trouble fighting down there ourselves!"

Hickman stared moodily at a wall map showing the world. "On the other hand, South Africa's increasingly isolated and bogged down in a racial mess of its own creation." He looked up at Forrester. "Nope, Mr. Vice President. As things stand now, these people can keep killing each other from now until doomsday without achieving much of anything."

Hurley added the final kicker. "And neither side has much reason to seek a political settlement. Having started this thing, Vorster can't afford to settle for anything less than all of Namibia. And Castro's pride won't let him aim for anything less than driving every single Afrikaner back across the South African frontier. Every bit of international support he's gained will disappear unless he ends the war with a clear victory."

Forrester understood the implications. It was going to be a long war. Worse than that, the conflict showed signs of spreading like a virus, affecting any country that bordered on South Africa or Namibia. The United States could not afford to let that happen. Besides the economic considerations, the loss of life would be tremendous. America would have to act, and act effectively, or she would be blamed for her inaction.

Forrester tapped his notepad impatiently with his pen. "All right, people, what can we do? The President is looking for specific recommendations."

Nicholson spoke first. "The Namibian invasion is the source of the problem. Stop the war and things will loosen up."

Hurley countered, "That's a noble sentiment, but how exactly do you propose we go about doing that soon enough to matter? It took eight years of trying and we never did pull the Iranians and the Iraqis apart. We don't have that kind of time here."

General Hickman snorted. "The key to this situation is that bastard Vorster. He's the one who started this friggin' Namibian war. Now we've gotta find a way to make him call it off."

"I'd have better luck teaching my cat to tap-dance." Hurley replaced his tortoiseshell glasses.

"Hold on, Ed. The general may have something there." Forrester sat back in his chair, head tilted up slightly toward the low ceiling. "Vorster's a stubborn son of a bitch, but he might listen to reason if we can find a way to cut him off at the knees. We know the military's in good shape, but South Africa can't go on fighting a foreign war if its civilian economy starts falling apart."

"You mean South Africa's whites won't be so interested in foreign conquests if they start going hungry," Hurley said.

Forrester hesitated and then nodded. "Yes, that's exactly what I mean. Let's speed up the process."

It seemed strange to contemplate accelerating South Africa's economic collapse in order to stave off a larger, bloodier catastrophe. Something like innoculating people with a weakened version of a deadly virus to protect them from the disease itself.

Forrester turned to the secretary of commerce. "Hamilton, I'd like your people to prepare an analysis of South Africa's greatest vulnerabilities. Where can we really turn up the heat on these people? As a start, we'll recommend to the President that we freeze South African assets in this country.

"I need something I can show the President within the week. Clear?"

The commerce secretary was obviously more comfortable

with fixing an economy than fouling one up, but he nodded and took notes.

Forrester glanced around the crowded, suddenly silent table. "Ladies and gentlemen, we are no longer talking about simple sanctions. Those are designed to show a government how we feel, or as a mild form of coercion. What we need is a hook we can sink into Vorster himself." He bared his teeth. "And I suspect the best kind of hook would be the threat that his own supporters will vote him out of office because they can't work and can't eat."

He looked across the table at Nicholson. "Chris, we may need to consider active measures by your people. Use Hamilton's list as a starting point, but have your Covert Action folks put together their own ideas as well. Again, we'll need to see whatever they can put together ASAP."

The CIA director nodded once, his high forehead creased by a worried frown. Covert operations were notoriously dangerous for any intelligence chief with political ambitions. Disgruntled political opponents and press cynics loved nothing better than to expose them to public scrutiny and congressional ridicule. Nicholson already knew that no covert action would survive the rigid test he planned to apply—risk of failure.

Hurley caught Forrester's eye. "I'd suggest additional consultations with some of our allies on these proposals. Especially with the United Kingdom. It has substantial military and economic interests in the region." He glanced in Nicholson's direction. "It also has a top-notch intelligence service. They may even have data we've missed."

The CIA director frowned slightly at that, but nodded his reluctant agreement.

Forrester held up a hand. "Let's hold off on that for a week or so, Ed. Just until I've had a chance to get some feedback from the President."

He scanned the table one last time. "Anyone else?"

General Hickman cleared his throat and leaned forward. "Let me get one thing straight, sir. Is our basic assumption now that things in South Africa are going to get a lot worse than they presently are?"

"Yes."

"Then I recommend we start moving out any U.S. citizens we can. Without delay. They could be a real liability for us if we have to take direct action against these bastards."

The room fell silent. Direct action. Nobody wanted to ask exactly what the chairman of the Joint Chiefs meant by that. Forrester wondered if the Pentagon had finished working up the contingency plans he'd asked for. He made a mental note to check later—when there weren't so many prying ears around.

Hurley frowned. "I'm not sure how much more we can do to persuade our tourists and businessmen to stay out of South Africa. We've already issued a travel advisory for the whole region. Anything more, like an outright ban on travel or a forced evacuation, would require either congressional action or a presidential National Security Decision Directive."

Forrester matched the shorter man's frown. A travel ban made military sense, but it might also fan the flames of hysteria in the world's financial markets. He turned to Hickman. "Look, General, your point's well taken. We certainly don't want too many of our people getting caught in the cross fire over there. I'll raise the issue with the President next time I see him. Fair enough?"

Hickman shrugged as though he hadn't expected immediate agreement.

"All right. Does anyone else have anything to add?"

Silence.

"Fine." Forrester flipped a small leather date book open and scanned it for a moment. "We'll meet again in a week unless events dictate a change in schedule. In the meantime, keep me posted on all significant developments. And let's move ahead at full speed on those options packages. The President'll expect us to have some concrete recommendations by then."

He looked up at the cluster of grim, worried faces around the table. Time for a quick pep talk. "Relax, people. I agree that what's happening in southern Africa isn't very reassuring.

But at least we have some idea of what's coming for a change.''

He was wrong.

SEPTEMBER 17—ARMY HEADQUARTERS, AVENIDA SAMORA MACHEL, MAPUTO, MOZAMBIQUE

The old stone fortress left by the Portuguese—Mozambique's former colonial masters—now housed the Army's main headquarters. Sentries carrying AK-47s ceaselessly patrolled the fortress's ramparts and bastions—looking strangely out of place on walls originally built to fend off muzzle-loading muskets and cannon.

Capt. Jorge de Sousa returned the crisp salutes of the guards and limped briskly into the fort's shadowy interior. A small, square-faced man with a tired smile, he had fought the Portuguese, and now Renamo. Although only in his early thirties, he had been a soldier for fifteen years.

The summons to appear at headquarters had come as no surprise. His convalescence was nearly over, and experienced officers were badly needed with a war going on. But he'd expected an interview with the staff flunkies of Officer Command, the bureau responsible for assigning officers to active-duty posts. Not a personal interview with General Cuellar himself.

De Sousa was confused. His wounding in a failed ambush had been honorable, and he knew of no cause for a reprimand—or for any special praise. Like many combat veterans, the Mozambican captain was a fatalist, so he decided to wait and see what the general wanted. After all, he didn't have long to wait.

Even in the Mozambican Army, which was small and poor, the chief of staff's office was richly appointed, almost to the point of opulence. De Sousa saw nothing wrong in such inequity. The general wielded almost absolute power over the Army, and such power was entitled to its rewards.

Cuellar wasn't alone. Another man stood at ease near the

chief of staff's beautifully polished teak desk—an item "liberated" from Mozambique's last colonial governor. Tall, with a swarthy complexion and a thick mustache, the man wore a civilian suit and tie. Nevertheless, his erect bearing marked him as a military man.

De Sousa saluted and Cuellar waved him in. "Greetings, Jorge, I am glad to see that you are active again. You are recovered, then?"

"Completely, General." De Sousa was lying, but it was the only answer he would give. His left leg hurt when it rained, and it rained a lot in Mozambique.

Cuellar arched an eyebrow in polite disbelief. He mentioned toward the man standing by his desk. "This is Colonel José Suarez of the Cuban People's Army."

A Cuban, eh? Interesting. De Sousa stepped forward and shook hands with the colonel. He was genuinely glad to meet the Cuban officer. Castro's long opposition to South Africa and Western imperialism made him something of a folk hero in lands where censorship suppressed unpleasant truths.

Suarez responded in kind. The two men had time to exchange compliments and a few pleasantries before Cuellar coughed lightly, cleared his throat, and came to the heart of the matter.

He motioned them into two leather-backed chairs placed squarely in front of his desk. "Captain de Sousa, while you were in hospital, the Cuban government approached us with a proposal that would dramatically alter our strategy against Renamo." He glanced sideways at Colonel Suarez. "I reveal no secrets when I say that this proposal has prompted considerable debate at the highest levels of our country's leadership."

Suarez nodded once, a thin, meaningless smile fixed on his narrow face.

Cuellar folded his hands. "Cuba's recent victories in Namibia made us want to listen. And South Africa's recent aggressions against us have compelled us to agree to President Castro's proposal."

De Sousa's questioning look was all the prompting the

general needed to continue. His voice grew deeper, more dramatic. "Essentially, Captain, we are going to cooperate with the Cubans and their other socialist allies in launching an attack against South Africa. We shall advance into their territory, capture their capital, and knock Vorster and his racist cronies from their thrones."

Stunned, de Sousa sat up sharply, ignoring the pain in his leg. The Mozambican Army was in a pitiful state, only able to mount occasional raids against Renamo strongholds. The idea of invading South Africa with such a ragtag force was so outlandish that Cuellar might as well have talked of invading Russia or North America.

Colonel Suarez saw his dismay and hastened to reassure him. "Cuban and other troops will be used to make the actual assault, Captain. Your men are needed too badly here, close to their homes. We understand this. But we do need your country's cooperation for bases, intelligence, and security. In return, we offer the material and training cadres needed to upgrade your forces. In addition, President Castro has promised that Mozambique will receive significant trade concessions from the new South African government—once we have installed it in power."

De Sousa stared from the Cuban back to his general, scarcely able to believe what he was hearing.

Cuellar's voice changed again, becoming sterner, less the voice of persuasion and more the voice of command. "Captain de Sousa, this decision has been ratified by both the President and the party leadership. You do not question their wisdom, I hope?"

"Of course not, General." De Sousa shook his head. Questioning orders was a fast track to oblivion, even for a proven combat veteran.

Cuellar smiled. "Good." He gestured toward the Cuban colonel. "You will serve as Colonel Suarez's liaison with our forces. We must arrange transport and security for all the Cuban and other military forces who will shortly begin arriving by air and sea. It will be a massive undertaking, Captain. A great responsibility."

De Sousa nodded, intrigued despite his misgivings. He'd never imagined having the opportunities now being laid out before him.

"For the moment, most of the Army will know nothing of this upcoming operation. They will be told that the Cuban forces are arriving to assist us in counterinsurgency operations and training. Other cover stories will be used to deceive outside 'observers.' " Cuellar didn't bother to conceal his contempt. The general never bothered to distinguish between diplomats, journalists, businessmen, and spies. They were all variations on the same theme as far as he was concerned.

Cuellar picked up a thick folder and pushed it across the desk. "This is the operational plan conceived in Havana. Study it with care. Your new office is two doors down from mine."

Thinking he had been dismissed, de Sousa started to get up from the chair, but Cuellar waved him down. "One final item, Jorge. This new assignment is too important to leave to a mere captain. Accordingly, you are now a major. Congratulations."

A major? Careful to keep a tight rein on his conflicting emotions, de Sousa shook hands with both men, saluted the general, and got out as quickly as he could.

CHAPTER 14

Investigations

SEPTEMBER 18—JOHANNESBURG, SOUTH AFRICA

Emily van der Heijden didn't hide her envy as she studied the busy newsroom. By rights, she should have been a part of this noisy, exciting chaos.

The staff of the *Johannesburg Star* was on final countdown—working frantically to put the afternoon paper's last edition to bed. Copyboys, harassed reporters, and red-faced, fuming editors threaded their way through a maze of desks, filing cabinets, and overflowing wastepaper baskets. Loud voices, ringing phones, and clattering typewriters and computer keyboards blended in a swelling, discordant clamor.

"Looks almost like the real thing, doesn't it?" Brian Pakenham said bitterly.

Emily looked up at the tall, gangly, balding young man beside her. When they'd been in classes together, Pakenham had been widely teased for his naïveté and innocent good nature. He'd never shown a trace of the cynicism so necessary to thorough reporting. Four years as a real journalist working under South Africa's press restrictions had changed him.

"But the *Star* is a fine paper, Brian."

Pakenham shook his head. "Wrong, I'm afraid. It used to be a fine newspaper. Now we're just cutting and pasting official press releases that are so full of shit I keep wanting to reach for toilet paper after I skim one."

He jerked his head toward a dour-faced man conspicuously alone at the far end of the newsroom. "And there's the bloody Cerberus who makes sure nothing like the truth leaks into our readers' minds."

Emily followed his angry gaze. "A security agent?"

"Uh-huh. One of your father's brighter thugs." Pakenham saw her hurt look and blushed. "Hey, Em, I'm sorry about that crack. It wasn't fair. I know you're not to blame for any of this mess."

She forced a smile. "Yes. One cannot pick one's parents, right?"

"Right." He took her elbow and steered her through the crowded newsroom, dodging coworkers, leering wisecracks, and a handful of pink telephone message slips fluttered at him by his shared secretary.

The noise level fell off dramatically as the newsroom's clear glass door closed behind them.

Pakenham glanced down at her as he led the way down a long, narrow hall toward a staircase posted with a sign that read EMPLOYEES ONLY. "I can get you into the morgue, but then I've got to get back to work." He hesitated. "Look, Em, is there anything I can do to help? What kind of material are you looking for?"

For an instant, Emily was tempted to tell him. The *Johannesburg Star*'s morgue, its reference library, was huge—a roomful of filing cabinets crammed with yellowing back issues, old photographs, and folders full of clippings from newspapers and magazines around the world. Scouring through it on her own for information about security chief Erik Muller would take hours or even days. And there was always a chance that she'd miss something vital. Getting Pakenham's help would make the task much easier. But it was also unwise.

Ian was right. The fewer people they involved, the fewer people they put at risk.

"I thank you for your offer, Brian, but there is really nothing very special in what I am doing. Just a bit of historical research . . . about my family, you see." She was glad that negotiating the steep staircase made it impossible to look Pakenham in the eye. She'd never been an especially convincing liar.

"Historical research. Oh, of course." Obvious disbelief vied with ordinary politeness. He sighed and shrugged. "Well, I suppose it doesn't matter very much anyway. I don't expect to be here much longer."

Emily came to a dead stop. "What do you mean, Brian? Are you in some kind of trouble?"

"No special trouble." Pakenham laughed harshly. "No more trouble than any other white male in this country."

Oh. The Army. "You've been called up?"

He shook his head. "Not yet. But I will be soon. In fact, with all the casualties, I'm surprised it's taken them this long to get around to me." A thin, humorless smile flitted across his face. "Vorster and his *broeders* must be reluctant to see too many damned English rooineks running around with weapons."

"Will you go?"

"Yes." It was Pakenham's turn to look away. "I'm not a hero, Em. I find it easier to face the thought of being an unwilling soldier than to go to one of the special camps as a prisoner."

The *Star*'s morgue occupied a windowless basement room, but powerful fluorescent lamps lit every corner. Scarred and stained worktables and chairs were scattered haphazardly around the room, seemingly moved wherever deemed convenient by the last reporter to use them. Two elderly, gray-haired women circulated through the morgue, carefully refiling clippings and old newspapers.

Pakenham introduced her to the older of the pair. "Miss Cooke's our own special genius. She'll help you find whatever it is that you're looking for." He turned to go.

Emily put a hand on his arm. "Good luck, Brian. I thank you for your help. Be safe."

Another sardonic half-smile surfaced briefly and then vanished. "I'll try my best, Em. I just hope they send me to Namibia and not anywhere else. I'd much rather shoot at some Cuban than at some poor black or student." He straightened to his full height. "Hey, who knows . . . maybe I'll run into your ex-fiancé out there. He's a soldier, isn't he?"

Emily nodded. "Yes. Perhaps you will." It surprised her that even the thought of Henrik Kruger still hurt. Not because of anything he'd done. Far from it. It was the memory of the anguish she'd caused him that was still painful. He'd been a good man, a kind man—just not the right man. Not for her.

She watched Pakenham take the steps two at a time until he was out of sight. Then she turned to find the helpful Miss Cooke hovering nearsightedly at her shoulder.

It was time to buckle down to work.

Emily van der Heijden straightened her aching back and rubbed at weary, bloodshot eyes. The low, persistent hum and white glare of the morgue's fluorescent lights had given her a pounding headache—a headache magnified by the hours spent combing through fading press clippings announcing births, store openings, and church outings. All the humdrum tedium that made news in the rural Transvaal.

So far she'd come up with nothing of any real use. The date of Erik Muller's birth, for instance. Something readily obtainable from public records. The fact that he was an only child. Unusual in an Afrikaner farm family, but not unheard of. Or the discovery that Muller's father had died in a car wreck when Erik was seven. Again, nothing strange there.

Back in the early fifties the northern Transvaal's roads had been rudimentary at best and accidents were common. At least the military expansion of recent decades had changed that. Now a web of multilane superhighways crisscrossed the high veld, more superhighways than the rural towns and villages in the region needed. Some cynics suggested they were intended as alternate airstrips for jet fighters in case of war. Some cynics were probably right.

Emily shook her head in exasperation. Her brain was wandering too far afield. Muller. Erik Muller. He was her target, her mission. She pushed the last yellowing scrap of newspaper aside and leaned backward, straining against the uncomfortable, straight-backed wooden chair.

"Miss van der Heijden?"

She opened her eyes.

Miss Cooke stood in front of her worktable, another pile of clippings clutched in eager hands. The librarian had proved an avid, enthusiastic helper. And one who seemed to possess an infallible, inexhaustible memory.

"I thought you might want to have a look through these. As background material for your project." Miss Cooke spread the handful of articles out across the table. "None of them mentions the Muller boy by name. But they all deal with events in the same town and from around the time he and his mother were still living there." Her thin lips pursed in disapproval. "There seem to have been some most unusual goings-on in that little place."

Intrigued, Emily sat forward. "Unusual, Miss Cooke? In what way?"

"See for yourself, Miss van der Heijden." The librarian tapped the first clipping with a delicate, wrinkled finger.

Emily scanned the story quickly, reading only for the essentials. The details could come later. The minister of the Dutch Reformed Church in Muller's hometown had been defrocked for a series of what were referred to only as "shocking misbehaviors." No specifics were provided.

And that meant the minister's "misbehaviors" must have involved some kind of sexual misconduct. She felt the beginnings of a smile. Nothing made an old-style Afrikaner retreat into embarrassed silence and sanctimonious circumlocution faster than the barest hint of sex. Especially when it was a member of the clergy who'd gotten tangled up between the sheets.

She checked the month and year. Muller would have been about eleven. Not much connection there. Still, the experience of seeing his family's minister, the dominie, drummed out of the church must have made some impression on him.

She jotted a rough note to herself and moved on to the next item.

A murder! Now that was more interesting. A young black boy, Gabriel Tswane, had been found dead in a field just outside Muller's hometown. Again, the details were sketchy, but Emily's reading between the lines left her fairly convinced that the young man had been beaten to death. The unbylined reporter hadn't bothered to hide his own belief that Tswane had been murdered by "black bandits and cattle thieves," but had also been forced to admit that the "police still had the case under investigation."

Emily noticed the date. October 22. Less than two weeks after the dominie's downfall. Was there a connection? If so, what kind of a connection?

She felt her temples pounding again and slid the article on top of her burgeoning pile for further study. Thirty-year-old mysteries and clerical misdeeds might make interesting reading, but they weren't moving her any closer to uncovering information about Muller's role—if any—in the Blue Train massacre.

"Were the articles of any use, Miss van der Heijden?"

Emily looked up into the librarian's anxious eyes and smiled. "They were very helpful, Miss Cooke. Very much so." She glanced at her watch. "But perhaps we'd best move on to Meneer Muller's early days in the security services. Have you been able to—" She stopped suddenly.

The thick stack of file folders the librarian plopped onto her desk answered her still-unasked question. Emily stifled a groan, converting it with tremendous difficulty into a simple, quiet sigh.

Who'd ever said a journalist's life was glamorous?

SEPTEMBER 24—JOHANNESBURG

Shelby's Olde English Pub wasn't very old and it certainly wasn't very English. Its chrome fittings and hard plastic tables reminded Ian more of a slapdash, drink-on-the-run airport bar back in the States. But at least Shelby's had all the elements so essential to a private, conspiratorial meeting: it was dimly lit, smoke filled, noisy, and crowded.

The government's new limits on the hours during which liquor could be served hadn't cut South Africa's alcohol consumption. They'd just forced people to drink their booze faster. A classic example of the law of unintended consequences, Ian thought sourly as he sipped the warm pint of beer in front of him.

He'd come here to play a hunch—a hunch backed by tidbits he'd picked up in an earlier, off-the-record conversation with the U.S. embassy's CIA station chief. "Political Counselor" Frank Price hadn't confirmed his belief that South Africa's security services had a high-ranking mole inside the ANC, but he had drawn Ian's attention to an operation that seemed to indicate it just might: the surgically precise SADF commando raid into Zimbabwe back in May.

Although Price hadn't been willing to say more than that, the mention of the attack on Gawamba had been enough to put Ian on what he hoped was the right track. He'd spent the several days since then arranging this meeting with a man he hoped could take him even further toward the truth.

The bar's front door swung open, briefly admitting a swirl of fresh, cool evening air along with a new customer. Ian watched through narrowed eyes as the man, self-conscious in an unfamiliar civilian suit, made his way through the tangle of portly businessmen and loud, off-duty soldiers. The newcomer was looking for someone.

Ian waited until the man's eyes focused on him and then tapped the empty place across the table.

Capt. Michael Henshaw, SADF, slid gingerly into the booth, sweat gleaming on his brow. "Are we safe here? Were you followed?"

Ian shook his head impatiently. He'd taken a lot of precautions to dodge any kind of a tail—feeling spectacularly silly all the while.

First, Sam Knowles had bundled their driver and suspected informer, Matthew Sibena, off on an all-day wild-goose chase across Johannesburg. The two were supposed to be filming a whole new slew of background shots for use as filler in news broadcasts. Ian only hoped Sibena didn't know that the network's files already held more footage of Johannesburg street scenes than could possibly be used in a dozen years.

Once they were gone, Ian had slipped quietly out of the studio and followed a long, roundabout path to the pub—one designed to shake loose anybody dogging his footsteps. Sudden changes in direction. Rapid taxi switches. Even a quick stroll through a department store teeming with late-afternoon shoppers. Hell, he'd used every trick he'd ever read about in espionage thrillers. And all without seeing any sign of anyone trying to follow him.

He signaled toward the bar. "A beer for my friend here, please."

Henshaw watched in silence as the white-jacketed barman deposited a tall glass in front of him. Once the man was safely out of earshot, he pushed the glass aside and leaned across the table. "Well, did you bring it?"

"Yeah." Ian risked a quick glance around the haze-filled room. Nobody seemed to be watching. He slid an envelope across into Henshaw's hands and looked away as the South African tore it open and riffled through the stack of crisp bank notes inside. Five hundred pounds' worth of tax-free British currency. Henshaw was one of those people who wanted to do the right thing, but only at a profit.

Ian frowned. He hated paying for information. Bribing somebody, even to tell the truth, always left him feeling soiled. He forced himself to smile. "Satisfied?"

The South African officer nodded abruptly and slid the envelope inside his suit coat. "You may ask your questions, Mr. Sherfield. I will do my best to answer them."

"Did you get a chance to check the records I mentioned earlier?"

"About the raid on the ANC's command center in Zimbabwe? Yes." Henshaw took a cautious sip of his beer. "It was a classic hit-and-kill op. Very well handled."

Ian grimaced. "I didn't ask you here to grade the damned thing for me." He lowered his voice. "What I want to know is, was there anything out of the ordinary about the raid? Anything that struck you as unusual?"

Henshaw hesitated and took another look around the crowded bar. Then he turned back to Ian. "There were three things, okay?"

He traced numbers on the table while he talked. "One, the paras who went in on the assault had a complete readout on the target before they went in. Enemy strength. Building plans. Everything. It was like they'd been talking to somebody who'd worked there. Right?"

Ian nodded his understanding.

"Okay, two. There weren't just paras on the op." Henshaw's voice dropped even lower. "I saw the orders for the mission. It listed a special intelligence-gathering unit besides the parachute company."

Curiouser and curiouser. "Who'd they work for?"

Henshaw looked even more nervous. He took another pull at his beer, this time a sizable gulp. Then he leaned forward. "For a man named Erik Muller. You've heard of him? The director of military intelligence?"

Jackpot. Ian nodded again, casually, as though the information were of little importance. "All right. What else?"

"Something very odd. The brass said this raid was an outstanding success. Medals galore for the paras involved. A unit citation. The whole works, right?"

"So?"

Henshaw shook his head. "So where were all the captured documents? Nothing came through my section. Not one scrap of paper!"

Ian shrugged. "Maybe your troops didn't find anything worth bringing back."

The South African officer looked annoyed. "No . . . no, you don't understand! We don't mount these kinds of commando assaults just to kill guerrillas. There are easier ways to do that! With bombs, for example." He shoved his beer aside again. "The reason you put troops in on the ground is to seize and hold buildings so you can search them for useful intelligence—for documents!"

Ian sat back, beginning to understand Henshaw's puzzlement. The commando raid on Gawamba had been intended to capture ANC documents. South Africa's high command viewed the attack as a stunning success. But nothing Muller's intelligence boys had found had come back through regular military channels. So what kind of information had they uncovered? And where was it?

He sat motionless for a long while after the South African left the pub. Muller had played some part in the Blue Train massacre. He was sure of that. Every piece of evidence pointed in the secret-service man's direction.

So far, so good. But all he had right now was a collection of what could be passed off as pure supposition, malicious rumor, and drunken barroom gossip. Turning any of that hodgepodge into solid, substantial proof was going to be tough—damned tough. Unfortunately, Ian didn't have the faintest idea of how he was going to go about doing that.

CHAPTER 15

Spreading Flames

OCTOBER 1—STATE SECURITY COUNCIL CHAMBER, THE UNION BUILDINGS, PRETORIA

Clusters of red pins dotting the topographic map of the Natal told their own story. The Zulu rebellion was growing, gathering strength day by day, despite the ever harsher measures adopted by Franz Diederichs and his security troops. It was a story matched in smaller scale across the length and breadth of Natal's neighbor to the west, the Cape Province. Student riots flared in Cape Town on a daily basis. Growing numbers of young men of draft age refused to report for induction. There were reports of increasing opposition to the war in Namibia among the province's business and labor leaders. There were even disquieting rumors that some of the police and soldiers stationed in and around Cape Town were increasingly reluctant to enforce the government's security decrees.

Karl Vorster's angry voice thundered through the room. "This situation is intolerable, Marius! You swore to me these nests of traitors and malcontents would be rooted out and utterly destroyed by now! And instead you come here to tell us that matters are worse than they once were?"

Erik Muller hid a satisfied smile as he watched Marius van der Heijden squirm under Vorster's tongue-lashing. His closest, most dangerous rival on the cabinet had finally bitten off more than he could easily chew.

Muller shook his head, remembering van der Heijden's proud recitation of kraals burned and Zulus shot down in fields or on rocky slopes. The man and his oafish subordinates really had no idea of how the game should be played—no sense of subtlety at all. Mass executions, indeed. Ridiculous! Much better results could have been achieved by a series of carefully planned assassinations and kidnappings.

Vorster whirled from his contemplation of the damning situation map. "Well, Marius? What do you suggest now?"

Van der Heijden cleared his throat. "Brigadier Diederichs and his men have fought well, Mr. President. But they are too few to adequately patrol the province. These Zulus have proven more stubborn than expected." He looked toward the tall, white-haired general sitting at one end of the table. "But we could subdue them if General de Wet could just spare three more battalions of motorized infantry. Diederichs assures me the extra manpower would let him form enough pursuit forces to track these guerrillas to their lairs and smash them there."

De Wet sniffed. "Impossible. The Permanent Force and those Citizen Force units already in Namibia are vital to our campaign there. We cannot spare units for what should be simple police work."

Better and better. Muller found it increasingly difficult not to laugh out loud. The two cabinet factions he disliked the most were now going for each other's throat.

"Then mobilize more troops! You still have Citizen Force battalions held out of the front lines. Let us make use of them where they are needed!"

Vorster held up a hand for silence, interrupting de Wet's retort. "Enough." He turned his grim, dark-ringed eyes on the general. "What of these men Marius speaks of, General? Are they all needed for Namibia? Truthfully, now."

De Wet hesitated for a moment before answering. "We need many of the Citizen Force troops as replacements for our regulars, Mr. President. Some of our best battalions have suffered serious losses that must be made good."

"But do you need them all?" Vorster's tone dropped toward a growl. He didn't like having to repeat himself.

The general lowered his eyes. "No, Mr. President. Not as yet." He nodded toward the map of Namibia now hung permanently on one of the room's windowless walls. "Our supply services are stretched to the breaking point as they are."

"I see." Vorster thumped a heavy hand onto the table and turned toward van der Heijden. "Very well, Marius. You'll have your three battalions. The Ministry of Defense will select which reserve units will be called up."

He glowered at the shorter man. "But I warn you, *meneer*. Do not fail me again. I expect you to crush this treacherous rebellion within the month. Is that quite clear, Marius?"

Van der Heijden nodded slowly, his normally plump red face now pale—almost ashen.

Muller was disappointed. He'd hoped for more fireworks, more angry shouting. He glanced covertly toward the man seated immediately to his right. Helmoed Malherbe, the minister of industries and commerce, sat rigidly in frozen silence. Too bad. He'd expected Malherbe to object again to the increasing drain on South Africa's civilian economy. Every battalion of reservists called to the colors meant one thousand fewer skilled white workers and managers in the nation's factories and mines.

But Malherbe seemed to have learned his lesson. Contradicting Vorster's cherished notions was one of the fastest ways known to end a promising government career, so the man stayed quiet.

Muller's lip curled upward in a tightly controlled sneer. Another toady in a cabinet of toadies. At times, the company his ambitions forced him to keep sickened him beyond all measure. But power brought its own rewards—rewards that made the bootlicking and petty infighting worthwhile.

Power. The very word stirred long-suppressed desires and appetites, sending them racing through Muller's mind and body. He shifted uncomfortably. It was October. He would need to make another secret journey—a pilgrimage of sorts—soon. Very soon.

OCTOBER 5—20TH CAPE RIFLES, REHOBOTH, NAMIBIA

Commandant Henrik Kruger had never been prouder of his men. Despite coming out of the line less than twenty-four hours before, they'd gone to great lengths to prepare for the brigade commander's last inspection. Somewhere they'd found enough water to wash and shave. Uniforms tattered, torn, and stained by weeks of trench warfare had been cleaned, pressed, and resewn. And vehicles once caked in dust and oil now gleamed in the spring sunshine.

But all the cleaning and polishing couldn't conceal the fact that the weeks of fruitless fighting had reduced his battalion to a shadow of its former self. Sergeants led infantry platoons now barely the size of squads, and two of his companies were commanded by second lieutenants scarcely out of school. Fewer than half the soldiers who'd marched into Namibia with him were still ready for battle. Wounds, deaths, and combat fatigue had stripped away man after man in a never ending round of artillery bombardments, outpost skirmishes, and massed assaults.

No, there couldn't be any doubt. The 20th Cape Rifles was fought out.

Now it was going home. Home to South Africa. Home to rest. Home to absorb new faces and new names as willing and unwilling replacements alike filled its shattered ranks. The battalion's mortar tubes and armored cars would remain in Namibia to equip the reservist units being sent to replace it.

"An impressive display, Henrik. Very impressive, indeed. Your men are a credit to our nation. It's been an honor to command them."

Kruger looked up sharply, suddenly aware that he'd been drifting along behind Brigadier Strydom in his own private haze. Sleep was a high-priced luxury in combat—one he'd rarely been able to afford over the past few weeks. With an effort, he gathered his thoughts. "Thank you, sir. I'll pass your commendation on. I'm sure the battalion will appreciate your kind words."

Strydom nodded. "Good." He studied Kruger carefully, a rare look of concern on his narrow face. "You may dismiss your men, *Kommandant*."

Kruger drew himself to attention, saluted, and held the salute until the *brigadier* returned it. Then he swung round, his weary, red-rimmed eyes scanning the officers ranked before him. "Captain Meiring! Dismiss the battalion!"

"Sir!" The bearded officer who'd replaced Forbes as Kruger's second-in-command stepped forward smartly, stiffened, and wheeled to bellow the order across the parade ground. Instantly, the battalion broke its ordered ranks—each man heading at a fast walk for his tent or for the crowded mess line.

Kruger grimaced as he caught sight of a familiar, loathesome, and fleshy face disappearing amid the sea of patched uniforms. So that damned AWB fanatic Hertzog was still here, eh? Still circling about like a vulture seeking easy prey—unarmed civilians or officers too tired to guard their tongues. Camp gossip told of continued mass executions and midnight arrests. Without realizing it, he took a step after Hertzog.

"Leave it, Henrik." Strydom took him by the arm. "You can't win a fight with that man. Hertzog has too many friends—too many powerful friends. Believe me I know." He sighed.

Kruger stared at him.

Strydom shook his head. "Go home, Henrik. Go home and rebuild your battalion. Concentrate on that. You are a soldier, not a politician."

A soldier? Perhaps. Kruger wasn't sure how much longer that could remain true. At what point did one stop being a soldier who simply followed orders and become something lower, something fouler—an accomplice?

He frowned. He'd read stories of the German soldiers who'd found themselves trapped between their patriotism and their code of personal honor. But he'd never expected to find himself caught in that same agonizing dilemma. Never.

Henrik Kruger turned slowly toward his tent—praying that, if it proved necessary, he would have the wisdom and the strength of heart to choose the right path.

OCTOBER 6—PORT SECURITY ZONE, MAPUTO, MOZAMBIQUE

Harsh white arc lights flared along the length of Maputo's inner harbor—turning night into eerie, shadowless day. Beneath their unwavering glare, dozens of stevedores swarmed around the long, rust-streaked hull of a Soviet freighter, the *Cherepovets*. Distorted images of the lights and bustling work crews were reflected in the oil-smeared waves gently lapping round the ship and against Maputo's old, cracked concrete quay. High above the water, massive cranes hovered, hesitated, and then dipped into the freighter's open cargo holds—each coming up in turn bearing an assortment of bulky crates and loaded pallets. All of the cargo was covered, either by tarpaulins or crates. Some of the crates were large enough to contain disassembled aircraft.

Most of *Cherepovets*'s cargo went onto a special twenty-car train waiting on a side track paralleling the waterfront. Other crates and cargo pallets went into warehouses just off the pier. They were packed with ammunition, small arms, and communications gear—the first promised installment payment for the use of Mozambique's largest port and its most important railroad line.

Soldiers patrolled the chain link fence separating the harbor from Maputo's darkened streets. Others behind them manned a deadly array of heavy machine guns, light antiaircraft cannon, and SAM batteries—all sweeping back and forth across preset sectors of the clear night sky.

Cigarettes glowed red near the front of the waiting train, marking the presence of more soldiers. The momentary flare of a match illuminated lighter-skinned faces and different uniforms. Cuba's generals didn't plan to entrust their valuable equipment to the safekeeping of Mozambique's slipshod army. Cuban troops would guard the train on its long journey north to secret assembly areas deep inside Zimbabwe.

Whistles blew shrilly across the harbor, urging the dock-workers to greater efforts. The *Cherepovets* was only the first of many Soviet cargo ships bound for Maputo.

OCTOBER 10—DIRECTORATE OF MILITARY INTELLIGENCE HEADQUARTERS, PRETORIA

= START = XMT: 12:26 Mon Oct 10 EXP: 12:00 Tue Oct 11

Soviet Union and Mozambique Announce New Trade Agreement

MAPUTO (October 8) UPI—A spokesman for the Mozambican government today announced the signing of a new three-year trade agreement with the Soviet Union. Under the agreement, which has an estimated value of approximately 40 billion metecais, roughly 88 million dollars, Mozambique will exchange its agricultural products for Soviet manufactured goods. When pressed, the government spokesman admitted that the agreement would include substantial shipments of Soviet military equipment.

Western diplomatic sources expressed no surprise at this revelation. Mozambique's armed forces, poorly armed and trained, have been on the losing side of a ten-year struggle against a South African–backed insurgency. New Soviet equipment and advisors are seen by Mozambique's ruling party as essential to reversing the worsening military situation.

-30-

"Here it is, *Kolonel*. Here is the piece of the puzzle we needed." Maj. Willem Metje knocked on the doorframe as he walked into his superior's office.

Col. Magnus Heerden looked up with irritation from his work. He was responsible for coordinating the SADF's intelligence-gathering operations in Mozambique, Zimbabwe, and Botswana. The job had once been time consuming and stressful. Now it was simply impossible. He'd once had five men, four of them trained analysts, under his command. Now four were gone—pulled out from under him to bolster the battlefield intelligence effort in Namibia. That left just himself—and Metje.

The major excitedly fluttered the thin piece of paper in his hand and laid it down in the center of Heerden's desk, obscuring the map of Zimbabwe he had been studying. "This explains it all, sir. It's just as I supposed. These reports you've found so troubling are simply a reflection of this new arms deal between Mozambique and the Russians."

The colonel scanned the UPI story and shook his head. "Major, I don't see how this trade agreement could account for all the unusual movement we're seeing in Mozambique, and"—he emphasized—"*in Zimbabwe* as well."

Heerden looked at the wire-service report again. "More importantly, the matériel we've already heard about has to be worth twice this much!"

A haughty frown creased Metje's lean, elegant face. "True, *Kolonel*. That's why I believe our agents must be overestimating the amounts of military equipment they have spotted."

"Are you saying they can't count?" Heerden picked up a manila folder from the side of his desk and opened it. "Take a look at this, for example. Windmill reports sighting thirty T-62 tanks and one hundred wheeled armored personnel carriers parked in a wooded area near Moamba—practically right on our border. And they're being guarded by nearly a brigade of Mozambican troops!"

Metje shrugged. "How close a look could Windmill get if these tanks were really under such a heavy guard? And would this kaffir know a T-62 tank from a T-55, or a T-72 for that matter?'' He shook his head contemptuously. ''The fool probably stumbled across a Red Cross convoy with ten or twenty trucks. At most, he might have seen a small group of new tanks parked in the jungle until the Mozambicans train troops to man them.''

He smiled. ''Come now, *Kolonel*. We can't base our analysis on the hallucinations of a few ignorant blacks.''

Heerden's powerful hands closed tightly around the edge of the folder, crumpling it. ''I'm not proposing that we do that. But I am suggesting that we've received too many unsettling intelligence reports from Mozambique and Zimbabwe. Reports that can't be explained by something so convenient as this.'' He flicked the teletypewritten copy of the wire-service report with a finger. ''Plane flights in at night to Harare and Maputo, security stepped up at the ports, increased troop activity . . .''

''All of which the President has seen, *Kolonel*. He is convinced that these movements are related to their own antiguerrilla efforts. They show that our destabilization strategy is working. The black states have been forced to beg for help from the Soviets—for equipment that is being drained away from the Cubans fighting us in Namibia! Even if they are accurate, these reports that frighten you so much are proof of our success!'' Metje's impertinence was caused by his enthusiasm, which Heerden tolerated, and safeguarded by his political credentials, which Heerden despised. As an active member of the AWB, the major had his own channels of communication with the political leadership.

Heerden sat motionless for a moment, uneasily considering the possibility that Metje's optimistic assessment was the right one. Certainly, it was what the new government wanted to hear. He shook his head. That alone made it suspect. The greatest intelligence failures occurred when analysts allowed their own wishful thinking to obscure inconvenient facts. Unfortunately, he didn't have enough of those inconvenient facts on hand. A few reports from paid agents. A scattering of intercepted radio transmissions and radar intercepts. Not enough.

The colonel frowned. What he needed were aerial photographs. Solid, undeniable, pictorial proof of the military buildup he feared was taking shape on South Africa's northern and eastern borders. But he couldn't get it. He'd put in request after request for Mirage IIIRZ reconnaissance overflights of Zimbabwe and Mozambique. All had been rejected. The Air Force's small photo recon squadron was already stretched too thin just trying to monitor Cuban movements inside Namibia.

Metje watched him carefully and then leaned forward to pick up the UPI news report. "Well, *Kolonel*, have you come up with any other explanation for these Soviet arms shipments?" From his tone he knew that Heerden hadn't—at least nothing that he could prove to anyone's satisfaction. "Then, sir, I recommend that we send the news of this trade agreement up the chain of command. It provides the obvious explanation of the activity we've spotted inside Mozambique. And I'm sure the President will be delighted to learn that his strategy has been vindicated."

His tone was soothing, almost patronizing, and Heerden struggled to control his temper. Metje was an ass, but he was a well-connected ass.

At last, with an almost inaudible sigh, Heerden nodded. Even if he submitted a different, more pessimistic analysis, the major would simply go behind his back. And the colonel didn't have any doubts about whose version Karl Vorster would choose to believe.

30TH GUARDS MOTORIZED RIFLE REGIMENT, MAIN ASSEMBLY AREA, NEAR RUTENGA, ZIMBABWE

Dozens of acres of the fly-infested, unproductive flatlands outside the small town of Rutenga were now covered by camouflage netting, barbed wire, and protective minefields. Trains from the south arrived almost daily, pulling flatcars crowded with Cuban tanks, armored personnel carriers, and artillery pieces. And day by day, the equipment parks outside Rutenga grew larger.

Hard-eyed soldiers of Zimbabwe's North Korean–trained Fifth Brigade patrolled the town's streets and railway station—on constant guard against South African spies or commandos. Travelers of every description were hauled in for questioning by local interrogators or taken north to the capital, Harare, for more rigorous investigation. Antiaircraft batteries dotted the surrounding landscape, ready to down any unauthorized plane that poked its nose into forbidden airspace.

Both Zimbabwe and Cuba were determined to prevent any word of their military buildup from leaking out. But their efforts were unnecessary.

South Africa's leaders weren't even looking in the right direction.

OCTOBER 11—CUBAN EXPEDITIONARY FORCE HEADQUARTERS, WINDHOEK, NAMIBIA

Col. José Suarez, Gen. Antonio Vega's chief of staff, looked tired. Three days of ground-hugging airplane flights, stomach-wrenching helicopter rides, and secretive movement all across southern Africa had taken their toll. Most wearing of all had been Vega's relentless questioning. He'd insisted on going over every last detail of the trip, and if Suarez hadn't known what to expect, he would have been shattered by the persistent probing.

Vega knew that his fierce, pitiless questioning was just a symptom of his own frustration. For security purposes, he was supposedly planning a new offensive in Namibia—all the while staying as visible as possible to draw South Africa's eyes away from the buildup in Mozambique and Zimbabwe. It was a necessary task, but it left him unable to monitor directly the unfolding of his own plan. It also left him feeling like a caged lion.

Suarez answered his last question and sat back, looking even more tired.

Vega nodded. The colonel was one of his best officers. He'd given a good, concise summary of his impressions and activities.

Suarez must have seen his pleasure because he risked a

question of his own. "Have the Soviets discussed a starting date for our operation yet, Comrade General?"

Vega scowled. "No, they haven't. And I understand that Castro's last inquiry came back with the damned standard line about the need to wait for a 'more favorable correlation of forces.' " If they hadn't been indoors, Vega would have spat to relieve the foul taste the bureaucratic nonsense left in his mouth.

"Our soldiers are dying, wearing down the South African Army with their blood, while the gutless Russians wait for the most opportune moment to promise us their continued support." Vega stood up and started pacing back and forth, in front of the map board. He'd been pacing a lot lately.

The casualty figures and the strain involved in running one campaign while planning for another, wider war were to blame for that. His nerves were also being stretched tight by the Soviet Union's continuing refusal to commit itself fully to the invasion of South Africa.

Abruptly, the room seemed too small, too stifling. He needed fresh air and open skies, if only for a few moments. "Colonel, walk with me."

Suarez rose with him and together they stepped out of the headquarters—a nondescript block of office flats that had once housed a car rental firm, an accounting firm, and a small printing shop. Now the brick building housed more than one hundred staff officers responsible for guiding the largest military operation on the continent.

A squad of armed guards at the entrance snapped to attention as Vega and his chief of staff emerged into the evening air. It was pleasantly cool, and Vega ambled across the street to a small municipal park, surrounded by a bubble of quiet and privacy that would be breached only by desperate emergency. He ignored the thin screen of security troops fanning out around the park. They, like the weight of the stars on his shoulders, were always with him.

"The Russians are using us, José, just as they always have."

Suarez nodded grimly, apparently unsurprised by his commander's disenchantment with the Soviet Union. It was a disenchantment shared by many in Cuba's higher political and military echelons.

They'd long looked to the Soviet Union as a source of spiritual inspiration, but Moscow's revisionist moves had shaken that faith. The Kremlin's political bosses were increasingly viewed as little more than corrupt, tepid socialists—not as the dynamic leaders needed by the international communist movement.

The military situation in southern Africa was widening that gap. The Soviets seemed perfectly content to sit back and reap all the benefits of Cuba's armed struggle, while avoiding any of the risks. It was intolerable.

After they had walked in silence for a few minutes, Vega spoke again. "Our buildup should be complete by the middle of November. Correct?"

Suarez nodded. All the troops, equipment, and supplies should be in place by then—poised within a hundred kilometers of South Africa's borders.

"Very well. If the Soviets don't give us their full support by then, we will attack without them."

Suarez started to exclaim, but Vega hushed him. "We won't be operating completely on our own, Colonel. We've received assurances of additional aid from Libya and North Korea—should it prove necessary. We could also cut the number of attacking columns from three to two. That would reduce the logistical load significantly, true?"

He could see his chief of staff running through the figures in his mind. Suarez's razor-sharp brain was one of the things about him that Vega most prized. They'd planned to have thirty days' worth of fuel, food, and ammunition stockpiled before striking into South Africa. Reducing the number of troops involved in the invasion would allow them to stretch those supplies beyond the thirty-day mark.

Vega's face lit up in excitement. "Think of it, Colonel. Think of the looks on those long, sad Russian faces when Cuba shows them their duty! And when we win, Cuba will gain the lion's share of the rewards—not just the crumbs allowed us by our so-called Soviet brothers!"

Suarez studied the ground for a few seconds before looking

up. "Such an attack is possible, General. But we'll be taking a tremendous risk."

"More than we are already taking? More than we will take when we launch the attack? High stakes are involved here, José, but it's a game I know. We will strike South Africa with such speed and such fury that we'll hold Pretoria before the damned Afrikaners can react. And before Moscow's caution can thwart us!"

Vega smiled. The war in southern Africa would spread, whether or not the Soviet Union really wanted it to.

CIA HEADQUARTERS, LANGLEY, VIRGINIA

Christopher Nicholson tried to make sense of the information in front of him. Operatives in Libya had reported battle tanks, armored personnel carriers, and artillery being moved from storage dumps and loaded on freighters. The numbers were impressive—enough for an army, literally. But where was it going?

The newest piece of information involved an increased level of diplomatic communications between Mozambique, Zimbabwe, and Cuba. Not disturbing in itself, since it just indicated they were talking a lot. Nicholson rubbed his burning eyes. But what were they talking about?

One more piece of the puzzle. Parts of it were scattered all over his desk. Or was it the same puzzle? What if it was more than one? And what if Pretoria's enemies had slipped some false pieces onto the table?

The director of the CIA, and by statute director of central intelligence for the U.S. national decision-making apparatus, worried the pieces for another hour or so, but in the end put them back in the box until more could be found.

CHAPTER 16

Full Exposure

OCTOBER 12—WOMEN'S STAFF CANTEEN, MINISTRY OF LAW AND ORDER, PRETORIA

In a desperate attempt to ward off utter boredom, Emily van der Heijden risked another glance away from the young woman chattering amiably at her from across the table. Unfortunately, her surroundings did nothing to dispel the growing feeling that she was trapped in a place where boredom reigned supreme and idle gossip passed for thoughtful conversation.

Certainly, the architects and interior decorators who'd crafted the Ministry's women's dining area had created a masterpiece of drab institutionalism. Fading off-white walls matched the canteen's fading black-and-white checkerboard-pattern tile floor. Narrow, unwashed windows opened out onto a small interior courtyard long since converted into a parking lot. The dresses worn by the forty or so women still eating lunch provided the only touch of color—and little enough of that. Most of the secretaries, typists, and other clerical workers clustered around identical, government-issue aluminum tables seemed content with plain white blouses and black or gray knee-length skirts. It was like staring at the bureaucratic soul made flesh.

"Really, Miss van der Heijden, I'm so glad you asked me to sit with you. It's such an honor. I mean, imagine me—Irene Roussouw—taking lunch with the deputy minister's own daughter. It's fantastic!"

Emily forced her wavering attention back on track. She smiled sweetly at the young, red-haired woman in front of her. "Come now, Irene. None of that 'Miss van der Heijden' nonsense. You'll make me feel old! My name's Emily, remember?" She hoped her real feelings weren't showing. Flattery was bad enough, but to be flattered and fawned over simply because she was her father's daughter was infinitely worse!

"Oh, yes, certainly . . . Emily." Roussouw still sounded breathless, exactly like one of those giddy, vacant-minded schoolgirls she'd always avoided whenever possible.

But it wasn't always possible, Emily reminded herself. She, Ian, and Sam Knowles were playing for high stakes now—stakes that made pretty but petty idiots such as this Roussouw woman worth tolerating.

She nodded. "That's the way, Irene. After all, we should be friends, right? Since we may wind up working together here?"

Roussouw looked puzzled. "But I don't understand . . . Emily. Why should you need to work at all?"

Emily gritted her teeth and hid her irritation by taking a sip of the iced mineral water in front of her. Her smile was back when she looked up again. "Oh, I don't need to work. But it's . . . well, it's a sacrifice I feel I should make."

Roussouw nodded, her bright blue eyes openly admiring.

Now for the hard part, Emily thought. She leaned forward and lowered her voice conspiratorily. "And besides, I didn't think it was fair for the rest of you girls to have all these eligible young men all to yourselves."

The other woman leaned forward herself, lowering her own voice to match Emily's soft, secretive tone. "Ah, if only it were true, Emily. There aren't too many prize catches left here. Most of the best have gone off to war. Off to risk their lives for us, and for the fatherland, of course.'' She sighed theatrically.

Emily winced inwardly. She suspected that Irene Roussouw's ideas of patriotism came straight out of trashy romance novels. She arched an eyebrow. "Come now. They can't all have gone. There must be a few handsome young fellows left to fight over, true?'' She tapped a finger gently on the table's plastic surface. "What about this Major Karlsen I hear so much about? Isn't he the one you work for?''

"Oh, no, Emily!'' Roussouw shook her head, laughing. "Major Karlsen is a nice man, I'm sure . . . but I don't work for him. I'm the personal secretary for the director.'' She looked quickly to either side before continuing proudly, "For Erik Muller. Have you heard of him? He's in charge of special operations.'' The way she said it made it clear that she had very little idea of exactly what Muller's "special operations'' entailed.

Emily pretended to be surprised. "Erik Muller? You work for him?'' She wagged a finger in Roussouw's face. "So now I know you were holding out on me! Why, I've heard that he's very handsome . . . and very much a bachelor.''

The other young woman blushed. "Well, he is quite good-looking.'' She seemed strangely uncertain. "But I think he must be one of those men who are married to their work, you know? He never seems interested . . .'' Her voice faded away as she blushed further, embarrassed at having admitted her evident failure to attract her superior.

Emily changed her tack. "Well, I'm sure it's simply that he's so busy. Believe me, I know what these government officials are like—my father, for instance. Work, work, and more work. That's all they care about!''

"Yes, exactly!'' Emboldened by Emily's evident sympathy, Roussouw had recovered her equilibrium. She leaned closer still. "Why if it weren't for his little trips, I'd think Meneer Muller was a completely cold fish. Like a priest, eh?''

Some instinct warned Emily to conceal her curiosity.

"Trips? Oh, hunting and hiking jaunts, I suppose." She waved them away as unimportant.

"No, no. Not hiking!" Roussouw shook her head impatiently. Her voice dropped even further until she was speaking just above a whisper. "The director goes to Sun City from time to time! I should know—I'm the one who makes all his arrangements and reservations!"

Sun City? This time Emily didn't have to pretend to be surprised. Sun City was a resort town about a two-hour drive away from Johannesburg and Pretoria—inside the nominally independent tribal homeland of Bophuthatswana. The homeland's black rulers had outlawed apartheid and rescinded many of the blue laws that still marked South Africa. As a result, Sun City was famous, or infamous, for its mixed-race casinos, hotels, and pornographic entertainments.

Certainly, it seemed the last place on earth that a high-ranking official in Karl Vorster's regime would want to visit. Unless . . .

My God! It was the perfect place for a covert rendezvous—assuming that their theory about a double agent inside the ANC was correct. Blacks could mingle freely with whites without arousing suspicion. Crowds were constant. And there were few police or security agents to elude. Muller and his agent could meet there in absolute safety.

She shook her head decisively. "Sun City? No, I can't believe it. No one in his position would risk such a sinful thing."

Irene Roussouw wrinkled her face up, obviously irritated at not being believed. "I tell you it's true! He's going again in less than a fortnight. I've made the hotel reservations to prove it! A Saturday night at the Cascades no less!"

A Saturday less than a fortnight away? That meant the weekend of the twenty-second. They had ten days to prepare. The twenty-second. Something about that date rang a bell in the back of her mind. What was it? Emily suppressed the thought for the moment. She had more important matters to pursue. "Perhaps he's going there on some kind of government business?"

Roussouw chewed her lower lip. Clearly, she'd never considered that possibility before. Finally, she shook her head —tossing her thick mane of red hair back over her shoulder. "Hah! That's just his excuse. He's really going there for the cards and the liquor . . . and maybe even those filthy movies people say they show there." She sat back primly, folding her arms. "It is a good thing that I am loyal to him. I tell you, if I weren't, I could get him in some kind of trouble and that's for sure."

Emily coughed, choking back a strained laugh. Irene Roussouw couldn't possibly have the faintest idea of the kind of man she was working for. Muller was a murderer and a traitor. He'd sooner kill the pretty young woman than try to explain away any imaginary peccadilloes.

She'd better pull the conversation away from Erik Muller and onto safer ground. What Irene Roussouw needed was the chance to fill her head with catty gossip. She shrugged. "Well, if Meneer Muller is out of consideration, what about Jan du Toit? He's unmarried, isn't he?"

The other young woman laughed softly and shook her own finger back and forth. "Oh, no, Emily. Jan du Toit isn't suitable at all. You see, I've heard . . ."

Emily leaned closer, a bright, interested expression plastered across her face as she prepared to exercise the twin virtues of patience and politeness. Inwardly, she exulted. She had it! She had the information Ian needed. She had the clue that could lead them to the truth—the truth about the Blue Train massacre and Karl Vorster's treachery. His exposure would mean at least his downfall, and maybe that of the entire government. No Afrikaner would be able to accept his authority.

OCTOBER 13—JOHANNESBURG

Johannesburg's towering steel-and-glass skyscrapers stood outlined in the pale glow of a new-risen moon. No lights gleamed behind any of their several thousand windows. Power cuts and nightly curfews were fast becoming a fact of life under the Vorster regime.

Ian Sherfield turned away from the window and looked carefully at Emily van der Heijden and Sam Knowles as they sat uncomfortably at opposite ends of his sofa. The three of them probably seemed a most unlikely group of conspirators, he thought. One would-be journalist who hadn't managed to get a single meaningful story on the air for months. One cameraman and technician shorter than his own gear if it were piled end on end. And a single, beautiful woman who probably had far more to lose than either Knowles or him if things went wrong.

He moved to a chair across from the sofa. They waited for him to speak. He paused, trying to find the right words. "I think we'd better take stock of exactly where we stand with this thing. To decide whether we should press on, or whether we should drop the whole damned business right here before we get in too deep."

Knowles looked puzzled. "Whattya mean, boyo? Why even think about giving up? Hell, we know what we're looking for now and we know who's got it. I say we go ahead and nail the bastard. Nothing could be simpler."

"It's not quite that simple." Emily shook her head slowly, her eyes fixed on Ian's somber face. "What he is saying is that up till now we've simply been engaged in a kind of academic game—a paper chase, I think you would call it? But the moment we step closer to Erik Muller, we step across the line into reality."

"So?" Knowles shrugged.

"So someone could get plenty pissed off at what we're trying to do—somebody who just might decide we're better off dead," Ian said, irritated. Sam Knowles wasn't usually so willfully stupid.

Knowles smiled broadly, letting Ian know that he'd walked into one of the shorter man's traps. "No shit, Sherlock." He turned serious. "Look, Ian, we're tracking big game here . . . maybe a whole gang of murdering creeps, from this Vorster guy on down. Stands to reason that's kind of a dangerous proposition. But it comes with the turf."

The cameraman shrugged again. "Sure, if we screw up, we could wind up dead or in jail. If I'd wanted to play life perfectly safe I'd have listened to my dear old mom and become an accountant."

Knowles ran out of breath and sat back, coloring a little under their astonished gaze. Neither Emily or Ian had ever heard him say so much at a single sitting. "Anyway, I've blabbered enough. I say we go."

Ian nodded and turned to Emily. She was his main concern. He and Knowles could look after themselves. And as the shorter man had said, this was the kind of job they'd signed on to do. But Emily was different. She wasn't getting paid to risk her neck for the news. Besides, she meant too much to him to risk losing in some damn fool race for a scoop.

Emily must have seen the thought on his face because she frowned. "I say we go, too. And I will go with you."

He shook his head. "Sam and I can take it from here, Em. You've put us on the right track, and now . . ."

"Now, what? Now you leave me behind like some sort of porcelain doll—too pretty and fragile for real work? Is that what you mean, Ian Sherfield?" Her eyes flashed dangerously.

Ian winced. Emily had always warned him that she had a sharp temper, but he'd never seen it aimed at him until now. The trouble was that she was pretty much on target.

"This is my country. These are my people, the people of my blood. One of them is my father." Emily's anger faded into sadness. "I must be a part of this, Ian. Do you understand? Please?"

She smiled crookedly—a smile that contrasted strangely with the tears brimming in her eyes. "Besides, I know where you're going. So even if you refuse to let me come with you, I will still follow."

"She's got a point," Knowles interrupted. "I'd say Miss van der Heijden's in on this little jaunt no matter what you say." He grinned. Emily appeared to have gone up several notches in his estimation.

Ian shook his head helplessly. "All right already, I give up. We're all in. And God help us all, because nobody else will!"

Knowles and Emily exchanged knowing looks that made

him wonder just how long they'd rehearsed their little speeches. They must have known that he'd try to give them an out. Was he really that predictable?

Maybe it was better not to know. Ian pulled his chair closer to the coffee table. "So have either of you two geniuses given any thought to how we go about catching Muller and our hypothetical ANC traitor in the act?"

Both of them looked blank. Good. At least he was ahead in something for a change.

Emily chewed at her lower lip. "I thought we'd follow Muller to Sun City and see whom he meets . . ." Her voice trailed off as she saw Ian shaking his head.

"Wouldn't work, I'm afraid. Muller's a professional intelligence guy. He'd be sure to spot us following him." Ian drummed his fingers lightly on the glass coffee tabletop. "Besides, we'd never get a camera close enough to them to shoot some usable footage. And that's the whole point of this exercise."

"What are you saying, then? That we cannot succeed?" Emily sounded frustrated. Sam Knowles looked thoughtful.

"Nope." Ian laced his fingers behind his neck and spoke with elaborate casualness. "I'm saying we don't need to follow Meneer Muller at all. We already know exactly where he's going. All we've got to do is be there well ahead of him. Get it?"

Understanding dawned on Knowles's face. "Yeah. Sound and Sight R Us. No problem."

"Well, I don't get it!" Emily stared from one to the other.

Ian explained.

Emily sat silently for a moment, clearly mulling over concepts and technologies she'd never before contemplated. Finally, she looked up. "If you say this is possible, then it must be so. But what of all the equipment you'll need? Do you have such things here in South Africa?"

Knowles glanced up from a piece of scrap paper he'd filled with hastily scribbled notes. "Not all of it. But I know where I can lay my hands on the stuff we don't have." He turned to Ian. "I'll have to have a few items FedExed over from the States through London. It's gonna cost an arm and a leg . . ."

Ian shrugged. "So we expense it! If this works, nobody'll begrudge a penny. If it doesn't, the network can bill our respective estates, right?"

Knowles showed his teeth. "I like the way you think, bossman." Then he frowned. "That still leaves us with one pretty big problem."

Ian nodded. "Sibena."

He'd been giving the problem posed by their full-time driver and part-time police informant a lot of thought. Even if the young black man was cooperating with the South African security services against his will, they still had to find a way to shock him into working with them—and not against them.

"Uh-huh. How are we gonna make a move on this Muller goon with Matt still on our tail?" The cameraman's frown grew deeper. "Shit, all he's gotta do is make one lousy phone call to the bad guys and we're toast!"

"Too true. But I've got a couple of ideas about how to get a handle on our friend, Matthew Sibena." Ian bent forward over the coffee table and added two more pieces of electronic gear to Knowles's scribbled list. Then he drew a quick sketch.

The cameraman pursed his lips in a soundless whistle. "You sure you've never thought about working for the CIA, boyo? You're just the kind of devious son of a bitch I hear they're looking for."

Ian looked back and forth from Knowles to Emily and then laughed. "Maybe I am. But I guess that makes us a matched threesome, right?"

At least they had the grace to blush.

OCTOBER 18—NEAR THE HILLBROW HOSPITAL FOR BLACKS, JOHANNESBURG

Johannesburg lay smothered in a dull yellow-brown pall of auto exhaust and industrial fumes. The smog had been building up for days, trapped by a ridge of high pressure that shoved any wind to the north or south.

Ian Sherfield sat staring out the backseat window as Matthew Sibena drove down Edith Cavell Street, careful to stay, as always, well within the posted speed limit. The young black man had insisted on locking all the Ford Escort's doors before venturing into the Hillbrow district, and it was easy to see the reasons for his caution.

Though officially a white residential area, Hillbrow had long been a bustling multiracial neighborhood—full of trendy cafés, inexpensive apartment buildings, and late-night jazz clubs. But time and the Vorster regime's return to strict apartheid had not been kind to the area. Now the district's cracked sidewalks, trash-filled alleys, and boarded-up windows stood in stark contrast to the walled mansions, swimming pools, and flowering gardens of the rich white suburbs north of Johannesburg. Though it was broad daylight, few people were on the streets. Most were at work, in the government's crowded detention camps, or staying close to their illegally occupied flats. And some of those who dared to venture out shook angry fists or spat contemptuously at the sight of white faces inside the Escort.

Sibena shook his head nervously. "I'm telling you, Meneer Ian, this is a bad place, a dangerous place. Surely you and Sam could find another area to take your pictures today?"

Ian leaned forward. "Don't sweat it, Matt. We'll be okay. But we got the word through the grapevine that there might be some kind of illegal demonstration at the hospital here. That's too good to pass up, right, Sam?"

Knowles winked back and then nudged him, pointing out a graffiti-smeared phone booth a few yards ahead.

Ian nodded. It was time to activate their plan. He could feel his heart starting to race. A lot depended on what happened in the next few minutes. If they couldn't turn Sibena against his masters, they'd have to abandon all hope of nailing Erik Muller.

Ian tapped Sibena on the shoulder. "Pull in right here, Matt. Sam and I can walk the rest of the way. We'll take a few back alleys to avoid the cops."

They popped the doors open as the Escort coasted into the curb and stopped. Ian shrugged into his favorite on-camera blazer as Knowles pulled his gear off the backseat and out of the trunk. Then he waited while Knowles bent low one final time, fiddled with something out of sight inside the trunk, and slammed the lid shut.

The little cameraman nodded once. They were ready.

Ian leaned in through the driver's side window. "Just take it easy while we're gone, Matt. We'll be back in a jiff."

He ignored the stricken look on the man's face and headed toward the phone booth, fingering his pockets as though looking for change. Knowles followed him with the Minicam and sound gear slung over his shoulder.

Once inside the phone booth, Ian waited until Sam stopped behind him—blocking most of Sibena's view. Then he picked up the receiver and hurriedly unscrewed the mouthpiece. A small metal disk lay nestled loosely inside—the microphone disk that ordinarily transformed sound waves into electrical impulses for transmission over the phone lines. He tapped it out into his cupped palm and slipped it into one of his jacket pockets.

"C'mon, boyo. I can't stand here looking like a barn door all day." Knowles's mutter showed that he was just as nervous.

"Almost done." Ian cradled the receiver between his ear and shoulder, pretending to make a call. He reached into another pocket and pulled out a microphone disk that looked very much like the one he'd just removed. But this disk had another, very special function built into its wafer-thin circuits. Over short distances, it worked like a miniature wireless transmitter. And any conversation over this telephone could now be picked up by the radio receiver and tape recorder hidden inside the Escort's trunk.

Ian fitted the new disk into place and screwed the mouthpiece shut. Sweat trickled into his eyes and he wiped it off on his pants leg. Done.

He backed out of the phone booth and waved toward the car where Matthew Sibena sat peering anxiously at them through the front windshield. Then Ian and Knowles moved away down a nearby alley, skirting heaped piles of rotting garbage—walking fast until they were out of sight.

The alley opened up onto Klein Street beside a small, shabby Dutch Reformed Church. Somebody had scrawled anti-Vorster slogans in white paint across its brown brick walls.

"This way." Knowles pointed off to the right. "There's another alley leading back a few yards up."

A minute later, Ian and his cameraman crouched near the side of a nightclub that had been raided and padlocked shut by the police. From their vantage point behind an overflowing Dumpster, they could just see the phone booth.

Matthew Sibena was in the booth, talking on the telephone and gesturing frantically while turning from side to side to see if they were on their way back.

"Well, I'll be damned. Your cockeyed plan worked!" Knowles shook his head. "He actually fell for it. Son, you're a frigging cloak-and-dagger genius!"

"Yeah, sure."

"There he goes!"

Ian risked another look. The phone booth was empty. Their driver was probably already back inside the car, waiting nervously for their return with that same helpful, friendly expression he always wore. Ian was staking a lot on the belief that much of Matthew Sibena's desire to help was quite genuine.

Ian glanced down at Knowles. "Okay, we'll let him stew for another couple of minutes and then head back acting disgusted . . . like the whole trip was just one more wasted afternoon. Then I'll pretend to make another call and switch the mike disks again. Right?"

The cameraman nodded. "Cool." He squatted down on his haunches behind the Dumpster. "So when are we going to spring our little tape on our pal over there?"

Ian squatted beside him, his forehead creased in thought. "Later today. At the studio. I've got a few pieces of file footage I want to show Matt first—to put him in the right frame of mind, if you know what I mean."

Knowles grinned suddenly and muttered something under

his breath. Ian didn't catch all of it—just the words "one devious son of a bitch."

Matthew Sibena sat awkwardly on a folding metal chair, intently watching the images flickering across a video monitor. Scenes of carnage shot at peaceful demonstrations turned into riots. Scenes of whip-wielding South African police and foam-flecked attack dogs. Clips of hate-filled passages from Karl Vorster's speeches. Pictures of black-on-red swastika banners and chanting, roaring brownshirts. All flashing by at a lightning-quick tempo.

The videotape ended with a simple shot of a teenaged black girl running in panic from the police, blood streaming from a cut on her forehead. The camera zoomed in and focused on her anguished face and froze—locking the image in place until Ian got up and turned the VCR off.

He swung round and studied Sibena's tear-streaked face carefully. "Pretty horrible stuff, huh, Matt?"

The young black man coughed, wiped the tears off his face, and looked away. "It is terrible, *meneer*. I wish it were not so."

"You do?" Ian sounded surprised. He hit the VCR's rewind button and pretended to watch the tape counter rolling back. His eyes, though, were really focused on Sibena's reflection in the darkened TV monitor. "Say, Matt, did you ever join the ANC or any of the other antigovernment groups?"

The young man shook his head slowly from side to side without looking up from the floor. "I was never political." Emotion choked his voice. "You must understand, *meneer*. Life in the townships is hard, impossibly hard. It's very difficult to find work to put food on the table."

He looked down at his hands. "I've never had time to work for freedom. And I am ashamed of that."

For an instant, Ian was tempted to drop the matter right there. Pushing Sibena to the wall felt uncomfortably like bullying a handicapped child. As a white, middle-class American, Ian knew he'd never been subjected to even a tenth of the subtle pressures and outright suffering inflicted on non-white South Africans.

A glance at the tape recorder lying beside the VCR hardened his resolve. Certain virtues had to be expected: honesty and loyalty to one's friends, to name two. It was time to remind Matthew Sibena of that.

He cleared his throat. "Matt?"

Sibena looked up.

"I've got one other thing I'd like you to listen to. Maybe you can explain it for me. Okay?"

The young black man nodded slowly, evidently unsure of just what the American had in mind.

Ian pressed the playback switch on the tape recorder and stepped back, watching Sibena's puzzled face as the first few seconds of static crackled faintly out of the recorder's speakers.

Suddenly, a series of high-pitched beeps cut through the static—the sound of a six-digit number being punched in on a touch-tone phone.

The phone rang twice before it was answered. A harsh, grating voice came on the line. "Monitoring station. Who is this?"

Ian actually saw the blood drain from Sibena's face as the young black man heard his own voice answering, "Sibena. Four eight five."

"Make your report, kaffir."

"The American reporters are near Hillbrow Hospital, at the corner of Cavell and Kapteijn. They're here to see if the rumors of an illegal demonstration are true."

A pause. Then the voice on the other end came back. "We have no word of such a thing. Report back if such a protest is planned or if the Americans take any interesting pictures. And do not fail us! You remember what is at stake, kaffir?"

Sibena's recorded voice dropped to a strained whisper. "I remember, *baas*."

"See that you do." The connection ended in a low buzzing hum.

Ian reached out and snapped the tape recorder off. Then he turned to look at Matthew Sibena.

The young black man sat crumpled in his chair, his face buried in his hands. Low moans and sobs emerged in time with his shaking shoulders. Ian felt sick.

He knelt beside Sibena. "Why, Matt? Tell me why you're working for these people. I know you hate them. So what hold do they have over you?"

Slowly, very slowly, Ian coaxed the whole story out between the young man's tear-choked coughs.

Like the parents of most black children growing up in Soweto's slums during the 1970s, Sibena's father and mother hadn't been able to keep paying the fees for his schooling. As a result, he'd gone to work just after turning fourteen—taking mostly odd jobs whenever and wherever he could find them. Few lasted long or paid a living wage.

Then, as South Africa's economy continued its long, slow slide toward collapse, Sibena found it increasingly difficult to get work of any sort. He had few salable skills—the ability to drive a car, to read and write, and to run a cash register, nothing much more. And he was too small and too weak to be seriously considered for any job in the Witwatersrand gold mines outside Johannesburg.

Finally, out of money and down on his luck, he'd drifted into petty thievery. Nothing serious and certainly nothing violent. Just small burglaries of untenanted rooms in white-run hotels or the glove compartments of parked cars. Sibena had existed that way for months—operating in the narrow fringe between legality and Soweto's organized criminal gangs.

And then he'd been caught breaking into a locked car. But the Afrikaner officers who'd arrested him hadn't taken him before a magistrate. Instead, he'd been hauled into a police barracks, savagely beaten, and told to choose one of two unpalatable alternatives—either work for the security services as a paid informer, or be sent to the rock-breaking, man-killing prison on Robben Island off South Africa's coast.

To his eternal shame, Matthew Sibena had chosen the role of police spy. Monitoring Ian and Knowles's activities while serving as their driver had been his first and only assignment.

Ian rocked back on his heels, considering his next move.

Sibena's story was an ugly one, but it was pretty much what he'd expected to hear. South Africa's police forces weren't famed for either their subtlety or their sensitivity.

"What will you do to me now that you know what I have done?" Sibena's voice quavered.

Ian felt a sudden surge of anger toward the bastards who'd turned Sibena into the weak and fearful young man cowering before him. He shook his head impatiently, fighting to conceal his anger. The kid would only think it was aimed at him.

He looked Sibena squarely in the eyes. "Nothing, Matt. We won't do a thing to you."

"Truly?"

Ian nodded. "Truly."

He paused, casting about for the best way to make his offer. Finally, he got up off his knees and pulled another folding chair over so that he could sit on the same level as Sibena. "But I would like you to make a decision, Matt, a difficult decision."

The young man flinched. He'd heard white men offering him tough choices before.

Ian saw the panic in the other man's eyes and shook his head. "No, Matt. This isn't like what those goddamned cops put you through." Jesus, I hope that's true, he thought.

Ian took a deep breath, unable to escape the feeling that he was about to bet his life savings on a single roll of the dice. "All I want to do, Matthew Sibena, is ask for your help—as one man to another.

"If you don't want to do what I'm asking, just say so. Sam and I will drop what we're planning and carry on as before—and you're welcome to keep making your reports to the police." He sat forward, keeping his eyes fixed on Sibena's face. "But I'll tell you this much for now. I think we're on the edge of a damn big story—a story that could blow the lid off this whole blasted country and tear the guts out of the Vorster government."

Sibena stared at him without saying anything.

Ian lowered his voice until it was just above a whisper. "We need your help, Matt. We need you to keep the security services off our backs while we ferret out the truth.'' He looked down at the floor and then back up. ''I won't lie to you. I can't promise you that we'll succeed. I can't promise you that even if we do it'll really help make life better here in South Africa. And I sure as hell can't promise you that we'll be able to protect you from the police if things go wrong—or even if they go right.''

Silence. A silence that dragged on for what seemed like hours but couldn't possibly have been more than seconds.

At last, Sibena sat up straight on his metal chair. His eyes were red rimmed, but they carried a new look of determination and of purpose. ''I will try, *meneer*. God help me, for I am a weak man, but I will try.''

Ian held out his hand and waited until Sibena shook it—tentatively at first and then with vigor. They were committed.

OCTOBER 22—THE CASCADES HOTEL, SUN CITY, BOPHUTHATSWANA

Sun City was surrounded by a vast expanse of the highveld —a barren plain of brown, withered grasslands, isolated groves of stunted scrub trees, and small, ramshackle villages. Bophuthatswana's poverty made the sight of the resort town even more startling. It was an oasis of wealth, privilege, and pleasure in the midst of an arid, sun-baked wilderness.

The resort area's hotel and casino complex rose around the paved shoreline of a sparkling, sky-blue artificial lake. Hundreds of picture windows gleamed in the summer sunlight—opening onto wide terraces full of greenery and purple-blossomed jacaranda trees. Outside the hotel, sprinkler systems swiveled to and fro, spraying a fine mist of fresh water over manicured lawns, towering palm trees, and an eighteen-hole golf course.

On the inside, though, the Cascades Hotel and Casino was abnormally quiet, almost lifeless. Most of the young South African men who normally frequented its slot machines, blackjack tables, and roulette wheels were off fighting in

Namibia, the Natal, or the country's black townships. And there were few foreign tourists arriving to replace them during these troubled times.

Ian and Emily sat restlessly in a small bar adjacent to the hotel's main lobby. Two untouched glasses of white wine warmed to room temperature on the table between them. With difficulty, Ian stopped himself from checking his watch for what seemed the thousandth time. Muller was already much later than they'd expected him to be. Had something gone wrong? Had the South African security chief canceled or postponed his meeting?

Ian felt cold sweat beading on his forehead. They'd only have one opportunity to pull off a stunt like this, and if the Afrikaner intelligence man didn't show tonight, they'd have to rethink everything from square one. He twisted around again to check the lobby. Nothing. No sign of the damned man.

In a brief puff of warm air, the automatic doors leading outside slid open and then closed behind a single lean, wasp-waisted man carrying a tan overnight bag slung over his shoulder. Ian started suddenly. He'd studied the few available file photos long enough to recognize the narrow, arrogant face and pale blue eyes of South Africa's director of military intelligence. Erik Muller had arrived.

The South African strode confidently across the lobby and stood waiting in front of the Cascades' teak registration desk. Seconds later, the hotel's main door slid open again and Sam Knowles ambled in and got in line behind Muller—acting like any other travel-weary tourist eager for his chance at the swimming pool and gaming tables. The cameraman rocked back and forth on the balls of his feet, shifted impatiently, looked at his watch, and then started whistling.

Ian held his breath as Muller turned round to look for the source of the disagreeable, off-key noise. Shut up, Sam, for God's sake, shut up, Ian thought desperately. But the South African simply ran his cold, hard eyes over the shorter man, taking in Knowles's open-collared green sports shirt, pleated plaid trousers, and white shoes. Then he scowled and turned back to the desk clerk to finish checking in—having evidently dismissed the American as nothing more than the annoying buffoon he appeared to be.

With a curt nod, Muller took his room key from the clerk, waved away the offer of a bellman's services, and vanished in the direction of the elevators without looking back. Ian heaved a sigh of relief and waited while his cameraman finished registering and sauntered across the lobby into the bar.

Knowles plopped onto a chair next to Emily and across from Ian. "The bugger signed in as Hans Meinert and they put him in Room three thirty-five." Then he grinned, dangling an oversize room key from his hand. "And we're in three thirty-seven—right next door."

Ian matched his grin. "And just how the hell did you manage that?"

Knowles shrugged. "The same way you get anything special in one of these swanky hotels—a kind word and a hundred-rand gratuity tucked in your registration card."

Ian chuckled and took the room key out of Knowles's outstretched hand. Then he stood up to go. They were as ready as they could ever be.

Room 337 overlooked Sun City's central artificial lake and swimming pool. A handful of elderly couples strolled along the tree-lined edge of the lake, enjoying the cool early-evening air. Lights were coming on all over the quiet compound, triggered into action by the gathering darkness. It all seemed too peaceful to be part of the South Africa Ian had seen so much of over the past few months.

He turned and looked at the two very different men waiting inside the room with him. Matthew Sibena sat bolt upright in a chair facing a small writing desk, his face a rigid mask of nervousness and underlying fear. Sam Knowles, on the other hand, seemed completely at ease—lounging carelessly on the room's queen-size bed beside a closed soft-sided suitcase.

Knowles looked up from his paperback. "You realize we're gonna look mighty stupid if this ANC mole you're expecting comes straight to Muller's room?"

Ian nodded without saying anything. That was a risk they'd

just have to take. Not that he believed there was much chance it would happen. Muller was too professional to bring a field agent to his hotel room without first making sure that the man hadn't been followed. No, the odds were that the South African would leave his room to make the initial rendezvous—returning only when he was certain it was safe. But Ian was betting that Muller's main business with his mole would be transacted inside the hotel room itself. The casinos were too noisy and too public. And the landscaped grounds outside were too quiet and too open for a clandestine meeting.

The sound of the door next to theirs opening and shutting brought them all to their feet. Muller was on his way. Ian moved to the phone and stood waiting, annoyed to find that his palms were damp. Seconds passed one by one, turning into minutes with agonizing slowness. Come on.

The phone rang. He grabbed it in midring. "Yes."

"He's outside. Walking toward the Entertainment Centre." Emily sounded breathless—frightened and excited all at the same time.

"Great. You know what to do if you see him coming back?"

"Yes." Emily's voice fell to a low, husky whisper. "Be careful. Please be very careful."

Ian swallowed past a throat grown suddenly tight. "We will, believe me. And stay out of sight yourself . . . got it?"

He waited until he heard her murmured acknowledgment and then hung up.

Knowles and Sibena were already lined up by the door. Ian edged past them and opened it just a crack—just far enough to glance down the long, carpeted hallway in either direction. It was empty.

Four quick strides put him opposite the door to Room 335, with Sibena tagging along right behind. Suitcase in hand, Knowles followed more slowly, pausing to pull their own door shut.

Ian knocked once and listened carefully, hearing his own heartbeat pounding in his ears. Nothing from inside the room. He stepped back and let Sibena past. The young black man slipped a thick plastic card through the narrow gap between the door and the doorjamb and worked it back and forth—trying to force the lock. As he worked, his lips moved silently, either in prayer or in stifled curses.

Ian checked the corridor again, mentally willing Sibena to get the damned door open before somebody saw them. He wasn't sure what the penalties were in Bophuthatswana for breaking and entering, and he didn't want to find out the hard way.

Click. The sudden noise seemed horribly loud over the soft, hushed hum of the hotel's air-conditioning. Sibena stuck the plastic card back in his pocket with a trembling hand and pushed in on the door. It moved, and they were in. Thank God.

Ian led the way into a room identical to their own. A large bed, writing table, lamps, a chest of drawers, television, telephone, and a private bath. All the comforts of modern civilization. Muller had closed his drapes, shutting out the view of the lake and landscaped grounds. Naturally. The paranoid bastard was probably afraid that he might be seen and recognized.

Knowles moved immediately to the wall shared by their adjoining room. He stopped near the drape-cloaked window and started tapping along the wall, listening intently for the hollow sounds of an area free of supporting beams. Satisfied, he swung round and started panning around the room with his arms outstretched and hands held apart—mimicking the field of view available to a video camera. "This'll do."

Ian handed him a small portable power drill from the suitcase.

Knowles thumbed the drill onto its highest setting and pressed the whining, spinning drill bit firmly against the wall. Fiberboard particles, sawdust, and fragments of insulation puffed out into the air and settled slowly onto the thick carpet. In seconds, the drill bored a tiny hole through the wall between their two rooms. A hole scarcely large enough to be seen, but just large enough to take a thin, flexible light tube hooked up to a VCR.

Ian glanced down at his watch. They'd been in the room for three minutes. It hardly seemed possible. It felt more like three years.

Knowles backed the power drill out of the hole and moved along the wall, tapping again, this time closer to the door.

Ian raised an eyebrow. "We need another lead into here?"

His cameraman nodded, still tapping away. "Uh-huh. One thing you can always count on: if you've only got one camera angle, some dumb bastard's sure to be facing the wrong damned way. Ah. There we go." He pulled his ear away and thumbed the drill on for a second time. "This'll give us coverage over the whole room. No blind spots except for the john."

More shredded fiberboard and sawdust drifted onto the carpet. Ian tried to calm his nerves by concentrating on catching every bit of the debris with a small portable vacuum cleaner.

Five and a half minutes down. Sibena stood fidgeting near the bathroom, afraid to move and too nervous to stand completely still.

Ian squinted at the wall, trying to judge just how obvious their spyholes were. Not very, he decided. Even knowing exactly where they were, he had a hard time spotting them.

Finally, Knowles finished and stepped away from his handiwork. "All set, bossman." He dropped the drill back inside his suitcase and zipped it shut.

"Terrific." Ian climbed to his feet, brushed a few stray particles of fiberboard off his knees, and headed for the door. Whoops. Idiot. He stopped so suddenly that both Knowles and Sibena cannoned into him.

"What the fu—" The little cameraman bit back the rest.

"Forgot to do something." Ian brushed past them and went straight to the queen-size bed. Working rapidly, he pulled the covers off the pillows on one side and tucked them back neatly. Then he scooped two foil-wrapped mint chocolates out of his shirt pocket and set them carefully on the top pillow.

It was Sam Knowles's turn to look surprised.

"Emily's idea." Ian gestured toward the door. "In case Muller had any telltales rigged to see if somebody came snooping when he was out. You know, hairs stuck in the door and that kind of stuff.''

Knowles smiled. ''So now all he'll know is that the maid came in and turned down his bed for him. Cute. Real cute.'' The smile grew into a full-fledged grin. ''It's no wonder that you and this Miss van der Heijden make such a perfect couple, boyo. You're both as sneaky as they come under those goody two-shoes exteriors. By God, it makes me proud to know you both.''

Ian laughed softly and pushed him out the door. ''Save the bullshit for later, Sam. We've still got a lot of work to do before Muller gets back here with his little friend from the ANC.''

Half an hour later they were completely ready. Two video monitors flickered in opposite corners of their room—each showing a different view of Muller's empty hotel room. And though the pictures coming back through the light tubes were grainy and dim, they were acceptable. Digital enhancement on the studio's computer-imaging system could remove any blurring and brighten anything too dark to be clearly seen.

Without breaking back into Muller's room, Knowles couldn't do a sound check, but he was confident that they'd be able to pick up enough audio. And if need be, the computer could be used to enhance voices, too.

Ian paced back and forth, glancing at the monitors from time to time. They were set. Now where was Muller? Had he decided to hold his secret meeting somewhere else in Sun City after all?

The phone rang. He jumped over a tangle of cabling and picked it up on the second ring. ''Hello?''

Emily's soft voice caressed his ear. ''He's back. And he's not alone. There is a black man with him.''

Yes! Ian couldn't hold back a small whoop of triumph. He'd guessed right. ''Wait until they're in the elevator and then come on up. You won't want to miss this.''

''I certainly don't.'' A faint trace of doubt warred with the joy in Emily's voice. ''But the other man seems awfully young to be someone of high rank in the ANC, Ian.''

He shrugged and then remembered she couldn't see him. "I've heard that some of their guerrillas start training as young as fourteen. And some of those kids throwing rocks in Soweto are even younger."

"Perhaps . . ." She paused and then came back on the line. "They're in the lift. I'm on my way."

The phone went dead.

Ian turned to his companions. "It's showtime, guys."

Knowles squatted by his equipment, hastily making one last check through slitted eyes. Sibena sat carefully in a chair facing the monitors, much calmer and obviously fascinated by the ease and assurance with which the American handled his high-tech gear.

Motion on one of the monitors caught Ian's attention and he saw the door to Muller's room swing open. Muller himself entered, followed by a very short, very skinny black youth. Despite his earlier words to Emily, Ian was puzzled. Though it was tough to tell for sure from the flickering, grainy picture, Muller's companion didn't look as though he could possibly be more than sixteen or seventeen years old.

A light, hesitant tap on the door to their room brought him to his feet. Emily came in through the half-opened door, gave him a quick kiss, and sat on the bed—all the while staring at the scene unfolding in the next room. Ian joined her.

Muller could be seen standing near the chest of drawers, apparently counting out pieces of paper into the young black man's outstretched hand. Ian squinted at the wavering picture, trying to make out the details. Were those pieces of paper money? Probably. The Afrikaner must be paying for more information on the ANC's operations.

But he didn't like the expression on Muller's narrow face—an odd mixture of contempt, self-loathing, and something even stranger. Something very strange indeed. Was it anticipation?

Apparently satisfied, the other man abruptly nodded and fumbled the thick wad of rand notes into his pants pockets. He muttered something indistinct.

Muller spoke for the first time. "No words, kaffir!"

Shit. Ian leaned forward, suddenly anxious. Could the South African intelligence officer have spotted one of their camera leads after all? He started to turn toward Knowles to ask . . .

And Muller erupted into action, viciously smashing a clenched fist into the young black man's stomach. As the kid doubled over in agony, the Afrikaner followed up with a short, stabbing jab to the face. Other blows landed in rapid succession, driving the young man down onto the carpet in a crumpled, groaning heap. Blood spattered from his broken nose and cut lower lip.

For a second, Ian sat still, shocked into immobility. Then he was on his feet and moving toward the door. This wasn't what he'd thought to see, and he'd be damned if they'd sit idly by and watch this murdering bastard Muller beat some poor kid half to death. To hell with the reporter's role as impartial observer! Sam Knowles was right behind him.

But Emily got there first and stood blocking the door. Her face was deathly pale but determined.

"Let me past, Em." Ian could feel the adrenaline roaring through his bloodstream.

"No." She shook her head firmly. "We've come too far to throw this chance away on a gallant whim. Trying to help that poor boy in there will only result in our deaths or imprisonment. You know that Muller is far more than a simple thug. We must follow your original plan."

"And besides, the kid's just a black anyway, is that it?" For the first time, Ian found himself wondering how much of the Afrikaner racial beliefs Emily had unconsciously absorbed.

She colored angrily. "That is not fair, Ian Sherfield, and you know it!"

Knowles cleared his throat. "I think she's right, boyo. We're playing for big stakes here. Bigger than what happens to any one person."

Ian glowered from one to the other. Knowing that they were both right didn't make it any easier to contemplate doing nothing as they watched Muller indulge his private sadism.

"Oh, my God . . ." Matthew Sibena's horrified whisper yanked their attention back to the scene still being played out on the video monitors.

The beating had stopped as suddenly as it had started. Now the young black man lay curled in a fetal position on the floor, moaning pitiably through a bruised throat. One eye was already swelling shut. And Muller, so full of rage a moment before, now knelt beside him, softly caressing his battered face!

Ian felt his stomach heave as the Afrikaner bent down and kissed the young black's torn lips, smearing the other man's blood over his own face. He felt cold. This couldn't be happening!

Through ears that seemed stuffed full of cotton, he heard Emily muttering to herself. "Of course, now I see it. The defrocked minister. Poor dead Gabriel Tswane. October twenty-second. It all fits. This is like a ritual for him. . . . Oh, how stupid of me!"

Ian couldn't look away from the monitors long enough to ask her what she meant. His image captured by both hidden cameras, Muller lifted the black teenager in his arms and carried him over to the bed. Then the Afrikaner stepped back and started unbuttoning his shirt.

God . . . Ian looked away, feeling sick. They'd failed. All their hard work and all their hopeful planning—all for nothing. No ANC mole. No truth about the Blue Train massacre. Nothing. Just a sordid, anonymous homosexual encounter. Just another dead end.

He turned back to the monitors. Muller had all his clothes off now. He grimaced. "Shut it down, Sam. We don't need to see any more."

"No. Leave the cameras on."

Ian looked at Emily, astounded by the stern, grim note in her voice. "C'mon, Em. Why waste more time here? We can't use this"—he gestured toward the bodies writhing on the twin screens—"this pornography."

She shook her head stubbornly. "Yes, we can. We must."

His face must have shown his confusion because she went on, "That man and his master, Vorster, knew of the ANC's plans in advance. They must have! Nothing else could explain what has happened to my nation.''

''Agreed.'' Ian spread his hands. ''But how did they know? And how do we prove it?''

Emily stared off into space for a moment and then snapped her fingers. ''The attack on Gawamba!''

Gawamba? Of course! Ian felt his excitement returning, along with a healthy dose of humility. The truth had been sitting right there in front of him all the time. He'd known that the ANC base inside Zimbabwe had been an important command center—a place where guerrilla operations inside South Africa were planned and supervised. Precisely the kind of place where you'd expect to find documents describing upcoming missions—missions such as the scheduled attack on South Africa's president and his cabinet.

And the South African paratroops who'd blown the shit out of Gawamba must have found those plans. Plans that had gone straight back to Erik Muller without passing through any of the normal SADF intelligence channels.

He frowned. The paratroops had to have removed the information without leaving a trace or else the ANC would simply have canceled the whole operation. Was that possible? He shook his head irritably. It must have been possible. Nothing else fit the facts.

But again, how could they prove it? Nobody in the world would believe the story without seeing some kind of evidence. And nobody connected with such treachery would ever dare admit it. He said as much to Emily.

She nodded toward the monitors. ''Erik Muller will prove it for us. I'm sure he has copies of those documents still. As insurance should Vorster find a new favorite.'' Contempt sharpened her words. ''So it is simple. We will use these videotapes to force him to give us those documents.''

Blackmail. An ugly word and an uglier idea. He hadn't become a journalist to twist people's hidden weaknesses and vices against them. Catching Erik Muller conferring with a South African spy inside the ANC leadership was one thing. Using the man's strange sexual preferences against him was quite another. Ian stared at her.

Emily was implacable. "I loathe the idea as much as you do, Ian. But it is what we must do. We have no choice." For an instant, her self-control slipped and her voice wavered. "Please . . . my whole nation is being destroyed before my eyes. Thousands are already dead and thousands more will die. And all because of monsters like that!" She pointed a shaking finger toward the closest screen.

Her voice sank, falling to a soft, sad whisper. "What choice do we truly have, Ian? We have been given a tool that could help put an end to all this madness. How can we refuse to use it?" Tears rolled down her cheeks. "How can we? No matter how it taints our own souls with its evil."

Without thinking, he reached out and took her in his arms, stroking her soft, sweet-smelling hair as she sobbed quietly. Over her shoulder, he saw the twinned images of Muller and his catamite writhing on the hotel bed. She was right. They didn't have any choice.

He stared grimly into the video monitors. Very well. They'd find out just how this bastard Erik Muller would react to the threat of having his secret sins laid out for all to see —to the threat of full exposure.

CHAPTER 17

Retaliation

OCTOBER 24—DIRECTORATE OF MILITARY INTELLIGENCE, PRETORIA

Erik Muller stared at the television screen in horror. What had seemed so natural—so wonderful—in that Sun City hotel room looked so sordid and depraved when seen on videotape. He shivered uncontrollably, feeling both feverishly hot and ice-cold at the same time. His worst nightmare had come to life and shown itself in broad daylight.

The tape had been delivered to his office earlier in the day—enclosed in an unsealed manila envelope and marked only by a typed card specifying that it was "personal and confidential." His idiotic secretary could remember nothing beyond the fact that it had been dropped off by a courier from one of the city's many delivery services.

As Muller watched, the grainy, half-lit black-and-white images vanished, replaced by a buzzing, static-filled test pattern that showed the tape was over. He sat motionless for several minutes, feeling sick and completely unable to summon up the energy needed to reach over and shut off the

VCR. His thoughts were far away, reaching back over time to the moment when surrendering to his physical needs had laid him open to this treacherous attack. Who could have known? And what did they want—his death or disgrace, or something else entirely?

Muller fumbled for the receiver as his phone rang. "Yes?"

"A call for you, Director. Something about that videotape."

He tried to suck in air and failed. The monster of darkness and blood he had feared for so long and so long denied had come for its payment at last. The monster he himself had created. And now death or worse stared him full in the face.

"Director?"

Through a roaring in his ears, Muller heard his own voice answer—a voice made harsher by unsuppressed panic. "Put the call through."

A new voice came on the line. A woman's voice speaking fluent Afrikaans. "Director Muller?"

"What do you want?"

"Copies of the documents seized by your special intelligence team during the commando attack on Gawamba." The woman paused briefly. "The documents revealing the ANC's intention to attack our president's train."

The Blue Train? Muller hadn't thought it possible that anything else could shock him. He suddenly realized that he'd been wrong. Dead wrong. An unexpectedly analytical part of his brain evaluated the woman's choice of words and decided that she was educated and probably a native-born Afrikaans speaker.

He tried playing for time. "I don't know what documents you are talking about. No such papers exist."

The woman's words were cold and uncompromising. "That's a great pity, Meneer Muller. Then I'm very much afraid that the videotape of your 'indiscretion' will find its way into the hands of your superiors."

Muller gripped the phone tighter, feeling dizzy as his office seemed to swirl around him. Time. He needed more time to consider his options.

She dashed any hope of finding that time. "You have ten

seconds, *meneer*. If I hear nothing from you by then, I will ring off—and the matter will be out of my hands."

The bitch! Muller sagged back in his chair. Whoever these blackmailers were, they had him in an unshakable grip. He had no illusions about how Karl Vorster would react to seeing his intelligence chief in bed with a black man.

He swallowed hard and croaked, "All right, damn you. I agree. You'll have the papers you want."

"An eminently sensible decision," the woman approved. "Now here is how the exchange will be made. At ten tonight, you will come alone to the . . ."

Muller jotted down her instructions with a shaking hand and then sat motionless holding the phone for long minutes after she'd hung up. His mind wandered back and forth, figuratively tugging at the bars of the cage in which he found himself. There seemed to be no way out—no exit that did not lead to inevitable disaster. Either he betrayed his leader or he betrayed himself. Unless . . .

Muller looked down at his notes. For all the cool, calm professionalism shown by the woman who'd called, the rendezvous site and procedures she'd outlined displayed a certain amateur touch. An amateurishness that might let him evade the noose he already felt tightening around his neck.

He made a decision and dialed a three-digit internal number. Even a slim chance of survival was better than none.

NETWORK STUDIOS, JOHANNESBURG

Four people crowded the cubbyhole that served as Ian Sherfield's Johannesburg office. Emily van der Heijden and Sam Knowles sat in a pair of chairs in front of his desk and Matthew Sibena stood behind them, still appearing faintly scandalized that the cameraman had offered him his seat. The notion that white men might actually regard him as an equal partner still seemed impossible for the young man to comprehend fully.

Ian glanced at his watch. Two hours to go before their scheduled meeting with Erik Muller.

Their gear for the night's outing stood in a separate pile on his desk. A pair of walkie-talkies, binoculars, the videotape, a small pen flashlight, and a set of keys to the car Emily had rented under a phony name. Not much to challenge one of the leaders of South Africa's state security services.

He unfolded a tattered city map showing Johannesburg and its surrounding suburbs. "Okay, here's how we'll run this show tonight. The three of you will follow me out to the site in our pool car. Make sure you stop a couple hundred meters or so away and stay out of sight." He circled an area around the map. "Probably about here—near the N-three interchange. From there you could make a quick getaway onto either the expressway or Lombardy Link if this stunt doesn't work out the way we planned."

He pointed to the walkie-talkies. "We'll use these to stay in touch. See any problems?"

Knowles nodded vigorously. "You bet I do. One big one. You can't be the guy who makes contact with Muller."

"Why the hell not?" Ian winced at the way that came out. Sounding like a petulant child wasn't the way to win arguments with either Emily or Sam Knowles.

The other man jabbed a finger at his face. "Your ugly mug is why, boyo. You're the on-camera talent in our little team. Odds are that this bastard's even seen one or two of your censored reports. You show up tonight trying to exchange dirty videos for secret papers and *whammo*"—he smacked his hands together—"we're all heading for jail and a bullet in the back of the neck."

Emily chimed in, "Sam is right, Ian. I will go in your place. Muller has heard my voice before anyway."

Knowles shook his head. "Nope. That's no good either."

Now it was Emily's turn to sound like a child deprived of its favorite toy. "And why not, Mr. Knowles?"

The cameraman smiled mirthlessly. " 'Cause our boy's just as likely to have seen your picture before, too. Your dad's his number one enemy inside the government, right?"

Emily frowned and then nodded reluctantly.

"So there's really only one person who can do this . . . and that's me." Knowles tapped himself on the chest.

Sibena cleared his throat and spoke, looking frightened but strangely determined. "That is not quite so, Sam. I could go in your place."

Knowles turned sideways in his chair to look the young black man in the face. "I'm afraid not, Matt. Muller's not only a bastard and a thug, he's a racist bastard and a thug. I doubt if he'd ever agree to hand anything important over to you."

Damn it. Ian clenched his hands below the level of his desk. Much as he hated to admit it, Knowles was absolutely, undeniably right. He was the only one of the four of them who had any chance at all of successfully pulling off this clandestine swap. Besides, the South African intelligence chief had already had a glimpse of Knowles once before in his guise as an annoying American tourist back at the Cascades Hotel. Letting him see Knowles again wouldn't expose them to any additional risk.

He swore one more time under his breath before looking up and catching his friend's eye. "All right, Sam, you win. You'll be the one who gets to go pick up our prize."

Ian just hoped there really was a prize for Knowles to collect.

MADDERFONTEIN MUNICIPAL REFUSE DUMP, JUST OUTSIDE JOHANNESBURG

A chain link fence surrounded the Madderfontein Municipal Refuse Dump, enclosing mounds of broken furniture, rusting food tins, old tires, and all the other assorted scraps left by a wealthy civilization. A flat, featureless plain stretched northeast beyond the dump—a plain marked only by scattered small reservoirs and the distant, floodlit smokestacks of the Klipfontein Organic Products Factory.

To the west, a multilane highway, the N3 Motor Route, paralleled the dump. Glaring headlights revealed traffic moving north and south along the highway at high speed. To the east, only a few of Madderfontein's separate, single-family homes showed dim lights glowing from behind drawn curtains. And barely one in three of the suburb's streetlamps were lit, leaving dark pools of shadow at regular intervals.

A battered Ford Escort sat idling quietly in one of the patches of darkness—parked near a collection of scarred and rusting trash haulers and maintenance sheds used by the refuse dump's work force. A man and a woman stood on either side of the Escort, their attention riveted on a car two hundred meters farther down the road.

Ian adjusted the focus on his binoculars, trying to make out more than the faint silvery outline of Knowles's rented Mercedes as it sat under one of the few lit streetlamps. Nothing, damn it. The stretch of two-lane road running alongside the garbage dump was just too dark.

On the other side of the Escort, Emily stirred as the walkie-talkie she held in her hand crackled into life.

"You guys awake? I think we've got company. Coming off the freeway . . ."

Ian swiveled his binoculars right, scanning the exit ramp. There. The twin headlights of another car moving off the highway, fast at first but visibly slowing. He nodded abruptly. It had to be Muller.

Emily pressed the talk button. "We see it, Sam. We're ready."

Ready. Sure they were, Ian thought bitterly. He'd had two hours to think of all the things that could go wrong with this secretive exchange. Two hours to realize just how much trouble they could be in if Muller didn't come through with his end of the bargain or tried to double-cross them.

The other car, a Jaguar, turned left off the ramp and pulled alongside Knowles's Mercedes.

Emily's walkie-talkie crackled again.

"It's him. I can see him through the windshield." Knowles sounded calm, with only the clipped endings of his words revealing any anxiety. Static hissed over the radio. "He's rolling his window down. Stand by."

Ian tensed and stared hard through the binoculars. No good. He still couldn't see anything but the bare shapes of the two parked cars. Seconds passed, dragging first into one minute and then into two. He could hear Emily whispering what he suspected was a prayer.

"I'm back. Did you miss me?" Beneath the banter, both of them could hear the relief in the cameraman's voice. "Transaction completed. Looks good so far."

Thank God. Ian felt his back and neck muscles starting to unknot.

Muller's Jaguar pulled out from the curb, turned left again, and rolled away down the dimly lit Lombardy Link—heading for the ramp leading back onto the highway. Ian followed the Jag with his binoculars until it vanished among the stream of other cars and trucks moving north to Pretoria. He turned and nodded to Emily.

She pressed the talk button again. "It's clear, Sam."

"Far out! I'm on my way. Get ready to pop the champagne corks, 'cause it looks like little Mrs. Knowles's boy has hit the frigging jackpot this time! Names. Dates. The whole schmear!"

Ian laughed aloud, caught up in Knowles's infectious enthusiasm.

Two hundred meters down the road, the Mercedes shifted gears and turned through a smooth half-circle to end up moving straight at them. Ian bent closer to the Escort's open driver's-side window. "We're almost ready to head for home, Matt. No fuss and no muss."

Sibena smiled up at him from behind the wheel.

Suddenly the Mercedes braked and came to a complete stop while still twenty meters away.

Emily thumbed the walkie-talkie button. "What's wrong, Sam? Why have you stopped?"

Knowles sounded puzzled. "I'm not really sure. There's something rattling around in the back. I'm going to check it out. Hang on for a sec." They both heard the click as his car door opened.

The Mercedes blew up in a spectacular rolling, billowing ball of fire—throwing pieces of glass, shards of metal, and shreds of rubber high into the air. For a split second, the explosion turned the night inside out—lighting up the surrounding landscape as though it were day.

Before the flash faded away, a roaring wall of superheated air knocked Ian off his feet and rolled him hard against the Escort's underbody. From the other side of the car, Emily cried out in terror as the shock wave threw her to the ground. Fragments pattered down all around, spanging off the Escort's chassis and starring its windshield in half a dozen places.

Then, as suddenly as it had come, the noise of the explosion died away—leaving only a crackling roar as the Mercedes burned. Ian and Emily climbed shakily to their feet and stared in horror at the flames leaping high into the night sky.

Sam Knowles was gone, and the evidence of Vorster's treachery had gone with him.

ALONG THE N3 MOTOR ROUTE, NORTH OF JOHANNESBURG

Erik Muller pulled onto the shoulder and braked sharply. Then he slid out from behind the wheel of his Jaguar and got out to smile in satisfaction at the funeral pyre blazing brightly to the south. He stood watching the flames with his hands planted squarely on his hips. Good riddance. The mind-numbing fear that had been his constant companion since he'd first seen the videotape was already vanishing.

A dark-colored sedan turned off the highway and halted ten meters behind his car. Its driver's-side door popped open and a tall, burly man clambered out. He glanced briefly at the fiery glow staining the southern sky and then trudged through the loose gravel until he stood before Muller.

"A fine job, Reynders. Very professional. I'll see that you get a commendation for this night's work." Muller resisted the temptation to pat the taller man on the shoulder.

Field Agent Paul Reynders acknowledged the compliment with a brief, almost bored nod. In truth, it hadn't been a terribly difficult or even interesting mission. The heaped mounds of trash had provided more than a dozen perfect hiding places within easy reach of what he had been told was an ANC agent's parked car.

He frowned. "There was another car, Director, with two

or three occupants. But no one else.'' Reynders shrugged. ''Definitely amateurs. I detected no signs of any other backups or surveillance teams.''

He glanced again at the fire still burning fiercely. ''I hadn't expected the second car, but I changed the timer to catch it inside the blast as well. We should have no more problems with these spies.'' He said it flatly, absolutely convinced that he spoke the truth.

Unfortunately for Erik Muller, Reynders couldn't have been more mistaken.

NETWORK STUDIOS, JOHANNESBURG

The studio's offices, workrooms, and broadcast facilities lay wrapped in silence and darkness—apparently utterly empty, abandoned for the night by a fast-shrinking American staff. Even the South African security guards who normally patrolled the hallways guarding valuable electronic gear were safe at home in bed.

The lights flickered on in the main editing room and stayed on—revealing banks of racked VCRs, monitors, reel-to-reel machines, and the squat, white-cased shape of the studio's computerized-imaging system. Ian shut the door leading into the main hallway and sagged back against the wall. ''We're clear.''

Emily looked up at him, her cheeks still stained by new-dried tears. ''For now.''

''Yeah. For now.'' Ian rubbed angrily at a smear of ground-in dirt from the road on his own face. It served as a grim reminder of the night's disaster. ''But when the police identify Sam's body and trace that car, they'll be down on us like a ton of bricks.''

Images of the burning Mercedes and of Muller's car speeding away to safety flashed into his mind and he slammed his fists into the wall, making both Emily and Matthew Sibena jump. ''Goddamnit! I should have known! I should have known that bastard was giving in too easily!''

He took a deep breath, fighting for control. ''We have a

day or so before things really start to cave in. Sam wasn't carrying any ID tonight.'' He looked somberly at Emily and Sibena. ''I'll call my friend at the embassy. He should be able to rig up some kind of temporary papers for the two of you. With luck, we can be on a plane out of this fucking country before they start looking for us.''

Sibena nodded gratefully, but Emily turned away without saying anything. She moved to the console where Knowles had spent so many of his waking hours splicing and resplicing tapes, bringing structure and theme out of a confusion of recorded sights and sounds.

Ian watched her quietly, praying that her Afrikaner stubborn streak wasn't about to erupt. They'd gambled and lost. Now it was time to back away before any more of them lost their lives. He felt his hands ball into fists. Damn. He didn't want to leave either. He wanted to nail Muller's head on a pole—personally. But there was a world of difference between wanting something and being able to make it happen.

''Ian!'' Emily's voice sliced through his increasingly morose thoughts. ''Look at this!''

She held out a single sheet of notepaper. ''I found it there.'' She pointed to a pile of videocassettes stacked neatly atop the computer casing.

He recognized Knowles's sloppy, almost illegible handwriting. ''Some extra copies of the hotel hijinks . . . just in case the creep cheats. Get him for me.'' Tears blurred his vision until he blinked them away. The little cameraman had known he might not come back, and he'd still gone through with it.

Emily touched his arm. ''We can't abandon this, Ian. It would mean that Sam's death was for nothing.''

He took her by the hand and looked deep into her eyes. ''Believe me, I don't want to give up. It's just that I can't see any way left for us to get those damned documents without getting killed.''

She started to nod and then stopped abruptly, sudden excitement creeping in past her sadness. Ian had seen that look before.

"You've got an idea?"

Emily answered by tugging him over to where they'd tacked up a spare city map of Johannesburg. She pointed to the site they'd picked for their disastrous rendezvous. "Tell me, what was wrong with the area around Madderfontein?"

Reluctantly, Ian mentally ran through the painful, frightening sequence of events yet again. As always, hindsight operated with perfect 20/20 vision. "It was too empty, too deserted. We thought that'd help, but all it did was make it easy for Muller to zero in on us."

Emily nodded seriously and pointed at another spot on the map. "So if we try again, but here this time . . ." She paused significantly.

Ian followed her finger and sucked in his breath, beginning to understand what she had in mind.

Emily saw the comprehension dawning in his eyes and motioned Matthew Sibena closer. He was going to have to be a full partner from now on. "This is how I believe we should proceed. . . ."

Both Ian and Sibena listened with mounting respect and confidence as she outlined her idea for snatching the Gawamba-raid documents out from under Erik Muller's nose.

OCTOBER 25—DIRECTORATE OF MILITARY INTELLIGENCE, PRETORIA

The early-morning phone call ruined what had begun as a delightfully routine day.

"Your cowardly treachery failed, *meneer*."

Muller gripped the phone so hard that the blood drained out of his knuckles. That same cold, arrogant, demanding woman's voice! Damn that idiot Reynders! He'd failed.

"Several of my friends wanted to distribute the tape immediately—to the President, your cabinet colleagues, and other interested parties."

Muller shivered, imagining the gleeful reaction of his enemies and the hatred of his former allies if they ever saw those pornographic images. He licked suddenly dry lips. "Well?"

"You are a fortunate man, Meneer Muller." Her sarcasm bit deep. "I persuaded them to give you one last chance."

He felt a faint stirring of hope. The fools were going to give him another chance to destroy them! He pulled a thick booklet of street maps closer to him and picked up a pencil. "Where?"

The woman's instructions were, like her voice, clear, clinical, and painstakingly precise. Muller frowned at the notes he'd scribbled. Whoever these people were, they'd definitely learned a thing or two from their failure the night before. It wouldn't be so easy this time. He cleared his throat. "And what about the tape? When will I get this duplicate copy you claim to have?"

"You'll get the tape when we are satisfied that you've given us the real documents. Not before."

Muller grimaced. "And how do I know that I can trust you?"

This time the woman didn't bother concealing her contempt and her hatred. "You don't know, *meneer*. It's that simple." Her voice hardened. "Do not attempt to double-cross us again, boy lover. You won't get a third chance to save your neck."

The phone went dead in his ear.

JOHANNESBURG RAILWAY STATION

The platforms of the Johannesburg Railway Station were jammed with a sea of irritable black and white faces.

Despite the Vorster government's best repressive efforts, strict apartheid had proven impossible to reimpose on the city's overburdened public transportation system—at least during peak commuting hours. A flood tide of tens of thousands of black store clerks, janitors, and factory hands leaving Johannesburg for their Soweto hovels mingled with thousands of white businessmen and wealthy, bored housewives heading for home in the rich northern suburbs. There wasn't enough space under the train-station roof for the evening commute to be anything but a deafening, sweaty, milling madhouse.

The crowding made it impossible for the detachments of uniformed soldiers and police assigned to enforce order to do more than deter the most obvious kinds of crime or troublemaking. And they weren't trained or equipped to carry out covert surveillance operations.

In a word, Erik Muller thought sourly as he watched from the station manager's second-floor office, the security troops were useless. He adjusted the office's venetian blinds again, opening them a fraction more to get a better view of the main station concourse below.

The sight of the swirling crowds brought a scowl to his narrow face. The six agents he'd posted around the concourse were going to have a damned hard time keeping the drop point in view. He lifted the field glasses hanging from his neck and focused them on the trash bin near a central pillar.

The papers were still there, stuffed awkwardly between the bin and pillar—held together only by a thin rubber band. Something that bitch who'd called him had insisted on as a precaution against hidden explosives or tracking devices.

Muller swore as a sudden surge of black day laborers heading for an arriving train blocked his view of the drop point. He lowered his field glasses, impatiently waiting for the small mob to pass by.

When he looked again, the papers were gone. For an instant, Muller stiffened in shock. Then he whirled, looking for the black workers who'd just swarmed past the drop point. They were several meters farther on, pushing their way through the milling crowds to clamber aboard the closest train. Muller swore again. Every one of the blacks was carrying a lunch pail or shopping bag of some kind—perfect for concealing documents. As he watched, they mingled with a throng of white commuters moving in the opposite direction.

Muller dropped his field glasses and reached for the walkie-talkie hooked to his belt. "Captain, order your men to stop those blacks trying to board at Platform Two! Stop them and search them for stolen state security papers!''

Shrill whistles tore through the air and boots slammed rhythmically on the train station's concrete floor as a platoon of heavily armed soldiers jogged forward through the crowds and deployed along the edge of the platform. In seconds, they were in position—patting down men and women alike and poking rifles into bags and lunch pails with brisk, impersonal efficiency.

Muller allowed himself a brief, humorless smile. So there were blacks involved in this little conspiracy, eh? So much the better. He knew how to extract information from blacks. A half hour's work in a well-equipped interrogation center should give him the names of the other plotters. And with luck, he'd have them all swept away into oblivion before they had a chance to post that damning videotape.

But his smile faded as the search went on and on without any sign of success.

Two people passed through the station's sliding doors and emerged, blinking, into the late-afternoon sunlight. The first, a stylishly dressed young white woman, carried only a gleaming leather briefcase. The thin, young black man following five paces behind her strained under a heavy load—the bags and boxes that seemed to represent the fruits of a day-long shopping expedition.

The woman glanced back once at the station and then strode confidently across Joubert Street to the parked car waiting for her—a battered Ford Escort. The black chauffeur hurried ahead to open the rear door for her. She slid gracefully into the backseat and kissed the man already there.

Ian Sherfield gently disentangled himself and asked, "Well, did you get them?"

Emily van der Heijden smiled happily and pulled the sheaf of papers out of her brand-new briefcase. They had the last piece of the puzzle they needed. Muller and his master, Karl Vorster, were about to be exposed as men who'd betrayed their sacred oaths and their own people in a quest for power and position.

NETWORK STUDIOS, JOHANNESBURG

Ian finished his photocopying and laid the last sheet of paper to one side. "All set."

Emily looked up from her reading. She pushed a loose strand of hair away from her eyes and shook her head slowly from side to side. "My God, even though I had some idea of what to expect, I still can't believe it! They knew everything that would happen. The time. The place. Even the weapons and coded signals that would be used. Everything!"

Ian nodded grimly and slid his copies into a manila folder along with a videocassette.

"Your recorded narration?" Emily pointed to the tape.

He nodded again. "Yeah. It's just a rough cut. Sam was going to . . ." He faltered briefly before continuing, "Sam was going to do the final editing, but I'll have to leave that up to the guys in New York instead."

He shrugged into his jacket and picked up the manila folder. "I thought I'd better drop this off at the embassy so my friend there can send it out in tomorrow's diplomatic bag." He reached over for one of the two remaining tapes showing Muller's Sun City encounter. "I'll leave this for that bastard to find at the same time."

Emily narrowed her eyes. "Why give it to him at all? He murdered Sam and he would have murdered us if he'd had the chance."

Ian sighed. "I know. But we made a deal . . . and a deal's a deal, even if you're trading with the devil himself." He waggled the tape. "Besides, we've got what we wanted. And I'll be damned if I ever stoop low enough to really use something like this against anyone for real—even someone like that son of a bitch Muller."

Emily didn't say anything more as he leaned forward, kissed her, and left on his errands. Instead she sat quietly, thinking furiously. Ian was a good man. Too good, perhaps. His sense of honor wouldn't let him seek revenge against Erik Muller—not even after the man had killed his best friend. She wiped away tears that rose unbidden as she remembered Sam Knowles's always cheerful, ever-irreverent face.

At last, Emily shook her head and picked up the last remaining copy of the videotape. She couldn't let Muller's treachery pass unpunished.

She opened the phone book. Another of Johannesburg's many messenger services would soon be delivering a sealed package to the Ministry of Law and Order.

CHAPTER 18

End and Beginning

OCTOBER 27—DIRECTORATE OF MILITARY INTELLIGENCE, SPECIAL SECURITY OPERATIONS BRANCH, PRETORIA

Even with the air-conditioning off, the office felt cold. Erik Muller stared in disbelief at the police report sitting faceup on his desk. A combination of forensic medicine and dogged detective work had finally identified the dead man found in the bomb-mangled Mercedes.

Samuel Knowles. Age: thirty-seven. Citizenship: American. Profession: television news cameraman.

My God. The very magnitude of the disaster was stunning. It couldn't possibly be any worse. He'd given the ANC documents seized at Gawamba to American journalists! And they'd already had them for nearly forty-eight hours—two precious, uninterrupted days to smuggle the information they contained out of South Africa.

Disaster indeed. Even the country's whites were growing increasingly dissatisfied and disenchanted with the Vorster government. A costly foreign war, bloody internal rioting, and a moribund economy had all taken a heavy toll on Karl Vorster's popularity. For the most part, though, the white opposition had been confined to isolated, angry muttering or an occasional ineffective and easily crushed student demonstration. But all that was bound to change when the true story of the Blue Train massacre broke overseas.

Muller smiled mirthlessly. Most Afrikaners and other white South Africans would forgive their self-appointed leaders almost any atrocity directed against blacks, coloreds, or Indians. Treachery and deceit aimed at fellow whites wouldn't be so easily condoned or overlooked.

He pushed the police report to one side and started fumbling through the drawers of his desk. South Africa's impending crisis didn't concern him—but his own fate did. He'd better be several thousand miles beyond Vorster's iron grasp when the American television network began broadcasting its story.

Muller spread an array of forged bank cards, passports, and traveler's checks across the desktop—enough to sustain the three or four false identities he'd need to disappear completely. He shoveled them off the desk into his open briefcase. There wasn't any point in dawdling. The first news of what he'd given those damned Americans would spread around the globe like wildfire.

He stood up, grabbed his jacket and briefcase, and strode briskly out into his outer office.

Red-haired Irene Roussouw looked up in surprise from her Dictaphone.

Muller patted his briefcase. "I'm taking the rest of the day off, Miss Roussouw. I have some personal business to take care of. Tell the garage to have my car ready."

He turned away without waiting for her acknowledgment. If he hurried, he could just make the afternoon flight to London. And by dawn the next day, he'd have vanished somewhere into one of Europe's crowded cities.

Wrapped up in his own thoughts, he missed Irene Roussouw's reluctant, uncertain reach for her telephone.

Muller took the steps down to the Ministry's garage two at a time. He was breathing easier already. Better to be a rich exile in Europe than a corpse in an unmarked grave in South Africa.

He was smiling when he emerged into the small underground garage reserved for the Ministry's senior servants.

The smile flickered and died when he saw the four men waiting close to his black Jaguar. The deputy minister of law and order, Marius van der Heijden, and three others—men whose grim, almost lifeless eyes quickly scanned him and as quickly dismissed him as any serious threat.

"Going somewhere, Erik?" Van der Heijden nodded at his bulging briefcase.

The fear was back. Muller moistened lips gone suddenly dry. "Just taking a bit of work home with me, Minister. Now, if you'll excuse me?" He took a step closer to his car.

At a barely perceptible nod from van der Heijden, two of the grim-faced men moved forward to block his path. The third stayed by the older man's side.

Van der Heijden shook his head. "I'm very much afraid that I can't excuse you just yet, Erik." He smiled unpleasantly. "There's a small matter the President has asked me to . . . well, let us say, discuss with you."

Muller realized his hands were shaking and he tried to hide that by moving them behind his back. "Oh?"

Van der Heijden nodded slowly, his smile twisting into a sneer. "A small matter of a videotape it seems, Erik. A videotape showing you and a kaffir boy."

They knew! Those bastard Americans had lied! They'd betrayed him after all. Muller's stomach knotted abruptly and he swallowed hard against the taste of vomit. Oh, God. They knew . . .

His knees buckled and he sagged forward, watching numbly as his briefcase clattered onto the concrete garage floor and broke open—spilling forged documents and traveler's checks out in a damning pile. Van der Heijden's agents grabbed his arms and hauled him upright.

The older man looked down at the multiple passports and money and then back up into Muller's horrified face. "Well, well, Erik. Your work is almost as unusual as your sexual habits. One would almost think you planned to flee our beloved fatherland.'' His smile disappeared, replaced by a disgusted scowl. ''Take this boy-loving pig away. I have some questions to ask him in more private surroundings.''

No! Muller felt his blood run cold. He knew exactly what van der Heijden had in mind. Torture. Lingering, mind-flaying torture. His knees buckled again. Pain was something to be inflicted—not suffered! Please God, he prayed for the first time in decades, grant me a swift bullet in the back of the neck. Anything but this.

''Marius, wait! Please!'' He squirmed in the grasp of the two men still holding his arms. ''You don't need to do this! I'll tell you everything! Everything! I swear it!''

Van der Heijden nodded again to his men. One of them shifted his grip and locked an elbow around Muller's throat—choking him into silence.

The older man leaned forward and took Muller's red, tear-stained face in one deceptively gentle hand. ''Oh, Erik, I know you'll talk. I know you will. But you mustn't deprive us of our little fun, eh?'' He shook his head in mock regret. ''In any event, the President has already ordained the manner of your death. You, *meneer,* have nothing left to bargain for, and soon you will have nothing left to bargain with.''

He stepped back and stood watching as his men dragged Erik Muller kicking and gagging toward a waiting unmarked van.

South Africa's onetime director of military intelligence was about to learn what it felt like to lie helpless and at the mercy of merciless men.

NETWORK STUDIOS, JOHANNESBURG

The photocopier flashed again and again, throwing rhythmic pulses of blindingly bright white light against Emily van der Heijden's tense, determined face. She stood close to the copier, watching intently as the ANC documents they'd blackmailed out of Muller fed themselves one by one into the machine, emerged, and then cycled through to begin the whole process over again. Complete sets joined a growing pile on one end of the copier table.

Ian Sherfield spoke from behind her. "I'm still not sure this is necessary. Or wise. I mean, to all intents and purposes, the story's out already." He glanced at his watch. "People all over the world are going to find out what really happened to the Blue Train and your government in a couple of hours or so. Vorster can't possibly put the cork back in this bottle."

Emily brushed a strand of hair out of her eyes and leaned forward to check the copier counter. Twenty down and twenty sets of duplicates left to go. Then she turned to face Ian. "He may not be able to stop the rest of the world from finding out what's going on, but he can certainly clamp down on the news here in this country."

Ian looked unconvinced, doubting whether any wall of censorship could hope to keep the story they'd so painfully and painstakingly pieced together from eventually leaking through to South Africa's restive populations. If nothing else, too many people owned shortwave radio sets that could pick up news broadcasts from around the world. He said as much to Emily.

"True enough." She pulled another collated and stapled set out of the machine's grasp. "Many will hear the news . . . but how many will believe it?"

She shrugged. "I'm afraid too many of my countrymen are all too used to ignoring foreign newscasts." Emily laid a careful hand on the unwieldy pile of copied documents. "I have the names and addresses of many influential men—men who could lead others against this government. But such men will need to see the proof of Vorster's treachery for themselves—this proof."

She stepped closer to him and took his hands in hers. "I ask this of you, Ian. I ask your help in what I must do."

He stared first into her serious, hope-filled face and then down at the pile of papers behind her. Emily had to know what she was asking. If he helped her send these documents to a cadre of potential rebels, he'd be stepping across an important line—the line between simply reporting the news and creating it. Did he want to go that far? Could he go that far?

Then he remembered a car burning fiercely in the night—the car that had been driven by Sam Knowles. And there was an entire government, murdered by a ruthless power-grabber. That same man had started a war and tortured thousands of people. Sam's death was tragic, but certainly not the largest of Vorster's crimes.

Somehow that put things back into focus. He'd already stepped across the line. Hell, he'd been shoved across it by the dawning realization of just what Karl Vorster had done to seize and maintain power. Thousands, maybe even tens of thousands, of innocent people had already died to satisfy that man's ambition and private hatreds. And a nation struggling to shake off its unsavory past had been pulled back into a nightmare of state-mandated racism and tyranny.

Ian shook his head. Other journalists might be able simply to grit their teeth and carry on just "observing" events in this troubled country. He no longer could. What happened to South Africa and its divided peoples mattered to him now.

Ian gathered Emily into his arms and held her tightly for a moment before whispering, "Okay, I'm in." He'd help her distribute the documents that could ignite a bloody civil war.

He'd go back to being a dispassionate observer when Karl Vorster and his cronies were where they belonged—dead or behind bars.

OCTOBER 28—BBC WORLD SERVICE

The recorded chimes of Big Ben faded, replaced by the smooth, honeyed tones of the BBC's leading radio announcer. "Good evening. Here is the news.

"American television news broadcasts claiming that South Africa's security services had advance warning of the plot to assassinate President Frederick Haymans and other members of his cabinet continue to send shock waves around the world. Although the reports, which first aired yesterday, are as yet unconfirmed, they have prompted emergency meetings at a very senior level in London, the other European capitals, and in Washington.

"Relations between the world's democracies and South Africa are already under tremendous strain owing to Pretoria's invasion of Namibia and its brutal reimposition of total apartheid at home. Confirmation that the nation's current president, Karl Vorster, knew beforehand of the ANC's plans to attack his predecessor and did nothing to thwart them would surely call into question the very legitimacy of South Africa's existing government.

"Official spokesmen in Pretoria have so far maintained a tight-lipped silence, refusing all comment on what they label 'communist-inspired propaganda.' "

The announcer's voice shifted down a notch. "In other news from Africa, Cuba's President Fidel Castro announced the dispatch of an additional motorized infantry division to Namibia. Castro made the announcement in the midst of a three-hour speech to Cuba's Communist Party Youth Congress, claiming that the additional soldiers would enable his forces there to crush South Africa's invasion army in a 'final battle of liberation.'

"Western military sources confirm that Cuba's expeditionary force does appear to be preparing for a renewed offensive against South African troops holding positions along the southern edge of the Auas Mountains—barely forty kilometers from the Namibian capital of Windhoek. . . ."

CHAPTER 19

Tailspin

OCTOBER 31—CNN HEADLINE NEWS

Four days after it first aired, the furor generated by Ian Sherfield's story showed no sign of fading away. Events in southern Africa continued to dominate newspaper front pages and TV nightly newscasts. CNN's half-hourly news recap was no exception.

As the computer-generated graphics signaling the start of the broadcast disappeared, the screen split, its upper right-hand corner showing a stylized map of South Africa, while the rest showed CNN's glittering, high-tech Atlanta studio and the familiar, grave face of its daytime anchor. "In the news at the top of the hour, the German government has just announced that its ambassador to South Africa is being recalled 'for consultations'—bringing to eight the number of major powers that have withdrawn their senior diplomatic representatives from Pretoria. Several more European nations, including France and the Netherlands, have actually broken all ties with the Vorster government and are closing their embassies completely.

"Western governments may hope this latest round of diplomatic saber-rattling will encourage their citizens living and working inside South Africa to leave before the situation grows any more violent. If that's the case, it may already be too late."

The map of South Africa expanded to fill the entire screen. "Despite a total foreign-press blackout, there are persistent reports of rioting in Cape Town, Port Elizabeth, Durban, and several other cities. An accurate casualty count seems impossible to obtain, but key members of the country's fragmented political opposition claim that hundreds have been killed by police and security units in just the past three or four days." Red stars sprouted on the map, highlighting each mentioned location. South Africa looked hemmed in, its entire coastline a sea of bright-red trouble spots surrounding a seemingly placid white interior.

The camera cut back to show the anchor's somber face and a file photo of Ian Sherfield. "In related news, the story filed by American newsman Ian Sherfield, now believed to be in hiding somewhere in South Africa, has been partially corroborated both by sources inside the ANC and inside the South African security forces. CNN has also learned that U.S. government officials have been given copies of the documents —presumably so that they can be authenticated.

"In Pretoria, the Vorster government continues to refuse to comment on the claim that it allowed the ANC's attack on the Blue Train to go forward without interference. And though black opposition groups have long campaigned against Vorster, sketchy reports of growing dissatisfaction seem to indicate that white opinion inside South Africa is finally turning against the regime—including many of the far-right groups ordinarily thought to be a source of political strength for the current government.

A picture of a scowling Karl Vorster took shape over the anchor's left shoulder. "President Vorster is scheduled to address his nation at eleven A.M. Eastern time tomorrow. CNN will, of course, carry that speech live."

Vorster's picture vanished, replaced by a drawing of a gold bar surmounted by an arrow rising at a steep angle. "South

Africa's worsening political, military, and economic crisis continues to send shivers through the world financial community. Gold closed today on the New York exchange at near six hundred dollars an ounce, and the price is expected to continue rising tomorrow. The gold price rise parallels similar price increases affecting all other strategic minerals exported by South Africa. We'll have more details on what that could mean for the average consumer in Dollars and Sense, later in this half hour.

"In domestic news, police in San Francisco refused to speculate on whether a bomb found near the Federal Building there this morning had any connection with a recent series of attacks blamed on radical environmental groups. . . ."

NOVEMBER 1—JOHANNESBURG

Ian, Emily, and Matthew Sibena sat uncomfortably close together on a small sofa facing a black-and-white television set. Even with all the drapes drawn, the late-afternoon sun turned the tiny, one-bedroom apartment into a sweltering hotbox.

Ian wiped the sweat off his forehead and resisted the temptation to complain about the heat and the lack of working air-conditioning. He suspected that the same adage that applied to gift-horse dentures applied to borrowed apartments—especially for those on the run from the police. They'd been lucky enough that Emily's reporter friend and reluctant Army reservist, Brian Pakenham, had agreed to lend her a key to his flat without asking too many inconvenient questions.

Lucky indeed. Ian didn't doubt that police guardposts now ringed his apartment, the network studios, and probably the American embassy in Pretoria. And he was quite sure that his picture had been distributed to every roadblock and checkpoint on the roads leading out of Johannesburg. No South African police commander was going to let the foreigner who'd so insulted his president escape his dragnet.

But after being cooped up for nearly ninety-six hours straight, Ian was almost ready to take his chances out on

Johannesburg's crowded streets and empty highways. Almost anything seemed better than staying here in sticky, fearful ignorance. He shook his head wryly at the suicidal thought and tried to concentrate instead on the halting English translation of Karl Vorster's harsh, grating Afrikaans phrases. Maybe he could piece together some idea of what was going on in the world outside South Africa.

". . . I know that my words will reach not only my fellow South Africans, but many others throughout the world as well. I welcome this opportunity to speak to those outsiders, those foreigners, who have had so much to do with the crisis we face."

The camera pulled back from its close-up of Vorster's strong, square-jawed face—backing away until it showed him standing proudly in front of a huge blue-, white-, and orange-striped South African flag.

"Many of these small-minded outsiders have opposed our struggle to build a South Africa on our own terms. They have opposed our fight against the Marxists and terrorists bent on pulling us down into shame and degradation. They do not understand the conditions we face here in South Africa. Most have never even visited our land—our beautiful fatherland! They ignore the chaos and corruption afflicting so-called Black Africa! Instead they yammer and whine at us. At *us!* They preach at the people of the Covenant! At men and women who have fought and bled and died to hold this land for God and for civilization!" The camera zoomed in again, focusing on Vorster's red, angry face and pounding fist.

Ian shivered. My God, the man was hypnotic! Even though he didn't understand the language, he could feel the raw power of Vorster's voice and rhetoric. He glanced at Emily sitting pale and tense by his side. Did she feel it, too? His eyes slid down to where her hands were clenched so tightly that all the blood seemed to have drained out of them. Yes, she felt it—the appeal to a common heritage of sacrifice and of suffering. The instinctive response to form a laager—to circle the wagons—in the face of overwhelming and alien forces.

He looked back toward the television. Vorster was still

speaking. He spoke more softly now, picking and choosing his words in a calm, dispassionate tone that seemed strangely at odds with his violent and bloody message.

"Well, we have words of our own for them—for these small-minded foreigners. No fight is ever desirable. And no fight is ever pretty. But this struggle of ours is necessary. We are fighting for the very survival of our society, of our people. And we will not submit. We will not give up. We will not surrender our sovereign power while a single enemy, a single communist, or a single rebellious black is alive to menace our wives and our children."

Vorster paused and stared grimly straight into the camera for a moment. "Many of you may have heard the foreign charges that my government came to power illegally." He snorted contemptuously. "Illegally! What does that mean? What could it possibly mean in the circumstances our beloved country faced when I took office?"

Ian sat up straight in shock, scarcely able to believe that he'd heard Vorster right. But the other man's next words hammered the point home. "Very well. I admit that extraordinary measures were used to resolve a dangerous political situation. The previous administration had embarked on a course that could only bring about South Africa's ruin."

Vorster lifted his massive, calloused hand toward the ceiling—as though he were seeking heaven's approval for his actions. "My fellows and I acted as patriots to restore a stable, right-thinking government. Outside the normal constitution, yes. But within the bounds of national need.

"Our efforts are not ended, and will not be ended, until we can guarantee a safe and prosperous society for every right-thinking citizen of South Africa. We will spare no effort to reach that goal." Vorster glowered into the camera. "And if you are not with us, you are against us."

He lowered his voice. "And finally, to the United States and the other know-nothings who try to tell us what to do and what to think, you can get out of our affairs and stay out—until you accept us on our own terms. If we uttered a mere tenth of the lies and falsehoods about your countries that you've uttered about ours, your diplomats would scream in protest. Well, we do not scream, we act. Your ambassadors can all stay home until you are willing to speak reasonably and let us run our own affairs our own way."

Vorster's smile grew smug, unpleasantly near a sneer. "Remember, you need us more than we need you. You need our gold, our diamonds, and all the precious metals that keep your industries alive. More than that, you need us to show you what no black has ever achieved—a stable and prosperous bulwark of civilization on the African continent."

The camera zeroed in on his stern, implacable face and held the image for what seemed an eternity. Then the picture faded to black before cutting back to the South African Broadcasting Company's main studio. Even the government's handpicked anchormen looked shaken by what they'd just heard.

Ian reached out and snapped the set off. He needed peace and relative quiet to think this thing through. Vorster hadn't even bothered to try denying his involvement in the Blue Train massacre. Instead, he'd practically thrown down a gauntlet—challenging anyone who dared to pick it up.

The question was, would anyone dare?

NOVEMBER 2—DURBAN, SOUTH AFRICA

From the air, Durban was now a city of strange contrasts—natural beauty, bustling commerce, and bloody, merciless violence.

To the northeast, the sun sparkled off the bright blue waters of the Indian Ocean stretching unimpeded toward the far horizon. To the northeast and southwest, long foam-flecked waves rolling in from the ocean broke on spires of jagged gray rock just offshore or raced hissing up wide sandy beaches. Closer to the city center, dozens of ships crowded Durban's deepwater port, South Africa's largest. Oil tankers, container ships, bulk ore carriers, and rusting tramp steamers—all waiting a turn alongside the harbor's crane-lined marine terminal.

The violence was all ashore. Durban's skyscrapers and streets were shrouded by a thick pall of oily black smoke hanging over the central city. Flames licked red around the edges of half-demolished buildings and roared high from the wrecked carcasses of bullet-riddled automobiles. Bodies littered the streets, singly in some places, heaped in grotesque piles in others. The flashes of repeated rifle and machine-gun fire stabbed from windows and doorways where armed rioters still fought with the police and the Army.

"Again." Brig. Franz Diederichs tapped his pilot on the shoulder and made a circling motion with one finger. The tiny Alouette III helicopter banked sharply and began another orbit over a city now transformed into a battleground.

Diederichs scowled at the smoke and flame below. He'd been taken by surprise and it wasn't a pleasant feeling. His networks of informers and spies had warned of increasing unrest among the city's predominantly Indian population—but nothing had prepared him for the sudden onset of outright rebellion and armed resistance.

In the first half hour of the revolt, Durban's palm tree–lined City Hall, its massive, barricaded police headquarters, and the SADF's fortified central armory had all been attacked by rifle- and pistol-armed groups of Zulus and Indians. That strange alliance was troubling in and of itself. In ordinary times, Natal's Zulu and Indian populations feared and hated each other almost more than they did the ruling white minority. Diederichs grinned sourly. If nothing else, at least his bungling political masters had managed to unite all the separate factions opposed to them!

The Alouette straightened out of its bank, bringing the burning city back into full view. The sight wiped Diederichs's twisted grin off his narrow face. Most of the rebels had been driven off after a few minutes of fierce fighting, but not before both sides had suffered heavy losses. For several hours since, his men had struggled to regain control of a city seemingly gone mad.

Unarmed women and children had thrown themselves in front of armored riot cars and APCs—blocking main roads and alleys alike until blasted out of the way. As troops on foot tried to bypass those human roadblocks, snipers hidden in office buildings, churches, and storefronts picked them off one by one, imposing delay and triggering panicked bursts of indiscriminate automatic weapons fire that only consumed needed ammunition and killed more civilians.

Resistance was finally beginning to fade—broken by superior firepower, training, and Diederichs's willingness to order the slaughter of all who got in his way. Still, even his most optimistic estimates showed that it would be several days before he had all of Durban's districts and suburbs firmly in hand.

Diederichs was thrown against his seat belt as the Alouette, caught in a sudden updraft of superheated air, bucked skyward and then fell toward the water like a rock before the pilot regained control. He glared left through the canopy to where sheets of orange-red flame more than a hundred meters high marked the site of one of the day's worst human and economic disasters—the destruction of the Shell Oil refinery's main tank farm.

Early in the fighting, stray cannon shells and mortar rounds had slammed into several of the storage tanks—igniting a conflagration that had already consumed at least fifty lives and precious oil worth tens of millions of rands. Hours later, the fire still raged out of control, kept back from the refinery only by a series of massive earthen berms and the heroic efforts of virtually every surviving firefighter left in Durban.

Diederichs stared at the man-made inferno roiling below, all too conscious of how narrowly he had escaped total disaster. The Shell facility alone supplied nearly 40 percent of South Africa's refined petroleum products—fuel oil, petrol, and diesel. The oil destroyed in storage could be replaced in days. But the refinery itself was essentially irreplaceable. And no government—especially not one headed by Karl Vorster—would have looked with favor on anyone even remotely connected with its loss. This rebellion was bad enough.

He shifted his gaze toward the city center. His best troops were down there, fighting their way from house to house through the heart of Durban's Indian business district. He spotted more smoke rising from stores and shops either set aflame by the rebels or demolished by armored-car cannon fire.

One enormous pillar of smoke stained the sky above a shattered pile of white stone.

Diederichs's lip curled in disgust. The Great Mosque of Grey Street was said to have been the largest Islamic religious site in southern Africa. The Moslems among South Africa's Indian minority had built it with their own money and hard labor over long years. Well, he and his troops had shown the *koelietjies*—the little coolies—how quickly and how easily Afrikaner explosive shells could knock it down. Hundreds of dead or dying men, women, and children lay sprawled among the mosque's shell-torn arched passageways and collapsed sanctuary.

Brig. Franz Diederichs nodded to himself, pleased by the sight of the carnage. Durban's mongrel population of blacks and coolies had surprised him once. They would not do so again. He'd see to it that they were too busy counting their dead to trouble South Africa's peace for a generation or more.

Rifle and machine-gun fire continued to rattle across Durban's corpse-strewn streets all through the night.

NOVEMBER 4—NATIONAL SECURITY COUNCIL MEETING, WASHINGTON, D.C.

A cold, driving rain soaked the capital's parks and public buildings, puddling on oil-slick streets and knocking dead and dying leaves off the trees onto the pavement. One by one, the city's streetlamps flickered on—triggered by simpleminded sensors that believed the dull-gray half-light must signal the approach of night.

In the Situation Room, two stories below the White House grounds, a shift from pitchers of iced lemonade to hot coffee marked the only concession made to Washington's worsening weather. There were differences, though. The Situation Room might remain untouched by the passing seasons, but it did reflect the changing world scene. On one wall, a map of sub-Saharan Africa had replaced that of the Soviet Union. And the faces of the men and women seated around the room's single table were as gloomy as the weather above.

The sardonic amusement generated by listening to a replay of Vorster's rabid speech had died quickly after the secretary of commerce's terse reminder that South Africa's president might well be as mad as a hatter, but his policies were still wreaking havoc on the economies of the world's industrialized nations.

The shadows and new lines on Hamilton Reid's handsome face showed his fatigue and concern. "Strategic minerals prices are rising even faster than we expected." He shook his head wearily. "Frankly, I think it's likely we'll see the cost of chromium, platinum, and the others tripling by the end of the month."

Christ. Vice President James Malcolm Forrester forced himself to nod expressionlessly as others around the table showed their dismay. All of those minerals were essential to a wide range of industries, and the drastically higher prices being paid for them meant a surge in inflation and interest rates around the world. The fact that it had been predicted earlier was no comfort. It still spelled disaster for the nation's economy.

Edward Hurley leaned back, the Situation Room's overhead lighting momentarily reflected in the thick lenses of his tortoiseshell glasses. "It's only going to get worse, Mr. Vice President. We've all seen the latest intercepts and smuggled video footage. South Africa's falling apart faster than anyone ever dreamed it possibly could." He shrugged. "Vorster seems to be on the verge of losing all control over the country's major ports. The equation's pretty simple—no ports means no exports. And no minerals exports coming out of South Africa means panic-buying around the world as companies and countries scramble to make up the difference elsewhere."

Forrester nodded and looked toward the paunchy, white-haired man sitting uneasily at the opposite end of the table. "Can you cast any further light on all of this, Chris?"

Christopher Nicholson, director of the CIA, shook his head

reluctantly—chagrined at being caught out in front of his peers. His subordinates were already taking bets about which of their colleagues' heads would roll because of the fiasco. "I'm afraid all my data has been overtaken by events, Mr. Vice President. My people had been trying to confirm the Blue Train massacre story aired by this reporter, but Vorster told the whole world last week that he did it and he's not sorry."

The CIA director paused briefly and then passed two documents down the table to Forrester. "Other than that, we have an updated list of arms shipments to both sides in the Namibian war, and a bio of Sherfield, the reporter who actually broke the story." Nicholson's embarrassed tone made it clear that he considered the information less than useful.

Forrester sat back, idly scanning the papers, then half-threw them down. "Any further word on this Sherfield character?"

Nicholson shook his head again. "I'm afraid not. We don't think the South Africans have him in custody, because they're still maintaining a round-the-clock surveillance on our embassy in Pretoria. Based on that, we think he's still hiding out somewhere in Johannesburg."

"Any chance of helping him get out of the country?"

Nicholson opened his mouth, but Hurley beat him to the punch. "I don't think that would be a good idea, Mr. Vice President." The short, bearded assistant secretary of state tapped his pen lightly against his glasses, thinking aloud. "Vorster's security boys have our intelligence assets inside South Africa pretty closely watched. If they spot us making a move toward Sherfield, they'd be bound to use that to bolster some kind of claim that he's nothing more than an American spy."

"So you're proposing that we just leave this guy dangling out there all alone?"

Hurley nodded somberly. "I don't see what else we can do, sir. We're not likely to be able to help him, and even the attempt to find him could draw South African security forces to his real location." He paused. "Wherever that is."

"Very well." Forrester looked down at his hands, feeling suddenly tired and a lot older than his years. As usual, Hurley's reasoning was impeccable, but that didn't make the decision any more palatable.

Well, so be it. Even though the buck ultimately stopped with the President, a lot of the spare change landed on his own desk. Making unpalatable decisions went with the territory. Forrester smiled inwardly, remembering his relatively carefree days in the U.S. Senate. Only congressmen had the luxury of speaking and acting out of both sides of their mouths at the same time.

In the meantime, the President expected concrete recommendations from this NSC session and he expected them soon. Forrester looked up, encompassing the entire group in one sweep of his eyes. "Okay. Let's move on to the broader problem: just what the hell are we going to do about this mess?"

He was answered by silence.

The Vice President frowned. Perhaps it was time for a small prod. "Come on, folks. The American people aren't paying us to sit around on our behinds." He pointed toward the map. "Now we know what's happening in South Africa is going to hurt us and hurt us badly. So what can we do about it? Ed?"

Hurley fiddled with his glasses, polished them quickly, and then slipped them back on his nose—plainly stalling for time. Finally, he shrugged. "Our people at State could draft a statement for the President's signature demanding that Vorster resign and schedule new elections under their constitution."

Forrester hid his disappointment. He'd expected something more direct and forceful from Hurley. Still, the suggestion was worth considering as a first step.

"Vorster will simply ignore it," Hamilton Reid interjected.

"Of course he will!" Hurley shot back. "But we need to tell the world just where we stand before we go any further."

That was true, Forrester thought. A clearly worded call for Vorster's resignation would also help take some of the political heat off the administration. Even more importantly, it would commit the U.S. government to finding some way to pressure Vorster out of power. He said as much to the group.

Reid persisted, "Maybe so, but how much can we really

do? Directly interfering in the internal affairs of a legitimate government . . ." The secretary of commerce paused, realization dawning on his face. "My God, they aren't a legitimate government. They grabbed power illegally!"

Nicholson continued the thought. "And Vorster was kind enough to tell everyone that on worldwide television." He turned to Forrester. "Mr. Vice President, I move that we recommend that the President withdraw our recognition of South Africa's government until voters there have elected new leaders according to their own somewhat lopsided constitution."

Forrester felt a little life returning to the group and smiled slightly. "We may reword the last bit of that, but I agree that we should explicitly label Vorster's government illegal and break off our relations with it."

He leaned forward and lowered his voice. "But let's face hard facts. We all know that Vorster won't capitulate or hand over power simply because we say he should. In fact, we may just be giving him more propaganda ammunition for the home folks. What the President needs to know is this—exactly what can we do to push the son of a bitch out of office?"

The secretary of commerce raised a hesitant hand. "I still think South Africa's economy offers the best avenue for attacking him. If enough of his white supporters see their livelihoods and businesses going down the drain, they'll try to pull the plug on Vorster themselves." Reid grimaced. "But conventional sanctions take a long time to work. And anyway, I'm not sure we can do anything that would wreck South Africa's economy faster than Vorster's own Namibian war and crazy security crackdowns."

Forrester frowned. "What about using a wider range of measures?"

"How wide?" asked Reid. Other heads around the table nodded, agreeing with the commerce secretary's push for a clearer definition. Few people were willing to commit themselves to any concrete recommendation without some firmer indication of the President's intentions.

Fair enough. It was time to drop a small bombshell, Forrester thought. "The President has authorized us to consider anything short of open war."

A deep bass baritone from near the end of the table cut through the stunned silence. "Then it's a blockade."

Forrester looked at the tall, lantern-jawed man in an Air Force uniform. Combat service ribbons and decorations added splashes of different colors to his dark blue jacket. "A blockade, General?"

Gen. Walter Hickman, chairman of the Joint Chiefs, nodded once. "We can move a carrier battle group down from the Indian Ocean and cut off South Africa's seaborne commerce."

Nicholson was shocked and didn't bother concealing it. "Use the military? That's insane! A blockade on South Africa's imports and exports would send world commodity prices into the stratosphere! And that's precisely what we're trying so desperately to stop!"

Others around the table muttered their agreement.

Forrester held up his hand for silence and got it. He tapped Reid's economic report. "I don't think there's anything we can do to stop these price increases, Chris. As long as those bastards in Pretoria are in power, we're going to be in trouble. So maybe it's worth some short-term pain to get rid of what would otherwise be a long-term problem."

Nicholson changed tack. "What if Vorster decides to retaliate against U.S. citizens still inside South Africa?"

"Highly unlikely, Mr. Director." Edward Hurley reentered the fray. "Vorster's already at war with the Cubans, the Namibians, and at least four-fifths of his own population. I doubt he'll want to add us to the list."

The bearded State Department official pushed his glasses back up his nose before continuing. "In any event, there aren't many Americans left in South Africa as targets. Fewer than three or four hundred as near as we can tell." He flipped to a page near the back of his briefing binder. "We've been tracking the numbers on a day-by-day basis. Most tourists left after we posted the travel advisory, and companies still doing business inside the RSA have been shuttling their American executives home for weeks. Plus, we're already down to a skeleton staff at the embassy."

"All right. But what if their navy tried to stop us?" Nicholson seemed determined to find reasons to scuttle the proposed blockade.

Hickman snorted. "The South African Navy has a few short-range missile boats, three old submarines, and no naval air capability. They're a fourth-rate naval power." He shook his head. "Hell, Libya's a bigger naval threat! Our ships can patrol well out to sea—beyond their range—and block all merchant ship traffic into and out of the country."

Nicholson purpled. "I don't doubt that we could establish such a blockade, General. That's not my point." He turned to Forrester. "The key question is, should we do such a thing in the first place?"

"What's your alternative, Chris?" Forrester asked, curious to see what the CIA director had in mind.

Nicholson opened his mouth and then shut it again, taken aback.

"I'm not saying there's any kind of a guarantee that a blockade will force the South Africans to dump Vorster and act more reasonably," Hickman explained, "but it would sure as hell boost the pressure on their economy."

"Just how much pressure?" Forrester directed his question to a still-stunned Hamilton Reid.

The secretary of commerce rubbed the bridge of his nose. "Quite a lot, Mr. Vice President. South Africa could still export by air and ground of course, but those are awfully narrow 'pipelines' for their major products." He nodded toward the map. "And some commodities, especially oil, have to come by sea. In fact, oil imports are their biggest Achilles' heel. It's about the only mineral resource South Africa doesn't have in ridiculous abundance."

Hurley frowned. "I'm not sure that's quite right, Mr. Secretary. Last time I checked, Pretoria was supposed to have a five-year strategic petroleum reserve stashed away."

"A five-year reserve in a peacetime economy," General

Hickman pointed out. "But there's a war on down there, and wars burn gas at a helluva rate."

Forrester nodded slowly. "True enough. And imposing a blockade on South Africa's imports would send a pretty goddamned strong shot across Vorster's bow—one he couldn't shrug off or just ignore." He felt a small, tight smile spread across his face. Even thinking about doing something real, something concrete, about the mess in South Africa made him feel better.

He looked at Hickman. "How soon could that carrier group reach South African waters?"

"We could have a carrier, her escorts, and eighty-six aircraft in range in eight days, Mr. Vice President."

"I still don't think sending a warship is the best course of action." Nicholson sounded worried, almost alarmed at the idea. "Using any kind of military force would be inflammatory."

"And just whose opinion would we be inflaming, Mr. Director?" Hurley didn't bother hiding his sarcasm. "The South Africans? Hell, I should hope so. That'd be the whole point of the exercise. The Europeans? I sincerely doubt it. If anything, most Europeans are even more outraged by Vorster's actions than people are here in the States."

Forrester mentally scored a point for Hurley. His reading of European political and public opinion seemed right on target. As an example, Britain's prime minister had long been one of the staunchest opponents of indiscriminate sanctions aimed at South Africa. But the revelation that Vorster had played a hand in the deaths of Frederick Haymans and his cabinet had swung him around almost one hundred and eighty degrees. In the last two days alone, he'd been on the phone twice with the President urging joint U.S. and British action against what he now called "Vorster's dastardly cabal."

Hurley faced him squarely. "In a nutshell, I think General Hickman's suggestion has merit, Mr. Vice President. We've been damned for not doing anything. Let's be damned for doing something constructive."

One by one, the others around the table nodded, some with

more enthusiasm than others, but all agreeing nonetheless. Only Nicholson shook his head angrily, evidently outraged at having been overruled. Forrester suspected that the CIA director's anger had more to do with his perceived loss of face than with any serious disagreement over policy.

He glanced at the wall clock. "All right, ladies and gentlemen. I'm meeting with the President in half an hour, and I'll pass along the recommendation that we dispatch a carrier battle group, with the eventual mission of establishing a maritime blockade of all South African ports." He smiled crookedly. "In the circumstances, I suspect he'll approve it wholeheartedly."

More nods. Everyone present knew only all too well how much heat the President was taking from the Congress and the media for his apparent inaction. With no economic or diplomatic options, the administration's carefully worded statements had only served as a point of departure for its critics. Action, easy to call for but hard to specify, was the only thing that made good PR.

Forrester glanced down at his agenda. One penciled-in item remained. He looked up. "Also, effective immediately, the President's asked me to establish a Crisis Group to monitor the southern African situation and to provide day-to-day control over our initiatives in the region."

Still more nods. Establishing a Crisis Group—a full-time team of junior NSC members and staffers—was the logical next step. Everyone in the room could see that events in South Africa were moving too fast for the ordinary processes of government to be effective. The cabinet officers who made up the regular National Security Council had too many other responsibilities to devote full attention to a single prolonged crisis—no matter how important or how dangerous.

Forrester stared down the table, focusing his gaze on Nicholson's red face. The CIA director had already proven surprisingly unwilling to back proposals made by other members of the President's inner policy-making circle. It was time to make sure he knew who held the reins on this issue. "I've recommended that Ed Hurley take charge of the group, and the President agrees. I expect deputies from all concerned departments and agencies to be assigned by this afternoon. Understood?''

Forrester noticed several ill-concealed looks of surprise on several faces around the table. With the crisis escalating, most of the NSC's members had undoubtedly expected him to name a military man or one of the intelligence agency deputies. Well, they'd reckoned wrongly. Hurley had the brains and background needed for the job. He'd also shown that he had the guts and political savvy needed to take on those above him inside the administration. Forrester had him marked as a serious contender for higher office in the near future.

Even better, Hurley was still low enough down on the totem pole to feel awkward about exercising his newfound authority without frequent consultation. Neither the President nor Forrester planned to relinquish any substantive part of their power over U.S. policy toward Pretoria.

The growing catastrophe in southern Africa was now much too important to be left solely in the hands of the bureaucrats and political appointees.

NOVEMBER 6—ABOARD THE USS *CARL VINSON*, SOUTH OF THE MALDIVE ISLANDS

The American battle group spread over a hundred square miles of the Indian Ocean, steaming west just long enough to allow its massive, Nimitz-class carrier to launch and recover her aircraft. Eight other ships ringed the carrier—two guided-missile cruisers, a pair of guided-missile destroyers, two more destroyers for antisubmarine warfare, and two bulky combat support ships carrying needed fuel, ammunition, and stores. Well ahead of the battle group, two Los Angeles–class attack submarines slid quietly through the water, their ultrasophisticated computers constantly sifting the sounds of fish and ocean currents—searching for telltale engine or propeller noises that might signal the approach of a hostile surface ship or sub.

Above the battle group, aircraft of various types orbited slowly in fuel-conserving racetrack patterns. Huge, twin-tailed F-14 Tomcats loitered on combat air patrol. A twin-engined E-2C Hawkeye provided early warning of any incoming plane or missile, and a boxy S-3 Viking swooped low now and again to monitor the line of passive sonobuoys it had dropped ahead of the oncoming carrier group.

Aboard the carrier itself, video monitors brought the sights and sounds of the busy flight deck to the *Carl Vinson*'s soundproofed flag plot. Radios muttered near control consoles, relaying conversations between the *Vinson*'s air wing commander, the CAG, his assistants, and pilots already in the air, landing, or awaiting takeoff. Glowing computer displays updated the position and status of every unit in the formation.

Rear Adm. Andrew Douglas Stewart ignored the constant hum of activity all around as he scanned the message flimsy that had just arrived. As he read, he rocked back and forth slowly on the balls of his feet—still as compact and trim as he'd been when he earned his living as an attack pilot over North Vietnam.

The creases around Stewart's cold gray eyes tightened as he skimmed through the various addresses that showed this order had originated with the Joint Chiefs of Staff—and presumably somewhere inside the White House before that. The real meat came in the second short paragraph.

". . . Proceed at best speed to . . ." The admiral eyeballed a nearby electronic chart. The latitude and longitude contained in the message marked a point approximately four hundred nautical miles east of Durban. "You will prepare for contingency operations off the South African coast on arrival."

It still read the same way the second time through. Contingency operations off South Africa. He whistled once and then swore under his breath. "Son of a big, bad bitch!"

"Trouble, Admiral?" His chief of staff hovered on the other side of the plot table.

Stewart handed him the message and watched his surprise.

The younger man unconsciously scratched at his balding scalp and shook his head. "I don't get it. What kind of ops are we supposed to prepare for?"

"Damned if I know exactly, Tom." Stewart shrugged. He'd read about the South African military situation in the daily intelligence summaries, and they were about as helpful as the out-of-date magazines the COD planes delivered. Certainly nothing he'd read seemed to warrant direct U.S. involvement. He smiled slightly to himself. Could it be that the Joint Chiefs and the political bigwigs were actually thinking and planning ahead for once? It was doubtful, but he'd seen stranger things in his thirty-odd years in the military.

He shook himself out of his reverie. They had a lot of work to do and not much time to do it in. Even with all the latest in instantaneous communications and computer navigation, a carrier battle group couldn't turn on a dime.

"Get your boys busy, Tom. I want to be ready to alter course in half an hour, after this ops cycle. Check the training schedule, and make sure it allows enough aircraft for air and sea surveillance missions." Stewart glanced at a row of clocks set to show local times at various points around the globe. "In the meantime, I'll be on the secure net back to D.C." He glanced down at the message still held in his chief of staff's hand. "I'd like to have somebody back there tell me just what the hell is going on."

The younger officer nodded once and hurried away in search of his staff—already pondering the most efficient way to continue the training cycle while the *Carl Vinson* and her escorts moved toward Durban.

For the first time ever, major elements of U.S. military power were being focused on South Africa.

CHAPTER 20

Civil War

NOVEMBER 9—STATE SECURITY COUNCIL CHAMBER, PRETORIA

Karl Vorster and his cabinet met in their windowless chamber for the tenth time in as many days. Caught between the twin pressures of a bloody, stalemated war in Namibia and escalating political chaos at home, the cabinet was starting to crack. Several chairs were empty, abandoned by men who'd resigned—men either unable to stomach Vorster's actions or who feared being held responsible for them by a new government.

Marius van der Heijden blinked rapidly, his eyes watering in the thick haze of tobacco smoke choking the small room. More evidence that sinful addiction could overcome the best intentions of weak-willed men, he thought irritably. Weaklings like Erik Muller, though on a smaller scale. Muller's pale, agonized face rose in his mind, and he shied away from the memory. The security chief's pain-filled death had been richly deserved, but not pretty.

He drove Muller's image away by concentrating on the situation maps tacked up on the chamber's otherwise bare walls. Clusters of multicolored pins dotting the map showed only the vaguest outlines of the disaster spreading with wildfire rapidity across the whole country. An open revolt crushed in Durban, but untamed elsewhere in the Natal. Secessionist movements springing up among the former Afrikaner faithful in the Orange Free State and the Transvaal. The entire elected city council of Cape Town under arrest for suspected treason. And so it went—each succeeding piece of news worse than the last.

"I tell you, my friends, we simply cannot go on like this. Not for another week, let alone a month! We must find a way to win peace before our nation burns down around our very ears!"

Reluctantly, van der Heijden turned his attention to the speaker, Helmoed Malherbe, the minister of industries and commerce.

Malherbe pointed to the sheets of trade figures and economic statistics he'd passed around the table. "Already the economy is a complete shambles. Inflation is at forty percent and climbing fast. Exports are running at scarcely half last year's level. . . ." He showed every sign of droning on for hours.

Van der Heijden scowled. He loathed Malherbe. The man was nothing more than a gutless, whining, rand-pinching economist. Always a pessimist, a naysayer, and a second-guesser. He looked toward the head of the table, hoping their leader would put this coward in his proper place.

But Karl Vorster sat silent, his head cradled in his hands as he listened to Malherbe's recitation of economic catastrophe.

Van der Heijden frowned. Since Muller's arrest and execution, Vorster had been quieter, less likely to take control of the meetings he called. Even worse, he hadn't yet named a replacement for the late and unlamented director of military intelligence.

And that was a crucial error. Muller had been a boy-loving bastard, but he'd also been a competent covert-operations specialist. Without anyone at the helm, his whole directorate was adrift—unable to plan, organize, or carry out the kind of selective assassinations and kidnappings that might have nipped some of these troublesome rebellions in the bud.

"All of these problems are only compounded when the police and security troops overreact in places like Durban." Malherbe waved a hand in van der Heijden's direction.

What? The newly promoted minister of law and order snapped to full attention. He glared back at Malherbe. "Brigadier Diederichs and his troops acted properly to restore order, *meneer*. Are you suggesting that they ought to have allowed those rebels to seize the city?"

"Not at all." Malherbe sniffed. "But I'm not sure what you mean by 'order,' Marius. Most of Durban's industries are idle. The port is almost completely paralyzed. The jails are full. The morgues are full, and do you know what? There are a lot of white bodies in those morgues—many of them Afrikaner bodies. Oil refinery technicians. Factory managers. Civil servants. Ordinary white citizens. People whose skills we desperately needed."

He turned toward Vorster. "Mr. President, by every objective measure, this nation is at the breaking point. Even white opinion is turning against us. We must take steps to regain their support or we will be left without any power at all."

For the first time in nearly an hour, Vorster looked up from his hands. "Nonsense, Helmoed! As long as we have the army and the security forces, we will have all the power we need."

Vorster rose and began to pace. "Those whites who have been killed were misguided, deceived by a lying press and by communist agitators." He shrugged. "Their deaths are a tragedy, but they will be avenged."

He eyed the remnants of his cabinet carefully. "Oh, I know what some of you want me to do. You want me to end our war against the communists of Namibia and to bend to the demands of these communists inside our own borders. You want me to do things that my very soul cries out against.

"Well, I say never! Never! Never!" Vorster's powerful fists crashed into the table one, twice, and then a third time. His face seemed carved out of stone. "This is the hour of crisis, when the danger is greatest. If we can survive this time of testing, if we can live through this purging fire, we shall emerge a stronger and cleaner nation!"

Vorster's tone grew sharper, angrier. "A few of you even want me to step down. To retire to some country home in the Transvaal. To vanish into obscurity so that you can step up one rung and make your own climb to power!"

His rough, grating voice rang through the entire room. "Well, my friends, it shall not be. I will not resign. I will not shirk this burden. I will not leave the duty God has called me to! Only I have the vision needed to save our beloved fatherland. I will not abandon my people!"

He finished speaking and stood glaring at them in the embarrassed silence that followed his tirade.

Van der Heijden caught several of his fellow ministers covertly exchanging appalled glances, and he made a mental note to tighten surveillance on them. Recent events had shown only too clearly that not all of his leader's enemies were black or colored or foreign.

Malherbe, pale and obviously shaken by Vorster's words, finally rallied far enough to ask, "And if the country abandons you? Even our own Afrikaners are rejecting your authority."

"You cannot say who accepts or rejects me!" Vorster pointed accusingly at the industries minister, his voice rising again in pitch and volume.

He paused, then spoke more softly. "As soon as I can, I will go to my fellow Afrikaners. I will speak to them and explain fully what has happened. And once they have heard me out, those who have foolishly allowed communist lies to confuse them will come streaming back to our open arms!"

More mouths around the table dropped open and then as quickly snapped shut. Too many of them had already learned the hard way not to challenge any of Vorster's cherished illusions.

"In the meantime, my friends, we must weather this storm of lies and vicious attacks with whatever measures are necessary." He turned to Fredrik Pienaar, the small, skeletal minister of information. "Schedule a television address for tomorrow morning. I am going to declare an even stricter National State of Emergency. We will forbid any assembly, any whatsoever, until this crisis has passed. And the security forces will impose a nationwide dusk-to-dawn curfew."

He paused, thinking. "Heitman."

The minister of defense warily met his leader's stern gaze. "Yes, Mr. President?"

"Expand the reserve call-up. I want every trained man in South Africa under arms as soon as possible! Use the new troops to restore order and build more detention camps—as many as are needed."

That stung Malherbe into speaking again. "Mr. President, we simply can't afford such a thing! Total mobilization would wreck our economy beyond repair. If you insist on this, we face a depression as well as defeat in war!"

Vorster's temper finally erupted beyond control. "And we do not need your negative ideas paralyzing this government! Minister Malherbe, you are relieved of your duties!"

Van der Heijden felt a moment's elation. First Muller and now Malherbe. Another of his enemies had managed to cut his own throat—though only figuratively this time. But his elation faded in the face of a whispering inner fear. The minister knew his job. What if Malherbe's dire predictions were accurate?

Vorster snarled at the shocked official, "Only my memory of your past service stops me from having you arrested." Contempt dripped from every word. "Go home, Helmoed, and rest. You are not equal to the struggle, but that is not your fault. This is not a task for ordinary men."

White-faced and shaking, Malherbe rose from his chair and left the room without looking back.

Vorster ignored his departure. Instead, he turned to the other men sitting in stunned silence and smiled. "Now, gentlemen, let us discuss a more joyful topic. I believe you've all seen Fredrik's proposal that we make Afrikaans, our sacred tongue, the nation's only official language. . . ."

Outside the chamber, an Army messenger trotted up with a manila folder stamped SECRET. He was about to enter when a sour-faced aide stopped him.

"You can leave that with me, Captain. I'll take care of it for you."

The officer shook his head. "I'm afraid not. I have orders to deliver this to the President personally."

The aide shrugged, unimpressed and eager to show it. "Then you'll have to wait. The President himself left orders of his own. No one is to be admitted until the cabinet meeting ends." He folded his arms and stared at the wall with studied indifference.

"And when will that be?"

The aide checked his watch and shook his head. "An hour more? Perhaps two? Who can say? They'll finish when they finish." He held out his hand again. "Come, Captain. Just give it to me and be on your way. No point in standing idle, is there?"

"You don't understand! This is an emergency!" The officer glanced quickly around and lowered his voice before continuing. "We've received rumors that troops in the Cape Town garrison may mutiny!"

"Rumors?" The aide arched a supercilious eyebrow. "I hardly think those are worth troubling the cabinet with. In any event, President Vorster has already said that he doesn't want to hear any more bad news for the moment. You'll have to wait until the meeting is over."

"But . . ."

"It can't be helped." The aide stood directly in front of the door, physically blocking it.

Muttering under his breath, the soldier stomped away.

Like their superiors, South Africa's lower-level government officials were learning to ignore troublesome realities.

NOVEMBER 11—HEADQUARTERS, 16TH INFANTRY BATTALION, CASTLE OF GOOD HOPE, CAPE TOWN, SOUTH AFRICA

Red-brick ramparts, bastions, and cobblestone courtyards marked the Castle of Good Hope as a relic of the seventeenth century. Patches of scarlet, pink, white, and yellow flowers, emerald-green lawns, and museums full of precious paintings, Cape silver, and delicate Asian porcelain identified that same old fortress as a center of beauty and culture. And the scattering of armored cars, khaki-clad soldiers, and sandbagged machine-gun positions marked it as a military garrison of South Africa's crumbling late-twentieth-century Republic.

Ordinarily, Maj. Chris Taylor found the sight of the castle's immaculately maintained grounds comforting. They gave him a sense of the permanence and order now in such short supply in Cape Town's troubled streets.

But not today.

Today, he decided that he hated the cold, gray fortress walls, hated his job, and especially hated his new commanding officer, Col. Jurgen Reitz. He stormed down the long hallway toward his own office, face tight with suppressed fury.

He'd just left Reitz's office with a new set of orders even more absurd than the last.

Taylor was a compact, stocky man, slightly shorter than average height, with sandy-blond hair and a long-jawed face. Despite being a reservist and in his late forties, he was in good shape. Long years of labor in his family-owned vineyards and fruit-tree orchards had seen to that.

As he walked, he twisted his neck from side to side, trying to ease the pain from tension-knotted muscles. Calm down, he thought, don't let the Afrikaner bastard get to you.

Any meeting with Reitz was irritating. Taylor's Citizen Force unit had been one of two mobilized last August and sent to Cape Town on security duty—allowing the Permanent Force battalion ordinarily stationed there to be sent north to Namibia.

It had been a hard job. The government's idiotic policies

had stirred up enough trouble in the city to make every reservist a veteran in less than a month. They'd put in day after day patrolling known trouble spots such as the University of Cape Town campus or suppressing full-fledged riots in the black townships. But the unrest had only grown worse, and Pretoria's politicians had insisted on laying the blame on someone else's shoulders.

The Ministry of Defense had picked the battalion's old commanding officer, Colonel Ferguson, as its sacrificial lamb.

Taylor frowned at the memory. Ferguson had been replaced two weeks ago by this Afrikaner orifice, Reitz, who claimed that he had been assigned to the 16th because of "his special experience in security matters."

Since then Reitz had been insufferable, more because of his attitude than his orders. He would speak only Afrikaans, though he understood English—and most of the men in the 16th Infantry were of English descent. He treated any order from Pretoria as gospel and ordered that it be executed "energetically," as he put it. But what does a soldier do when the order reads "prevent disruptive assembly"? Ask for amplification from Reitz and he'd bite your head off.

And the battalion's officers and men desperately needed clarification of their orders. When they first arrived, they'd been needed to police the black and colored townships. But now they were being ordered into more and more white suburbs and city areas to cope with steadily escalating political protests, rock-throwing, and other incidents of "antistate" agitation—mostly small groups or individuals caught defacing government propaganda posters and the like. The troops didn't like that at all. It was bad enough being asked to club unarmed blacks and coloreds, but using the same tactics against fellow whites left them feeling queasy.

The last few days had been especially tense. First the all-too-believable reports of Vorster's involvement in Frederick Haymans's assassination. Then the sudden wholesale arrest of the City Council—an act that placed Cape Town under combined military and police rule overnight. Taylor had heard the increasingly discontented muttering from his men and junior officers and he sympathized. If Karl Vorster had really seized power by allowing Haymans and the others to be killed, he had no constitutional authority. And the orders they'd been following were manifestly illegal. But what could they do about it?

Taylor shied away from the obvious answer.

Reitz refused even to discuss the question of Vorster's legitimacy or the men's concerns. That was troubling. Taylor hadn't been especially close to his old colonel either, but it was important that the battalion's executive officer understand his superior's intentions. He remembered long talks with Ferguson, sharing opinions, discussing battalion matters—a professional relationship based on mutual respect.

Not with Reitz. The Afrikaner treated him either as an idiot child or as the enemy. It was a rare day when he said anything good about the battalion or the men in it. No, this was a matter beyond clashing command styles. This was a case of active and mutual contempt.

So Taylor stormed down the hall, inwardly raging at the idiocy of his commander, the government, and his latest orders. Dusk curfew for everyone? No exceptions for emergency crews? No assemblies at all? Two people walking down the street together couldn't be made illegal. Such an edict was insane and utterly unenforceable.

He stopped short in the hall, drawing curious glances from the few other officers passing by. He could not work this way. He might be a reservist now, but he was still a professional, an officer with ten years of active service and an honorable record, and he would not let himself be intimidated by an overbearing . . .

Taylor spun around and stalked up the hallway back to the colonel's office. He knocked once, ignoring a pale, overweight orderly who stared in surprise at him before wisely deciding to concentrate on his typing.

He heard a snapped "*Kom*" from within and stepped through the door, mentally rehearsing the Afrikaans phrases for what he had to say. It was a little absurd, but he sometimes thought that Reitz deliberately spoke quickly to make it hard for him to understand.

As he entered the room, Taylor already had his mouth open to speak, but Reitz was on the phone. The colonel saw him and scowled, but waved him all the way in as he continued shouting into the phone. "I don't care what they are doing, Captain! They are violating the law. Disperse them and be quick about it. I'm holding you personally responsible!"

Reitz slammed down the phone and glared at Taylor. "Captain Hastings has let a situation at the Green Point Soccer Stadium get out of control. Another communist riot brewing, no doubt."

Without bothering to explain any further, the Afrikaner strode quickly toward the door, buckling on a pistol belt and grabbing his cap from a hook. Taylor followed automatically.

Reitz stopped briefly in his outer office to snap an order at the pudgy corporal staring up anxiously from his typewriter. "Find Captain Kloof and tell him to get his company to the stadium immediately. He is to report to me when he arrives."

"At once, *Kolonel!*" The orderly hurriedly picked up his phone. One did not dawdle in Colonel Reitz's presence.

Reitz turned and regarded Taylor. "Another foul-up by one of my officers! You'll come with me, Major."

The colonel's personal Land Rover was parked near the Castle's main gate. A command flag fluttered from a long, thin radio aerial. Reitz slid behind the wheel, and Taylor jumped into the passenger seat, knowing the Afrikaner wouldn't bother to wait for him. He fumed quietly.

Reitz continued his lecture. "I want you to see how I deal with this riot. I've been trying to make you and the other officers in the battalion understand my policies for well over two weeks now. If you can't or won't understand, it's not my fault, but I'm going to keep trying until you do—or until I find men who can. If my orders were executed more energetically and with less insubordinate discussion, this would be a very quiet, peaceful city."

Taylor nodded curtly, hating himself for having to appear to agree even that much.

The Castle of Good Hope was located across from the main train station and near the city center, and the streets were already packed with cars and pedestrians on their way to lunch or early-afternoon shopping. Reitz scowled, turned on his Land Rover's siren and flashing light, and began weaving recklessly in and out of traffic.

In minutes, they were headed at high speed along the Western Boulevard toward Green Point—a bulge of level ground pushing northward out into the Atlantic Ocean. A thousand-foot-high rock outcrop called Signal Hill towered above Green Point's sports grounds, golf course, beaches, and soccer stadium.

Ordinarily, the area would be full of people enjoying the warm spring weather, but barricades, police vehicles, and SADF APCs now blocked every road and path. Most Cape Town residents, wise in the ways of such things, were giving the place a wide berth.

As the Land Rover roared past two hospitals built on the eastern edge of Green Point, the buildings on either side fell away to an open grassy area. Taylor held on tight to the dashboard as Reitz wheeled the vehicle through a traffic circle and onto a small access road. The soccer stadium was visible now, almost straight ahead and surrounded by hundreds of small figures, vehicles, and wisps of white that had to be tear gas.

Noises filled the air. An amplified voice, with the words confused and indistinguishable, could be heard from the direction of the stadium. Some wild-eyed, impractical agitator, Taylor thought coldly. Some idiot who still believed the Vorster government gave a damn about public opinion in the Cape Province. Shouts and breaking glass, mixed with occasional thumping shots from tear gas launchers and the high-pitched, screaming sirens of arriving ambulances, all added to the overpowering din.

Reitz braked the Land Rover beside a roadblock manned by a squad of armed troops. He had to shout to make himself heard. "Where's your captain, Sergeant?"

The noncom stiffened at the unexpected sight of his battalion's two most senior officers and pointed toward the company's command post, set up on an open stretch of ground northeast of the stadium.

Capt. John Hastings stood in the shade of a Buffel armored personnel carrier, surrounded by several lieutenants and sergeants, all studying a city map. They looked tired, and one sergeant had a bandaged forearm. The gut-twisting, acrid smell of tear gas clung to their rumpled, sweat-stained uniforms.

Reitz leaped from the Land Rover and strode over to the group. "What the devil's going on here?" he shouted.

Hastings and his command group spun round, startled. They came to attention and saluted.

"Orders group, sir." Hastings pulled his blue beret off and ran a nervous hand through tousled red hair. "We're trying to determine the best way to clear the stadium."

Another Buffel pulled up, the wheeled vehicle's angular armored body towering over them. Andries Kloof, a lean, black-haired officer, climbed out of the troop compartment and ran over to join Reitz. More APCs arrived behind Kloof's command vehicle and halted, engines still turning over, adding yet more noise to the din all around.

"Captain Kloof and C Company, reporting as ordered, Colonel."

Taylor snorted, but quietly. This wasn't a parade ground, but Reitz returned the younger Afrikaner's salute with snap and precision—just as though it were. "Glad you're here, Kloof. Stand by for a moment."

The young officer moved closer and studied the map with the rest of the group.

Reitz, looking impatient, turned back to Hastings. "Well, Captain? What's this mess you've managed to create?"

Hastings's snub-nosed face paled beneath its light dusting of freckles, and Taylor saw his jaw muscles twitch as he fought to control his temper. "We estimate there are two to three thousand people in and around the stadium, sir. Mostly white students from the university, but there are a lot of blacks and colored there as well."

He gestured to the map. "We've sealed off all entrances and exits to the commons area . . ."

Taylor listened intently. Hastings and his company were following standard crowd control tactics designed to minimize civilian casualties and protect his own men at the same time. They were using tear gas to break up organized groups of demonstrators outside the stadium. Once the demonstrators were dispersed and fleeing the gas, a platoon armed with Plexiglas riot shields and batons moved in to haul them off to waiting trucks.

Unfortunately, it was a slow and tedious process. The soldiers carried more gear than the protestors and were finding it difficult to capture more than a handful with each sally. Most managed to evade arrest and reformed—only to be dispersed by new salvos of tear gas grenades. It was a frustrating cycle that seemed to go on and on.

"And what about the stadium itself?" Reitz asked.

Hastings shook his head. "I haven't wanted to fire tear gas inside because of the panic it would create. Too many people could be trampled. We've been using loudspeakers to order them to disperse or face detention."

"And whenever they are ready to leave, you'll arrest them?" Reitz's voice was laced with sarcasm. "Your concern for these hooligans is touching, but misplaced. These people are breaking the law and should be treated as such.

"Now listen to me closely, Captain! I will not have you"—Reitz raised his voice—"or any man in this battalion babying these troublemakers."

He jabbed the map. "Have your grenadiers start firing tear gas into the stadium. And form the rest of your men into a cordon. Once the gas goes in, start sweeping the area on this side of the stadium. Arrest everyone, and if they run, shoot them!"

Hastings stared at Reitz, shocked, but he quickly concealed it. Taylor noticed the captain's eyes flicker in his direction. He controlled his own expression, masking his true feelings behind an impassive countenance.

Reitz smiled for the first time. "You will see, gentlemen. A few bullets will convince these ruffians to stop running and surrender."

For an instant, Taylor thought about protesting the trigger-happy order to open fire without serious provocation. It would be a useless gesture, though. Even at the best of times, South African law enforcement was a pretty brutal business. And Reitz was within his rights as commander on the scene.

But that didn't mean Taylor liked the situation. It also didn't mean that he could forget that Colonel Ferguson had never found it necessary to have unarmed civilians shot. He stiffened.

Reitz's smile faded and he glared at the group. "Well?"

Galvanized into action, A Company's lieutenants and sergeants went flying off under a new string of orders from Captain Hastings.

The colonel turned to C Company's eager commander. "Kloof, take your men to the far side of the stadium and clear these communists away. Arrest anyone who stops, shoot anyone who moves."

The younger man saluted again and ran off to his waiting APC. Taylor heard him shouting orders in a high-pitched, excited voice.

Reitz strolled over to Taylor's side. His tone was pleasant, almost light. "There, Major, that's what I mean by my orders being energetically executed."

He glanced at his watch. "I expect we'll have this little tea party broken up in an hour or so." His voice turned harsher. "When we get back to the office, I want you to draw up court-martial papers for Hastings. He's obviously incompetent and may actually be in sympathy with these rioters."

Reitz frowned at his stunned look. "I will not have anyone under my command who harbors soft feelings for these people. Our president has made it quite clear that we should use strong measures to maintain law and order."

Taylor said softly, "The president has also admitted seizing power illegally."

"That will be enough, Major!" Reitz shouted, outraged. "I won't have you questioning our government's authority, or mine. You are here to learn how to do your job, which I should think is humbling enough. A court-martial would be even more humbling."

Taylor heard Kloof's shouted command to move out and

turned to see C Company's three platoons formed in a giant wedge. With assault rifles at port arms, they started trotting toward the far side of the oval soccer stadium.

A panting corporal ran up to Taylor and saluted. "Sir, Captain Hastings says his men are in position and he's ready to fire the tear gas."

Taylor started to speak, but Reitz cut him off. "Well, what does he want us to say? What is he waiting for? Tell that incompetent fool to fire. Let's get to it."

My God. This Afrikaner bastard was insulting his fellow officers in front of enlisted men. Taylor felt his rage returning, overcoming the fear his erstwhile colonel had tried to instill by threatening him with a court-martial.

Unnerved by the dispute between his superiors, the corporal backed away and then ran off carrying Reitz's message. The colonel watched him go and then muttered, "I wish it were nerve gas. Just wipe out the lot of them, that's what we should do."

A Company was deployed about fifty meters away, facing the stadium. A long line of men knelt on one knee with face shields down. Alternating soldiers carried assault rifles and riot batons, held at the ready. One group of four men armed with grenade launchers waited behind the line.

Hastings and his company sergeant had posted themselves near the four grenadiers.

Taylor watched as the corporal rejoined them and saw Hastings's head snap in their direction before turning back to his men. The captain's arm lifted and then dropped sharply.

Thummp! Thummp! Thummp! Thummp! Tear gas projectiles arced through the air and fell into the soccer stadium, trailing a thin white haze behind them. Wisps of gas started to rise slowly, drifting inland on a light breeze. The troops stood and started to move forward at a trot.

Reitz was beside himself. "Four grenades? My God, that's a stadium, not a public toilet!"

"He's trying to give them a warning, a chance to leave without causing a panic."

"Damn it, man, I want them panicked!" Reitz exclaimed. "I want them terrified, especially of us!"

Still swearing, the colonel ran after the advancing company, and when he was in earshot, he started shouting, "Fire more tear gas. Fire now!"

Screams and the sounds of dozens of people choking and retching almost in unison were drowning out the muddy, indistinct voice bellowing over the stadium's public address system.

Hastings looked over his shoulder when he heard Reitz, scowled, and passed the order on to the four men carrying grenade launchers. Another salvo of tear gas grenades arced into the air and fell inside the crowded stadium.

The colonel grabbed Hastings by the arm and swung him around. "Have these men fire and fire again until they do not have any more projectiles! Then tell me and I will find more for them to use! Is that clear?"

Hastings nodded silently and after half a beat, saluted. Reitz ignored him. Instead, he turned away and followed the advancing troops, staying about five meters behind the command group.

More grenades soared through the air and fell into a growing haze. A few scattered and landed outside the stadium walls, but most went straight in. Taylor noticed that the loud voice on the loudspeaker had stopped, but that the screams and half-choked shouts from inside kept growing in volume.

Small bands of brown, black, and white protestors milled in confusion around the entrances to the soccer field—still unsure of the Army's exact intentions.

Suddenly the screaming in the stadium moved outside. A mass of people, individuals indistinct at a hundred meters' distance, surged out the door nearest to Hastings's troops. Other throngs of fleeing demonstrators were pouring out the other exits, eager to escape what must be chaos among the tear gas–filled bleachers and soccer field.

Hastings motioned to a sergeant, who raised a bullhorn and yelled, first in Afrikaans and then in English, "Halt and surrender! If you flee, you will be shot." As if to add substance to this threat, Taylor heard rifle fire from the far side of the stadium. That bastard Kloof and his men were already at work.

The mob ignored the sergeant's warning. A few men and women near the edges seemed to hear, but even they ran. Taylor could see several people with bloodied limbs or heads, undoubtedly injured in the crush to get out through the narrow, body-packed exits. He shook his head slowly in dismay. The colonel's tear gas barrage had driven this crowd beyond reason.

A few rocks and bottles flew in the soldiers' direction as some of the more militant protestors tried to retaliate. None landed very close.

Reitz took it all in and smiled thinly again. "That's one way to stop a show. Now fire a warning burst over their heads."

Tight-lipped, Hastings nodded and gave the order. His men lifted their assault rifles and fired a ragged volley into the air. The stone throwers fled, but panicked protestors continued to stream out of the exits and away from the soldiers.

That was enough for Reitz, who shouted, "Fire again, damn it, and this time aim for the crowd!"

What? Till now, Taylor had hoped against all the evidence that the colonel's ugly threats were mere bravado and bluster. Too late, he realized that Reitz had meant every word. He stepped forward to countermand the order. . . .

A hundred rifles cracked as one, this time pointed straight at the disordered mass of people streaming out of the stadium.

Almost every bullet struck home—puncturing lungs, shattering bones, or ripping through arms and legs. Taylor saw dozens of people jerk and fall as they were hit. Hundreds of others fell flat as well, trying desperately to find cover on the open ground. A few people kept running, but most stopped, shocked and stunned by the blood and death around them. Ominously, in the sudden silence after the volley, they could still hear steady firing from the other side of the stadium.

Taylor stared from Reitz to the broken and bleeding bodies littering the trampled green grass and back again. Incredibly, the Afrikaner wore a small, pleased smile. Enough!

He moved in front of Reitz and yelled, "Cease fire!" Hastings immediately echoed him.

"These poor people are no further threat to us or anyone,

Colonel.'' Taylor ground the man's rank out between clenched teeth. ''I'll order the men to move in and start making arrests.'' Taylor turned to issue Hastings new orders and felt himself spun back round.

The colonel's face was red, almost purple with rage. ''Rooinek swine! I will not have one of my orders countermanded. You and Hastings are both under arrest! Report to headquarters at once and stay there until I have time to deal with you!''

Then, his voice rising, he shouted, ''Since you love these people so much, you can join them in prison! I'm taking personal command of this company, and I'll do what you are apparently unable and unwilling to do—put an end to this lawbreaking!''

Taylor stared at Reitz in amazement. Had the man gone utterly mad? ''What lawbreaking?'' He pointed toward the blood-soaked lawns and gravel paths outside the stadium. ''It's over! Finished! My God, can't you see that?''

Reitz was still in a rage. ''Major, I don't want to hear any more from you! You don't know how to deal with these criminals, and you don't want to learn. Get out of my sight—and take that weakling Hastings with you! By the time I'm through, you'll both be lucky if you're not hanged!''

Taylor stared at his colonel a moment longer before trained reflexes and ingrained discipline took over. He stiffened to attention, turned, and started walking back to the command post with Hastings trudging silently at his side. He felt strangely empty of emotion, unsure of whether he should feel shock at the slaughter he had just witnessed, anger at Reitz, or shame at his relief. No, not shame. He'd done nothing wrong.

Behind him, the demonstrators were beginning to stir. Many knelt weeping by dead or dying friends. Others sat shaking, unable to move. A few were crawling away in a futile search for better cover or escape. People were still trying to get out of the gas-filled stadium, but those in front, who saw the horror before them, were trying to turn around. Being choked and blinded by tear gas must have seemed preferrable to being butchered on the open ground.

The long, thin line of South African soldiers looked numbly at the carnage in front of them, each obviously trying to reconcile his own actions with his conscience. Murder was not a part of the soldier's code, and this had been a kind of murder. Their lieutenants and noncoms glanced uneasily at each other—shocked by the open break between their colonel and the battalion's second-in-command. Taylor was one of them—a fellow reservist and a peacetime neighbor.

Reitz swept the formation with an ice-cold glare, and they all turned to face forward. Deliberately, he called out, "A Company, at the rioters, fire!"

Taylor turned in horror. Reitz was not satisfied. He intended to kill and go on killing.

Obedient under orders, most of the men raised their rifles, aiming at the crowd. But when only one of the company's lieutenants echoed the colonel's order, instead of all three as was customary, they lowered their weapons again and looked back at their officers in confusion.

Reitz walked closer to the line. He drew his pistol, worked the slide, and held it in front of him, muzzle pointing up. "Damn it, I gave an order, and I'll shoot the next man who doesn't obey instantly! Now fire!"

"No!" Taylor shouted. He sprinted toward the colonel. The personal consequences and discipline be damned. Discipline meant following lawful orders, not committing cold-blooded murder at the whim of a madman.

He was still ten meters away when Reitz turned and saw him coming.

Pure hatred on his face, the Afrikaner swung his pistol in Taylor's direction. Without thinking, he fumbled for his own sidearm as Reitz aimed and fired.

Automatically, he threw himself to the ground, thumb cocking the hammer of his own weapon. The pistol's blinding flash and the crack of a bullet racing close overhead reached Taylor at almost the same instant. Out of the corner of his eye, he saw Hastings charging forward, and Reitz turned, drawing down on the running officer.

No! Taylor squeezed the trigger, something inside him seeming to leap out along with the bullet.

Reitz staggered back, agony on his face as bright-red blood spread across the chest of his uniform jacket. He tried to hold his aim on Hastings and failed. Then his legs folded and he crumpled to the grass. One hand clawed briefly at the sky and then fell back.

Hastings skidded to a stop and knelt beside the fallen Afrikaner.

Taylor rose to one knee, stunned by the speed with which he'd moved from officer to prisoner to mutineer. He wanted to stop and think, to understand what he had done, but there wasn't time. He levered himself to his feet and ran toward Reitz, shouting, "Get an ambulance!"

It struck him as odd that nobody was calling for help for all the protestors who'd been shot, but that the colonel's wounding brought an instant reaction from him.

Hastings laid the colonel's head down on the ground. "We don't need an ambulance, Major."

Taylor could see Reitz's unseeing, open eyes and shuddered. But he didn't feel ashamed, or even sorry. He'd killed before, in battle, and this felt no different. Reitz had been bent on murdering unarmed civilians, not because of what they had done, but because of who they were.

He looked from the corpse to find many of Hastings's soldiers and all of A Company's officers surrounding him. One of the lieutenants, Kenhardt, said, "You're in command now, Major. What are your orders?"

The other officers and noncoms nodded eagerly.

Again, Taylor had the sensation of being pulled along by events instead of shaping them. Was he in command? Despite shooting his own colonel? He shook his head, trying to clear it. Someone had to take charge. In the circumstances, the battalion's senior captain would be a better choice—but that was Kloof. The crackle of automatic weapons fire drew his attention to the far side of the stadium. Kloof and his men were still shooting unarmed protestors.

Right, first things first. He grabbed the nearest enlisted man and ordered, "Tell Captain Kloof to cease fire and report back here on the double. Nothing more than that, understand?"

The private nodded and ran off.

Hastings looked troubled. ''Chris, that damned Afrikaner will just order you, me, and everyone else in reach arrested. We'd probably be shot after the kind of trial these people would give us.'' His junior officers nodded their agreement.

Taylor's mind raced. *These people*, Hastings had said contemptuously. As though the men in Pretoria weren't worth obeying. Well, was that so far off? Vorster, his cabinet cronies, and pet generals certainly weren't the Army and the government he'd sworn to serve. Everyone in authority seemed to have gone mad.

He shook his head. Hastings was right. Vorster's Afrikaner fanatics would kill him, they'd kill Hastings, and anyone else who crossed their path. And they would just keep on killing.

All right. He'd stopped Reitz from killing. Now he'd see how much more killing he could stop. Or start, he reminded himself. Crossing the line from personal disobedience to armed rebellion could not possibly be a bloodless journey. But perhaps it was a journey that should have been begun long ago, he thought, remembering all the wasteful violence and death he'd seen these past few months.

Taylor took a deep breath and nodded to Hastings. ''Form your troops, Johnnie. I have new orders for them.''

Five minutes later, Kloof trotted up to see two soldiers carrying Reitz away, and A Company formed by platoons near its armored personnel carriers. Paramedics from neighboring hospitals were already moving slowly through heaped bodies outside the stadium—sorting the dead from the wounded and those who might live from those who would surely die.

He ran the last twenty meters to where Taylor waited. ''Good God, Major! What's happened to the colonel?''

It was the first time Taylor had ever seen the younger Afrikaner officer forget to salute.

The major nodded to Hastings, who silently walked away toward his waiting troops. Guiding Kloof by holding his upper arm, Taylor moved in the opposite direction.

"Unfortunately, Captain, Colonel Reitz was killed while attempting to commit murder."

Kloof drew back in shock, able only to exclaim, "What?" and stare at him.

Taylor put steel into his voice. It was essential that this Afrikaner hear no sign of weakness or fear. "Reitz ordered our troops to continue firing at the protestors after they had dispersed. I countermanded his illegal order, and when he attempted to murder Captain Hastings and myself, I was forced to shoot him in self-defense."

Kloof's eyes flicked down to the now-holstered pistol, and then up to meet Taylor's steady gaze.

"Major, there is nothing illegal about shooting protestors who try to resist arrest by running." The Afrikaner's eyes narrowed. "I heard the colonel talking to you earlier. And I know that he ordered my company here because he did not trust Hastings or his men."

Kloof stepped closer. "In fact, Major, I think he was going to have you and Hastings arrested, for dereliction of duty, disloyalty, or both.

"Therefore, I'm placing you under arrest for the murder of Colonel Reitz." The captain started to reach for his sidearm, but paused when he saw Taylor slowly shake his head. He frowned and pulled the pistol from its holster. His frown grew deeper as Taylor stood motionless, apparently unconcerned.

The major merely looked over his shoulder, nodded briefly, and said, "I think not, Captain. I suggest that you drop your weapon and turn around slowly. Very slowly."

Kloof heard several metallic clicks behind him. He paled. He'd heard that sound nearly every day of his professional life. It was the sound of safeties being released.

He let his pistol fall from nerveless fingers and turned to see half a dozen rifles aimed at his stomach, all held by men of A Company.

The Afrikaner licked lips gone suddenly dry. "Is this a firing squad, Major?"

Taylor shook his head, almost amused. He didn't doubt

that it would have been a firing squad if the Afrikaner captain had held the upper hand instead. "Just a guard detail. We're making a few changes, Andries. You and some of your like-thinking friends are going to jail. And we're letting the elected officials of this city out to form a new government."

"What? That bunch of traitors?"

"Yes, Captain Kloof, that's right. That bunch of 'traitors' and my bunch of 'traitors' and a lot of other 'traitors' are going to bring this country back to some semblance of sanity, starting with Cape Town."

Motioning to the guards, Taylor said, "Get him out of here."

As Kloof was led away, Taylor ordered Hastings and his platoon leaders to bring C Company over, one platoon at a time. They would either join the rebel force or be detained. He was sure of two of C Company's junior officers, and the third might side with them as well.

Then, with two rifle companies firmly in hand, they'd see how many others in the city's military garrison and police force would join them to throw off Pretoria's dictatorial control.

Sighing, he looked at his watch. It was already one-thirty in the afternoon, and he had a lot to do before dusk.

STATE SECURITY COUNCIL CHAMBER, PRETORIA

Messengers kept bringing in new reports from Cape Town, none of it good. Radio stations off the air. Contact lost with the international airport. Telephone lines down. It was always news of some strand's being cut, some part of the fabric of government lost to their control.

The room was filled with government officials and military and police officers. Maps of Cape Town and Cape Province hung on the wall, and colored circles showed the known extent of the revolt. Vorster and his civilian ministers sat at one end of the table, while military aides under General de Wet's somewhat confused direction tried to manage the few forces still under their control.

It was clear those forces were shrinking fast. Only one battalion, the 16th Infantry, had officially mutinied, but reports from the two other battalion commanders near Cape Town indicated that their units were not "completely reliable." Commandos had formed in the city and the surrounding townships, and many were siding with the mutineers.

Government strength seemed to be coalescing around Table Mountain, the three-thousand-foot high escarpment dominating the city skyline and the southern Cape Peninsula. Honeycombed with caves and bunkers, it had been always been designated as the final defensive position for South African forces holding Cape Town. Now infantry companies and fragments of infantry companies were reported regrouping atop the mountain.

Marius van der Heijden found himself clasping his hands as though in prayer as he listened to the steady stream of bad news streaming in and forced himself to pry them apart. He glanced toward the end of the table where Karl Vorster sat white-faced and immobile. His eyes, once so impressively cold and clear, were now shadowed and rimmed with red from too many sleepless nights.

Van der Heijden frowned. More and more these days, as people outside Vorster's immediate circle challenged his authority, the President withdrew into himself—as though he could shut out the very events he had triggered. It was a bad sign.

As the aide who'd borne the latest news of disaster left, Vorster stirred himself enough to ask, "Well, General? Can we hold the city?"

De Wet swallowed hard. "I'm afraid not, Mr. President. Not without more troops."

"Troops we do not have?"

De Wet nodded reluctantly. "That's correct, Mr. President. All our available forces are tied down in Namibia, Natal, or other trouble spots."

"Then perhaps it's high time we began withdrawing from Namibia, General." Fredrik Pienaar still retained enough of Vorster's confidence to speak bluntly. And the propaganda minister had never liked de Wet or his plans.

"That would be disastrous!" De Wet appealed directly to Vorster. "Intelligence reports indicate that the Cubans are planning a major offensive sometime in the next few days. Abandoning our defenses there now would be against all military logic!"

"Then what do you suggest, General? Shall we sit idly here in Pretoria while the Republic collapses around our ears? Is that the militarily sensible thing to do?"

De Wet turned red as he listened to Pienaar's scathing sarcasm. "No, Minister." De Wet breathed out noisily and refocused his attention on the silent, brooding figure of Karl Vorster. "I suggest a temporary delay, that's all. Let us absorb this Cuban offensive, bleed them white in fruitless attacks against our trenches and minefields, and send them reeling back toward Windhoek. Then we can safely pull forces out of Namibia to deal with these traitors!"

Van der Heijden nodded to himself. Surprisingly, de Wet made sense for once.

Vorster made an impatient gesture with one massive hand. "Very well, de Wet." He glowered at the general. "But do not fail me as so many have of late. I will not forgive treason or ineptitude."

De Wet paled, murmured his understanding, and turned back to his uniformed aides.

Vorster looked at the rest of his cabinet, his weary gaze moving from face to face until it settled on van der Heijden. "Marius?"

"Yes, Mr. President?"

"Have you captured that American swine yet?"

The minister for law and order felt his stomach lurch. For personal reasons, he'd been keeping the police search for Sherfield low-key. In the confession his men had ripped out of Erik Muller, the former security chief had babbled about the young, Afrikaans-speaking woman who'd been blackmailing him. And now Emily was missing—not at the farm or at her friend's home in Cape Town. Van der Heijden could add two and two to get four. Somehow his own beautiful, foolish, and headstrong daughter had been gulled into helping this American reporter. For her sake, he'd kept investigators from following up on several promising leads—hoping that she'd escape South Africa before he was forced to act. Now it appeared that time had run out.

He shook his head. "Not yet, Mr. President. But we're hot on this man's trail. I expect an arrest at virtually any moment."

"Good." Vorster stroked his chin. "When we have him in custody, your people can undoubtedly 'persuade' him to recant this foolish story of his—true?"

Warily, van der Heijden nodded again. This Ian Sherfield was only a journalist after all. A few hours of rigorous torture should render him malleable to almost any suggestion.

"Excellent, Marius." Vorster smiled at the rest of his uncertain inner circle. "There you are, my friends. Soon, we'll have this American admitting that his whole story was nothing but a communist plot to sow confusion in our beloved fatherland. And on that day, all these minor difficulties will begin to fade away like the bad dreams that they truly are. Our strayed brethren in the Orange Free State and the Transvaal will return begging for our forgiveness."

Vorster's smile turned ugly. "And the rooineks of the Cape and the kaffirs of Natal will weep for the days before they dared to oppose our power!"

Van der Heijden and the others stared back in open disbelief. How could their leader really believe that matters could still be so simply resolved? Mere words wouldn't douse the fires of revolt and rebellion now burning in almost every corner of South Africa.

How could any sane man hope to avert Armageddon here?

FORWARD HEADQUARTERS, MILITARY FORCES OF THE PROVISIONAL GOVERNMENT OF CAPE TOWN, NEAR THE HOUSES OF PARLIAMENT

Maj. Chris Taylor crouched behind a bullet-scarred Buffel armored personnel carrier, studying the hastily scrawled markings on a map of the city. He ducked as a mortar round exploded a hundred meters away, blasting leaves and bark off an ancient oak tree and sending white-hot shrapnel sleeting through the shattered front doors and windows of the Houses of Parliament.

Smoke from burning buildings and vehicles swirled across the street and billowed high into the air—joining a dense pall produced by fires raging out of control all across Cape Town. Taylor coughed as he breathed in the acrid stuff. He tilted his helmet back up off his forehead and looked closely at his new second-in-command, Capt. John Hastings. "You're sure about this, Johnnie? It's not just another damned rumor?"

Hastings shook his head. "I talked to the new base commander myself. It's official. Simonstown has come over to our side!"

Both men ducked again as another mortar round landed in the botanical gardens close by, showering them with dirt, grass, and pieces of mangled plants.

Hastings spat dirt out of his mouth and continued, "The Navy boys said they'd had some fighting with a few diehards, but they've got everything under control for the moment."

"Damage?"

"A few fires, but no damage to the docks or ships."

That was welcome news. Taylor had been hoping for support from the naval officers and ratings stationed at the Simonstown base. The Navy had always been the most "English" of all the South African military services. And even though its total strength didn't amount to much more than a few aging ships, holding South Africa's main naval base would give the provisional government's claims to independence needed national and international credibility.

He refolded the map and rolled out from behind the APC, seeking a better view of the house-to-house fighting raging up ahead. Hastings followed suit.

Cape Town, once arguably the most beautiful city on the African continent, now looked more like wartime Berlin.

The ugly debris left by war marred the long, broad expanse of Government Avenue and its adjoining botanical gardens. Buildings were pockmarked by bullets, mortar and grenade fragments, and cannon shells. Bodies lay here and there—some crumpled on the street or pavement, others draped over rose bushes and park benches or sprawled on gravel paths. Some of the dead wore civilian clothes, others were in uniform. Strips of white cloth fluttered in a light sea breeze, tied around the outstretched arms of those who'd fought against Pretoria.

A wrecked APC blocked part of the avenue, orange flames licking skyward as its fuel tanks burned. A single charred corpse hung half in and half out of the commander's hatch.

Taylor swallowed hard against the taste of bile, forcing himself to ignore the butchery before his eyes. Despite all the signs of slaughter, he and his men were winning. The flickering, pinprick flashes of rifle and machine-gun fire that marked his battleline were farther away than when he'd last looked. And he could see an Eland armored car moving slowly forward, stopping briefly from time to time to shell buildings farther down the street. Small figures clustered along each side of the armored car, sometimes crouching for cover, but always advancing.

He nodded to himself. Vorster's loyalists were definitely giving ground, falling back toward Table Mountain.

Taylor lifted his eyes to the flat-topped mountain rising south of the city. The escarpment loomed ominously over Cape Town's tallest skyscrapers—a massive edifice of jagged rock covered by what looked like a thick layer of fluffy white cloud. A rippling series of red and orange flashes from the summit reminded him that the white haze wasn't cloud at all. It was smoke from an artillery bombardment—a barrage so intense that it shrouded the entire top of the mountain.

He frowned. His gunners were firing everything they had at the fortified caves and bunkers held by government troops, hoping to knock out the artillery pieces emplaced there, but it seemed likely to be a vain effort. Those fortifications were too strong to be suppressed by long-range bombardment. They'd have to be taken in a bloody succession of set-piece infantry assaults.

And that was the problem. Taylor now had enough men under his command to clear the city of Vorster's troops. But he didn't have enough infantry, armored vehicles, or artillery to finish the job by seizing Table Mountain. As a result, the battle seemed headed for certain stalemate. He and his fellow rebels might control Cape Town, but loyalist artillery batteries and troops trapped on the escarpment would dominate both its harbor and international airport.

Taylor hugged the pavement as more mortar rounds rained down on the gardens ahead, knocking down trees and smashing already shattered greenhouses. Windblown dust, dirt, and smoke cut visibility to a matter of meters in seconds.

He rolled back into cover, reaching for his command phone. Table Mountain would have to wait. He had more immediate problems.

Behind him, the setting sun dipped lower, dropping steadily toward the western horizon. Night was falling across a South Africa now fully engulfed in bitter civil war.

CHAPTER 21

Flight

NOVEMBER 11—HEADQUARTERS, 20TH CAPE RIFLES, VOORTREKKER HEIGHTS MILITARY CAMP, NEAR PRETORIA

Furnace-white arc lights burned all along the perimeter of the Voortrekker Heights Military Camp—stripping the night away from barren brown hillsides. No trees, clumps of brush, or even patches of tall grass remained either to soften the outlines of those rugged slopes or to conceal an approaching enemy. Together, the perimeter lights and the empty kill zones they lit made it impossible for anyone to mount a successful surprise attack on South Africa's major military headquarters. But the dazzling glare also washed out any glimpse of cold, clear stars speckled across a pitch-black sky or the warm, golden glow of Pretoria's streetlamps and cozy homes.

Commandant Henrik Kruger regretted that. Any reminder of life outside this sterile military encampment would have been welcome.

Since leaving the Namibian front more than a month before, his battered battalion had been penned up among Voortrekker Heights' drab, look-alike barracks, parade grounds, maintenance sheds, and vehicle parks. Some high-ranking nitwit in the Ministry of Defense had ordered all enlisted personnel and noncommissioned officers restricted to base.

He and his officers had stayed with them, determined not to let a piece of bureaucratic idiocy endanger bonds of trust and loyalty forged in combat. Still, he had to admit to himself that he also had other, more personal reasons for avoiding Pretoria or nearby Johannesburg.

He was afraid that even the sight of their bustling streets, shops, and restaurants might awaken painful memories of his brief, happy time with Emily van der Heijden—memories that were three years old now. True, he'd known that their engagement was mostly her father's idea, but he'd hoped that he could reconcile her to the thought of their marriage. In retrospect, it had been a foolish hope. The gaps between their ages, their politics, and their interests were simply too wide to be easily bridged.

Kruger smiled crookedly. He'd been alone and aloof for most of his adult life—content in the masculine, monastic world of the professional military. Given that, it was strange that he should have found the one woman of his heart, only to learn that she had no room in hers for him.

He gripped the wood railing of his veranda until his knuckles stood out white against the surrounding blackness. With an effort, he forced his mind away from lasting personal grief to professional concerns.

Such as this absurd decision to keep his battalion confined to Voortrekker Heights. Vorster and his minions must fear that exposure to the political dissent and economic hardship sweeping the country might tempt their soldiers to commit treason or desert. So they'd denied his troops and the other weary combat veterans returning from Namibia promised home leaves, weekend passes, and any other opportunity to escape the rigid confines of a military life for even a short while.

Kruger relaxed his grip and flexed his aching fingers. Anybody brighter than a brain-dead Defense Ministry bureaucrat could have predicted the result. Weeks of bloody fighting followed by more weeks of mind-numbing routine—drill, calisthenics, drill, spit-and-polish inspections, and still more drill—had produced a battalion practically boiling over with resentment and barely suppressed rage.

More than a dozen of the 20th's veterans were in punishment cells right now—locked up on charges ranging from simple insubordination to being drunk while on duty. Kruger shook his head angrily. He'd rather chance the desertion of a few men than watch this slow, steady disintegration of what had been a proud fighting unit.

As matters stood, the 20th Cape Rifles was now effectively a weaker battalion than it had been in Namibia. Citizen Force replacements were filtering in slowly, fleshing out skeletal companies and platoons to something near their authorized strength. Unfortunately, most of the reservists were short on needed training, experience, and esprit de corps.

Kruger frowned. His companies were also short of heavy weapons and vehicles. They'd left what remained of their old gear in Namibia to equip the battalion replacing them on the line. In return, his troops had been promised first pick of the new armored personnel carriers, mortars, and heavy machine guns that were supposed to be rolling off the ARMSCOR production lines. So far, at least, they'd had little to pick from. Strikes and skilled-labor shortages had cut production well below required levels. And as a result, he had barely enough APCs to mount one of his three infantry companies. The other two could move only by truck or on foot.

The sound of guttural laughter emanating from the nearby bachelor officers' quarters turned his worried frown into a scowl. Tanks, artillery, APCs, and antitank weapons might be in short supply—but not, it seemed, junior staff officers with strong political ties to the Vorster government. They'd arrived in eager, interfering droves.

So though the 20th was short of trained troops and weapons, it had a battalion staff bloated to a size more suitable to a brigade. Kruger didn't have any illusions about why the Defense Ministry had seen fit to dump so many fanatics in his lap. They were there to keep tabs on him—to make sure that he and the other officers didn't lead their men into rebellion.

His scowl grew deeper. He didn't mind their prying and spying so much. He could cope with that. But the overabundance of inexperienced, inept, and arrogant Afrikaner officers was yet another source of friction in a battalion already rubbed raw. "Vorster's pets," as they were known, tended to treat the 20th's enlisted men—most born and raised in the Cape Province—as nothing more than would-be traitors and renegades.

Well, perhaps that wasn't too far off the mark, he thought wryly, remembering the news passed on by his friends inside the Ministry. It was incredible. Cape Town in flames and armed conflict spreading across the whole province like wildfire. Natal torn by guerrilla war, atrocity, and revenge. And antigovernment commandos roaming vast stretches of the Transvaal and the Orange Free State virtually at will. Karl Vorster's criminal stupidity and his ill-fated Namibian invasion had combined to tear South Africa to pieces in the space of a few short months.

He raised his eyes again, scanning the night sky above the low hills rising to the north for some sign of the city just beyond them. Nothing. Only the glaring lights and the elongated, ugly shadows cast by armored cars patrolling the perimeter. But even at this distance, he could tell that several of the armored cars had their weapons turrets pointing inward—toward the base's barracks and armories. He smiled sourly. Vorster's loyalists were taking few chances. And rightly so.

Kruger started to pace slowly up and down the darkened veranda. Many of his friends and fellow soldiers had already joined those rebelling against Pretoria's authority. Soon it would be his turn. Very soon.

JOHANNESBURG

The unmarked police minivan sat on a narrow side street, wedged between a silver Astra and a dark blue Toyota pickup.

Two uniformed officers slouched in the front seat with their ties hanging loose and collar buttons unfastened. One, a big, beefy man with thinning, straw-colored hair, sipped moodily at a styrofoam cup half-full of lukewarm coffee. His partner, smaller and darker-haired, sighed briefly and stubbed his cigarette out in the door ashtray. Both men were silently cursing the trick of fate that had saddled them with such a worthless assignment.

"I tell you, man, this just proves that the captain's got it in for you and me." The big man gestured with his cup and frowned as a few drops sloshed out over the steering wheel. "Some big deal, eh? We drive here. We drive there. And then we sit like this for fucking hours. And all for what?"

He answered his own question. "So some smart-ass lieutenant can come up and tell us to go drive somewhere else. That's what for."

The smaller policeman sat up sharply. "Man, speak of the devil! There's Baumann now." He unrolled his window as the much-younger police lieutenant, trim and self-assured in his blue-gray jacket, gray trousers, and peaked cap, appeared on the sidewalk beside them.

The lieutenant leaned in through the open window. "This is the right place, boys. I'm sure of it." He tapped the list of addresses taped to a clipboard. More than half had already been crossed off. "I spoke to several of the neighbors and there's definitely somebody living there now. Lights on from time to time. Cooking smells. Trash dumped. All the signs of occupancy."

The larger policeman frowned. He bent forward and checked the name written next to the address. "Couldn't it just be this Pakenham bastard . . . Lieutenant?"

For an instant the younger man flushed angrily. Then he controlled it and smiled silkily. "Not possible, Kowie. The rooinek's been on combat duty in Namibia for weeks. I checked this morning."

The smaller policeman nudged his partner into silence with a bony elbow. "That's great, sir. Just great." He straightened up and checked his holstered pistol. "Shall we pick him up right away?"

"I think so." The lieutenant stepped back from the van and watched as they climbed out onto the pavement, moving awkwardly on legs cramped from sitting still for so long. "From what I hear, Pretoria wants this fellow pretty badly."

The bigger policeman rubbed thick fingers through his thinning yellow hair and shoved his uniform cap back into place. "Right, Lieutenant, you can leave it to us, eh? We'll winkle the pig out without any trouble at all. Isn't that so, Arrie?"

His smaller partner nodded confidently while making sure his baton hung loose in its own holster. The man they were after wasn't supposed to be anything special, but it never hurt to be prepared.

Inside Brian Pakenham's borrowed apartment, the single lit table lamp cast a small circle of light over the man and woman entwined on a tattered sofa.

Ian Sherfield sat with one arm draped around Emily's shoulders, reading the same mystery novel for what must be the seventh or eighth time in as many days. She murmured something unintelligible and squirmed deeper into his grasp—dozing lightly. He kissed the top of her head and turned the page with a practiced thumb, stifling a yawn. Damn it. As always, the main character had just walked straight past the story's most crucial clue without noticing it.

He set the paperback down and tilted his head back against the sofa. It had been damned decent of Emily's friend and former classmate to volunteer the use of his apartment, but he wished the guy had been a little more widely read. Five so-so mysteries, a travel guide, and three college-level political-science textbooks weren't much of a library with which to while away the passing hours and days.

Emily was the lucky one. She could make occasional, lightning-fast trips outside to pick up supplies. He and Matthew Sibena were trapped in this tiny apartment—unable to so much as show their faces in public lest they be recognized and arrested. Every scrap of news Emily could pick up on her trips to the neighborhood market seemed to indicate that they were still at the top of South Africa's Most Wanted list.

Soft snores drifting through the open door into the apartment's only bedroom showed that Sibena had again taken refuge in deep, uninterrupted sleep. Ian felt the trace of a smile flicker across his face. Over the last two weeks, the young black man had astounded them by being able to sleep through anything and at any time. He could sleep through the noise of the morning rush hour, in the sweltering heat of a sun-lit afternoon, or even on a night that seemed far too quiet. It was a talent Ian often envied.

"Oh!" Emily sat up suddenly, looking pale and frightened.

"Bad dream?" He gently stroked her shoulder.

She shook her head, puzzled. "No, I do not think so." She sat listening for a moment. "I thought I heard something just now. Soft footsteps right outside the door."

Ian cocked his head, listening for himself. "I don't know, Em, I don't hear anyth—"

A savage kick smashed the front door open and left it dangling from one set of bent hinges. For one terrifying second, Ian felt his heart stop beating. He sat frozen in shock.

"Police! Police! Nobody move! Nobody move!"

Men in blue-gray uniforms poured into the apartment from the outside hallway. Two charged past the sofa, splitting up and spreading out to search the other rooms. A third policeman slid to a stop in front of them, aiming a Browning Hi Power pistol very precisely at an imaginary point right between Ian's eyes.

The barrel looked ten feet across.

"Do not even think to move, man, or I will blow your *blery* brains across the girl there." The pistol didn't waver. "You are the American reporter, Ian Sherfield?"

Still in shock, Ian nodded.

"Then I arrest you on charges of espionage and violation of the National Emergency decrees." The smug note of triumph in the man's voice was unmistakable.

Ian flushed bright red, ashamed to have been caught so quickly and apparently so easily.

"Lieutenant!" One of the other policemen emerged from the bedroom, dragging Matthew Sibena along in an iron-fisted grip. The young black man looked dazed, frightened, and completely disoriented. "Look what else I've found!"

The officer arched a single finely sculpted eyebrow. "A black?" He sneered at Ian and Emily. "ANC, eh? Your controller, perhaps?"

Sibena twisted helplessly in the larger South African policeman's locked arms. "No! That's not so! I'm not ANC, I swear it, *baas*."

"Shut up, kaffir!" The police lieutenant still hadn't lowered his gun. "Well, American?"

Ian looked back and forth from Emily to Sibena to the pistol, thinking fast. Right now, the three of them didn't have the slightest chance to wriggle out of this nightmarish situation. The police were too alert, too ready for trouble. The odds and ends of martial arts training he'd picked up for physical and mental exercise wouldn't be of any use if they thought he might be dangerous. He needed to divert their attention away from him—to convince these policemen that they had him thoroughly cowed and under control.

He let his face crumple in abject terror and allowed a whining note to creep into his voice. "That's right. He's an ANC guerrilla. The ANC was supposed to get us out of the country before any of this happened."

Emily breathed in sharply suddenly, but stayed silent. Good girl, he thought. She knows me too well to think I've suddenly cracked.

He glared accusingly at Sibena's stunned face. "Your people failed us, comrade! And I'll be damned if I'll take the fall for them!" Watch it, Ian, he told himself. No need to lay it on too thick.

"That's enough." The lieutenant smiled in satisfaction. "You can make a full confession later. In the meantime, just stay still and keep your mouth shut."

Another policeman, smaller than the one holding Sibena, wandered back into the living room. "All clear, Lieutenant. There's nobody else here."

"Good." The lieutenant waved Ian and Emily up from the sofa with his pistol.

They rose cautiously, with Ian's right arm still wrapped around Emily's shoulders. He could feel her shaking uncontrollably and squeezed gently with his right hand, trying to offer some assurance that all was not lost.

"Take these three to headquarters. I'll stay here and look for documents." The lieutenant holstered his pistol and stepped aside as the larger policeman hauled Sibena toward the door. "And keep an eye on that kaffir! He's probably had some kind of combat training."

Ian hid a thin-lipped, humorless smile as he followed Emily out into the hallway with his hands up in the air. They had a small chance after all.

Maybe these two South African policemen weren't going to be looking the right way at the right time.

MARKET STREET, NEAR JOHN VORSTER SQUARE, JOHANNESBURG

The police minivan wasn't designed for comfort—just efficiency. The smaller of the two policeman sat behind the wheel, separated from his companion and their three prisoners by the front seat itself. His four passengers perched on fold-down plastic benches that ran the length of each side of the vehicle.

Matthew Sibena sat on the right, immediately behind the driver, swaying uncomfortably from side to side as the minivan turned or changed lanes. Steel handcuffs pinioned his wrists behind his back. The beefy policeman with thinning hair sat next to him, his gaze shifting periodically from Sibena to Emily to Ian and back again. He cradled a pump-action shotgun in his lap.

Ian sat directly across from the guard, with Emily to his left. Like Sibena, he was handcuffed, but the policemen had left her hands free. He wasn't sure if that was because they viewed Emily as just a "helpless" woman or because of her father's importance in the government. Whatever the reason, he didn't plan to complain. Only the fact that she could still use her hands made any escape attempt even remotely feasible.

But so far no opportunity had presented itself. Traffic on Johannesburg's streets was light at this time of night, and their driver was proving dangerously efficient. He'd managed to time every light perfectly—only having to slow gradually without ever coming to a complete stop.

Ian could feel ice-cold sweat beading on his forehead and soaking the shirt under his arms. He shivered. Time was running out.

In five or six minutes at the most, they'd be trapped inside Johannesburg's heavily fortified police headquarters. And he didn't have any illusions about the kind of treatment they'd receive at the government's hands. Men who'd allowed their own countrymen and colleagues to be gunned down by terrorists wouldn't show any mercy to a foreigner, a member of a despised race, and a woman accused of high treason. Under the circumstances, even Emily's father wouldn't be able to save her. He was sure that their lives inside a South African interrogation center would, at best, be "nasty, brutish, and short."

Christ. The very thought of Emily under torture was unbearable. He tensed, ready to spring even while the minivan was moving. Maybe it would be better to die fighting than to be meekly led to a protracted slaughter.

The van braked sharply to a complete stop. Unable to use his hands, Sibena slammed into the front seat and rocked back. The rest of them had to hold on tightly to avoid following suit.

"Ho, man, we've got some trouble up here." The driver sounded suddenly tense. "A *verdomde* riot starting, maybe."

Rhythmic, shouted chants filtered in from the outside, building slowly in volume as they were repeated over and over again. Ian craned his neck out into the middle of the van's passenger compartment, trying to see through the front windshield.

Traffic along Market Street was at a standstill. The cars and trucks in front of them were jammed in bumper to bumper—unable to go forward and unable to reverse. Farther ahead, thousands of angry demonstrators milled around in front of the police station. Dozens of colorful banners and posters waved over the crowd, rising and falling in time with their chanting.

"Shit." Still holding the shotgun, the big policeman heaved himself to his feet and stood hunched over, staring through the windshield. "We'll never get through that *blery* mess. We'll have to try the back—"

Ian saw his chance and took it.

He rocketed off the bench, trying to ram the top of his head under the policeman's outthrust chin and up. He wanted to slam the Afrikaner's own head squarely into the van's metal ceiling. It was just the kind of crazy stunt he'd seen work in films. The only trouble was, making such a move work in real life would take perfect positioning and even more perfect timing. Too late, Ian realized that he didn't have either.

The adrenaline pouring into his bloodstream seemed to slow time itself.

The policeman saw him lunging upward and yanked his head backward, twisting right and away from him. At the same time, he swung his shotgun around through a narrow arc. Not far. Just far enough so that Ian's head grazed the shotgun's steel barrel instead of his vulnerable chin.

Red-hot pain blossomed. Jesus. He stumbled back against the bench.

The guard kept spinning to his right, trying to slam the butt of his shotgun into Ian's exposed stomach.

React! Counter! Trained reflexes took over when conscious thought seemed to crawl. Everything around him blurred to a halt—an image held frozen in time between the blink of an eye.

The big policeman's left leg was now straight, bearing all his considerable weight as he pivoted right with the shotgun poised for a crippling blow.

Perfect.

In one strangely calm corner of his mind, Ian remembered a dry academic voice saying, "The human knee, Mr. Sherfield, is a marvelously fragile mechanism. Momentum and the proper application of mass can maim any man—no matter how big or strong he might be."

Without thinking, he rocked back on his own left foot,

spinning sideways to the left. His right foot came up as though he were pedaling a bike. Now! He kicked out and down with vicious speed and force.

His right foot smashed home two finger widths' above the policeman's left knee and kept going. With a sickening, audible *crack,* the policeman's leg snapped like a dried stick. The big man flopped forward against the bench and screamed in sudden agony.

Ian stumbled against the van's rear door, thrown off-balance by his kick and by a painful, glancing blow from the shotgun butt. He could see the smaller, darker-haired policeman clawing for his pistol. No, damn it!

He tried to turn, already knowing he wouldn't make it.

Emily exploded into action. She scooped up the injured policeman's fallen shotgun, snapped the safety off, and had it aimed squarely at the driver's face before he had his own weapon more than halfway out of the holster.

Time accelerated back to its normal speed.

"Don't tempt me, *meneer*." Emily's voice was calm, even cold. "I will not hesitate."

The driver paled, and he dropped the pistol as though it were scalding hot.

Ian winced at the pain pounding through his head and turned to the other guard. No problem there. The beefy South African lay where he'd first fallen, cradling his broken leg in both hands. And Matthew Sibena had his feet planted firmly on the man's throat—ready to step down hard at the slightest sign of trouble.

Ian could feel his pulse starting to slow to something near normal. He grinned at Emily and took a shaky breath. "Jeez. Remind me not to ever piss you off on a date!"

She glanced down at the shotgun gripped tightly in both her hands and looked up with a somewhat shamefaced grin of her own. "My father insisted I learn about firearms when I was a small girl. But I must admit that I never thought such knowledge would be useful."

Ian started to laugh. He had the strangest feeling that Marius van der Heijden wouldn't be at all happy to learn how well his daughter had learned her lessons.

TOP STAR DRIVE-IN, JOHANNESBURG

The minivan was as isolated as any vehicle could possibly be in the middle of a vast, modern metropolis. More than one hundred meters of empty, oil-stained gravel stretched in all directions—empty except for row after row of splintered wooden posts holding detachable speakers. Giant, off-white movie screens and a high fence blocked any view from the houses and small office buildings around. Even more important, trains roaring along a railroad line to the south and trucks grinding their way along a motorway to the north should muffle any noises made by the two handcuffed policemen locked away in the van.

Ian slammed the van's windowless rear door shut, pointedly ignoring the smaller policeman's hate-filled glare. The other cop lay still, driven into unconsciousness by the pain from his broken leg.

"Got everything?"

Matthew Sibena nodded eagerly and held out the assortment of paper money, coins, and identification cards they'd filched from the two policemen.

Ian noticed that the young man's hands were still shaking. Well, he thought wryly, so are mine. "And their weapons?"

Sibena answered by silently pointing toward the rusting trash Dumpster backed against the drive-in theater's small cinder-block concession stand.

"Good." Ian had vetoed the idea of taking the pistols or shotgun along when it became clear that neither of the two police uniforms would fit him. They were going to be conspicuous enough as it was without walking around in civilian clothes while armed to the teeth.

"Ian! Come take a look at this!"

He followed Emily's voice around to the front of the minivan. She stood motionless by the open passenger-side door, pointing to a piece of paper taped to the dashboard.

She shook her head in disbelief. "My God! So that's how they found us!"

"Huh?" Ian looked over her shoulder at the typewritten list crammed full of names and addresses.

"My father must have given this to them. It's a compilation of all my closest friends." She sounded troubled. "Are they in trouble now?"

He shut the door and led her away from the van. "More to the point, how do we avoid getting nabbed by your dad's goons a second time?" He squinted, trying to see the numbers on his watch against the orange glow of the Johannesburg skyline. "They're going to start looking for this van any minute now, and they'll find it in a matter of hours . . . even if we're lucky."

Sibena joined them. "All set. The doors are locked and"—he grinned and dangled a set of keys from one finger—"they'll stay that way for a time."

Ian thumped him on the shoulder. "Good going, Matt." He paused and looked seriously at his two companions. "So where to now, folks?"

Sibena smiled shyly. "How about America?"

A joke. The young black man was telling jokes now! Ian shook his head in wonder. After only three months around people who treated him as a man instead of two-legged livestock, Sibena was turning into a someone who could make light of danger—instead of cowering in fear. He wished Sam Knowles were here to see it.

He smiled back. "Maybe we should shoot for somewhere a little closer. Just for the time being, of course."

Emily pulled nervously at separate strands of her long auburn hair. "I think perhaps there is one person who may be able to help us." She glanced quickly at Ian and then looked away. "But it may be risky."

"Hold on there." Ian shook his head. "Remember your dad's little list? We can't count on any more of your friends. It'd be too dangerous for them as well as being suicidal for us."

She shook her head, her expression unreadable in the darkness. "Oh, no, Ian. This one whose help I must beg wouldn't be on my father's list of my friends." Her voice fell to a whisper. "Nor am I at all sure that he will come again when I call."

And with that, Ian had to be content. She would say nothing more for the moment.

NOVEMBER 12—BRAAMFONTEIN CEMETERY, JOHANNESBURG

The sun was coming again to South Africa, warming the air and earth below, and coloring the once pitch-black eastern sky a faint shade of mingled gray and pink. Inside the Braamfontein Cemetery, tall trees, headstones, and squat marble mausoleums that had for so long been nothing more than darker shadows among a lesser darkness took on line and form and hue as night faded slowly into day.

Ian yawned uncontrollably, rose, and stretched aching muscles. He looked warily around for signs of movement where there should be none. Both Emily and Sibena had protested his choice of temporary sanctuary. But superstition worked both ways. Who would hunt for the living in a land of the dead?

He turned in a complete circle, studying every piece of ground in view.

And froze. A car, headlights on, moving slowly along the wide avenue running beside the cemetery. He sank back to the grass, listening now instead of looking. An engine growing louder—definitely coming closer.

Emily leaned closer and whispered, "I think it has to be the man we are waiting for. Who else would come here so early?"

"The police? A caretaker?" Ian shrugged. Emily's reluctance to name this mystery man both irked and worried him.

He risked another glance at the oncoming car. It was close enough to make out details now. A Land Rover painted a uniformly drab green. That was odd.

The Land Rover stopped just outside the graveyard's wrought-iron gate and sat idling.

Emily rose unsteadily to her feet. "It's him. It can't be anyone else." Ian and Sibena started to get to their feet, but she waved them back down. "Come when I say . . . not before. Right?"

They both nodded their understanding and watched her make her way carefully downhill to the gate. Ian felt cold and damp and knew he was sweating again. What if they'd been betrayed? He studied the Land Rover through slitted eyes, ready to make a mad dash downhill if his worst fears were realized.

The driver's door popped open and a tall, slender man stepped out onto the pavement. A man wearing an Army uniform.

Ian forced himself to breath. Emily wasn't running away in panic—at least not yet.

She came to the waist-high stone wall separating the cemetery from the street and stood waiting. The soldier stepped closer, until he stood just across the wall. His shoulders seemed curiously rigid, almost as if he were holding himself at attention—or in check.

Emily said something too quietly to be heard at this distance, and the soldier leaned closer still before abruptly straightening up. Ian frowned. For an instant this other man had seemed ready to embrace her. What the hell was going on here? Who was this guy anyway?

Part of his mind laughed at his own ridiculous pride. It was absurd to be jealous when half of South Africa's police force must be busy hunting high and low for them. But a deeper, more primitive side wanted to go down there and beat the hell out of that damned soldier. Yeah, right. Me Ian, you Emily—you my woman. Somehow he didn't think she'd appreciate the caveman approach to love and commitment.

"There's the signal!" Sibena tugged at his arm.

Ian glanced toward the gate. Emily was waving them down with short, sharp, urgent gestures.

Despite the jealous mutterings of his subconscious, his first impressions of this South African soldier were favorable. The man had a firm-jawed, weather-beaten face and open, intelligent gray eyes.

Ian lengthened his stride, aware that he'd also squared his shoulders. He stopped just across the wall from the soldier.

"Ian and Matthew, this is Kommandant Henrik Kruger." Emily's voice faltered, almost as though she'd been about to add something and then couldn't think of the right way to say it. She recovered. "And Henrik, these are my two friends, Ian Sherfield and Matthew Sibena."

Friends? Ian nodded toward the South African, his face kept carefully blank. Kruger inclined his own head, acknowledging the introduction. Neither man offered to shake hands.

"You are the American reporter the police are hunting?" Kruger's voice was deep, almost melodic despite a clipped Afrikaans accent. An easy voice to hear amid the noise and confusion of a battle, Ian judged.

"That's right."

The South African soldier frowned. "Then perhaps you can tell me why I should risk my career and my life to help you? Miss van der Heijden is a woman of my people—reason enough for my aid to her . . . even if there were no other."

Kruger glanced at Sibena. "But this man is an enemy of my blood . . . and you are nothing more than an interfering Uitlander. Why then should I lift a finger to save you?"

Ian felt Emily stir and laid a gentle hand on her shoulder, cautioning her to stay out of it. This was his fight.

He looked steadily into Kruger's eyes. "There's no reason you should, *Kommandant*. No reason at all." He heard Emily gasp softly in surprise and distress. "Matt and I will take our chances on our own. But you've got to promise me that you'll keep Emily safe or get her out of the country."

He pressed on, anger making his voice harsher, rougher. "And if I ever hear that you've broken your word or hurt her, I'll come after you myself. Is that clear enough, *Kommandant?*" He stopped talking, afraid that he might have gone too far and endangered even Emily.

But then slowly, almost imperceptibly, a tight, thin smile appeared on Kruger's sun-browned face—spreading from his firm mouth to the crow's-feet around his steel-gray eyes. "You make yourself very clear, Meneer Sherfield."

The South African officer offered his hand. "And you can all count on my help." He shook his head, amused at some private joke. "God help me, but I must have a weakness for romantic idiots."

Ian shook his outstretched hand—an action imitated, after a brief hesitation, by Matthew Sibena.

"Now what?"

Kruger helped Emily climb over the wall and stepped back, allowing them to cross as well. He laid a hand on the Land Rover's open door and smiled again. "Now, *meneer*, we make arrangements for the three of you to hide someplace where Vorster's police and spies will never think to look."

"And just where would that happen to be, sir?"

Kruger's smile blossomed into a full-fledged grin. "Why, inside South Africa's largest military base, my friend. Where else?"

CHAPTER 22

Green Light

NOVEMBER 12—SUPPLY BASE FIVE, IN THE HILLS NEAR PESSENE, GAZA PROVINCE, MOZAMBIQUE

The corpses were laid out in a neat, orderly row. Even their clothes had been straightened, but nobody could rearrange the bodies where they'd been torn apart. Each bore several bullet wounds in the chest or face.

Maj. Jorge de Sousa had seen bodies before—hundreds, it seemed. Like these, most of the dead had been simple, unarmed Mozambican peasants, but these villagers hadn't been shot by Renamo guerrillas. They'd been gunned down by so-called "allies"—guarding a Cuban supply depot.

There were a dozen such depots, each carefully hidden among the low, brush-choked hills surrounding Pessene. Each supply dump held a sizable fraction of the food, fuel, and ammunition needed to support the Cuban tanks, motorized rifle troops, and artillery moved into Mozambique over the past four weeks.

Each was guarded by a platoon or more of soldiers, a mixed

unit of Cubans and Libyans stationed together to foster "fraternal socialist awareness." Or so their political officers had claimed. Well, de Sousa thought coldly, these troops certainly didn't look fraternal. They stood clumped in distinct national groupings while he and Lieutenant Kofi inspected their victims.

There were five bodies—two men, two women, and a teenage boy. All were pathetically thin, almost skeletal, dressed in rags that passed for clothing. They'd been shot for trying to steal a fifty-kilo sack of rice. The rice bag, no different from hundreds of others piled high throughout the supply dump, lay nearby, also displayed as evidence. Apparently it had taken all five of them just to pick it up and carry it, a sign of their weakened condition.

The Cuban lieutenant in charge of this detail explained in Spanishaccented Portuguese, "We heard a noise last night and fired a flare. Then we saw these thieves trying to make off with the rice, so we arrested them. And then we shot them." Smiling, he motioned toward the row of corpses, slowly lowering his arm when he saw no praise forthcoming from de Sousa.

The Mozambican major turned on his heel and walked over to the Libyans. Their uniforms were the same dark khaki color, but had a different cut, and they wore billed caps instead of the soft, floppy "sun hats" of the Cubans. Both groups were armed with AK-47 assault rifles.

Their apparent leader, if de Sousa understood the Libyan's rank insignia, was a sergeant whose dark-skinned face seemed locked in a perpetual scowl. Without saying anything he looked the major up and down as he approached. Finally, prompted by a glare from the Mozambican officer, the Libyan reluctantly came to attention and tossed off a salute that was almost grounds for a charge of insubordination.

De Sousa tried Portuguese, then English, even Tsonga, without getting any intelligible response. As a Moslem from one of Mozambique's northern provinces, Kofi had more luck with his Tsonga-accented Arabic. The sergeant gave slow responses to the lieutenant's questions.

Kofi turned to de Sousa. "He says they have orders to

execute anyone who tries to steal from the supply dumps, Major."

De Sousa sighed wearily. His orders had been to guard the dumps, using force only if necessary. Someone else had obviously amplified those orders considerably.

When he'd been made responsible for the security of these supply dumps, he'd thought he would be protecting them from Renamo attacks—not from his own countrymen. But the guerrillas had stayed clear, scared off by each depot's defenses. Instead, starving villagers had flocked to the area—drawn by rumors of vast stockpiles of foodstuffs.

Everyone in Mozambique was starving. If you chased peasants away, twice as many would return. If you arrested them, you'd have to feed them with food you didn't have, or dip into the supplies you were supposed to protect. And if you used up these supplies, the Cuban column slated to attack South Africa from Mozambique might not be able to reach its objectives.

It was what an American would call a catch-22, de Sousa thought. Then he shrugged. Americans always thought every problem had to have a solution. As a Mozambican, he knew that wasn't true.

The men in Maputo had thrown in their lot with Cuba's grand strategic gamble. And that meant that almost every truck, every railroad car, and every cargo plane coming into their country carried military supplies—not foodstuffs for civilian consumption. Until the Cubans completed their logistical buildup and launched their attack, Mozambique's peasants would suffer.

De Sousa ordered the bullet-riddled bodies returned to their nearby village for burial, knowing only too well that the Cuban and Libyan guards would probably just dump them out in the brush, somewhere out of sight and smell.

This massacre was the third such incident. De Sousa hoped it would be the last, but doubted it. He could only hope Vega's planned offensive would start soon, not only so that the South Africans would be defeated, but also so that starving peasants wouldn't have these sources of fatal temptation dangling in front of their faces.

His eyes wandered over row after row of stockpiled rations, fuel drums, boxes of small-arms ammunition, and stacks of shells. The Cuban Brigade Tactical Group concealed in the surrounding hills had to be almost ready to move. His friends in Maputo told him that the flow of Soviet ships and cargo planes had slowed to a trickle. And inspection visits by high-ranking officers had dramatically increased—all sure signs of impending action.

Good, he thought, returning the guard detachment's careless salute, the sooner these "socialist brothers" of ours are busy killing Afrikaners, the sooner we will have our country back. Nevertheless, as he climbed into his jeep for the long ride back to headquarters, de Sousa couldn't help wondering if this Cuban "cure" wouldn't turn out to be just as bad as the South African "disease."

CNN HEADLINE NEWS

The satellite feed from Windhoek had all the elements of good television news: a sweeping analysis of the military situation in Namibia by a veteran reporter, the panoramic backdrop of a war-menaced city, and even the grim image of a T-62 tank parked in full view. Millions of viewers around the world were being given a real-time glimpse of what a commentator had already called "one of the century's most bizarre military conflicts."

Clad in a belted khaki field jacket with his press credentials prominently displayed, the CNN correspondent looked almost more like a soldier than did the openly curious Cuban tank crewmen perched atop the T-62's turret and rear deck. "After weeks of comparative openness in its dealings with the Western news media, Castro's army has begun cracking down. Security at Namibia's busy ports and airfields has been increased. All frontline passes for journalists have been revoked. And the commander of this growing army, Gen. Antonio Vega, has dropped completely out of public view. Sources close to the Namibian government report the general is now at his forward field headquarters—somewhere in the mountains outside this capital city."

The reporter pointed toward the Soviet-made tank behind him. "Other sources report seeing large columns of armored vehicles like this T-62 rolling south on Namibia's highways or parked in heavily defended staging areas. And everyone in Windhoek has grown used to hearing the constant, day-and-night roar of massive Soviet cargo planes ferrying still more men and equipment into this small African nation."

He faced the camera squarely. "One thing seems clear: the preparations for Cuba's long-expected counteroffensive are in their final stages. Though only Fidel Castro and his generals know the precise day or hour, no one can doubt that their soldiers will soon strike south, trying to drive South Africa out of this battered and bleeding country."

Vega's elaborate deception plan was working. The Western news media, like South Africa's intelligence services, were seeing exactly what they expected to see.

STAGING AREA ONE, NEAR BRAKWATER, NAMIBIA

Staging Area One lay nestled in a broad valley between barren, boulder-strewn hills. Empty cornfields stretched to either side, abandoned by their owners under orders from Cuban security troops. Only a few scrub trees dotted the low hills, each blasted by the heat, and shade was something to think about, not to find. The main highway connecting Windhoek with Angola ran right past the camp.

A barbed-wire fence two meters high encircled the entire compound, pierced only by one gate where it crossed a side road connecting with the highway. Rows of tents and vehicles were visible beyond the fence.

Col. José Suarez, chief of staff of the Cuban Expeditionary Force, strode slowly through the staging area trailed by an array of nervous officers. He was so tired that he almost had to force himself to take each new step.

He'd been up since five, with only a few hours' sleep the

night before. Managing the Namibian campaign in Vega's absence, even while holding along a relatively static front, was more than exhausting. Battlefield and intelligence reports. Staff conferences. Decision after decision. And inspection tours such as this one. They all drained a man of energy continuously—giving him no chance for any real rest.

Suarez frowned. If this was how he felt after just a week in temporary command, he didn't see how Vega managed his own, much greater, responsibilities. Where did the older man find such a seemingly inexhaustible source of personal energy? He shook his head, realizing he'd probably never find out. The general, like most good commanders, kept a large part of his inner self unknown and unknowable—even to his closest friends and subordinates.

In the meantime Suarez reminded himself, he had his own work to do. He straightened up, concentrating on his inspection.

The equipment park sprawled over several acres. Row after row of long, angular sand-colored shapes sat motionless, their appearance deceptively real even at this distance. Suarez actually smiled, his mood lightened by seeing such a successful ploy.

He walked closer to inspect what appeared to be a BTR-60 armored personnel carrier. It had the right shape and dimensions, but a rap of his knuckles revealed a fiberglass shell instead of an armored hull. Though the decoy lacked brackets and hatches and vision blocks, from a hundred meters away it was arguably a BTR-60.

Its eight wheels were actually painted cement cylinders, designed to keep the rest of the decoy from blowing away in the valley's ever-present wind.

Suarez continued, striding past rows of fiberglass APCs, T-62 tanks, artillery pieces, and even trucks, all made of fiberglass in local factories. Brought in at night in threes and fours, American intelligence satellites and South African reconnaissance planes recorded what appeared to be a slow and steady buildup of troops and armor just north of Windhoek.

Six other phony staging areas, along with two real ones, cluttered the mountain valleys around Namibia's capital. Security for all of them was as tight as he could make it with the limited resources at his disposal. The reason for that was obvious. If the South Africans ever learned that Cuba's buildup inside Namibia was one part reality to three parts charade, they'd start asking themselves hard questions about where all those tanks, troops, and guns really were.

And that would be disastrous.

Suarez hoped his political masters would make up their minds soon. Every day they delayed gave their enemies more time to realize just how badly they'd been fooled.

NATIONAL SECURITY COMMAND BUNKER, OUTSIDE HAVANA, CUBA

DCI Intelligence Estimate—
Southern Africa #846 (Revised)

Most Secret

Summary: The open rebellion in South Africa's own armed forces, combined with the reactionary government's ongoing and inevitable political disintegration, offers Cuba and its socialist allies a correlation of forces more favorable than at any other time in recent history. In addition, all available information confirms the complete success of our efforts to deceive the enemy's military intelligence apparatus. . . .

Fidel Castro flipped from page to page, skimming rapidly through the report prepared by his spy service, squinting in the harsh glare of overhead fluorescent lights. Its conclusions mirrored his own deeply held beliefs. Pretoria's white regime was on the verge of total collapse. Now was the time to strike and to strike hard.

At irregular intervals, he glanced up at the row of clocks set high on one of the bunker's reinforced-concrete walls.

One showed the local time. Another the hour in Moscow. A third had been reset to show the correct time in southern Africa.

Behind each clock's clear glass face, hands marked the passage of yet another hour. And still nothing! The Teletype machine linked to the Soviet Union remained obstinately silent. The staff officers grouped around a tabletop display of Namibia and South Africa stood idle.

Castro scowled darkly and watched with secret amusement as his uniformed generals and sober-suited bureaucrats looked quickly away—frightened that Cuba's absolute ruler might be tempted to vent his frustration and anger on them. His amusement faded as more minutes dragged slowly past.

The long delay irked him. Castro's lips thinned. To be kept waiting like an impoverished beggar was bad enough. To be slapped down like one would be even worse.

He bit down hard on the unlit cigar stuffed into one corner of his mouth. Those gutless fools inside the Kremlin's red-brick walls had already all but utterly renounced Marxism-Leninism as a scientific creed. Would they also throw away a grand opportunity to restore their own economic and military power? It seemed unthinkable. Of course, much that had happened over the past several years had once seemed unthinkable.

The Teletype chattered suddenly, spitting out line after line of a message encoded in Moscow microseconds before and now being decoded with the aid of computer technologies "borrowed" from the Americans. Castro controlled the urge to stand over the machine reading the Soviet reply as it emerged. That would be undignified.

Instead, he sat waiting with studied patience as the flimsy sheet of paper worked its way round the crowded bunker, quickly climbing the ladder of seniority until it landed in front of him. Cuba's leader raced through the message once, then read it a second time more carefully.

A muffled buzz of avid conversation and eager speculation died away—leaving only the faint hum of the bunker's ventilation system.

At last Castro looked up, his dark, hooded eyes seeking

out the officer responsible for military communications. "You have General Vega's headquarters on standby?"

"Yes, Comrade President."

"Good." Castro pulled a pad of paper closer, shifted his cigar from one side of his mouth to the other, and began writing. He finished in thirty seconds, ripped the top sheet off his pad, and held it out between a thick thumb and forefinger. "Then encode that signal and send it immediately."

After weeks of procrastination and uncertainty, Moscow had finally given Vega's planned offensive the green light. South Africa's white capitalists were going to learn about war the hard way.

HEADQUARTERS, CUBAN EXPEDITIONARY FORCE, RUTENGA, IN SOUTHERN ZIMBABWE

Dozens of officers were gathered in the sweltering heat beneath the central headquarters tent. They represented a dozen different service branches—air and land operations, supply, intelligence, political instruction, combat engineering, and others. Most of the men were Cuban, though a scattering of unfamiliar uniforms signaled the presence of a few token Libyan, Zimbabwean, and ANC commanders. Mesh screens kept most of Rutenga's biting flies outside.

"Attention!"

Gen. Antonio Vega strode into the crowded tent and stepped briskly up onto a small dais at one end. A large map of southern Africa dominated the wall behind him. He stared down at his officers for a few moments longer and then broke the silence. "I will not waste your time with fancy speeches, comrades. The Soviets have given their consent and promise of continued support. We attack at first light tomorrow."

Excited murmurs rose throughout the tent. Most had never really believed they'd be permitted to carry out their general's ambitious and audacious plan.

Vega held up a single hand, instantly silencing every voice. "I do not intend to forget what the delay imposed by the Soviets has cost us in Cuban blood, but they are with us now—as are our Libyan and African friends. We go forward together as true comrades-in-arms."

He nodded toward the map behind him. "We will attack as planned. There will be no modifications, no further delays, and no excuses. I've already cabled Colonel Suarez. At oh one hundred hours tomorrow morning, our remaining forces in Namibia will engage a South African army three times their size. They will do this to buy time for us. It is our job to make sure that their sacrifices are not in vain."

Vega's voice grow louder. "You've all seen the intelligence reports. Pretoria's thugs are reeling, torn and divided against one another. Let there be no doubt in your minds. These arrogant Afrikaners are ours for the taking. Our comrades in the ANC stand ready to lead their people to freedom. South Africa is ripe for liberation. Together, we stand on the threshold of victory. A victory for Cuba. A victory for the oppressed peoples of the world. A victory for socialism!"

With deep satisfaction, he watched his words send a sudden surge of pride and confidence through the tent. Years of retreat and self-doubt had come close to crippling his country and its allies. But all those doubts and defeats would be forgotten when his tanks rolled into Pretoria in triumph.

FORWARD ASSEMBLY AREA, FIRST BRIGADE TACTICAL GROUP, NEAR BUBI, ZIMBABWE

Cuba's First Brigade Tactical Group lay scattered in half a dozen camouflaged encampments around the tiny village of Bubi—sixty kilometers south of the road and rail junction at Rutenga and sixty kilometers north of Beitbridge, a town on the northern side of the Limpopo River. The "great, gray-green, greasy" Limpopo formed the border between Zimbabwe to the north and South Africa to the south.

Now, thousands of soldiers and hundreds of vehicles were stirring from their hiding places—from small clumps of trees, shallow trenches covered by dried brush and camouflage, and civilian huts and houses seized for military use. Engines roared to life as drivers revved their vehicles up to full throttle and then let them slide back to idle.

Helmeted infantrymen formed up under shouted orders and waited patiently to board their APCs. In a high-pitched, howling whine of powerful gas turbines, Mi-24 Hind gunships taxied out from under camouflage netting and sat ready for takeoff.

Trucks, their curved sides streaked with diesel fuel, moved from unit to unit topping up mammoth T-72 tanks, and wheeled BTR-60 and tracked BMP-1 armored personnel carriers. Ammunition carriers trundled along behind the diesel trucks, piled high with cannon shells, mortar rounds, and boxes of small-arms ammo. Tank crewmen swarmed over their armored monsters, tightening and adjusting tracks and engines. Engineers and medical personnel worked beside them, bringing their own vehicles to full war readiness.

Hours slipped by as the men of Cuba's First Brigade Tactical Group shook off the lethargy imposed by weeks of concealment and forced inactivity. At last, shouted orders brought the Tactical Group's battalions out onto the highway—hundreds of vehicles forming slowly into a kilometers-long stream of dense traffic flowing south. They would spend the rest of the day in the "hurry up and wait" cycle of armies everywhere, inching forward as the brigade made the long road march to its assault positions—just north of the Limpopo gorge.

This first of Vega's striking forces left behind an abandoned tangle of camps, already rusting coils of barbed wire, and fields scarred by tank tracks.

SECOND BRIGADE TACTICAL GROUP, NEAR PESSENE, MOZAMBIQUE

Dust clouds lit red by the late-afternoon sun hung low over southwestern Mozambique's hills, all converging on a single main road running west. Engine noises rumbled over the hills like a rolling, unending peal of man-made thunder.

Maj. Jorge de Sousa stood off to one side of the highway, watching in awe as hundreds of Cuban tanks, trucks, and other vehicles lumbered past on their way toward South Africa. He'd never seen so much combat power assembled in any one place. From time to time, pairs of Soviet-made helicopters flew overhead, adding to the general, ear-numbing din.

He stiffened to attention as the lead T-72 rolled by with its commander, a lieutenant colonel, saluting as though he were on parade in Havana's Revolution Square. More tanks followed, clattering down the highway in column. Ten. Twenty. Thirty. De Sousa lost count. Close behind the tanks came combat engineering units with special bridging and mine-clearance equipment, armored personnel carriers packed with infantry, ZSU-23-4 antiaircraft guns, and trucks bulging with ammo, food, fuel, and water.

The Mozambican major shook his head from side to side, caught in a sort of euphoria-induced daze. It all seemed unreal somehow, like a dream. He'd never imagined that his earnest wish earlier that same morning would come true so quickly. All his misgivings about Cuba's intentions and capabilities faded away—overwhelmed by this display of power.

THIRD BRIGADE TACTICAL GROUP, OUTSIDE BULAWAYO, ZIMBABWE

Bulawayo's rail yards had never been so crowded. Hundreds of flatcars, passenger cars, and boxcars pulled by dozens of diesel and steam locomotives rattled slowly past the city's idle meat-processing plants, automobile factories, and textile mills. At precisely timed intervals, train after train rolled out of the main station and headed for neutral Botswana—clanking southwest at a steady thirty kilometers an hour.

Canvas tarpaulins covered the squat, ugly shapes of armored vehicles and artillery pieces mounted on each flatcar, without doing much to disguise them. Cuban troops jammed every available seat and aisle on every passenger car. Machine-gun crews and hand-held-SAM teams occupied sandbagged fighting positions atop boxcars crammed with munitions and other supplies.

Commando teams and reconnaissance units were already in place along Zimbabwe's border with Botswana. If necessary, they would use force to secure safe passage for the troop trains ferrying Cuba's Third Brigade Tactical Group around onto South Africa's northwestern flank. Still, fighting shouldn't prove necessary. Botswana's tiny army was little more than a glorified police force.

Cuba's powerful armored right hook was on its way.

HEADQUARTERS, CUBAN EXPEDITIONARY FORCE

Gen. Antonio Vega stood near the main map table in his headquarters tent, listening as movement reports from his three tactical groups crackled over the radio. Junior staff officers stayed busy, constantly updating each column's position and deployment.

On paper, each tactical group was a brigade-sized formation containing three motorized rifle battalions, a tank battalion, and an artillery battalion. But its attached antiaircraft, signals, and supply troops actually made the formation almost as strong as a small division.

As a true "combined arms" unit, each of Vega's brigades had all the tools of its deadly trade massed in a single, highly mobile striking force. He'd used a battalion-sized tactical group to take Walvis Bay. Now he planned to use three forces, each five times as large, to attack the South African giant itself.

He smiled happily down at the map. More than fifty thousand Cuban and allied troops were on the march, closing steadily on South Africa's virtually undefended frontiers.

Naturally, all of this activity did not go completely unnoticed.

HEADQUARTERS, SOUTH AFRICAN DIRECTORATE OF MILITARY INTELLIGENCE, PRETORIA

DMI Flash Traffic

Eyes Only

Time: 211012 Nov From: DMI North To: HQ, SA DMI

1. Asset N13 reports seeing Gen. Antonio Vega in Rutenga, Zimbabwe, this morning, approximately 0900 local time, while engaged in surveillance of local military garrison. Asset also reported increased activity, including soldiers in uniforms not familiar to the asset. As described, the soldiers could be from any number of communist or socialist Arab countries.
2. A roll of film taken by the asset will be delivered by special courier no later than 1800 hours, 13 November.
3. Asset has been ordered to continue surveillance.

Maj. Willem Metje stood almost physically blocking his immediate superior's path as he tried to leave his office. "*Kolonel*, I can't let you take this information to General de Wet. It's too outlandish. Too impossible to believe!"

"You can't let me, *Majoor?*" Col. Magnus Heerden asked scornfully, his voice filled with a mix of utter amazement and outright anger. "I am the head of this section. Do I have to instruct you in the rank structure of the Defense Forces?"

Metje shook his head stubbornly.

"*Majoor*, you're entitled to your opinion. And I would be the first to admit that there is always room for professional differences in intelligence work, but you seem to forget that I command here. Even if your assessment of these new reports is right, which I doubt, our superiors have a right to see them."

Heerden glanced at the handful of flash messages he'd received only ten minutes earlier. "Listen to this: Renamo spotters report an armored column moving toward our border with Mozambique. A column containing at least fifty vehicles, including main battle tanks and mobile antiaircraft guns!"

"And this!" Heerden flipped to a new page. "One of our deep-cover people reports seeing General Vega in Zimbabwe. What the hell's he doing there on the eve of what's supposed to be a big offensive in Namibia?"

He shook his head. "I tell you, Willem, these reports can only mean one thing. Castro's planning a big push all right, but along our borders with Mozambique and Zimbabwe—not in Namibia. And this attack is imminent."

"*Kolonel* . . . sir." Metje added the last word for emphasis. "The President and General de Wet have already decided that Cuba's offensive will be launched in the near future—in Namibia. Our staff's Official Estimate predicts a divisional attack on one or two axes near Windhoek, with diversionary attacks from Walvis Bay and possibly elsewhere." He nodded contemptuously toward the papers in Heerden's hand. "Those reports obviously refer to the enemy's diversionary attacks."

The younger man didn't bother to hide his patronizing tone, and Heerden felt his blood pressure rise.

"Damn it, man, I know how de Wet's 'Official Estimate' reads, even if his staff ignored my reports when they wrote it. But that doesn't mean we should ignore new information."

Metje shook his head almost pityingly. "I'm afraid, *Kolonel,* that the General Staff ignores your conclusions because you are widely regarded as having been taken in by a Cuban deception plan."

Heerden felt his jaw drop open.

The major continued, hammering his point home remorselessly. "As a result, General de Wet and his officers have been using other sources of intelligence lately. They have decided that you are"—he paused—"unreliable."

Heerden felt a dozen questions bubbling up inside. The

first one to take definite shape reflected the basic curiosity of an intelligence officer. "So where are they getting their intelligence then?"

Metje smiled modestly. "From me."

The colonel could only stare at him, taken completely by surprise.

Metje continued, "So you see, *Kolonel*, I've already evaluated these reports you claim are so significant." He waved them away with one dismissive hand. "They are clearly nothing more than Cuban disinformation."

Heerden sat down heavily on the edge of his desk. "When did you see them?"

"About an hour ago."

"I see." Heerden's shoulders slumped. "Then there is nothing more I can do here."

"No . . . there isn't." This time Metje pointedly abandoned any reference to his rank.

Heerden made a sudden decision and threw the collection of reports onto his desk. He sighed once and apparently exhausted, reached for his uniform cap. In a tired voice, he said, "In that case, I think I'll go home now, *Majoor*."

Metje nodded carefully and moved away. "A wise decision, I believe." He turned sharply on his heel and strode in triumph down the hallway.

Heerden watched him go through narrowed eyes. Then he swept his gaze around his office, looking for anything he might need. There was nothing.

He shut the door, tucked his cap under his arm, and walked slowly in the opposite direction from that taken by Metje.

There wasn't much point in going back to his home. No sense in making it easy for Vorster's brownshirted Brandwag goons to find him. He'd have to call his wife and children from a pay phone. They could meet him at some inconspicuous public place—Botha's statue in the park on Church Street should be perfect. By the time his arrest order percolated down through the bureaucracy, he and his family could be well on their way to Cape Town.

Mentally, he started making a list of things Greta would have to bring. Civilian clothes for him and all the maps they had. She'd also have to take the time to get the car filled up, along with an extra petrol can if possible. He smiled thinly. Fortunately, his status as an officer entitled them to enough ration coupons for all of that.

He stepped out of the building into early evening. The air was a little cooler, and the outside sights and sounds broke his train of thought. As he walked toward the corner phone, he found himself wondering if this was the right thing to do.

His Army career was obviously over, finished by these politicians in uniform. But did that justify an act most would call treason? Joining a civil war on what might be the losing side? And why not leave his family here, out of danger? They would be safe. After all, Vorster's security police would only be looking for him.

Heerden paused with his hand on the phone, suddenly uncertain.

Then he shook his head angrily. His family wouldn't be safe. Even if de Wet and the rest of those fools didn't believe him, he could tell what was going to happen. He'd seen the evidence piling up until only an idiot or a blind man or Willem Metje could ignore it. At least two brigade-sized Cuban columns were going to come thundering in from the north and east—daggers aimed right at the heart of South Africa's government and industry.

And South Africa had almost nothing in their path to stop them.

Every soldier worthy of the name was already crouched in the mountains south of Windhoek, out breaking heads in black townships, or, he thought, in rebellion against a government that seemed bent on destroying its own people.

Heerden lifted the phone and punched in his own number. When he heard his wife's voice, he said, "Greta, listen carefully. I can't talk for very long . . ."

With less than ten hours left to go before Vega's tanks rolled across the frontier, South Africa's military intelligence service had lost its head.

CHAPTER 23

Afrikaner Nightmare

NOVEMBER 13—SADF HEADQUARTERS, PRETORIA, SOUTH AFRICA

Achieving surprise is the first goal of every military operation. Given ample warning, a well-prepared defending army can defeat an attacking force many times its own size. An alerted defender may have time to move units, call up reserves, or use other tactics to alter the odds in an upcoming battle.

Surprise prevents that. It guarantees an attacker the initiative, allowing him to set the pace of combat, forcing his victim to react—often in a predictable manner. But if a defender's response is unpredictable, then the mantle of surprise—the initiative—may be transferred from one side to the other, and the cycle begins again.

Surprise also has one other effect. When a commander confronts an unexpected situation, he naturally takes more time to react because he has to discard all the preconceptions and prejudices that allowed him to be surprised in the first place. And if he delays too long, his enemy is able to attack a disorganized, leaderless force—presenting the luckless commander with yet another set of problems before he has even begun to solve the first.

The result is command paralysis, a sense of shock and helplessness that has lost many battles and many wars. The best commanders, the "great captains" of history, are those men who "keep their heads when all around are losing theirs."

Newly promoted Kommandant Willem Metje hid a yawn as he watched staff officers plotting military movements on a large-scale map of Namibia. Fluorescent lights and a lack of sleep were giving him a headache that not even a general, bubbling sense of triumph could completely dispel. De Wet's headquarters staff had been up since midnight, barraged by incomplete and contradictory reports of ANC guerrilla and Cuban commando raids in Namibia and all along South Africa's northern border.

Several minor incidents near Pretoria—a grenade thrown at a police station and a few mysteriously downed power lines near Voortrekker Heights—had prompted de Wet's first positive order: an urgent call for more troops to guard the headquarters building and complex.

All in all, thought Metje crossly, it seemed a lot of effort for so insignificant a result.

But now at least things were finally moving in Namibia. Commanders on the front were reporting heavy air attacks, artillery bombardments, and ground assaults—all concentrated near the tiny town of Dordabis. And though South Africa's forward battalions were expending massive amounts of ammunition, they were holding their ground with relative ease. Castro's vaunted offensive was failing.

Tall, white-haired Adriaan de Wet moved closer and thumped Metje on the shoulder. "Congratulations, Willem, the Cubans are doing exactly what you predicted."

The younger man smiled back weakly and resisted the urge to rub his shoulder. Both his new rank insignia and his upset stomach seemed to settle a little in response to de Wet's praise. And any qualms he might have had about orchestrating Colonel Heerden's downfall vanished.

De Wet drew him forward to the edge of the map. "So now we let our enemies ram their heads into our brick walls a little longer, eh?"

Metje nodded. The general always liked to see complete agreement from his subordinates.

De Wet leaned far out over the table. "And when they are weak and reeling . . . then we strike, and strike hard!"

The other staff officers grouped nearby muttered their unreserved enthusiasm.

De Wet's eyes shone with excitement as he pointed to a single unit counter positioned on the main highway leading to Windhoek. "The Eighty-first Armored should be able to punch through their lines in a matter of hours! After the slaughter at Dordabis, the Cubans can't have much left to stop our tanks!"

More nods. The 81st was a crack outfit. Its two armored and two mechanized battalions contained practically every Olifant main battle tank left in South Africa's inventory. And when it attacked, its tanks and APCs would be backed by the concentrated firepower of more than fifty G-5 and G-6 155mm guns. Cuba's shattered forces shouldn't stand a chance. The long, out-of-control war in Namibia might be over within weeks.

De Wet and his staff stood contemplating their upcoming counterattack, basking in the glow of anticipated victory.

KOMATIPOORT BORDER POST, IN THE CROCODILE RIVER VALLEY, WEST OF MOZAMBIQUE

Late-spring days were always hot and humid in the wooded lowlands separating South Africa from Mozambique. And though it had barely begun, this day promised more of the same.

A dense, damp haze already lingered motionless over citrus orchards, sugarcane fields, and the slow, eastward-rolling waters of the Crocodile River. National Route 4, the main highway between Johannesburg and Maputo, stretched empty as far as the eye could see. High overhead, birds circled lazily through the still, warm air, their wings spread wide to generate every possible ounce of lift.

The only human activity seemed centered around a small wooden building adjacent to the highway and fifty meters back from a signpost marking the border. Shovels and pick-axes rose and fell together in a strange sort of rhythm as men in full combat gear dug foxholes and firing pits.

In a land as torn by violence as South Africa, border guards weren't sleepy policemen checking for insects in contraband fruit. They were soldiers.

The commander of the Komatipoort Border Post, gray-haired Sgt. Uwe Boshof, laid his shovel aside and breathing heavily, plopped down on the edge of his shallow, hastily dug foxhole. Sweat stains soaked his short-sleeved khaki shirt—black patches of wetness spreading from under his armpits and across his broad back. The sergeant was a tall, big-boned man, and he carried a lot of meat on those bones. Too much, perhaps.

If so, he thought with weary amusement, he'd undoubtedly worked some of that excess weight off during the past several hours.

Boshof mopped his brow with a handkerchief and squinted east into the rising sun—an enormous orange-and-red orb flattened and distorted by the low-lying haze. Despite the clinging, sticky heat it was sure to bring, he was glad to see the day proper begin.

His night had been long on confusion and wild rumor and short on needed sleep.

First, that idiot Private Krom had woken him up after hearing what he claimed were radio reports of some big guerrilla attack way up north along the Limpopo. When the story wasn't repeated in the SABC's next hourly broadcast, Boshof vaguely remembered going back to bed—but only after chewing Krom out for being a blithering, gutless moron.

He'd scarcely had time to drift off again before the first phone call came in—from the Army's Eastern Transvaal Command, no less. Some staff flunkie wanting to know if they'd spotted any "unusual activity." For a second, he'd been tempted to mention the pair of blesbok, or antelope, he'd seen wander by earlier that evening. But only for a second. Staff officers had a notoriously poor sense of humor.

After that, he'd only been able to grab one fitful, restless hour of shut-eye before the *kak,* the shit, really started to hit the fan.

At two in the morning, reinforcements arrived—six more men dropped off from a truck making the rounds of every guardpost along this stretch of the border. A hurried phone call to Battalion revealed only that both his captain and lieutenant were "unavailable." They'd probably been comfortably asleep, he thought irritably.

His new men had been full of tales, though: blabbering all over creation about the whole base being put on alert, all leaves being canceled, and frantic quartermasters rushing around issuing field rations and a basic load of ammunition to every combat soldier. They were sure something big was happening.

Right. The Afrikaner noncom snorted at the memory. God save him from raw recruits who couldn't tell the difference between real war and a *blery* drill.

Still, nobody was going to watch the grass grow under Sgt. Uwe Boshof's feet. Drills were always followed by inspections. And who could tell? This alert might even be real. Maybe the higher-ups had warning of an imminent ANC raid. Or maybe some farmer had spotted a rebel commando moving into the area.

Whatever. Even though nothing much was likely to happen at Komatipoort, he always believed that preparation for the worst was a wise precaution. That was why he'd ordered his small twelve-man garrison to stand to. And that was why he'd ordered them to dig fighting positions around the border post itself.

If any of those murdering ANC bastards do come sniffing around here, Boshof swore silently, they'll feel as if they've tried to bite into a buzz saw. It was a promise he felt sure he could keep. Besides their R-4 assault rifles, his men had a heavy caliber Vickers machine gun, grenades, and even a hand-held 60mm patrol mortar. His garrison would be more than a match for any kaffir raiding force.

And if there were white rebels out and about recruiting, the traitorous swine would get short shrift from him. He'd spent twenty-five years in the SADF—long enough to know how to take orders, even if they did mostly come from a pack of fools.

He yawned once. And a second time. Then his stomach growled, an unwelcome reminder they weren't likely to eat anytime soon. Meal trucks wouldn't make the rounds during an alert. Should he tell the boys to open some of their canned rations? Or was Battalion likely to call this whole thing off soon?

Boshof shrugged. Maybe his erstwhile superiors would tell him what the devil was going on when they bothered to get out of bed. He looked toward the guard shack, silently willing the phone to ring.

"Sergeant!"

Boshof turned toward the shout. He saw a slender, youthful figure climbing down out of a tree overlooking the border fence. As punishment for all his assorted sins and radio antics, Private Krom had spent the night in that tree, watching the Mozambican side of the frontier through a night-vision scope. Now he was scrambling down, waving one arm to attract his sergeant's attention.

Christ on a plate, now what? He stood up and brushed the dirt off his trousers. Then he slung his assault rifle and ambled toward the border.

Krom ran to meet him. "Sergeant! I can see vehicles on the highway! Dozens of them!"

Boshof groaned inwardly. Another pile of bullshit from the young idiot. "Nonsense."

"No, really, I swear it!" The younger man pointed back in the direction he'd just come from. "I'm telling you, I could see them passing between those two hills there. Moving in convoy. They can't be more than five klicks away."

What? Privately, Boshof thought the young recruit was out of his tiny mind. Still, it might be better to make absolutely sure of that before putting him up on a charge.

He focused his own binoculars on the spot Krom had indicated and grimaced. The sun's glare made it tough to make anything out. If I go blind, he thought, I'll kill the little son of a . . .

His hands tightened around the binoculars. He'd just seen sunlight glinting off glass or polished metal. Krom hadn't been hallucinating. There were vehicles on the highway out there. Vehicles headed this way. And that might mean trouble—big trouble. One thing was sure, Uwe Boshof hadn't made it to sergeant by taking unnecessary chances.

He grabbed Private Krom by the arm and ordered, "Get on the phone to headquarters. Report 'many vehicles approaching.' Go!"

Krom nodded and ran off.

Boshof swung round and bellowed, "Listen up, boys! I want everybody down in those fucking holes! Now!"

For a split second his squad stood frozen, shocked into immobility by the sudden order.

"Move!" Boshof was already lumbering back toward his own foxhole.

His men threw their shovels and pickaxes to one side, grabbed their weapons, and dropped flat in half-dug fighting positions. Boshof followed suit seconds later.

And not a second too soon.

Crouched low, with his binoculars glued to his face, the Afrikaner sergeant heard the clattering, howling roar of twin rotors and twin gas turbine engines an instant before he saw them—a pair of helicopters darting around the side of a low hill, racing westward just over the treetops.

At first they were just oval specks, black dots against the rising sun, but they quickly grew in size and shape until he could identify them as Soviet-made Mi-24 helicopter gunships. Big ugly monsters, he thought. He'd never seen a Hind up close before, but he'd seen enough photos and drawings to know what they were. Odd. Mozambique's armed forces weren't supposed to have any gear that sophisticated.

What were these gunships doing so near the border? No, strike that. What were they going to do, now that they were here?

His own orders from headquarters were clear. As long as the Mozambicans stayed on their own side of the line, they could do as they pleased. He did note, however, his men were tracking the two helicopters with every weapon they had. He just hoped some hothead didn't open up without his say-so. He'd hate to get killed just because some kaffir pilot couldn't resist showing off his brand-new, shiny toy.

The Hinds were still nose-on, closing fast just ten meters above the ground at two hundred kilometers an hour. They flew steadily, changing neither course nor speed. Orders or no, Boshof knew he couldn't wait much longer. They'd be across the border in seconds. He tensed, readying a shouted command to open fire . . .

And held it in as the Hinds pulled up, glass-canopied noses wobbling as they suddenly slowed. The two gunships came to a complete stop, hovering twenty meters above the ground and about a hundred meters away, still inside Mozambique.

Boshof studied the two craft closely while waiting for his pounding heart to slow down. Their sloping front fuselages were almost completely glassed in. He could clearly see each Hind's gunner, seated low and close to the nose. Their pilots were seated slightly higher and behind.

Both gunships hovered, motionless. Dust whirled away to either side, blown skyward by powerful rotors.

The Afrikaner sergeant shook his head angrily. What in God's name were these kaffirs playing at?

Boshof trained his binoculars on the gunner in the left-hand Hind, noticing that, whenever he turned his head, the gunship's chin-mounted rotary cannon pivoted—mimicking the man's movements. Interesting. And frightening. It made the helicopter seem more like a living, breathing predator than a simple machine.

Long seconds passed before he realized that both the gunner and the pilot were white. He snapped his binoculars over to the other Mi-24. Both its crewmen were white as well. Advisors? Mercenaries?

Boshof's unspoken question was answered sooner than he would have wished.

The left-hand gunship started to swing right, moving across his front. As soon as it turned, he saw the insignia on its side. A blue circle covered by a red triangle—with a white star in the center. Jesus! That was the insignia of the Cuban Air Force!

He dropped the binoculars and grabbed his rifle. "Fire! Fire! Fire!"

Boshof's scream was all it took to free his troops from their paralysis. Assault rifles cracked all around his small perimeter. Half a second later, their Vickers machine gun opened up with a hoarse, full-throated chatter—spraying steel-jacketed rounds toward the left-hand gunship.

At such short range, the South African machine gun couldn't miss. Sparks jittered and bounced off the Hind's streamlined fuselage, boxy heat suppressor, and tail rotor—visible signs that its bullets were slamming home. But they were hitting without effect. The Mi-24 was just too well armored.

A fraction of a second later, both gunships cut loose—hammering the shallow foxholes surrounding the South African border post with hundreds of 12.7mm machine-gun bullets. Dust and dirt billowed high into the air, hiding a scene of sheer butchery.

Sgt. Uwe Boshof and his men were cut to pieces before they could figure out how to shoot down armored gunships with weapons meant only for infantry combat.

ADVANCE HEADQUARTERS, CUBAN EXPEDITIONARY FORCE, NORTH OF MESSINA, SOUTH AFRICA

Two bridges spanned the rugged Limpopo River gorge, soaring high above a vista of sheer rock walls, foam-flecked rapids, and mist-cloaked waterfalls. One, a steel-girder railroad bridge, was empty. In sharp contrast, the highway crossing next to it was full—choked by bumper-to-bumper columns of Cuban tanks, APCs, and trucks streaming endlessly south along South Africa's National Route 1.

Dozens of SAM launchers and turreted ZSU-23-4 antiaircraft guns were parked on both sides of the gorge, their radars ceaselessly scanning the sky for signs of South African aircraft. To the north, sunlight winked off the sleek, missile-studded wings of MiG-29s orbiting in slow, fuel-conserving racetrack patrol patterns.

Gen. Antonio Vega stood watching his First Brigade Tactical Group wend its way deeper into enemy territory. From time to time, he turned to study the southern horizon. Pillars of black smoke rising there marked several burning buildings on the outskirts of the copper mining town of Messina—fruits of the brief and hopeless resistance put up by a mixed force of South African reservists and policemen.

"A glorious day, isn't it, Comrade General?"

Vega turned toward the shorter black man standing at his side. "Indeed it is, Colonel."

He carefully controlled his irritation at the other man's appearance. Col. Sese Luthuli, commander of the ANC's military wing, Umkhonto we Sizwe, wore camouflaged battle dress, a blue beret, a polished leather pistol belt, and a bayonet-tipped AK-47 slung over his shoulder. It all struck Vega as being ridiculously theatrical.

Luthuli's presence was also a reminder of unwelcome political constraints imposed on him by Havana and Moscow. Leaders in the two capitals were eager that Cuba's invading armies should be seen as liberators by both the black South Africans themselves and by the larger world public. As a result, they'd insisted that each of his three attack columns be accompanied by ANC guerrilla units.

Vega frowned at the memory. Most of the ANC troops he'd inspected seemed poorly disciplined, badly led, and ill prepared for full-scale conventional warfare. Even worse, they filled trucks and personnel carriers he desperately needed for more effective units and supplies.

Luthuli missed the frown and grinned. "I'm looking forward to leading my men into battle beside your troops, Comrade. Together, I'm sure that we can crush these white fascists once and for all."

With their engines howling, two shark-nosed Su-25 attack aircraft flashed past at low altitude, sparing Vega the need to reply through suddenly clenched teeth. Fifty meters away, the long columns of tanks and armored personnel carriers kept clattering south along the highway—moving steadily past the tall, grim-faced figure of their commander.

ADVANCED GUARD, FIRST BRIGADE TACTICAL GROUP, ON NATIONAL ROUTE 1, SOUTH OF MESSINA

Senior Capt. Victor Mares leaned far forward in the hatch of his BTR-60 as though he could somehow urge the wheeled command carrier to go faster. Although his men were already advancing at a tremendous pace, at this moment, even a jet aircraft would have seemed much too slow.

Sooner or later, he knew, those buffoons in Pretoria were going to wake up. So far their stupidity had cost them more than twenty kilometers of their territory. With any luck, it would cost them far more than that by the time this day was through. Still, this joyride was bound to end sooner or later.

And Victor Mares wanted to be deep inside South Africa when that happened.

"Scouts report men working on the road five kilometers ahead." His radio operator poked his head out of a top hatch, grateful for the excuse to get some air. "They may be setting up a roadblock."

Mares calculated rapidly. His BRDM scout cars were only lightly armed, and he didn't know what kind of weapons the South Africans up ahead possessed. It might be more sensible to call his scouts back and advance with the BTRs and BMPs.

No. It would take at least half an hour to deploy his lead company for a hasty—very hasty—attack. By that time, those bastards might have finished their defensive preparations. In any case, time was too precious. Even slowing long enough to deploy his troops would give the South Africans a minor victory. Certainly, if Vega heard about it, he would have his ears.

"Pass control of Axe and Dagger flights to the scouts. Have them attack as soon as the Su-25s have finished one pass. And tell the Hinds to back them up. Clear?"

"Yes, Comrade Captain." The radio operator nodded his understanding and ducked back inside.

Two minutes later, two Frogfoot attack jets screamed down the length of his column, headed for the reported enemy position, waggling their wings as they passed.

"Damn show-offs," Mares muttered. He could put up with a little aviator strutting, though, if they could blast the Afrikaners loose before they took root.

He scanned the horizon with his binoculars—eager to see signs that his advance units were going into action.

A prolonged, rattling boom filled the air, the sound rising above the growling roar made by his BTR's noisy diesel engine. The Frogfoots were already at work plastering the enemy force. Rippling cracks and explosions echoed over the treeless veld.

"Scouts are attacking, sir. They report heavy resistance."

Sure, Mares thought. When you're in a tin can with only a small gun on top, three farmers on donkeys looks like heavy resistance.

Five minutes passed with maddening slowness. Come on. Mares was getting ready to joggle his scout commander's elbow when the radio operator spoke again. "Lieutenant Morales says the Boers are running. Our gunships are in pursuit."

Mares smiled grimly at the thought. An Mi-24 Hind helicopter, armed to the teeth, made a good pursuer.

"Excellent. Tell the scouts I want prisoners if possible."

Twenty-five minutes later, Mares and his armored personnel carriers rolled past the shattered South African roadblock—a pile of old railroad ties, rusting civilian cars, and farm machinery. Smoking bomb and shell craters dotted the ground and the road.

His vehicles had to stop briefly as soldiers pushed the last of the wreckage off the road. Mares made out the twisted remains of an antiquated antitank gun and a single light machine gun. Bullet-riddled bodies wearing South African uniforms were heaped among unfilled sandbags.

A young lieutenant, Morales, ran up to Mares's BTR and

saluted. "We took two prisoners, Captain, and killed more than ten others." His smile faded. "But I lost three men myself—one killed and two wounded."

Mares nodded. Losing men in battle was never easy. But it was inevitable. He kept his own voice dry, businesslike. "A small price to keep the brigade moving, Lieutenant. Were the Frogfoots effective?"

Morales grinned, his good humor restored by the memory. "They blew those bastards clear off the road, Comrade. After that it was all broom and shovel work."

Mares chuckled inside. Right now the war was going their way. Let the boy have his fun. The tough going would start soon enough. He leaned forward. "Very well, Miguel. Get this mess cleaned up as soon as you can, then join up. We'll need you for the victory parade when we reach Pretoria."

The lieutenant laughed and moved off at a run.

Mares spoke into his microphone. "Second Platoon, take the point. All units, move out."

He studied the wrecked South African roadblock with contempt.

It would take more than that to stop Cuba's advancing armies.

SADF HEADQUARTERS, PRETORIA

Commandant Willem Metje stared back and forth from the reports he held in his hand to the strategic map showing the northeastern Transvaal. Something was wrong. Horribly wrong.

He'd expected the Cubans to launch a series of carefully planned diversionary attacks. Militarily, that only made common sense. After all, raids and other feints would tie down South African troops needed in Namibia. Vega's planners might also have hoped they could conceal the real axis of their attack. A successful raid could even do real damage, forcing South Africa to spend valuable time and resources repairing a vital radar station or supply depot.

But the Cubans seemed to be putting a lot of effort into

their diversionary attacks. More effort than seemed either reasonable or even possible.

Metje moved closer to the map, consumed by a growing sense of panic. Enemy contacts were represented by color-coded pins. Yellow meant a simple sighting. Orange indicated skirmish-level combat—small-arms fire, nothing more. And red meant a determined attack, with heavy weapons or rockets. A small tag attached to each pin showed the time of the contact.

Now, for the first time since the Cuban offensive began shortly after midnight, he was beginning to see a pattern emerging from all these "diversionary" contact reports—a damning and disastrous pattern. Although there were reports of enemy activity along all of South Africa's borders, major enemy attacks were being reported in just two sectors—those containing the two major highways aimed at Pretoria and Johannesburg. Red pins were sprouting along those roads with frightening regularity.

To Metje's suddenly very worried eyes, those two lines of red pins were beginning to look as though they were marching straight toward his nation's administrative capital and industrial heartland. He glanced down at the sheaf of reports clutched in his hands. They all told much the same story:

"061513 Nov—EASTERN TRANSVAAL MILCOM—Contact lost with Komatipoort border post at 0610. No word from relief patrol dispatched 0625."

"081513 Nov—NORTHERN TRANSVAAL MILCOM—Fragmentary call from SAP HQ in Messina reports attack by hostile armored car units and unidentified aircraft. Report unconfirmed. Unable to reestablish contact with Messina." Below the text of this message, someone had scribbled, "Phone lines probably cut."

He flipped from sheet to sheet. Each succeeding report showed enemy units pushing deeper into South African territory.

"Kommandant?"

Startled, Metje looked up into the somber face of one of his officers. The man handed him two more telexed reports. "I think you should see these, sir."

"101513 Nov—NORTHERN TRANSVAAL MILCOM—Helicopter-borne infantry attacking Wyllie's Poort. Infantry confirmed as Cuban, repeat, Cuban."

"101613 Nov—NORTHERN TRANSVAAL MILCOM—Louis Trichardt Air Base under heavy enemy air attack. Losses and runway status as yet unknown."

"My God . . ." Metje's voice trailed away in shock and disbelief. More than eighty kilometers inside South Africa, Wyllie's Poort was a narrow pass across the Soutpansberge—a chain of wooded mountains, ridges, and lichen-covered cliffs just north of Louis Trichardt and its military airfield. Two highway tunnels, each several hundred meters long, carried National Route 1 through the mountains at this point. Whoever held the pass held the key to the whole northern Transvaal.

"I think General de Wet should know about this, don't you, sir?"

What? Tell de Wet? But de Wet and the others were in another room, busy crowing over reports of rapid progress in Namibia. None of them were paying much attention to anything happening beyond the front lines outside Windhoek.

Metje struggled upward from his contemplation of complete and unmitigated failure. "I'll take care of these, Captain. Stick to your own knitting, if you please. Dismissed."

Without saying another word, the younger officer stalked rigidly away—hurt, angry, and resentful.

Metje ignored him. He had problems of his own.

His body temperature seemed wildly variable. One minute he was shivering, chilled to the bone, and the next he was sweating profusely, convinced he was burning up. No matter how hard he tried to fit the pieces together into another, less threatening pattern, he kept coming face-to-face with a single, horrifying conclusion: Colonel Heerden had been right all along. The Cubans were attacking from the north and east—driving hard for the undefended heart of the South African nation.

Metje could see that now. And in that realization he saw the certain end of his military career and all his political ambitions.

He ran a clammy hand over his face. It was so unfair. De Wet and the other generals would need a scapegoat, and he certainly filled the bill. Any court-martial would be swift and sure—able to reach only one conclusion and one sentence.

For an instant, just an instant, Metje was tempted to stay and play the farce through to its appointed end. Doing his duty up to the last possible moment was the only honorable course left open to him. But doing his duty would not mitigate his punishment.

Metje dropped the sheaf of contact reports on a nearby desk, turned on his heel, and left the room. His staff watched him go without saying anything. They probably imagined he was on his way to report to de Wet.

Good. That would buy him time—the time he needed to get clear of the headquarters complex and Pretoria.

Metje suddenly understood how Heerden must have felt while fleeing this same post.

Sometimes it felt good to give in to impulse.

It took de Wet and the others almost an hour to realize that their new chief of military intelligence had vanished. It took them several minutes more to realize just how big a disaster they were facing.

And all that morning Cuba's armored columns advanced.

BLOCKING FORCE, 2ND TRANSVAAL INFANTRY, ON NATIONAL ROUTE 4, NEAR HECTORSPRUIT, SOUTH AFRICA

Commandant Neils Bergen stood on a low hill looking out over a panorama of bright green sugarcane fields and small square groves of orange trees. Off to his right, the Crocodile River wound its lazy way east toward Mozambique. His shadow, lengthened by the setting sun, stretched east as well.

He shifted his binoculars, gazing downslope at his small team of engineers as they scurried to and fro—planting mines and building hasty, improvised barricades across the four-lane highway running east to west.

With the double-tracked railroad line paralleling it to the

north, National Route 4 was ordinarily a supply officer's dream and the best way to move an army fast from one place to another, unless that army happened to be Cuban. Now the highway was more like a dagger pointed straight at South Africa's heart.

Bergen still couldn't quite believe the chain of events that had landed him in this predicament. His Citizen Force battalion had been called to active duty just days ago—summoned to the colors as the mutinies and other insurrections spread. They'd mobilized quickly, caught up in a sense of wartime urgency that soon found them pressed into service hunting down ANC guerrillas and rebel commandos.

He hadn't enjoyed that at all. Shooting or arresting fellow South Africans was unpleasant duty. Unfortunately, the presence of brownshirt Brandwag "special units" left him little freedom for maneuver. As it was, he'd nearly lost his command after refusing to execute several white prisoners found guilty at a "summary court" held by the area's senior AWB representative.

That had been bad enough. But now he faced total disaster.

When the emergency orders from the Eastern Transvaal Military Command arrived, his three infantry companies were spread out over a hundred-kilometer square, dispersed in patrols and detachments. Just gathering the company-sized force he had here had taken most of the morning and afternoon.

The rest of his troops were digging in forty kilometers farther back—deep in the rugged foothills of the Great Escarpment. Bergen's tiny blocking force was supposed to buy time for them, maybe even delaying the oncoming Cubans long enough for reinforcements to arrive from Pretoria.

Sure. The commandant scowled. At least Leonidas and his Three Hundred Spartans had fought with a terrain advantage. He didn't have crap. Under ideal conditions, a well-supported, dug-in company might be able to fend off an armored brigade for a short time—with the emphasis on *short*. But conditions were far from ideal. This was a fragile force, poorly supplied and lightly armed. My God, he only had mortars for artillery and machine guns for protection against enemy aircraft.

Boots scraped on rock somewhere behind him. Bergen turned to see an elderly man in jeans and a plain white shirt climbing the hill. The man carried an R-4 assault rifle slung over his shoulder. Clearly having trouble climbing the slope in this heat, he paused once, then made it to the crest with a final surge of energy. "Andries Kaal, of the Hectorspruit Commando, reporting."

The old man didn't bother saluting, but he did come to attention—smiling slightly at some private joke.

Bergen wasn't surprised by the man's sudden appearance. The Boer tradition of the commando, or local militia, went back to the very roots of Afrikanerdom. Even so, he considered Kaal coldly for several moments. He needed solid, dependable soldiers, not fat farmers who might run away in panic at the first shot. With that in mind, would the "Hectorspruit Commando" be an asset or a liability?

At least this fellow's bearing showed he was a veteran, Bergen decided. He nodded toward the distant town. "How many men in your commando?"

"Fifty, with more coming in all the time." Kaal smiled, showing a mouthful of extraordinarily bad teeth. "We all have rifles, though most of them are not so new as my friend here." He patted his R-4 with real affection.

Fifty men, Bergen thought. He could have used five thousand. And since almost all white men of military age were already in uniform, Kaal's commando was undoubtedly made up mostly of older men and teenage boys. He shrugged. No matter, this was a static defense. All they had to do was shoot straight. And die.

He pointed to the canvas-sided truck doubling as his command post. "Talk to my operations officer. Tell him I said to put your men on the left flank, reinforcing the platoon I've already posted there."

Kaal nodded once and skidded slowly down the rise.

Bergen lifted his binoculars and looked east again. The Cubans were out there somewhere—and closing fast. He wasn't surprised that his hands were shaking, jiggling the view through the field glasses. He fought to hold them steady.

One minute later, the irregular, pulsing *whup whup whup*

of a rotor sounded behind him. The noise came from a tiny Alouette III utility helicopter practically skimming the ground on its way toward his position.

Bergen ran back down to the command truck, catching and passing Kaal as he plodded in the same direction.

He was still only halfway there when the Alouette flared out and landed in a swirl of dust and hot exhaust. Its engine whined down slowly—fading in time with its slowing rotor blades. The helicopter pilot, a young, stick-thin man with straw-colored hair, jumped out and hurried forward to meet him.

The young man's clean, pressed uniform contrasted sharply with Bergen's rumpled clothes, already filthy after several days in the field. "Lieutenant Bankkop, reporting for duty."

"Where the devil have you come from, then?" asked Bergen as he returned the pilot's salute and then held out his hand.

Bankkop smiled ruefully. "Normally I'm the shuttle pilot for VIPs, but the *brigadier* thought you might be able to use me today."

Bergen nodded emphatically. "He thought right, for once. You're all the reconnaissance I'm going to get forward of my own positions. Understand?"

The pilot nodded back.

"Good, then get aloft and head east along the highway. See if you can locate the enemy column. I need to know how much time I have."

Bankkop paused just long enough to agree on radio frequencies and to pick up a map before sprinting back to his machine. Less than a minute later, the Alouette was aloft, nose down and engine screaming as it gathered speed. It raced east just above the ground, darting around or over obstacles like some giant insect.

Bergen climbed into the back of the command truck and found a spot where he could sit and listen to the radio without getting in the way. A wise commander doesn't disrupt his headquarters staff unnecessarily.

Nevertheless, he wanted to hear Bankkop's radio reports for himself—the instant they came in. It was vital that he know the Cuban column's exact position and approximate strength. In the meantime, he could rest.

He leaned back against the truck's canvas wall and closed his eyes.

At two hundred kilometers an hour, the little helicopter should reach the Cuban column's last reported position in minutes at most. But every minute Bankkop flew east was another twenty minutes of preparation for his men.

Far too soon, the lieutenant's voice came over the radio. "I can see a group of scout vehicles. Roughly ten klicks from your position. I don't think they've seen me. Continuing east. Out."

Bergen kept his eyes closed, but his mind was racing at high speed. The Cuban scouts were probably several kilometers ahead of their main force. Given that, he tried to calculate when he could next expect to hear from the dapper young helicopter pilot. Even at cruising speed, it shouldn't be more than a few seconds.

Then he remembered that the Alouette wouldn't fly a straight-line course along the road. Like any scout advancing in hostile territory, Bankkop would move from cover to cover, searching carefully from a protected position before darting forward.

The speaker crackled with static: ". . . signs of . . . no fire . . . forward." Bergen frowned. Broken, static-laced transmissions were a common problem during low-altitude flight. Hills, trees, even the curvature of the earth itself could block a short-range radio signal.

Now they'd have to wait for the helo's return before they got any information.

Suddenly it felt hot and stuffy inside the canvas-topped truck. Bergen stepped outside for a smoke. As he lit up, he scanned the hills to the east again. He heard a shout, saw one of the lieutenants pointing, and raised his binoculars.

There. A wisp of dust floating above the railroad line, half-obscured by the raised embankment the tracks rested on. Searching slowly, he saw another, about fifty meters back. The Cuban scout cars Bankkop had spotted earlier were arriving.

But what else had the Alouette pilot seen?

Bergen quickly scanned his positions. His engineers were out in the open, still frantically building obstacles across the highway. They'd probably be under fire in another five or ten minutes. Were a few more mines and barricades in place worth risking their lives for? He shook his head and ordered them back in cover.

Someone shouted from the command truck. "*Kommandant!*" He ran the few steps back and quickly climbed inside.

Bankkop's voice was on the speaker again, loud and clear, but hurried: ". . . overcome interference, am at medium altitude. Main column coordinates Romeo three six, Yankee one five. Thirty plus tanks, large number APCs, self-propelled artillery, and SAMs in support." The engine noise underlying Bankkop's voice stepped up in pitch and he paused for a moment. "Enemy aircraft in the area. Returning to your position now. Out."

Bergen silently thanked the pilot for the information, and for his bravery. By climbing he'd restored radio contract, but he'd undoubtedly also drawn unwelcome attention to himself.

The *Kommandant,* along with most of his staff, went outside.

He knew it would be only moments before the helicopter arrived back over his position. He could hear his operations officer relaying the order for all platoons to hold their fire.

They waited, and word quickly filtered down through the men until everyone watched the eastern sky.

Suddenly, Bankkop's gnat-sized helicopter popped over a hill several kilometers away. It was moving fast, adding the speed from a shallow dive to that from its overworked engine.

Two specks appeared close behind the Alouette, weaving from side to side in what looked like a lethal dance. Then, as Bergen and the rest of his men watched in horror, a puff of white smoke appeared under one of the specks and stabbed out toward the fleeing South African helicopter.

He raised his binoculars in time to see the missile pass clear of the Alouette. Christ, that was a near-run thing!

Bergen swept his binoculars back to the two enemy helos

closing in on the South African scout. They were Mi-24 Hind gunships. His heart sank. Smaller, slower, and unarmed, the Alouette was completely outclassed. Bankkop dove right, racing for cover behind a grove of orange trees.

Two more missiles flashed out from under stubby wings of each Hind. They closed the narrow gap in seconds. One missed the violently maneuvering Alouette—arcing aimlessly off into thin air. The other guided, though, homing in on the South African scout craft's hot exhaust. It detonated in a short, sharp ball of orange flame, and the explosion blew the tiny helicopter's tail boom clear of the shattered airframe.

The Alouette's cabin section, boom, and blades all spiraled to earth separately, taking only seconds for the short trip. Then, without even decelerating, the two Soviet-made gunships gracefully turned away, careful to stay well out of machine-gun range.

As they disappeared behind the railroad embankment, Bergen heard a roaring, whooshing sound arcing down out of the sky. Oh, shit. "Down!"

He dove for cover in a slit trench next to the parked truck.

Artillery started to land all over the place, churning the earth in a rapidfire succession of enormous explosions. Big stuff, one fifty-twos and one twenty-twos, he thought. That meant at least two batteries supporting the Cuban brigade, more, probably three, with one moving forward while the other two fired.

At least half the shells were fuzed to airburst, exploding overhead and showering lethal fragments down on his men. Since only part of them had found the time to construct overhead protection, most were going to take a heavy beating.

He could see enemy aircraft, loitering off to the east. Once this barrage lifted, they'd come roaring in with cannon and rockets. He'd heard about what Frogfoots and Hinds could do, and he knew that his piddling light machine guns stood one chance in a hundred of piercing their armor.

And after that, he could expect a ground attack by at least one battalion of Cuban tanks, with infantry in support.

He didn't stand a chance.

SECURITY CHECKPOINT 36, ON NATIONAL ROUTE 1, NEAR VENTERSBURG

Floodlights lit the highway from one side to the other, revealing cars and trucks backed up in both directions—their engines idling as drivers waited for their turn at the security checkpoint up ahead. Two canvas-sided trucks, a command jeep, and a wheeled Hippo personnel carrier were parked off to the left side of the highway. Soldiers in full combat gear stood chatting in small groups near their vehicles—utterly bored with what seemed a completely routine job.

Few of them paid much attention to the flashy red Astra stopped right in front of their barricade.

Commandant Willem Metje was sweating again. He was tired, hungry, and scared. Even nearly three hundred kilometers south of Pretoria, he still felt too close to both the Cuban offensive and his own government's brownshirted enforcers, the Brandwag. He'd already bluffed his way past two other checkpoints by using a combination of rank, his AWB pin, and an overbearing manner. But doing that had left him a physical and mental wreck. He was not a good actor.

And in this case, the third time was most definitely not proving to be a charm.

He stared through his rolled-down window at the thin, sour-looking officer who'd refused to let him through the checkpoint without seeing either a travel authorization or an identity card. "Look, Lieutenant, we're both busy men. After all, this is wartime. We have to expect these small irregularities to crop up occasionally. Just let me pass, and I'll make sure your paperwork's brought up-to-date as soon as I can. Right?"

The younger man's face darkened in anger, and Metje winced inwardly, aware that he'd blundered badly. He'd meant to use his most cordial senior-officer-to-junior-officer tone. Instead, he'd sounded more like a smarmy, whining panhandler.

"And once again, *Kommandant*, I have my own orders. I cannot allow you to proceed without verifying your identity."

The lieutenant's eyes narrowed and he stepped back a pace from the car door. "Give me your ID card, sir . . . please."

Metje saw the man's hand drifting toward his holstered pistol. His heart fluttered once, then twice, and the sweat running down his back felt ice-cold. A loud clicking noise told him that one of the other soldiers at the barricade had just taken the safety off his assault rifle.

He folded. With his hand shaking uncontrollably, Metje passed the card through the Astra's open window.

"Thank you, *Kommandant*." The lieutenant slid the ID card into his shirt pocket. "Park over there, off the road, while I call this in. Sir."

Thoroughly cowed, Metje obeyed. He reversed the Astra and pulled off onto the highway's gravel shoulder—stopping just ahead of the mammoth Hippo. His heart sank as he watched the officer walk over to his radio-equipped jeep and pick up a microphone, standing with his back to Metje.

His mind raced through the options left open to him, raising and discarding them in almost the same instant. Doing nothing was not an option. The Defense Ministry was sure to have an alert out with his name on it by now. Resisting arrest seemed even more absurd—pitting his poor pistol marksmanship against a squad of rifle-armed soldiers would be simple suicide. And escape . . .

Metje thought about that. The Astra was a fast car. If he could swerve around the single Army truck parked ahead, he might gain a large enough lead to evade any pursuit. It seemed worth trying. He reached for the ignition key with trembling fingers.

He glanced at his rearview mirror. The young lieutenant had just spun round, his face a mask of anger. Oh, God. He knew.

Metje gunned the engine and felt his tires spin wildly in the loose gravel. Come on! The Astra shot forward in a cloud of dust and thrown gravel, accelerating rapidly. For a millisecond, he felt a wild surge of exhilaration. He'd done it. . . .

Flames stabbed out of the darkness—muzzle flashes from rifles firing at point-blank range. The Astra's front windshield starred and then shattered, shot out by the same bursts that shredded its front and rear tires.

Metje felt himself thrown forward against the steering column as his car skidded to a stop in a cloud of dust, torn rubber, and exhaust.

He was still recovering from the abortive ride when the car door slammed open. Rough hands yanked him out of his seat and out onto the road. Two grim-faced soldiers grabbed his arms, while a third quickly pulled his pistol from its holster.

As his hands were cuffed behind him, the lieutenant strode up, finally stopping with his face only centimeters away from Metje's. The normal deference shown by a junior officer toward his superiors had vanished entirely. "I checked with my headquarters, Kommandant Metje. They informed me that you are charged with dereliction of duty and desertion! Those charges have been confirmed by General de Wet himself!"

Metje tried to protest, but the younger officer's outraged voice rode roughshod over his words. "Save your lies, man! It's too late."

The lieutenant jerked a thumb toward the darkness. "Take him away."

With a burly soldier pulling on each arm and his hands secured behind him, Metje was led, stumbling, toward the Hippo. As he walked, he tried vainly to put his shattered mind back in some kind of order. He'd have to get his story straight for the court-martial.

But the two soldiers led him straight past the personnel carrier and out to a small tree twenty meters away. Metje looked around, suddenly unsure of what was happening. The lieutenant and another two men were following along right behind him.

They dragged Metje over to the tree and roughly turned him around to face the parked APC. They took the handcuffs off just long enough to pull his hands around its slender trunk, then snapped them shut again. *Oh, my God . . .*

The lieutenant waved his men back and walked over to where Metje writhed, straining futilely against his bonds. "We don't have time for the pointless formality of a court-martial. In any event, I've received direct orders as to the disposition of your case. Sentence will be carried out immediately."

He turned to leave, stopped, and whirled back to face the shaking, white-faced officer. Wordlessly, he reached out and ripped the AWB pin from Metje's uniform. Then he strode over to where the four soldiers stood in a group.

Without even bothering to form them in a straight rank, the lieutenant barked, "Ready!"

Four assault rifles snapped up, aimed directly at Metje.

Metje looked at the leveled barrels in horror. His knees buckled and he sagged forward against the handcuffs holding him to the tree. He started sobbing. "*Nooooo!* You can't! I am an Afrikan—"

"Fire!"

Four bullets slammed into Metje's head, chest, and abdomen. He died instantly. His nation's death wouldn't come so easily.

CHAPTER 24

Commitment

NOVEMBER 14—THE WHITE HOUSE, WASHINGTON, D.C.

The once steaming-hot cup of coffee sitting on the President's desk had long since grown stone cold. Now it sat off to one side, pushed aside and abandoned after a particularly abrupt hand gesture threatened to spill its contents across an important stack of telexes, reports, and maps.

"Indeed, Prime Minister, you're absolutely right. The situation is quite intolerable."

Vice President James Forrester slid his own empty cup onto the low side table by his chair and leaned forward. The President's sudden formality was a sign that the hour-long, early-morning conversation with Britain's prime minister was drawing to a close. Until now, everything had been on a strictly first-name basis.

"Exactly. My people will be meeting within the hour." The President arched an eyebrow at Forrester, looking for confirmation.

He nodded back. Most of the NSC's key players had already been at their posts for more than twenty-four hours—ever since the first unsettling reports of the new Cuban offensive started pouring into official Washington. And a Marine Corps helicopter was already parked out on the White House lawn, on standby to fly him across the Potomac to the Pentagon.

"Yes, Prime Minister, I'll call you the moment I have more detailed information from this end. Yes. And thank you, too." The President put the phone down, his expression grim.

Forrester couldn't control his curiosity. "Well?"

The President looked up. "It's a go, Jimmy. The British are in." He seemed older somehow. "I don't like it. I don't like it at all. But I just don't see that we have any other real choice."

Forrester felt his pulse accelerating. He rose from his chair. "In that case, Mr. President, I'll be on my way. Hurley has his group waiting for me."

He glanced behind him as he left the Oval Office. The President sat still behind his desk—staring sadly at nothing in particular. Not for the first time, Forrester realized that it was a hell of a lot easier to follow orders than it was to give them.

EMERGENCY CONFERENCE ROOM, THE PENTAGON

At the President's direction, the NSC's Southern Africa Crisis Group had shifted its day-to-day operations over to the Pentagon. The basement Emergency Conference Room there was larger, had better communications facilities, and allowed faster access to the latest intelligence data from the region.

Almost as important, the Pentagon had more parking and entrances and exits than the White House. And that, in turn, made it easier to hold a serious meeting without creating a three-ring media circus. The print and TV reporters who prowled through the White House looking for fast-breaking news had limousine-counting down to a science.

Besides, the Conference Room looked a lot more like a

high-tech command center than did the rather dingy White House Situation Room. A bank of six-foot-high computer display screens, most of them blank at the moment, lined one whole wall, three across and two rows high. The length of a T-shaped table accommodated Crisis Group staffers and aides, while members of the Crisis Group sat across one end. A microphone stood in front of every seat at the table. Podiums, with as much audiovisual equipment as a small high school, allowed the entire group to be briefed on developments.

Doors led to the basement hallway outside, an adjacent communications center, a pair of small apartments with beds and washrooms, and a carefully guarded cubicle crowded with terminals linked directly to the mainframe computers at every major U.S. intelligence agency.

The Conference Room was supposed to be filled with organized chaos. Instead, it was just chaos. Cuba's attack into South Africa had caught the Crisis Group in midmove, turning what was supposed to be a smooth transition into a frantic scramble.

Officers and enlisted personnel from all four military services came and went in a steady stream, mixing with little knots of harried-looking civilian aides. Technicians clustered on one side of the room, trying to get the right images displayed on the room's wall-mounted computer screens. Maps for southern Africa were on file, but they hadn't yet been converted to the Pentagon's new computer format.

More enlisted men staggered in, carrying sealed boxes of highly sensitive intelligence reports. An extremely tense Air Force captain stood in the doorway to the tiny intel cubicle, checking off each report's title and serial number. Under normal circumstances, he would have counted every page of every report to make sure that none were missing—but circumstances were clearly not normal.

A low whistle broke across all the activity. The assorted technicians, officers, and enlisted men scattered through the chamber turned to see a short, bowlegged Army sergeant major waving them out. "Meeting's on, gents. Secure the room."

In the sudden exodus, pen flashlights, tech manuals, tools, and reams of paper were all left lying in place. They'd be needed again once the politicos and higher brass were done jawing at each other.

Flanked by his military aide and civilian chief of staff, Forrester entered at a fast walk—his hair still windblown after a wild, rain-drenched helicopter landing outside the Pentagon. Shrugging off his wet overcoat, he moved to the spot marked for him at the conference table. He nodded once to red-eyed Edward Hurley, plainly weary after a long, sleepless night spent monitoring developments, and took his seat.

All conversation around the T-shaped table died away.

Forrester glanced to either side, unsurprised to see that the Crisis Group's membership had expanded overnight to include the Joint Chiefs, the CIA director, the secretaries of defense, treasury, and commerce, and a small army of high-ranking assistants. So much for the original idea of a small, manageable group. Washington's political and military leaders were drawn to international crises like moths to a flame.

He rapped once on the table. "I'll make this short and sweet. I met with the President this morning."

Everyone at the table opened notebooks and grabbed pens. Guidance from the Man would make their task a lot clearer. Not easier—just clearer.

Forrester paused briefly before plowing straight ahead. "The President has decided to authorize direct American intervention in southern Africa. Direct military intervention."

He raised his voice, overriding the surprised murmuring coming from around the table. "We have three objectives: One, bouncing Vorster and his goons out of power. Two, preventing Cuba from gaining control over South Africa's strategic minerals. Third, and most important, securing world access to those resources by restoring some kind of civil order over there." He glanced at the wall clock showing local time. It was already ten forty-five A.M. "The President's scheduled a full cabinet meeting for seven o'clock tonight. He wants our recommendations and preliminary plans by then."

"Good God." Christopher Nicholson broke the stunned

silence. The CIA director had been fiddling uneasily with the cap of one of his pens, pulling it off and pushing it back on. "Mr. Vice President, we are still gathering information on the invasion, on Cuban intentions and capabilities. We don't know how many troops are involved, we don't know where they are located. We can't possibly act without a better idea—"

"I'm sorry, Chris, but we can't wait for you to produce some glossy intelligence product." Forrester's tone combined urgency and impatience. "We just don't have time to dot every i and cross every t. Hell, you've all seen the financial news this morning."

Most of the men and women around the table nodded grimly. The world financial markets were in an uproar. Prices for South African–produced minerals were skyrocketing. Gold alone was trading at more than a thousand dollars an ounce. The New York, Tokyo, London, and other stock markets were all in sustained free-fall. Several governments had shut down their exchanges in a frantic effort to slow the collapse. Commentators and self-proclaimed economic experts were openly predicting a new world recession. Others were using the word *depression*.

Forrester looked down the row of stunned faces. "We simply don't have any choice, folks. The President wants a solid plan he can present to the nation by this time tomorrow morning. Not a 'spin' and not a 'slant.' " He nodded toward the one lit display screen—a map showing the known war zones in Namibia and South Africa. "The world's too small a place for this kind of crap."

More nods. This wasn't America's first reminder that the nominal end of the Cold War hadn't automatically ushered in a millennial age of peace and prosperity.

Forrester turned toward the Air Force general sitting to his left. "Walt, the President has one key question he needs answered right away. Can the Cubans win if we don't intervene?"

The chairman of the Joint Chiefs didn't hesitate. "Yes."

The civilians around the table were openly surprised by Hickman's blunt answer. Senior military officials, like their civilian counterparts, tended to be more comfortable with carefully hedged assessments.

Nicholson spoke up first. "How can you be so sure, General? My analysts estimate that the total Cuban attack force is still smaller than the whole South African army. They're outnumbered by at least two to one. How can Castro hope to beat those kind of odds?"

Hickman shook his head impatiently. "The overall numbers don't matter worth a damn, Director. What counts is combat power on the front line. And right now the front lines are in South Africa itself—not Namibia. Cuba's probably got a ten-to-one force ratio there."

He left the conference table and moved to the display screen. "Look here. Half of Vorster's reliable troops are dangling out here in Namibia—more than a thousand miles away from the real action. Most of the rest are scattered around in penny packets, chasing down black guerrillas and rebel commandos." He faced Forrester directly. "So the question is, can Pretoria shift its heavy armor and infantry units out of Namibia fast enough?"

Hickman shook his head again, answering his own question. "I doubt it." He traced a sparse network of red and black lines shown on the flickering display map. "South Africa's road and rail net is just too limited. Plus, Cuban MiGs have achieved almost total air superiority. They can pound the hell out of troop trains or truck convoys moving by day."

"So?"

"So South Africa's troops are going to arrive piecemeal—if at all. They'll slow the Cubans down some, maybe even a lot, but they're not going to stop them. Not short of Pretoria anyway. And they'll be cut to pieces in the process."

Hickman stalked back to his seat in the silence that followed.

Nicholson cleared his throat. "I still believe we should offer the President some alternative to an ill-conceived and unilateral commitment of U.S. forces."

Forrester stopped him there. "Hold on, Chris. The British have agreed to send troops as well."

"Are their troops going to stop every bullet the South Africans or Cubans fire, Mr. Vice President?" Nicholson shot back. "We're talking about going to war against a country that has more than a hundred thousand men under arms—a country that's already at war with Cuba and itself. This isn't going to be a walk in the park. We're talking about a casualty list that could run into the thousands."

Forrester's eyes narrowed at the unsubtle dig, but he kept his temper under control. Beneath all his bluster, the CIA chief spoke for a sizable fraction of the cabinet, the Congress, and the American people. Nobody wanted to rush into another bloody, unwinnable quagmire like Vietnam. "The alternative to military action is another Great Depression—tens of millions of people out of work, hunger, riots.

"Neither the President nor I claim to be infallible, Director. Do you see an option we've overlooked?"

"Yes. Why not press for action by the UN Security Council instead. Get a resolution calling on all parties to withdraw to—"

For the first time, Edward Hurley spoke up. "Won't work, I'm afraid. The Soviets would veto any such resolution like that!" He snapped his fingers for emphasis.

The secretary of commerce backed him up. "That's true. Moscow has too much power and prestige invested in a Cuban victory. They can't afford to let the UN intervene."

Again, the men and women seated around the long table nodded gravely. A Cuban victory meant de facto Cuban control over South Africa's mineral wealth. That, in turn, meant the West would have to pay sharply higher prices for the strategic minerals it needed. For the first time in decades, Cuba wouldn't need annual billion-dollar infusions of Soviet economic and military aid.

Even more important, from Moscow's point of view, the prices paid for the USSR's own chromium, titanium, gold, and other mineral resources would climb dramatically—pouring badly needed hard currency into the State Treasury. And if those higher prices produced a worldwide economic slump, so much the better. A depression in the industrial giants of the West would level the playing field. Power is relative—not an absolute.

For the first time since the Cold War's supposed end, the strategic interests of the Soviet Union were again opposed to those of the Western democracies.

Nicholson backed down and tried another angle. "Then why not impose a blockade on Cuba? Cut off Castro's ability to feed his troops and we end the war."

"For the simple reason that they're not being supplied from Cuba itself. As you should know, Director." For the first time that morning, Forrester showed his irritation openly. "I assume you're not proposing that we risk an even wider war by stopping Soviet merchant ships on the high seas?"

Wisely, Nicholson kept his mouth shut.

"In any event, even forcing a Cuban pullback would still leave us facing this nutcase Vorster." Forrester grimaced. "The President is absolutely convinced that we cannot guarantee the free flow of the minerals, and a stable international economy, without installing a democratic government of some sort in South Africa."

He glared down the table toward the sullen, silent CIA chief. "We've tried diplomatic pressures. They've failed. We've tried economic pressures. They've failed. And now we're facing a situation that could wreck every economy from here to Tokyo. I'll ask you this just one more time, Director Nicholson: What other option do we have?"

Silence.

"Right. None." Forrester shifted his gaze toward the Joint Chiefs. "Gentlemen, I think it's time we started talking seriously about the use of military force. You've heard the President's three objectives. Now I need to know what kinds of troops and hardware we'll have to commit to achieve those objectives."

His question created a stir among the Joint Chiefs as they talked among themselves for a moment or two.

Finally, General Hickman leaned forward. "Mr. Vice President, one thing is very clear—the carrier battle group we've got sitting off the South African coast can't handle this on its own."

Forrester nodded and motioned him on, knowing that Hickman and the other chiefs were talking the problem through out loud.

The Air Force general stared hard into space for several seconds and then glanced at his colleagues. Finally, he looked back at Forrester. "Even sending another carrier battle group won't do much good, sir. We're going to need more than just air and sea power to impose our will on South Africa. To do that, we're going to need men on the ground—lots of them."

HEADQUARTERS, SECOND MARINE EXPEDITIONARY FORCE, CAMP LEJEUNE, NORTH CAROLINA

Lt. Gen. Jerry Craig, USMC, squirmed in his chair as the briefer droned on and on. His intelligence officer, Col. George Slocomb, had pieced together a summary of the military situation in South Africa, but it wasn't a straightforward military campaign. There were essentially three separate wars raging, all rapidly turning into one giant furball. Hard data on any of them was tough to come by.

Slocomb was trying to fill in the gaps by concentrating on South Africa's confused political situation, but Craig was uncomfortable with that kind of stuff. He was a military professional—one ordinarily only too glad to leave politics to the "power tie" boys in Washington.

The general squirmed again, running his hand slowly through close-cropped red hair. It was impolite to go to sleep during a briefing you had ordered. Besides, South Africa was the hottest part of the world right now, and he had to know what was going on.

"General?" One of his aides leaned next to his ear.

"What?"

"Washington's on the line, sir."

Irritated at the interruption, Craig got up and walked over

to a side table that held a phone. The lights came up and a low buzz of conversation started. His irritation faded, though, when he heard the voice on the other end.

"Jerry, this is Wes Masters." Craig knew Wesley Masters's voice well. Two classes ahead of him at the Academy, Masters had served with him in several posts, fought with him near the DMZ in 'Nam, and partied with him in some of the wildest ports in the world. Masters was also one of the few men in the Corps senior to him—the head honcho, in fact, commandant of the whole everlovin' Marine Corps.

Craig automatically stiffened to attention. "Yes, Commandant. What can I do for you?"

When his staff saw Craig's response, all talking stopped as though it had been cut off by a switch, and every ear listened to Craig's side of the conversation.

"Yes, sir, we're as ready as ever. We're prepping for Gold Eagle next month, but . . .

"Aye, aye, sir. I understand." Craig shook his head. Jumping Jesus. Had he heard that right? "I'll be there ASAP. I'll radio my ETA to Andrews. Good-bye, sir."

Craig hung up the phone and turned to face his openly curious staff. "Listen up, people. Drop everything in the plan of the day. Implement the recall bill and start preparations for embarkation."

Jaws dropped all around the room. Well, he knew exactly how they felt.

He turned to his operations officer. "Terry, call Cherry Point. I want a two-seat Hornet prepped with a pilot standing by in twenty minutes. I have to make a fast trip to Washington—real fast. And get my helicopter over here."

Craig raised his voice slightly so that it would carry through the crowded room. "When I get back, I want a meeting with every officer on the staff. Everyone. Have a list of anything that might interfere with a fast embarkation."

He smiled slightly, but there was a grimness to it. "And it better be a very short list."

CHERRY POINT MARINE CORPS AIR STATION, NORTH CAROLINA

Craig barely noticed the helicopter ride to the Air Station. He spent the entire trip pretending to go over routine paperwork. Reading and signing trivial memos and authorizations helped him conceal an inner whirlpool of thoughts and emotions. Marines, generals especially, were not supposed to act like giddy schoolboys. And he'd been fighting to control his expression and his demeanor ever since the commandant's phone call.

An order to embark was not given lightly, or routinely. It was only issued in a time of serious crisis, when the President's list of options had shortened so much that using military force wasn't just possible, it was probable.

It had to be South Africa. There were hot spots aplenty elsewhere, but the world's only serious shooting war was going on down there. And Masters had asked him to ready his entire expeditionary force! Not just a battalion or one of his two brigades. Whatever was up was big, and again that pointed to South Africa.

Combat in Africa. He shook his head. His Marine career had already included a lot of combat duty, always in godforsaken places nobody sane would ever want to live in, just fight over. But he'd never had the opportunity to command so many men in battle. At full strength, a Marine Expeditionary Force could muster up to forty thousand sailors and Marines, two hundred fighters and attack jets, four hundred -plus helicopters, and hundreds of tanks, light armored vehicles, and artillery pieces. In Craig's admittedly biased view, it was the world's most perfect combination of strategic mobility, firepower, and pure guts.

Just thinking about handling all that in the noise and confusion of battle was enough to make a man sweat bullets, Craig thought. You couldn't just lead your boys forward in a head-on slashing attack. You had to know how to mass air, land, and sea power into a single, flexible whole. Still, he was ready for it—ready for anything. Or so he told himself.

During a long and distinguished Marine Corps career, he'd

held a variety of staff assignments, not just troop commands. Every Marine officer, even the most gung ho, had to spend plenty of time commanding a desk. And his time at the Pentagon and at various duty stations around the world had shown him to be a good planner—a thinking soldier who never lost sight of the shortest, least costly route to the objective.

Despite what at times seemed an inordinate number of people shooting at him, Craig had stayed healthy and moved up the hierarchy, one slow rung at a time. Now he'd reached the penultimate step of his career—commander, Fleet Marine Force Atlantic and commanding officer of the Second Marine Expeditionary Force, one of only three such forces in the Marine Corps.

The general looked up as the helo came over Cherry Point Marine Corps Air Station. He started packing up his paperwork. Once overhead, it took several more minutes to reach the flight line, a huge expanse of bare concrete bordered on one side by a row of boxy, metal-walled hangars. The runways themselves seemed like a study in perpetual motion. Of turboprop cargo planes taking off with supplies for carriers at sea. Of fighters practicing touch-and-gos in a howling roar of powerful engines. And over it all, the pervasive, biting tang of raw jet fuel.

His helo landed near a twin-tailed F/A-18 parked next to a grimy yellow starter cart. A long hose ran from the starter cart to the Hornet, blowing air into its jet engines to get their turbines spinning. A small group of men in camouflage uniforms came to attention as the engines stopped. They saluted Craig as he stepped out.

Leaving his briefcase for his aide, Craig returned their salutes and walked quickly over to the senior officer, a lieutenant colonel.

"Good afternoon, General. I'm Steve Walker, squadron commander." He pointed to a lieutenant wearing flight gear. "This is Tom Lyles, your chauffeur for this trip."

Lyles was a short, stocky man with a broad, clean-featured face. Craig liked him immediately. Their eyes were on the same level.

He held out his hand. "Lieutenant."

An enlisted man ran up carrying a pile of flight gear, and they quickly fitted Craig with coveralls, g-vest, and a helmet. He noticed that there were several sets of equipment, all in different sizes, lined up on a nearby jeep.

As the sailor helped him lace up his g-vest, Craig asked, "How long a flight to Andrews?"

"About thirty minutes, sir." The young Navy flyer grinned at his surprised expression. "We'll be at Mach point nine five as soon as we get to altitude."

Though he did his best to hide it, Craig was impressed. Just driving from Andrews to the Pentagon around Washington's traffic-choked Beltway would probably take twice that long. In his case, though, another helicopter would carry him to the Pentagon.

His aide ran up. "Your gear's stowed in the baggage pod, General."

"Great." Craig pulled the helmet onto his head. "Signal my ETA to the commandant. And I'll need another fast ride back after this meeting."

"Aye, aye, sir."

Ten minutes later, the Hornet roared off the runway, climbing fast on full throttle. At twenty thousand feet over the wooded Virginia countryside, Lyles leveled off. He kept his throttle shoved forward, though.

Most Navy pilots spend their lives computing flight profiles that give them the longest possible time aloft. Lyles evidently planned to make the most of a mission that let him fly almost as fast as he wanted to.

The Fighter roared on, boring a hole through the air at over six hundred knots. Craig's mood soared along with the plane.

THE PENTAGON

Craig strode briskly up the wide set of steps to the Pentagon's River Entrance, greeted by a forest of salutes snapped his way by officers and enlisted men coming and going through the set of double doors.

A Marine major hurried forward. "General Craig, sir. Right this way. They're waiting for you downstairs."

Craig had expected to go straight to the commandant's office in the Navy Annex, but had found himself deep inside the Pentagon instead—midway along a poorly lit basement corridor he'd never seen before. His guide stopped in front of an anonymous metal door. "In here, General."

The man punched in a four-number security code on a keypad and pulled the door open.

Hat under his arm, Craig stepped through into a wood-paneled conference room, complete with a long mahogany conference table and beautifully upholstered furniture. Even the room's utilitarian fluorescent lights had been tastefully enclosed.

His first glimpse of the men waiting for him wiped away any lasting impression of the room. He'd been expecting to see Wes Masters, of course. But he sure as hell hadn't expected to see a group that included the rest of the Joint Chiefs, the secretary of defense, and the Vice President. He stopped dead in the doorway.

"Come on in, Jerry. Take a pew." Masters stepped around the table, shook Craig's outstretched hand, and steered him toward an empty chair.

Oh, boy. Although some of the glitter had worn off those in high places as he advanced in rank, Craig still found himself a little awed in such company. Here he was, the commanding general of a Marine expeditionary force—the absolute lord and master of nearly forty thousand men—and he was still the junior man present in this small, secret room. He wasn't used to that.

Also, just what kind of orders was he going to get? There was an old rule in the Corps that the higher a job started, the tougher it got.

Wordlessly, he nodded to the assembled group and sat down.

Masters took the seat next to him and nodded to an Air Force officer standing near the wall. "All right, Colonel."

A projection screen slid down from the ceiling, and the lights dimmed.

For twenty minutes, Craig sat through another briefing on South Africa. Though shorter than his G-2's version, the data was a little more timely and a little more complete. Nevertheless, Craig made a mental note to tell Slocomb he'd been pretty close to the mark.

The lights came up, and General Masters looked at him. "Jerry, we want you to take the Second MEF to South Africa."

Bingo. His earlier guesses had been on the mark, too.

"Our people are still putting a plan together, but right now we anticipate an initial landing at Cape Town—followed by extensive operations inland and east along the South African coast."

With two briefings under his belt, Craig understood exactly what this entailed. Cape Town was eighty-five hundred miles from the Marine amphibious base at Camp Lejeune—an incredible distance for an operation of that kind. Automatically, he glanced at the map still displayed on the screen.

Masters anticipated his question. "We understand the distance problem, Jerry. But we've got several factors working for us. First, South Africa's Navy is practically nonexistent, so we don't have to worry about an opposed transit." The Marine Corps commandant nodded politely toward the admiral sitting across the table and said, "The Navy's promised us a fast trip.

"Second, we think you'll only need one brigade loaded for assault. Cape Town's well away from the path of the Cuban invasion, and our contacts among the rebels there tell us they'd welcome American intervention as a stabilizing influence."

Swell. Craig hated the thought of relying on men he didn't know—men who'd already betrayed one trust. He made another mental note to make sure his staff did their damnedest to combat-load more than one brigade.

"This is a major operation, Jerry. To get the job done, we think we're going to need your boys, the Seventh Light, the One oh One Air Assault, and the Twenty-fourth Mechanized. We're gonna back you up with two or three carrier battle groups and a whole slew of Air Force tac air squadrons."

Craig swallowed hard. They were talking about committing more than a quarter of a million men. Jesus Christ. He hadn't even begun to imagine what "big" really meant. He tried a tentative joke. "Is that all, sir?"

Masters smiled briefly and looked toward the Vice President. "Not quite. We're expecting the British to join in, too."

Craig felt everyone's gaze converge on him. This was probably a historic moment, he thought, but no memorable oratorical gems came readily to mind. "My Marines are ready, Commandant. When do we ship out?"

"As soon as you humanly can, Jerry. We're on one helluva tight timetable for this op," Masters replied.

"So who's in command?" Craig needed to know whom he'd be working for. Some grunt, probably. It might even be someone he knew.

For a split second Masters looked exactly like Lewis Carroll's Cheshire Cat at its most insufferable—all smiling teeth. "You are. We're making you Joint Task Force commander . . ."

Masters's voice faded, and Craig suddenly felt hollow and a little dizzy. Him? In charge of a combined operation? My God, they were offering him the equivalent to a corps command—no, better—a unified command. He'd be leading a mix of U.S. Army, Navy, and Air Force units, plus those of at least one other nation, into almost certain combat on the other side of the ocean. . . .

He suddenly realized he was woolgathering, and that it wasn't a good idea to play space cadet in front of the Joint Chiefs. Might adversely affect his chance of promotion, he silently joked, and he realized he was a little euphoric.

". . . amphibious operation so a Marine should be in overall command. You have a reputation for aggressiveness and energy, and you'll need every bit of it. The President is planning to go on television tomorrow night, so we'll be committed from the start. You can expect a lot of press attention, Jerry, and we need good press."

Masters leaned toward him. "We know you can fight. Can you handle the rest of the job? We're the only ones who know you've been tapped for overall command." The commandant nodded to the men seated around the table. "If you turn down the top slot, you'll still take the Second MEF overseas. We'd be disappointed, though, because we think you're the best man for the job.

"This isn't an order, it's a request. Will you take command?"

Not an order, Craig thought. The big ones never are. They always give you a chance to back out, with honor. Of course, backing out would mean he could kiss any further promotion good-bye. He wouldn't stand a chance at taking the top slot after Wes retired. The theory was sound, though. Some men would find it easier to risk losing a promotion than a whole war.

Craig sat quietly for no more than a second. He tried to think objectively, to weigh his own strengths and limitations dispassionately. But he already knew his answer. It was impossible for him to say no.

The flight back seemed even shorter than the trip north. Strapped into the Hornet rear seat, he could barely open the briefing book they'd given him. Nevertheless, what he saw as he leafed through summaries of his force structure and the latest intelligence strengthened his original belief that he could do the job.

Then he got to the thick annex labeled "Political Considerations." For the first time since receiving his orders, Lt. Gen. Jerry Craig began to have doubts.

NOVEMBER 15—HEADQUARTERS, 3 COMMANDO BRIGADE, ROYAL MARINES, DEVONPORT, ENGLAND

Brig. Neil Pascoe was sound asleep when his bedside command phone rang. It trilled loudly six times before his hand fumbled past the nightstand lamp and found the receiver. "Yes. What the bloody hell is it?"

The brigade's duty officer sounded properly contrite. "Major General Vaughn on the line, sir."

Pascoe came fully awake instantly. The commander of

Great Britain's Commando Forces wasn't known for calling his subordinates without good reason. Most especially not at half past two in the morning.

The line hummed and clicked. "Pascoe?"

"Yes, sir."

Vaughn came right to the point. "I'm afraid events in South Africa have taken rather a nasty turn for the worse. I've just spoken with the PM, and he's asked us to come to seventy-two hours' notice to move."

CNN MORNING WATCH

The reporter stood in front of the main gate to the U.S. Marine Base at Camp Lejeune, North Carolina. Behind him, a small crowd milled outside the base—workers entering or leaving, well-wishers waving small American flags, curiosity seekers, and a thin scattering of fringe-group protestors with signs. A mixed force of Marine MPs and North Carolina state troopers kept the two tiny groups apart—skinheads and KKK supporters to one side, leftists and aging Spartacus Youth League members to the other. Green-painted trucks lumbered in and out of the gate, mixing with civilian cars and semitrailers. It made a picturesque background for his narrative.

". . . catapulted into furious action by the events of the last forty-eight hours. Camp Lejeune, North Carolina, home of the Second Marine Expeditionary Force, has erupted as the Marines prepare to embark on every available Navy hull and on several commercial vessels chartered by the Military Sealift Command. The container ship *Gulf Galaxy* and several bulk cargo carriers are only the first of many that will be needed to carry the Marines and their equipment across the Atlantic to South Africa.

"Ships are loading at Navy and commercial ports all along America's Atlantic coast, and overseas in Southampton, England, as the Royal Marines embark as well."

The image cut away to an aerial view of Wilmington. It was normally busy with merchant traffic and warships bound for the shipyard or for the naval base there. Now it was choked with traffic, with dozens of ships literally filling the marked channels leading in and out of the busy waterway.

The camera zoomed in on the Navy base itself, showing cluttered gray ships pulled up to several piers, all the centers of frantic activity. "These Navy ships will carry what official sources describe as 'the leading elements of the Allied peace-keeping force.'

"Other Marines we've talked to used the term 'assault echelon.' "

CHAPTER 25

Thunderhead

NOVEMBER 18—ADVANCE HEADQUARTERS, CUBAN EXPEDITIONARY FORCE, LOUIS TRICHARDT AIR BASE, SOUTH AFRICA

The South African air base showed all the signs of fierce resistance and thorough demolition. Mile-long concrete runways were peppered with craters torn and gouged by heavy artillery fire. The control tower, hangars, and storehouses were all pounded into burnt-out masses of scorched aluminum, twisted steel girders, and broken shards of brick, concrete, and rock. Hanging over everything was the sickening, pungent tang of death, decay, and thousands of gallons of jet fuel poured out and left to evaporate or go up in flames.

Louis Trichardt Air Base had died an ugly and lingering death. But now its new owners were hard at work resurrecting the freshly captured corpse.

Four six-wheeled vehicles were parked at various points along the main runway, each mounting four "Romb" surface-to-air missiles. NATO called them SA-8A Geckos. An acquisition radar mounted on each vehicle scanned the skies above for any indication of an incoming air raid. The SAM battery had a conventional backup—eight towed 23mm antiaircraft cannon spaced at regular intervals along the rest of the airfield perimeter. Their long, twin gun barrels pointed toward the sky, ready to throw a fiery curtain of high-explosive rounds at any attacking plane.

Behind this protective screen of SAMs and automatic weapons, teams of Cuban combat engineers supervised sweating gangs of black South African laborers filling in craters and clearing away wreckage by hand—"volunteers" in the service of their own liberation. Other blacks were busy carting off the last few dead Afrikaners for disposal in a mass grave beside the main runway.

Gen. Antonio Vega watched the blacks working with a practiced eye, a slight, worried frown on his stern, narrow face. There were fewer genuine volunteers than he'd hoped for. His political officers and ANC liaisons blamed the dearth of willing labor on civilian casualties caused by artillery and air bombardments directed against SADF positions inside the black townships surrounding Louis Trichardt.

Well, perhaps that was so. The Cuban general shrugged. Did these South African blacks expect to win freedom and a proper political structure without loss? If so, they would be bitterly disappointed. Wars and revolutions were always brutal and bloody affairs, he thought. And he should know. He'd fought through enough of both during more than thirty years of service to Fidel Castro and his people.

Some of the ANC officers assigned to him reported that a few of their people believed the Cubans to be nearly as racist as the Afrikaners they displaced. And why? Simply because the army of liberation needed their strong backs and unskilled hands. Vega scowled. Racism! What nonsense. Why, he had black Cuban officers on his own staff. Brave and competent men—every one of them.

As for the charge that he used South African blacks only for manual labor, what of it? Hadn't Karl Marx himself said it best? "From each according to his abilities, to each according to his needs."

He dismissed the problem from his mind. Let the rear-area

commissars worry about such matters. He had a war to fight and win.

Vega turned to the stout, mustachioed colonel of engineers waiting silently beside him. "Well, Luis? How soon before our planes can land here?"

"Twenty-four hours, Comrade General." The colonel sounded certain—always a safe tone to use around Vega. "My heavy equipment should arrive before sundown, and when it does . . ." He waved away the waist-high piles of debris still littering the runways as though they were nothing more than dust before a broom.

Vega patted him on the shoulder and glanced at the shorter, thinner Air Force officer attached to his personal staff. "You hear that, Rico. Twenty-four hours. That's good news, eh?"

"Yes, sir." The Air Force major pointed toward the sweating work crews. "Once they've got the main runway cleared, we can start flying in ground elements of the brigade. And once they're here, we'll have this base back in full operation within half a day."

Vega nodded his understanding. Cuban forward air-base operations were organized around special brigades made up of all the skilled troops needed to keep jet aircraft flying and combat ready—air traffic controllers, mechanics, armament and fueling specialists, planning staff, and pilots. Even more important, Cuba's fighters and transport aircraft, like all Soviet-made planes, were able to use captured NATO rearming, refueling, and maintenance equipment. And the South Africans used NATO standard gear.

How thoughtful of them, Vega mused.

He stared beyond the airfield toward the multilane highway running south. South toward the vital road junction and minerals complex at Pietersburg, one hundred and twenty kilometers away. And south toward the enemy capital of Pretoria, two hundred and eighty kilometers beyond Pietersburg. A hint of yellowish dust and gray-white smoke on the horizon marked the position of his First Brigade Tactical Group—tanks, armored cars, and APCs driving steadily forward despite slowly stiffening Afrikaner resistance.

Vega allowed himself a short moment of self-congratulation. Capturing this air base would breathe new life and vigor into this portion of his grand offensive. Urgently needed supplies and spare parts could be flown in with ease instead of being trucked south from Zimbabwe over hundreds of kilometers of dangerous road. Even better, MiG fighters and fighter bombers based here would be only a few short minutes' flying time from the battlefront—drastically increasing their time on station and the number of missions they could fly as they hunted for Afrikaner targets on the ground and in the air.

It all added up to one thing: Pretoria was going to have to commit an ever-increasing number of its own troops to this front. Troops that would have to be stripped from other parts of South Africa.

Vega smiled grimly. Karl Vorster and his generals were about to learn another painful lesson in logistics, careful planning, applied air power, and deft footwork.

Abruptly the Cuban general turned on his heel and headed back to his command vehicle. Small victories were worth gloating over only if they brought total victory in sight. Time to look at the big picture.

FIRST BRIGADE TACTICAL GROUP, NEAR BANDELIERKOP, SOUTH AFRICA

More than twenty wheeled and tracked Cuban armored vehicles rumbled across the Transvaal countryside—smashing through barbed-wire fences meant to pen in cattle, flattening fields of tall grass, and grinding new-planted wheat and corn into the damp earth. No revealing plumes of dust rose today to mark their passage. A late-spring storm had come and gone earlier in the morning—tearing out of the east in a drumbeat barrage of wind-tossed rain and thunder.

Now a barrage of human making hammered the veld.

Whaamm! Dirt fountained high into the air two hundred meters ahead of the advancing Cuban column, and newly promoted Maj. Victor Mares ducked behind the steel hatch cover of his BTR-60. He clicked the transmit button on his radio mike. "Any sign of that OP, Lieutenant?"

"Not yet, Comrade Major." The voice of the advance guard's scout commander crackled through his earphones.

Mares ducked and swore as another South African shell ploughed into the fields off to the left. Closer this time. Steel splinters whined overhead. The damned Afrikaners had to have somebody with a radio and a map guiding their fire. But where?

"We may have found it, Major!" Excitement made the scout lieutenant sound even younger than he was. "We're closing on a stone farmhouse about three kilometers ahead of your position. Will investigate."

Mares let the mike fall free to dangle on a cord around his neck and raised his binoculars. Low hills. Dark, cloudy sky. Magnified views of vehicles only a few score meters ahead. The sky again. Curse it, the BTR's rocking and rolling motion made it almost impossible to focus on anything for more than a fraction of a second. He braced himself and tried to ride with the vehicle as though it were a bucking bronco like those he'd seen in American cowboy movies aired on the officially forbidden and periodically jammed TV Marti.

He steadied his binoculars and looked again. Yes, that was better. The tiny image of a whitewashed, gabled farmhouse leapt into view. Mares scanned left and then back right. The high cylindrical shape of a grain silo rose behind the farmhouse. Two separate barns were set off to one side, surrounded by wire enclosures for cattle or other animals. A row of tall trees planted for shade and as a windbreak lined the eastern edge of the Afrikaner farm. A tidy little place, he thought. Much more prosperous looking than the agricultural cooperatives and collectives back home in Cuba.

He lowered his binoculars a fraction, looking for the squat, four-wheeled shapes of his recon platoon's BRDM-2 scout cars. They were about five hundred meters from the farmhouse, spread out in a rough wedge formation and moving fast. Maybe too fast.

After all, that farm might house more than just a South

African artillery OP. Its stout stone walls and barns would make a good defensive strongpoint for troops assigned to hold this sector. Too good for any sensible South African commander to pass up, Mares thought.

The first few days of the offensive had been a cakewalk, a lightning drive against scattered opposition by lightly armed Afrikaner commandos. But that couldn't continue forever. Pretoria must be going mad trying to redeploy its forces from Namibia.

Another shell burst fifty meters ahead of the column. Mares ducked again and made a quick decision. Where the South Africans had heavy artillery they were also likely to have regulars—regulars armed with their own APCs and armored cars. He lifted his radio mike to order the scouts back.

Too late! A sudden flash from near the farmhouse, followed seconds later by a blinding explosion and a billowing column of oily black smoke. The lead BRDM lay canted at an angle, mangled and on fire. Its two companions were frantically wheeling away at high speed.

Mares focused his binoculars hastily. Shit. An Eland armored car armed with a 90mm cannon. He'd been shot at by too many of the damned things in Namibia to make any mistake about that. More than just one, of course. He could see another ugly, snouted turret poking out from behind one of the barns. Small figures scurried into position in windows and doors and in hurriedly dug foxholes.

A second sun-bright flash erupted from the first Eland's main gun. Mud sprayed high beside one of the fleeing scout cars, and both took wild evasive action, twisting and turning sharply as they raced north.

Mares stood high in his commander's hatch, studying the approaches to the South African–held farmhouse. It didn't look good. The farm occupied a commanding position, perched precisely at the crest of a low rise and surrounded by open fields. No orchards. No convenient hillocks offering cover and concealment. No sunken roads. Nothing but the wide open space of a ready-made killing ground.

He swore softly to himself. If the South Africans held that farmhouse and its outbuildings in force, he and his men were in for a bloody and protracted fight. And his brigade commander would not be pleased. Well, the sooner they started, the sooner they'd finish.

Mares dropped down through the hatch into the BTR's crowded interior. He stabbed a finger at the young corporal strapped to a seat in front of the radio. "Get me Brigade HQ!"

The radioman nodded and started changing frequencies on his bulky, Soviet-made set.

Mares whirled to the rest of his staff—a captain, two baby-faced lieutenants, and a tough, competent-looking sergeant. "We're going to have to dig the bastards out. Order the column to reform in line abreast. And remind everyone to keep at least fifty meters between vehicles. I don't want any idiots bunching up like cowardly sheep."

Another near-miss rocked the BTR from side to side, pounding his point home.

They nodded seriously. Dispersing your vehicles under artillery bombardment was only common sense. Every meter of extra open space dramatically complicated an enemy's attempts to adjust his fire and reduced his odds of scoring a direct hit. Unfortunately, too many soldiers under heavy fire abandoned common sense in favor of the age-old pack instinct that screamed out, "When in danger, join together."

"I have Brigade on the line, Major."

He took the offered handset. "Tango Golf One, this is Alpha Two Three."

"Go ahead, Two Three." Mares recognized the dry, academic tones of the Brigade's operations officer. Good. The man wasn't very personable, but he did his job damned well.

The major outlined his situation in a few terse sentences.

"And your recommendation?"

Mares thumbed the transmit button. "I can attack in twenty minutes, but we'll need an airstrike to soften the place up first."

"Impossible." The operations officer didn't bother sounding apologetic. Facts were facts, and courtesy couldn't change them. "The Air Force reports a new storm front moving in. They expect all their attack aircraft to be grounded from now until sunrise tomorrow."

Damn it. Mares wished that Cuba had all-weather bombers like those available to the United States. He hunted for an alternative. "What about artillery?"

The dry, matter-of-fact voice doused that hope as well. "Our batteries won't be up for another three hours. Can you try a hasty attack?"

"Negative, Tango One." Mares shuddered inwardly at the thought. Charging across that killing zone out there without air or artillery cover would only lead to disaster—a sure and certain harvest of wrecked and blazing personnel carriers and dead and maimed men. He took the map offered by his staff sergeant. "We'll look for an alternate route, but I don't think we'll find one. This country's too open. We may need that artillery deployed yet."

"Understood, Two Three. Tango Golf One, out."

Mares got busy with his map. He couldn't see any way for his two remaining BRDMs to pick their way around the farmhouse strongpoint without being spotted. The South Africans had too good a view from their commanding hilltop. And he wasn't sure that he had enough men and vehicles to take that strongpoint—even with artillery support. He might need help from the heavy tank and infantry units lumbering along with the main column.

In fact, he was sure of only one thing. The First Brigade Tactical Group's easy romp through the northern Transvaal was over.

They'd pay in blood for every kilometer gained from here all the way to Pretoria.

NOVEMBER 19—SECOND BRIGADE TACTICAL GROUP, NEAR THE MPAGENI PASS, SOUTH AFRICA

The rattle of heavy rifle and machine-gun fire echoed oddly through the night air, bouncing off high rock walls and mingling with the whispering rush of water tumbling downstream. With a screaming hiss and a soft *pop*, a parachute flare burst into incandescent splendor a thousand meters over the pass and began drifting slowly downwind.

The flare cast strange shadows among the giant ferns and tall yellowwood trees crowding the valley floor, and it lit small, shaggy clumps of aloe and thorn scrub dotting the rugged cliffs above. A troop of wild baboons, already frightened by the gunfire and sickly sweet odor of high explosives, scurried frantically up the cliffs—seeking shelter from this eerie, horribly bright sun rising where there should be only welcome, restful darkness.

Five hundred meters farther down the winding road, men trying desperately to sleep beside camouflaged T-62 tanks, BTR personnel carriers, and towed artillery pieces stumbled out of their bedrolls and stared west toward the slowly falling flare. Did the small-arms fire and illumination round signal an unexpected South African counterattack? Some, less experienced than their comrades, groped for assault rifles or swung themselves into their vehicles. Others, older and wiser in the ways of war, noted the conspicuous lack of frantic activity around the Brigade Group's lantern-lit command tent, swore bitterly, and settled back to snatch a few hours of needed rest.

"Acknowledged, Captain. Keep me posted. Out." Col. Raoul Valladares slipped the headset off and tossed it back to a yawning radioman.

"Well?" Gen. Carlos Herrera glared at his trim, dapper subordinate while he struggled into his jacket and strained to button his tunic collar. Unfortunately, not even the most creative military tailor could design a uniform that made the general look anything less than grossly overweight. Spiky tufts of black hair sticking straight up offered clear proof that Herrera had been sound asleep when the shooting started.

"Nothing more than an outpost skirmish, Comrade General." Valladares ran lean fingers through his own tousled hair. "One of our sentries thought he saw movement and opened fire."

Herrera grunted sourly and left his collar hanging open. He moved closer to the situation map and stood frowning at the portrait it painted.

Valladares understood his commander's irritation. In the first four days of Vega's offensive, the Second Brigade Tactical Group had driven deep into the eastern Transvaal—plowing forward more than one hundred kilometers through the low veld's orange groves and banana plantations. But the past day's progress had been painfully slow and costly as the brigade's tanks and infantry fought their way up steep hills and across rugged river gorges on a front sometimes only one road wide.

The colonel shook his head wearily. They'd planned to punch through the two-thousand-foot-high escarpment separating the low veld from the high veld before the South Africans could mount an effective defense. Crystal-clear hindsight showed how wildly optimistic they'd been. Even a small number of determined defenders can delay an attacker advancing through rough country. And the South Africans were nothing if not determined.

They'd probed and harassed the oncoming Cuban column at every opportunity. An ambush here. A stoutly defended roadblock there. No major engagements. No set-piece battles that would allow the brigade to use its superior firepower. Just a never-ending series of skirmishes that left one or two men dead, several others wounded, one or more vehicles in flames, and slowed the Cuban advance to an anemic crawl.

Not that General Vega was displeased, Valladares knew. Even though its daily gains were now measured in kilometers instead of tens of kilometers, the Second Brigade Tactical Group was still advancing—still drawing South African troops away other fronts. His eye fell on a red arrow designating the third of Vega's attacking columns. Transshipped by rail the long way round through neutral Botswana, the Third Brigade had shot its way onto South African territory three days after its two counterparts.

This third Cuban column was driving hard—advancing east

rapidly against weak opposition. Confronted by two more immediate threats to its vital northern and eastern Transvaal mining complexes, Pretoria had stripped its border with Botswana of almost every trained man able to bear arms.

Exactly as Vega had planned.

NOVEMBER 20—THIRD BRIGADE TACTICAL GROUP, NEAR BODENSTEIN, SOUTH AFRICA

Dozens of Cuban armored cars, APCs, and self-propelled guns rolled steadily eastward along a two-lane paved highway. The sun stood high overhead, beating down mercilessly on grasslands just starting to turn from yellow-brown to a lush, rich green. Wisps of dark cloud on the far horizon hinted at the possibility of more rain later in the day or evening.

Four BRDM-2 scout cars led the column, their turrets spinning continuously from side to side as gunners sought out potential targets. Scouts who grew sloppy and complacent were scouts who were soon dead.

So when the lieutenant commanding the lead BRDM saw movement in a clump of brush just off the road, he didn't hesitate before screaming a shrill warning. The heavy machine gun in the scout car's turret was already firing as it slewed on target. And more than a hundred rounds of 14.5mm machine-gun ammunition slammed into the patch of brush.

The scout car and its companions swept on past in a swirl of dust and torn vegetation.

Ten minutes later, the first BTR-60 troop carriers thundered by. Cuban infantrymen riding with their hatches open turned curious eyes on the site of the attempted ambush. Two old men dressed in ill-fitting South African uniforms lay bloody and unmoving, entwined around a dull-gray metal tube—an ancient World War II–era bazooka.

The road to the small farming town of Bodenstein lay open and undefended. And Cuba's Third Brigade Tactical Group was just one hundred and seventy kilometers from Johannesburg.

NOVEMBER 21—STATE SECURITY COUNCIL CHAMBER, PRETORIA

Fear has its own peculiar smell—the sour stench of sweat triggered by sheer, gut-twisting panic and not by hard manual labor.

It was an odor Marius van der Heijden knew well. As a young policeman and later a senior security official, he'd smelled fear in dozens of small, sterile interrogation rooms. He'd witnessed the terror of men confined in brutal prisons or awaiting death on a gallows.

But now he caught its unmistakable scent in a room full of South Africa's self-proclaimed leaders. The men seated around Karl Vorster were, quite plainly, frightened almost out of their wits.

The arrows and lines drawn on the large map at one end of the room explained their growing panic.

"In sum, Mr. President, we face an impossible military situation." Gen. Adriaan de Wet looked haggard and worn, aged beyond his years by a series of unprecedented disasters. "We simply do not have the manpower or equipment to hold Namibia, crush local rebellions, and fend off this Cuban offensive. It cannot be done." His hand shook as he tried to hold the map pointer steady.

Van der Heijden listened with a sinking heart. The battalions rushed back from Namibia to face the Cuban columns driving on Pietersburg and Nelspruit were fighting hard, slowing the enemy's advance. But they were being destroyed in the process. Reinforcements and replacements sent to them were swallowed up within hours.

Even worse, the SADF had almost nothing left to throw at the third Cuban invasion force—now within one hundred and fifty kilometers of Johannesburg. Many of the Afrikaners who'd rebelled against the government were returning to the fold—willing to bury their own grievances to fight a foreign enemy. But it was all too little and too late. Hastily assembled task forces made up of understrength infantry companies, ill-equipped commandos, and outdated artillery pieces had either been smashed to pieces or swallowed whole. South Africa's back door was wide open.

De Wet finished his grim briefing and stepped away from the situation map. Every head swiveled toward the dour-faced man seated at the head of the table. But as always of late, Karl Vorster sat silent and unapproachable.

An uncomfortable silence dragged. De Wet shifted his pointer nervously from hand to hand.

Finally, Fredrik Pienaar, the minister of information, waved a thin, bony finger at the map. "What about the troops garrisoning Voortrekker Heights and other bases? Can't they be used to defeat this third Cuban force?"

De Wet shook his head. "Most of those battalions are badly understrength themselves. And they're needed to defend vital installations in and around Pretoria against possible guerrilla attack. We can't afford to fight one fire by leaving our enemies free to set others."

Heads around the table nodded in hurried agreement. De Wet's definition of "vital installations" included their own homes and offices.

Pienaar reddened. "Very well, General. Then what about the rest of our army? What about the troops and tanks you've managed to leave dangling uselessly in Namibia?"

De Wet turned red himself, his fear almost submerged by anger. "We're shifting forces as quickly as we can, Minister. But our air, rail, and road transport capabilities are stretched to the limit. We simply can't move soldiers, equipment, or supplies fast enough to matter!"

"And whose fault is—"

"Enough!" Karl Vorster slammed the table with one clenched fist. "Enough of this childish squabbling!"

He turned angrily on his cabinet. "Start acting like men, not whimpering schoolboys. Or worse, like cowardly kaffirs!"

The deadly insult stiffened backs throughout the room.

Vorster shoved his chair back and rose to his full height, towering over every other man in the room. He strode over to the situation map, pushing past a startled de Wet.

He turned. "You look at maps, at scraps of paper, and see the end of the world!" A contemptuous hand thumped the map, almost toppling it off its stand. "I look at the same drawings, the same lines of ink and pencil, but I do not see defeat and disaster! I see our final victory!"

Marius van der Heijden shivered. Had the man he'd followed blindly for so many years gone mad? Others around the table stirred uneasily, grappling with the same fear.

Vorster shook his finger at them like a sorrowful father chiding unruly children. "Come now, my friends. Can't you see God's design in all of this?"

His voice dropped, becoming softer and more persuasive. It was less the voice of a politician and more the voice of a preacher. "Like the ancient Israelites we stand surrounded by our foes—outmatched and seemingly overpowered. But just as God raised up David to smite Goliath, so God has given us the weapons we need to destroy our enemies. Weapons of awesome power and cleansing fire."

He turned and pointed to a small dot on the map—a dot just outside Pretoria. "Weapons that wait there for our orders, my friends."

His finger rested on the hill called Pelindaba—the "place of meeting."

ADMINISTRATION CENTER, PELINDABA RESEARCH COMPLEX

The atomic research site called Pelindaba sat high on a bluff overlooking a tangle of winding valleys and low hills just south of Pretoria. Lush green lawns and immaculately landscaped rock gardens gave its laboratories, living quarters, and gleaming steel-and-glass administration building the look of a quiet college campus. In such surroundings, the squat, square, windowless bulk of Pelindaba's uranium-enrichment facility and the tall smokestacks of an adjacent coal-fired power plant seemed alien—obtrusive reminders of the intrusion of a hostile industrial machine into what appeared to be a placid academic world.

Inside the Administration Center, Col. Frans Peiper stared out an upper-floor window to hide his irritation from the young woman receptionist. A face marked by cold gray eyes, a straight, pointed nose, and a tight-lipped mouth scowled back at him. He clasped his hands behind his back to avoid the embarrassment of unconsciously looking at his watch again.

As usual, Pelindaba's civilian director was late. For a man of great learning, Peiper thought savagely, Dr. Jakobus Schumann had such an imperfect concept of time.

He turned as the rotund, white-haired administrator came bustling in through the door, an apology already tumbling out through a smiling mouth. "Terribly sorry for the delay, Colonel. Afraid I got myself tangled up in a small liquefaction problem over at the labs."

Peiper nodded stiffly, unsure whether Schumann's "small problem" involved uranium enrichment or a drunk technician.

"But here I am at last, eh?" The older man ushered him into his office. "Now then, Colonel, what can I do for the esteemed commander of our garrison?"

Peiper came to attention. His news required a formal delivery. "It is more a question of what you will do for me, Director. I have received new orders from Pretoria." He paused, watching Schumann's face carefully. "Headquarters informs me that the State Security Council has issued a Special Weapons Warning Order."

Schumann paled. "Are you sure of that, Colonel? That would mean . . ."

"Quite sure, Director." Peiper nodded in grim satisfaction. "All scientists, engineers, and other personnel at Pelindaba are now under my direct command. Further, effective immediately, this facility is on full war alert. No one goes in or out without my permission."

He glanced out the window over Schumann's shoulder and caught a glimpse of soldiers in full battle dress scattering throughout the compound. Good. He didn't expect any trouble. All the South African scientists and engineers working here were handpicked Afrikaners of proven loyalty. Still, it never paid to take chances. "Do you have any questions?"

Schumann moistened suddenly dry lips. "Just one, Colonel. Have they told you how many weapons will be assembled or where they might be used?"

"No." Peiper looked down at the nervous old man, secretly rejoicing in a welcome sense of power and control. "And I haven't asked. Such questions are beyond our need to know."

He fingered the AWB button pinned to his uniform jacket. "One matter remains, Director. These Israeli scientists of yours . . ."

"They are not mine, Colonel. They're invited guests of our government." If anything, that was an understatement. The atomic weapons programs of Israel and South Africa had been closely linked for decades. It was an alliance of convenience—not conviction. Israel had much of the essential scientific and engineering expertise, while South Africa had the vast expanses of unpopulated wasteland needed for weapons tests.

Peiper waved away the distinction as unimportant. "I want their names, pictures, and dossiers delivered to Captain Witt as soon as possible."

Schumann's eyes widened. "My God, you're not planning to hold them as prisoners here, are you?"

"Of course." Peiper grimaced. "We can't allow these Jews out to broadcast our plans to the world. They'll be kept under close guard until Pretoria decides their fate.

"In the meantime, we have work to do." He leaned closer. "A special Air Force team will be here within the hour, and I expect your best technicians to be ready to offer them any necessary assistance. I trust that is perfectly clear?"

The older man nodded in a daze.

Peiper smiled scornfully at Schumann's pudgy, quivering face. "Cheer up, Director. You and your colleagues have worked diligently for many years to make this moment possible. You should give thanks and be glad that you've lived to see such a day."

He spun on his heel and left, amused at the old man's

sudden display of nerves. Academics! They lived so far outside the real world.

To Peiper, the equation was perfectly simple. Communists and rebels of all races threatened South Africa's existence as a white-ruled nation. But South Africa possessed a stockpile of nuclear weapons.

And weapons were meant to be used.

CHAPTER 26

Safety Play

NOVEMBER 22—THE WHITE HOUSE, WASHINGTON, D.C.

The White House Rose Garden looked dead in the dull gray light. Bare rose bushes and patches of brown, withered grass stretched beyond the covered walkway outside the Oval Office—a gloomy vista made more depressing by the dark, overcast day. Unsmiling pairs of White House policemen or Secret Service agents trudged through the garden at irregular intervals, bundled up against the cold and damp of a late-fall morning.

"I quite agree, Mr. Prime Minister. Yes, it's extremely unfortunate."

Vice President James Malcolm Forrester held his hand cupped over the extension's mouthpiece and looked across the Oval Office. The President, a tall, lanky man, sat rigid behind his desk, fingers drumming angrily as he spoke. The President's voice was a far cry from his usual mix of the clipped, nasal New England accent of his boyhood and the lazy drawl adopted later in life. Every word seemed to hang in midair, chosen coldly and precisely to convey an impression of tightly controlled wrath.

Forrester listened intently to the voice emerging from the phone—crystal clear despite being scrambled at one end, bounced halfway round the world via satellite, and then unscrambled at the other. Israel's prime minister sounded embarrassed, unusually meek, and only too well aware that his news wouldn't win any new friends for his country inside America's highest policy-making circles.

"I see. Yes, yes, we'll have people standing by to meet this scientist of yours." The President stabbed an impatient finger at an aide listening in on the second extension. The man nodded hastily and punched to another phone line to begin making arrangements.

"No, I think that's all we need discuss for the moment, Mr. Prime Minister." The President swiveled round in his chair, stared out the window at the bleak, barren view, and then spun round again. "Yes, I'll pass this information on to London as soon as possible. Good-bye, Mr. Prime Minister." He put the phone down with slightly more force than was necessary to cut the connection.

Forrester hung up at the same time and moved to a chair across the President's desk.

The President rubbed tired eyes. "Well, what'd you think of our Israeli friend's little bombshell?"

"That we've got even more trouble than we thought we did," Forrester said evenly. "CIA estimates have always said it was likely that South Africa had nuclear weapons stored at Pelindaba, so we'd been doing some contingency planning to eliminate them. But now we know for sure that the South Africans have a real nuclear capability. And we know they've got ten twenty-kiloton devices—five or six more than we hoped."

The President nodded. "Hell, even one nuke going off would be too damned many."

He stared grimly off into space for a moment, obviously remembering the pictures he'd seen of the devastation at Hiroshima and Nagasaki. So Karl Vorster and the other madmen in Pretoria controlled ten weapons capable of causing that kind of destruction. That was bad enough. The fact that a joint Allied task force was already at sea, steaming toward Cape Town, made the situation even worse.

Forrester coughed lightly, catching his attention. "In a way, though, I'm more worried by Israel's sudden inability to contact its people at Pelindaba."

"Yeah." The President's face looked as bleak as the lifeless garden outside his office. "That kind of a communications blackout could mean . . ."

Forrester finished it for him. "That Pretoria's actually planning to use one of those damned bombs."

The President picked up his phone for the second time that morning. "Marge, get me General Hickman, pronto." He looked at his vice president. "I hope like hell we're wrong about this, Jimmy, but we'd better be ready for the worst."

Forrester nodded in silent agreement. Any situation involving South Africa seemed to slide inexorably from bad to worse. The U.S. Rangers preparing for a possible assault on Pelindaba were about to get a high-level hurry-up call.

HEADQUARTERS, 1ST BATTALION, 75TH RANGER REGIMENT, HUNTER ARMY AIRFIELD, GEORGIA

The clatter of helicopter gunships and troop carriers practicing landings and takeoffs filtered into the crowded, smoke-filled briefing room. More than forty Ranger officers lounged on metal folding chairs, their eyes riveted on the black-and-white satellite photos and maps pinned to a chalkboard behind the short, sturdy figure of their temporary commanding officer. Despite their carefully casual poses, no one could miss the tension crackling through the room.

Lt. Col. Robert O'Connell ran his left hand through thick black hair cropped too short to curl, realized what he was doing, and forced it back to his side. This was going to be tricky, he thought.

He'd been brought in to command the 1st Battalion because its old CO, Lieutenant Colonel Shaw, was still in the hospital, nursing a badly broken leg. Logically, that shouldn't present a problem for any of the assembled officers. He'd had the full dose of Ranger training, and he'd commanded a battalion in the 10th Mountain Division before this. But taking charge of a unit on short notice was always tough—even under peacetime conditions. Those difficulties were compounded by the fact that he'd been asked to lead them on the most dangerous and daring Ranger raid ever conceived. Especially when that operation seemed likely to be a one-way ride for most, if not all, of the men in the room.

Not that he doubted his own ability to lead the battalion into combat. Far from it. For the O'Connell clan, self-doubt stood right next to sloth on a list of the seven deadly sins. And as the fifth of six children, he'd learned early on that you didn't get what you wanted by standing around waiting for it to be handed down on a silver platter. You worked hard for it, and you even fought for it when necessary.

The resulting combination of fierce determination, stubborn pride, and considerable talent had earned him an appointment to West Point and pulled him through a miserable plebe year. From there, he'd seen only one logical career path. The Rangers were regarded as the Army's elite fighting force, and Robert O'Connell had never wanted to be anything less than the best. Now he was being given the chance to prove his real worth.

A slight smile flitted across his face. It would have been nice if the opportunity carried higher odds of survival. On paper, this mission looked impossible. Fly two Ranger battalions and their support units seven thousand miles over the Atlantic Ocean and enemy-held territory without being spotted. Conduct an airborne assault against more than a battalion of crack South African troops. And then hold out long enough to fly every captured nuclear weapon out of the country. Sure.

He buried his doubts deep inside and strode forward to the edge of the foot-high dais. "It's official, gentlemen, we have a 'go' order for this op."

Faces around the room tightened.

"High-level intelligence sources have now confirmed the existence of these South African nukes. And their location."

O'Connell nodded toward the mosaic of satellite photos showing a network of military airfields, supply bases, troop barracks, and vehicle parks near Pretoria—a mosaic centered on a single high bluff called Pelindaba. Red circles drawn in grease pencil ringed identified bunkers and gun positions surrounding both the South African uranium enrichment plant and the suspected bomb storage site.

"The code name for this mission will be Brave Fortune."

"Looks more likely to wind up as Big Damned Fuckup." A twangy Texas drawl lifted from out of the back row, prompting several nervous chuckles.

O'Connell grinned. Trust Lieutenant Colonel Carrerra to say what was on everybody's mind. The 2nd Ranger Battalion's commander was a master of ambush, assault, and patrol tactics—skills he'd learned during a career that stretched all the way back to service as an enlisted man in Vietnam and as an officer in both Grenada and Panama. But Mike Carrerra had never been noted for his tact.

Carrerra's half-joking outburst opened a path for others.

"Mike's right, Colonel. I don't mind taking risks to accomplish a mission, but this thing's nothing but risks." Charlie Company's CO, Capt. Tom Keller, shook his head. "Why can't the flyboys plaster the frigging place with a few precision-guided munitions? Or why not hit it with a Tomahawk strike?"

"Good question, Tom." O'Connell remembered raising the same objections three days ago when he'd first heard about this crazy stunt. It felt as if a lifetime had passed since then. "Unfortunately, our lords and masters have a very good reason for wanting our very special services. Aside from thinking we look swell in our black berets, that is."

That drew a quick laugh.

He stepped closer to the collection of satellite photos and pointed to a rectangular cluster of squat, camouflaged bunkers labeled WPN STOR (N). "Right now, the South Africans have ten nukes stashed away in these bunkers—protected by several meters' worth of dirt, concrete, and reinforced steel. Navy or Air Force planes could hit the site hard. No doubt about that at all. Trouble is, we'd never know for sure whether or not all ten bombs were actually destroyed—or simply buried.''

O'Connell let the officers mull that one over for a moment, waiting until their murmurs died away. ''You've got it. As long as there's the slightest chance that Pretoria still owns a working nuke, we can't risk bringing our ships and Marines within range of their coast. If even one bomb got through, we'd be looking at ten or twenty ships sunk and thousands of our guys dead.''

He rapped the taped sheet of satellite photos. ''Nope, gentlemen. There's only one hundred-percent-guaranteed way to be sure these bastards don't have any nukes left.'' He bared his teeth. ''And that's to lay our own hot little hands on 'em and take 'em away. Right?''

Several heads nodded, Carrerra's and Keller's among them. All of the assembled Rangers looked more determined—not much more confident—but definitely more determined.

One of the younger lieutenants raised a hesitant hand. ''What about air support, sir?''

''F-14 Tomcats will be covering us during our extraction. Plus the Navy plans to launch diversionary air attacks on several major South African bases and command posts just as we're going in.'' O'Connell jerked a thumb toward a succession of black-ringed facilities that included the Voortrekker Heights Military Camp.

''But that's not all the help we're going to get, gentlemen. Apparently, the Israelis have offered us the services of one of their top nuclear scientists.'' He checked a note card. ''The prof's name is Esher Levi, and he's supposed to be an expert on the design, use, and safe handling of the kind of bombs we're going hunting for.''

O'Connell paused, looking for the dour face of his Support Platoon commander. ''He'll be training your special teams, Harry.''

The lieutenant nodded.

''What's more, this Levi character worked at Pelindaba for more than two years. So let's pump him dry once he gets here. Find out where the weak spots are, okay?''

Heads nodded vigorously throughout the room. Access to someone with detailed knowledge of Pelindaba's buildings, grounds, and security procedures would make it much easier to plan the assault. Satellite photos and out-of-date maps were a lousy substitute for firsthand experience.

O'Connell scanned the rows of tough, young faces in front of him. Nobody looked wildly optimistic, but mission success didn't require optimism—just competence and professionalism. He'd accomplished as much as he could reasonably hope for in a single briefing/pep talk.

Now it was time to get back to the grind of actually putting this crazy operation together. Brave Fortune existed as a skeletal outline, but the 1st and 2nd Battalions' officers and men still had a tremendous amount of work left to do. Board and computer simulations to test variations of the basic attack plan. Dry runs through full-scale mock-ups already being built by the base engineers and service troops. And they'd need to hold a seemingly endless series of conferences with Air Force and Navy liaisons to make sure that units of all three services understood their assigned roles.

He moved forward again to the edge of the dais. "Very well, gentlemen. That's it for now."

He held up a hand to still a sudden buzz of comment. "Brave Fortune is slated for December sixth. So we have less than two weeks to get this plan and our Rangers whipped into shape. That's not much time. Don't waste it."

Carrerra, already standing to go, nodded gravely.

HEADQUARTERS, 20TH CAPE RIFLES, VOORTREKKER HEIGHTS MILITARY CAMP, NEAR PRETORIA

Commandant Henrik Kruger was a troubled man. At first, he'd thought it would be easy to shelter Emily, the American reporter, and their black driver for a short while before slipping them off the base and away to safety. Cuba's surprise invasion had wrecked that first plan.

With Voortrekker Heights on continuous full alert, his three fugitives were trapped. Emily was no real problem. She'd simply become his new civilian secretary, a Miss ter Horst. And he'd put the black, Sibena, to work as a camp servant. Nobody in the South African military thought twice about seeing a black engaged in menial labor. But Sherfield, the American, was a problem. He'd been forced to spend the last nine days hiding inside Kruger's own quarters—moving into the bedroom whenever junior officers or others visited their commanding officer.

Kruger smiled thinly. He wasn't sure who would go mad first—the American or him. Their natural friction over Emily was bad enough, but wildly varying attitudes, opinions, and habits only made matters worse. Neither of them was really suited to life as anything but a self-sufficient bachelor, he decided—all too aware that Emily had other plans for this Ian Sherfield. He veered away from such thoughts. Jealousy was a corrosive emotion.

Better to focus on more concrete matters, on military matters.

Cuba's invasion hadn't just made it impossible for Emily and the others to escape, it had also ended his own tentative plans to rebel—at least for the time being. Despite all of the Vorster government's crimes, no Afrikaner could contemplate abandoning his fellows to the savagery of a communist attack.

Given that, he couldn't understand why he and his men hadn't already been sent into combat against the Cubans. True, the 20th's rifle and heavy weapons companies were still understrength and woefully underequipped, but they were proven fighting units. And South Africa needed every available man, gun, and armored vehicle up on the firing line.

Vorster's propaganda broadcasts claimed that the Cubans were being driven back in disarray. Kruger knew the truth. His friend on de Wet's staff, Brig. Deneys Coetzee, kept him fully informed. The Cuban columns, though slowed in the north and east, were still pushing hard for Pretoria and the mines. So why not send the 20th Cape Rifles and the other battalions held around the capital into battle before it was too late? They might not be able to stop Castro's advancing armies, but they could certainly buy time for more troops to arrive from Namibia.

What was Karl Vorster planning? Had the man abandoned all hope and military common sense?

He stared eastward, away from the setting sun and into the gathering darkness. Something very strange was going on at Swartkop Air Base—just across the broad, multilane strip of the Ben Schoeman Highway connecting Pretoria with Johannesburg.

Lights were on all around the outer airfield perimeter, painfully bright against the twilight sky. Wheeled Ratel APCs and cannon-armed Rookiats were stationed at regular intervals along the length of the highway—their guns pointed out to the east and west. Kruger recognized the unit insignia painted on each vehicle—the stalking leopard of Frans Peiper's 61st Transvaal Rifles.

His mouth tightened. He didn't like Peiper at all. The 61st's colonel was a very nasty customer indeed—an AWB fanatic to the core, and a murderous bastard if even half the stories of his atrocities in Namibia were true.

Kruger stood up straighter as four canvas-sided trucks appeared on the highway, moving slowly south. What? All that firepower as security for four vehicles? Then he remembered where Peiper's battalion was stationed, and he grew colder by the second.

The trucks rolled past his vantage point and turned left through the main gate into Swartkop Air Base.

Two of South Africa's ten nuclear weapons were already outside Pelindaba's bombproof storage bunkers.

CHAPTER 27

The Fourth Horseman

NOVEMBER 23—THIRD BRIGADE TACTICAL GROUP, ALONG ROUTE 47, BETWEEN BODENSTEIN AND MAKOKSKRAAL

The cool desert night would fade into full day soon, much missed by the Third Brigade Tactical Group's Cuban and Libyan soldiers. The days were pure hell—long hot stretches of driving through a region short on potable water and long on thick, choking dust that clung to everything. South Africa's highveld was moving into summer, with daytime temperatures soaring to over ninety degrees Fahrenheit—climbing quickly from midnight lows in the sixties.

The Libyans were more used to it than the Cubans, but enlisted men from the two nations had few chances to mix or share their knowledge. Aside from the basic problems of language and culture, the Cuban and Libyan political officers were feuding over everything from supply allocation to Marxist-Leninist doctrine. As a result, separate units went their separate ways, connected only by liaison officers at the brigade headquarters—a kind of socialist apartheid.

It also reduced efficiency. But then the brigade didn't really have to be very efficient. It just had to keep moving. The Afrikaners still hadn't managed to scrape up much more than a thin corporal's guard to oppose its steady advance on Johannesburg.

The Third Tactical Group contained five battalions, plus a number of "attachments"—smaller specialist units. Three of the five were motorized rifle units, one of them Libyan. One battalion each of T-62 tanks and self-propelled 122mm howitzers completed the force.

When the brigade halted for the night, each battalion formed its own "strongpoint"—a defensive position with all-round fields of fire. This deep in enemy territory, an attack could come from any direction.

At the moment, the Third's battalion strongpoints were strung out along the highway like a succession of huge oval beads several hundred meters across. Gaps of two or three hundred meters between them made it impossible for any would-be attacker to strike one strongpoint without taking fire from its neighbors.

This pattern of separation and mutual support was repeated inside each battalion strongpoint. Individual rifle and tank companies had each "laagered" their vehicles in separate formation. Ironically enough, the very word *laager* came from Afrikaans. It had slipped into worldwide military usage after South African troops reinvented the old Boer tactic during World War II.

In laager, tanks and APCs were parked nose-out in a rough oval, their turrets turned outward against the hostile landscape while the men slept inside the ring. Once the vehicles were parked, it only took a little digging to create a first-class defensive position.

So went the theory, anyway. Right now, the Third Brigade Tactical Group lay camped on an arid plateau, rising in elevation to the north. Covered with low scrub and tufts of grass, the ground was dust dry. The rocky soil complicated digging in, but at least their foxholes weren't muddy.

Supply and maintenance units also sheltered inside these

company laagers, ensuring that the entire brigade was protected by an armed and armored fence.

The brigade's surface-to-air missile batteries and antiaircraft guns were scattered throughout the battalion encampments. And while the rest of the Third Brigade Tactical Group caught a few hours of desperately needed sleep, several SAM radar operators rubbed red eyes and stared at their scopes. Nighttime air raids had become a part of life, and they were sure they'd be hit before dawn.

JERICHO FLIGHT, SOUTHWEST OF PRETORIA

Four Mirage aircraft flew west at one thousand meters over the darkened South African countryside, heading straight for Cuba's Third Brigade Tactical Group. Capt. Jon Heersfeld piloted the lead plane. He was nervous, almost to the point of distraction.

Well, he thought, who wouldn't be on a mission such as this?

Heersfeld was a professional. He'd flown combat missions over Angola during the long, undeclared war there. In recent months, he'd seen more combat in the skies over Namibia. And in just the past week, he'd flown a dozen-plus sorties against the Cuban forces invading the Transvaal. In short, he knew his business as well as any attack pilot in the Air Force.

Which was probably why he had been picked for this mission. But did the Air Force higher-ups have to make such a production out of it? First he'd been pulled off combat operations without any explanation and ordered to sleep. Then the wing commander himself issued the attack order, leaving his poor squadron commander standing there like a fifth wheel.

And the briefing! My God, every major, commandant, and colonel on the base, along with the de Wet himself, had wormed his way into the auditorium. Didn't the brass have any work to do?

Heersfeld scowled. It was a good thing they were flying immediately, because any chance of secrecy was shot.

Even his preflight had been bizarre. The tired old Mirage, which he'd sometimes been forced to fly with only basic flight instruments working, had been groomed and tweaked and even cleaned until it gleamed. Technicians had spent most of the day installing special weapons control equipment in its cockpit.

His squadron commander, the maintenance officer, and one of the government's brownshirted fanatics had all accompanied him as he circled the aircraft, looking for the smallest fault. There hadn't been any, thank God.

He'd inspected the weapon itself, of course, not that looking at it told him much. It hung from the Mirage's centerline hardpoint, under the fuselage. One drop tank hung under each wing, and the plane carried two Kukri heat-seekers—one on each wingtip. The missiles were there almost out of habit. Considering the heavy fighter escort assigned to this mission, he shouldn't need them. Still, they didn't weigh much, and his wing-tip rails couldn't carry anything else. Besides, Heersfeld hated to fly naked. He'd already downed one Cuban MiG-23 during an attack mission.

The weapon was shaped like a standard low-drag bomb, a little bigger than most, but no heavier. Its surface was simply polished aluminum or steel, with a few small black patches near the nose and tail. It was totally unremarkable, and Heersfeld had been forced to depend on the technicians to tell him it was ready to go.

His wingman's Mirage had received a similar going-over and had also been pronounced mission-ready. Mulder's plane carried a second bomb as a backup in case he was shot down or forced to abort.

Heersfeld had almost expected a band to serenade him as he climbed in the cockpit, but instead the majors, commandants, colonels, and the general had just watched as he strapped himself in, connected the leads, and started the Mirage's Atar engine.

Takeoff had been clean, and he'd hoped that once away from the confusion at the airfield, he could treat this as just another mission.

He'd been wrong.

The nature of his payload preyed on his mind. Nobody had asked his opinion on whether or not this kind of weapon should be used, or where. The fact that it was being dropped inside South African territory had raised more than a few eyebrows at the briefing. Still, the nearest inhabited town was more than ten kilometers away from his aim point—and upwind.

Heersfeld shook his head and checked his instruments. Militarily, South Africa really didn't have much choice. His squadron alone had lost a third of its planes and pilots, without doing much more than slowing the enemy advance. Rumor said the ground-pounders were being hammered even worse.

So what was left to his people? How would they explain building such weapons and then losing a war because they were too frightened to use them? No, South Africa must use all its weapons, all its strength, in this conflict. Too much was at stake for anything less.

Heersfeld scanned the air behind and beside him again. There, outlined against the star-studded night sky, he could just make out the shape of a Mirage F1.CZ fighter, this one armed purely with missiles. Another fighter escorted Mulder's aircraft, a few hundred meters in trail.

The fighters were ready to protect his valuable plane from any air attack, although none was expected. So far, the Cuban Air Force hadn't shown much taste for night intercepts. Heavy air attacks and fighter sweeps were being launched farther north—all designed to draw off any enemy aircraft capable of attacking them.

Other South African planes had already played a vital role in this attack.

Two precious reconnaissance aircraft from South Africa's diminishing fleet had overflown their target earlier in the evening, so prestrike data was good, for a change. And good data allowed the mission planners to calculate both the weapon's aim point and its release point with special care.

Heersfeld checked his kneeboard once more. There were few landmarks in this part of the country, and fewer still that were visible at night. Watching the map, he could only steer as well as his aircraft's antiquated avionics allowed. No inertial trackers, no moving map displays in this beauty. The arms embargo by the West hadn't been entirely without effect.

Ten minutes to target. Heersfeld was flying down Route 47, using the road as his compass. He glanced down and saw a pattern of parallel lights leading west. Although the small town of Ventersdorp was normally blacked out against Cuban air attack, security forces there had turned on the streetlights along the main highway to help him verify his position.

He clicked a switch on his microphone. "Springbok, this is Jericho Lead. Over initial point."

Heersfeld tapped a button on his control stick, jettisoning the two now-empty drop tanks. Two heavy clunks, one right after the other, confirmed that the fuel tanks were gone—spinning down toward the ground below. Then, after aligning his Mirage carefully on the correct compass heading, he advanced his throttle to maximum. The aircraft kicked forward, accelerating smoothly through calm air.

Two clicks in his earphones told him that Mulder and his escort were turning away, starting a series of long, lazy circles. They wouldn't come any closer to the target unless something happened to him. And right now the air raid sirens in Ventersdorp and every other town for fifty kilometers around were supposed to be going off—warning civilians to get down and stay down.

He started a shallow climb, calculating the appropriate variables in his head. Both speed and altitude at release were critical. A few practice runs over the veld yesterday had helped build his confidence for this mission, but they'd also convinced him of the importance of precision.

THIRD BRIGADE TACTICAL GROUP

Sgt. Jorge Jimenez stared at the radar scope. He took his job seriously, but he'd been battling sleep all through the second half of this night. He looked forward to dawn, when the column would be moving again. His radar could only be deployed while the vehicle was stationary, so it was then that he slept.

Jimenez kept watch in one of the tactical group's four "Romb" air defense vehicles. A lightly armored wheeled box, it carried four surface-to-air missiles code-named SA-8 Gecko by NATO, and a search radar NATO called Land Roll. Each vehicle was a self-contained firing unit, and all four vehicles in the battery were deployed in a flattened diamond that provided complete coverage over the Cuban position.

A blip appeared on the edge of the scope, and despite what it meant, the sergeant was secretly relieved. Finally, something to break up the boredom of a night watch.

He spoke into his intercom. "Comrade Lieutenant, I have an inbound target at thirty kilometers. No response on IFF. The target appears to be four fighter-sized aircraft."

The SAM battery's assistant commander shook off sleep and leaned over his shoulder. "What's their speed and altitude?"

"Medium altitude, sir." There was no direct readout of speed on the scope, but the blip's movement was clear. "It's moving fast!"

"Right. No time to be subtle. Turn on your tracking radar and warm up the missiles."

While Jimenez acknowledged the order, the lieutenant alerted his battery commander and the other SAM vehicles. "Watch your sectors. This may be a feint to distract us from the real attack."

Outside, he heard warnings being shouted throughout the camp. "Air alert!"

He remembered the flyby earlier. Although they'd done their best, both South African reconnaissance planes had escaped unharmed. This attack was almost certainly the result. Jimenez nodded to himself, watching his radar screen with hawklike intensity. The going had been far too easy.

He leaned forward as the pattern on his radar scope changed. "Separation, Comrade Lieutenant! Two aircraft turning away." But two blips were still closing. "Speed is up over one thousand KPH. Altitude now four thousand meters."

"Probably going for another reconnaissance pass at maximum speed. This may not be an attack after all,'' the lieutenant speculated.

Jimenez shrugged. Reconnaissance run or an actual attack, it didn't really make much difference. They'd still shoot the bastards out of the sky. Numbers flashed on a display next to his scope. ''The computer says firing range is eight and a half kilometers.''

''Shoot when they're in range.''

JERICHO LEAD

Heersfeld was juggling several balls at once. Airspeed and altitude had to be maintained within precise, narrow limits, course had to be held exactly, and meanwhile here he was hanging out at medium altitude where every Cuban all the way back to Havana could see him.

He could almost feel the SAM radar beams sweeping over his Mirage. Normally, attack runs on a target were made at altitudes of just one or two hundred meters. Pilots used terrain masking and violent maneuvers to evade or confuse enemy antiaircraft defenses. This straight-and-level stuff gave him the willies.

Well, his wingman escort was supposed to watch for incoming threats. Heersfeld hoped the fighter jock had his eyes open wide. He pulled his eyes back inside the cockpit and activated the special weapons console. The indicators were all green. Great. He kept one eye on the flight instruments and punched in a five-digit security code on the keypad.

He was rewarded with a new set of lights, whose significance was both exciting and frightening. The weapon was armed.

Passing twenty kilometers. He was high and a little fast, so he throttled back slightly. With only a thousand meters to go, he hit the transmit switch on his radio. ''Springbok, this is Jericho Lead. At alpha point.''

Glancing right, he saw his escort flash his formation lights and break hard right. As the fighter turned, Heersfeld saw the glow of its afterburner. The other pilot was trying to get as far away as he possibly could. A wise man, he thought.

The Mirage shuddered slightly as it punched through a whirl of disturbed air. He checked his instruments again.

His speed was good and he was still on course. In a useless gesture, Heersfeld tightened his straps and settled himself in the seat. Reaching over to the weapons panel, he selected CENTERLINE and watched the gauges. Now!

In a carefully practiced motion, he pulled back on the stick, pulling his plane up into a loop. The Mirage's nose snapped up toward the zenith. Needles spun round on the aircraft's altimeter as it thundered high into the dark night sky.

At seventy-seven hundred meters, eleven hundred kilometers per hour indicated airspeed, on a course of two seven five degrees magnetic and at a forty-five-degree angle, Heersfeld stabbed the release button on his control stick. He felt a solid thump under the aircraft as the bomb separated—cleanly, he hoped.

The mission was out of his hands now, and it was high time he looked after Jon Heersfeld's immediate future. He pushed the throttle all the way forward and yanked back on the stick, even harder than before. The Mirage roared upward and over, finishing the loop—inscribing a vertical semicircle through the air.

At ten thousand meters, the plane's nose passed the horizon and kept going. He was upside down now, hanging from his straps staring "up" at the earth below.

Heersfeld quickly rolled from inverted to wings-level in a steep dive and watched his airspeed indicator climb higher. He was already moving at over Mach one, and he intended to wring every possible ounce of speed out of his old mount.

Behind him, the bomb traveled through its own arc.

THIRD BRIGADE TACTICAL GROUP

Sergeant Jimenez counted down as the lone South African aircraft approached. "Fourteen kilometers. Twelve kilometers. Ten kilometers. Ten kilometers!'' He sat up straighter, staring at the screen. ''It's turning away! Range is now twelve kilometers. Comrade Lieutenant, the other aircraft is turning away, too!''

His eyes followed the blips as they moved blinking toward the top of his radar scope. His outstretched finger slid away from the fire button next to his console. It looked as though the South Africans weren't going to test the accuracy of his missiles—not tonight at any rate.

Jimenez had never seen a ''lob-toss'' delivery on his scope before. He'd never get another chance.

Too small to be picked up by radar, the South African bomb arched up to twelve thousand meters before descending in a gentle curve across the ten kilometers between its release point and target.

After fierce debate, Pretoria's mission planners had picked the Cuban T-62 tank battalion as their primary target. Ordinarily, two battalion strongpoints could have been included in the bomb's inner kill zone, but the tanks represented most of the Third Brigade Tactical Group's combat power. The planners were willing to accept ''minimal'' damage to the rear of the column in order to guarantee destruction of the Cuban armor.

As the weapon fell earthward, a pressure fuse sensed its passage through the one-thousand-meter mark and closed a switch. Thousandths of a second later, it ceased to be.

Counting both vertical and horizontal distance, the bomb had traveled almost sixteen kilometers in its arc, totally unguided. While Heersfeld's delivery had been within norms, high-altitude winds and pressures had changed the tiniest bit since the last reading. As a result, South Africa's twenty-kiloton atomic bomb fell slightly off target—three hundred meters long and to the right.

Fused for airburst, it detonated over and just outside the northwest edge of the tank battalion's laager. A boiling, white-hot fireball, more than two hundred meters in diameter, speared through the night—turning darkness into flickering, man-made day for several deadly seconds.

Anyone who could see it clearly died instantly. Heat and radiation raced outward from the detonation point at the speed of light, and troops who weren't under some sort of cover suffered second-degree burns, their skin blistered and reddened wherever they'd faced the fireball.

Inside five hundred meters from the fireball, though, men suffered third-degree burns as their clothing and hair smoked and then caught fire in the intense, blood-boiling heat. Half a second later, a roaring pressure wave arrived, ending their agony. The shock wave crushed lungs, picked men up bodily, and tossed them through the air. Simply being shielded from the radiant heat and radiation couldn't save the Cuban tank crews. Most struck a hard object at high speed and died instantly.

The tanks themselves were "hard" targets, able to resist massive overpressures before their armored bodies were broken, but the intense heat ignited external fuel drums, paint, and in many cases, even the ammunition stored inside. Multiple blasts shattered armored vehicles that were already on fire. Any that were broadside to the blast were scooped up by the wall of dust, gases, and debris and literally rolled and tumbled along the ground.

Sergeant Jimenez's SAM carrier sat near the head of the brigade column, only five hundred meters from ground zero. His vehicle was much easier to kill than a tank.

First, the electromagnetic pulse spreading outward with the bomb's heat and radiation knocked the launcher's electronics out—showering Jimenez, the lieutenant, and the rest of his crew with sparks. At the same time, its SA-8 missiles started cooking off in their launch tubes—set off by the intense heat. But that took several tenths of a second, and by the time the missiles began exploding the pressure wave arrived.

The shock wave tore the fragile radars and missile launcher right off the vehicle's chassis and then crushed the flimsy steel body with the men still inside. Jimenez and the others were already dead.

The shock wave kept going—expanding outward in an ever-widening, ever-deadly circle.

The brigade tactical group's T-62 tanks were low, squat,

heavily armored targets, but its BTR-60 personnel carriers were actually designed to float and had much more surface area. The nearest infantry battalion, within a thousand meters of the fireball, had its troop carriers pulverized and flung like shattered toys through the air. Anyone who'd gained momentary shelter from the blast inside the vehicles died quickly.

The next battalion was only five hundred meters farther back, but that was far enough to halve the force of the shock wave. A few heavy engineering vehicles survived intact, but its boxy personnel carriers and unprotected infantrymen still suffered crippling losses.

Next came the Cuban artillery, three batteries of 122mm self-propelled guns. At this distance, the blast flipped over howitzers, command vehicles, and ammo carriers that were facing the wrong way. Sights and other delicate instruments were stripped off or smashed. It also scattered the ammunition of the one battery deployed and ready to fire. Shells stacked near the guns began exploding.

Only the men of the trailing battalion had any real chance to survive. Troops who were asleep in their APCs or who'd dug a little deeper than the rest were screened from the first deadly flash of heat and radiation. They woke up to see an angry ball of fire rising skyward more than three kilometers away. Anyone who didn't duck immediately suffered painful burns.

And then the shock wave hit them—buffeting and blasting BTR-60s with pressures still strong enough to knock over an ordinary house. Debris rained down on the helpless Libyan soldiers—man-killing pieces of rocks, boulders, trees, and torn, twisted, and smoldering metal.

The two forward battalions in the Third Brigade Tactical Group were wiped out in one swift, merciless moment. The middle two battalions lasted only five seconds longer. Ten seconds after the South African fission bomb went off, the brigade's fifth and final motor rifle battalion lay shattered in its debris-choked laager.

Several thousand men lay dead or dying among the

hundreds of wrecked vehicles littering Route 47. Gen. Antonio Vega's Third Tactical Group had been annihilated.

DECTECTION AND TRACKING CENTER, NORTH AMERICAN AIR DEFENSE COMMAND

Maj. Bill O'Malley, USAF, sat bolt upright in his chair as one of the red phones buzzed. Throwing down the duty schedule, he grabbed the receiver. "Watch officer."

"Sir, this is Sergeant Ohira. We have a Nucflash. Detonation appears to be over South Africa."

O'Malley leaned over the row of consoles in front of him. Looking down from the watch officer's elevated position, he saw Sergeant Ohira waving from his station on the operations floor below.

"I'll be right down." He hung up and raced downstairs.

Ohira's panel normally showed a map of the world with the positions of America's DSP Early Warning satellites displayed. But it was computer generated so he could modify and expand the image as needed. Right now it showed the southern third of the African continent. A glowing circular symbol flashed repeatedly near the center of the screen.

"Let's see the numbers," O'Malley ordered.

Ohira replaced the map with a screen showing the data they'd received from one of their satellites. While hovering in geosynchronous orbit over the Indian Ocean, it had sensed the infrared signature of a nuclear detonation and instantly relayed the data to NORAD's computers. Sophisticated processors evaluated the available information and assessed the blast as being that of a relatively small weapon—one in the twenty-kiloton range. Other numbers showed that it had exploded at latitude 26° 15′ south and longitude 27° 45′ east.

From what O'Malley could see, the Nucflash looked reliable. Ohira called up more data, this time from seismic stations around the world. The seismic data matched that provided by their satellite.

"Give me a map overlay." Roads and cities appeared with

the location of the detonation marked. Three concentric circles surrounded the point, showing projected zones of total, heavy, and light damage. An arrow showed wind direction.

"Goddamn it, they've really done it. They've really frigging done it."

"Why would the Russians bomb South Africa?" Ohira asked.

O'Malley shook his head. "The South Africans did it, Sergeant. They've used a goddamned nuke on their own goddamned territory." Aware that he sounded rattled, he tried to bite down on the stream of profanity rolling out over his tongue.

Ohira looked puzzled. "Doesn't make any sense to me, Major." The sergeant's interests included mystery novels and computer games. He wasn't really up on current events.

O'Malley sighed. There were more checks he could run, but first there were a few phone calls he had to make. The only reason that he'd delayed this long was that the blast posed no immediate threat to the United States, even from the fallout, and he'd been sure his superiors would want to know more than just the time of detonation and the size of the blast.

Returning to his watch station, the major picked up another handset, this one labeled JCS. As soon as he picked it up, he heard ringing at the other end. "Colonel Howard, watch officer."

"Sir, this is Major O'Malley at Cheyenne Mountain. We have a nuclear detonation . . ."

CNN SPECIAL REPORT

CNN's normal cycle of news, sports, and entertainment gossip was interrupted in midsentence. The anchorman, who'd been introducing a piece on a sports figure's tax problems, suddenly stopped, distracted by something off screen.

A paper was passed to him, adroitly, so that the camera never caught a glimpse of the passer. The anchorman scanned it quickly, and for a moment his carefully shaped mask dropped—replaced by stunned shock and disbelief.

He glanced off camera again, looking for reassurance, then made a visible and successful effort to regain his composure.

"This just in. For only the third time in history, a nuclear weapon has been used in anger. About an hour ago, Cuban troops invading South Africa were attacked by South African Air Force warplanes, which dropped one atomic weapon, inside its own borders.

"Department of Defense sources have confirmed the detection of a nuclear explosion in South Africa, describing it as a 'low-yield' burst. Cuba's foreign ministry, though quick to point out that it has no independent confirmation of this attack, strongly condemned the use of nuclear weapons as 'an act of barbarism' that 'revealed the true nature of Pretoria's racist and fascist regime.'

"The White House, while saying the President is 'deeply concerned by recent developments,' is reportedly awaiting definitive information before releasing an official statement."

Another message slid across the desk. This time the anchorman took it in stride.

"In a new twist, South Africa has admitted that it has used a nuclear weapon. According to a statement released simultaneously by the South African Broadcasting Corporation and by Pretoria's embassies worldwide, 'South Africa will use its special weapons at times and places of its own choosing —without regard for the hypocritical squeamishness of other nations.' "

The screen divided—one-half still showing CNN's Atlanta studio, the other showing a crowded, noisy room as reporters milled around a small, flag-draped dais.

"We're going live to our Pentagon correspondent for a Defense Department briefing . . ."

CHAPTER 28

Vengeance

NOVEMBER 24—HEADQUARTERS, CUBAN EXPEDITIONARY FORCE, PIETERSBURG, SOUTH AFRICA

Military traffic moving south filled Pietersburg's wide streets—rumbling past burned-out homes, crater-choked public parks, and barren, blasted jacaranda trees. Smoking piles of charred blue and pale-purple blossoms littered the ground beneath each tree. Stray dogs, some unfed for days, roamed side roads and alleys in packs.

The advancing Cuban troops had appropriated a small, two-story brick office building as Vega's new forward headquarters. Col. José Suarez walked into the splinter-scarred building past piles of discarded papers and wrecked furniture heaped outside.

The building's outer offices had been taken over by the expeditionary force's supply, communications, and other support sections. Worried-looking staff officers bustled back and forth from room to room as they tried, sometimes in vain, to manage the advance of Cuba's two remaining columns.

Others sat stunned, still horrified by the split-second annihilation of the Third Tactical Group.

Suarez knew the confusion he saw here was only a fraction of the chaos sweeping the dead brigade's rear areas. A dozen different supply, maintenance, and medical units, working to support what had been a spectacularly rapid advance, now found themselves suddenly fighting for their lives against local Afrikaner commandos. At the same time, they were working hard to save those few dazed survivors found wandering back down the highway. Well, he thought sadly, there won't be any survivors left by tomorrow. Heat, a lack of potable water, and Boer bullets will see to that.

He moved deeper into the building and knocked quietly on a closed door. No answer. He turned the knob quietly and peered inside.

Gen. Antonio Vega, Liberator of Walvis Bay, victor of a dozen battles, the man who held a knife to South Africa's throat, sat staring at a map. He held a sheaf of papers in his hands, the air reconnaissance photos taken over the site of the Third Brigade Tactical Group's destruction. Suarez knew what those photos showed. He had given them, and the rest of the data on the column's death, to Vega over two hours ago.

Daylight had revealed a crater a hundred meters wide and fifty meters deep near what had once been the brigade's lead battalion. Mounded debris spread far and wide past the rim of the crater itself, creating a scene that looked as though it belonged on the surface of the moon—not on earth. Blackened vehicles and bits of equipment littered the gray landscape, mixed with the scorched remains of men, brush, and trees. For the most part, the vegetation had burned itself out, but some of it was still smoking, and a pall lay over the desert floor, dimming the harsh sun.

Only about fifty men had been found alive from the first four battalions, mostly extended scouts or pickets. All were hurt—burned or blasted and in shock. The fifth battalion, a Libyan motorized rifle unit, had lost ninety percent of its equipment and three-quarters of its men. Only the brigade's supply battalion, strung out fifty kilometers behind, had survived as a unit. Altogether, more than three thousand men were dead, and another thousand or so were badly wounded—emergency-room cases who weren't expected to live out the week.

Winds from the southeast were pushing the fallout across a dozen small towns and villages scattered over the plateau. Lichtenburg, with its art museum, bird sanctuaries, and farms, would be the largest town to suffer. It would have to be evacuated. Suarez smiled grimly. How the Afrikaner bastards were going to do that wasn't his concern, but if they didn't, many people were going to die slow, nasty deaths from radiation sickness.

Some of the fallout would fall in Bophuthatswana, as well, eventually fanning out into the unpopulated wilderness. Another nuclear bomb for the scientists to study, he thought.

The colonel shook his head. His musings were almost as bad as Vega's. He'd stood in the door patiently for several minutes now, waiting to be noticed. This had happened before when the general was working or thinking, and Suarez was sure they could stand like this the rest of the day.

"Comrade General . . ." He spoke softly, as if he were trying to wake Vega, or avoid startling him.

Vega didn't even look up. "Colonel, I am a fool. You told me that South Africa had nuclear weapons. I'd seen their order of battle. So what made me think they would not use them?"

"You stated that they would be unlikely to use them inside their own borders," Suarez answered quietly. "You also thought that the instability and confusion in their government reduced the odds of their successfully employing such weapons."

"Dry words to cover wishful thinking, José. These people seem willing to do anything to stop us, even if they destroy their own lands in the process. I know that now."

Vega suddenly stood up. He made a visible effort to master his dismay. "We confront two related problems, Colonel. First, how do we continue our attack with only two-thirds of our forces? And second, how can we avoid being annihilated by South Africa's atomic weapons?"

Suarez looked uncertainly at his commander. "Perhaps a reinforced air defense network could—"

"Insufficient." Vega shook his head. "All the SAMs in the world can't guarantee the destruction of every attacking aircraft. No, Colonel, we must take measures that are more aggressive, more active."

Suarez knew his face revealed his bewilderment.

"Read this." Vega pulled a message form out of the papers in his hand and gave it to him.

The chief of staff read: *President Castro shares your anger and outrage. The South Africans have joined the United States, their bankrupt leader, as the only nations in the world ever to use nuclear weapons against other human beings. Use any means at your disposal, or any means you can obtain, to wipe this regime from the face of the earth.*

Suarez looked puzzled. Stripped of the rhetoric, Castro's message just said to fight harder. "What can we do that we haven't already done?"

"While you've been busy trying to bring order out of this mess, I've been talking with our socialist allies." Vega's voice turned grim. "Two cargo aircraft are already in the air, en route to us. One is from Libya, the other from North Korea. By the end of this day, I expect to have enough nerve gas on hand, in 152mm artillery shells and aircraft bombs, to destroy a significant part of the South African Army. From now on, we're making chemical weapons a part of our arsenal."

Suarez felt a hundred questions welling up inside him. Like their Soviet counterparts, Cuban troops were trained in the use of chemical weapons—up to a point. But, except for limited bombardments in Angola, they'd rarely used chemicals in combat.

For one thing, chemical weapons sometimes created almost as many problems for an attacker as they did for the defender. There were special protective suits for the assault troops, decontamination procedures, special reconnaissance vehicles . . .

Vega reassured him. "I know what you are thinking, José. Do not worry. We will be using nonpersistent nerve agents, and every weakness we have in chemical arms is mirrored in the enemy twofold. They have no training and very little equipment."

Suarez spoke slowly, still troubled despite his commander's sudden assurance. "But this will simply escalate the war, Comrade General. Even if these weapons are effective, their use will only enrage the Afrikaners. They may actually incite further atomic attacks on our forces."

"I had thought of that, Comrade Colonel."

Suarez shivered inwardly. He'd never heard Vega's voice quite so cold and forbidding.

"For that reason, I want every base and higher headquarters moved immediately. We will plant our flags squarely in the middle of South Africa's own towns and cities." Vega stressed every word. "I also want you to round up several thousand civilians—white civilians, they don't care about blacks or other races—for use as shields around every unit headquarters above company level."

The Cuban general's face darkened with anger. "If need be, we will send photographs to this madman Vorster—daring him to bomb our units under those circumstances. If they want to butcher tens of thousands of their own women and children, we will make it easy for them. This war has changed, Colonel. We will match these Afrikaners threat for threat. Escalation for escalation."

Suarez shook his head. "These precautions may protect our men from nuclear attack, sir, unless our enemies are truly insane. But I still have reservations about using chemical weapons. Residues, decontamination, these are all things we are not prepared for. Our own casualties could be high."

"For once we have had a little luck, Colonel." Vega smiled thinly. "Our Libyan comrades-in-arms have more experience in this than we do, so their troops will lead the assault."

Suarez nodded sagely. The Libyans had used poison gas many times during their unsuccessful attempts to conquer Chad. By rights, they should know enough about such weapons to avoid killing themselves.

"Both cargo aircraft also carry technicians and extra protective equipment." Vega faced his chief of staff squarely. "Cheer up, José. These chemicals will help us break the back of South Africa's remaining defenses. They'll replace the combat power we lost yesterday. With luck, we'll destroy the Afrikaner army in its foxholes!"

"Let us hope so, Comrade General."

Vega stared at him, obviously unsure whether his subordinate's flat, impassive tone signaled continued doubt or growing confidence. Vega walked over to the map and pointed to it. "The planes are scheduled to arrive later this afternoon. Ensure that our best people are in the tower. We do not want a landing accident today." He smiled grimly. "I want those munitions moved to our forward units tonight. Tighten security, both on the ground and in the air. Clear?"

Suarez nodded.

"Good. Tomorrow, at dawn, we will use the weapons in preparatory bombardments against the enemy's main line of resistance." Vega pointed to a spot south of their position on National Route 1. "There."

HEADQUARTERS, 1/75TH RANGERS, HUNTER ARMY AIRFIELD, GEORGIA

Frowning, Lt. Col. Robert O'Connell flipped from page to page of the wargame after-action report. Board games and computer simulations couldn't predict real-world battle results with total precision, but they were useful tools. Done right, they could highlight unexpected glitches or weaknesses in plans. Sometimes, they offered valuable insights into possible enemy countermoves. Right now, though, he thought, the battalion's simulations were just depressing.

So far, each of the three mock battles fought using the 1/75th's initial attack plan had ended in unmitigated American disaster. Casualties over 75 percent, no objectives seized, complete loss of command and control—the list of foul-ups went on for more than four pages. He shook his head in frustration. It was pretty clear that the battalion's command team would have to rethink drastically the Brave Fortune operations plan all the way from landing to extraction.

Someone knocked on the doorframe.

"Come."

Maj. Peter Klocek, the 1/75th's operations officer, poked his head through the open doorway. "I just got off the phone with Cheyenne Mountain, Colonel. It's for real. No media hype. They're already using those nukes we're supposed to grab."

"God." O'Connell had been praying it was all a mistake ever since he'd heard the first panicked reports from South Africa.

"But I'm sure you'll be glad to hear that the world community is up in arms over this." Klocek didn't hide his cynicism. "I understand there are reports of protest notes, peace demonstrations, and threats of further unspecified sanctions rolling in from all over."

"Great. Just great." O'Connell scowled. Sanctions, demonstrations, and protests didn't matter a damn now. Not when the Afrikaners had already shown they were prepared to wage total war—nuclear war. The only real way to stop Pretoria's madmen would be to take the bombs away from them.

He glanced down at the reports littering his desk. At the moment, that scarcely seemed possible.

NOVEMBER 25—POTGIETERSRUS

The shattered remnants of several South African battalions held Potgietersrus like a drowning man clinging to a rope.

The bushveld mining town wasn't quite the last bastion before Pretoria itself, but there weren't many such spots left along National Route 1. With its mixture of excellent defensive terrain, a strategic road junction, and important economic assets, Potgietersrus was a good place to make a stand.

The city sat overlooking a dry, rocky plain, its offices and smelters and homes rising out of the ground like an island of civilization in the wilderness. In ordinary times, thirty thousand people called Potgietersrus home—ten thousand of them white, fifteen thousand black, the rest mixed and other races.

Naturally, the whites lived in the center of town and ran the mines and businesses that kept the city alive. Their homes were mostly spacious, tree shaded, and expensive.

Many of the blacks in Potgietersrus were single men who lived in migrant-worker barracks adjacent to the mines themselves—one hundred men crammed into each long, one-room building. They lived there while fulfilling year-long labor contracts. At the end of each year, they were free to visit families, wives, and children who'd been left behind in South Africa's tribal homelands—or even in Mozambique or Zimbabwe. They returned as soon as possible, though. The mines were usually the only work to be had.

Some lucky blacks, either mine workers or laborers elsewhere in town, managed to bring their families with them. They crowded into the same kind of squalid shantytown visible just outside every South African city. Technically, blacks were not allowed to own land or even live near white-populated areas, but necessity drove them to settle wherever they could—existing as squatters for white convenience and at the government's sufferance.

Applying the word *township* to Potgietersrus's slum gave it a dignity it did not deserve. No water, no electricity, and no sewage system would ever serve the tin and wood shacks that were home to the bulk of the city's labor force.

Potgietersrus was an important mining center—nickel, tin, copper, and platinum were all found in profitable quantities close by. The Cubans might say they were fighting to liberate their black brothers and end apartheid, but the mines would be their reward if they won. Capturing them would also immediately deny vital resources now flowing to Pretoria.

South Africa's military mobilization had already reduced mine output by stripping away most white supervisors and craftsmen. Only a fraction of the explosives experts were black. Even fewer of the machinery operators were nonwhite. Black laborers were starting to fill those roles, but they had little training and even less guidance.

Much of the white population had fled Potgietersrus before the Cubans even reached the city's outer defenses. Most blacks were still there. They had nowhere else to go. The mine workers were actually being held under guard in their barracks whenever they went off shift. Since so many were foreign workers, the Brandwag felt they were a security risk. Considering their treatment, that was probably right.

So mining operations continued, even with Cuban armor and infantry units less than thirty kilometers away. Huge trucks carried refined metals and other valuable ores south toward Pretoria. They moved without interference.

Vega had ordered his artillery and air commanders to avoid firing on the mines and smelters. Leaving them untouched would reduce the time needed to get them back into full swing once they were captured.

In any case, the Cubans had more than enough military targets for their artillery. Potgietersrus sat on the western slope of a rugged mountain more than two thousand meters high, and its defenders had been preparing a new defensive line for several days. There were no shortages of digging tools in a mining town.

The South African garrison contained several understrength infantry battalions, Air Force personnel who'd abandoned the base at Pietersburg, and men of the local commando—a sizable force, though one with little heavy equipment. Defeated farther north, they'd collected themselves in this town, all survivors of at least one battle and hasty withdrawal. This time, though, they were dug in on good ground. This time, they would hold.

HEADQUARTERS, POTGIETERSRUS DEFENSE FORCE

Brig. Piet Boerson had retired from the SADF years ago, but Vorster's full mobilization had reactivated his commission and placed him in command—defending the town where he had lived for more than half his adult life. The tall, thin man's face was craggy from a life of hard work. He hadn't always sat behind a desk.

He'd been perfectly happy as a senior manager responsible for production in one of the area's most successful copper mines. Now he fought to protect his home, his job, his way of life. Thank God, his wife and children were gone, though they'd only fled as far as her sister's place in Pretoria. Well, if they didn't stop the Cubans soon, there wouldn't be anywhere that was safe.

Boerson stared at the map and sighed, taking another swig of lukewarm coffee. He should be grateful. Considering his country's disastrous strategic situation, he'd been dealt a fairly strong hand. In the three days since the fall of Pietersburg, he and his men had fended off three separate Cuban assaults, and he was confident he could hold his ground for some time to come.

But he was also sure the Cubans would try again—and soon. Probably at dawn.

Emergency reinforcements, scraped together from God knew where, had arrived shortly after midnight. He snorted. Reinforcements. A battery of World War II–vintage artillery pieces and two companies of boys barely old enough to carry rifles. Barely enough men to replace those lost during the previous day's fighting. Still, he'd thrown them into the line. Even boys with rifles were useful.

So far, Boerson's "composite" brigade had survived air attacks, artillery barrages, and commando raids. And he'd used the last twenty-four hours of comparative quiet to rest his men and bolster their defenses. They'd even managed to rig mining explosives as command-detonated land mines.

The brigadier leaned over his map, studying his defenses for what seemed like the thousandth time. Was there anything more he could do?

Emplaced in an arc facing north and west of the city, his infantry were dug in deep in the stony soil, grimy and tired. Minefields and barbed wire covered the easiest approaches to their lines. He'd deployed the brigade's single battery of G-5 155mm guns on a low hill close to his front lines. From there, their shells could reach almost all the way back to Pietersburg. His two remaining missile launchers, each with three Cactus SAMs left, guarded the guns. The newly arrived artillery battery, with British-manufactured 5.5-inch guns that were half the size and five times the age of his 155s, covered the highway itself. Finally, Potgietersrus's local commando, unreliable as line infantry, were acting as scouts and snipers. They knew the area, and Boerson hoped to use their local knowledge to his advantage.

Yes, they could hold, but not to protect those fools in Pretoria, Boerson thought. They got us into this mess, and if we can survive, those idiots will be the first ones against the wall—Vorster's brownshirted Brandwag notwithstanding.

Boerson turned to look at the other officers in the room. Two commandants and a colonel, each commanding a battalion, sat discussing the details of troop employment and artillery allocation, while a Brandwag monitor listened to every word, as though one of them were going to stand up suddenly and shout, "Long live the ANC."

Groote Kempe, the commandant of the local commando, sat quietly in a corner. His men didn't have radios or any heavy weapons except for some old Lewis machine guns. Their rôle was simple. Snipe at the enemy for as long as possible, then fall back to the main line of resistance.

The distant rumble of artillery fire served as a constant backdrop to their discussion. Harassing fire had been falling for the past twenty-four hours—small salvos designed to pin the South Africans in their positions, inflict a few casualties, and keep them short on sleep.

The tempo of the Cuban barrage suddenly picked up—shells seemed to be raining down at the rate of three or four a minute. At the sound, the South African officers looked up from their maps and discussion.

Boerson checked his watch: 0527 hours. A little early, he thought, but the Cubans probably plan to give us one hell of a pasting before they attack. Wonderful.

"Everyone, stand your units to. And tell your boys to make every shot count," he ordered. Grabbing a helmet and a flashlight, he ran out into the night. Behind him, his battalion commanders scattered to their posts.

His headquarters occupied a two-story stone vacation home

built near the mountain's summit. In daylight, he had a view that stretched from one end of his line to the other. On a clear day, he could even make out Cuban-held Pietersburg as a blur far to the northeast. Potgietersrus itself lay behind him. His staff officers kept complaining that he'd picked a spot too close to the front lines, but Boerson liked to see things for himself.

Night was just beginning to fade, with a thin line of pink appearing to the east. He could already make out the rugged landscape falling away to his front. Individual infantry positions were still cloaked in darkness, but he knew their locations. Bright flashes lit the skyline as Cuban shells burst over them.

The Cuban gunners were going for airbursts, he noted, a reasonable tactic considering how well his troops were dug in. Shells fused to explode on impact with the ground were ineffective against men in deep holes, unless one happened to land in the hole itself. But shells exploding twenty meters up could shower dug-in infantry with high-velocity fragments—forcing them to keep their heads down while armored troop carriers and tanks attacked.

It was light enough now for binoculars, and Boerson scanned the ground between Pietersburg and his positions. Yes, there they were. A dark wedge of dots moving toward him. Time to release the guns.

Stepping back into his headquarters, he said, "Order the one fifty-five battery to engage the enemy formation. Fuse for airburst." That would give the swine a little of their own back, he thought. It wouldn't hurt their tanks much, but it would disrupt that pretty formation and give them something to think about.

He waited while the operator called the battery, located about eight hundred meters away. The man jiggled his receiver. "Sir, there's no reply,"

What? Boerson moved back outside, sweeping his binoculars toward his nearby artillery emplacements. He pursed his lips. Yes, they were being shelled, too, and by more airbursts. So much for concealment. The Cubans knew right where he'd hidden his guns.

Still, his gunners should have their battery fire-control center under cover. Had an explosion cut the telephone line?

Then, staring at the enemy barrage, he noted that the airbursts looked a little different. The explosions were smaller. Mortars, maybe? If so, when were the Cubans going to use their bigger guns? Each shell was also throwing off a tremendous amount of red-colored smoke. That was unusual. Mixing smoke with high explosive was a common tactic, but not against artillery.

His signalman appeared in the doorway. "Sir, Commandant Salter is on the line!" Traces of barely suppressed panic crept into his voice. "He says his men are all dying."

The brigadier leapt for the phone. What the hell was going on? "Boerson here."

"It's gas . . . poison gas, bursting over us!"

My God. Gas. Of course. That explained the red mist and the small explosions. Each Cuban shell contained just enough explosive to scatter its deadly cargo over a wide area.

"Only a few of us have masks, and they don't help anyway! Most of my men are already dead! I've got a mask on, but if I open up my vehicle, I'll die from skin contact!" Salter's abject terror came through clearly over the phone line.

"Pull back, George. Save yourself and anyone you can." It was an automatic response, sensible in the circumstances but no less distasteful. Pulling back from the mountain meant abandoning Potgietersrus to the communists.

The phone line went dead.

Boerson stood rooted in place, his mind in a mad, dizzying whirl. What could he do now? Salter's infantry battalion and his best artillery battery were both gone. How much of the brigade had the Cuban poison-gas barrage hit?

He heard the *crump* of a muted explosion overhead, quickly followed by a handful more. His heart sank, and for the first time in his career, he hoped he was under fire by enemy high explosive.

Then he saw the mist drifting down toward him. Boerson wheeled to the white-faced, shaking signalman. "Order a general retreat!"

He was too late.

* * *

The red-tinted cloud settled slowly around the headquarters building and all up and down the South African defense line. It was not a true gas, but an aerosol, a spray of extremely fine droplets created by the small charge in each shell. An artillery airburst wasn't as uniform or efficient as a spray nozzle, but it worked well enough.

The chemical itself was named GB, or sarin. A complex organic substance, it had been available since World War II. Unlike chlorine gas, which affects the human respiratory system, or mustard gas, a blister agent, sarin directly affects the human nervous system.

Chlorine has to be inhaled to kill or maim, and mustard gas must come in contact with a large area of exposed skin before it can seriously injure. But a tenth of a gram of sarin, touching the body anywhere, is a lethal dose.

Troops who have the training and equipment to deal with chemical weapons must wear respirators and protective suits. Every piece of equipment touched by the chemical must be thoroughly washed before it can safely be used by anyone without protection.

But these suits are hot and heavy. Even in temperate climates, a soldier's efficiency can be halved after only a few hours in his gear. On the highveld, wearing chemical protection gear led to heatstroke—not lost efficiency.

The South African Defense Force had never worried much about the threat posed by chemical weapons. Faced with limited funds and a severely limited threat, they'd concentrated on other areas. Most of the SADF's real-world experience with chemicals involved the ubiquitous CS, or tear gas. Line troops were only trained to use gas masks, and commandos and other defenders weren't issued any protection at all.

The men defending Potgietersrus never had time to complain.

When the first shells burst over their trenches and foxholes, those few regulars who still carried them quickly donned their gas masks. But by the time they turned to face the oncoming enemy, the sarin was already killing them.

A nerve agent works by interfering with the nervous system, causing signals to be blocked, amplified, and generally scrambled. In seconds, hundreds of men were dying—staggering around wildly in their foxholes and tearing at their masks in a futile effort to breathe.

The brigade died in a five-minute bombardment.

Boerson knew what was happening, but he couldn't control the panic flooding over him as he saw his death approaching. He ran inside, searching frantically for a room whose windows hadn't been shattered by the bombardment. The mist finally found him crouched in the cellar, trying to seal a leaky door with tape.

He suddenly felt dizzy, and his skin was instantly covered by a thick sheen of sweat. He felt sick to his stomach. His hands were already growing heavier as he struggled with the roll of tape. Then they took on a life of their own, and he fell, legs and arms twitching, onto the floor. His lungs were bursting. He had to breathe. He needed air. Clean air. The South African brigadier vomited onto the floor.

Random bursts of pain surged through him as his synapses fired uncontrollably, mixing with sensations of heat, cold, and motion. Every sensor his body had was going wild.

Piet Boerson had just enough coordination left to roll over. With one last desperate gesture, he grabbed for the tape he'd dropped, but then the sarin reached his brain cells. He flickered mercifully into unconsciousness. A few seconds later his brain stopped telling his heart to beat. From beginning to end, he had taken less than thirty seconds to die.

PEOPLE'S GUARD MOTOR RIFLE BATTALION

Col. Hassan Mahmoud stood high in the commander's hatch of his armored personnel carrier—calculating the distance separating his battalion from the outer South African defenses. One thousand meters, perhaps. It was time to deploy.

He lifted his radio mike. "All units. Form line. Continue the advance."

Jubilant acknowledgements flooded into his earphones. Mahmoud scowled. Young idiots. They were acting as though this were some kind of peacetime joyride.

Luckily, there wasn't much left out there to oppose them. The defending fire had been light, very light. These peasants might actually be able to execute the maneuver, he thought.

The gas appeared to be working. In this heat it would only be effective for another ten minutes. After that, it would begin breaking down—decomposing into harmless compounds.

Other nerve gases, such as Soman, or GD, would have lasted for days—true "persistent" agents. Vega had chosen sarin precisely because it was "nonpersistent." With proper care, Mahmoud's battalion ought to be able to seize its objectives without suffering any self-inflicted losses.

The Libyan colonel was optimistic. The Afrikaners appeared to have been taken completely by surprise. Even the wind favored them, a light breeze from behind and to his left that should push the poisonous mist completely clear of his men.

POTGIETERSRUS

The wind blew from the northeast, moving at between ten and fifteen kilometers an hour. In the fifteen minutes that the nerve gas remained effective, it drifted a little over three kilometers—mixing and fanning out over Potgietersrus in a deadly cloud.

Most of the city's remaining white population had taken refuge in improvised bomb shelters when they heard the Cuban barrage echoing down the mountain. A sizable fraction did not bother, however. Three days of living within earshot of constant fighting had made war seem almost routine.

People outside—especially those working or breathing hard—were immediately affected. And the residents of the black township, living in windowless shacks, might just as well have been outside. There were no bomb shelters for them.

The gas was starting to break down, though, so it was

somewhat less lethal. The very young and very old were vulnerable, as was anyone with respiratory trouble—a common ailment among miners. And even when weakened, sarin can still paralyze and blind its victims. Once destroyed, nerve tissue does not heal.

Six-year-old Alice Naxula lived in a one-room hut with her mother, grandmother, and uncle. A typical black child in the townships, she was about to go out, to play and to forage for food. Wartime chaos had emptied store shelves, so she and her mother had to split up and hunt in the city, while her uncle worked in the mine and her grandmother sat quietly in the shack's one chair, remembering.

Her uncle was already awake, ready to catch the six-o'clock bus to the mine. They all rose early to see him off each day, sharing the leftover porridge from last night's dinner. In the darkness, none of them saw the gas seeping in through their tattered, rusting walls and a blanket-draped doorway. Even in the daylight, it was spread so thin as to be invisible, but still lethal.

The first sign of trouble came when her grandmother started coughing uncontrollably. She had bronchitis, common among the old, brought on from scores of winters spent living in unheated shacks. Suddenly, the old woman howled once in agony and threw herself out of the chair. She landed on the dirt floor in a writhing, twitching heap.

Alice's own eyes were stinging. Her mother started to scream something, pointing at her grandmother. With an instinct born from years of police sweeps, the little girl dove under a pile of bedding in one corner and froze, lying motionless. Her mother had taught her this years ago, so that the adults could flee from the township police when they made one of their sporadic sweeps. Alice looked on the pile of patched bedding as a place of refuge.

She waited in terror, hearing screams and thumps all around, but she knew she would be safe. The rags smelled, and the air was stifling, but the police had never found her in here.

The screams stopped, and she wanted to get up and see what had happened, but Alice remembered her mother's instructions. There was a silly song about a monkey and a rhinoceros that she was supposed to sing three times, and so she sang it to herself, always enjoying the part where the monkey tricked the rhino.

Then she finished and scrambled out from her hiding place, shaking off the rags and blankets.

Her mother lay on the floor, next to her grandmother and uncle. Shaking her only elicited a faint moan. Alice ran for water. The police had whipped her mother once during a raid—leaving her bruised and bloody. And her uncle had told her to fetch water. That had helped.

She was halfway to the pump when she heard her mother screaming, "I cannot see. I cannot see!"

Alice ran back and tried to rouse her uncle or grandmother to help her, but they were both dead. She knew how to check, and she answered her mother's questions about them. Neither had any wounds, but their staring, horrified expressions showed that they'd died in agony.

"Momma, what should I do?"

There was no answer.

Several thousand South African civilians—blacks and whites alike—lay dead or wandered maimed through Potgietersrus.

NOVEMBER 25—HEADQUARTERS, CUBAN EXPEDITIONARY FORCE, PIETERSBURG

Jonathan Sasolo served as Gen. Antonio Vega's liaison with the African National Congress. Classified by South Africa's laws as "mixed race," he was a wide man, with big hands and a loud voice. He held the rank of major in the ANC's military arm, Umkhonto we Sizwe, and theoretically was accorded that rank here at headquarters. Vega's staff hadn't treated him with enough respect, though—an injustice that only served to amplify his anger and outrage.

"Is this how you liberate us? Kill half of our people and let the rest starve?"

Vega was trying to be diplomatic, and both Suarez and Vasquez were present to lend their arguments as well. "Comrade Sasolo, please understand. We had no control over the wind."

"But you knew its direction and strength. And you ignored the very predictable results of a nerve gas barrage!" Sasolo leaned over Vega's desk, yelling at him in a way that left his staff aghast. "More than a thousand dead, Vega, and thousands more maimed. There are so many dead that we haven't yet had time to count them. What kind of a victory is this?"

"An important one," Vega retorted. "Our forces, which include your men, I might add, lost only fourteen dead and thirty-seven wounded while annihilating an entire enemy brigade."

Vasquez nodded. "Think of the shock in Pretoria, Comrade Major. Think of how much closer this brings us to victory."

Sasolo scowled angrily. "Victory? I tell you, man, there will be far fewer people to celebrate this victory of yours if you continue like this. Especially if your troops confiscate every scrap of food in the city! What are my people supposed to live on?"

"We only took food from stores in the white areas, Major." Suarez's tone was calm.

"All the *blery* food is in the white districts, you bastard! There *is* no food anywhere else."

Vega answered him this time, clearly losing patience. "The supply echelon will bring up more food soon, comrade. Our own logistics have been snarled by air raids and commando attacks. Fuel and ammunition have first priority anyway. That's why we had to collect food in the first place."

"Letting my people starve."

Vega's tone began to harden. "Major, I am concerned only with the rapid, efficient advance of my forces. My men are fighting and dying to liberate your people from this fascist regime. I am sorry about the deaths here. Many others will no doubt die before we are done. But their deaths will not be in vain.''

Sasolo stood his ground. ''Pretty speeches won't change the masses' minds, Vega. They've seen the Boers, and now they've seen you. They say, 'Where is the difference?' '' The ANC major stepped back from the desk. ''I have been discussing this matter with our executive committee.''

Vega nodded. Vasquez had told him of several coded communications passing back and forth between ANC headquarters in Lusaka and Sasolo—codes that the Cubans hadn't been able to break.

The major continued, ''I now believe that we should withdraw from this alliance. That we must chart our own course for the liberation of South Africa. You are using us . . . just as the Soviets once used you.''

Vasquez went to the door. ''That's enough, Major.''

Sasolo turned to see two Cuban soldiers, rifles pointed at him.

Vega pointed to the ANC guerrilla. ''Arrest him.''

Sasolo's astonished protests quickly faded away as they grabbed him and hustled him out of the room.

Vasquez shook his head. ''He's not alone, Comrade General. Many of the ANC troops are grumbling. We may have trouble with them over this matter.''

''I know, Vasquez, I've read the reports, too.'' Vega sighed. ''Weaklings. They can't see the need for sacrifice.'' He shook his head. ''True socialism does not come easily. It must be earned with blood and hard work.''

The general stood up and looked over at Suarez. ''Very well, Comrade Colonel. Disarm and detain any group of ANC guerrillas you think may be disloyal.''

His face darkened. ''I will not tolerate mutinies among my forces. Not when we stand on the threshold of victory. Dismissed.''

He stood brooding, staring out the window as his officers filed out the door. Sasolo's cowardice and treason left a bitter taste in his mouth.

ABOARD USS *MOUNT WHITNEY*, BETWEEN ASCENSION ISLAND AND CAPE TOWN

Long columns of gray-painted ships steamed through the night at high speed, bow waves and trailing wakes gleaming pale blue in the dark. Aboard the ships, thousands of American and British Marines ate or slept or played cards. And they talked. They talked about sports and women and anything at all except South Africa.

Their officers weren't so fortunate.

"General Craig?" The orderly softly called him away from a knot of officers in the command center. It was hard to get his attention in the bustle and noise of the crowded compartment, but it was considered rude to shout at a lieutenant general.

Finally, Craig turned and nodded to the corporal, who approached and handed him a single sheet of paper. The enlisted man saluted and left as Craig absentmindedly returned his salute, reading the message while his staff waited expectantly.

Craig's posture sagged a little, but he recovered quickly. He turned to face Brig. Gen. Clayton Mauer. As his J-3, Mauer was in charge of operations for the invasion force. "Clay, revise the training schedule. I want at least one full day spent on chemical warfare training. Drills, protective suits, the works."

Mauer whistled softly. "You mean . . ."

"Yeah. The Cubans gassed a town north of Pretoria that was putting up a stiff fight. The message doesn't say what they used, but total casualties are several thousand. Hit the civilians pretty hard, according to our intel."

"Shit." Mauer sat down heavily, letting out his breath in a whoosh. "First, nuclear protection drills, now this. Sir, the men are liable to acquire a negative attitude about this operation." He smiled to hide his concern, but the message was all too real.

Craig nodded somberly, his thoughts several thousand miles away.

Mauer didn't know about the planned Ranger raid on Pelindaba. In fact, only five officers outside the Ranger battalion itself, Craig included, had even heard it mentioned.

His staff would only be told about Brave Fortune when it was under way. The security classification "need to know" didn't include a separate category for those who needed a quick morale boost. Besides, he wasn't sure knowing the details of what sounded like a suicide mission would make anyone any happier.

Craig only prayed that this harebrained Ranger attack would be successful. He'd never seen an amphibious task force turn tail and run before, but that would be the only sensible course if the Afrikaners held on to their nukes.

CHAPTER 29

Countdown

NOVEMBER 25—HEADQUARTERS, 1ST BATTALION, 75TH RANGER REGIMENT, HUNTER ARMY AIRFIELD, GEORGIA

Lt. Col. Robert O'Connell was on a secure line to Washington, listening grimly as his regimental commander, Col. Paul Geller, threw ten days' worth of mission planning into the shitcan. The fact that it was a phone call he'd been half-expecting since the news of Pretoria's nuclear strike was no consolation.

A stray beam of pale, watery sunshine briefly brightened his office without brightening his mood. Just once, he wished that he could get a telephone call from the Pentagon containing good news. It seemed likely to be a wish that would never come true.

"No, sir, I understand. . . . Yes, sir. This is one helluva way to run a railroad. We'll see you here tomorrow. Goodbye." He bit back the urge to say more—a lot more. Instead, he replaced the red secure phone on its cradle and sat staring out the window.

"Trouble?"

O'Connell turned slightly and looked across his desk at the lean, tanned face of Maj. Peter Klocek, the battalion's operations officer. "You could say that, Pete." He nodded toward the phone. "We just lost a week. This is now D minus four. Washington wants us to go in on the twenty-ninth—not December sixth. Plus, they've upped the target list. The Joint Chiefs want us to take out Pelindaba's enrichment plant, too. They don't want to give South Africa the slightest chance of prepping a weapon before our Marines go ashore at Cape Town."

"Jesus Christ!" The S-3 couldn't hide his consternation. Attacking a week ahead of schedule would mean abandoning a series of full-scale rehearsals designed to test a complicated plan so far worked out only on paper and on computer. Even worse, the last-minute addition of a major target such as the uranium enrichment plant would spread the 1st Battalion's already thinned-out resources even further. "How the hell are we supposed to do all that?"

O'Connell shrugged. "Any way we can. We stage to Ascension Island the day after tomorrow."

"We're screwed." Klocek looked sick. Mounting an airborne operation required careful planning and thorough preparation. Skimping on either dramatically increased the odds against success and for bloody disaster.

"Yeah, maybe so. But doing this kind of stuff is what the taxpayers are paying us for." O'Connell forced himself to sound confident.

Klocek nodded toward the secure phone. "Is the colonel still planning to jump with us?"

"Uh-huh." O'Connell said it flatly, not yet sure how he felt about the situation.

The 75th Ranger Regiment's commander had made the decision to drop with the 1/75th several days before. In theory, he was going along to provide higher command and control for both Ranger units, but O'Connell didn't have any illusions about how the colonel's presence would affect his battalion's chain of command. In practice, Geller would wind up running the whole show, and he'd be relegated to the sidelines.

Despite that, he couldn't really fault the colonel's decision. O'Connell's 1/75th had the toughest and most critical assignment in Brave Fortune, and Carrerra, the 2/75th's CO, was a veteran Ranger—someone Geller had worked with for years. So naturally, the colonel wanted to be where he was likely to be needed most.

O'Connell frowned, irritated with himself for having wasted even a second of precious time worrying about something he couldn't control. He looked up. "Round up the guys, Pete. I want to see all company commanders here at thirteen hundred hours. And tell Professor Levi I'd like to talk to him—now."

Prof. Esher Levi eyed the short, dark-haired American officer warily. In the two days since he'd arrived at Hunter, he'd met O'Connell only briefly—at meals and once after a rigorous session with the Rangers he was training to handle South Africa's nuclear weapons. And each time, he'd sensed two conflicting emotions vying with each other inside the American officer: gratitude for Levi's help and deep outrage at the fact that Israel's cooperation with South Africa made it necessary for his men to risk their lives in the first place. It made for a somewhat complicated working relationship.

"You wanted to see me, Colonel?"

"Yeah. For two reasons." O'Connell pushed an enhanced satellite photo across his desk and watched as Levi picked it up. The photo showed a squat, square building in the center of Pelindaba's scientific complex. "Recognize that?"

Levi nodded. He'd spent two years of his life in and around Pelindaba's centrifuge uranium-enrichment plant—the key component of South Africa's top-secret nuclear weapons program.

Only slightly more than seven-tenths of one percent of raw uranium ore is actually U-235—the uranium isotope needed for bomb-making. The other ninety-nine-odd percent is U-238, an almost identical isotope. Separating the two to produce enriched, weapons-grade uranium is an extraordinarily difficult, costly, and time-consuming process. And only the fact that U-235 weighs slightly less than U-238 makes it possible at all.

In centrifuge enrichment, uranium hexafluoride—a gaseous combination of natural uranium and fluorine—is whirled round and round at high speed inside a tall, thin centrifuge. A small fraction of the slightly heavier U-238 is thrown to the outside of the centrifuge and can be removed, leaving behind gas with a slightly higher concentration of U-235. The process is repeated over and over and over again until more than ninety percent of the remaining uranium is U-235.

Levi smiled to himself. In many ways, he thought, uranium enrichment closely resembled the fabled infinite series of monkeys pounding away on an infinite number of typewriters to produce the complete works of William Shakespeare. Obtaining usable quantities of bomb-grade material required a great many machines working at high speed for a very long time.

He scanned the photo of Pelindaba's enrichment plant again, marveling at the technical achievement the picture represented. Despite being taken by an American satellite orbiting several hundred miles above the earth's atmosphere, it looked as though it had been snapped only a few feet off the ground. Details of the facility's heavily guarded doorways and rooftop air-conditioning system were plainly visible. Nevertheless, the shot of the plant's square, windowless exterior revealed nothing of its inner complexity.

Like an iceberg, most of the South African uranium enrichment plant was below the surface—a design feature that made it easier to maintain a constant temperature inside. A central cascade hall housed more than twenty thousand centrifuges—each only thirty centimeters wide and seven meters high—arranged and mounted in rows and connected to form ninety distinct enrichment stages. Tens of kilometers of small-bore piping ran through the plant—feeding in fresh uranium hexafluoride, carrying off U-238 waste, and moving batches of ever more enriched uranium from stage to stage.

Levi passed the photo back to O'Connell. "You have some question about the facility, Colonel?"

"Not exactly." The American frowned. "I need a quick, efficient way to destroy the damned place."

Levi wasn't surprised. It was a logical step. Seizing South

Africa's nuclear stockpile without wrecking its uranium enrichment plant made little long-term sense. Why go to a lot of trouble to take a few bullets away while leaving the whole ammunition factory behind?

Levi steepled long, graceful hands—hands his ex-wife had thought more appropriate for a surgeon than a nuclear physicist. It was an intriguing problem. What was the best way to wreck thoroughly Pelindaba's enrichment plant? Placing conventional demolitions meant capturing the facility itself and then spending a fair amount of time wiring a large number of charges together. You'd need a lot of explosive power to destroy everything.

Power. That might be it. Levi sat up straighter, a series of half-formed ideas and concepts floating through his brain. He looked across at O'Connell. "There could be a relatively simple way to do such a thing, Colonel." His fingers beat a quick, distracted beat on the desk. "However, I will need a little time to work out all the details."

O'Connell nodded briskly. "Good. Because a little time is all we've got." His eyes narrowed. "Which brings me to my second reason for wanting to see you. Can you get Lieutenant Vaughn's special weapons team ready to go by the twenty-ninth?"

"Impossible." Levi shook his head decisively. "Your Rangers are good students, Colonel, but even they cannot learn everything they will need to know in anything less than a week."

"I see." The American officer sounded disappointed, but not particularly surprised. He glanced down at a manila folder in front of him. Levi saw a small tag that bore his name. "I understand you're an Israeli Defense Force reservist, Professor."

"That's correct. Just like any other adult male in my country." Levi looked curiously at the folder. Had Jerusalem given the Americans his whole personnel record?

"Paratrooper?"

Levi smiled and shook his head. "Nothing so glamorous, Colonel. As a senior scientist, I now have an exemption from active duty, but I wasn't quite so fortunate as a young student.

Consequently, I spent several long months as a lowly infantryman. Why do you ask?"

O'Connell slid a telex across the desk. "Because your government's called you back to the colors, Professor. As of six hundred hours tomorrow, you're to consider yourself attached to my battalion in a military capacity."

Levi stared at the message form for several seconds. "But why? I don't understand."

Now it was O'Connell's turn to smile. "It's pretty simple, Private Levi. Washington's changed the timetable. We're jumping into Pelindaba on the twenty-ninth—a week ahead of schedule. And I need a special weapons team led by an expert. Unfortunately, you've just confirmed that my troopers won't be ready by then. So you're going to be my expert."

Levi felt his mouth drop open and stay open.

Visibly amused, the American officer nodded briskly and stuck out his hand. "Welcome to the Rangers, Professor." His thin smile turned into a wide grin. "You're just lucky that learning how to jump out of airplanes isn't quite as complicated as learning how to assemble and disassemble A-bombs."

NOVEMBER 26—STATE SECURITY COUNCIL CHAMBER, PRETORIA

Karl Vorster glared at the ashen-faced South African Air Force officer standing at attention before him. "I am not interested in listening to your meaningless technical babble, General! I want to know when you can be ready to attack again! Nothing else, understand?"

The officer drew a quick, shaky breath and tried to explain. "The planes and weapons themselves can be readied in a matter of hours, Mr. President. But target selection isn't so simple a matter."

Vorster's eyes seemed to flash fire and he turned slowly red, working himself into a towering rage.

White-haired Gen. Adriaan de Wet recognized the danger signs and interceded. "What General Roefs is trying to say,

Mr. President, is that the Cubans are taking steps to make it impossible to use another nuclear weapon on them."

"What steps?" Vorster's voice was dangerously calm.

"The remaining fighting units are staying as close as possible to our own defending forces. And their support units stay just as close to captured towns filled with our own civilians."

"So?"

De Wet took great care to control his own temper. Three of the several empty chairs in the council chamber had belonged to men who'd angered Vorster at the wrong moment. "As things are, Mr. President, we cannot strike the communists without killing hundreds or thousands of our own folk in the same instant. We can gain no military advantage under these conditions."

Vorster signaled his understanding with a curt nod and sat brooding at the end of the table. From time to time he glanced up at the situation maps hung at one end of the room, a sour frown fixed on his face.

"Even if it were possible, we cannot use another such weapon!" Tiny, wasp-waisted Fredrik Pienaar, the minister of information, lifted a haunted face. He'd seen pictures showing the results of Cuba's nerve-gas attack. "Castro would only retaliate . . . perhaps against our cities this time."

Propaganda and boastful proclamations of imminent victory were proving no match for hard reality.

Vorster snorted. "What of it? Let the communists spray their poisons on cities full of kaffirs, coolies, and rooinek traitors! Our people are spread across the veld, made safe by distance and dispersion." He shrugged. "And if some should die, so be it. We fight for the survival of our whole nation—not for a few individuals."

He rose from his chair and stood facing de Wet, grim and utterly implacable. "I give you three days, General, to select suitable targets for our remaining weapons. If you cannot find them in South Africa, then I suggest you look elsewhere. If we cannot strike our enemies in the face, then we must cut them off at the knees." He moved closer to the situation map and pointed to the port at Maputo, Mozambique's capital, and the airfields around Bulawayo, Zimbabwe's second-largest city.

The men seated around the table turned pale. Maputo's piers were crowded with Soviet merchant shipping, and Soviet cargo aircraft jammed Bulawayo's runways. Dropping an atomic bomb on either would mean killing hundreds of Russians along with thousands or tens of thousands of blacks.

Vorster silenced them with a single stern look. "We strike again on the thirtieth. Two weapons this time. And four more on the day after that." He scowled. "We will hammer these communists until they either flee outside our beloved fatherland or until they are reduced to mere grains of radioactive dust, scattered across our soil."

NOVEMBER 27—WIDEAWAKE AIRFIELD, ASCENSION ISLAND

Prof. Esher Levi emerged blinking from the darkened interior of an American C-141 Starlifter into bright sunshine. He stared for a moment at the barren, alien landscape in front of him before walking stiffly and awkwardly out onto the tarmac. His first impressions from the air had been accurate—Ascension Island was a thirty-four-square-mile piece of hell planted smack in the middle of the vast South Atlantic.

The whole island was a jagged assembly of black and gray, sharp-edged volcanic rock and mounded ash. The only touch of living color came from a small tropical rain forest atop a mountain above the airfield. A murmuring, muted roar echoed everywhere—the constant thunder of long, rolling, gray-green South Atlantic waves breaking on a rugged shore.

Then a man-made roar drowned out the sound of the surf.

Levi turned and watched as another C-141 lumbered in out of the sky, touched down in a puff of black wheel smoke, and rolled on past—all four engines screaming as it braked. The Starlifter turned ponderously off the runway and parked close by its nine companions.

Work crews, a mobile staircase, and fuel trucks were already on their way to meet the transport aircraft. Ascension Island's sole military asset—Wideawake Airfield's 11,000-foot runway—had again proven its value. The island had served as a vital staging area for the British during their 1982 campaign to retake the Falklands. Now it would play the same role for U.S. Rangers preparing for a raid into South Africa.

" 'Scuse me, Prof. Hot stuff coming through."

Levi moved aside as a file of heavily laden Rangers started thumping down the stairs onto the tarmac and then across to the hangar apparently selected as temporary quarters for the battalion. Under their distinctive black berets, the soldiers looked more like pack mules than men—each piled high with his personal weapons, extra rifle ammunition, grenades, spare ammo belts for machine guns, mortar and recoilless rifle rounds, canteens, medical supplies, and anything else the battalion quartermasters thought might be needed.

The Rangers, already tired from days and nights of back-breaking practice and drill, were exhausted—worn-out by a grueling ten-hour plane flight in cramped conditions. Looking at their weary faces, Levi began to understand O'Connell's and Carrerra's absolute insistence that their battalions spend at least a full day on Ascension to rest, recuperate, and make final preparations.

The Israeli scientist's own aching muscles and bruises were a constant reminder of the last two hectic days. The Ranger battalion's jumpmasters had driven him hard, almost mercilessly, through an accelerated course of classroom instruction and drill—everything except a real parachute drop from a real plane. O'Connell had vetoed this final step because he did not want to risk Levi's suffering a jump-related injury. Even a sprain would scratch him from the mission.

Levi shuddered. Jumping out of a perfectly sound airplane in broad daylight had sounded bad enough. Jumping out of one into pitch darkness, without any practice, seemed utterly insane.

His teachers hadn't been the least bit sympathetic. "You need to know this stuff cold, Mr. Levi," one hard-bitten sergeant had said, " 'cause a nuclear expert who breaks his neck on landing ain't much of an expert and he ain't much use." Well, that was true enough, he thought wryly. At least the Americans wanted him alive long enough to identify the South African nuclear weapons and to prepare them for the airlift out.

He spotted O'Connell striding purposefully toward the airfield's small terminal and control tower, keeping pace with the taller, older man beside him. Seemingly agreeing with something the other man said, the American lieutenant colonel nodded once. His face was strangely blank, as though all his emotions and feelings were being held rigidly in check. Levi suddenly realized that the taller Ranger officer must be this Colonel Geller he'd heard so much about—the 75th Ranger's fire-eating regimental commander.

He shook his head, understanding O'Connell's apparent constraint. Although the lieutenant colonel had spent the past week preparing his battalion for this raid, now that they were finally on the way, Geller had shown up with every apparent intention of exercising de facto command.

Levi frowned. The U.S. Army operated under a strange concept of command and control. In Israel, the conduct of an important operation was always left in the hands of the unit commander. It was the best guarantee of victory and efficiency amid the bloody confusion of combat. But it seemed as though some in the American military treated combat command as nothing more than a routine way station on a career path—as a simple résumé box to be inked in or crossed off and promptly forgotten.

He shrugged halfheartedly. Israel's armed forces undoubtedly had their own weak spots. Of course, those weren't quite so likely to get him killed in the next few days. With that cheery thought to keep him company, Levi hoisted his own small bag and walked toward the hangar that would be his home for the next day or so. He had a feeling that sleep would be difficult to come by—despite his mind-numbing fatigue.

A deeply tanned man in a lightweight tropical suit came out of the terminal building and moved to intercept him.

"Professor Levi?"

Levi stopped. The other man's accented English identified him. He answered in Hebrew. "That's right."

"My name's Eisner. I'm attached to the Washington, D.C., embassy. I have several routine messages from home to pass on to you. Can we speak privately?"

Routine messages? Levi didn't buy that for a moment. He'd seen too many other hard-eyed men like this one to be fooled. Diplomats were never in such good shape or so obviously humorless. But what did the Mossad, Israel's foreign-intelligence service, want with him? Or perhaps more importantly, what did his country's spy service expect him to do?

He had a feeling he wasn't going to like whatever it was.

ABOARD USS *CARL VINSON,* IN THE INDIAN OCEAN

The normal buzz of good-natured banter and friendly insult died away completely as Rear Adm. Andrew Douglas Stewart entered the ready room. Even aviators knew better than to ignore an admiral.

Stewart waved them back into their chairs and took his place behind a podium. He scanned the rows of suddenly tense young faces before him. These men might pretend to be carefree and untroubled, but every one of them had to have a pretty good idea of what was in the wind.

The clues were all around. First, there was the fact that the *Vinson* and her escorts had been loitering a bare two hundred miles off the South African coast for nearly two weeks. Second, the carrier's air group had been run through a series of increasingly intense and realistic exercises over that same period. And finally, all communications with the outside world were being closely monitored and controlled. It all added up to a single inescapable conclusion: Washington was on the edge of committing the *Vinson*'s aircraft to a real shooting war. A war where one side had already dropped an atomic bomb without any show of regret or remorse.

"Good afternoon, gentlemen." Stewart focused his attention on the pilots and naval flight officers in the room with him, knowing that video cameras would relay his words and image to the other squadron ready rooms and briefing rooms scattered throughout the *Vinson*'s vast hull and superstructure. "I'll make this short and sweet. Your respective squadron commanders and ops officers will go over the details after I'm done."

He nodded to his chief of staff. The lights began dimming. "I'm here to brief you on our part in a strike against South Africa's nuclear capability."

The room filled with a buzz of conversation, and a waiting aide laid a map overlay on the ready room's overhead projector. The map showed a series of red lines converging on Pretoria. Most emanated from a tiny dot marking the *Vinson*'s position, but one line slanted in across all of southern Africa—coming east out of the Atlantic. A tag identified it as the flight path of Air Force transports carrying the two Ranger battalions and elements of the 160th Aviation Regiment.

Brave Fortune was just thirty-four hours away.

HEADQUARTERS BUNKER, 61ST TRANSVAAL RIFLES, PELINDABA RESEARCH COMPLEX

Col. Frans Peiper stood still for a moment, watching the rise and fall of hundreds of picks and shovels as his troops worked frantically to complete their fortifications.

Since its designation as a nuclear research center and weapons storage site, Pelindaba had been surrounded by a barbed wire fence and military guardposts. Now it more closely resembled a fortress. Thirty meters inside the barbed wire, slit trenches now circled the entire compound, connecting an array of twenty-two concrete bunkers. Each bunker was large enough to shelter a reinforced rifle squad and sturdy enough to withstand heavy mortar fire. Minefields were being laid on the slopes outside the wire to channel attacking ANC guerrillas or Cuban commandos and armored vehicles into previously selected kill zones for the battalion's recoilless rifles, machine guns, and mortars. Deadly looking armored fighting vehicles prowled outside the wire—Rookiats of the Pretoria Light Horse hunting for enemy infiltrators.

At the eastern end of the compound, more barbed wire surrounded a group of five camouflaged mounds—the nuclear weapons storage bunkers that were his main responsibility. A separate slit trench ran from north to south just west of the weapons bunkers, further isolating the storage site from the rest of the Pelindaba complex. Beyond the trench, firing pits for 120mm and 60mm mortars dotted a patch of open ground stretching west to the rock gardens, shade trees, and buildings of the research center. Shoulder-high earth and sandbag walls provided some protection for the four Cactus SAM vehicles parked in and among the rock gardens.

"Our chemical protection gear is arriving, Colonel."

Peiper turned. His adjutant, Captain van Daalen, pointed to a line of five-ton trucks pulling up to the peacetime battalion-headquarters building.

"Excellent, Captain. Have each company draw its gear as it comes off work detail. And inform all commanders that I plan to hold our first gas-attack drill early this evening."

Van Daalen saluted and hurried away.

Peiper watched him go, knowing that the order wouldn't be popular with his men. The gas mask, hood, gauntlets, suit, and boots needed to fully protect a man against attack by poison gas or nerve agents were cumbersome, clumsy, and confining. Even worse, they trapped body heat and quickly became unbearably hot even in cool weather—let alone on a warm spring evening.

He scowled. His soldiers' complaints and comfort were completely unimportant. In fact, only one thing mattered: fending off the inevitable Cuban attempt to destroy or seize South Africa's nuclear stockpile.

Peiper turned on his heel and headed back toward the cool, dimly lit recesses of his command bunker. The Cuban attack could come at almost any time; certainly within days, possibly even within hours. But Castro's minions were bound to unleash a choking, burning deluge of chemical weapons first—weapons against which his troops were now protected.

The Afrikaner colonel smiled wolfishly. When the communists and their kaffir allies came charging in, expecting to find most of his men dead or disabled, they'd be met instead by a hail of small-arms and artillery fire. It would be an easy victory.

He trotted down the steps into his bunker with that cold, cruel smile still on his lips.

NOVEMBER 28—WIDEAWAKE AIRFIELD, ASCENSION ISLAND

Nearly one thousand men crowded around the low raised platform. Green camouflage paint robbed each man's face of its individuality, but did nothing to cloak the air of grim expectation permeating the entire hangar. Each Ranger stood waiting in absolute silence, together with his friends and comrades and yet strangely alone.

Up on the platform, Lt. Col. Robert O'Connell caught a glimpse of movement near the hangar doors. Geller was coming back from the communications center. O'Connell straightened up, feeling the first trickle of cold sweat under his arms. This was it. "Ah-tench-hut!"

The Rangers snapped to rigid attention as their colonel threaded his way through them and bounded onto the platform.

Geller nodded once to O'Connell, his eyes alight with excitement. Then he turned to face the waiting battalions. "At ease!"

A tiny, almost invisible, wave of relaxation rippled through the hangar.

The colonel pulled a single sheet of thin paper out of a pocket and held it up so that every man could see it. "This signal came in from Washington five minutes ago. It's official, gentlemen! Brave Fortune has a green light! We go in tonight. Exactly as planned."

O'Connell felt some of his nervous tension evaporate as the mission became a reality. No one had really been sure that Washington had the guts to risk trying such a stunt, and in many ways, that uncertainty had been the worst part of the wait. From now on each man's fate was out of the hands of unknown politicians and generals and in the hands of God, impersonal chance, and the team's fighting skills. Somehow that was easier to take.

Geller lowered the message form and studied the sea of camouflaged faces in front of him. "Before Lieutenant Colonel O'Connell goes over the ops order with you, I just want to say one thing. And that's that I'm damned proud to be fighting with you boys. Damned proud. Rangers, I salute you." He brought his hand up in a sweeping, almost exuberant, salute and held it as every soldier in the vast hangar returned the gesture.

The colonel dropped his hand, spun on his heel, and looked at O'Connell. "They're all yours, Colonel."

Yeah, right. At least until we hit the ground, O'Connell thought. He moved to the edge of the platform. Two noncoms wrestled a large map into position behind him. Circles, arrows, and dotted lines marked drop zones, objectives, and approach routes. He half-turned toward the map, feeling the pressure of nearly one thousand pairs of eyes watching his every move.

"At oh one hundred hours tomorrow, the First and Second battalions, plus elements of the regimental HQ, will make airborne assaults on the following targets inside the Republic of South Africa. . . ."

O'Connell was sure that all of his men already knew the entire attack plan both forward and backward. Some could probably repeat it back word for word. But it wouldn't hurt to go over the highlights one last time. Airborne landings in darkness and against opposition were full of sound and fury—glowing tracers in the night, blinding explosions, and dead men entangled in still-falling parachutes. In the midst of such brain-numbing confusion, it was vital that every Ranger know exactly what he was supposed to be doing at any given moment. And since there were bound to be casualties, he should know exactly what his comrades were supposed to be doing as well.

In what seemed like no time at all, he was finished. O'Connell let the last map page fall back and turned to face the waiting battalions. ''This is it, gentlemen. We've worked hard together preparing for this op. But now you're as ready as we can make you.''

He lowered his voice, speaking quietly now so that every man had to strain to hear him. ''This mission won't be easy. And it sure as hell won't be a bloodless cakewalk. But remember that this mission *is* strategic. And when we're done, these Afrikaner bastards are gonna know exactly who's jumped down their throats and kicked their guts out.''

He swept the black beret off his head and lifted it high in one hand. His voice grew louder, more confident. ''And who's that gonna be?''

The answer came flooding back, shouted from a thousand throats. *''Rangers! Rangers! Rangers!''*

O'Connell grinned. He let them yell awhile longer and then held up a hand for silence. ''First and Second battalions of the Seventy-fifth, board your aircraft.''

In seconds, companies and platoons were forming up into march columns—each heading for one of the ten C-141 jet transports waiting outside on the tarmac.

Brave Fortune was under way.

CHAPTER 30

Brave Fortune

NOVEMBER 28—ABOARD SIERRA ONE ZERO, OVER THE SOUTH ATLANTIC OFF THE COAST OF ANGOLA

The MC-141 Starlifter known as Sierra One Zero flew east toward Africa at thirty thousand feet, surrounded by a man-made constellation of winking navigation lights. Those ahead and slightly higher belonged to four huge SAC KC-10 tankers. The lights behind and to either side belonged to Sierra One Zero's four companions.

"All right, disconnect." Sierra One Zero's pilot, a full Air Force colonel, glanced across the darkened cockpit at his copilot.

"Roger," the aerial tanker's boom operator responded over the intercom. "Pumping stopped. Good luck and give them hell." They were operating under conditions of strict radio silence, but the boom connecting them to the KC-10 also allowed them to talk to the tanker directly. "Released."

The refueling boom snapped up and away from the Starlifter in a white puff of jet-fuel vapor.

The colonel eased back very gently on the throttles, watching carefully as the huge tanker pulled farther out in front. Satisfied that he now had enough room to avoid a midair collision, the colonel banked the MC-141 gently to the right and slid back into place at the head of his formation.

Sierra One Zero's pilot watched the tankers slide past his side window and disappear from sight. Then he pushed his throttles forward again, listening as the roar from Starlifter's four engines grew louder. An indicator showed the plane picking up airspeed, accelerating from the 330 knots used for in-flight refueling toward its normal cruising speed of 550 knots.

The five jet transports carrying the 1/75th now flew in a tight arrowhead, with one Special Operations MC-141 out in front and four standard Starlifters behind and to either side. The 2/75th's C-141s, another MC-141, and more tankers were several miles behind the formation. The MC-141s, designed for long-range penetration missions deep in enemy territory, carried just about every piece of special electronic gear known to man—terrain-following radar for low-level flight, infrared TV, and jamming systems to boggle hostile radars if they were detected.

With luck, they'd be able to lead the less capable C-141s all the way in to Pretoria.

The SAC tankers altered course and began pulling away fast, heading back for their own refueling stop at Ascension Island nearly sixteen hundred miles to the west.

He toggled his intercom switch. "Bob?"

"Yes, Colonel?" Lt. Col. Robert O'Connell answered immediately from his position in the crowded troop compartment below and behind the cockpit. His regimental commander, Colonel Geller, was in Sierra One Three—flying in a separate aircraft to make sure that no single crash or mishap would leave the 1/75th leaderless.

"We're gassed up and heading in. Estimate we'll cross the coast in twenty minutes."

The Air Force colonel could hear the tension in the Ranger battalion commander's voice. "Thanks, I'll pass the word."

The five C-141s continued east, flying high above an unbroken layer of cloud and beneath a sky full of bright, unwinking stars.

ABOARD USS *CARL VINSON*, IN THE INDIAN OCEAN

Rear Adm. Andrew Douglas Stewart stood watching from the *Vinson*'s bridge as her four steam catapults threw plane after plane into the night air. F-14 Tomcats, A-6 Intruders, F/A-18 Hornets, and EA-6B Prowlers screamed aloft, tailpipes glowing orange in the darkness. Others, engines idling, waited their turn to taxi onto the catapults. Navigation lights blinked in the sky, aircraft orbiting slowly around the task force while waiting for the whole strike to form up.

"Admiral?"

Stewart turned toward a waiting lieutenant. "Yes."

"Washington's on the secure phone, sir."

Stewart brushed past him into the darkened enclosed bridge. Enlisted men and officers alike bent over their work, with only the nearest ones acknowledging his presence with deferential nods. He moved immediately to the red secure phone and took the handset from his portly communications officer. "Stewart here."

There was no apparent delay, even though a computer scrambled his words, converted them into a radio signal, beamed them twenty-four thousand miles straight up to a satellite in geosynchronous orbit, and then down to the Pentagon. Then the process was repeated in reverse and Gen. Walter Hickman's gentle Oklahoma twang sounded in his ear. The chairman of the Joint Chiefs was brief and to the point. "Sierra Force has reached Point Yankee. Execute Phase Two."

Stewart was equally brief. "Acknowledged. Out." He replaced the red phone.

His imagination reached out toward Sierra Force—the C-141s carrying the Rangers and their attached Army Aviation units. Point Yankee was a computer-designated spot over the barren Kalahari Desert where the Air Force transports would begin a planned steep descent out of the now-normal African-airspace traffic pattern of Soviet cargo planes and civilian airliners. At less than five hundred feet, well below the coverage of South Africa's remaining ground radar stations, the C-141s would turn sharply southeast—toward Pretoria and the Pelindaba Nuclear Research Complex.

The admiral picked up a plain black ship's phone. "CAG? This is Stewart. Execute Pindown." Through the receiver, he heard the *Vinson*'s air wing commander relaying his order to the strike leader already orbiting overhead.

They were committed.

NOVEMBER 29—ABOARD SIERRA ONE ZERO, NORTH OF RUSTENBURG, SOUTH AFRICA

Sierra One Zero's pilot kept his eyes moving in a regular pattern—shifting from his terrain-following radar display to the flight instruments to the low hills and flat grasslands flashing past the MC-141's cockpit and then back again. His hands were poised on the controls, ready to take instant evasive action should it prove necessary. Sweat trickled down his forehead despite the cockpit air-conditioning. Flying the large, four-engined transport barely three hundred feet off the ground required intense concentration. A second's inattention could all too easily prove fatal for the more than one hundred men aboard.

"Point Zulu." His copilot looked up from the computer-generated map.

"Roger." The colonel reduced his throttle settings, hoping the four planes following close behind were paying careful heed to their spacing. "Inform our passengers."

Sierra One Zero's copilot pushed a well-worn button.

A red light came on over the Starlifter's large rear door. Lt. Col. Robert O'Connell was already rising from his seat as the plane's jumpmaster bellowed, "Six minutes! Outboard personnel hook up!"

Rangers seated along the C-141's fuselage clambered to their feet.

"Inboard personnel stand up!"

The troops seated in two rows facing outward scrambled upright.

"Hook up!"

The Rangers hooked their parachute harnesses on to the static lines running the length of the MC-141's troop compartment. A very pale Prof. Esher Levi imitated them.

Outside the compartment, the droning roar of the Starlifter's engines began fading as the big plane slowed to jump speed.

HEADQUARTERS, NORTHERN AIR DEFENSE SECTOR, DEVON, EAST OF JOHANNESBURG

The South African Air Force flight sergeant yawned once, and then again, wishing he could slip outside for a quick cup of coffee and a smoke. Night radar-watch duty was invariably boring. Lately, neither the Cubans nor his own air force had shown much willingness to risk precious aircraft in combat operations after dark. Both sides had already lost too many planes in raids against strategic and tactical targets.

He leaned forward to study the glowing screen again, his face green in the light emanating from the radar repeater. He didn't see anything out of the ordinary. Just blips at the far edge of his coverage showing a steady stream of Soviet air transports and cargo planes ferrying men and matériel into Zimbabwe and Mozambique. A smaller number of blips closer in represented South African transports moving units out of Namibia.

The sergeant shrugged, deciding that he was lucky to be able to see that much. South Africa's radar net, already inadequate before the war, was in even worse shape now. Mafikeng, the site of one of its three permanent stations, had already been overrun by the Cubans. And Ellisras, the northernmost station, was expected to fall any day now.

A large blip appeared suddenly on his screen—close to the center, near Pretoria—and then vanished as quickly as it had appeared. What the devil? Was that a scheduled flight he'd forgotten about, or was his equipment acting up? The sergeant fumbled through his logbook while keeping one eye on the glowing radar screen.

More blips appeared—coming from the southeast this time and moving fast. He stared hard, trying frantically to get an accurate count. Five. Ten. More than twenty planes racing in from out of nowhere! He spun round in his chair, his eyes wide in alarm. "Lieutenant!"

PROWLER LEAD, SOUTHEAST OF JOHANNESBURG

Ten miles behind the A-6 and F/A-18 attack squadrons, the EA-6B Prowler electronic warfare aircraft bounced and shook as it ploughed through choppy air. Rolling ridges and valleys emerged out of the darkness ahead and then blurred past and aft. Flying low at five hundred knots left little time for sightseeing.

One of the two officers seated side by side behind the pilot and navigator listened to a series of tones sounding in his earphones and watched as a signal intensity indicator climbed higher. He spoke into the intercom. "SA radar's got us, Curt."

"Right." The pilot broke radio silence on the strike frequency. "Tiger flights, this is Prowler Lead. They know we're here. We're lighting off."

He clicked back to the intercom. "Okay, guys, let's do it. Radiate and blind those bastards."

The two backseaters flipped a series of switches, activating the Prowler's ALQ-99 jamming system. Current started flowing from windmill turbogenerators on the three jamming pods slung beneath the EA-6B's fuselage. In seconds, the Prowler was punching kilowatts of power into the same frequencies used by South Africa's air-search radars.

NORTHERN AIR DEFENSE HQ

"Shit!" The blips on the flight sergeant's radarscope vanished in a coruscating swirl of bright green blotches and a solid strobe line. He switched frequencies frantically and ineffectively. The jamming followed him across the wavelengths—effortlessly matching every shift.

After several failed tries, he stopped frequency-hopping and tried turning down the radar's gain instead. It worked—after a fashion. By trading range for visibility, he was able to break through the jamming . . . and see nothing.

The flight sergeant swore again. The bogies were outside his radar's reduced range. He knew there were enemy aircraft over South Africa, but he couldn't tell how many, where they were, or most important of all, where they were headed.

The Air Force lieutenant watching over his shoulder turned pale and grabbed a red phone by the radar console. "Put me through to Number Three Squadron!"

ABOARD SIERRA ONE ZERO, OVER PELINDABA

Lt. Col. Robert O'Connell took a deep breath, held it for a second, and let it out—trying to shake off a case of last-minute jitters. Literally last minute, too, he thought. They couldn't be much more flying time than that from the drop zone.

The drop zone was one of his concerns. Their need for total surprise had ruled out the use of pathfinders to mark the DZ. As a result, the aircraft carrying the Rangers were relying entirely on navigational data supplied by Navstar GPS—Global Positioning System—satellites. The GPS program managers claimed their system was accurate to within a few feet, and O'Connell hoped like hell that they were right.

He staggered slightly and braced himself as the MC-141 began a steep climb, popping up to five hundred feet for its run over the Pelindaba complex. Any second now

Without stopping to think much about it, O'Connell found

himself muttering a prayer from his childhood. "Hail Mary, full of grace, the Lord is with thee . . ."

As the MC-141 leveled out, its two side doors whined open and twin blast shields deployed to provide pockets of calm air outside the doors. Cold night air and howling engine noise swept through the crowded troop compartment. O'Connell watched as the plane's jumpmaster leaned out through the open door, checked the shield and jump step, and made sure they were approaching the drop zone.

The jump light over the open cargo door flickered and went green. "Go! Go! GO!"

Conscious thought faded and thousands of hours of training and preparation took over. Rank by rank and row by row, the Rangers shuffled rapidly to the open side doors and threw themselves into empty air.

Five C-141s swept low over Pelindaba spewing out hundreds of Rangers and their equipment.

COMMAND BUNKER, 61ST TRANSVAAL RIFLES, PELINDABA

Col. Frans Peiper spilled his mug of hot coffee onto the bunker's concrete floor as his phone buzzed. He grabbed the phone on its second buzz. "Pelindaba CO."

He didn't recognize the panic-stricken voice on the other end. "Air raid warning! This is an air raid warning!"

"What?"

The roar of large aircraft passing directly overhead drowned out any reply.

Peiper dropped the phone and ran to one of the bunker's firing slits, trying vainly to catch a glimpse of these attacking planes. Nothing. Nothing. There! Something huge and black—more a shadow than a discernible shape—flashed past and disappeared beyond the eastern end of the compound. They *were* under attack!

He whirled and slammed a shaking hand down on the alert button.

Sirens screamed across the complex in a rising and falling wail designed to wake the dead, or in this case, the two-thirds of Pelindaba's garrison who were off duty and fast asleep in their barracks. At the same time, arc lights around the perimeter began winking out to deny incoming enemy bombers easy aiming points.

1/75TH RANGERS

More than five hundred men of the 1/75th's three companies and its headquarters came drifting down out of the night sky into the Pelindaba atomic research and weapons storage complex. Some never made it farther than that.

Three Rangers, the first men out of the lead plane, landed too far to the west—outside the barbed wire and inside a minefield. One hit the ground and rolled right onto the pressure plate of an antipersonnel mine. A white-orange blast tore him in half and spewed fragments that scythed the other two paratroopers to the ground, bleeding and unconscious.

More Americans came down hard in the middle of Pelindaba's ornamental rock gardens—breaking legs or arms or fracturing collarbones. Near the power substation, a Charlie Company sergeant slammed face first into a steel pylon at more than twenty miles an hour. The impact broke his neck and left his corpse draped across a steel girder forty feet off the ground.

Two groups of Rangers had the worst luck of all.

Six men landed in a tangle of billowing parachutes and loose gear on open ground—less than thirty feet away from mortar pits occupied by South African troops who'd been on duty. The Americans were still struggling out of their chutes when a fusillade of automatic weapons fire mowed them down.

Four others came down right in the middle of a South African infantry squad patrolling inside the compound. Flames stabbed through the darkness as R4 rifles and M16s were fired at point-blank range. Seconds later, all four Americans and three of the South Africans lay dead. One of the

Rangers wore the silver eagle insignia of a full colonel over his chest pocket. Paul Geller, commander of the 75th Ranger Regiment, had made his last combat jump.

HEADQUARTERS COMPANY, 1/75TH RANGERS

Lt. Col. Robert O'Connell hit the ground with his legs bent and rolled—his hands already fumbling with the release catch for his parachute harness. A light wind tugged at his chute, threatening to drag him along through the open grassland between the research center and the weapons storage bunkers. Done! The catch snapped open and he shrugged out of his harness. He got to his knees to get a better view of what was going on.

Most of the compound was in darkness, but enough light remained to make out the pitch-black outlines of a slit trench only twenty yards away. Good. The trench was ready-made cover if he could get to it without being shot. It also ran from north to south, separating the nuclear weapons storage area from the rest of Pelindaba.

More men were coming down all around him—slamming into the ground with teeth-rattling force. Automatic weapons fire rattled from somewhere close by, kicking up a spray of bullet-torn grass and dirt. Two Rangers who'd just scrambled out of their chutes screamed and folded in on themselves.

O'Connell threw himself flat. Too many of the damned South Africans were wide awake and ready for a fight. His troops needed protection—any kind of protection—or they were going to be slaughtered while still landing.

He yanked a smoke grenade off his combat webbing, pulled the pin, and lobbed it toward a half-seen bunker. Others around him were doing the same thing. Wargames played during the planning for Brave Fortune had shown that the immediate use of smoke might save a few lives. That was why every Ranger in the assault force had been briefed to throw a smoke grenade as soon as possible after landing. The more smoke in the air, the more confusion. And the more confusion, the better.

White tendrils of smoke started to swirl and billow, spreading in the wind to form a light haze that grew thicker as more and more grenades were thrown. South African machine guns and assault rifles chattered from bunkers around the perimeter, stabbing through the haphazard smoke screen. More Rangers were hit and thrown back—dead or badly wounded.

"Goddamnit!" O'Connell unslung his M16 and started belly-crawling toward the South African slit trench. The soldiers who'd landed near him followed, some dragging injured comrades. From all appearances, his battalion was being cut to pieces before it could even get organized.

COMMAND BUNKER, 61ST TRANSVAAL RIFLES

Peiper stared through the narrow firing slits of his headquarters bunker, trying to piece together some idea of just what the devil was going on. If this was an air raid, where were the bombs? And if it wasn't, what were his troops firing at?

Then he saw the first wisps of white and gray smoke rising from the open ground beyond Pelindaba's science labs and uranium enrichment plant.

Peiper expected to be attacked by the Cubans. He expected the Cubans to use chemical weapons as part of that attack. And now he saw what could only be the first nightmarish tendrils of nerve gas drifting toward his bunker.

He staggered back and grabbed a young lieutenant who still looked half-asleep. "Sound the gas alarm!"

"Colonel?"

Peiper shoved the officer aside and ran for the alarm control panel himself. He chopped down at the right button and then whirled to find his own chemical gear.

The wailing rise and fall of Pelindaba's air raid sirens faded—replaced instantly by the high-pitched warbling of its poison gas alert.

In wooden barracks buildings all around the compound, several hundred newly wakened South African soldiers who'd been grabbing rifles and helmets dropped them and started fumbling for gas masks, gauntlets, and chemical protection suits instead. Two or three extra minutes would pass before they could hope to join the bloody battle now raging throughout the camp perimeter.

Col. Frans Peiper had just given the U.S. Rangers the time they so desperately needed.

HEADQUARTERS COMPANY, 1/75TH RANGERS

O'Connell crouched just below the lip of the slit trench and stared at the wide-eyed, panting men clustered around him. More of his headquarters troops and officers had survived the landing then he'd first thought possible. Even Professor Levi had come through unwounded, although the Israeli scientist now sat huddled on the trench floor, nursing an ankle he'd sprained on impact. "Weisman!"

His radioman pushed through the crowd. O'Connell took the handset he offered. "Sierra One Zero, this is Rover One One. Atlas. I say again, Atlas." The MC-141 still orbiting somewhere overhead would relay the news that the Rangers were on the ground and attacking. And men waiting in the Pentagon and the White House could push new pins in their maps.

He passed the handset back and stood listening to the noise of the battle. M16s, M60 machine guns, and squad automatic weapons were being fired in greater numbers, their distinctive crackle and chatter beginning to blend with the heavier sounds made by South African rifles and machine guns. The Rangers were starting to fight back.

RADAR CONTROL VEHICLE, CACTUS SAM BATTERY, PELINDABA

Panicked by the gas alert siren, the lone corporal manning the Cactus battery's jammed and useless fire-control radar tore his headphones off and scrambled out of his chair. He'd left his chemical suit back in the barracks. He moved toward the vehicle's rear hatch.

It clanged open before he got there, and the South African stared in surprise at the figure outlined against the night sky. Odd, that didn't look like any uniform he'd ever seen before. . . .

Three M16 rounds threw the radar operator back against his equipment in a spray of blood and torn flesh.

Outside the hatch, the Ranger sergeant lowered his rifle and pulled the pin on a fragmentation grenade. He tossed the grenade in on top of the dead man and then slammed the hatch shut.

Whummp! The Cactus battery command vehicle rocked slightly and then sat silent—its delicate electronics smashed by bullets and grenade fragments. The radar dish on top stopped spinning.

Bent low, the sergeant sprinted across a stretch of open lawn near Pelindaba's main science lab. Rifle rounds whip-cracked over his head—fired at long range from a bunker on the compound's northern perimeter. He dove for cover behind a row of young saplings planted as shade trees. Leaves clipped off by stray bullets drifted down on the five men waiting there for him. Two carried a Carl Gustav M3 84mm recoilless rifle.

"You get 'em?"

"Yep." The Carl Gustav gunner patted his weapon affectionately. "Hammered 'em real good."

The sergeant lifted his head an inch or two, risking a quick look. The three Cactus SAM launch vehicles were cloaked in flame and smoke. As he watched, one of the burning launchers blew up in a blinding flash of orange light. Must've been a missile cook-off, the sergeant thought.

Time to report in. He squirmed around and found his radioman. "Rover One One, this is Bravo Two Four. Diablo One, Two, Three, and Diablo Dish are history."

Pelindaba's air defenses were down.

B COMPANY BARRACKS, 61ST TRANSVAAL RIFLES

The red, flickering glow of burning buildings and vehicles dimly lit a scene of mass confusion inside the barracks building. Half-dressed South African soldiers scrambled frantically to put on protective gear they'd only been issued the day before. Others, faster or better trained, were already suited up and trying to ready their weapons with clumsy, gloved hands. Lieutenants and sergeants roved through the crowd, trying to sort their squads and platoons into some sort of order before leading them outside and into battle.

Captain van Daalen, the battalion adjutant, felt more like a spaceman than a soldier in his chemical protection suit. The suit itself was hot and difficult to move in, and the gas mask limited both his vision and his hearing. He scowled. Going into combat while practically deaf and blind didn't strike him as a particularly sane act, but the thought of nerve gas made him check the seals.

He crouched by an open window, trying to spot a reasonably safe route to the battalion command bunker. He wasn't having much luck. The bunker lay more than two hundred and fifty meters away across a flat, open field. Perhaps it would be more sensible to carry out his duties from the barracks, van Daalen thought. After all, there wasn't much point in dying in a quixotic and suicidal dash through machine-gun fire.

Movement outside caught his eye. Soldiers, silhouetted against a burning SAM launcher, were fanning out into a long line less than fifty meters away. As each man reached his place, he dropped prone facing the barracks.

Van Daalen rose. That was damned strange. It was almost as though those troops were planning to attack . . .

"Let the bastards have it! Fire! Fire! Fire!" The shout from outside echoed above the staccato rattle of gunfire and the crash of explosions all across Pelindaba.

Van Daalen froze in horror. That shout had been in English, not Afrikaans. He started to turn . . .

Half a dozen rockets lanced out from the line of enemy troops, tore through thin wood walls, and exploded inside—spraying fragments and wood splinters through the tightly packed South African soldiers. Machine-gun and M16 fire scythed into the building right behind the rockets, punching through from end to end. Dead or wounded men were thrown everywhere—tossed across bloodstained bunks or knocked into writhing heaps on top of one another.

Capt. Edouard van Daalen clutched at the jagged edges of what had once been a window frame in a vain effort to stay standing. Then his knees buckled and he slid slowly to the floor, pawing feebly at the row of ragged, wet holes torn in his chemical protection suit.

The Americans outside kept shooting.

HEADQUARTERS COMPANY, 1/75TH RANGERS

Lt. Col. Robert O'Connell listened with growing satisfaction to the reports flooding in from units around the compound. The enemy's Cactus SAM battery permanently out of action. Barracks after barracks reported on fire or collapsed by salvos of light antitank rockets, HE rounds from recoilless rifles, and concentrated small-arms fire. A 120mm mortar position overrun at bayonet point by survivors from Bravo Company's 1st Platoon. Brave Fortune was finally starting to go according to plan.

But the battalion's casualties were heavy and growing heavier with every passing minute. Colonel Geller hadn't been seen since the jump. Three of eight platoon leaders were down. He didn't even want to guess how many noncoms and other Rangers lay dead in Pelindaba's barbed wire, rock gardens, buildings, and open fields.

He ducked as a grenade burst close by, showering dirt and fragments across the open lip of the slit trench. A Ranger beside him screamed and fell back in a tangle of thrashing arms and legs. Blood spattered across O'Connell's face. Other soldiers were already up and shooting back—pumping rounds into the flame-lit darkness.

"Medic!"

Rangers dragged the wounded man farther down the trench to where the 1/75th's senior medic had set up an impromptu aid station for the headquarters company. It was already overflowing with badly wounded men.

O'Connell spat out the salty, coppery taste in his mouth and grabbed the handset from his radioman. They had to move. It was time to go after the first of Brave Fortune's two key objectives. "Bravo Two One and Charlie Two One, this is Rover One One. Execute Thor and Erector Set."

2ND PLATOON, BRAVO COMPANY, 1/75TH RANGERS, NEAR THE POWER PLANT

Pelindaba's small coal-fired steam plant had been built to a simple design that stressed function over pleasing form. Turning coal-heated boiler water to high-pressure steam—steam used to drive turbines generating electricity. In turn, that electricity powered the uranium enrichment plant, science labs, and every other building inside the compound's barbed wire fence.

One hundred yards south of the power plant, two Rangers lay flat in an open field. Their sergeant's bullet-riddled body sprawled bloody and unmoving behind them.

Cpl. Mitch Wojcik squinted through the recoilless rifle's night-vision sight. Piping of various thicknesses girded the outside of the plant, carrying feedwater into its boiler, steam out to propel its spinning turbines, and steam cooling and condensing into water back again to the boiler. One tall stack carried away the smoke produced by burning high-sulfur soft coal.

Wojcik swung the Carl Gustav slightly to the right, seeking his target. Bingo. Hours spent studying every available photo of the power plant paid off. "Load HEAT."

His loader slid a seven-pound high-explosive antitank round into the breech and slapped him lightly on the helmet. "Up!"

Wojcik squeezed the trigger.

Whanng! The HEAT round slammed into a jumble of piping and exploded—peeling open thick, insulated pipes as though they were tinfoil. One was the conduit carrying feedwater into the boiler. Superheated water and steam sprayed out through the torn edges of a rapidly growing hole. With their lifeblood pouring out into the atmosphere, the power plant's boiler and turbines ran dry in seconds.

Pelindaba's primary electric power source went dead.

2ND PLATOON, CHARLIE COMPANY, 1/75TH RANGERS, NEAR THE PELINDABA POWER SUBSTATION

Steel transmission towers spaced three hundred meters apart carried thirteen-kilovolt power lines connecting the Northern Transvaal–Pretoria electric grid to Pelindaba. One of the thirty-meter-high towers stood just across a road running between the nuclear weapons storage bunkers and the rest of the complex. Rows of canvas-sided trucks and civilian automobiles filled a parking lot on the other side of the road. Several were already ablaze—set on fire by tracer rounds buzzing through the complex.

"Christ!" Second Lieutenant Frank Miller threw himself flat as another burst of machine-gun fire cracked over his head and slammed into the steel tower. Sparks cascaded down onto his Kevlar helmet. He looked back over his shoulder toward what was left of his first rifle squad—five men, one carrying a squad automatic weapon. The rest were dead or dying, strewn across the drop zone and the road. "Hernandez, gimme some covering fire, goddamnit!"

The squad automatic weapon cut loose again, spewing steel-jacketed rounds into the darkness. M16-armed Rangers joined in, trying to pin down the South African infantry occupying a bunker one hundred meters away. The odds of actually hitting any of the enemy troops were vanishingly small, but enough bullets spanging off the bunker's concrete walls might make the South Africans flinch away from their firing slits. One of the Rangers threw another smoke grenade upwind.

Miller got to his knees and looked at his handiwork. He needed one more demolition charge in just the right place. He held out his hand. "More C4, Steve."

No response.

The Ranger officer frowned and turned around. Corporal Lewis lay flat on his back, with his arms thrown out wide and a gaping hole where his forehead used to be. Miller swallowed hard and pried the last charge of plastic explosive out of the dead man's right hand.

Working fast now, almost in rhythm with the sound of the firing behind him, he molded the C4 onto one of the steel supports steadying the power pylon and stuck a line of detonator cord into it. Satisfied, he crawled away, unreeling detcord as he went.

A shallow drainage ditch running beside the road offered the only piece of real cover for more than a hundred meters. Miller calculated distances and angles and swore viciously. He was well inside the minimum safe distance for setting off the C4, but he didn't have time to crawl farther. He glanced over the edge of the drainage ditch. Flashes showed where Hernandez and his men were still firing toward the South African bunker. "First Squad! Break it off and reform here!"

Working quickly and carefully in the darkness, Miller attached a blasting cap, fuze, and fuze igniter to the end of the cord. As he worked, he tried to forget that det cord was itself an explosive. If he rushed the job, it would go off in his face.

Wire and electrical detonators were out of the question for this job. There was too big a chance of their picking up stray voltage from the transmission tower.

One by one, the Rangers stopped firing and raced over to the drainage ditch. One screamed suddenly and flopped forward, clutching at a leg that had been shot out from under him. Two others hauled him upright and half-pulled, half-carried him to the ditch.

Miller took one last look around. None of his men were still out in the open. He took a deep breath and pulled the pin out of the fuze igniter. Throwing it back toward the tower, he yelled, "Fire in the hole!"

The Rangers went prone, facedown in the dirt. Nobody fucked around when explosives were about to go off. Miller buried his face in the ditch.

Whummmp. Whummmp. Whummmp. Three separate blasts sliced through the supports holding up the transmission tower. Torn pieces of metal whirled away overhead.

Slowly at first and then faster, the tower leaned drunkenly far over to one side. Bolts and struts popped and then snapped off under immense and increasing weights and pressures. Abruptly, everything gave way at once. With a grating screech of tortured, twisting steel, the tower crashed to the ground. Downed power lines danced and sparked like ghostly flickering blue snakes.

Pelindaba's backup power source had been knocked out of commission.

PELINDABA CENTRIFUGE URANIUM-ENRICHMENT PLANT

Indifferent to the outside world, the South African technicians monitoring twenty thousand rapidly spinning centrifuges inside the enrichment plant's central cascade hall moved through their own universe of high-pitched, howling noise. None of them could hear the alert sirens and nobody in the garrison had yet taken the time to warn them of the attack. Then the lights went out.

Disaster struck instantly.

The scientists and engineers who'd designed the enrichment plant had taken precautions against an accidental loss of one or the other of Pelindaba's two independent electric power sources. An automatic transfer system stood ready to shunt electricity from either the coal-fired steam plant or the thirteen-kv transmission line connected to the Pretoria grid. Unfortunately, the South African design team had never imagined the deliberate and simultaneous destruction of both. Esher Levi had found Pelindaba's Achilles' heel.

Like any highly sophisticated and fragile machine, a uranium-enrichment centrifuge carries the seeds of its own destruction inside itself. To successfully and efficiently separate fissionable U-235 from nonfissionable U-238, each centrifuge's carbon-fiber rotor must spin at nearly thirty-five thousand rpm—producing peripheral velocities of up to five hundred meters per second.

Reaching that kind of rotation isn't easy. An enrichment centrifuge must be carefully balanced and precisely controlled as it spins faster and faster. Several critical speeds—speeds where the rotor will begin to vibrate dangerously—must be negotiated before it can reach its operating rpm. End dampers can help reduce these vibrations, but they become uncontrollable if the machine contains a significant amount of uranium hexafluoride gas as it cycles through any of these critical speeds.

All of Pelindaba's spinning centrifuges were full of uranium hexafluoride gas when the plant lost power.

In fractions of a second inertia and drag were at work. Rotors spun slower and slower. And as the machines decelerated, their carbon-fiber walls began to flex, wobbling about like wet noodles—distorted by the gas trapped inside.

Most of the twenty thousand uranium-enrichment centrifuges shattered simultaneously—hurling carbon fiber fragments spinning at more than a thousand miles an hour into the protective casings surrounding each machine. Each crashing centrifuge sounded exactly like a large-bore shotgun being fired just a few feet away.

Some of the casings ruptured, and other machines were thrown off their floor mountings, tearing violently away from the piping connecting each enrichment cascade. Immediately, yellow clouds of highly corrosive uranium hexafluoride gas began spewing out into the cascade hall—spraying from the mangled centrifuges themselves or from hundreds of ruptured feed, waste, and product pipes dangling overhead.

The gas started turning into a solid as soon as it hit room temperature and pressure, but not soon enough for some of the technicians unlucky enough to be trapped inside the darkened maze of broken piping. Several scientists and engineers ran screaming for the emergency exits clutching badly burned faces. Others died moaning, crushed beneath fallen equipment.

South Africa's uranium-enrichment plant had been wrecked beyond repair for years.

HEADQUARTERS, 2/75TH RANGERS, NEAR THE SWARTKOP MILITARY AIRFIELD CONTROL TOWER

Scarcely a kilometer south of Pelindaba, Swartkop Military Airfield was also under attack.

Bullets had smashed every window in the Swartkop control tower, and grenades had ignited several fires that were slowly taking hold inside—filling rooms and corridors with thick, choking smoke. Bodies littered floors and stairwells. Most of the dead wore the dark blue uniform of the South African Air Force.

Lt. Col. Mike Carrerra ran out the control tower door with one hand holding his helmet on and the other clutching his M16. His radioman and headquarters troops were right behind him.

Swartkop Airfield was a mess. Three turboprop transport planes and a fuel truck sat ablaze at the far end of the flight line. Closer in, wrecked cars and trucks dotted the base's parking lot and access roads. Parachutes fluttered in the breeze, abandoned wherever his men had landed. Collapsed mounds of torn, smoking sandbags showed where the Rangers had overrun South African positions in bitter, hand-to-hand combat.

Carrerra frowned. The Citizen Force company assigned to defend Swartkop had put up one hell of a fight. Bright white flashes and the harsh rattle of machine-gun fire near the airfield's huge, aluminum-sided hangars reminded him that his assessment was somewhat premature. South Africa's reservists were *still* putting up a hell of a fight.

"Colonel, Sierra One Zero's on the horn." His radioman ducked as a mortar round burst on the tarmac ahead of them.

He took the offered mike. "Go ahead, Sierra One Zero."

"Do you have that runway clear yet?" Carrerra recognized the clipped Northeastern accents of the colonel flying the lead MC-141. The ten American jet transports were circling in a tight pattern over Pretoria and its adjoining airfield, waiting for confirmation that it was safe to land.

"Negative, One Zero. Estimate five minutes before we can bring you in. Will advise. Out."

Karrumph. Another mortar round tore up dirt and gravel one hundred meters to the left. Carrerra took his thumb off the transmit button and motioned his senior sergeant over. "Ike, get on the platoon net and tell Sammy I want those goddamned mortar pits cleared pronto. We've got some birds up there anxious to get down on the ground. Got it?"

Carrerra led his headquarters troops across the tarmac toward the fighting raging near Swartkop's aircraft maintenance hangars. He'd brought five hundred men into this battle. He had a lot fewer left now, and the 2/75th needed every rifle it could bring to bear.

CACTUS SAM LAUNCHER, SWARTKOP MILITARY AIRFIELD

The last surviving SAM launcher assigned to defend Swartkop from air attack sat motionless on a low bluff overlooking the airfield. Brown, tan, and black camouflage netting softened the four-wheeled vehicle's rectangular, boxy shape—making it look more like a boulder or a clump of dried brush than a missile carrier.

Three men crowded the launcher's tiny red-lit control compartment.

"Well?"

The short, tight-lipped South African Air Force warrant officer manning the vehicle's target acquisition and firing board flicked one last switch and shook his head. "Nothing, Lieutenant. I'm not getting any data from Cactus Four. Either they're dead or the cable's been cut."

"Damn it!" His taller, younger commander pounded the darkened instrument panel in frustration. Then he took refuge in standard procedure. "Switch to optical tracking, Doorne."

"Yes, sir." Warrant Officer Doorne's nimble fingers danced across his control console. A TV monitor slaved to a camera mounted atop the vehicle lit up, showing a wide-angle view of the star-studded night sky outside.

Something moved ponderously across the sky, blotting out stars in its path. Doorne tapped a key and and focused his

TV camera on the airborne intruder. A big, four-engined jet was already turning away for another orbit over the city. "Target locked in, Lieutenant!"

His commander stared at the image on his screen. South Africa didn't have any planes that looked like that. The bogey must be an enemy. "Fire!"

The vehicle shuddered and rocked back as one of its missiles roared aloft on a pillar of glowing white flame, accelerating rapidly toward its maximum speed of Mach 2.3. The missile arced toward its target, guided by Warrant Officer Doorne's joystick.

Optical tracking permitted South Africa's Cactus SAM launchers to attack enemy aircraft even if their fire control radars were out of action or being jammed. The system worked very much like a child's video game. An onboard digital computer translated a human controller's joystick movements into flight commands and radioed them on to the missile. All he had to do was hold the cross hairs of his TV sight on the target and the computer would steer the SAM directly into its target. Best of all, optically guided missiles couldn't be jammed or spoofed away by flares and showers of chaff.

The system wasn't much use against fast-moving attack aircraft or fighters coming in head-on or crossing at a sharp angle. Human reflexes simply hadn't evolved to cope with closing speeds measured at nearly two thousand miles an hour. But the C-141 known as Sierra One Four was a huge, lumbering target flying in a wide circle at just four hundred knots.

Two hundred meters downslope, a Ranger fire team leader saw the missile launch and dropped the data cable he and his men had been following uphill. "Incoming!"

The American soldiers dove for the ground as the SAM flashed past not far overhead—trailing smoke and fire. Spitting out dirt, the fire team leader reared up onto his knees. "Get the bastards!"

One of his men nodded grimly and squeezed the trigger

on his LAW. The 66mm antitank rocket ripped through the South African SAM vehicle's camouflage netting and punched through its hull before exploding in an orange-red ball of fire and molten steel.

Warrant Officer Doorne and the others inside were killed instantly. But it was too late to save Sierra One Four.

SIERRA ONE FOUR, OVER PRETORIA

The South African missile detonated just fifty meters behind the C-141. Fragments lanced through the plane's port wing, puncturing fuel and hydraulic lines. Flames billowed out of its inner port engine, streamering away into the darkness.

"Jesus!" Sierra One Four's pilot fought to bring his crippled aircraft under control. Warning lights glowed red all around the cockpit. The Starlifter was dying. He wrestled with the controls, trying desperately to keep the plane in some semblance of level flight and headed away from the city below.

With its port wing engulfed in flame, the C-141 fell out of position in the formation. For a second, it staggered onward through the air, seemingly determined to fly on despite all the damage it had sustained. Then the huge plane tipped over and plowed into the ground at four hundred miles an hour.

The Starlifter's tumbling, burning, and rolling wreckage tore a swath of total destruction through Pretoria's southern suburbs. Houses vanished—reduced to piles of smoldering rubble and shattered wood. Century-old oak and jacaranda trees were uprooted and splintered in the same instant, and automobiles were ground under and crushed—mangled into heat-warped abstract sculptures of metal, fiberglass, and molten rubber. More than one hundred South African civilians lay dead or dying beneath the debris.

Burning jet fuel set a quarter-mile stretch of Pretoria on fire and lit the night with an eerie, orange glow.

2/75TH RANGERS, SWARTKOP

Lt. Col. Mike Carrerra crouched beside his radioman, watching as the nine remaining C-141s touched down and taxied off Swartkop's main runway. One by one, the planes turned around and came to a stop with their noses pointed back down the runway—ready for instant takeoff.

The rear cargo ramp of the last C-141 whined open, settling slowly onto the tarmac. In less than a minute, Air Force crewmen emerged from the plane's dimly lit interior, pushing two small helicopters ahead of them—McDonnell Douglas MH-8 gunships belonging to the Army's 160th Aviation Regiment. Aviators called them "Little Birds" with good reason. Even carrying a full combat load—four TOW antitank missiles and a GE 7.62mm Minigun—each weighed just over a ton and a half. Technicians were already swarming around the two choppers, frantically prepping them for flight. Special blade-folding and stowage techniques developed by the 160th were supposed to allow both gunships to be assembled, loaded, and in the air within seven minutes.

Carrerra hoped those estimates were accurate. O'Connell and the nearly four hundred Rangers still fighting at Pelindaba would need those helicopters overhead by then, covering their withdrawal to Swartkop. He clicked the talk button on his radio mike. "Rover One One, this is Tango One One. Icarus. I say again, Icarus."

Swartkop Airfield had been captured. He and his troops were holding the way home open—at least for the moment.

HEADQUARTERS COMPANY, 1/75TH RANGERS

O'Connell snapped a full magazine into his M16 and eyed his closest subordinates. "Right. You heard Carrerra. We've got Swartkop. Now we need those goddamned nukes." He looked at his radioman. "No word from Bravo Three?"

Weisman shook his head. The radioman had a droopy, sad-eyed face made mournful by nature. He looked gloomy even at the best of times. Right now he looked heartsick.

O'Connell made several quick decisions. The Rangers of Bravo Company's Third Platoon were supposed to have dropped right on top of the weapons storage complex and its guard bunkers. It was beginning to look as though they'd been wiped out. Either that or all their radios were on the fritz. Sure. In any case, he'd have to go find out what had happened. South Africa's nukes were Brave Fortune's prize—its only prize. Without them, this whole operation was nothing more than one big bloody disaster.

He started issuing orders. "Fitz, you and Brady stay here with Doc and the wounded. Keep an eye peeled for anybody using that to come down on our backs." He pointed north along the trench. Several of the bunkers along Pelindaba's northern perimeter were still in South African hands, and the slit trench would offer cover and concealment for any counterattacking force.

Sergeant Fitzsimmons, a linebacker-sized Ranger from Colorado, nodded once and moved down the narrow trench with his M16 out and ready. Brady, a smaller black man who delighted in a thick, almost impenetrable Southern drawl, followed him, cradling an M60 light machine gun. He looked eager to try his weapon out on the first available Afrikaner.

O'Connell watched them go and turned to the rest of his able-bodied headquarters troops. There weren't many. Maybe half of those who'd jumped. He made a quick count. Seven officers and roughly twenty enlisted Rangers—and with only two M60s for support. He shook his head, impatient with his own pessimism. He'd have to make do. "Okay, let's mosey on down this trench and see what the hell's holding up Bravo Three."

He caught Esher Levi's anxious eye. "Can you make it with that bum ankle of yours, Professor?" Jump injuries were always painful, and the Israeli scientist's injury had probably already had time to swell inside his boot.

Surprisingly, Levi smiled—a brief flash of white teeth. He leaned on an M16 he'd taken from one of the seriously wounded. "I have a crutch, Colonel. And I suspect that I can hobble with the best of you."

O'Connell decided that he liked the man. Levi was a lot

tougher than he looked. Having a sense of humor was vital when all you really felt like doing was screaming. He nodded briefly and turned to Weisman. "Spread the word that we're going after the nukes."

He checked his watch. It felt like an eternity, but they'd only been on the ground for eight minutes. Those Navy fly-boys ought to be joining the party at any moment now.

"All set, Colonel." Weisman looked as unhappy as ever.

O'Connell tapped the assault rifle slung from the radio-man's shoulder. "Cheer up, Dave. Who knows, you may even get a chance to use that thing."

Weisman looked just the tiniest bit happier.

O'Connell gripped his own M16 and stepped out into the middle of the trench. Rifle and machine-gun fire crackled nearby, punctuated by muffled grenade blasts. Alpha and Charlie Company platoons were busy wreaking havoc on South African barracks and silencing enemy-held bunkers one by one. The sky to the west and north seemed brighter, lit by the fires of burning buildings and vehicles.

He glanced over his shoulder. Tense, camouflage-painted faces stared back at him from beneath Kevlar helmets. "Okay, let's do it."

The Rangers trotted south down the trench, with a determined Prof. Esher Levi limping in their midst. As they moved, a sound like ragged, rolling thunder rumbled overhead. The *Vinson*'s carrier-based planes were winging into action.

TIGER FOUR, OVER WATERKLOOF MILITARY AIRFIELD, NEAR PRETORIA

The F/A-18 Hornet came in low from the southeast, roaring two thousand feet above Pretoria's suburbs at almost five hundred knots. Lights appeared ahead of the speeding American plane—a string of widely spaced lights running east to west for more than a mile.

The Hornet's pilot, Lt. Comdr. Pete "Pouncer" Garrard, keyed his mike. "Tiger Lead, the runway is lit."

"Roger that."

Garrard concentrated on his flying, lining up for what he fervently hoped would be a perfect attack run. Tonight's show wasn't just for some intersquadron trophy. This was for real. Six Durandal antirunway weapons hung beneath Tiger Four's wings, ready for use on one of South Africa's biggest military airfields. The F/A-18 angled left half a degree, edging onto the imaginary flight path its computer calculated would produce the best results.

Garrard spotted movement on the runway off to his right. Two winged, single-tailed shapes were rolling down the tarmac, still on the ground but picking up speed fast. The South Africans were trying to get fighters in the air. Too late, *mi amigos,* he thought, using fragments of the street "Spanglish" he'd picked up during a boyhood spent in southern California.

The word RELEASE blinked into existence in the lower left-hand corner of his HUD. Aggressive instincts and years of training paid off as he stabbed the release button twice and yanked the Hornet up into a forty-degree climb. Two separate shudders rippled through the plane as a string of Durandals tumbled out from under its wings—falling nose-down toward the runway below.

Grunting against g forces that quadrupled his effective weight, Garrard pulled the climbing F/A-18 into a tight turn and craned his head all the way around to stare at the scene now behind and to his right. He wanted to see what happened when his bombs went off.

Small drogue parachutes snapped open behind each bomb. At a preset altitude above the runway, rocket motors inside the Durandals fired. All six weapons accelerated straight down, smashing into the earth below before exploding. Six flowers of flame, smoke, and spinning chunks of shattered concrete blossomed in a ragged line, angled across Waterkloof's primary strip. Two actually struck the narrow runway, heaving and buckling the thick concrete for eight or ten meters, in addition to a five-meter crater.

One of the two South African fighters racing down the runway ran into a smoking, jagged crater at more than one hundred miles an hour. The jet slammed nose first into the concrete in a fiery shower of sparks, broke in half, and blew up. Garrard whooped into his oxygen mask. Scratch one Mirage! One down and one to go.

But the other South African interceptor emerged from the wall of smoke and tumbling debris apparently unscathed. Afterburner blazing, the Mirage F.1CZ soared off the runway—clawing frantically for altitude.

Garrard clicked his mike button. "Tiger Lead, one hostile airborne. Engaging."

He shoved his throttle forward and pulled the Hornet into a rolling, vertical climb, groaning involuntarily as the Hornet's g force meter flickered past seven. At the same time, he switched his HUD to air-to-air mode. Two concentric circles leapt into view in the middle of the display. The circles identified cones of vulnerability—areas of the sky in front of his plane where his heat-seekers had the best odds of scoring a hit.

The sky and ground seemed to spin around, changing places, as Garrard pulled his F/A-18 inverted. Just a little more. Almost . . .

The climbing Mirage came into view in his HUD's upper left corner. A target designation box appeared around the South African jet's dim, wavering shape. Garrard rolled his plane back upright and accelerated. The Hornet streaked after its opponent.

As the F/A-18 closed, the box surrounding the enemy plane moved slowly down and across its HUD—sliding toward the center. Garrard's finger poised over the fire button on his stick. Come on, you bastards, lock on! It might not make much sense to swear at the simpleminded circuits inside the two AIM-9L Sidewinders his plane carried, but somehow it did make him feel better.

One of the missiles growled suddenly in his earphones—letting him know that its IR seeker had finally locked on. A flashing diamond appeared over the South African jet now barely a mile ahead and starting to turn.

Garrard squeezed his fire button and felt a small shudder

as the Sidewinder mounted on his plane's starboard wingtip dropped off and ignited. A streak of orange flame arced across the sky. The heat-seeker flashed across the gap between Tiger Four and its prey in less than five seconds. It exploded just yards behind the F.1's brightly glowing tailpipe.

The South African Mirage seemed to disintegrate in midair—tearing itself apart as fuel, ammunition, and missile propellant all went up in a thousandth of a second. Burning bits and pieces of torn metal and plastic fell earthward beneath an ugly, drifting cloud of oily black smoke.

Garrard doubted that the enemy pilot had even known he was under direct attack. Nothing unusual in that. Most air-to-air kills were scored on planes that never saw their attackers. And getting bounced just seconds after takeoff was every fighter pilot's nightmare.

He keyed his mike again. "Tiger Lead, this is Tiger Four. Splash one hostile. Runway is out of action."

The strike commander's laconic voice carried well over radio. "Roger, Four. Nice work. What's your fuel state?"

Garrard took a quick look at his fuel display. "Approaching Bingo." The Hornet was a shit-hot fighter and attack plane —much better than either the F-4 Phantom or the A-7 Corsair, the two aircraft it had replaced. But the F/A-18 was short on legs. Pretoria, three hundred and fifty miles inland, was near the limit of its unrefueled combat radius.

"Okay, Four. Head for Gascan flight at Point Tango."

Garrard clicked his mike twice to acknowledge and turned southeast, flying back toward a rendezvous with KA-6D tankers topped full of aviation fuel.

Behind him, the rest of the *Vinson*'s aircraft went to work with a vengeance.

VOORTREKKER HEIGHTS MILITARY CAMP, NEAR PRETORIA

A stick of four 500-pound bombs landed just two hundred yards away from the small officer's cottage assigned to Commandant Henrik Kruger. They exploded in a thunderous, thumping blast that instantly shattered every window, toppled bookcases, and threw pictures off rippling walls.

Ian Sherfield dived for cover behind a sofa as flying glass sleeted across the living room. He lay flat until the floor stopped rocking and then looked up.

Dust knocked off the walls and ceiling swirled in the air. Razor-edged pieces of glass littered the floor, mixed in with fragments of loose plaster and with splintered pieces of wood that had once been slats for the cottage's venetian blinds. Several deadly looking shards of glass were actually embedded in the far wall itself. He shivered suddenly, realizing that those bomb-made daggers must have passed within an inch or less of his unprotected head.

The building swayed again—rocked this time by bombs landing farther off. Ian scrambled to his feet, driven by an intense desire to get outside and into a bunker or trench. He'd stayed inside when the air raid sirens had gone off, more afraid of being recognized as a fugitive on the run from South African "justice" than of missing out on what he'd thought was only another drill. But it was beginning to look as though his calculations of relative risk were greatly in error.

More bomb blasts shook the cottage.

Ian bolted out the front door and into a scene that might have been lifted straight out of the most frightening parts of Dante's *Inferno*. A thick cloud of smoke and dust from burning buildings and repeated explosions hung low over the base, making it almost as difficult to see as it was to breathe. What he could see was terrifying.

One bomb had slammed into a nearby barracks and blown it apart—leaving only a ragged, smoking skeleton of roofless walls and heaped rubble. Other bombs had rained down all over the South African camp. Armories, maintenance sheds, and guardrooms alike were either in ruins or in flames. An eighteen-ton Ratel armored personnel carrier lay on its side in the middle of a parade ground—torn and twisted as though it had been first squeezed and then hurled there by a careless giant's hand.

As he scuttled across the road in front of Kruger's quarters, Ian was surprised to find that part of his trained reporter's mind was still busy jotting down details and impressions—even though the rest of him just wanted to dive into some nice safe hole. Christ, he must be going mad. This wasn't the right time to contemplate winning a prize for war reporting. But his brain wouldn't turn off.

Despite all the destruction, he couldn't see many bodies. The ten-minute delay between the time the first air raid sirens sounded and the first bombs cascaded down must have given everyone a chance to find cover. Everyone but him, that is. He dodged a blazing five-ton truck still rolling down the road with its driver slumped behind the wheel.

Another stick of bombs rained down on the barracks row just across the parade ground—exploding one after the other in rippling series of blinding white flashes. Shock waves slapped him in the face and punched the air out of his lungs. Ian ran faster, heading for the shelter Kruger said had been dug in front of his quarters.

There! A dark hole seemed to rise up out of the parade ground's flattened grass and tamped-down dirt. Without slowing, Ian threw himself through the entrance and tumbled head over heels down into a low-roofed bomb shelter. He lay still for a moment, facedown on the dugout's earthen floor and very glad to be there. Three other people were there ahead of him—Kruger, Matthew Sibena, and Emily van der Heijden.

As he rose to his knees and spat out a mouthful of dirt, Emily's worried face brightened. "Ian!"

She rushed over and he felt a pair of wonderfully warm arms tighten around him. She didn't say anything more. She didn't have to. He could feel her shaking.

Ian buried his face in her sweet-smelling, auburn hair. When he looked up, he found Henrik Kruger's sardonic gaze fixed on him.

"A rough night, Meneer Sherfield?"

A near-miss rocked the bunker. Dust sifted down through gaps in the timber roof. Kruger's expression didn't change.

This guy was a damned cool customer, Ian thought, deciding to reply in kind. He nodded abruptly. "Perhaps a bit loud, *Kommandant*."

Surprisingly, Kruger smiled. "That is the trouble with war, my friend. It's very hard on your hearing."

Emily and Sibena stared at the two of them, half-convinced that both of them were beginning to slide over the edge into total insanity.

In the air above them, jets roared back and forth, strafing or bombing any target still visible through pillars of rising smoke. And two battalions of crack South African infantry cowered in bomb shelters and foxholes—pinned down by American air power.

Pelindaba's garrison was on its own.

HEADQUARTERS COMPANY, 1/75TH RANGERS, NEAR THE WEAPONS STORAGE SITE, PELINDABA

"Jesus!" Lt. Col. Robert O'Connell yanked his head back below the trench parapet as a sudden burst of machine-gun fire ripped past. The goddamned South Africans were on their frigging toes. Still, he'd seen enough—more than enough.

The enemy had a heavy-caliber Vickers machine gun ensconced in a reinforced concrete bunker barely thirty meters north of the nuclear weapons storage area—covering every possible approach from the western side of the Pelindaba compound. Other bunkers guarded the eastern approaches. Bravo Company's Third Platoon had found that out the hard way.

Dead Rangers were strewn across the ground between the trench and the barbed wire fence surrounding the storage site. Most lay within a few feet of the trench—mowed down only seconds after they'd climbed out of cover. Some were draped over the wire, butchered as they tried to cut their way through. Several bodies still tangled in blood-soaked parachutes lay crumpled inside the weapons storage area.

O'Connell felt sick. Many of his best Rangers lay dead out there. A few of Bravo Three's forty-two men were probably still alive, huddled behind scraps of cover or playing possum in the middle of that murderous field, but the platoon itself had ceased to exist as a viable fighting force.

He gritted his teeth and motioned his officers and senior noncoms over for a quick conference. Regrets could come later. Right now, he and his thirty or so headquarters troops had to find a way to knock that damned machine gun out. Until they did, nobody was going to be able to get inside that storage site, and more importantly, nobody was going to be able to haul the nukes themselves out.

"Well, anybody got any brilliant ideas?" O'Connell looked from face to worried face.

His executive officer, Maj. Peter Klocek, pursed his lips and tilted his helmet back a few inches so he could wipe his sweat-streaked forehead. "Can we get a Gustav here?"

"No time." O'Connell shook his head regretfully. The battalion's recoilless rifle teams were scattered over a wide area—busy knocking out other enemy bunkers and strongpoints. The Carl Gustav team attached to Bravo Three had disappeared. They were probably among the dead piled up in the field just beyond the trench.

"What about Navy air? Why not let a couple A-6s pound the shit out of those SOBs?"

O'Connell considered that for a second. It was tempting—too tempting. And too likely to cause them more problems. He shook his head again. "That bunker's too close to the storage area. One near miss and we'd have to try digging those nukes out with our bare hands."

"Then I guess we gotta take our lumps and do it the hard way, Colonel." Sergeant Johnson growled, hefting his M16 in one massive paw. The assault rifle looked small in comparison.

O'Connell's fingers drummed a brief tattoo on the plastic butt of his own M16. Johnson had never been known for either his tact or his fancy tactical footwork. He had both the physique and mental attitude of a bare-knuckle brawler. But basically the sergeant was right. They'd have to throw subtlety out the window.

He grimaced. This was another of the decision points

dreaded by any sane combat commander—the moment when you came face-to-face with an awful and unavoidable truth about battle. Sound tactics and sufficient firepower were vital, but there would always be a time when all options narrowed down to one horrible choice—the decision to put men into a position in which a lot of them were sure to be killed.

O'Connell slid down to squat on his haunches. His officers and NCOs followed suit. "All right, people, listen up. Here's how were gonna play this thing." He quickly traced movements in the dirt, outlining the only plan open to them.

Two minutes later, O'Connell and four of his Rangers crouched below the edge of the slit trench. Two more soldiers stood ready to boost them up and into the killing ground. Another group of six led by Sergeant Johnson waited one hundred meters south along the same trench. The rest of his headquarters troops—thirteen officers and men—were spaced at five-meter intervals between the two assault groups.

A tight-lipped Peter Klocek worked his way up the narrow trench to within whispering distance. "We're set, Rob."

O'Connell nodded. He knew Klocek thought he was crazy to lead this attack himself, but he'd grown tired of sending other men into danger. For too long on this op, he'd been forced to lead like the faith-filled New Testament Roman centurion, saying to one man, "Go," and to another, "Come." Well, no more.

This suicidal bunker hunt was make or break for Brave Fortune. And that meant his battalion had a right to expect to see him out in front, yelling the infantry-school motto, "Follow me!"

Enough pissing around, he told himself. Every second counted. He took a deep breath and then let it out in a bull-voiced roar. "Fire! Fire! Fire!"

Rifles and machine guns chattered all along the length of the American-held trench, pouring bullets toward the distant, half-seen shape of the South African bunker. M16-mounted M203 grenade launchers thumped once, twice, and then a third time—lobbing 40mm grenades onto the open area right in front of the bunker.

Bright orange flashes stabbed out of the rising smoke. The South Africans were shooting back, trying to lay down a curtain of steel-jacketed slugs across ground they could no longer see.

O'Connell's hands closed tight around his M16. "Let's go!"

Two of the six Rangers in his assault group stooped and locked their hands together to form a makeshift stirrup. Without hesitating, O'Connell stepped forward and up into their interlocked hands and immediately felt himself being tossed upward—literally being hurled out of the trench. He landed in the grassy field outside, rolled over, and scrambled to his feet already running. Rifle in hand, he moved north, angling away from the heavy machine-gun fire now pouring out of the South African–held bunker. Four Rangers hurtled up and out of the trench after him.

All five men sprinted forward, dispersing on the move—spreading out in the hope that a single enemy burst wouldn't hit them all. This gauntlet could only be run alone.

Burning buildings and vehicles added an eerie orange glow to the black night sky and sent strange shadows wavering ahead of them across the corpse-strewn, half-lit ground. O'-Connell kept going, speeding past crumpled bodies, scattered gear, and torn, bullet-riddled parachutes. In an odd way, he felt almost superhuman, with every sense and every nerve ending magnified and set afire. He squinted through sweat toward the smoke-shrouded enemy bunker. Two hundred meters to go.

Movement flickered at the edge of his vision, far off to the right. Sergeant Johnson and his five Rangers were there, making their own headlong dash for the bunker. He lengthened his own stride.

One hundred and fifty meters. One hundred. O'Connell felt his pulse accelerating, racing in time with his pounding feet. My God, he thought exultantly, we might really pull this crazy stunt off after all!

Suddenly, the ground seemed to explode out from under him. Dirt sprayed high in the air as a machine-gun burst hammered the area. One slug moving at supersonic speeds tore the M16 right out of his hands and sent it whirling away into the darkness. Another bullet ripped through a fold of cloth over his right shoulder, leaving behind a raw, bleeding line of torn skin.

O'Connell threw himself prone, scarcely able to believe that he'd escaped without more serious injury.

Agonized screams rising above the crashing, crackling sounds of gunfire and grenade explosions told him that the rest of his men weren't being so lucky. He swiveled to look to the rear.

The four Rangers who'd been following him had vanished—cloaked behind a curtain of smoke and dust. As it settled, another burst of South African machine-gun fire stitched across the open ground—sweeping back and forth across the bodies of men who'd already been hit several times. No one moved or cried out in pain.

He was alone.

O'Connell clenched his teeth and tried to bury himself in the earth as more rounds whipcracked low overhead. Pebbles, sand, and torn bits of grass pattered off his helmet and neck. He lay motionless as the machine-gun fire traversed right. The South Africans, firing blind, had gone back to working over corpses heaped in front of the American-held slit trench.

He started crawling toward his rifle, careful to stay flat on his stomach. It took him nearly half a minute to reach it.

Hell and damnation. O'Connell stared at the useless lump of plastic and metal lying on the grass before him. The same bullet that had torn the M16 out of his grasp had smashed its firing mechanism. He fumbled for the pouch clipped to his combat webbing and relaxed momentarily as his fingers encountered the small plastic V-shape of his only real remaining weapon. He still carried a couple of grenades, a knife, and a holstered 9mm Beretta, but they wouldn't be much use against a concrete-walled bunker. No, clearing that out was going to take something considerably more powerful.

He snapped the pouch flap shut and started crawling forward again, worming his way toward the enemy machine-gun position.

It seemed to take forever to cross the roughly one hundred meters still separating him from the South African bunker. Long periods of lying frozen as bullets slapped through the air right over his helmet were interspersed with frantic flurries of motion as he wriggled closer. By the time O'Connell got within five meters of the bunker's north side, his battle dress was soaked in sweat and coated with ground-in dirt and loose blades of sun-dried grass.

He lay panting quietly for a moment, studying what little he could see of his target. The Rangers left behind to provide covering fire had long since stopped shooting—afraid that they might hit any of their own men who'd survived that last death-or-glory charge. Several of the Americans were still lobbing smoke grenades, though. A thick pall of gray-white smoke hung over the immediate area, blinding the South African machine-gun crew and their lookouts.

The bunker itself was a squat, square slab sticking less than three feet above ground level. Its reinforced concrete walls and roof offered complete protection against small-arms fire. In fact, they were designed to withstand all but a direct hit by heavy mortar or artillery shells. Narrow slits cut through each of the four walls gave the troops inside close to a 360-degree field of observation and fire.

The South African machine gun chattered again, pouring a steady stream of bullets out the firing slit facing west. O'Connell nerved himself to move. It was time.

He eased the pistol out of his holster and thumbed its safety catch off. Slowly, almost infinitely slowly, he raised his head to get a better view of the northern firing slit. There wasn't anything there. Just an empty black gap in the gray concrete wall. No R4 assault rifles aimed at his face. The South Africans inside were busy shooting in the wrong direction.

Go! O'Connell jumped to his feet, lunged forward, and scrambled onto the bunker's flat roof. Nobody took a shot at him. Seconds passed while he waited for some kind of reaction from inside the enemy gun position. Nothing happened.

By God, he'd actually done it! Now any enemy soldier who wanted to clear him off the bunker would have to come out in the open to try it. And the odds were that the South Africans didn't even know he was up there.

He laid his 9mm pistol to one side and started making his final preparations. One hand scrabbled inside the pouch hooked to his combat webbing while the other reached inside his shirt pocket for the wires and detonator he'd stowed there. He ignored the two fragmentation grenades he still carried. The bunker was bound to have a grenade sump—a small, sandbagged hole designed to smother a blast and deflect fragments—somewhere inside. If he simply tossed a grenade in through the firing slit, all the South African soldiers had to do was kick the grenade into the sump and duck. Sure, one or two of them might be wounded, but they'd know they had trouble on their roof.

O'Connell smiled grimly. He had something more assuredly fatal in mind for the enemy machine-gun crew.

He pulled the small, curved Claymore out of his pouch and unscrewed the shipping plug from the fuse well. Inserting a blasting cap in the recess, he connected it to the leads from an electrical detonator. His hands relaxed. All set.

The machine gun rattled again, firing out of the bunker beneath him. Defiant yells in Afrikaans echoed above the gunfire. Bastards. One . . . two . . . three . . .

O'Connell leaned out over the edge of the bunker, jammed the Claymore into its northern firing slit, and rolled away back onto the roof. Now! He pressed his face into the cool concrete and squeezed the detonator.

Whammm! The Claymore exploded with an ear-shattering roar. Driven by a powerful charge of C4 plastic explosive, hundreds of tiny steel ball bearings sleeted through the narrow opening—killing everyone in their path as they ricocheted and rebounded off solid walls. No one inside the bunker even got the chance to scream.

As O'Connell sat upright, still stunned by the force of the

blast he'd unleashed, wispy coils of acrid, yellow smoke and the awful smell of burnt flesh eddied out through the bunker's firing slits. The last outpost guarding Pelindaba's Nuclear Weapons Storage Site had fallen.

COMMAND BUNKER, 61ST TRANSVAAL RIFLES

Col. Frans Peiper stared helplessly at the map showing his battalion's few surviving fighting positions. Bunker after bunker and barracks after barracks had been hurriedly crossed out as they were reported overrun or destroyed. Although events were unfolding too fast for him to keep pace, one thing was increasingly clear: the 61st Transvaal Rifles was being gutted.

Peiper breathed out heavily through his gas mask and swore as his clear plastic eyepieces fogged over for the tenth time. These damned chemical-protection suits made even the simplest actions difficult! He grabbed at a grease pencil near the map and cursed again as it slipped between his thickly gloved fingers. A young lieutenant standing at his side handed the pencil back.

For an instant longer the colonel stood still, his eyes fixed on the map. Now what? Well, for a start, he had to take charge. He had to find a way to reorganize the broken fragments of his battalion into some semblance of a fighting force. Unfortunately, he didn't have the faintest idea of how to go about doing that. Enemy units now occupied key positions all across the compound. The situation seemed hopeless.

"Sir, Captain Karel's asking for instructions. What should I tell him?"

"Tell him to wait, goddamnit!" Peiper looked up, angry at what sounded very much like a reproach. The sergeant manning the command bunker's communications setup stared back at him without flinching.

Damn the man. His insubordination would have to be dealt with later. Assuming, of course, there was going to be a later.

Peiper wiped the steam off his gas mask eyepieces and

scrawled a rough circle around the single bunker and stretch of trench apparently still held by Capt. Anton Karel and the remnants of A Company. Karel's troops covered the northwestern end of the compound, well away from either the main road or the nuclear weapons storage area. Too far away in fact to do any good.

Peiper threw his pencil down and moved to the bank of field telephones. "Let me talk to him!"

The sergeant gave him the handset.

"Karel? This is Peiper." The colonel frowned. Blast it, he could scarcely hear or talk inside this wretched suit. "Listen carefully. I want you to counterattack—"

A yell from one of the soldiers manning the bunker's southern firing slit interrupted him. "Movement along the access road, Colonel! Trucks! Ten or twelve of them!"

Peiper threw the phone down and joined a general rush over to the narrow opening. He squinted toward the access road linking Pelindaba's military and civilian sectors. Dim shapes rumbled slowly along the road, silhouetted against a row of burning buildings. He recognized the distinctive outlines of canvas-sided Samil trucks made only in South Africa. Were these reinforcements from Voortrekker Heights? They must be.

With trembling fingers, he raised his binoculars and focused them carefully. The trucks and the men riding on them leapt into closer view. That was odd. Their helmets were strangely shaped—almost exactly like the old-style coal-scuttle helmets worn by the German Wehrmacht during World War II.

Despite the sauna-bath heat of the chemical protection suit he wore, Peiper felt a cold shiver run down his spine. The soldiers aboard those trucks were the enemy—not a friendly relief force. Even worse, they were driving straight toward the special weapons bunkers.

The Fates were not kind to Col. Frans Peiper. He had just enough time to savor his utter and absolute failure before an American recoilless rifle round burst against the edge of the firing slit—just twenty centimeters in front of his horrified face.

HEADQUARTERS COMPANY, 1/75TH RANGERS, AT THE WEAPONS STORAGE SITE

Prof. Esher Levi surveyed the frantic activity around the five weapons storage bunkers with increasing satisfaction. After what had seemed a most unpromising and bloody start, the Americans were finally getting Brave Fortune back on track. Pelindaba's uranium enrichment plant had been wrecked. His fellow countrymen had been rescued. Even more important, survivors from O'Connell's headquarters and the other Ranger units were busy loading several of the South African trucks they'd hot-wired and "liberated" from the Pelindaba vehicle park. Sleek, metallic cylinders, each carried by ten men, were carefully being hoisted up and into their rear cargo compartments.

"We've got that last bunker open, Professor. The colonel's waiting for you there."

Levi turned. Smoke and sweat had stained Maj. Peter Klocek's lean, tanned face. "The weapons are there?"

Klocek nodded wearily. "Yeah. The last two. But the colonel'd like you to make sure of that."

"Of course."

Levi hobbled after the much younger American officer through a maze of hurrying soldiers. The entrance to the last storage bunker lay down a set of steps. A thick door sagged to one side—blown off its hinges by small charges of plastic explosive.

The two men ducked down and into the bunker. Several unbroken, battery-powered emergency lights illuminated a single chamber measuring roughly twenty feet by fifty feet. Steel racks lined each concrete wall. Four metal half-cylinders—twin halves of two twenty-kiloton fission bombs—rested in separate sections of the racks, kept physically apart to preclude what technicians referred to as "premature weapon criticality." Levi smiled to himself, remembering his first appalled reaction to the technobabble term used to describe what might, in the worst case, be an uncontrolled chain reaction—a runaway nightmare of hellish temperatures and deadly neutron radiation.

He moved to where O'Connell stood examining one of the four bomb halves. The American lieutenant colonel looked just about out on his feet—bruised, bedraggled, and bloodstained. The Israeli scientist suddenly felt a wave of admiration for this brave man. It was an uncomfortable feeling, especially since the orders he'd received from his own government would soon force him to lie to the Ranger officer. Though not about these bombs themselves, thank God.

"Have we got them all, Professor?" O'Connell sounded as tired as he looked.

Levi nodded. "These two weapons make a total of nine. Every fission bomb the Afrikaners had left." He leaned past the American officer and examined a printed manifest taped to the rear half of one weapon. "It would appear that your attack came just in time."

"Oh?"

Levi pointed to the manifest. "Those codes indicate that this weapon has been thoroughly checked, certified ready for detonation, and prepped for movement within the next twenty-four hours."

O'Connell looked grim. "So those bastards were going to drop another nuke? This one?"

Levi nodded again and tapped the bomb's exposed core—a smooth piece of dark metal about half the size of a small grapefruit. "It seems hard to believe that this little lump and its twin over there could kill thousands or even tens of thousands, doesn't it? But believe me, this is really all one needs—a few kilograms of highly enriched uranium. That and the proper arrangement of a few more kilos of high explosive."

O'Connell took an involuntary step backward. "Christ! That stuff's U-235?"

Levi nodded a third time, inwardly amused. Like many laymen, O'Connell obviously had some serious misconceptions about nuclear materials. He'd also been too busy planning the operation itself to attend Levi's technical training sessions. The temptation to lecture, just a bit, was simply too strong to resist.

The Israeli scientist laid his palm flat on the bomb's metallic core. "As a solid metal, U-235 is not dangerously radioactive, Major. It's mainly an alpha emitter, and even your skin can stop alpha particles." He stroked the smooth black surface. "You could even hold this in your lap for a month or more without suffering any significant ill effects."

O'Connell took the unsolicited science lesson with good grace. He grinned suddenly, appearing years younger for a brief instant. "Hell, Professor, I'd curl up to sleep with every one of these damned things for a year if it meant getting 'em safely out of this frigging country."

Ten Rangers led by the leader of the battalion's Support Platoon trotted down the steps and crowded into the bunker. "Okay to take these now, Colonel?"

"You bet. Carry on, Harry." O'Connell moved toward the entrance with Levi in tow.

The Israeli scientist risked a quick glance at his watch. So far so good. He'd helped the Rangers find and capture South Africa's nuclear arsenal. Now he had to try completing the most difficult part of *his* mission—the part he'd kept secret from the Americans. He cleared his throat. "Your troops hold most of the compound, don't they?"

"Yeah." Small elements of Pelindaba's garrison still fought from sections of trench along its northern perimeter, but almost all the rest of the South African soldiers had been killed or wounded. O'Connell paused just outside the bunker doorway andlooked down at him. "Why do you ask, Professor?"

Levi swallowed hard. Now for the lie. "Because I'd like your permission to search the Administration Center for certain scientific documents of interest to both our governments. Records of nuclear experiments and weapons design blueprints, among others." He scanned the men hurrying to and fro outside the storage complex—carrying wounded, collecting weapons, and checking corpses. Bomb blasts echoed off in the distance as carrier-based planes kept pounding away at other South African military installations and air bases. "All I need are a few minutes. Five at most."

O'Connell walked away without answering, his face hard and remote.

Levi limped after him. "Please, Colonel, it's important."

The American stopped and turned around. "I agree, Professor. But your personal search isn't necessary. Captain Kelly already has a team going through the Admin building. They know what to look for. We need you here with the weapons."

Levi choked. The Americans were ahead of him? He tried again. "But my technical expertise could be invaluable. I should be there—"

"So you can destroy any records showing the size and composition of your own country's nuclear stockpile? I don't think so, Professor."

Levi felt his jaw drop open in shock.

O'Connell smiled wryly. "You and your compatriots should have known better, Esher. Americans are sometimes naive, but we're not stupid. Naturally, we're grateful for your country's help with this operation, but that doesn't make us blind or deaf." He shook his head slowly. "I'm afraid Jerusalem's just going to have to live with the knowledge that some of its best-kept secrets aren't so secret anymore."

Levi stood openmouthed for a moment longer and then shrugged, accepting his defeat with good grace. So much for the Mossad's rather Byzantine plot. Washington would soon know exactly how much weapons-grade uranium Israel had received from the Pelindaba enrichment plant. And that, in turn, would allow the United States to calculate exactly how many nuclear bombs his country had manufactured for its own deterrent force.

Well, he hadn't been that keen on deceiving the Americans anyway. "In that case, Colonel, what else can I do to help you? Your men will soon have the bombs loaded, but you still have wounded to be collected. My conscript service included rudimentary first aid courses . . . perhaps I can assist your medics?"

O'Connell's weary eyes lit up with approval. "Thank you. My men and I would appreciate it." He broke off abruptly as several of his noncoms moved past, checking dog tags on bodies scattered around the storage site.

The Ranger watched them for a moment before shaking

his head sadly. "I expected losses, but I never thought it would be this bad."

Levi tried to offer some comfort. "But you've won, Colonel. And your battalion's sacrifices have saved many thousands of lives."

O'Connell shook his head again. "We haven't won yet. We've still got to get these damned bombs down the road and out through Swartkop."

The Israeli stared at a horizon lit red and orange by dozens of fires raging out of control. Jets thundered low overhead, crisscrossing Pretoria in search of new targets. He spread his hands in confusion. "But what kind of fighting force can the South Africans possibly have left to throw against us?"

"I don't know, Esher, and what I don't know could still kill us all." He raised his voice. "Weisman!"

The sad-eyed little radioman came trotting up. "Colonel?"

"Inform all commanders that we're pulling out in five minutes. I want every truck or car they can lay their hands on at the main gate ASAP. We've got a lot of wounded to move. And tell Carrerra we're on our way. Got it?"

Weisman nodded vigorously, obviously already mentally running over the list of code phrases needed to transmit O'Connell's instructions.

"Good. After you've done that, put me in touch with Night Stalker Lead and Tiger Lead. I want solid air cover over us all the way to Swartkop!"

Levi moved away, looking for a medic to whom he could offer his services. O'Connell's depression had vanished for the time being, washed away in a flood of work still to be done.

Galvanized by their commander's radioed orders, small groups of Rangers moved into high gear all across the Pelindaba complex. Some helped wounded comrades into stolen trucks. Others carried boxes of captured documents down the Administration Center's bullet-riddled stairwells, past bodies sprawled in the building's central hallway, and out through a set of double doors blown open by recoilless rifle rounds.

To the north, other American soldiers kept up a withering

fire, trying to pin down those few South Africans who'd survived the initial assault. But slowly, one by one, men slipped away from the firing line, joining skeletal squads and platoons assembling by the compound's main gate. The Rangers were getting ready to leave Pelindaba's corpse-strewn lawns and wrecked, burning buildings behind.

ROOKIAT TWO ONE, A TROOP, 1ST SQUADRON, PRETORIA LIGHT HORSE, ALONG THE BEN SCHOEMAN HIGHWAY, NEAR PELINDABA

South of Pelindaba, a lone diesel engine growled softly as an eight-wheeled South African armored car ground its way into cover.

Dried twigs and branches rustled and snapped as the Rookiat's long 76mm gun poked slowly through the clump of dense brush and low scrub trees. Riding with his commander's hatch open, Capt. Martin van Vuuren leaned far forward over the AFV's turret, sighting down the length of the main gun barrel, trying to judge the exact moment at which its muzzle would clear the surrounding vegetation.

The Rookiat lurched upward over a tiny shelf of rock and then dropped level again. At the same moment, its gun tore through the last fringe of brush and emerged into open air.

"Halt!"

Van Vuuren's whispered order brought immediate results. The muted roar of the Rookiat's diesel engine died as it came to a complete stop. He swiveled through a complete circle, carefully scanning the terrain around his vehicle. A thin, humorless smile creased the South African captain's lips. Perfect.

The Rookiat lay hidden inside a small, thick patch of woods overlooking the Ben Schoeman Highway—the expressway connecting Pretoria with Johannesburg. It was also the main road between the Pelindaba Nuclear Research Center and Swartkop Military Airfield. More importantly, the dense canopy of brush and tree branches would conceal his vehicle from what he was sure were Cuban ground attack aircraft roaming the night sky over Pretoria.

It seemed an ideal position, even though van Vuuren still wasn't sure of just what the hell was going on. His A Troop had been on routine patrol when the enemy air strikes began—moving slowly along a wide circuit outside the perimeters of both Pelindaba and the Voortrekker Heights Military Camp. Now his radios were out—jammed across every possible frequency. And the two other Rookiats under his command were gone. He'd seen one blow up, shredded into a blazing fireball by cannon shells from a strafing enemy plane. The other had simply vanished, lost somewhere in what had quickly become a confused, harrowing race through a deadly gauntlet of smoke and flame.

Fresh scars on Rookiat Two One's turret, souvenirs of steel splinters sprayed by a near miss, showed how close a race that had been. Van Vuuren's fingers lightly brushed a bruise spreading across his left cheek. He winced, remembering the tremendous, ringing impact that had thrown him face first into the Rookiat's ballistic computer and laser range-finder readout. The enemy bomb couldn't have landed more than thirty or forty meters away.

He shuddered. That had been too damned close. For the moment, he was content to wait here—safely hidden and out of the line of fire. A muffled cough from below reminded him to check his crew.

He lowered himself into the vehicle's crowded, red-lit turret. Anxious faces stared up at him.

"Now what do we do?" The pressure lines left on Corporal Meitjens's face by his gunsight made him look something like a raccoon.

"We wait." Van Vuuren's own uncertainty added a bite to his tone. "And you keep your damned eyes glued to that night sight!"

Meitjens hurriedly obeyed.

Minutes passed, dragging by one by one. Van Vuuren had left his hatch open for comfort. Even when sitting idle, a four-man crew generated a lot of heat inside the Rookiat's turret. And the cool night air pouring in through the open hatch provided a bit of welcome relief.

Sound also poured in through the hatch, and the South African captain sat with his eyes closed, listening to the noise of a one-sided battle. Bombs echoed in the distance—dull, thumping explosions that seemed to shake the very air itself. Jet engines roared past from time to time as enemy planes came in on strafing runs against some poor sod stupid enough to show himself. But the bombing seemed to be tapering off.

The bastards up there must be running out of targets, van Vuuren thought sourly. The steady crackle of heavy small-arms fire rose from off to the north—audible now over the diminishing noise of the air bombardment.

The Rookiat's commander opened his eyes and sat up straight. Small-arms fire? Were soldiers in the Pelindaba garrison actually trying to shoot down jets with rifles and machine guns? If so, they were braver than they were wise.

"Sir! Trucks moving south on the highway. Many of them." Meitjens sounded as surprised as van Vuuren felt. What kind of idiot would try to run a truck convoy down a multilane highway in the middle of an enemy air attack?

He motioned the corporal aside and pressed his own face against the thermal-image sight. Bright green shapes moved into view, hot against cold hillsides and an even colder night sky. By God, they *were* trucks!

Van Vuuren found himself counting aloud. "Ten, eleven, twelve . . . eighteen, nineteen . . . " He shut his mouth abruptly. More than two dozen vehicles were out there, rolling past his position at twenty kilometers an hour. A sizable convoy even under ordinary circumstances. And the circumstances were scarcely ordinary. He couldn't understand it. Why weren't those trucks being blown to pieces by enemy air attack?

A nagging fear suddenly crystallized into certainty. The aircraft weren't attacking those trucks because they were all on the same side. He couldn't figure out how the Cubans could possibly have moved their troops so close to Pretoria so fast, but that would have to wait. All that mattered now was that he had what must be a communist truck column under his Rookiat's 76mm gun.

"Target! Five hundred meters! Load HE!" Van Vuuren kept his eyes glued to the night sight. By rights he should sit back and allow Meitjens to man the gun, but he couldn't resist the temptation to do it himself. In the past thirty or so minutes, he'd been bombed and strafed and generally terrified half out of his mind. Now he wanted the pleasure of personally killing some of the Uitlanders whose airborne comrades had been responsible for all of that.

Besides, this was going to be easy—what an American would call a "turkey shoot." Two or three shots to the front and two or three more to the back would trap this tightly bunched truck convoy on a ready-made killing ground. Hundreds of enemy infantrymen would meet death on a wide, empty expanse of asphalt and concrete.

Van Vuuren gripped the gun controls and traversed the turret to the right in one smooth, whirring movement. Bright yellow cross hairs centered on the green image of the lead truck. He tapped the laser range-finder control with his thumb and numerals appeared on the screen—382 meters. Practically point-blank. He ignored Meitjens's resentful muttering behind his back. His gunner would just have to learn that rank had its privileges and this was one of them.

"Up!"

"On the way!" Van Vuuren squeezed the trigger.

Klaanng! A bright white flash erupted out of the Rookiat's main gun. The whole vehicle rocked back as it recoiled. Dust swirled through the air, kicked up by the 76mm cannon's muzzle blast.

The South African captain pressed his face into the night sight, swearing softly as he waited for the dust to settle. Come on. Come on. Clear. Let me see, blast it!

Vision returned. Shit! Van Vuuren snarled at the view his screen showed. The truck he'd fired at was still moving, and a glowing hot spot two hundred meters farther up the opposite hillside showed where his shot had landed. He'd either missed entirely or the HE round had passed right through the enemy vehicle without slamming into anything solid enough to set off its warhead.

"Up!" Rookiat Two One's loader was still on the job.

Van Vuuren traversed right again, bringing the truck back under his cross hairs. This time you die, he promised. He reached for the laser range-finder button. . . .

The night sight went blank. Cross hairs, glowing green images, and digital readouts all faded out and disappeared.

Van Vuuren stared at his darkened screen in dismay. Both the Rookiat's ballistic computer and its thermal-imaging system were down. One part of his panicked mind remained calm enough to guess that the vehicle's delicate electronics had taken shock damage in the same bomb blast that had scarred its turret armor.

"Meitjens!" He scrambled out of the other man's seat in frantic haste. Only the gunner had the technical know-how needed to get their ballistic computer up and running again. He collided head-on with the corporal in a confused tangle of arms and legs and curses.

Van Vuuren's attempt to do everything himself cost Rookiat Two One precious time it did not have.

NIGHT STALKER LEAD, 160TH AVIATION REGIMENT, OVER PELINDABA

One hundred and fifty feet above the highway, the MH-8 helicopter gunship, known as Night Stalker Lead, spiraled downward in a tight turn to the right. Ghostly images of trucks, hillsides, and patches of brush spun past at dizzying speed.

While the AVS-6 night-vision goggles worn by the gunship's two crewmen made them look a bit like pop-eyed insects, the goggles also turned night into lime-green-tinted day inside a narrow forty-degree arc. Pilots and gunners using NVGs could pick out tremendous detail—the difference between thin, harmless tree branches and thick tree trunks for example. That and years of intensive training gave the crews of the 160th Aviation Regiment a combat symbolized by their motto: "Death waits in the dark."

The 160th's gunships had proven themselves invaluable in combat over Panama and the Persian Gulf. Now they were proving it again in the darkness over South Africa.

Night Stalker Lead's pilot, a U.S. Army major, leveled out of his turn at fifty feet. "You see where that shot came from, Dan?"

"Looking." His gunner, a middle-aged warrant officer going prematurely gray, stared straight ahead—scanning the eerie, cartoonlike world visible through his goggles. A low hill rising steeply ahead. Hard-to-see clumps of scrub brush and scraggly trees. Painfully bright fires raging just over the horizon. There! "Target! One o'clock! AFV!"

Now the pilot saw it—the solid box-shape of an armored vehicle parked in a copse of trees overlooking the highway. He pulled back on his controls, decelerating to give his gunner a better shot. "Nail him!"

"Doing it!"The gunner swiveled his fire control to the right. Cross hairs settled over the enemy AFV and stayed there. "Locked on!"

Night Stalker Lead's pilot dropped the gunship's nose.

"Firing."

The helicopter's last remaining TOW antitank missile leapt from its right stores pylon and raced through the sky trailing fire and an ultrathin control wire. It crossed the six hundred meters separating the gunship from its target and exploded against the South African AFV's turret. The Rookiat's top armor had been designed to stop 23mm cannon rounds—not heavy weight antitank missiles.

Fuel and ammunition went up in a rolling blast that threw torn and twisted pieces of Rookiat Two One more than fifty feet into the air. Oily black smoke boiled out of the vehicle's shattered hulk, spreading slowly across a barren hillside now dotted with small fragments of flaming wreckage.

Night Stalker Lead's missile had annihilated South Africa's last organized opposition to Brave Fortune. The 1/75th Rangers had a clear road to Swartkop.

SWARTKOP MILITARY AIRFIELD

Swartkop Airfield's vast stretches of oil-stained concrete were deserted—almost entirely abandoned to the dead and the dying. Fires guttered low in burnt-out hangars and workshops. Smoke and flame rose from the wreckage of the two MH-8 "Little Birds." As part of the plan, they'd been abandoned and blown up by their own crews rather than let the South Africans capture them intact. The only signs of life were concentrated near one end of the flight line where Rangers hurriedly unloaded wounded men from captured trucks and carried them into the huge cargo bay of the last waiting C-141. More soldiers lay prone in a rough semicircle around the aircraft, ready to provide covering fire if any South African troops appeared. Two weary officers stood watching off to one side of the Starlifter's cargo ramp.

Jet engines howled from the other side of the tarmac where the other C-141s taxied toward takeoff. Abruptly, one swung through a sharp 180-degree turn, came to a brief stop on the runway's centerline, and then accelerated—rolling past with a thundering, rumbling roar.

Lt. Col. Robert O'Connell watched his battalion's lead transport lumber heavily into the air with a profound sense of relief. Three nuclear weapons were safely off South African soil and bound for American-garrisoned Diego Garcia—the first stage on a long flight back to the United States. Another C-141 followed a minute later, lifting off just as the third Starlifter flashed past down the runway. One after another, the huge transports took off.

"Rob, we're done! Now I suggest we get the hell out of here!"

O'Connell turned toward the hoarse shout. Lt. Col. Mike Carrerra pointed toward a collection of empty trucks. The wounded they'd carried were all inside the C-141. O'Connell nodded vigorously. "Amen to that, Mike. Get your people aboard!"

"Right." Carrerra whirled round and yelled through cupped hands, "Let's go, Alpha Two!"

Moving fire team by fire team, the Rangers of the 2/75th's

Alpha Company scrambled upright and ran for the open cargo bay. As the last man's combat boots thudded onto the steel ramp, Carrerra signaled the Air Force crew chief waiting eagerly by the door controls. "Close and seal!"

He turned back to O'Connell with a wide, punch-drunk grin plastered across his face. "Well, I'll be dipped in shit, Colonel. I gotta admit I never thought we'd pull this fucking thing off. Congratulations."

O'Connell smiled wanly and glanced over his shoulder at the rest of the C-141's crowded cargo bay. Dozens of men lay motionless on either side of the central aisle, swathed in bloodstained bandages. Others, apparently uninjured, sat silently along the Starlifter's metal walls, clutching M16s and light machine guns in hands that shook uncontrollably. Carrerra's battalion had taken heavy losses while seizing and holding the South African airfield. His own unit's casualties were even higher. Preliminary casualty reports showed the 1/75th's losses running at more than 50 percent. His Ranger battalion had been wrecked while accomplishing its mission.

He looked up at Carrerra's tired face. "Yeah. We did it. I just hope to God it was worth the price."

Carrerra eyed the pillars of smoke and flame rising in a great arc from the west to the north. "Well, one thing's for goddamned certain. These bastards will sure as hell know we've been here!"

O'Connell found himself nodding in agreement as the cargo ramp whined shut, blocking their view of South Africa. The huge C-141 was already in motion, turning rapidly onto the runway leading home.

Karl Vorster's government had just lost its nuclear option.

CHAPTER 31

Foothold

DECEMBER 7—SIMONSTOWN NAVAL BASE, CAPE TOWN

"There's the helicopter." Brig. Chris Taylor, commander of the Independent Cape Province Defense Forces, pointed out over the water. At first, the shape was visible more by the starlight it blocked than as a concrete form—visible just as a small patch of blackness racing low across white-capped water. But the whupping sound of rotor blades made it real.

The helicopter was headed for a pier at the Simonstown Naval Base, an area controlled by his troops, but still in range of the guns on Table Mountain. In fact, all of Cape Town was in range of those guns, and that was a problem. Vorster's troops, holed up in the mountain, had made the liberation of Cape Town a hollow victory, because any movement, any sign of organized activity, quickly ended in a storm of shell-fire.

For more than three weeks, the whole city had taken a terrible beating. Its citizens now moved only at night, without lights, and as much as possible, without noise. All those who could had fled to the countryside—something that wasn't an option for Cape Town's black population.

The black and colored population lived in Alexandra township, south of the city, and they depended on the normal commerce of the city for their income. Servants, cleaners, and laborers, they'd been hit the hardest when the daytime shelling started.

Now bands of blacks roved the city, looking for food, money, or anything of value. Transportation was rigidly controlled, and Taylor's forces were once more employed in trying to preserve order. Those that weren't busy chasing looters escorted food convoys or formed a perimeter around Table Mountain—guarding against a sortie by the besieged forces.

Vorster's troops were deeply entrenched in a network of improved caves and tunnels bored into solid rock. With little more than a single infantry battalion plus artillery, they'd stood off two determined attacks by Taylor's much larger forces. Those assaults had claimed so many of his men that he'd given up trying to take the place by storm.

Unfortunately, a conventional siege was certain to be both costly and protracted. He wasn't completely familiar with the defenses, but it was common knowledge in the Army that the mountain held food and ammunition for several months. Ammunition in abundance, including plenty of shells for their heavy G-5 howitzers. The G-5s, massive 155mm artillery pieces with a forty-kilometer range, were the centerpiece of the holdouts' defenses.

Well, he thought, with luck and some tact, they could end the siege with American help. Taylor, his second-in-command, Adriaan Spier, and Deputy Governor Fraser were all going out to meet the American invasion fleet steaming toward the Cape Town coast.

Making sure that his hooded light was pointed out to sea, one of the soldiers escorting Taylor's party shone a beam toward the advancing aircraft. As if making sure that was the proper recognition signal, the helicopter paused about fifty meters away, hovering over the water. Phosphorescent foam showed where its powerful rotor wash hit the surface. It waited, hanging almost motionless in the air, until the South African signalman pointed his light at a clear section of the pier. Then the aircraft slid forward and came in to land.

The concrete pier was ten meters wide at this point. In earlier days, Simonstown had served as a base for the Dutch, then the Royal Navy. Now it served what was left of the South African Navy—a force that had shrunk from scores of ships to the present handful of missile boats. Some of those had been lost in the fighting. The rest were hidden along the coast against future need. They would be of little help in assaulting the Mountain.

As soon as the helicopter settled, Taylor shook a few hands, received heartfelt best wishes from his men, and trotted toward the aircraft, ducking under the still-turning blades. Spier and Fraser were close on his heels, and as they approached, a side door opened, revealing a red-lit interior.

The three men quickly clambered aboard, helped by experienced hands. Crewmen, expressionless beneath bulky flight helmets, strapped them in. As soon as they were secure, Taylor felt a steady pressure on his seat and spine. They were airborne.

Just as the helicopter started moving forward, a flash and the roar of an explosion broke the night's calm. Taylor felt the machine shudder. Spier, seated beside him, said, "It's a ranging shot. They must have seen something."

True. The smallest flicker of movement could attract the attention of the guns hidden in Table Mountain's tunnels. Even sound could prompt an attack.

A second shell landed closer to the pier than the first. White water spouted high in the air. Taylor swore softly. Even a near miss could tumble the slow-moving helicopter into the ocean.

He felt the helicopter's engines roar as the pilot fire-walled the throttle. It skimmed over the water, gathering speed. A third round landed almost on top of their landing site, but they were well away, and Taylor was sure that the men they'd left behind were long gone. You didn't live long in Cape Town these days without knowing how to take cover.

The helicopter was a troop carrier, a Nighthawk version

of the Sikorsky UH-60, equipped with navigation and night-vision gear. Taylor and the other two rubbernecked for a few moments until an enlisted man handed each South African an intercom headset. Removing his beret, Taylor put it on and heard, "Good morning, gentlemen. Lieutenant Colonel Haigler, U.S. Marine Corps, at your service."

Sure that lieutenant colonels did not normally pilot helicopters, Taylor replied, "Good morning, Colonel."

Taylor, who still thought of himself as a major, fought the urge to call Haigler "sir." His commissions as commandant, colonel, and finally brigadier had been earned in combat, in response to the new province's desperate need for an organized military force. His deputy, Adriaan Spier, had been a lieutenant and was now a colonel.

"How far is it to your flotilla, Colonel?" asked Fraser.

The American officer's slow, confident voice filled his earphones. "About sixty miles—nautical miles. ETA over the task force is in roughly forty minutes."

Taylor looked back. The dark coast behind them was invisible, and the Nighthawk skimmed over the dark waves only twenty meters below them. There were no marks to navigate by, and only fading starlight to see by. He trusted the pilot's navigational skills, though. He had to.

After about thirty minutes, the helicopter started climbing. The eastern horizon was already visibly lighter, and the three South Africans heard Haigler say, "I thought you'd like to have a look before we set down."

Taylor and his two companions peered out the port windows. They were climbing steadily. His ears popped uncomfortably, and he kept yawning, trying to clear them. Now he knew why so many American fliers seemed to chew gum all the time.

The sun was also climbing to meet them, casting its pale early-morning light farther and farther to the west. Suddenly, what had been a dark and empty seascape was full of gray-painted ships.

Taylor was sure they were in some sort of formation, but all he could see was a mass of ships—some small, many large. He picked out what had to be a carrier, and as if to reinforce the point, two F-14 fighters flew past the helicopter, close enough for a good look but just far enough away to avoid buffeting their craft.

The brigadier began to smell a setup. No doubt the Americans and their British allies thought an initial display might influence the attitudes of their South African guests. Still, he appreciated the show. If nothing else, Taylor now had a much better idea of the task force's size and fighting power.

The Nighthawk angled down, and Taylor realized they were not heading for the carrier, but for what had to be a battleship. He had heard and read of these vessels, but he had never seen one, certainly not like this. The warship seemed to symbolize the American intervention. It was massive, powerful, even pretty to look at. He was genuinely impressed.

In a long, slow, smooth arc, the helicopter came in to land on the battleship's fantail. As soon as it touched down, two lines of Marines ran up, dressed in camouflaged battle dress but still looking crisp and neat despite that.

Fraser stepped out first, followed by Taylor and then Spier. Boatswains' pipes shrilled, and they stopped momentarily as the Marines lined up to either side presented arms. Taylor and the others were escorted over to a group of officers drawn up on the fantail.

He consciously squared his shoulders. The ceremonies were almost over. Now they'd get down to work.

Lt. Gen. Jerry Craig eyed the approaching South Africans carefully. They were potential allies, but that alliance was far from automatic. His mind sorted out names, faces, and first impressions while his ears listened to the routine introductions—the *Wisconsin*'s captain, the commander of the Marines Expeditionary Force, and so on.

He liked what he saw of Taylor. The South African commander was a weathered-looking man, a little younger than Craig, weary, with that same thousand-mile stare he'd seen in Vietnam—the look of a man who'd seen too much combat. Spier was similar, but more enthusiastic. It was clear the mantle of responsibility was a heavy burden for the young brigadier.

Fraser was a different sort. Smooth, self-assured, he looked as if he hadn't missed many meals—despite the shortages Craig had heard about. Although Fraser was a South African, the general thought he could have stepped out of any city hall or state house in the States. He hated the politician instantly.

Well, it was time to start the festivities, Craig thought. As senior officer he was master of ceremonies. "Will you gentlemen accompany us to the wardroom? We thought you might like some breakfast before we get down to business."

Although billed as a training exercise, the gunnery drill was really a demonstration of the battleship's firepower. An ample, "American-style" breakfast had been followed by a quick tour of the *Wisconsin*, capped off by this "exercise" firing. Taylor didn't need the demonstration, but he was happy to watch. He'd be too busy when the *Wisconsin* actually fired her guns in anger.

The *Wisconsin* was the centerpiece of Taylor's plan for clearing Table Mountain—the answer to his prayers. Air attacks had proved futile against the recessed, heavily armored gun positions. The battleship's one-ton shells were both precise and powerful enough to knock out the guns. In addition, sixteen-inch shells were cheap, and the *Wisconsin* could pound the battery again and again, until it was gone.

Craig and Capt. Thomas Malloy, the *Wisconsin*'s skipper, were having an animated discussion about gun safety and backblast, and Taylor sagged against the railing and tried to rest. His morning on the battleship had been his first day of relative peace since the civil war started.

He looked up as Craig nodded to his guests. "Gentlemen, I recommend that we remain inside the bridge during the firing."

Taylor was reluctant to leave the bridge wing's fresh air and wider view, but he sensed that Craig knew his business.

As soon as they stepped inside the bridge, sailors rushed forward to swing the armored doors shut, dogging them tightly. During their brief tour, Taylor had noticed the heavy steel forming both the doors and the bulkheads they were set in. With its six inches of all-around steel protection and splinter-proof glass windows, Malloy referred to the bridge as part of his ship's armored "citadel," a term that seemed highly appropriate.

Responding to Malloy's orders, the *Wisconsin* changed course. As the ship turned, Taylor saw its massive forward gun turrets start moving. A ringing alarm bell warned anyone foolish enough to be on deck to keep clear of the moving machinery.

Each turret swung out to starboard, pointing harmlessly out to sea. Craig explained that an artificial target was being fed into gunnery plot, many decks below, and that the guns would fire a salvo at this imaginary enemy.

Muzzles whined upward on the two forward turrets.

Taylor heard a "Stand by!" from the phone talker, followed by a shrill beep-beep, and the second beep ignited an explosion that filled his world with sound.

Smoke and flame splashed off the armored glass windows in front of him, and his feet carried the firing shock up his legs and spine until it shook inside his head. Nine sixteen-inch shells, each weighing one ton, howled twenty miles downrange. Each shell was twenty times larger than those fired by the guns on Table Mountain. For a brief instant, the whole battleship seemed to stagger and rock back under the force of its broadside.

The bridge windows cleared as the *Wisconsin*'s motion carried it out of the smoke cloud. Mist still streamed from the gun tubes. In the silence following the explosion, Taylor turned to the Marine general and nodded firmly. "That should do the job, I would think."

WARDROOM, USS *WISCONSIN*

Lt. Gen. Jerry Craig wanted to rub his eyes, get up and walk around, and take a breath of fresh air. He wanted to leave, to get back to his command center where the only problems he faced involved killing an armed and alert enemy.

Fraser was speaking. "General Craig, I must insist that your government has already recognized our government by our reception here. We welcome that recognition and ask only that you formalize it before we proceed with any military planning."

Fraser had been insisting on the same thing for the past two hours, using fine points of international law, the Bible, and his own rhetorical skills to hammer his point home: the Cape Province was now an independent nation.

But Craig had other things he wanted—no, needed—to discuss: logistical support, communications, intelligence on the enemy forces. Fraser's insistence on diplomatic recognition had come as a complete surprise. There had been no indication to anyone that this would be on the agenda.

The politician wanted Craig's assurances that any civil affairs personnel landed would act in accordance with Cape Province law. He wanted Craig's promise that the U.S. consulate would be reopened soon as a full embassy, and he asked for the general's agreement in principle on an aid and mutual defense treaty—all prior to landing any American or British troops.

Internally, Craig fumed. It was a stickup, plain and simple. His forces had to land at Cape Town, and quickly, if there was going to be anything left to save in South Africa. Instead, the Cape Town authorities seemed to be more concerned with assuring their own political survival.

Fraser wasn't leaving much doubt about that. "The Cape has always had a different cultural makeup and a different political philosophy from the rest of South Africa. We've no use for these stiff-necked Boers. And this is a historic opportunity to chart the course of our country. Free of outside control, free to develop as we want. I tell you, General, apartheid has already ended here."

That might be true, Craig thought, but he wasn't buying it. He'd seen the hard numbers during his Pentagon briefings. The Afrikaners had been working to fragment their population for years—the old divide-and-conquer rule. So it was natural that the English-descended Cape Towners should want to go it alone. Facts didn't take much notice of wishes, though. The provincial economies were too interdependent. South Africa's separate pieces simply could not stand on their own.

Fraser's quiet, impassioned, and utterly self-interested tirade went on and on.

So far, the two military officers, Taylor and Spier, had sat quietly and uncomfortably throughout the entire discussion. At one point, Craig asked Taylor for his views.

Fraser had interrupted as the brigadier opened his mouth to speak. "We have the full support of our military in this matter, General."

Right. Craig remembered the fat briefcase that Spier had carried aboard under his arm. It lay on the table now, next to Taylor's elbow, and he had to force himself to stop staring at it. Everything his men needed was in there, he was sure of it.

He was also sure these two soldiers were ready to talk business, but Fraser wanted his deal first.

Craig cleared his throat. "Look, these are all points that you can iron out with our State Department later. Right now, I need to work with Brigadier Taylor and his people, coordinating the military aspects of this operation."

Fraser was obstinate. "And I insist, General, that before you can help us you must state whom you are going to help—and to what end."

Craig bristled. Deputy governor or not, who the hell did this guy think he was? "And I am not empowered to recognize a foreign country, Mr. Fraser."

"But you already have, by receiving us in our official capacity."

Aaarrggh. Craig unclenched his teeth long enough to spit out a quick, "Excuse me, gentlemen. Back in a moment." He left the wardroom for his own sea cabin. As he stepped into the passageway, his chief of staff, Gen. George Skiles, intercepted him.

Skiles was an Army brigadier general, part of the "joint," all-service staff Craig had inherited as part of his new post. A good administrator, he'd taken a lot of the paperwork load off Craig's shoulders.

"Well?"

"I just got off the secure phone with the State Department. They say that they have almost no information on the 'Independent Cape Government,' and that they have every confidence in your judgment."

Nuts. Twenty-five years of micromanagement and the one time he needed them, the Foggy Bottom boys left him alone. He shook his head. Two things were certain. They'd show up again as soon as he worked out an acceptable deal. And if he screwed up, he'd hang alone.

"All right." Craig walked down the passageway and entered his cabin. He thought for a few minutes, washed his face, took a deep breath, and summoned Skiles. "Get Taylor out of the wardroom, by himself, and bring him up to the bridge wing."

"Fraser won't like you talking to him alone."

Craig frowned. "I don't care. Tell Taylor he's got a message from his wife. Think of something. Keep the good deputy governor busy. I won't be long."

Skiles nodded and left.

Craig climbed the two decks up to the bridge wing and waited, but not for long. Metallic footsteps clattering up the ladder preceded Taylor. The South African joined him at the railing, his uniform tunic fluttering in the wind.

Taylor's tone was stiffly formal. "I came because you requested it, sir, but I will not negotiate with you separately. Mr. Fraser is our sole voice in these matters."

Craig nodded quietly. "I understand, Brigadier."

"And even if I were to come to some sort of separate agreement, I would not have the power to impose it on the civilian authorities."

"Is that true, Brigadier?" Craig asked. "After all, you control Cape Town's military forces."

"I will not use those forces to interfere with civil authority again." Taylor's tone softened. "I am sure we share a certain dislike for politicians"—he smiled—"but they hold the reins, and any other way leads to chaos."

Craig matched his smile. "I agree. But I asked you up here because I want you to understand my situation. To give you information that only a military man can appreciate.''

Taylor arched an eyebrow.

Craig spoke carefully, picking his way through a verbal minefield. He wanted this man as an ally—not pointing a rifle from the other side of the beach. ''I have at my disposal an immense force—more than a division of embarked Marines, air, and artillery. At least two more divisions are at airfields in the States waiting for word that D. F. Malan airport is open. Those men can begin arriving within twenty-four hours of the time I give that word.''

Taylor nodded. America's rapid deployment capabilities were widely known.

''You also know we're on a timetable—a tight one. And that timetable was drawn up in response to allied needs, not the needs of the 'Independent Cape Province' or the rest of South Africa. We're burning precious time right now.''

Again Taylor nodded. The Cubans were already hundreds of kilometers inside the Transvaal region. Unless Craig and his men got ashore soon, Castro's two remaining armored columns would reach Pretoria, Johannesburg, and the Witwatersrand minerals complex well ahead of them.

Craig paused. Now for the hard part. ''I'll be blunt, Brigadier. You know the strengths and abilities of your forces, and you've seen some of our capabilities. Now, I want your forces working with us, but if we can't reach agreement soon, I'll land my troops without your approval and proceed on my own.''

''We would have to fight you.''

''Yes. And you and I would both lose men. And time, which would cost more lives, later on. And I'd win.''

Taylor nodded, not bothering to hide the truth. His forces, short on everything except confusion, could not stop the Americans. He could slow them down, inflict casualties, and bog them down in house-to-house fighting—but to what end?

Cape Town had always been a beautiful city. He hated the holdouts on Table Mountain for what they were doing to the city and its people. That would be nothing compared to a full-scale invasion. Unbidden, pictures of the damage the *Wisconsin*'s shells could cause flashed into his mind.

Craig had been leaning on the rail. He turned now to face Taylor, and he moved half a step toward the younger man. "The only reason I've put up with Fraser's bullshit this long is because I want to avoid bloodshed between people who should be friends. But I can't stall out here forever. We're getting close to the point where lost time means more than lost lives."

Taylor stared back at him, his face held rigid.

"All I need is the airfield. I don't care what shape the rest of the town is in." Craig paused. "That sounds cruel, but the alternative is even worse. Brigadier, you're a professional, and I respect professionals of any nation. You know the score, and you know your duty. But I can't afford to waste any more time."

Craig stopped speaking and turned back to the rail. There was a somber expression on his face, and Taylor wrestled with words, looking for the best reply. Finally, he said nothing and turned to go back to the wardroom.

A few seconds after Taylor's footsteps faded, Skiles appeared on the ladder. "General, do you need anything?"

"Ask for a recess. Give the South Africans about fifteen minutes alone, then we'll start again."

Craig walked into the wardroom at the appointed time to find a circle of expectant faces waiting for him. His staff looked weary but hopeful, confident that he could find some solution. Taylor and Spier were clearly worried. Fraser, on the other hand, seemed genuinely angry, but he also seemed able to control his rage with a politician's skill.

Craig sat down heavily, and Fraser spoke, carefully choosing each word. "General Craig, we have been discussing the issue of the Cape Province's sovereignty. While we feel it is vital to our interests, we do not wish to delay your essential military operations any longer. Are you willing to state that you are at least unopposed to the concept of an independent Cape Province?"

Craig was tempted to throw him a bone, but he was angered that this politician was still attempting to drag him into some sort of last-minute commitment. "Mr. Fraser, I will only state that the political status of the Cape Province is of no concern to me, one way or the other." He leaned toward Fraser, looking him in the eyes. "My only responsibility is to my men and the accomplishment of my mission here."

He leaned back. "State Department negotiators can discuss the matter with you at length—once we are ashore."

Craig caught a flash in the man's eyes, but Fraser only nodded. "Very well. Then we are agreed."

There was a sudden bustle in the room. Skiles slipped a typed agenda in front of the general, and Craig spotted Spier handing Taylor a fat folder. Time to get down to business.

DECEMBER 8—C GUN, 1ST CAPE ARTILLERY, TABLE MOUNTAIN GARRISON

Sgt. Franz Skuller slept next to his gun. It wasn't devotion to the thing. After weeks of being besieged, and thousands of rounds fired, the sergeant secretly hoped the blasted piece would break—split its barrel from muzzle to breech, or something else so catastrophic it would be beyond repair.

But the garrison was badly overcrowded, and space was at a premium. Alerts were constant, and there wasn't time to run through a maze of passages and still get the first shot off quickly. No, sleeping next to his gun was really the path of least resistance. Anyway, he was so tired he could have slept anywhere.

Skuller stirred in his sleep, reacting to a noise, but it was only Langford and Hiller, performing one of the countless maintenance tasks that kept the gun in working order. Once the clank of tools and the men's voices would have awakened him, but he had long since ceased being a light sleeper.

During the initial confusion of the mutiny, he and his gun crew had fought for three days straight. Skuller was part of the existing garrison. He'd watched from above as troops loyal to Vorster's government had fought for control of the city—using Table Mountain's commanding position as the anchor of their defense. But they'd been defeated, and he'd also seen their fighting withdrawal turn into a scramble for cover in the mountain's underground complex.

Since then his crew had been kept hopping by constant alerts, raids, bombardments, and fire missions. His gun was one of six buried in Table Mountain, and not a night had passed when he hadn't fired at some target in the city below.

His gun had begun life as a standard G-5 artillery piece. It had a 155mm bore—just a little wider than six inches, moderately big as artillery goes. The G-5, built by South Africa's ARMSCOR, was probably the best weapon of its class in the world. A special shell design, stolen from the Americans, combined with other improvements, had resulted in a gun of phenomenal accuracy and range. Some G-5s had even scored first-round hits on targets forty kilometers away.

Normally, the G-5 was towed from place to place, but since these guns were "static," permanently emplaced, its wheels had been removed. Now it sat on twin rails that ran the length of the tunnel. Electric motors ran the weapon forward and back on those rails. They also elevated and traversed the gun automatically, in response to signals from a fire control computer buried deep in the complex. Laser range finders and fire control radars sited around the circumference of the mountain fed target ranges to the computers, ensuring that if the first salvo didn't hit, the second would.

When not in use, C Gun was pulled back into the tunnel and an armor-steel blast door covered the tunnel mouth. As soon as the gun was needed, the counterbalanced door swung up and the gun ran out. Its own shield neatly fitted the opening, providing some protection for its crew.

There were motorized ammunition hoists, a filtered ventilation system; everything needed to defend Cape Town—or hold it at bay.

Skuller smiled grimly in his sleep, wrapped in his blankets. Yes, they'd been driven in here, but he'd seen the storerooms and magazines. They could hold out for months, maybe another two or three if the officers he'd heard were right. He and his comrades had more food than the citizens below.

Successive assaults and raids had all failed to dislodge them, and Skuller knew that once the Cubans had been wiped out in the north, Vorster would deal harshly with Cape Town's rebels. All they had to do was hold out until then.

An earth-shattering clanging filled the tunnel, echoing off the rock walls and filling his head. It was mercifully short, but Skuller still took his time rolling out of his blankets and stretching. Just because he could sleep on a rock floor didn't mean that it felt great. The kink in his back felt as if it would never go away.

Privates Langford and Hiller quickly finished their work as the rest of the gun crew arrived at a dead run. Skuller hooked up his headset at the front of the tunnel as the gun began rolling forward down its rails.. "C Gun on line, sir."

"Look alive down there, Sergeant." Lieutenant Dassen's voice carried excitement. "There are American ships approaching."

The Americans! So the rumors had been true. Skuller smiled. This would be different. A moving ship would be a real challenge, although Table Mountain's guns had never had problems engaging trucks or other moving targets.

C Gun whined forward and tripped a release built into the rail. Smoothly, the inches-thick blast door swung up, letting in sunlight. Skuller filled his lungs with the cool morning air. Once the gun started firing, the ventilators wouldn't keep the stink of the gun's propellant from filling the tunnel.

The 155mm gun's muzzle and then the front two-thirds of its tube emerged into the sunlight. His brief dose of sunlight ended as the shield skid into place, and he heard latches on the rail lock the gun carriage into firing position.

"C gun is in battery," Skuller reported over the intercom. "Ready to fire."

USS *WISCONSIN*

Capt. Thomas Malloy, USN, wished he'd been able to persuade Craig to leave the ship with the South Africans. Most of his staff had gone back to the *Mount Whitney,* but the general had insisted, as only generals can, that he needed to observe the bombardment firsthand. In fact, only a tour of the Mk40 gun director had convinced him that there wasn't room inside for him to watch from there. Of course, Craig might just have wanted to see the director, but Malloy didn't think the general was pulling his leg.

"Twenty-seven miles to Green Point, Captain," reported the phone talker.

"Very well, sound general quarters." The Klaxon's echoes throughout the ship were almost an anticlimax. Having been warned earlier about the upcoming bombardment, most of the crew were already at their stations. Gunner's mates had been sweating over their machinery half the night, making sure that every piece of equipment functioned perfectly, and practicing the countless actions necessary to send a one-ton shell twenty miles with pinpoint accuracy.

A boatswain's mate handed Malloy his helmet, mask, and gloves. Every crewman was required to wear protective equipment at battle stations, and Malloy believed in setting a good example. The cloth hood and gloves were good protection against flash burns, and even in the summer heat, nobody with any sense complained about wearing them.

The face mask covered the wearer's features, but Malloy knew the officers and enlisted men on the general quarters bill well by voice alone. If he did forget, the helmets were labeled with the wearer's position, HELMSMAN or NAVIGATOR, for example. Malloy's helmet read SKIPPER.

Craig accepted a spare set, and with the boatswain's help, donned the gear. Someone had turned a spare helmet over to the *Wisconsin*'s Marine detachment, and the steel pot had been painted in camouflage colors to match his fatigues, then adorned with three black plastic stars and the Marine Corps insignia. As Malloy watched, the short, stocky Marine general donned the helmet with a smile and a shake of his head.

The phone talker turned his phone set over to the man who held the position at general quarters, and the new talker reported the *Wisconsin*'s progress toward battle-ready status. "Damage control is on the line. Engineering reports all boilers lit off, ready to respond to all bells. Gunnery reports all turrets manned, all mounts manned, all guns in automatic." His tone was calm, cold, clear, and completely factual. A good talker never let emotion cloud his repeated messages.

A final report was more immediate. "Electronic Warfare module reports a J-band radar bearing zero nine five."

Probably a gunfire control radar, Malloy thought. The bearing was consistent with the mountain. Well, he hadn't really expected to catch them napping.

Malloy watched the clock. Three and a half minutes after he'd ordered general quarters, the talker reported, "All stations manned and ready. Damage control reports condition zebra set throughout the ship." They were ready, all right. Clearing for action usually took five minutes or more. Still, his crew was helping him look good in front of the general.

Malloy needed to take control of the ship's movements. "This is the captain. I have the deck and the conn. Navigator, what's the range to Green Point?"

"Twenty-five point four miles to Green Point, sir, twenty-eight point two to Table Mountain. Recommend we come right three degrees to zero nine seven true."

"Very well. Helm, come right to zero nine seven." Malloy turned to the 21MC intercom and pressed the button that allowed him to talk to the combat information center. "Harry, tell our screen to split off as planned."

The radio speaker came to life as his coded signal was transmitted. The *Wisconsin*'s screen of three frigates and two destroyers normally surrounded her, protecting the battleship from air and submarine attack. They wouldn't be able to help with this job, though, and some of them couldn't even keep up with the battleship at top speed.

As his escorts turned away, Malloy ordered, "All engines ahead flank."

The four ships of the Iowa class were rated at thirty-three knots, but his engineers had promised him thirty-five, and the captain believed them. He planned to close on Table Mountain at high speed, firing as soon as his ship came within maximum range. There wasn't any point in messing about. Malloy wanted to go in fast, hit the Boers hard, and get it over with.

Even the weather was helping. The sea was relatively smooth, with waves no more than four feet high and the wind at less than fifteen knots—conditions the Navy labeled Sea State Three. They wouldn't interfere with the big ship's progress or rock the vessel beyond the capabilities of its gun stabilizers.

Malloy stepped out on the bridge wing and looked aft. Four sleek warships, tiny when compared to his battlewagon, were falling away behind. One ship remained. USS *Scott*, a Kidd-class guided-missile destroyer, would fall in astern and to seaward of the *Wisconsin*—to protect her from air attack while she worked. Picked for her high speed, *Scott* had five-inch guns that couldn't possibly reach Table Mountain, so she'd just have to wait and watch.

The navigator reported, "Range to Green Point is twenty-one point two miles. On course."

Table Mountain was a little under three miles from Green Point, which showed up clearly on radar and thus made a better place from which to mark the ship's position. Table Mountain's guns, if intelligence reports could be believed, had a range of twenty-one and a half miles.

The *Wisconsin*'s current course took her straight toward the mountain. On this heading, her rear turret, one-third of her firepower, could not be brought to bear. When she was in range, Malloy planned to turn his ship's bow thirty degrees to one side. That would bring the aft turret into play, while still letting the *Wisconsin* continue to close with her target. Anytime enemy fire got too hot, he would put the ship's rudder over—"tacking" to the other side of her base course, continuing to close.

A fountain of white and gray water erupted to port, almost drowning out the navigator's latest report. "Range twenty-one point five miles." The shell burst was close, no more than a hundred yards away.

Right on the money, Malloy thought. He was in the maddening position of being outranged by a six-inch-gun shore battery. It was time to give them a harder target. "Left standard rudder. Steady on course zero eight eight."

At thirty-plus knots, the eight-hundred-and-ninety-foot

ship responded quickly to its helm. She would never be as nimble as a destroyer or a frigate, but Malloy loved his ship's feel as she turned.

The rules were simple. Head toward the last shell splash so that the enemy's corrections would move his next shot off-target. Occasionally make small turns, since they might not be noticed and the enemy might assume you were still on your old course. Finally, stay off the cardinal points of the compass, since that might let an enemy guess your course.

At least running through standard tactics kept his mind busy while he waited for the next ranging shot. Time of flight at this range was almost a full minute—a fact that gave every potential target plenty of time to think about the next salvo between corrections.

A second shell splash appeared, this time to starboard, and closer. Malloy waited approximately twenty seconds, then ordered, "Right full rudder, steady on course one two six."

The massive vessel actually heeled over in the hard high-speed turn and quickly steadied up on her new course. Half a minute later, a ragged line of shell bursts tore the sea apart, well off to port. Those bastards would have to work harder than that to catch him. Malloy felt as if he were in a pitchers' duel. He looked over at Craig, who nodded in approval.

A loudspeaker mounted on the overhead carried the gunnery officer's voice. "Director reports we are in range, all turrets unmasked. Request permission to fire."

Malloy pressed the intercom switch. "Batteries released."

Nine sixteen-inch guns fired simultaneously, bellowing in a thundering crack of noise and smoke that made him think he'd unleashed a thunderstorm. But would the lightning strike where he wanted it?

Normally a ship twenty miles away would be invisible from the bridge, hidden by atmospheric haze and the curvature of the earth. During World War II, big-gun ships like the *Wisconsin* had all carried their own spotter planes, launched from catapults, to adjust their gunfire.

The target this time, though, was Table Mountain, with a recorded elevation of 3,566 feet. Its rocky, barren cliffs rose straight up out of the sea, visible to the naked eye. Malloy watched the summit carefully through his binoculars—waiting for his shells to arrive.

Another Afrikaner salvo landed, a half dozen splashes a hundred yards behind them. Ordering their speed down to thirty-three knots, Malloy also changed course to zero three three. That should throw them off, he thought, and he continued to watch the target.

At the *Wisconsin*'s stern, its aft turret swiveled around, its guns now pointing forward and to starboard. The crews inside worked frantically, bringing massive shells into alignment with gun bores and ramming them home. Bags of propellant powder were carefully loaded behind each projectile. Finally, the heavy breech was closed and locked. It took over a hundred men, working in close harmony, to serve the guns of each three-gun turret.

Malloy heard "Splash" over the loudspeaker just as the upper third of the mountain disappeared—enveloped in a cloud of smoke, flame, and dust.

Cheers filled the bridge. Malloy turned round. "Quiet down. Did you really think we couldn't hit a mountain?" He kept his tone light, but the message was clear.

Malloy heard a Klaxon and braced for his battlewagon's second salvo. It roared out and he hoped his guns were having an effect. Time to start thinking about a course change again.

TABLE MOUNTAIN

For the first time during the siege, Sergeant Skuller was worried. They'd endured artillery bombardments, commando raids, even attacks by aircraft. The Mountain and its garrison had withstood all of them—sometimes with ease.

They'd never fired at a naval target, though. During peacetime, his battery had trained against target barges, but they'd been slow-moving creatures, towed in a straight line by a civilian tug. This battleship, though, maneuvered and dodged and worst of all, shot back.

And what shots! In five minutes of action, they'd received seven or eight tooth-rattling salvos. Lieutenant Dassen reported that they were being hit by sixteen-inch shells! The Afrikaner artilleryman looked at his own gun and tried to imagine the size of such a projectile. His eyes widened when he visualized the size of the gun you'd need, and the crew you'd have to have to serve such a weapon.

Skuller shook off his speculation and concentrated on the job at hand. At least his G-5 could fire twice as fast as those on that ship, and rate of fire counted for a lot in a gunnery duel. After all, he told himself, they only needed one or two hits.

USS *WISCONSIN*

Malloy had long since ceased bracing himself for each salvo from the guns. Keeping one arm wrapped around a bracket, he stayed close to the 21MC intercom speaker and concentrated on dodging the increasingly accurate shell bursts.

After a little more than ten minutes, they'd closed another six miles on the target, dropping the range to about thirteen and a half miles. His guns grew more accurate as the range decreased, but the enemy's accuracy was improving as well. A shorter range meant a smaller time of flight, less dispersion in the fall of shot, and even reduced error in the range-finding equipment.

The *Wisconsin*'s guns fired again, and Malloy ordered another course change, this time back to a starboard "tack." The trick was to get the ship's rudder over and steady up quickly. The turret crews were reloading while the guns pivoted to the opposite side, and if everything went by the numbers, rate of fire wasn't affected in the slightest.

Another line of shell bursts tore up the ocean, close aboard, just off the port side. A fraction of a second later, the water on either side of the *Wisconsin* vanished in tower columns of yellowish spray. The ship shook violently as a ball of black smoke and orange flame cloaked her forecastle. They'd been hit!

Malloy leaned forward, peering out through the bridge windows. He couldn't see the damage. Even with the wind created by the battleship's speed, the shell smoke streamed astern only slowly.

As if to reassure him, all three turrets fired on schedule, and Malloy ordered a change in speed and direction almost by reflex. When the gun smoke cleared, the site of the shell hit was visible—a small, ugly hole forward of the *Wisconsin*'s Number One turret, slightly to port.

It was a solid hit, and he shuddered to think of the damage their escort destroyer, the *Scott,* would have suffered from that impact. The *Wisconsin,* though, had three armored decks. The top deck, the one penetrated, was three inches thick. A second right below the first was twice as thick. All told, nine inches of solid armor had easily stopped the force of the 155mm exploding shell.

But not all of his ship's vital areas were so well protected. Malloy could only hope there wouldn't be many more like that.

TABLE MOUNTAIN

Sergeant Skuller listened to the news with incredulity. The A Gun had taken a direct hit on its gun shield. The impact had pushed the thirteen-ton artillery piece twenty meters back down the tunnel, killing its crew instantly and mixing them with their weapon in an unholy tangle of metal and flesh.

Another enemy salvo shook C Gun's tunnel. The mountain could absorb a lot of punishment, thank God. The little bit that reached them was bad enough.

"Calling C Gun. Are you all right?" Lieutenant Dassen sounded shaken.

Skuller waited a beat as Hiller pressed the firing switch. The gun's breech leapt backward. Even when wearing protective earphones the noise was almost deafening. "We're fine here, sir."

"D Gun is out of action. A shell in that last salvo collapsed the tunnel on them."

D Gun was right next door. Skuller's eyes leapt to the rock ceiling above them. The rough surface was covered with air ducts, water pipes, and electrical cables. He scanned the ceiling for any sign of damage. Nothing was visible.

Another salvo from the American battleship hammered the mountain above them. Skuller was too busy readying his gun for its next shot to notice the network of fine cracks spreading through the ceiling overhead. They'd been invisible when he looked before, more weaknesses in the rock crystal than actual cracks. But the sledgehammer pounding created more and more fractures. Every linked crack weakened the overhead rock's ability to support its own weight.

Skuller continued to listen on the headphones and report to his crew while he supervised the gun's firing. Dassen, in his observation bunker, was calling the fall of shot, making adjustments, and informing his surviving crews of the results. Isolated in rock holes, with only a small sighting telescope for each gun, they needed the big picture to do their best.

The picture wasn't improving. Dassen had reported three hits, so far, and several near-misses, but without visible effect. The Afrikaner gun crews were beginning to realize the power of the floating fortress that had decided to attack them.

Another salvo from the battleship rocked the mountain, and Skuller heard a scream on the line.

"We've lost E Gun." Dassen didn't elaborate further.

The cracks in the ceiling continued to grow. They were clearly visible now, if only Skuller had taken the time to look up.

Forty seconds later, nine more shells arrived, streaking in at more than 1,900 feet per second. Each armor-piercing projectile weighed 2,700 pounds and bored thirty feet into the hard rock before exploding. Adding to the tremendous kinetic energy already possessed by each shell, 4,500 pounds of TNT detonated in nine separate explosions, sending pressure waves surging outward through the rock.

One shell slammed into the cliff just ten meters away from C Gun and almost directly overhead. The shock was strong enough to rattle the gun on its rails. Without the locks holding it in place, the G-5 would have leapt off and smashed into one of the tunnel walls.

Thrown to the floor by the pounding, deafening impact,

Skuller and his men scrambled to their feet and raced forward to check their weapon for damage. But as the sergeant bent over C Gun's delicate sighting mechanism, a small piece of rock pattered off his shoulder. As he looked up at the ceiling, reacting to the impact, a second chunk rattled off the gun barrel, followed immediately by a third. Realization came, and on its heels, panic.

He ripped off his phone set. "Out! Get out, now!"

But as he looked up to see how much time they had, the web of cables and pipes overhead was already falling—torn from the ceiling by man-sized chunks of rock. Skuller managed just two steps before his head and chest were crushed. Only Private Hiller made it to safety to report on the fate of C Gun and its eight-man crew.

USS *WISCONSIN*

"Sir, the gunnery officer reports no firing from the mountain for five minutes now."

"Very well. Cease fire." A rolling blast from the battleship's three gun turrets punctuated Malloy's order, and the talker quickly relayed his command before the guns were reloaded.

The last wisps of gun smoke trailed away, and Malloy took a deep breath. It would be a long time before the acrid powder smell was out of his nose, or his clothing. But he had other things to worry about right now. He turned from the bridge windows. "Navigator, course to the mountain?"

"Zero eight three, sir."

"Helm, steer zero eight three. Indicate flank speed. Director, keep mounts one and two trained on the target." Malloy wasn't going to give Table Mountain's defenders a chance to surprise him. He planned to run in fast. The *Wisconsin* would take station ten thousand yards off the beach. If anyone on the mountain fired again, he'd give them all nine guns at point-blank range.

Besides, his job wasn't finished yet.

Malloy looked away from the gyro repeater to see Craig

studying the mountain. Dust and the smoke of fires started by their bombardment still obscured most of its heavily scarred surface. The Navy captain raised his own binoculars to the area.

Men and vehicles were visible between the columns of smoke, advancing slowly up the mountain along winding roads—Taylor's Cape Province infantry were making their assault.

There were still defenders up in the tunnels and bunkers, though. The Cape troops were moving slowly—pinned down from time to time by heavy machine-gun and rifle fire. Even without its heavy guns, Table Mountain would be a tough nut to crack.

"Sir, lookouts report aircraft approaching from astern."

Craig and Malloy stepped out onto the bridge wing to watch as a cloud of aircraft appeared over the horizon. As they closed, Malloy identified them as Marine Ospreys. The amphibious assault ship *Saipan* had launched two dozen Ospreys carrying two companies of U.S. Marines. The tilt-rotor aircraft were headed for the top of Table Mountain.

A flight of four AV-8B Harriers screamed past the battleship. Loaded with bombs and gun pods, they would hit any remaining defenders on top of the mountain—covering the LZ while the Marines landed.

Malloy's grim smile matched Craig's. Caught between two advancing forces, with the *Wisconsin*'s guns and Marine fighters in support, the Afrikaners would have nowhere to go. They'd have to surrender—or die in place.

For all practical purposes, the battle for Cape Town was over.

DECEMBER 10—TRANSIT CAMP, 101ST AIR ASSAULT DIVISION, NEAR THE D. F. MALAN INTERNATIONAL AIRPORT, CAPE TOWN

The Marine helicopter touched down in a cloud of hot dust and wind. Its rotors were still turning as Lt. Gen. Jerry Craig, flanked by his chief of staff and intelligence officer, jumped from the machine and marched over to a knot of men waiting near a long barbed wire fence. Craig noted that there were Marines, Army personnel, and South African soldiers present. He hoped that was a good sign.

"Good morning, sir." The senior officer, an Army lieutenant colonel, saluted, and Craig returned it quickly, still walking. The officer, a slim man with a carefully trimmed crew cut and a small scar on his chin, fell in beside him.

Ahead lay a massive tent city, still growing if the frantically working construction teams were any indication. Some men were erecting tents while others built more-permanent structures—mostly prefab hangars and maintenance sheds for the 101st's helicopter fleet. Other troops were digging emplacements for heavy weapons at regular intervals along the fence line—an action prompted by last night's incident.

"Over here, sir." The party followed the fence line to a stretch of wire that had a six-foot gap cut in it. A row of bodies lay off to one side, covered by a green, Army-issue tarpaulin.

As Craig's group approached, a young Army private standing near the fence came to attention and saluted. The lieutenant colonel nodded in his direction. "This is PFC Moffett, General."

Then he turned to the private. "At ease, Moffett. Tell the general about last night."

Clearly nervous in the presence of so much rank, Moffett tried his best to report. "Sir! I was assigned the midnight-to-oh-four-hundred guardpost last night, the ninth of December, when I detected unauthorized personnel near the fence. When I ordered them to halt, they engaged me with unauthorized small-arms fire. So I was forced to return fire while calling for the corporal of the guard."

Craig fought down a sudden grin. "Unauthorized" small-arms fire? He'd have to remember that one. "Good work, son. You did the right things at the right time. Were you nervous?"

The private relaxed slightly and turned his head to look at

Craig. "Nervous, sir? I was scared shitless!" Suddenly remembering whom he was speaking to, he braced, exclaiming, "Oh, fuck! I mean, excuse me, sir!"

Craig's grin broke out into the open. "Don't worry, Corporal. We need men who do their job even when they're scared." He glanced at the Army officer beside him. "I think we can forgive Corporal Moffett's language, this time. We need NCOs who can think on their feet. Right, Colonel?"

The man nodded. "Definitely, sir." He jerked his head to one side. Moffett took the hint, saluted again, and sidled away, grinning at his good fortune.

Craig turned his gaze on the row of dead men. There were four of them, and the bare feet sticking out from under the tarpaulin showed that they were black.

Soldiers pulled back the sheet, revealing four young African men, all dressed in fatigue-style uniforms of mixed cut and color. Moffett had shot three of them, the Army officer explained. The fourth had been killed by another guard as he attempted to flee. "All our sentries are equipped with night-vision gear, General. I don't think they were ready for that."

And Craig was not ready for black guerrillas. "Who were they?" he asked. "What were they trying to do?"

The lieutenant colonel shrugged. "We didn't find any documents, but one of them had an ANC pin on his shirt. Other than that slim link, nothing." He frowned down at the row of corpses. "As for what they were up to? Well, they had three AK-47s, one RPG launcher, and some satchel charges. And this part of the wire is opposite our helicopter park. That's a pretty juicy target for a sabotage attack, sir."

Craig nodded reluctantly. "Double your guards. We shouldn't expect them all to have Corporal Moffett's aim."

He turned to the staff officers with him. "Increase security at all our camps. I don't want any frigging Beiruts on my watch, understand?"

They nodded. Nobody in the U.S. military took the threat of terrorist attacks lightly.

Craig spun back to face the Army lieutenant colonel. "Send out a tracking party right away. See if you can pick up any further information about these guys—where they came from, if they had any help.'' Addressing the party as a whole, he said, ''We're not here to hunt down the ANC, but by God, we will protect our own people.''

Turning away, Craig headed for the helicopter. Shaking his head, he muttered under his breath, ''Sounds good, anyway.''

Another complication.

As his helicopter lifted off and headed back to the *Mount Whitney,* he cursed his luck. Cape Town was supposed to be a safe haven, a place where his men could prepare for their real job. While he didn't view his primary mission as ''liberating South Africa's black population,'' certainly booting out Vorster should be good news for them. Were these guerrillas working with the Cubans, or did they just hate armed strangers in their country?

New contingents of troops were landing constantly, crowding camps that were springing up like plants after a desert rain. Every airfield in the area was so choked with military aircraft that the precious engineer units had been diverted to expanding one of them.

Craig closed his eyes for a brief moment's rest. Just coordinating this buildup was an exhausting, but vital, job. And now he faced this new distraction. Ashore among a fragmented and violent population, he longed for the relief of open combat.

DECEMBER 12—CNN HEADLINE NEWS

A blond, thirtyish announcer sat before a now-familiar map of sub-Saharan Africa. ''The American buildup in South Africa continues, amid criticism both at home and abroad. For different reasons, Senator Steven Travers of Nevada and Soviet foreign minister Alexei Tumansky both released statements today condemning U.S. involvement in the region.''

The scene shifted to show Tumansky in front of the United Nations building, surrounded by aides and reporters. Bundled in an elegant overcoat and fur cap, the minister spoke earnestly. ''Our resolution is intended to call world attention to the West's intervention in support of the South African government."

As if on cue, one of the reporters surrounding him asked, "Washington has stated that it intends to remove the Vorster regime from office. Don't both you and Washington have the same goal?"

"Washington merely intends to restore its own version of 'law and order' to South Africa. The socialist armies now liberating the country intend to let the people decide their new government."

The scene changed again, this time to show Senator Travers at a podium, in front of an applauding crowd. The anchor's voice-over said, "And at a recent fund-raising dinner for TransAfrica, Senator Travers castigated the administration for involving the U.S. in a 'dangerous foreign adventure.' " Travers's voice became audible as he said, "Instead of starting our own private war, we should be assisting those forces in the area that are already fighting Vorster's regime. The cold war is dead. If the President can't get used to the idea of joining hands with old enemies in a common cause, then it's time for new leadership in the White House." More cheers and applause greeted his words, which faded along with the senator's image.

The anchor's face returned, and in a calm, reassuring voice, he read a statement by the British foreign minister, speaking after a particularly noisy question period in the House of Commons. "Britain remains committed to intervention in South Africa, both as a way of protecting our extensive commercial interests in the region, and to ensure that a democratic government is created, one that can end the frightful bloodshed now under way."

Looking up from his script, the anchor let a little excitement creep into his voice. "Meanwhile, the buildup continues."

CHAPTER 32

Gauntlet

DECEMBER 12—VOORTREKKER HEIGHTS MILITARY CAMP

Commandant Henrik Kruger's bungalow still showed signs of the damage it had suffered during the American attack on Pelindaba. Rough plaster patches covered cracks in every wall, and sheets of plastic were tacked over empty window frames. His standard-issue furniture hadn't come through in any better shape. Thick pieces of canvas now covered a small sofa and three high-backed chairs whose upholstery had been torn to pieces by flying glass and steel splinters.

Brig. Deneys Coetzee paused in the doorway and made a show of carefully surveying his surroundings. "What a pigsty, Henrik! You'd be more comfortable living in a tent or inside your Ratel!"

"Perhaps I would." Kruger smiled briefly and then glanced over Coetzee's shoulder. None of his "trusted" junior officers were in sight. Good. He motioned the older man inside and shut the door behind him.

By the time he turned around, the brigadier had already

doffed his peaked officer's cap and plopped himself down on the closest chair. "We're alone?"

"Yes." Kruger felt it might be better not to mention Ian Sherfield's presence in the room next door. What Coetzee didn't know, he couldn't be forced to reveal if the security forces chose to interrogate him.

As always, the shorter man came straight to the point. "You're about to receive new orders—marching orders."

Kruger nodded. He'd been expecting that for some time now. His battalion hadn't suffered many casualties during the American air and commando raid—just a few wounded and even fewer dead. True, they were still short of heavy weapons and APCs, but so was almost every other Army unit. And with South Africa being invaded from every direction, keeping a veteran unit such as the 20th Cape Rifles sitting immobile and useless outside Pretoria made less and less sense with every passing day. If anything, he was surprised that it had taken General de Wet and his incompetent toadies this long to reach that conclusion.

Coetzee looked him straight in the eye. "You and your men are being sent north tomorrow. To fight the Cubans."

"I see." Again, that wasn't very surprising. He and most of his men had been born and bred in the Cape Province. Even Karl Vorster wasn't crazy or foolish enough to trust soldiers to put down a rebellion in their own homeland.

Coetzee shook his head sadly. "No, I don't think that you do see, Henrik. You and your battalion are still under suspicion. There are some at the Ministry who believe your troops failed in their duty during the American attack on Pelindaba."

Kruger's temper flared. "What in God's name was I supposed to do? Order my men out into the open so they could be bombed with greater ease? We were under continuous air attack! Would de Wet's bootlickers be happier if we'd been slaughtered like Peiper and his sixty-first?"

His friend grinned cynically. "Probably. Don't forget Peiper is being mourned as a hero of the Afrikaner people. An incompetent hero perhaps, but a *blery* hero nonetheless."

"Good Christ." Kruger fought to regain control over his

anger. Weeks and months of frustration and pent-up rage threatened to boil over in seconds. He spoke tightly through clenched teeth. "If we are under such suspicion, why are they even willing to trust us in combat against the Cubans?"

"You're not going to be trusted, man. You're going to be used." Coetzee opened his briefcase and handed him two photocopied sets of orders. "Read those."

Kruger obeyed. One was addressed to the head of the Far North Military Command. The other had been sent to the officer commanding the SADF's Logistics Branch. Both were signed by Gen. Adriaan de Wet himself. And both contained instructions effectively sentencing his seven hundred officers and men to death.

De Wet wanted the 20th Cape Rifles destroyed—but he wanted to make some use of its destruction. Essentially, Kruger and his men were to be thrown in front of Cuba's advancing columns as cannon and tank fodder. Brigade commanders along the northern front were supposed to assign them to every possible dirty and dangerous mission—to place them in the most exposed defensive positions and to use them as spearheads for every suicidal counterattack. Even worse in a way, the Rifles were marked as dead last on the list of units slated to receive chemical warfare gear. De Wet wanted protection against Castro's poisons restricted to battalions and rear-area headquarters of "proven loyalty and dependability."

Naturally, exceptions were to be made for a certain number of junior officers and a small scattering of known AWB loyalists among the enlisted men. Kruger studied their names with some care. A thin, humorless smile flickered onto his face. It was decent of de Wet to provide him with a ready-made list of those who would willingly abandon their comrades to near-certain death.

He waved the documents at Coetzee. "I can keep these? And show them to men I can trust?"

"Yes. But don't get caught with them. I have to pay some attention to saving my own skin, eh?" The brigadier snapped his briefcase shut and rose to his feet. "So what will you do now, Henrik?"

Kruger pondered that for a moment. Even though he'd contemplated rebelling against Vorster's illegal authority for months, it still felt unnatural. Helping Emily and her friends escape the security police had been a personal decision with solely personal risks. But leading his whole battalion into action against Pretoria might mean dragging several hundred others in front of a firing squad beside him.

Still, what other choice did he have? Vorster's government had already tried and convicted his troops—men who were guilty only of being born in the wrong place. Kruger stared down at the orders he held crumpled in his hands and made his decision. He would choose the path that left some of his honor intact. He would lead the 20th Cape Rifles out from under Vorster's illegal authority.

Coetzee read the determination in his eyes and nodded his own understanding and agreement. "You'll have to move decisively when the time comes, Henrik. No dawdling. No second thoughts. And no coddling for those who'll try to betray you to the government."

"You speak true. As the wise man said, see a snake . . . kill a snake." Kruger's right hand lingered over the pistol holstered at his hip. He looked up sharply. "Come with us, Deneys. Get out while you still can."

Coetzee shook his head. "Not yet, Henrik. Not just yet." He cleared his throat. "You see, I haven't given up all hope for our country. There are still some of us, a few of us, in the Army who know what is right and what is wrong. We may still be able to salvage something for South Africa from this disaster."

He took a pen and notepad out of his pocket. "If you need to reach me for any reason, call one of these two places." He jotted down two phone numbers. Both had a Pretoria prefix. "Neither is tapped, and you can speak freely to those who will answer."

Kruger took the folded piece of paper from him and carefully stowed it away in his tunic. "I thank you for all that you have done, Deneys. No man could have a better friend."

Coetzee gripped his outstretched hand hard and then stood back. "I wish you and your troops a good journey, Henrik."

Kruger blinked away an uncomfortable feeling of moisture in his eyes. Officers did not cry. Instead he stiffened slowly to attention and saluted.

Coetzee returned the salute in perfect silence.

Both men knew it would probably be the last time Commandant Henrik Kruger showed his respect for a superior officer of the South African Army.

DECEMBER 13—20TH CAPE RIFLES, ALONG THE N1 MOTOR ROUTE, NORTH OF PRETORIA

More than fifty trucks, jeeps, and armored personnel carriers moved steadily northward along the highway—spread single file in a column more than a kilometer long. Machine gunners aboard each Ratel and Buffel APC kept both hands clamped firmly to their weapons and both eyes fixed firmly on the sky. They were only forty kilometers beyond Pretoria's northernmost suburbs, but Cuba's MiGs ranged far and wide across the Transvaal these days.

Ian Sherfield sat uncomfortably in the cab of a five-ton truck stationed right behind Kruger's Command Ratel, feeling awkward and all too visible in a crisp, brand-new South African Army uniform. Emily van der Heijden and Matthew Sibena rode out of sight in the back—crammed in among boxes of ammunition, concentrated field rations, and twenty-gallon drums of water. So far, the truck driver, a close-mouthed sergeant, had pointedly ignored all three of his passengers. Ian wondered how much longer the man would be able to restrain his evident curiosity.

Without thinking, he fingered the single stripe that identified him as a lance corporal—whatever that was. Just what did Kruger have in mind? Did the Afrikaner officer really believe he could impersonate a South African soldier for any length of time? Especially in combat against the Cubans? Because if he did, the whole idea was a nonstarter from the word go.

Ian knew that he'd give himself away as an American the very first time he opened his mouth. Even after spending almost a year in this country, the odds of his being able to successfully fake any kind of a South African accent could best be summed up as zero. Kruger must know that, he told himself. So the man had to have some other plan up his sleeve. But what was it?

He remembered the strange late-night meeting the South African had held with his veteran officers. He'd been forced to stay concealed in the bedroom while they slipped into Kruger's quarters by ones and twos. The assembled officers had spoken only Afrikaans—a rapid-fire, guttural Afrikaans far beyond his comprehension. But he had been able to sense their shifting emotions. Shocked disbelief at something their colonel had shown them had slowly given way to deep, abiding anger and fierce determination.

Ian sat up straighter. This morning's frantic rush to get ready and on the road hadn't left him much time to think about that meeting, but it had pretty clearly been important. Kruger and his officers had obviously made a crucial decision of some sort. But about what? He held his breath as the first inkling of what they must be planning flashed across his brain. My God, maybe they were going to . . .

Squealing brakes broke his train of thought. He looked up through the front windshield. The lead Ratel had pulled off onto the left shoulder—an action being imitated by every other vehicle in the battalion column. Dust plumes rose as tires left the asphalt road and rolled over dirt and loose gravel.

The sergeant brought the truck to a complete stop just a few feet behind Kruger's command vehicle and switched off. Then he unrolled his window, looked briefly at his perplexed passenger, and then looked away again. His expression was as unreadable as ever.

Ian shook his head. Why were they stopping now? The battalion had only been on the move for a little more than an hour. And why stop here? He studied the flat countryside surrounding the long line of trucks and APCs without finding any answers. Empty grazing lands stretched to either side for as far as the eye could see. Two or three hundred meters farther on, a narrow, unpaved track crossed the motor route, winding west toward nominally independent Bophuthatswana. The main highway itself ran north, passing straight through the open savannah of the Bushveld Basin until it vanished in a wall of shimmering heat waves.

Up ahead, a boyish-looking lieutenant swung himself out of the Command Ratel, dropped lightly to the ground, and moved down the length of the stalled column shouting, "Orders group! All platoon and company officers report for an orders group in ten minutes!"

Kruger himself clambered out of the command vehicle a minute or so later, followed by a tall, bearded officer Ian recognized as Capt. Pieter Meiring, the battalion's second-in-command. Both men looked tense.

Slowly, other officers joined them. Soon Ian realized that he could sort the arriving captains and lieutenants into two distinct groups. Most greeted Kruger with friendly informality and wore comfortable-looking uniforms wrinkled and creased by long service in the bush. But a sizable minority, mostly young and mostly sour faced, seemed insistent on exchanging rigid parade-ground salutes with their commander and each other. Their pressed, immaculate uniforms showed the same insistence on punctilious formality. Ian disliked them on sight.

Kruger dropped to one knee and unfolded a large map. His officers grouped themselves into a semicircle around him—apparently intent on whatever he was saying. Ian frowned suddenly. That was odd. Each of the battalion's veteran officers seemed to have stationed himself next to one of the younger men.

He leaned forward, trying to get a better view through the dust-smeared windshield. Maybe he could see more outside the truck—

"Please stay put, Meneer Sherfield. *Kommandant*'s orders." The sergeant sitting beside him didn't even turn in his direction. One of the man's hands still rested on the truck's steering wheel, but the other lay conspicuously near the assault rifle clipped to his door.

Ian sat back, stunned. The man knew who he was! Was Kruger turning them over to the security police despite all his promises to Emily?

The sergeant saw his surprise and grinned. He patted the rifle. "Don't worry, *meneer*. This is not for you. We have enemies somewhat closer at hand. You see?" He gestured through the windshield.

Ian followed his pointing hand and stared in shock. Kruger had risen to his feet and now stood with a grim, cold expression on his face, watching with folded arms as his veterans roughly disarmed their younger counterparts. More soldiers were coming down the line of trucks and APCs, herding several of their onetime comrades ahead of them at bayonet point.

The sergeant nodded in satisfaction. "A good clean sweep of all the AWB trash. That's what the *kommandant* said he wanted. And that's what we're giving him."

No kidding, Ian thought, still amazed by the speed of Kruger's move to rid himself of Vorster's toadies and spies. As he watched, the prisoners were stripped of all their weapons and rank insignia and crammed into three of the battalion's troop trucks. R4-armed guards scrambled atop Ratels stationed to the front and rear—perched there to deter any escape attempts. The rest of the battalion's junior officers and staff were already scattering—trotting toward their own APCs and trucks.

Engines roared to life from one end of the column to the other. The men and vehicles of the 20th Cape Rifles were ready to move again.

Kruger appeared at the open window on Ian's side of the truck with Emily beside him, her eyes blinking rapidly against the harsh light of the bright sun. "You have room up front for another passenger, I trust?"

Ian smiled faintly, still not sure what to make of this man who seemed able to swing so swiftly and easily between cold ferocity and warm companionship. He popped the door open and slid over into the middle of the seat. "Any time, *Kommandant*."

Kruger helped Emily up and stood back as she pulled the door shut. Then he leaned in through the open window. "Both of you may now move about more freely. I do not think you need fear Pretoria's informants. Not in this battalion at least.

My men and I are no longer subject to Vorster's illegal orders."

"And Matthew Sibena?" Emily asked. "What of him?"

Kruger looked taken aback for a moment. He'd obviously forgotten all about the young black man. "He can also come out of hiding." He paused, apparently searching for the right way to say something. "However, it would be best if he does not call too much attention to himself. My soldiers may not like what they have seen of the AWB and its fanatics, but that does not make them 'liberals' in matters of race. You understand?"

Emily nodded once. "We understand. And we thank you for all your help, Henrik."

Ian felt her warm hand slip into his and relaxed. He studied the other man's calm, weather-beaten face. "So I guess we're not heading north to the Transvaal, then?"

Kruger nodded. "You guess right, *meneer*." He pointed toward the narrow dirt track ahead of his Ratel. "That road will take us west and then southwest—the beginning of what I am sure will be a long journey to the Cape."

They were going to try driving all the way to the Cape Province? Ian whistled softly. A long journey indeed! The last reports he'd seen had claimed the nearest rebel forces were in Beaufort West—more than a thousand kilometers away over unpaved back roads scarcely worthy of being called by that name. "Assuming we make it, *Kommandant,* what will you do then?"

"Who can say? Join the new government? Surrender to your newly arrived American army of occupation? Scatter to our homes?" Kruger shrugged. "I truly do not know."

Ian asked, "And your AWB prisoners? What will happen to them?"

"We will keep them with us for a while. Any of those *verdomde* traitors would gladly shoot me or you, especially you, Meneer Sherfield. They would also certainly betray the Twentieth's position to their masters."

"But are we taking them all the way to Cape Town?" Emily asked.

The *kommandant* shook his head. "No, I don't want those

jackals with us, but I cannot afford to turn them loose. Certainly in a few days our defection will be noted at headquarters. After that, we can discard them at some small town as we pass. We will be commandeering any gasoline we find, and if we cut the telephone lines, they will do us no further harm.''

He glanced south, down the highway to Pretoria. ''In any event, my friends, I am not at all sure we will survive long enough to worry about such matters.''

Neither Ian nor Emily needed to ask what he meant by that.

Suddenly, Kruger showed his teeth in a lightning-quick grin. ''Still, we shall have a few hours' head start on the hounds. I plan to make the most of them.''

And with that, he swung away, striding quickly and confidently toward his waiting command vehicle.

In minutes, the trucks and APCs of the 20th Cape Rifles were rolling north along the highway. One by one they turned left onto the tiny dirt road heading west into Bophuthatswana—west toward the Cape Province, the U.S. intervention force, and safety.

DECEMBER 14—STATE SECURITY COUNCIL CHAMBER, PRETORIA

Fifteen men, half of them in uniform, crowded around an array of maps spread out on the chamber's large teakwood table. Small colored flags and numbered blocks of wood represented the ground units and air squadrons locked in combat across South Africa. Their positions were plotted with extreme care since shifts of half an inch in any direction could indicate either a stunning victory or a disastrous defeat.

Marius van der Heijden tried hard to hide both his boredom and his increasing frustration. As always of late, the State Security Council's morning briefing showed every sign of dragging on into the late afternoon. He risked a quick, irritated glance at the tall, haggard man bent over the maps. There stood the sole reason for this absurd waste of time.

As the nation's battlefield situation worsened, Karl Vorster's interest in military minutiae only grew more pronounced. Not content with the kind of broad overview needed to make vital strategic decisions, he seemed obsessed with comparatively unimportant details—combat reports from individual infantry companies and tank squadrons; fuel and repair states for individual aircraft; even raw, unfiltered data gathered by recon units probing enemy positions or occupied territory.

We don't have a president anymore, van der Heijden thought sourly, we have just another incompetent brigade commander. He grimaced. While Vorster fiddled with his maps and wooden blocks, the rest of the government bumbled along on a sort of automatic pilot—hobbled by increasingly bitter personal and departmental rivalries. And all at a time when the wars with Cuba, its allies, and the United States and Great Britain were strangling what remained of the Republic.

Even in loyalist-held areas, key industries were at a standstill. Basic munitions and armaments production goals weren't being met. Fuel shortages were crippling both civilian transport and power production. Outlying rural regions and the black townships were running low on food.

Much as van der Heijden hated to admit it, his own Ministry of Law and Order reflected the chaos sweeping through South Africa. Hundreds, perhaps thousands, of his police and Security Branch troops had gone over to rebel forces in the Cape and the Orange Free State. Hundreds more were trapped in enemy-occupied territory—either dead or captured or in hiding. Communications across the rest of the country were so poor that his surviving police commanders were largely forced to administer their districts on their own initiative, acting more as feudal magnates than as cogs in a smoothly functioning bureaucratic machine.

"What? What do you mean they've disappeared? How could such a thing be possible? How can a whole battalion vanish into thin air?"

Van der Heijden looked up sharply as Vorster's harsh voice snapped his bleak train of thought. What had he missed?

The President stood upright, glaring down the length of

the table at Gen. Adriaan de Wet. One of his powerful hands grasped a single wooden block.

Van der Heijden squinted, trying to read its identifying label. He could just barely make out a sequence of two numbers and two letters. The block represented a unit tagged as the 20CR—whatever that was.

De Wet opened his mouth to speak and then shut it again in evident confusion . . . or was it fear?

"I have asked you a simple question, General. I expect a simple answer. At once!" Vorster's voice rose in volume, climbing steadily toward an enraged bellow.

De Wet turned pale. "I do not know how to answer you, Mr. President. Kommandant Kruger and his battalion were ordered to report for duty with the Far North Military Command. But they did not arrive last night as scheduled. Nor have they answered our radio messages asking for their current position and status." The general hesitated, clearly afraid to say anything more.

"Go on."

Vorster's angry growl shattered de Wet's reluctance to speak. "My staff does not believe the Twentieth has fallen victim to enemy action, Mr. President."

"Then you believe this Kruger of yours has turned traitor?" Vorster's tone was dangerously calm. He tightened his grip on the tiny piece of wood representing the 20th Cape Rifles.

De Wet nodded unhappily. "It is the strongest possibility, Mr. President. We have had Kruger and his officers under close scrutiny for some time."

"Clearly not close enough, damn you!" Vorster's closed fist crashed down on the table, bouncing other wooden blocks and unit flags out of position. Two red-tabbed staff officers scrambled to put their situation maps back in order.

Van der Heijden shivered involuntarily. First his own daughter had betrayed her land and her tribe. And now the man he himself had handpicked as his future son-in-law had followed her into treason. His enemies inside the government would make much of such damning misjudgments if they learned of them. The Minister of Law and Order shivered again. He could not allow that to happen. No one must know that he had once considered Henrik Kruger a friend.

Vorster slowly opened his clenched fist, revealing the piece identified as the 20th Cape Rifles. When he spoke again, his voice was calm and coldly precise. "Listen to me carefully, General. I want this unit of renegades hunted down and exterminated. I want no survivors left to flaunt their treason in our faces. Is that understood?"

Surprisingly, de Wet shook his head. "I understand your anger, Mr. President, but I do not believe it would be wise to waste valuable forces searching for these men. We face far more powerful enemies on several fronts. Six or seven hundred fugitives can do us little real harm."

Privately, van der Heijden agreed. With the Americans preparing some new amphibious strike at South Africa's coastline, and the Cubans pressing hard for Pretoria, they could ill afford to scatter needed troops across the countryside in a vengeance hunt.

Vorster disagreed. His voice grew colder still. "Do not even think to dispute this matter with me, General de Wet. Your pronouncements and predictions have too often been wrong." He looked sternly around the now-silent circle of officers and cabinet members. "Never forget, my friends, a rebellion unpunished is a rebellion that will spread. That is why those who would betray our sacred fatherland must pay a heavy price. And that is why they must be *seen* to pay a heavy price."

He laid the wooden block marked 20CR down on the table and pointed to it with a thick, calloused finger. "I want Kruger and his men killed before their example tempts other cowards and weaklings into disobedience." He studied de Wet and the other assembled officers for a moment longer. One by one, they dropped their eyes, unable to meet his grim, unyielding gaze.

"One word of warning, General." Vorster turned back to a white-faced de Wet. "I will not tolerate any further failure."

The general nodded stiffly. "You may rely on me, Mr. President. The Twentieth Cape Rifles will be annihilated."

He clasped his hands behind his back to hide the fact that they were shaking.

Marius van der Heijden stared down at the map-covered table to conceal his own growing uncertainty. Cuba's communists and the capitalists of the West might not have to work very hard to destroy the Afrikaner nation. Karl Vorster seemed only too willing to do their work for them.

HEADQUARTERS, 44TH PARACHUTE BRIGADE REACTION FORCE, NEAR VILJOENSDRIF, SOUTH OF JOHANNESBURG

The setting sun cast long, red-tinted shadows over the orange groves and green, irrigated lawns surrounding Jan Bode's whitewashed two-story farmhouse. Flocks of bright-plumed birds circled overhead through a cloudless sky before landing along the banks of the nearby Vaal River. Faint traces of dirty-gray smoke lingered on the western horizon—visible signs of Vanderbijlpark's iron and steel plants and clear proof that not all of South Africa was a pastoral and peaceful land.

But there was more than enough evidence of that closer to hand.

Three hundred South African paratroops in full combat gear lounged beside the sixteen helicopters dotting the farmhouse's open lawns. Assault rifles, boxes of ammunition, and fuel drums were stacked under the brown-and-green camouflage netting covering each helicopter. Mechanics and air crews in grease-stained overalls clustered around several of the helicopters—performing routine maintenance work on Puma and Super Frelon troop transports.

Maj. Rolf Bekker paused in the farmhouse door, waiting for his eyes to adjust to the sunlight. He nodded slowly to himself, glad to see his men seizing every opportunity for both rest and needed repair work. They were all combat veterans, and veterans knew the value of time.

He stepped out onto the lawn, wincing slightly at a momentary twinge in his left leg. The doctors had assured him that he'd made a full recovery from the wounds he'd received during the battle for Keetmanshoop Airfield. Right. Know-it-all bastards.

Bekker spotted the man he'd been looking for and instantly forgot all about the pain from his old wounds. "Sergeant!"

Staff Sergeant Roost hurried over from the pile of supplies he'd been inspecting. "Sir?"

"Find Captains Reebeck and der Merwe and tell them I want to see them at the farmhouse in fifteen minutes."

"Yes, sir." The short, wiry noncom turned to go and then turned back. "Are we going to see some action soon, Major?"

Bekker nodded.

Roost smiled, a fierce, quick grin. "Do we kill Americans or Cubans this time?"

"Neither, Sergeant." He shook his head grimly. "This time we hunt our own kind."

If the thought of killing fellow South Africans bothered Roost, he certainly didn't let it show on his face. Instead, he just touched his hand to his beret in a casual salute and moved off to obey his orders.

Bekker stood motionless for several moments, watching as the sergeant headed away in search of his two company commanders. At least this once, he thought, Pretoria's orders were clear and concise. The men and helicopters of the Parachute Brigade's Reaction Force were to find, attack, and destroy Commandant Kruger and his traitorous 20th Cape Rifle battalion.

And Maj. Rolf Bekker always obeyed his orders.

CHAPTER 33

Invasion

DECEMBER 14—FORWARD HEADQUARTERS, CUBAN EXPEDITIONARY FORCE, POTGIETERSRUS

Gen. Antonio Vega tried not to let his anger and frustration show. It was important that his staff, and all his men, think that he was in absolute control, but inside, his inner drive was locked in its own private war with his patience. Damn it, they had to get moving again!

Castro's latest message lay on his desk, an unwelcome reminder of his progress. The tone was encouraging enough: *The presence of the Western imperialists shows that the South Africans must be on their last legs, otherwise their masters would not have to rescue them. Press on to victory! Cuba has every confidence in you.*

Press on with what? Despite an apparently overwhelming victory at Potgietersrus more than two weeks before, his offensive had ground almost to a halt. The Afrikaners were proving unexpectedly resilient. And his own problems seemed to multiply with every passing day.

His own slow progress was especially galling in the face

of the Americans' removal of South Africa's nuclear option and their successful landing at Cape Town. He had to move fast—his window was closing.

The loss of South Africa's nuclear capability had not overly helped him, since his tactics of dispersion and civilian masking had worked well. It simplified his movement plans, but you had to be moving for that to matter.

His First Brigade Tactical Group had begun squandering the first fruits of its triumph in the first hours after its attack. When Colonel Mahmoud's Libyan motorized rifle battalion entered the city, it had stumbled into what its poorly trained, poorly paid soldiers regarded as their own private treasure trove. Hundreds of homes abandoned by their white owners—homes packed with portable radios, television sets, and stereo systems. Stores and shops crammed with rich foods, automobiles, and other luxury items. Even with assistance from Cuban troops following close behind, it had taken Mahmoud precious hours to bring his rioting, rampaging men to heel.

Then, when Vega's troops were finally able to resume their drive south, they'd run headlong into more Afrikaner troops hurrying north—the first significant numbers of tanks and guns to arrive from the stalemated Namibian front. So what should have been a cakewalk had turned into a bloody, bruising, two-day fight that left both sides exhausted and about where they'd started from. Even worse, the battle had consumed the Cuban tactical group's carefully hoarded stockpiles of ammunition and fuel.

Supply. Vega rubbed his temples, feeling the start of another pounding headache. He'd always known that logistics would be his largest problem—especially for the First Brigade Tactical Group. He had a Soviet-supplied airhead at Pietersburg, but cargo aircraft alone couldn't carry the massive quantities of diesel fuel, ammunition, and spare parts a modern mechanized army needed to keep moving and fighting. Most of the supplies he needed had to go by sea to Maputo, then northward along the railroad to Rutenga, and from there south into South Africa—an overland distance of more than one thousand kilometers.

The distance alone presented his supply officers with an almost insoluble problem. The constant hit-and-run attacks on his truck convoys and freight trains only made things worse. Not only were white South African commandos attacking his columns, but breakaway guerrillas from the ANC and other black groups were making separate raids. He smiled grimly. It was probably the first time that the two sides had ever agreed on anything.

Vega remembered the early days of the offensive, when his men had been welcomed by villages they passed with gifts of food and beer. Now they got rocks if they were lucky, bullets if they were not.

He scowled. Whether he liked it or not, the First Tactical Group's days of easy victories and rapid advances were over. The supplies it needed to go back on the offensive were coming in steadily—but only very slowly. And until he had enough fuel and ammunition, his northernmost attack column was reduced to simple skirmishing—company-strength probes of the Afrikaner defenses at Naboomspruit, fifty kilometers south of Potgietersrus.

Farther south and east, his Second Brigade Tactical Group found itself in a similar situation. Closer to the port facilities at Maputo, its supply problems were less pronounced. But the Second had to fight its way up the tangle of mountains, ridges, and chasms called the Great Escarpment. Despite heavy losses, its daily gains were often only measured in hundreds of meters.

And the Third . . .

Vega's headache intensified. The split-second destruction of his third attack column had been even more disastrous than he'd first supposed. The Third Tactical Group had been the striking arm that was supposed to outmaneuver the Afrikaner defenses. Without the "three" in his "one-two-three" punch, he was reduced to this damned crawling advance, attacking South Africa's strongest defenses head-on. It was a formula for losing the war.

Maneuver was the way to win a war in Africa, but he didn't have any units to maneuver with. At the moment, his sole reserve consisted of two companies of infantry, one of tanks, and a battery of self-propelled artillery.

Stripped of his strategic mobility and tactical flexibility, he'd counted on using chemical weapons to break open the war again. Unfortunately, since that first devastating attack, their effects hadn't matched his hopes and expectations.

There were several reasons for that. First, the battle for Potgietersrus had used up most of his hastily obtained stocks of sarin. Acquiring more had proven unexpectedly difficult and time consuming. International condemnation and pressures were making even Castro increasingly reluctant to approve its use.

These political restrictions were matched by military difficulties. Weather was sometimes a problem. To minimize self-inflicted casualties and delays, chemicals were best used when the winds blew from the northeast—toward the enemy lines and away from his own positions. At the same time, Vega knew the Afrikaners were learning how to fight in a chemical environment. They'd doled out a limited supply of protective gear to their frontline troops and artillery crews. Unprotected troops were kept dispersed and well hidden. And accurate counterbattery fire by long-range G-5 and G-6 155mm guns often wreaked havoc among his own artillerymen when they tried to fire chemical shells.

The Cuban general grimaced. Supply shortages. Commando raids. And the growing fear that his grand offensive might grind to a halt far short of its objectives. All of that was bad enough, however he looked at it. Very bad. But now he had to worry about the damned Western allies—the Americans and their British lackeys.

With the forces at his disposal, he didn't have the slightest chance of interfering with the Western troop buildup in Cape Town. He'd never planned to fight a war that far away from South Africa's northern and eastern borders. His strategy had always been to capture the centers of government and let the distant provinces fall into his lap.

Still, he thought, the important regions were within reach. Cape Town was famous for its wine and its wool. Well, he'd rather have Pretoria's diamonds and gold. Let Washington and London squabble over South Africa's dregs.

"Colonel Suarez!" His chief of staff's office was always next door, well within earshot. Suarez appeared immediately.

"Send a message to Havana," Vega ordered. " 'The Western presence means we must accept a limited, but still significant, victory—liberation of the Transvaal and the Orange Free State. I am sure that you will see the necessity of this decision.' "

Vega paused briefly, wondering if there was anything else he should add. Nothing came immediately to mind. "Send it. And call a staff meeting in five minutes. We have to get this offensive moving again."

DECEMBER 15—USS *MOUNT WHITNEY*, SIMONSTOWN NAVAL BASE, CAPE TOWN

One thousand miles west of Durban, several anxious-looking staff officers crowded one of the *Mount Whitney*'s conference rooms. The U.S. and Great Britain had a secure foothold in the Cape Province, but Cape Town had never been viewed as anything more than a stepping stone toward South Africa's industrial and political heartland—Pretoria and Johannesburg. Going overland would take too long. Going by sea meant making another landing somewhere farther up the Natal coast—an opposed landing, where they would have to fight their way ashore. The sea route, in spite of its risks, had always been part of the plan, but it might not be fast enough.

"I just don't see how we can be ready in time, General. The buildup's just too far behind schedule." Brig. Gen. George Skiles, Craig's chief of staff, was adamant, but also distressed. He was a hard worker, with a "can do" attitude, and it hurt Skiles's professional pride to admit failure.

Lt. Gen. Jerry Craig sat glowering, a man unhappy with the news he'd received but unable to shoot the messenger. Shipping delays, bad weather in the Atlantic, and tired air crews had already put his buildup nearly three days behind its original schedule. That wasn't bad when you considered how many tens of thousands of troops and pieces of heavy equipment were en route—streaming across thousands of miles of empty ocean and airspace. But it wasn't good enough. Neither the Cubans nor Vorster's men showed any signs of adhering to the timetable established in Washington.

Photo recon missions over the Potgietersrus area showed massive and unmistakable signs of a Cuban supply buildup. This Vega character was planning to jump-start his own stalled offensive first. At the same time, Afrikaner commanders up and down the Natal coast were doing what they could to strengthen their own defenses against an allied amphibious assault.

Craig frowned. The schedule for his own planned landing in Durban was looking more and more like a nonstarter.

The original plan called for a full division of U.S. Marines and a Royal Marine Commando to make the landing, supported by a battalion-sized air assault on Durban's Luis Botha airfield. Two Army divisions—the 7th Light and the 101st Air Assault—would move in once the airfield had been secured. Heavy armor units still sailing from the U.S. were scheduled to off-load directly at Durban—once its harbor was secure.

The operation was precisely timed and hard to change once the units were in motion. Craig remembered how carefully they'd all considered the date of the landing back in Washington. Tides, weather, and phases of the moon all had to be folded in along with the strategic situation. How quickly could American forces be ready? How fast could the Cubans move?

To allow some flexibility, he'd ordered alternate staff plans prepared. One assumed landing a day early, one a day late. But by December 24, the planned D day, Vega could be drinking Cape wine in Pretoria, thumbing his nose at the Western allies from the Union Buildings.

Craig lowered his chin onto his chest, thinking hard. Like all good staffs, his people tended to be cautious and conservative—"risk averse" in DOD lingo. They often followed a general rule in putting together operations—figure out how much firepower you thought you'd need and double it. And usually they were right. An amphibious landing was the riskiest kind of operation in military art. You had to assemble overwhelming firepower, with enough force to shove the bad guys off the beach. But what if your invasion was too late?

Sometimes, you needed to cut corners. Sometimes you had to take more risks. Such as now.

He looked up. "Okay, here's the way we play it. We're landing in Durban on the twentieth, but with only two brigades plus the Commando. The third will have to follow when it can." He looked at his shocked staff. "All right, gentlemen. We're under way in three days for Durban. Start loading."

DECEMBER 17—HEADQUARTERS, CUBAN EXPEDITIONARY FORCE, POTGIETERSRUS

"Every piece of data we have indicates the imperialists will land at Durban, Comrade General." Colonel Vasquez pointed to the map. "It has the best beaches and port facilities in all of South Africa. Plus, we know that the Boers have had a very difficult time with civil unrest and guerrillas in the area."

He hesitated and then went on, "Durban is also too far away for us to do anything to interfere with their invasion."

"Agreed, Colonel. An excellent analysis." Vega looked disgusted. "Now tell me what we can do with this fact."

Up to now, this war had been fought on land and in the air. By adding a naval dimension, the Western allies had given themselves a freedom that neither Cuba or South Africa could hope to match. Operating without interference off the coast, the Allies could cause both belligerents great pain.

Even the Soviet Navy could not challenge the Western ships off the Natal coast. The Soviets did not want to risk a direct war with America and Britain. They were willing to spend a few rubles and out-of-date equipment, but spilling Russian blood was out of the question.

Part of their reluctance to confront the West was certainly because of the distance from Russia's ports. Their navy was structured for operations close to Soviet shores, in combination with land-based aircraft. Their chances of success against two carrier battle groups were just about nil.

Vega suspected that Castro hadn't even bothered to ask for the Soviet Union's help. Just as well, anyway, he thought. They would only have refused us.

Vega pursed his lips. "The devil of it is, Colonel, that I don't even know if we should help the Americans or try to stop them."

Vasquez took his commander's statement as a request for information. "Certainly, an Allied landing would draw off some of the Afrikaner troops now facing us."

The Cuban general nodded sharply. "Precisely, Colonel." He slapped a hand down hard on the desk. "Right! We cannot stop this invasion . . . so we'll make use of it for our own ends. We'll delay our own attack until after the Americans and British land."

He laughed harshly. "Let us allow the capitalists to stop Afrikaner bullets for a change. Once they're ashore, we'll crush what's left at Naboomspruit and drive hard for Pretoria." He noticed Vasquez's dutiful smile. "Something troubles you, Comrade Colonel?"

"Yes, sir." Vasquez pointed to the waters off South Africa's southeast coast. "Soviet satellite photos show that the American carrier *Independence* has already left Cape Town to join the *Carl Vinson*. Soon they will be in easy striking distance of Durban, Pretoria—perhaps even our lines here. If we get too close to Pretoria, planes from those carriers could hit us."

Vega's tone was final. "We are running out of options. All we can do is push as hard as we can and leave the rest to the uncertainties of war."

DECEMBER 18—PROVISIONAL HEADQUARTERS, NATAL MILITARY COMMAND, DURBAN, SOUTH AFRICA

Worried-looking men in military uniform hurried back and forth through the halls and offices of Durban's fortified police headquarters. Phones rang, maps were updated, and defense plans were changed in a dizzying cycle of ever-increasing urgency. Vorster loyalists still hiding in the Cape Town area had confirmed their worst fears—America's aircraft carriers and amphibious ships were steaming eastward, preparing for another landing somewhere along South Africa's coast.

Brig. Franz Diederichs stood in his office, watching with cold, detached contempt as his subordinates tried desperately to find ways to stop the unstoppable. Intelligence estimated that the Americans and British planned to storm ashore with at least a reinforced Marine division—backed by more than two hundred carrier-based planes and the guns of more than a dozen warships.

In contrast, he had scarcely a corporal's guard to oppose them. Five understrength companies of security police. Three artillery batteries of superb G-5 and G-6 guns. And three weak infantry battalions already worn down by months of guerrilla war with the Zulus and by days of bloody street fighting during the city's November rising. All were short on men and heavy weapons.

He grimaced. Common sense alone should tell the idiots on his staff that they had no chance of achieving victory—at least not victory as it was ordinarily understood.

Logic argued that the Allies were moving on Durban itself. The city's airfield and harbor were perfect staging points for an all-out Allied drive on Johannesburg and Pretoria. In fact, they were the only possible staging points. Essentially, all main roads on the Natal coast led to Durban. Only there did they blend together into a single superhighway stretching north to South Africa's mineral-rich interior.

Logic also argued that the Allies, though long on men and matériel, were short on time. Even capturing the city would still leave this General Craig and his men more than six hundred kilometers from their final objectives. And before the Americans and British could push farther inland, they'd need a secure supply line—the kind one could only build with unimpeded access to a major port.

Diederichs nodded slowly to himself. He and his soldiers

couldn't win the upcoming battle, but they could at least deny their enemies a quick victory. He leaned over his desk, studying a series of charts and diagrams showing Durban's port facilities.

For more than a week now, his engineers and gangs of conscripted black and Indian laborers had been working night and day to wreck the harbor beyond easy repair. Some had planted demolition charges to destroy cargo-handling equipment along the waterfront itself. Others stood ready to scuttle freighters and tankers already trapped by the American blockade—blocking both the harbor's narrow entrance and all its docks and anchorages.

Once the first waves of the Allied invasion force touched down, Diederichs planned to pull the bulk of his small garrison into a perimeter enclosing most of Durban's central city. Even with their overwhelming numbers and firepower, it would take the Uitlanders days to dig his troops out of their fortified skyscrapers and beachfront hotels. And until they did, they couldn't possibly begin repairing the damage to the all-important port facilities. At the same time, his artillery—well hidden among the forested foothills of the Drakensberg Mountains—would interdict the Louis Botha Airport. Periodic barrages of high-explosive shells would make it impossible for the Americans to land their huge C-141 and C-5 cargo planes.

With any luck, the Allied drive on Pretoria would soon sputter and stall—strangled at birth by a lack of food, fuel, and ammunition.

The Afrikaner *brigadier* smiled crookedly at that thought. Whatever the result, he wouldn't be alive to see it. He planned to die fighting with his soldiers. Retreat out of the city was unthinkable and unsurvivable. He didn't have any illusions about his own government's attitude toward unsuccessful officers. Pretoria's firing squads would soon make short shrift of the man who'd lost Durban.

Surrender to the Americans or the British was equally unthinkable. He had no intention of appearing as chief defendant at a so-called war crimes trial. If necessary, he'd kill himself first. His thin lips creased in an ugly snarl. Better by far to die by one's own hand than to stand in chains before swaggering, kaffir-loving conquerors.

Diederichs straightened his shoulders and turned back to his work. Durban's barricades, trenches, and fortified buildings would make the city more than just a graveyard for his own ambitions and dreams. They would end Allied hopes for a quick and bloodless end to the war in South Africa.

DECEMBER 19—SEAL TEAM ONE, ABOARD HMS *UNSEEN*

Boatswain's Mate First Class Joe Gordon, USN, left the *Unseen*'s hatch in a silvery cloud of bubbles. The three other men in his SEAL detachment were already out. They signaled him with a small light, dimly visible through the water.

After closing the diesel submarine's hatch behind him, Gordon swam over to them and pointed to the compass on his wrist. If they were in position—and the *Unseen*'s skipper had assured them they were—their target lay two thousand yards to the north.

Gordon heard a dull, muffled clank behind him and turned to see the hatch opening again. His wasn't the only raiding party going out tonight. The *Unseen* also carried another party of SEALs and one of SBS, Britain's Special Boat Service.

His three men all looked at him, legs and arms paddling slowly to keep them in place against the offshore current. Even in their face masks and other scuba gear, Gordon knew them all, and knew what they could do. Motioning, he pointed north. They started swimming.

He was glad to be out of the British submarine. He'd ridden subs often enough, but he decided that he didn't like the British variant. They talked funny, ate funny food, and the thing always stank of diesel oil. And they were too tight. A U.S. nuclear sub was crowded, but after a full day in a British boat, Gordon had wanted to ask for a marriage license. All they could do was talk. He chuckled inwardly. At least those SBS guys told some fascinating lies.

The sub's small size was perfect for this job, though. The Sturgeon-class U.S. nukes couldn't get any closer to shore than the sixty-fathom curve, dumping them miles from their objective. Here, it was just a short swim—only a mile underwater.

Swimming felt good, stretching out the muscles, burning off some of that adrenaline flowing through his veins. He kept a sharp lookout for sharks. The waters off Durban were famous for them, and he didn't want an encounter to screw up the timetable. They were supposed to be ashore just after midnight.

The water was dark and the shoreline empty. Gordon could only rely on his compass and skills honed by long years of training to get him ashore. He certainly wouldn't find any friends on the beach. Not that he expected any. SEALs were always the first in, and that was exactly what he wanted.

SECOND MARINE EXPEDITIONARY FORCE, SEA ECHELON AREA, OFF DURBAN

Fifty American and British ships lay shrouded in darkness fifty miles off the Natal coast. Massive, flat-decked amphibious assault vessels mingled with smaller ships carrying landing craft, tanks, and tracked LVTP-7 amphibious vehicles. Destroyers and frigates steamed back and forth, screening the formation against air or submarine attack. Inside each ship, Marines and Navy crewmen worked through the night stowing gear, readying aircraft, cleaning weapons—making all of the thousands of last-minute preparations necessary for survival on a hostile shore.

SEAL TEAM ONE, NEAR THE LOUIS BOTHA INTERNATIONAL AIRPORT, SOUTH OF DURBAN

Boatswain Gordon lifted his head above the surface of the water. The shoreline was a smooth expanse of sloping sand, perfect for amphibious ships, but lousy for SEALs. He quickly scanned the area. They couldn't be that far off.

There, off to the right. Reunion Rocks, a jumble of boulders jutting out from the shore, verified his navigation. Signaling silently to the rest of his men, Gordon submerged and without surfacing again, headed straight for the place where a small stream emptied into the Indian Ocean.

The roar of surf as he emerged from the water matched his mood. He was in hostile territory and ready for trouble.

The three other swimmers were only steps behind him, and they quickly moved into the cover provided by the rocks. Once there, they stripped off their swim gear and tore waterproof coverings from the rest of their equipment. It was a warm night, but all of them wore dark-colored clothing from head to toe, including balaclavas.

A roaring scream ripped through the quiet night, and for one fraction of a second, Gordon thought they'd been ambushed. Instantly he and his three comrades hugged the ground, tearing at the coverings on their weapons and wondering what had gone wrong.

Then, as he frantically scanned the immediate area, his ears recognized the sound. It wasn't gunfire, it was the sound of revving jet engines echoing off the airfield in front of them.

Their targets—the airfield's runways and control tower—were separated from the beach by a short strip of industrial buildings. At this time of night, the warehouses and factories would be empty, and the buildings should provide the cover they needed to reach their objectives safely.

Gordon had been given a general brief on the invasion plan. Nothing specific—he was too far into enemy territory to be risked with detailed information. SEALs, though, were expected to act with initiative, and that required knowledge.

The main landing beaches lay just south of Durban. The Navy and Marine brass aboard the *Mount Whitney* had chosen the southern side of the city to stay close to Louis Botha Airport—only about ten kilometers from the city center.

The first Marines ashore would fan out to secure the beachhead for follow-on waves. At the same time, other Marines would come in by air, dropping right on top of Louis Botha itself. From there, the American and British troops would push inland—surrounding the city itself. Seizing Durban's airfield and capturing its port facilities were the first steps on the long road to Pretoria.

Reconnaissance photos had shown that the port was already blocked. The American naval blockade had already put an end to South Africa's maritime trade, so the Afrikaners had nothing to lose by wrecking it.

But the airfield was still in constant use. Although it no longer served as an international airport, military transports and cargo aircraft landed and took off on a regular basis. Gordon looked at his watch and smiled. In a little over an hour, Navy aircraft were going to close the airport, violently.

So far, U.S. carrier-based aircraft had stayed far away from the Durban airport. Allied commanders didn't want to spook the Afrikaners into destroying its runways, control tower, and refueling facilities prematurely.

Gordon's mission was simple. In the few hours remaining before the first assault waves touched down, his and the other two SEAL teams had to find any explosive charges and disable them. If possible, they had to do all that while making the Afrikaners think they still had the airport wired for demolition.

The SEAL smiled grimly. The airport garrison three kilometers from here was going to have one hell of a rough night.

COMANCHE FOUR, ABOARD THE USS *CARL VINSON*

Comanche Four leapt off the deck. Even when it was fully loaded with fuel and bombs, the *Vinson*'s portside catapult still had the strength literally to throw the A-6E attack jet into the air.

Lt. Mark Hammond quickly lowered the Intruder's nose, depending on instinct more than the instruments to keep the big plane in the air. The cat could get him into the air, but it always took a few seconds for the A-6E to decide if it liked it or not.

Hammond felt the machine steady under him, and for the first time he looked for the rest of his flight. The three other Intruders had been launched from the carrier just minutes ahead of Comanche Four. He scanned the still-dark night sky ahead. There! He spotted their navigation lights blinking low over the water.

The three Intruders were already heading west—toward the city just sixty or so miles away. This close in to their target they didn't have to worry about tanking up from the KA-6Ds already aloft. But they weren't going downtown just yet. The air commanders aboard the *Carl Vinson* and the *Independence* planned a coordinated alpha strike on key military targets scattered throughout the Durban area. So Comanche flight's four A-6Es would orbit at a predesignated point until all the fighter and attack aircraft were launched. Both carriers were launching full deckloads—putting more than one hundred and twenty warplanes in the air.

The four planes of Comanche Flight quickly reached their holding point, Sierra Twelve, and orbited slowly—circling round and round at low altitude. Night formation flying kept Hammond busy enough, but his bombardier/navigator, Rob Wallace, was even busier checking out the Intruder's complex electronic suite. Even with built-in test equipment, making sure everything worked took a while.

"This is Overlord. Execute." The order to move came after only a few minutes. Watching his flight leader carefully, Hammond followed his movements automatically, without radio conversation.

The four attack jets had been orbiting at two thousand feet, but now they eased down to a tenth of that as they made their run in toward Durban. Hammond felt his heart pounding faster. This was for real. They'd been assigned to take out the 20mm and 30mm antiaircraft guns ringing Louis Botha Airport.

About twenty miles out from the shoreline, the Intruder's thermal imager started picking up buildings and other heat sources. The heat-sensitive TV camera allowed them to navigate and find their target in total darkness. The camera didn't need light, just heat.

As they closed the beach, taller structures appeared, and bright, glowing spots appeared on the screen. Hammond squinted at the screen. Fires? He nodded to himself. Yeah. Big ones burning out of control. Set by other strikes, maybe. Then he realized that they were too widespread and too well developed. The city was already burning.

It looked as if an invasion could only improve things.

USS *MOUNT WHITNEY*

Silhouetted against the rising sun, Lt. Gen. Jerry Craig leaned over the rail, staring through binoculars at the crowded ships steaming slowly to either side. Helicopters and other aircraft were already spooling up, engines howling across the water. A strong offshore breeze tugged at his jacket, whining through the *Mount Whitney*'s massive arrays of radio antennas and satellite dishes.

By rights he knew he should be down in the ship's comfortable, computer-display-lit Fleet Command Center. But he couldn't resist the chance to take one last look at the forces under his command.

"Sir?"

Craig turned to find a Navy lieutenant commander standing behind him. "Yes, Commander?"

"General Skiles wanted me to tell you we've gotten word from the *Vinson*. Our initial air strikes are complete." The Navy officer's face broke into a sudden smile. "We pounded the hell out of 'em, sir."

Craig nodded. "Good." He headed for the ladders leading down to the command center. "Signal all ships. Land the landing force."

USS *SAIPAN*

Columns of heavily armed Marines were still climbing aboard their waiting planes when the order came to launch. Barely heard over the howling rotors and jet engines, cursing sergeants and officers of all ranks hurried the camouflaged soldiers aboard. Men piled into seven Ospreys at the run. And as their hatches slammed shut, the heavily loaded troop carriers skittered forward and off the deck, their rotors straining to pull them skyward.

Even as the first wave of aircraft lifted off, the *Saipan*'s elevators brought up another set, which taxied into takeoff position. With well-practiced movements, more men emerged from the island and in snaking columns trotted up to their assigned aircraft just as they reached position.

The evolution was being repeated on the USS *Wasp* and *Inchon*. Clouds of fighter and attack aircraft covered them as twenty-one Ospreys orbited, assembling, then turned and headed inland.

Skimming the wavetops at almost three hundred knots, the formation hurtled toward the smoke-shrouded beach. Troops in the cargo compartment sat strapped in, facing each other on crash-proof seats, but they still had to hang on as the Ospreys plowed through the bumpy, low-altitude air.

The Osprey pilots, most of them converted over from the old Sea Knights helicopters, looked out to either side, gratified to see loaded attack aircraft and armed fighters pacing them.

When riding shotgun, the "fast movers" normally looped over and around helicopter troop carriers, but the Ospreys were fast enough to keep up with a cruising jet. That made for tighter control, better support, and a warm, fuzzy feeling for the Osprey drivers. Higher airspeed also meant the vulnerable troop carriers were exposed to enemy flak for a much shorter time.

In fifteen minutes, five of them spent assembling, the assault formation was over the Louis Botha International Airport. Over, in this case, was a relative term, since the Ospreys came in low and hot—screaming in no more than a hundred and fifty feet off the ground.

As their wings tilted upward to vertical flight mode, the Ospreys bucked and shuddered—dumping speed. In less than a minute, three-hundred-knot turboprop planes became fifty-knot helicopters, gently settling down on the runways and taxiways and any other paved areas. The second their gear touched down, rear ramps dropped and Marines poured out onto the airfield.

They fanned out across the tarmac in an almost eerie silence broken only by whining rotors, shouted commands, and crackling flames. Nobody was shooting at them.

The airport's antiaircraft batteries and ground defenses had been thoroughly pasted. A-6E Intruders dropping dozens of five-hundred-pound bombs had turned them into crater-riddled, smoking piles of torn sandbags and mangled metal. Now orbiting AH-1 Sea Cobras and Harriers waited for any sign of serious opposition, but columns of thick black smoke billowing into the air were the only signs of movement.

Despite the terrific aerial pounding it had taken, however, Louis Botha's runways were still intact. The Allied invasion force had uses for them.

Empty now, the Ospreys lifted off, buzzing low over abandoned factory buildings and warehouses as they headed back to the formation, fifty miles distant, to pick up the second wave.

The freight-train roar of heavy artillery broke the silence. Shells began bursting among the Marines scattering across the open tarmac—exploding in huge fountains of earth and flame. Three batteries of Afrikaner guns pounded the airport mercilessly, killing American Marines with every carefully directed salvo.

USS *MOUNT WHITNEY*

Craig stared at the computer-generated map, wishing it were a wide-screen TV. He wanted to see what was going on. Trouble was, if he left the *Mount Whitney*, he wouldn't be able to do his job. The ship carried the sophisticated communications and computer systems he needed to control all his forces—those already onshore and those still waiting to hit the beach.

"How bad is the shelling?" he asked Skiles.

"Hayes says his men are completely pinned down. He's taken moderate to heavy casualties. He also reports that the LZ's way too hot for the second wave."

Craig nodded. "I concur. Hold the second wave twenty miles out, and let's see what we can do about the artillery."

"We're getting nothing on radio intercepts," Skiles reported. "We don't know where the guns or the observers are."

Skiles scribed a forty-kilometer arc on the map, centered on the airfield. Craig sighed. The damn guns could be two-thirds of the way to Pietermaritzburg. It was rough country, far too big an area to search.

Thinking out loud, Skiles said, "They must be using land-line, regular telephones to communicate. In a big city like that, they've got a built-in secure communications system."

"The initial bombardment was supposed to hit the phone centers along with the radio stations. Every target was reported to be pasted." Craig took off his hat and rubbed his forehead. "Damn it, the only part of the system we know about is the comms. Hit the communications target list again," Craig ordered. "And do it fast."

NAVAHO FLIGHT, OFF THE NATAL COAST

"Navaho One, this is Overlord. Target." The radio call was a welcome relief for Lt. John "Rebel" Lee and his wingman. Everyone in the world was hip deep in the war, but his flight was "in reserve," assigned to orbit forty miles off the beach until the right target appeared.

It took time to arm, launch, and fly aircraft to targets, so pairs of strike aircraft had been place "on call"—ready to hit targets of opportunity on command. Navaho Flight was one of six launched by the two American carriers after they'd flown off their first strike planes. And he'd listened anxiously as first one flight, then two more, were given missions by their carriers. Now it was his turn.

Continuing to circle, Lee clicked his mike. "Overlord, this is Navaho Lead. Say target."

The strike controller aboard the *Carl Vinson* responded with a string of coordinates—and a quick description. "Target is a telephone switching station—concrete structure."

Lee repeated the information back to Overlord.

The *Vinson* signed off. "Roger your last, Navaho Lead. This is urgent priority. Hit it fast."

Lee punched the coordinates into his flight computer, and as soon as he hit the ENTER key, a course indicator appeared on his HUD.

His earphones carried Overlord's voice again as the remaining pairs of aircraft were given their missions, all urgent. Something was up, he decided. Well, he'd hold up his end, at least.

Lee checked his armament switches. Since the carriers were so close to Durban, his F/A-18 Hornet was fully armed, with Sidewinders on the wingtips, a single drop tank on the centerline, and eight five-hundred-pound bombs under the wings.

The map display showed his target, buried deep in the city. It also showed each leg of his plotted course. Lee whistled. Luckily, Afrikaner flak had been light and enemy fighters nonexistent, because this was one bitch of a route. Lee hit the radio switch. "Turning to first leg, Panther."

Lee heard two clicks in his earphones. He glanced to the right and saw his wingman, "Panther" Lewis, turning to follow. Lewis was changing formation, sliding from aft and right of Lee's Hornet to dead astern, in preparation for what was certain to be an "E" ticket ride.

USS *MOUNT WHITNEY*

"The strike coordinator says he'll have aircraft on top of the targets momentarily," Skiles reported. He frowned. "But I'm worried about the second air assault wave, sir. We're going to start cutting into their fuel reserve in a few minutes. We may have to bring them back, refuel, and launch them again."

Craig shook his head. "Hell, George, we do that and we'll

be delaying the whole operation.'' He glared angrily at the map. ''But I agree, we can't land any more men until we've knocked those guns off target.'' Visions of burning aircraft caught while landing haunted him.

He turned to the admiral commanding the amphibious task force. ''Steve, take your ships closer to the beach. If the Ospreys don't have to fly so far coming back, we can buy ourselves a few extra minutes.'' Of course, it would also bring them all closer to the South African shore defenses.

As the admiral reached for the command phone by his chair, Craig added, ''And be sure the carriers are rearming all their aircraft as soon as they land. We'll need them.''

NAVAHO FLIGHT

''Coming up on the IP, Panther. Slow to four fifty knots.''

Lee heard his wingman acknowledge with two clicks just as he turned the Hornet over to its attack heading.

Throttling back, he watched his airspeed fall. They'd made a fast trip from their holding station to the initial point, but from here on, he wanted to take it slow and careful. Flying in a built-up area, against a nonbriefed target, he needed to look the situation over.

Lee switched his HUD to air-to-ground mode and made sure that his bombs were selected. He always took extra care with the ordnance panel—especially after an incident in training. He'd made a perfect bomb run on the target, only to find that he'd dropped his centerline tank instead.

The uneven surface of Durban's rooftops flashed beneath him, individual homes and buildings blurring by too fast to make out much detail. His HUD showed the range to the target, which at this speed looked just like any other structure. An open box was centered over the computed position of the building, and Lee kept one eye on the box while he used the other to make sure he didn't fly into anything.

An F/A-18 ordinarily attacked at six hundred knots or more, but that was usually at sea or over open terrain. Here, the buildings rushing by made even a slower speed seem more like Mach two.

There still wasn't any fire from the ground, and with a little relief, he concentrated on pinpointing his target. His targeting box seemed centered on a thick smoke column billowing high into the air. In a flash the scene filled his windscreen.

Lee's eyes narrowed. He hadn't seen what he'd expected to see. The target was obvious, an already-bombed building in the exact center of the box. It was in ruins, no more than a pile of dirty brick and twisted steel. With an error of less than one foot, he couldn't argue with the coordinates. That was the target.

During his one split second overhead, he saw people pointing up at his aircraft, running for cover. He had a momentary image of sandbags in front of the building next door, and men among them, and then he was past.

Lee checked his wingman. Panther Lewis was still in position. He waved a gloved hand as he spotted Lee looking him over. "What's the plan, boss?"

"Proceed as ordered, I guess."

Panther's voice revealed his doubts. "There's not much left to hit."

"I know, but we don't know the story, so we stick to plan A."

By this time the two aircraft had "extended" away from the target—gaining enough distance to turn and line up on their programmed target again. Lee clicked his radio switch again. "Reverse course, turn left in place. Now."

Both Hornets dropped their left wingtips and neatly pivoted one hundred eighty degrees. Lee lined up on Lewis, the new leader, and pushed the throttle forward as his wingman said, "Accelerating."

A four-fifty-knot stroll looking over the target was one thing, but they'd make the real attack run at full speed. Flying faster would make their bomb drop more accurate, increase their separation from the explosions, and make them harder targets for the now-alerted defenders.

The rooftops flashed by below them, and Lee followed his partner in.

MAIN TELEPHONE EXCHANGE, ON WEST STREET

The soldiers guarding the phone exchange watched the American planes scream past. They had a fleeting impression of sharp noses and gray, square-cut wings, combined with a roar that filled their heads.

The enemy planes were dangerous, but seemingly random in their destruction. Less than two hours before, they had bombed the office building across the street into oblivion, while leaving the telephone building unscathed.

One soldier had suggested that there must have been secret military work going on in there, and that was why the Americans had bombed it. Among the laughter, the consensus had been that they were just poor shots. They had been lucky. That was something soldiers could understand.

NAVAHO FLIGHT

Rebel divided his attention between the rooftops, the cues on the HUD, and his wingman, now a mile in front of him. At six hundred knots, that distance became a six-second separation, barely enough time for the fragments from Panther's bombs to clear. The idea was to do this in one quick pass, in and out before the enemy recovered enough to shoot back.

Rebel's HUD was filled with lines and numbers. Altitude, airspeed, weapons settings, steering, and aiming cues covered the angled glass in a confused jumble. Compared to air-to-ground attacks, dogfighting was simple. His target box was still centered on the ruined building, but the target itself was obscured by the surrounding buildings.

Panther's Hornet bobbed, and Rebel worried that something was making him break off the run. In the time it took him to think that, though, the plane in front of him steadied and then dove sharply, its nose pointing at the ground for a few short seconds.

He saw bombs fall from the wings, and in the same moment, tracers flew up from the ground, narrowly missing Panther's aircraft. It was hard to tell, but they seemed to be coming from the building he had noted earlier. It was impossible to tell the exact type of weapon. It was probably just a machine gun, but it was the first flak they had seen.

A split second later, the bombs hit, and as Rebel closed on the target, he gauged Panther's pattern to be a direct hit.

Fuck it, Rebel thought. The rubble's been bounced and someone in that building shot at my wingman. Mentally, he reclassed his mission from "strike" to "postattack flak suppression."

He lowered his nose.

MAIN TELEPHONE EXCHANGE

The soldiers were congratulating themselves. Once again, the American planes were bombing the other building, not them. Crouched behind their sandbag barriers, they smiled at their continued good fortune.

Their luck was running low.

A second screaming roar filled their ears as something big and gray streaked low overhead. Dark objects came off its wings, and eight five-hundred-pound bombs exploded in the street and on the building. Those who were not killed by the fragments or the blast were finished when the telephone center collapsed on top of them.

LOUIS BOTHA INTERNATIONAL AIRPORT

The artillery fire slackened momentarily, and Sgt. Jim Cooper looked out across the airfield. Most of his squad crouched nearby—taking shelter inside a hangar near the LZ, hiding from the relentless Afrikaner barrage. But four of his men, the slower ones, lay out on the tarmac, wounded or dead. He couldn't tell which—not from this distance.

Cooper faced a serious dilemma. If he ran out to recover them, he might attract unwelcome attention to the hangar and the rest of his men. Aluminum sheeting offered concealment—not protection.

But he couldn't leave the guys lying out there, maybe bleeding to death. He couldn't.

Cooper slipped off his pack and laid his M16 down. If he moved fast enough, he might be able to get any survivors under cover while the unseen enemy gunners were shifting targets.

The barrage stopped.

Cooper sprinted out, gut-twisting fear pushing him the dozens of meters in record time. He skidded to a stop by the nearest man—PFC Olivera. He gagged. Ollie was gone, a hole in his neck the size of a fist. The next two he checked were dead, too. But the last Marine, Ford, was still alive.

The sergeant scooped his squadmate up in one clean motion and slung him over his shoulder like a side of beef. Then he started jogging and trotting back toward the hangar—expecting the first deadly shell burst at any moment.

It finally came, screaming in far off to the left—on top of a cluster of earlier craters. What the hell? Whatever or whoever had been there earlier was long gone to ground.

Cooper didn't know why the Afrikaner artillerymen were wasting their rounds tearing up an empty piece of real estate, but he didn't need to be told what to do next.

He made it back to the hangar, and as eager hands lifted Ford gently off his shoulders, he said, "You people waiting for an engraved invite? Stand to while I find the LT. We got work to do."

USS *MOUNT WHITNEY*

General Skiles's tone was filled with suppressed excitement. "Sir, Colonel Hayes reports that artillery fire in the LZ is landing off target. And it isn't being adjusted."

Craig grinned and stood up. "Looks like the air strikes did the trick. Land the second wave before those damned gunners figure out what's going on. We're back in business."

Minutes passed—minutes filled with increasingly optimistic reports from the landing area.

"Second wave is ashore, General. No casualties."

Craig nodded. With their telephone net scrambled, the Afrikaner guns were in a world of hurt. His people had been waiting on their secondary radio frequencies when the perplexed gunners came on line. And now direction-finding and jamming would make short work of the South African artillery.

Meanwhile, his first LVTP-7s and landing craft were heading for the beach, and on-scene commanders reported that the airfield would be cleared in half an hour. Some units were already moving inland on foot—securing strategic hilltops overlooking the assault beaches and the roads leading into the city itself.

Craig stared at the constantly updated computer displays in sober satisfaction. His Marines were winning. True, they hadn't won yet. He still expected some hard fighting for the city over the next day or two. Urban combat was never easy and always bloody.

Nevertheless, he was confident of final victory in the battle for Durban. He planned to hammer the Afrikaner defenders with overwhelming force, and he knew they wouldn't be able to talk to each other.

Craig let himself relax a little. He and his troops had their second foothold in South Africa.

CHAPTER 34

Slowdown

DECEMBER 20—FORWARD HEADQUARTERS, CUBAN EXPEDITIONARY FORCE, NEAR POTGIETERSRUS, SOUTH AFRICA

Dozens of Soviet-made T-72 tanks, BTR and BMP armored personnel carriers, and 152mm self-propelled guns sat motionless beneath a blue, cloudless sky. Dust stirred up by passing trucks hung suspended in midair, blown east by a fitful breeze. Weary, bedraggled soldiers moved slowly under the summer sun—fixing broken equipment, cleaning weapons—or were simply catching up on much-needed sleep. Worn down by weeks of constant combat and operating at the end of an increasingly vulnerable supply line, Cuba's First Tactical Group had ground to a halt along a high ridge just south of the mining town of Potgietersrus.

Gen. Antonio Vega stood off by himself, scanning the lowlands to the south through a pair of field glasses. Vasquez and his other aides waited nervously near a small convoy of BTR-60 command vehicles and GAZ-69 jeeps. He heard their worried mutterings and smiled. What they saw as their general's pigheaded insistence on seeing things for himself never ceased to trouble them. Fears that he might be killed by a South African sniper while touring the front had already caused several ulcers among his staff.

But Vega liked to visit the front lines. His troops needed the lift they got from seeing their general sharing the same difficulties and dangers. He, in turn, needed firsthand knowledge of how his troops and tanks were standing up to the rigors of the campaign—not abstract reports filed by self-serving unit commanders.

What he saw so far was reassuring. Despite heavy losses and growing fatigue, his men were still confident, still sure they were nearing a final victory over an increasingly desperate Afrikaner foe. Few had the time or information needed to worry about the West's imperialist intervention in the conflict. Fewer still worried about the fading support for Cuba's "liberation" force among South Africa's black population. With Pretoria scarcely more than two hundred kilometers away, they were ready to attack again.

Vega adjusted the focus on his binoculars, sweeping his gaze southward across a landscape of sparse, scattered trees, open grazing lands, and green tobacco fields. The savannah looked empty, as though it had been utterly abandoned by its human inhabitants. That was almost literally true, he knew. Cuban reconnaissance units had been probing ahead for the past several days. Except for a few small artillery observation posts, Vorster's northern field commanders had pulled their troops back to defend the vital road junction at Naboomspruit—a prosperous farming and mining community fifty kilometers south of Potgietersrus.

He lifted his binoculars, seeking the far horizon. There it was—Naboomspruit. A purplish smudge at the very limits of his vision. By any reasonable military standard, the town was the last easily defended choke point on the road to Pretoria, Johannesburg, and the almost unimaginable mineral wealth of the Witwatersrand.

Vega frowned. Naboomspruit would be a tough nut to crack.

A drowned morass of swamps and bogs ran just east of

the highway all the way south from Potgietersrus to the Afrikaner-held town. The swamps blocked any possible flank attack to the east by his tanks and armored vehicles.

If anything, the terrain north and west of Naboomspruit offered even fewer alternatives for bold maneuver. The Waterberg Mountains rose sharply there—climbing high in a sweeping panorama of vertical cliffs and rugged pillars of rock. That was bad enough. Worse yet, Boer infantry companies and artillery batteries were reported dug in on Naboomspruit Mountain, only a few kilometers west of troops entrenched in the town itself. Together, they served as interlocking parts of a much stronger defense.

It all added up to another bloody and bruising head-on assault against prepared Afrikaner defenses. To take Naboomspruit, Vega's tank and infantry units would have to come down off their own high ground, cross the open savannah, and then charge straight down the highway.

He shook his head. Pretoria and Johannesburg, South Africa's political, economic, and industrial centers, were within his grasp. But many more of his soldiers were sure to die before he could close his fist around them.

"Comrade General!"

Vega turned to face Vasquez. "What is it?"

The colonel held out a notepad. "Radio intercepts confirm that the Americans have landed! At Durban, as we expected!"

Vega fought to control two conflicting emotions. While they were busy trying to pacify Cape Town, the capitalists hadn't represented any immediate threat to his plans. Allied troops on the Natal coast were another matter entirely. They would be fighting toward the same objectives—fighting for prizes only one side could win.

On the other hand, the threat of another Allied amphibious invasion had already forced Vorster's generals to shift battalions to Natal—troops, tanks, and guns that would otherwise have been facing his two surviving Tactical Groups. Now the Afrikaners would have to redeploy even more forces in an effort to contain the American and British Marines pouring ashore at Durban.

Slowly, almost imperceptibly, one corner of Vega's mouth lifted in a thin smile. He'd spent the past two weeks preparing for just such an opportunity. With South Africa's intelligence services and remaining reconnaissance aircraft focused almost entirely on the approaching invasion fleet, he'd quietly stripped his Second Tactical Group—transferring armor, infantry, and artillery units northward to reinforce the First Tactical Group.

From now on, the Second, still bogged down in the mountains west of Mozambique, would confine its operations to raids and noisy feints designed only to pin down the South African troops facing it—not to gain ground. The real push, Cuba's final offensive, would come from the north.

He looked up. "Inform all commanders, Colonel. We attack again at oh four hundred hours on the twenty-second."

Gen. Antonio Vega would give his enemies another twenty-four hours to weaken their formidable defenses.

TRANSVAAL COMMANDO "GOETKE," THORNDALE, ON NATIONAL ROUTE ONE

Generations of hardworking Afrikaner farmers and cattle ranchers had known Thorndale as simply "the town"—as the closest center of commerce and culture. But the small collection of houses and shops had slowly been withering on the vine for years. Business and people alike were drifting southward to booming Pietersburg, forty kilometers away along the new N1 superhighway. By the time of the Cuban invasion, there were only two generations in Thorndale's tiny white population—the very young and the very old. Almost everyone else had gone, lured away by the opportunities and excitement of South Africa's big cities.

Like many small towns in similar circumstances, Thorndale had been dying a slow, inexorable, and almost painless death. Then the Cubans had come.

At first, the invasion had been more a matter of inconvenience than of terror. Of day or night curfews imposed while armored columns roared past on the highway. Of newly paved streets and fertile fields crushed by tank treads. Of growing shortages and increasing humiliation.

All that had changed when Castro's rear echelon and support troops arrived. They'd rolled through Thorndale like mechanized locusts on the march—stealing food, looting shops, and terrorizing those who'd stayed behind to watch over homes and farms.

Most of the men were already gone, off on commando harassing Cuban supply lines and killing isolated stragglers. Much of the rest of the white population had fled into the countryside with them rather than risk the tender mercies of their enemies.

They'd been right to flee. The local commando was too good at its job, and the Cubans had decided to make their friends and families pay in blood for their success.

One night, in reprisal for what they called "acts of terrorism," three batteries of Cuban artillery shelled the town with poison gas and white phosphorus. Five minutes of wholesale, indiscriminate slaughter had turned Thorndale's wood and brick buildings into fire-blackened shells filled with horror.

Now fourteen-year-old Jaime Steers lay silently in the burnt-out ruins of his own home and watched the campfires lit by enemy soldiers. He'd lain there for hours, hidden behind a pile of rubble and covered by a sheet of black plastic. Despite the darkness he could see moving shapes and occasionally, faces illuminated by the fires.

The Cuban supply convoy was camped in what had once been the town's main square. Ten trucks escorted by almost as many armored cars and personnel carriers had driven into Thorndale just before dark. The ruined town made a good resting place after the wearying, day-long journey from Cuba's main supply depot at Bulawayo—deep inside Zimbabwe. And this was the fourth convoy in as many days to laager there.

The Boer commando led by Erasmus Goetke planned to make them pay dearly for their lodging.

In more peaceful times, Goetke had been a prosperous

farmer, a lean, wiry man who many said could coax wheat out of dry sand. When the Cubans burned his farm and stole his crops, he had sworn a solemn oath to destroy this newest enemy of his people. He was a religious man, well versed in his Afrikaans Bible, and his rage was of biblical proportions.

So Goetke had gathered not only his commando, but every man and boy old enough to carry a gun. Their women were spies and messengers. Children too young to fight hid in the hills with their grandmothers and listened to stories of other battles. But Jaime Steers was just old enough to play an active role in this act of vengeance.

It was his birthright. A remembrance of deadly struggles against powerful enemies was etched deep in the heart of every Boer. All of Afrikaner history had been a story of bullheaded perseverance—against the elements, the Zulus, the British, world opinion, and now the Cubans. With a tradition of resistance, they bounced back from hardship and tragedy like steel springs.

Jaime kept his eyes glued to the binoculars his father had given him—studying the men Commandant Goetke had promised would die.

The Cubans moved confidently, strutting through the twisted wreckage left by their incendiary shells. Most squatted around the campfires, heating rations or brewing coffee. Several amused themselves by urinating on a mass grave dug for those who'd died in the bombardment.

The sight brought tears of frustrated anger and hate to Jaime's eyes, clouding his vision. His uncle, his smiling, bright-haired aunt, and three young cousins lay entwined in that grave—butchered without warning or pity. His hands balled into fists. He wanted to kill and kill and kill again.

He took a deep, shuddering breath. Simple thoughts raced through his mind in a dizzying succession. Calm down. Don't let them hear you. They mustn't hear you. Not yet.

Jaime choked back a racking cough. The smell of smoke and other burnt things still clung to the ashes.

Slowly, very slowly, his hands unclenched. He kept watching the Cuban camp, wanting desperately to hear or see his father and the other commandos as they closed in, but knowing that if he could spot them, so could the enemy sentries. No, it was better by far to wait in silence and seeming isolation.

So he lay flat, trying hard to cultivate the stoic patience of the fighting man. He glanced once at the luminous dial of his watch: 2010 hours. The others should be in position by now. It would be his honor to signal their attack with a single, well-placed bullet.

He lowered the binoculars and fumbled for the rifle by his side. It was not a modern assault rifle, but a bolt-action British .303 Enfield, fitted with a telescopic sight. Jaime was rated a good shot by both his friends and his father, which among Boers made him very good indeed.

The rifle's smooth wooden stock felt good against his cheek and shoulder—a solid, reassuring promise of vengeance. No man with such a weapon in his hands and an enemy in sight was truly impotent.

He scanned the distant shapes outlined against the campfires.

His father had told him what to look for, and he'd picked his own target—a tall, black-haired man whose uniform was neater than the others. Although Jaime couldn't speak Spanish and was too far away to hear it even if he could, it was clear that when the tall man spoke, other men listened, and obeyed. He had to be an officer.

Scraps of charred paper fluttered in a sudden gust of cold night wind. The breeze was across his line of fire. Not the best situation, he thought, but at least it would carry sounds away from the Cuban sentries. His father's team, led by Commandant Goetke, was stationed downwind, hopefully close by.

A bird chirped suddenly, barely audible over the noise of the wind rushing over ruined homes. It was time.

Carefully, slowly, silently, Jaime Steers lifted his rifle and swung it onto the brace he'd half-buried in the pile of rubble in front of him. Then he squinted through the telescopic sight and settled into firing position.

Although the sight was more powerful than his binoculars,

it had a narrower field of view. For a heart-stopping moment he thought he'd lost his target. But then he found the Cuban again, sitting in front of a small fire by himself, sipping cautiously from a steaming cup held in his right hand.

Through the sight, Jaime could actually see the Cuban's smiling, clean-shaven face clearly. A cold sensation rippled down his spine. He'd hunted game often enough and had even stood guard over their house when his father had been worried about unruly blacks in the town, but he had never had to kill a man before.

Then, remembering what had happened to his uncle's family, he realized it wouldn't be too difficult. He checked the wind and adjusted his grip a little. Holding the Cuban officer in his sight, he took a deep breath and let it out. Another quick, shallow breath. His cross hairs settled over the man's uniformed chest and steadied.

He pulled the trigger.

The Enfield cracked once, sounding very loud in the darkness, and the Cuban looked up just as Jaime's shot struck him. He fell forward, folding inward as though the bullet had let all the air out of him. His coffee cup dropped out of his hand and rolled onto the ground.

Through the scope, Jaime saw stunned men looking at their fallen leader. Most seemed frozen in place.

A sudden chorus of other shots rang out, and Jimmy knew his brother, Johann, and his other friends were also in action. Sentries and other soldiers all around the laager began falling—cut down by well-aimed rifle fire.

Goetke had placed Jaime and the other snipers all around the encampment. They were supposed to force the Cubans to go to ground, to hunker down inside their defensive circle.

Jaime squinted through his sight at the fire-lit scene of confusion, remembering Commandant Goetke's strict orders: "Do not shoot unless you will kill your target. I don't want a lot of fire. I want deadly fire." The commando leader's tactic was working. With only a few shots coming in from many directions, the Cubans weren't shooting back, reluctant to expose themselves to an unseen enemy.

Most of the Cubans were behind cover now, and with a

hunter's instinct, he swung the rifle left—scanning for an armored vehicle he'd noticed parked on his side of the laager. It hadn't moved for hours. If its crew were still outside, he knew they'd want to get back inside their nice, safe, armored box.

He didn't have to wait more than a few seconds. First, a head slowly peeked up over the BTR-60's hull, and then hands slid along the fender. Someone was trying to get in through the open driver's hatch.

Jaime let the Cuban expose most of his body and then shot him through the heart. The man crumpled against the hull, his outstretched arms just short of the hatch. Jaime looked for other soldiers to kill.

A shout from the left rang out. He turned his head in time to see a ball of flame envelop "his" BTR. Bright light and a tremendous roar surged through the night air. More blasts followed in rapid succession, all centered on vehicles or among groups of Cuban soldiers lying prone in the open. Agonized screams echoed above the explosions as men turned into blazing human torches.

He gasped in relief. The commandant, his father, and the other commandos were attacking. The older men had crept stealthily to within fifty meters of the Cuban laager. Then, while Jaime and his friends suppressed the sentries, they'd moved in to lob their "Thunderbolts."

Thunderbolt was an accurate term for the homemade bombs, he thought, watching in awe as they set the Cuban camp afire. He'd helped make them, though he had been threatened with dire consequences if he ever made one on his own. The recipe was simple: glass and plastic containers filled with a mixture of gasoline and soap flakes—a combination that quickly turned into a smelly, half-liquid concoction. His father had told him the mixture was similar to napalm. That hadn't meant much to him—not until now.

Each Thunderbolt had one of the commando's precious grenades securely taped to the outside as an igniter. Goetke had assured his men that their gasoline bombs would incinerate any vehicle, no matter how thick its armor. As always, Jaime thought, the commandant had been right.

He watched the battle rage through his rifle scope—wanting to join in, to rush forward and help the commando, or at least to snipe at the Cubans as they fled. His father had been strict, though, and had ordered him not to fire a shot once the gasoline bombs went off. After that, the men of the commando would be inside their enemy's camp, doing God's work.

Shouts, screams, and bursts of automatic weapons fire rose above the sound of roaring flames. From time to time, the ammunition or fuel stored in a burning vehicle would explode—spraying white and yellow streaks of fire high into the dark sky. In less than a minute, smoke rolled across the scene, hiding everything in an oily black mist.

Slowly, the sounds of firing died down and the shouting faded away. Soon, all Jaime could hear were flames crackling as Cuban trucks and armored cars burned. He waited, following his orders, and kept watch through his field glasses.

A hand on his shoulder startled him, and he whipped around, reaching for a rifle he suddenly realized was too far away. His father's voice stilled his panic, though, and the warmth and praise he heard filled him with pride.

"You did well, Jaime. We were watching as you dropped that officer. You killed a captain."

"You are all right, Father?" Jaime could see that he looked healthy, but he wanted to hear it with his own ears.

"I'm fine." His father held out one arm, a little reddened, with the hair singed. "I got a little too close to one of the commandant's Thunderbolts, but otherwise I'm in good shape."

His smile disappeared. "We lost two men, though, and three others are hurt." He saw sorrow cross Jaime's face and quickly added, "It's the price of our struggle, son. Those who live must remember them and carry on."

The elder Steers's face grew grim. "And the enemy paid, son. We got them all." He jerked a thumb at the smoke-shrouded laager ahead of them. "Every vehicle there burns. No Cubans have escaped. No Cubans survived, and we took no Cuban prisoners. They are all in Hell."

Jaime Steers's eyes followed his father's pointing finger

toward the burning encampment. Rumor said that the Cubans had sworn to conquer South Africa or turn it into a depopulated wasteland. Well, he thought, with a newly adult grimness that matched his father's tight-lipped expression, the communists were finding out there was more than one kind of scorched earth.

DECEMBER 22—20TH CAPE RIFLES, NEAR GENYESA, INSIDE BOPHUTHATSWANA

The sun rose fast over the barren lands of the Kalahari Basin—a fiery red ball that turned night into day in one blinding instant. Shadows fled westward across a desolate, sandy plain stretching north toward the vast Kalahari Desert itself and south to the rugged, treeless peaks of the Langberg and the Asbestos mountains. Sunlight glinted off the tin roofs of several dozen one-room shacks clustered around the junction of two roads—one tarred, the other little more than a dirt track. Small herds of scrawny cattle and sheep were already on the move, ambling outward in what would be a long search for sparse grass to graze on. Dogs barked and a lone rooster crowed, signaling the start of what seemed like just another day for the people of Genyesa.

But things were different.

Genyesa's population had more than doubled overnight. Camouflage netting strung between clumps of twisted scrub covered an array of nearly forty trucks, jeeps, and armored personnel carriers. Armed sentries in khaki South African battle dress stood guard along each road entering the town. Others lounged beside the central, flat-roofed stone building that served as Genyesa's post office, telephone center, and police station.

Henrik Kruger and his 20th Cape Rifles now controlled the tiny black town.

With his back propped against a tire, Ian Sherfield sat cross-legged in the shadow cast by a large, five-ton truck. From time to time, he glanced up from the notebook he held open in his lap, gazing skyward without seeing anything at all as he searched for the words or phrases he wanted. Whenever he moved, he moved carefully, determined not to wake Emily van der Heijden as she slept curled up on an old Army blanket by his side.

Matthew Sibena and their driver, a young Afrikaner sergeant, lay back to back beneath the truck itself, snoring peaceably in counterpoint. Everywhere Ian looked he could see men sleeping or trying to sleep—snatching every moment of rest they could while the battalion laagered for the day. Flies droned through the artificial gloom created by their camouflage netting.

He forced his eyes open and yawned hugely, fighting to stay awake at least long enough to finish scribbling a few quick notes describing last night's trek. Keeping a daily record of their long flight westward from Pretoria to the Cape Province had been Emily's suggestion. A damned good one, he thought wryly.

Assuming they lived long enough to tell somebody about it, the details of Kruger's rebellion against his government would make an exciting story—a kind of modern-day anabasis with the 20th Cape Rifles standing in for Xenophon and The Ten Thousand, Vorster's troops playing the vengeful, pursuing Persians, and with assorted independent Boer commandos in the roles originally held by wild Anatolian tribesmen.

At any rate, Ian felt sure the classical analogy would amuse Kruger himself. God knows, they all needed something to laugh about.

The Afrikaner soldier had pushed his men hard over the past several days, evidently determined to put as much distance as possible between Pretoria and his battalion. They'd driven only at night, taking side roads and back-country lanes to avoid towns that might harbor informers or AWB loyalists. Vehicles that broke down were ruthlessly stripped of all useful spare parts and supplies and then abandoned. Where the battalion's quartermasters couldn't buy or beg enough gasoline or diesel fuel, they'd stolen it. One constant, unchanging set of orders governed every action and every decision: move and keep moving. Don't stop. Don't give Vorster's hunters an immobile target. And don't blunder into unnecessary combat.

Last night's march had been by far the worst of all. Warned by scouts of a sizable government force garrisoning the road junction at Vryburg, they'd been forced west and north over a rugged chain of hills and ridges separating the Cape Plateau from the Kalahari Basin. And stretches that could have been covered in minutes on a freeway took hours to traverse on the narrow, unpaved tracks available to them.

So far, though, Kruger's insistence on speed and discretion had paid off. They'd come more than four hundred kilometers without stumbling into any government roadblock or time-wasting firefight. Not bad, Ian thought. Then he remembered the maps he'd seen. They were still at least seven hundred kilometers from the nearest American or Cape Province outposts. Plenty of time yet for disaster to strike.

Beside him, Emily suddenly muttered something in her sleep and rolled over onto her stomach. He put down his pen for a moment and softly stroked her hair. She sighed once, moving closer.

Suddenly, and with surprising intensity, he found himself praying, please, God, no matter what happens to me, protect her. Surprising, because he'd never been especially religious. His ambitions had already gotten Sam Knowles killed. He didn't want them to cost Emily her life or her freedom.

A polite cough warned Ian that someone else was near. He looked up from Emily's auburn hair and saw Commandant Henrik Kruger standing outlined against the rising sun—his pale gray eyes and weather-beaten face a mask of unreadable shadow.

"I hope I am not interrupting, *meneer?*" Kruger kept his own voice low, as though he, too, wanted to avoid breaking into Emily's rest. But Ian could hear the carefully controlled bitterness in his words.

My God, the man's still hopelessly in love with her, he realized. Suddenly embarrassed, he took his hand away from Emily's hair. There wasn't much point in ramming the loss down Kruger's throat—especially not after he'd already risked so much to save their lives. Ian shook his head and gestured to the ground. "Take a pew, *Kommandant*."

"My thanks." Kruger squatted on his haunches, still with his back to the sun. He cleared his throat, sounding strangely tentative. "Your companions are resting, then?"

"Yeah." Moved by an unexpected urge to pick a fight with this man from Emily's past, Ian nodded toward the still, silent, companionable figures of Matthew Sibena and the Afrikaner sergeant lying asleep back-to-back. "Too bad that's as close to real peace as you people ever get."

Kruger smiled sadly. "Yes." Then he shrugged. "Who knows, *meneer*. Perhaps this hellish war of ours will do the trick. Perhaps those who still hate each other will finally weary of all this blood and pointless waste."

The Afrikaner shrugged again. "And perhaps I am dreaming foolish dreams, eh?" He grew more businesslike. "In any event, such things are beyond our control for the moment. We must concentrate on staying alive from day to day. True?"

Ian acknowledged the point with a rueful nod.

"Good. That is what I have come to talk to you about. After all, I would not want the chronicler of my deeds left ignorant of what we face."

Despite himself, Ian grinned. Kruger could take a verbal punch and throw one back without flinching. Plus he didn't take himself too seriously. It was hard to dislike a guy like that—no matter how awkward things got around Emily.

Kruger's news wiped the grin off his face. They were almost out of fuel. The long, unplanned detour around Vryburg had virtually drained the battalion's gas tanks and spare jerry cans. And Genyesa's lone service station didn't have the thousands of gallons needed to refill them. The 20th Cape Rifles had come to a sudden, screeching halt in the middle of nowhere.

"Christ! So what do we do next?"

Kruger frowned. "The only thing we can do. I'm sending special teams to each of the surrounding towns and villages. With luck, they'll be able to obtain enough fuel to get us moving again."

He spread his hands. "In the meantime, the rest of us can only dig in here and wait . . . and pray."

Ian felt himself grow cold. Until now, the battalion had stayed undiscovered and alive by staying mobile. Now they'd lost their only edge against the forces arrayed against them. His hand strayed back to Emily's hair.

Henrik Kruger watched them both in silence.

DECEMBER 23—44TH PARACHUTE BRIGADE REACTION FORCE, KIMBERLEY, SOUTH AFRICA

Two hundred and fifty kilometers south of Genyesa, helicopters circled high over the urban sprawl of open-pit mine museums, factories, and homes known throughout South Africa as "the diamond city." Other helos practicing assault landings hovered low over the soccer fields now serving as a headquarters for Maj. Rolf Bekker and his paratroops. Most of the Puma and Super Frelon troop carriers sat motionless on the ground, surrounded by small groups of fully armed soldiers on five-minute alert.

Maps cluttered the walls of Bekker's command tent. Each showed a fifty-by-fifty-kilometer piece of the Cape Province's northeastern corner. Grease pencil notations indicated loyalist garrisons holding important towns and road junctions. They blocked every road going west or south—every road but one. Voices crackled through a high-powered radio set up in one corner.

"Roger, Zebra Four Four. Good work. Out." Twenty-five-year-old Capt. Kas der Merwe pulled off his earphones, his eyes shining with excitement. "We have them, Major! Reconnaissance units report sighting small enemy units. Here. Here. And here!" He checked off several villages in a wide circle around Genyesa. "And all of them are apparently gathering as much fuel as they can carry!"

Bekker nodded thoughtfully. "Petrol. I knew that would be Kruger's Achilles' heel. They've run out of petrol." He leaned closer to der Merwe's map and tapped Genyesa. "The Twentieth has to be laagered somewhere close to there."

The younger officer tapped the radio mike he still held clutched in one hand. "Shall I ready our strike force?" He measured distances with a quick, practiced eye. "We can reach the village in less than an hour."

Bekker laughed. "No, Captain, you have it backward. This is not a fox hunt. We are too few for such a thing, and besides"—he smiled thinly—"I do not entirely trust the abilities of all my hounds.

"No, we must model this operation on a lion hunt. The Citizen Force units and commandos will act as our beaters—driving these traitors south . . . toward us. When we face Kruger and his troops, we will face them on ground of our own choosing. Near there." He circled a spot on the map labeled Skerpionenpunt—Scorpion Point.

Der Merwe looked troubled. "But how do we know they will come? They may not be able to collect enough petrol even to make it that far."

Bekker shook his head. "I've heard of this man Kruger. He's a tough soldier. A real Boer. Don't you worry, der Merwe, he'll find a way to get his people south."

The major's handsome face twisted into an ugly, sardonic smile. "And we will be there waiting for them."

Rolf Bekker contemplated his plans in growing satisfaction. For the time being he would seek victory in his own mission. The rest of Vorster's shrinking domains would have to look after themselves.

DECEMBER 24—NABOOMSPRUIT

The setting sun lit a battlefield crowded with scenes of death and destruction.

Gen. Antonio Vega looked down out of his Hind gunship at the still-smoldering ruins of Naboomspruit. Burnt-out vehicles blocked almost every intersection, and mangled corpses littered every stretch of open ground. Shell craters pockmarked the highway south.

Naboomspruit and its defenses had fallen to the Cubans.

Better late than never, he thought angrily. Fuel and ammunition shortages caused by Boer commando raids on his supply lines had forced him to postpone his assault against the town. They'd also forced him to send several valuable units back north along the highway in what would probably be a futile effort to crush the elusive commandos. Units he could have used in the battle for Naboomspruit.

It had taken his troops and tanks several hours of hard fighting to clear the Afrikaner-held town, but the outcome had never really been in doubt. The Boer defenses had been strong but brittle, and once he'd broken through their front line, they hadn't had any reserves left to launch a counter-attack.

Vega had also been forced to fight without a reserve. He hadn't liked that very much. Combat units held back for use in the right place at the right time were all too often the margin between victory and defeat, but he hadn't had any choice. His casualties had simply been too high in the six weeks since he'd crossed South Africa's frontiers.

The Hind gunship landed on the northern edge of Naboomspruit, near a small cluster of officers who stood shielding their eyes from whirling sprays of rotor-blown grit.

Vega debarked to a chorus of greetings and salutes, most of which he ignored. Instead, he walked directly over to Vasquez, who stood off to one side. "Let's have a look at these secret weapons of theirs, Comrade."

With Vasquez at his side and the rest of his officers trailing along behind, he walked about a hundred meters to what appeared to be just a low mound of dirt—at least until one looked closely.

The earthen mound had a regular, shaped appearance, and as they curved around to approach it from the front, Vega saw the long barrel and large muzzle brake of a G-5 155mm artillery piece poking out through a gap in the front.

Vasquez nodded toward the mound. "Each gun emplacement is completely roofed over, Comrade General, and open only in back and in front. The Boers knew we could only attack from the northeast, so the opening in front is limited to that arc."

Vega nodded his understanding. Thus concealed and protected, the G-5 was a powerful antitank weapon. Used as an indirect fire weapon, it could fire a high-explosive shell forty kilometers. Used in a direct fire mode, it far outranged the 115mm cannon mounted on his tanks.

Vasquez walked forward far enough to lay a proprietary hand on the G-5's monstrous barrel. "As you suspected, Comrade General, the Boers were short on ammunition. They wanted to make every shell count. But these guns aren't normally rigged for antitank work, so they have separate projectiles and charges." He inclined his head toward the sandbag-covered magazines visible behind each gun position. "That makes them fire more slowly than ours. And even a one fifty-five millimeter shell will not stop one of our tanks every time."

Often enough, though, Vega thought moodily, surveying a field crowded with wrecked T-72s and BTR-60s. Still, the Afrikaner decision to use their G-5s as antitank weapons explained the lack of artillery fire during his approach march. It also indicated a growing sense of desperation. No commander used towed artillery that way unless he had no other option.

Abruptly, he turned toward Suarez. "What are our casualties?"

The colonel consulted his leather-bound notebook. "We lost twenty-eight vehicles—ten of which can be repaired." He cleared his throat. "Plus about a hundred and fifty men killed, with another two hundred seriously wounded. We believe enemy casualties were very heavy, almost twice ours."

Vega sighed. He'd won another victory, and at what Havana would call a reasonable cost. But any price was high when he was this poor in resources. He looked south, wondering if the American Marines fighting their way inland from Durban were faring any better.

CHAPTER 35

Bloody Ridge, Bloody Forest

DECEMBER 25—MOBILE HEADQUARTERS, ALLIED EXPEDITIONARY FORCE, NEAR THE OCEAN TERMINAL, DURBAN

Trailed by a small security detachment of fully armed U.S. Marines, Lt. Gen. Jerry Craig made his way through the wreckage littering Durban's waterfront. What he saw was not making him happy. A freshening sea breeze had blown the stench of cordite and sun-bloated corpses inland, but all the clean salt air in the world couldn't hide the damage inflicted by days of bitter fighting and deliberate sabotage.

Out in the harbor, oil-coated waves lapped gently against the rusting superstructures of ships sunk to block the main channel. Other burnt-out hulks sagged against the docks themselves, entangled in the torn and twisted skeletons of fallen cargo-handling cranes. Mounds of fire-blackened rubble from bomb- and shell-shattered buildings choked off the spiderweb of streets and rail lines spreading out from the port into Durban proper.

Bulldozer engines, chain saws, and acetylene torches

roared, howled, and hissed as the nine hundred men of Craig's Marine combat engineer battalion tried frantically to clear paths through the debris. But the sheer volume of work remaining seemed to make a mockery of all their efforts. Although Diederichs's garrison troops had failed to hold the city, their stubborn defense had left it a smoking ruin.

Two days after all significant Afrikaner resistance had collapsed, South Africa's largest deepwater harbor remained closed to Allied shipping. And until its docks and access roads could be reopened, Craig's British and American forces would remain dependent on whatever supplies and equipment could be brought in over the beach or by air. Most of his main battle tanks and self-propelled guns were still parked offshore—crowding the decks and cargo spaces of fast transports waiting impatiently at anchor.

Craig frowned. A few heavy vehicles had been ferried in one at a time by the U.S. Navy's overworked air-cushion landing craft. Not enough to make an appreciable battlefield contribution, just enough to impose even more strain on a supply system already laboring to provide the fuel, ammunition, and food the expeditionary force needed.

All of which left the advance inland toward Pretoria in the hands of a few infantry battalions backed by light armor, artillery, and carrier-based air power. He quickened his pace, skirting a trio of bomb craters pockmarking the quayside road. His men were pushing forward as fast as they could, but every hour's delay in opening the harbor gave Vorster that much more time to rush additional troops into the Drakensberg Mountains—a rugged band of steep mountains and forested ridges separating Natal's lowlands from the open grasslands of the highveld.

The chubby, straw-haired lieutenant colonel commanding his combat engineers saw Craig coming and hurried over.

"Sir." He saluted wearily. Sweat stains under his arms and dark rings under his eyes showed that he'd been working side by side with his men for nearly forty-eight hours straight.

"Colonel." Craig casually returned his salute and gestured at the mess visible on all sides. "I need your best guess, Jim. How much longer before we can start off-loading here?"

The younger man stared at the controlled chaos along the waterfront as though seeing it all for the very first time. "Three days. Maybe four." His shoulders slumped. "My boys are pretty near the edge, General. Some of 'em are so tired they're starting to walk right into booby traps a five-year-old could've spotted."

Craig nodded. He'd watched the casualty reports climb steadily. In the two days since Durban had officially been "pacified," the engineer battalion had lost more than ten men killed, with another forty or so seriously wounded. Snipers, explosive booby traps, and fatigue-related accidents were eroding the effectiveness of a unit he was sure to need later.

He raised his voice as a bulldozer rumbled by, shoving a burned-out car away from the road. "We're bringing in some help from the Cape. Sort of a Christmas present. The One oh one's putting its engineers on C-141s right now. Air Force says they'll be here by the end of the day."

It took several seconds to sink in. Then the lieutenant colonel nodded gratefully. The Army air assault division's combat engineers wouldn't have their equipment with them, but they could be used to spell his own men. Even without bringing in extra gear, doubling the number of skilled people working might cut up to twenty-four hours from the time needed to clear the port.

The battalion commander saluted a second time, this time with more vigor and enthusiasm. The news that he'd be getting reinforcements seemed to have stripped years off his age. "We'll get these goddamned docks open ASAP, General. You can take that to the bank."

"I already have, Jim. I already have. Now you get some rest yourself when those Army pukes show up, you hear me?" Craig patted the other man on the shoulder. "I need a smart, tough engineer in charge of this operation—not a walking zombie."

"Yes, sir."

Craig turned away, already moving back to his waiting helicopter. He'd come to the waterfront himself to show the colonel and his men just how important their efforts were to the whole expeditionary force—not to try micromanaging every last detail of their work. In his book, you found the right man for the job, gave him the tools he needed, and then got the hell out of his way.

As he neared the camouflaged UH-60 Blackhawk serving as his command transport, an aide hurried over—bent low to clear the helicopter's still-turning rotor. "General! Sixth Brigade HQ reports our guys outside Pietermaritzburg are taking fire from heavy arty!"

Craig grabbed the captain by the arm and spun him back around. Their free ride was over. Vorster's generals had a blocking force in place.

With one hand clapped onto his helmet to hold it in place, Craig raced ahead and hauled himself aboard the Blackhawk. The Marine riflemen assigned to protect him followed at a dead run.

Thirty seconds later, the command helo rolled forward on its wheels, lifted off, and raced low over the harbor—moving south at a hundred knots toward the shell-scarred runway at Louis Botha International Airport. Radio reports of the fighting continued to crackle through Craig's headphones. His American and British troops were securely ashore on the Natal coast, but Vorster's Afrikaners were clearly serving notice that any further gains would have to be paid for in blood.

3RD BATTALION, 6TH MARINE EXPEDITIONARY BRIGADE, SOUTHEAST OF PIETERMARITZBURG, SOUTH AFRICA

The Victorian homes and quiet suburban streets of Natal's provincial capital, Pietermaritzburg, lay eerily at rest below steep wooded hills rising on all sides. No cars moved down the wide N3 Motor Route or rattled along the narrow roads winding off to the farms and small clusters of houses that dotted the forested hollow. Clouds sent patches of shadow rippling over the ground, drifting almost idly from east to west.

A clock chimed the hour from a tall, red-brick tower over the city hall. Its ringing, melodic tones echoed from building to building before dying away among the dense groves of mopane and acacia trees spread across the slopes above the city. Drawn curtains or blinds in every window made Pietermaritzburg and its suburbs look deserted.

They weren't.

One thousand meters south of the open green fields of the Scottsville Race Course, soldiers wearing full packs and carrying M16s were visible—moving steadily north along the highway. The U.S. Marines were entering Pietermaritzburg on foot.

Backed by a platoon of four LAV-25s, Bravo Company's three rifle platoons trudged grimly in single file along either side of the road. Except for a thin screen of four-man recon teams, they were the advance guard for the whole Allied expeditionary force—one hundred riflemen probing far ahead of massive air, sea, and ground contingents already numbering more than fifty thousand men.

Craig's field commanders were using Bravo Company's Marines in much the same way that a man would use a stick to poke carefully through the branches of a tree while looking for a hornets' nest. The trouble was that, in this case, any hornets found were likely to be very hard on the stick.

Whooosh. The long columns of marching Marines reacted instantly to the high-pitched, screaming whirr of a shell arcing overhead. Men scattered into the empty fields to either side of the road. The LAVs spun round in a semicircle and accelerated, racing for the shelter offered by a nearby overpass.

"Incoming!"

Capt. Jon Ziss dropped flat by the left side of the highway. His radioman and the others in the company command group threw themselves down on the dirt beside him.

Whaammm. Flame, smoke, and shattered pieces of roadway fountained high into the air barely one hundred meters ahead. Fragments spattered down all around, clattering off Kevlar helmets and backpacks.

As the smoke and dust thrown by the shell burst rolled past, Ziss slowly raised his head. Although his ears were still ringing from the blast, he could hear agonized screams rising from men of his First Platoon. Three or four Marines lay huddled on the pavement, scythed down by splinters. He risked a quick glance at the surrounding terrain.

To the west, a row of wood-frame, one-story houses offered the only possible cover. The flat fairways and shallow sand traps of a golf course to the east would be a killing ground for enemy artillery. And the same could be said of the racetrack to the north. He and his troops could only run west.

Whooosh. Another round howled in out of the sky, landing farther back this time.

Whaammm. The 155mm South African shell slammed straight into the rearmost LAV and blew it apart. Pieces of armor and mangled rubber tires spiraled off the road.

Jesus. For several seconds, Ziss stared in horror at the blazing wreck, unable to move. Then reason took over. The Afrikaners had to have an OP, a hidden observation post, directing their fire. So either he and his troops got out of sight or they'd be slaughtered out here in the open.

He scrambled to his feet, shouting, "Let's move it, people! Into those houses! Over there!" He waved an arm to the west.

All up and down the freeway, individual Marines rose and ran for cover, each bent forward at the waist as though he were pushing forward against high winds. Another shell burst behind them and several more men were bowled over—left lying dead or badly wounded.

Ziss found himself running side by side with his radioman, Lance Corporal Pitts. He grabbed the handset Pitts offered. "Mike One Two, this is Bravo Six Six, over."

"Go ahead, Six Six." Ziss recognized the deep Southern drawl of his battalion commander. "Give me a sitrep."

The two men charged through an open garden gate and slid to a stop beside one of the houses. Panting Marines from Bravo's First and Second Platoons pushed in after them. The artillery barrage ended—leaving behind a strange silence broken only by moaning from the wounded sprawled across the highway.

Ziss moved across the backyard of the house and crouched low next to a row of rose bushes planted as a hedge. He punched the transmit button on his handset, noticing with some detachment that both his hands were shaking. "We took some arty, One Two. Big stuff. They've got the N3 zeroed in and spotters out there somewhere."

"Do you want fast movers? Over." The Navy had bomb-laden flights of F/A-18s and A-6s circling overhead on call, just itching for the chance to blow South African guns or troops to kingdom come.

The Marine captain shook his head impatiently, realized what he was doing, and punched the talk button again. "Negative, One Two. I don't have any observed targets. We're gonna have to hunt for their damned OP."

"Understood." His battalion commander paused and then came back on line. "The Navy says their flyboys didn't manage to spot any of those guns firing."

No kidding. The South African artillery battery was probably parked almost forty klicks away—well hidden among the Drakensberg's woodlands and narrow mountain valleys. A plane would practically have to pass right over an artillery piece while it was firing to see anything. Even then the Afrikaner gunners were undoubtedly moving their weapons from camouflaged firing position to firing position—employing the classic battlefield tactic of "shoot and scoot."

Ziss shook his head in frustration. They needed counter-battery radar to pinpoint the enemy artillery—and all of the MAF's target acquisition units were still tied down providing protection for the Louis Botha Airport.

That left the Marines with just one unpalatable option: they'd have to scour every inch of Pietermaritzburg and its surrounding hills in what was very likely to be a vain search for the enemy observation team calling down the artillery. Until then, South Africa's big guns could sweep the N3 and block any significant advance toward Pretoria. Heavily armored main battle tanks might be able to roll right through a barrage, but fuel tankers and troop trucks would be sitting ducks.

He staggered upright, trying to get a better look at the terrain ahead. Once past this small spur of residential development and the racetrack, the ground sloped down toward a small stream before rising again into the city proper. Church spires and the tower of a Moslem mosque were sharply outlined against the tree-lined escarpment.

Terrific. A single rifle company couldn't even begin to cover that much territory. "We're going to need some help on this, One Two."

"Understood." Another brief pause while the battalion CO evidently tried to unscramble what had suddenly become a very confused situation. "Alpha and Charlie companies are closing on your position now. Plus Brigade has released another platoon of LAVs and some M60s for support. I'm shifting the HQ forward now, so hold up until we get there."

"Will do." Ziss saw a medic go by at the run, medkit and bandages in hand. Oh, Christ. He'd almost forgotten about his wounded. "I need a dust-off here, One Two. I've got several wounded for immediate evac."

"Roger that. Dust-off is already en route. ETA is five minutes." His commander's businesslike tone shifted, becoming more concerned. "Hang on, Jon. We're coming. Out."

Ziss acknowledged and signed off, not sure which of the two emotions warring within him was stronger—relief now that help was on the way, or irritation at being treated a little like a panic-stricken teenager. He handed the mike back to his radioman and moved off in search of his platoon leaders. They had some planning to do.

"Captain!" He hadn't taken more than five or six steps when Pitts caught up with him. "Rover Three One reports hostile movement on the western slopes of Signal Hill." Rover Three One was the call sign for one of the recon teams scouting the ground in front of Bravo Company.

Signal Hill? Now just where the hell was that? He flipped open a tattered topographical map. There it was. A nine-hundred-foot high, wooded hill just west of the city. He almost smiled. The Afrikaners were starting to show themselves. Fine. Time for an air strike. He grabbed the handset again. "Mike One Two, this is Bravo—"

A sudden loud popping sound made him look up just as a

window in a nearby house shattered. And for the second time in only a few minutes, Ziss threw himself prone. "Sniper! Hit the dirt!"

He wriggled back to the line of rose bushes as M16s opened up from houses all around—punching rounds in the general direction of Pietermaritzburg. The company's M60 machine-gun teams were next, indiscriminately hosing down buildings and treetops that might conceal Afrikaner troops. Parked cars hit by gunfire started going up in flames.

Capt. Jon Ziss gritted his teeth and checked the clip in his own rifle. This was going to be one bitch of a day.

DECEMBER 27—FORWARD HEADQUARTERS, ALLIED EXPEDITIONARY FORCE, TOWN HILL, NORTH OF PIETERMARITZBURG

Town Hill rose nearly nine hundred feet above the Natal lowlands, and more than three hundred feet above Pietermaritzburg's central business district. For years, the city's wealthiest families had been building their homes on its slopes, drawn by its spectacular views and easy access to the Durban-Johannesburg highway. And now the same factors made Town Hill the perfect site for the forward headquarters of the Allied expeditionary force.

In the middle of a street once reserved for Mercedes and other luxury automobiles, four camouflaged command vehicles sat parked back-to-back in a rough circle. Tarpaulins covered the open spaces between them, essentially creating a single large headquarters tent. Staff officers from two countries and all four branches of the armed forces crowded the tent—receiving reports from fighting units scattered all across South Africa, planning the next day's operations, and generally getting in each other's way.

Lt. Gen. Jerry Craig stood outside, ignoring the controlled chaos of his forward HQ. His binoculars were focused on the N3 Motor Route as it wound northwest through a narrow valley. He frowned. Right now the road looked more like a serpentine parking lot than a superhighway.

Long columns of trucks, APCs, and other vehicles were backed up all the way south through the city—evidently brought to a dead stop by more fighting somewhere up ahead. An ambush? More harassing fire from South African heavy guns? A roadblock? Craig shrugged. It didn't really matter. What did matter was that Vorster's troops were slowing his advance to a nightmarish crawl.

Just securing Pietermaritzburg had taken a full day, three infantry battalions, air strikes, artillery bombardments, and dozens of casualties. Since then, his men had been forced to fight for every kilometer they gained on the only main road from Natal to Pretoria.

The pattern was always the same. Units moving along the highway would take sudden fire from enemy troops hidden on a hill, behind a ridge, or in a side canyon. In response, they had to deploy off the road, call in air or artillery to pound suspected Afrikaner positions, and then peel off platoons or companies to drive any survivors back into the mountains.

Craig lowered his binoculars and shook his head in frustration. There were enough trails and dirt roads running through the Drakensberg to support small Afrikaner units operating against his flanks—but not enough to sustain his own, larger force. Getting to Johannesburg and Pretoria with a powerful mechanized army meant driving straight up the N3.

Two AV-8B Harrier jump jets suddenly howled past at low altitude, heading for a battlefield somewhere farther along the highway. Bombs bulked large beneath their stubby wings.

Craig silently urged the Harrier pilots on. C'mon, boys, give the bastards hell, but give it to them fast.

Time, as always, was an enemy. His intelligence officers claimed that the Cubans weren't advancing any faster. But the Cubans were just 160 kilometers away from South Africa's capital and its richest minerals complex. His own troops were still more than 500 kilometers away. You didn't have to be a mathematical genius to realize that was a prescription for a losing race.

The sound of squealing brakes drew his attention away

from his strategic problems. He turned around. A U.S. Army Hummvee had just pulled up in front of his improvised command tent.

The Hummvee's sole passenger, a dapper, bantamweight general whose gray, crew-cut hair still showed flecks of black, climbed out and headed straight for him. The man's lean, suntanned face showed signs of intense anger and irritation.

Craig stood his ground, preparing himself to exercise a little-used virtue—patience. Holding a unified command sometimes meant having to coddle and cajole fractious subordinates from all the service branches. He returned the other man's rigid salute. "Sam."

"General."

Uh-oh. Formality between near-equals almost always spelled trouble. "What can I do for you?"

Maj. Gen. Samuel Weber, commander of the 24th Mechanized Infantry Division, tried valiantly to keep the anger out of his voice. He failed. "I'd like to know why the ships with my tanks are still sitting off the goddamned port. I've got a hundred and fifty M-1 tanks out there—all set to come ashore and blow the shit out of these frigging Boers. And I've got the crews to man 'em, but they're just sitting on their butts at Cape Town waiting to fly in to the airport here. So what gives?"

Craig bit back the first words that came to mind. Treating a two-star Army general like an unruly Marine second lieutenant probably wouldn't be the best way to foster interservice cooperation. He took a deep breath and let it out slowly. "The engineers have only been able to clear enough room to dock one ship at a time, Sam. And right now I need that space to off-load more essential material."

"More essential?" Weber nodded toward the stalled columns crowding the highway below. "Christ, Jerry, you need some heavy armor to break this thing loose and gain some running room. Otherwise we're still gonna be slogging to Pretoria come the Fourth of July."

Craig shook his head forcefully. "Your M-1s couldn't do

much for us right now, Sam.'' He motioned toward the panorama of rugged, broken ridges and patches of forest spreading west, north, and northeast from Pietermaritzburg. ''We have to push through another hundred klicks like that before we'll reach anything resembling good tank country.''

''Hell.'' Weber scuffed at the pavement with one highly polished combat boot. He looked up. ''I'll tell you what, Jerry. You and I both know the Boers don't have much that can even scratch the paint on one of my tanks. So bring my M-1s ashore, and I'll go tearing up this goddamned highway so fast we'll be in Jo'burg before Vorster takes his morning dump.''

Craig chuckled, pleased by the Army general's aggressive instincts. For a second, he was half-tempted to let the man try his proposed high-tech cavalry charge. Then reality stomped back in bearing a few ugly and unfortunate facts.

Weber was only half right. His tanks could probably break past Vorster's blocking force without much trouble or many losses. But just running the Afrikaner gauntlet of ambushes and artillery fire with an armored column wouldn't accomplish much of anything. Tanks had to have infantry support to hold any ground they gained, and they had to have gas to keep moving. And neither the infantry's APCs nor convoys of highly flammable fuel trucks could advance until his lead brigades finished doing what they were already doing—securing every hill and ridge overlooking the N3, meter by bloody meter.

Craig shrugged, unable at the moment to see any practical alternative to a prolonged slugging match through the mountains. And given that, the Allied expeditionary force needed fuel, ammo, artillery, and infantry replacements even more than it needed the 24th's main battle tanks. Weber's M-1s would only come into their own once his American and British troops broke out onto the flat, open grasslands of the veld.

The sound of distant thunder—heavy artillery—echoed down the highway. Both officers turned and hurried into the command tent, their argument forgotten and unimportant in the face of yet another Afrikaner attack.

DECEMBER 29—A COMPANY, 3RD BATTALION, THE PARACHUTE REGIMENT, EAST OF ROSETTA, SOUTH AFRICA

Though the late-afternoon sun seemed to set the far-off slopes of the Drakensberg Mountains aflame, it left northern Natal's narrow valleys and tree-lined hollows cloaked in growing shadow. Ten kilometers south of the Mooi River, real fires glowed orange in the gathering darkness. Soldiers wearing red berets and green, brown, and tan woodland-pattern camouflage uniforms clustered around the fires sipping scalding-hot, heavily sugared tea. Men born and reared in London's crowded East End, the isolated West Country, the rusting, industrialized north, or southern England's rich farmlands and suburbs stood chatting together—their mingled voices and different accents rising and falling beneath overhanging mopane and acacia trees. After a hard day's march north along National Route Three, 3 Para's A Company was having a last "brew-up" before digging in for the night.

The muted roar of diesel engines drifted up the road as convoys of overworked trucks ferried supplies inland from the Durban beachhead, now nearly ninety kilometers behind them. The Paras could also hear the muffled thump of mortar rounds landing somewhere back along the road, audible proof that some of their "follow-on" forces were again catching hell from stay-behind Boer commandos.

Most paid little attention to the noise. A weeks' worth of combat in the Drakensberg's rugged foothills had taught them how to ignore the sound of gunfire not aimed in their direction.

Maj. John Farwell, A Company's tall, hook-nosed commander, moved from campfire to campfire collecting his officers and senior NCOs. His two signalers followed close behind, made easy to spot by the thin radio antennas rocking back and forth over their heads. Soldiers who saw them go past muttered uneasily to one another and began checking their weapons out of long habit. As a general rule, the major disliked formal meetings and avoided holding them whenever possible. So an orders group such as the one they saw forming probably meant action was imminent.

The Paras's instincts were on target. New information had generated new orders. The six hundred soldiers of 3 Para were being committed to a night attack.

Five minutes later, Farwell had his platoon leaders and sergeants assembled in a small clearing by the side of the road. He looked up into a semicircle of fire-lit faces. Some of the men seemed surprisingly eager, almost elated by the prospect of a real "set-piece" battle. Others, more imaginative, wiser, or simply more experienced, looked grimly determined instead. All seemed horribly young to their thirty-five-year-old company commander.

He unfolded a map and spread it out in the light thrown by the campfire. "All right, chaps. Here's the gist of what we're up to. . . ." He spoke rapidly and with more confidence than he felt, outlining the situation they faced and the broad plan of attack passed down from battalion HQ.

Two hours before, elements of D Company, the parachute battalion's special patrol unit, had contacted what appeared to be a company-sized Afrikaner infantry force digging in along the last ridgeline separating the Allies from the broad Mooi River valley. They showed no signs of being willing to withdraw without exacting a steep toll in lives and lost time. And by daylight their defenses might be strong enough to delay the expeditionary force's advance for several hours—hours the Allies could not afford to lose.

So the British paratroops were going to attack immediately, accepting the inherent risks and confusion of a night battle in order to strike before the Boers finished building their bunkers and fighting positions. To minimize the inevitable confusion, 3 Para's battalion staff had laid out a simple and straightforward plan. After a brief artillery barrage, Farwell and his A Company would storm the ridge east of the highway. Its counterpart, B Company, would drive on the heights to the west at the same moment. The Support Company's machine-gun and Milan antitank missile teams would be positioned along the Start Line, ready to move up and "shoot in" both assaults. If all went well, they'd be able to crush the enemy blocking force and unbar the road for a faster advance in the morning.

"And the colonel will hold C Company in reserve . . . here." Farwell's finger pointed to a tiny stream shown meandering along the base of the enemy-held ridge. "That should allow those Charlie Company layabouts to reinforce either axis of the attack . . . if anybody needs their rather dubious help."

As he'd intended, this last comment prompted a few quick, nervous grins. A and C companies had a long-standing but friendly rivalry.

Farwell sat back on his haunches and studied his subordinates. "Well, that's it then, gentlemen. Are there any questions?"

"Yes, sir." The freckle-faced lieutenant commanding 2 Platoon leaned forward, his expression troubled. "Why not use D Company to make a flanking attack? I mean, going straight up that slope seems likely to be a bit sticky."

Farwell nodded. It was a good question, one that deserved a straight answer. He traced the tangle of gullies and ravines shown extending to either side of the highway below the ridge. "I'm afraid we simply don't have time for such subtlety, Jack. It might take D Company hours to work its way into position through that mess." He shook his head. "And who knows what the blasted Boers might have waiting for them when they got there?"

The lieutenant nodded slowly, reluctantly conceding the point. No one else spoke up.

Farwell let the silence drag on a few seconds longer and then climbed to his feet. The other men hurriedly followed suit.

"Very well, gentlemen. You have your orders. You may brief your platoons at your leisure." He smiled broadly. "But make sure that happens to be sometime during the next five minutes. We're moving up to the Start Line in ten, so don't be late. Dismissed."

As the orders group broke up, Farwell moved among his officers and NCOs—shaking hands with one, clapping the shoulder of another. It seemed the least he could do. Privately, he didn't expect many of these young men would be alive to see the next sunrise. And since he planned to lead the attack personally, he counted himself among the likely casualties.

BLOCKING FORCE, NORTHERN NATAL COMMANDO BRIGADE, ON THE RIDGE SOUTH OF THE MOOI RIVER VALLEY

The scraping and rustling noises made by men digging in rocky soil carried far in the blackness under the trees carpeting the ridge. Foxholes and bunkers were being dug more by feel than by sight, and any necessary orders were passed along the chain of sweating, middle-aged soldiers in harsh, piercing whispers.

One hundred meters east of the spot where the N3 Motor Route cut through the ridge, short, broad-shouldered Sgt. Gerrit Meer laid his shovel to one side and straightened his aching back. *Ag*, he thought disgustedly, this whole thing was *blery* stupid—the product of some foolish staff officer's diseased mind.

He didn't object to fighting the Uitlanders, far from it. Meer came from the town of Mooirivier itself, and he didn't want to see a horde of black-loving invaders swarming freely through his hometown streets. But he did object to being asked to commit suicide.

And that was what his commanders seemed to have planned. He'd spent six years fighting along the Republic's borders before coming home to his family farm. So he knew enough about tactics to view the ridge as a potential death trap. The same trees that sheltered the commando from observation by enemy aircraft would provide cover for any attacker moving upslope. Even worse, with the open countryside of the Mooi River valley behind them, he and his comrades wouldn't have anywhere safe to retreat to when the time came.

As if that weren't bad enough, the sergeant didn't think there were enough men here to hold the ridge for long against a determined assault. It might have been different if the full commando had mustered, but more than half hadn't even bothered to show up at the assembly point.

Meer hawked once and spat. Traitorous rooinek swine. His English neighbors loathed the blacks as much as he did. He knew that for a fact. So what did they do the moment the going got tough? They ran away to save their own skins. He scowled. When this war was over, there would have to be a reckoning with such cowards.

He picked up his shovel again and leaned into his work—stabbing the broad, sharp blade into the ground with short, powerful strokes. After all, a good deep foxhole might just keep him alive long enough to kill some of his people's enemies.

A sudden, blindingly bright flash lit up the crest ahead and sent his shadow racing away downslope. The ground rocked. For an instant, Meer froze. Then he dove for cover.

"Down! Everybody down!"

More shells burst in the treetops—spraying jagged steel and wood splinters downward in a deadly rain. Some men dropped without a sound, killed instantly by blast or concussion. Others fell screaming, torn open and bleeding but alive.

Through it all, Sgt. Gerrit Meer and other veterans like him lay huddled in their shallow holes, waiting impatiently for the enemy barrage to end.

A COMPANY, 3 PARA

Maj. John Farwell crouched beside his signaler, ten meters behind the shadowy, motionless shapes of 2 Platoon. All eyes were riveted on the dark mass of the ridge rising above them.

Dozens of bright-white explosions flickered from east to west along the crest line, leaving in their wake a maelstrom of noise, smoke, and blast-thrown debris. Three full batteries of 155mm howitzers were pounding the Afrikaners—pouring salvo after salvo of HE onto defensive positions pinpointed by 3 Para's patrols.

Then, as suddenly as they had begun, the shell bursts stopped. Silence settled back over the night.

Farwell checked his watch: 2315 hours. The barrage had lifted.

He jumped to his feet, waving his men forward with one arm while the other clutched his Enfield L85A1 assault rifle. "Let's go, lads! Up and at them! Up and at them!"

Platoon leaders and their sergeants were already repeating his orders. A Company's whole line began to move ahead at a fast walk, separating into squads and sections as the men scrambled uphill.

Farwell followed, scrabbling up a slope that seemed to grow steeper with every step. Darkness closed in as they entered the treeline. He couldn't see more than ten or fifteen meters in any direction, but he could hear gasps, muffled swearing, and the sound of boots sliding and slipping on loose, rocky soil as his men fought their way toward the summit. Jesus, he thought, this bloody ridge is a damn sight higher than it looked on the map.

With a hissing *pop,* a parachute flare soared into the night sky and burst high overhead—spilling an eerie, white light over the men struggling up the ridge. Oh, shit. The barrage hadn't annihilated the Boers. They were still there and ready for battle. Farwell lengthened his stride. No point in loitering about.

One after another, three small explosions rippled across the hillside behind the British paratroops. Mortars! Hell's teeth. They were going to need more suppressive fire from their own artillery. Farwell angled over to his signaler and snatched the offered handset. "Red Rover One, this is Alpha Four—"

The next Afrikaner mortar salvo fell squarely on target. One 60mm bomb landed barely five meters ahead of the British major and his radioman.

Time and space, in fact everything, seemed to vanish in a single, searing blast of white fire and ear-shattering fury. Farwell felt himself being tossed backward like an unwanted rag doll. Conscious thought fluttered briefly and fled.

He came to only seconds later, propped awkwardly against the trunk of a small, gnarled tree. Small, bloodstained tears in his battle dress and the pain stabbing through his right side told their own story—he'd taken a load of white-hot shrapnel across his ribs. His rifle was gone, ripped out of his hands and thrown somewhere out into the surrounding darkness.

Farwell tried to stand up, failed at first, and looked down to see why. Christ. His signaler must have taken the full force of the explosion. The younger man's mangled body lay across his legs, pinning him to the ground.

He rolled the corpse to one side and staggered upright.

More mortar bombs rained down on the slope—lighting up the tangled landscape in brief, deadly flashes. Dead and wounded Paras were scattered across the hillside in bloody heaps. Others, uninjured, lay prone behind fallen trees or half-buried boulders. Some were firing blindly, spraying bullets uphill toward the crest.

Farwell swore violently. His attack was breaking down, losing its cohesion and force. He had to get his men moving again or they'd all die under the Afrikaner mortar barrage. Ignoring the pain in his right side, he hobbled onward. "Come on, A Company, on your feet! Close with the bastards! Close with them!"

A man rose from behind a splintered tree trunk and grabbed at his left arm. "Are you all right, Major?"

Farwell recognized 2 Platoon's senior NCO and yelled back, "I'm fine, Sergeant!" He ducked as another mortar round landed close by. Fragments whined past. "Where's Slater?"

"Dead, sir."

Unbidden, an image of the freckled lieutenant rose in Farwell's mind, momentarily blotting out the present. He remembered meeting an aging and widowed mother who'd been so painfully proud of her handsome young soldier son. He blinked the memory away. There might be time for sorrow later. If he lived.

He leaned close to the platoon sergeant's ear. "We must get the men moving. You understand?"

The other man nodded vigorously. The Paras either had to close with their enemies or admit defeat and fall back down the ridge.

"Right. Then take your platoon forward, Sergeant." Farwell bared his teeth, camouflaging a sudden blaze of pain as a fierce, tigerish grin. "Flush 'em out, Bates. I'll be right behind you with the rest of the lads."

The new commander of 2 Platoon nodded once more and moved away at a steady lope—briefly silhouetted by another explosion. His bull-voiced roar could be heard even over the noise of the barrage. "On your feet, you Terrible Twos! Come on! Let's go kill those Boer bastards!"

By ones and twos, British soldiers rose from cover and followed their sergeant up the slope. To the left and right, other voices rose above the shelling, echoing his call. One and Three platoons were rallying as well.

Farwell knelt beside a dead Para, tugged the man's assault rifle free, and hobbled after his men.

BLOCKING FORCE, NORTHERN NATAL COMMANDO BRIGADE

Twenty meters below the ridge's jagged crest line, Sgt. Gerrit Meer lay flat on his stomach, sighting down the length of his R-1 rifle. At any moment now, he thought grimly, the *verdomde* English will come swarming over the top. For a few seconds they'd be silhouetted against the skyline—easy to spot and easy to shoot. The sergeant's finger tightened on his trigger. He and his men would cut the rooineks to pieces.

One of the wounded men they hadn't had time to evacuate moaned softly behind him.

"Shut up." Meer didn't take his eyes off the top of the ridge.

Another parachute flare burst into life high above the battlefield, turning night into half-lit day.

Something small and round flew through the air and thudded onto the ground beside his foxhole. It rolled on past and came to rest against a fallen tree. Meer's heart stopped. "Grenade!"

He buried his face in the dirt.

Whummmphhh. A muted, dampened blast sent fragments whirring over his head. Other small explosions echoed from either side. Nothing more.

The Afrikaner looked up into the gray and swirling mist created by a volley of British smoke grenades. He moistened lips that were suddenly dry, peering frantically toward a skyline that had all but disappeared in the man-made fog.

Sounds were amplified by his inability to see anything clearly. Time slowed and finally seemed to stop entirely.

Damn it, where were they? Meer could feel his heart pounding again, feeling as though it might break out of his body with every separate beat.

There! Howling, yelling, defiant shapes raced out of the concealing smoke, lunging forward with fixed bayonets. He saw one man coming straight for him—all glittering eyes and a hate-filled, blackened face beneath a steel helmet.

God. He shot and shot and shot again. The Englishman stumbled, folded in on himself, and fell facedown in the dirt.

Meer's panic vanished in that same instant. He laughed aloud in exultation and rose to his knees, swinging from side to side—looking for more foreigners to kill.

Another small, round shape sailed out of the smoke and landed behind him.

Whummp. The blast threw him forward against the lip of his foxhole and left him lying there for a split second, bleeding and dazed. Some instinct told him to stay down, to accept defeat.

No! It would not be! Meer spat pieces of gravel and sand out of his torn mouth and pushed himself to his knees again. Vague shapes wavered in front of his watering eyes. He fumbled for his rifle.

He never really saw the British paratrooper who came screaming out of the mist and swirling dust. He was conscious only of a sudden, sharp, tearing pain as the man's bayonet slammed into his chest, reaching for his heart.

Gerrit Meer fell backward into his half-dug foxhole. He didn't feel the point-blank shot the Para fired to extract his bayonet. The Afrikaner sergeant was already dead, staring up at the smoke-shrouded night sky with sightless eyes.

The ridge guarding the Mooi River valley had fallen.

CHAPTER 36

End Run

DECEMBER 31—IN NATAL

Special Forces duty always surprised him. Capt. Jeff Hawkins knew that "unconventional warfare" was much more common and covered a lot more combat than "conventional warfare," but the longer he fought, the fewer rules there seemed to be.

Hawkins was dressed in U.S. Army battle dress, festooned with equipment, especially extra cans of water. Tall and slender, he was better suited to the heat than the massive Sergeant Griffith. Still, nobody wanted to risk dehydration. He carried the load easily, with a wiry strength that matched his thinness. His face was thin and angled. Even his fingers were skinny.

Captain Hawkins was the leader of a U.S. Army Special Forces "A" Team. Along with his eleven other comrades, he had landed in the Durban area with the invading forces and was now operating "behind the lines," assisting the black resistance.

Jeff's skin was only a shade lighter than the Africans he

walked with. He had always considered himself an American black, but in this color-conscious country, he would actually be classed as "colored," since he had both black and white ancestors. Looking at the Sotho and Zulu tribesmen walking with him, he decided the term *Afro-American* was a good way of describing himself.

Special Forces teams supported the local resistance with specialized skills, gathered intelligence, and coordinated operations with "conventional" U.S. forces. Except for Lieutenant Dworski and himself, all the men on the team were sergeants, noncoms with years of training and experience. It was a touchy matter, working with a different culture, advising and assisting without giving orders. And there were always complications.

They were on their way back from a two-day patrol. Jeff had led Lieutenant Dworski and Sergeants Griffith and Lamas on an engineering reconnaissance of the Tugela River bridge. It was a potential choke point on the Allied route of advance, and they had received orders to see if it could be seized and held in advance of the attacking Allied forces. This was only one of the missions his team was performing.

The answer was an exhausting and definite no. Jeff had learned enough to know when to walk away from a posthumous medal, and this was the time. Well defended, with a screen of patrols and scouts for twenty kilometers around, it had been an adventure just getting a look at the bridge.

No, headquarters would have to find some other way out of the Drakensberg. Those rugged mountains were coming to symbolize the South African defenders and the difficulty of the advance.

Hawkins's feeling of disappointment was mixed with his frustration with the African soldiers he was supposed to be training and leading. These people were supposed to be allies. He seemed to remember something about allies being people who didn't shoot at each other, but did shoot at the same enemy. In history, this had resulted in some strange alliances, but as long as the wars had lasted, so had the alliances.

Not here. Not at first, anyway. Hawkins and the other three

Americans had shown up at a nighttime rendezvous with local resistance forces, mostly ex-ANC guerrillas now fighting with the Allied side.

Any meeting at night, deep in enemy territory, was risky, and even after almost two weeks of operations in Africa, Jeff was keyed up. They had approached the site, an isolated grove of trees, in single file, with Ephraim Betalizu, their best scout, in front by fifty meters.

Ephraim had disappeared into the copse and a few minutes later had called out, in Zulu, "All clear."

Relaxing a little, Jeff had hand-motioned the file of soldiers forward. He had only taken two steps, though, when he heard thrashing and the sounds of a fight. Breaking into a run, Hawkins sprinted for the trees ahead, weapon ready. He heard shouts, the sound of metal on wood, and then a muffled shot.

Jeff took the final few steps through the trees and saw Betalizu on the ground with three men standing over him. A fourth lay facedown to one side. A pistol lay on the ground near Betalizu's outstretched hand, and two of the men held AK-47 assault rifles. Both weapons were pointed at the scout, and one man's pose made Jeff think he had been about to pull the trigger.

Shit. Time to sound American, Jeff thought. "What the hell is going on here? Ephraim, get up."

Stiffly, he turned to face his scout's attackers. Controlling the anger in his voice, he said, "Which one of you is our contact?"

One of the three, one with an AK-47 but not the man ready to fire, lowered his rifle and looked at Jeff. The American wore a standard-pattern U.S. camouflage uniform and green beret, with black plastic insignia. Although Jeff was not fully loaded with combat gear, he appeared lavishly equipped compared to the guerrilla.

The African wore camouflage pants, a ragged T-shirt, and sandals. A big man, he had a short beard and close-cropped hair, flecked with gray.

"I am George Nconganwe, leader of this cell. You look like the Americans we expected." He gestured to Betalizu, slowly standing up. "But you have brought this traitor with you."

Jeff felt himself bristling and tried to fight it. "If I brought him with me, he is not a traitor." Jeff heard the rest of the team coming through the brush behind him. "I will vouch for every one of my men."

Jeff's move was dangerous but necessary. Americans had no political currency in this area, and linking his reputation with that of the Zulus could work either way. Jeff was betting that Cape Town and Durban marked them as friends, not potential oppressors or collaborators.

Even in the weak moonlight, Jeff saw Nconganwe's eyes move to someone behind him. Hawkins followed his gaze and saw the guerrilla was looking at Dworski, then Lamas.

Jeff introduced the lieutenant as his second-in-command, and then the rest of the team. The idea of an armed white man and a Hispanic being allies seemed to disturb Nconganwe almost as much as the Zulu. Whites were the oppressors. Hispanics were Cubans, first friends, now enemies. He knew these men were Americans, and technically allies, but a lifetime of struggle made it hard to see past their race.

Jeff cursed his own complacency. Zulu and Xhosa had been historical enemies and also political rivals. Most of the now-shattered ANC's membership had been Xhosa, while 95 percent of the Inkatha movement had been Zulu. Inkatha had preached a more conservative line, while the ANC had ties with communist and socialist political groups.

Black South Africans had little experience with the idea of political dialogue. Any difference of opinion in this bloody land was cause for violence. The white government of South Africa had used this difference, and many others, to keep the two strongest opposition groups feuding between themselves. Now, even with the enemy in front of them, it was hard to forget old hatreds.

Dworski and Griffith had tended the fourth man—only knocked down and not shot, thank goodness. Only by being very businesslike had Hawkins managed to convince Nconganwe to continue with the mission. They still had many kilometers of hostile territory to cover, and a dangerous enemy was looking for them.

Jeff's original plan had been to place one of the local fighters with Betalizu on point, but that was now out of the question. Betalizu did not know the area and could not scout alone. Hawkins would have to depend on strangers for his team's security.

As they had set out, another conflict arose, with neither group willing to bring up the rear. Feeling like a schoolmaster, the American had ordered two separate side-by-side files, with the command group spread among them, keeping the peace.

The rest of the mission, successful but fruitless, had been a continuous string of compromises. Only after Betalizu and Lamas had gone forward together to survey the bridge, under the Boer sentries' noses, had Nconganwe said anything good about the Zulu.

They had slept that night in a hide about five kilometers from the bridge. Before sleeping, Nconganwe and Jeff had talked, first about the struggle in South Africa, then about America's multiracial society. The Xhosa had trouble with the concepts that made American society work.

Jeff explained his own upbringing. While he had seen and experienced discrimination during his life, there had been nothing like apartheid. Even more so, American society as a whole seemed committed to the idea of the races living together on an equal basis. This was something few South Africans, white or black, had actually seen. Nconganwe had trouble accepting that it actually existed.

In African culture, the family and extended family were everything. Loyalty to one's clan was far more important than any feeling of nationhood. America had forged her own borders. South Africa's had been drawn by European colonists, with no thought to the peoples already living there.

Jeff's own family was important to him, but he thought of himself as an American, not a Hawkins or a Chicagoan. Some of that was his upbringing, but the American ideals of one man, one vote and the rule of law were a basic part of his beliefs, and his loyalty went to the country that represented those beliefs.

And what nation should the Xhosas or Zulus feel allegiance to? The government was the enemy and the South African nation was a collection of peoples kept deliberately apart. There was no concept of the "melting pot" or a pluralistic society. That much of apartheid had taken root.

A hundred-plus years after the Civil War, Americans were still sorting out race relations. Jeff wondered how long it would take in South Africa.

He and Nconganwe had talked for over an hour, and like most Africans Jeff had talked to, Nconganwe seemed willing to take part on faith, but would have to see the rest for himself. Jeff decided to settle for that.

The following day they had marched home through enemy territory, although the Boers' grasp on it was weak and fading.

It was rough country, in the foothills of the Drakensberg Mountains. The paths rose and fell, passing through brown hills that broke into green only near a river or stream.

The team was headquartered in Tlali, a large village whose chief had been delighted to host Hawkins and his team, since the armed Americans would protect him from the lawless bands that now preyed on the population.

Tlali's population was Sotho, another tribe common in South Africa, but one not as antagonistic to the Zulu.

The Sotho had actually managed to maintain their own independent nation within the territory of South Africa, mostly by virtue of being on top of an escarpment, surrounded by steep walls. Lesotho was still in the thrall of South African power, but it was also a source of pride. Tlali lay outside its borders, but still maintained the cultural links.

The patrol was walking southeast, toward Tlali, when they came over a small rise and saw the village ahead. It lay nestled on a steep hillside, as if to keep the flatter land clear for farming. Fields of maize surrounded the neat thatched huts, and Jeff felt almost at home as he walked toward the village. It made him feel closer to his unknown ancestors. . . .

JANUARY 1—TLALI

Hawkins awoke with a start. Even in relatively safe quarters, a part of him always was on edge. His hand was halfway extended toward a pistol nearby when he saw it was Griffith leaning over him.

Relaxing, he glanced at his watch. It was four in the morning. His body was still sore from two days' march, and Hawkins said, "This had better be good, Mike."

"It is, Captain, sir. Very, very good." Griffith's exuberant mood intrigued Hawkins, and the officer quickly rose and dressed, then stepped out into the cool darkness.

A small fire was burning in an open space between the huts, and Jeff saw several figures crouched around it, including George Nconganwe. He and Dworski and Betalizu were all speaking in low voices. He could hear the lieutenant telling the Xhosa about growing up in a Polish neighborhood in Philadelphia.

Nconganwe greeted Jeff and said, "I wanted to bring this information myself. I do not understand it all, but the man who passed it to me said that your people would understand."

Jeff sat down next to the fire. "Thank you for bringing this information. I am sure it will be very useful."

"I am supposed to tell you that the surveillance radar covering Ladysmith has just broken down. Its 'transmit-receive relay' has failed, and they are having difficulty obtaining another. They continue to 'radiate,' but they cannot see anything on the radar screen. I know the man who overheard this. The Boers did not think he would understand.

"Additionally, some of the garrison was seen leaving town, moving north in trucks."

Jeff felt his chest tighten a little and fill with excitement. This might be the big break the Allies needed. Ladysmith was a strategic town past the Drakensberg Mountains. If its defenses were weakened . . .

Nconganwe continued, "You are helping to free South Africa. The Xhosa remember their friends." He scowled. "The Zulu may not be our friends, but as long as they are your allies, we will be their allies as well."

Jeff's excitement was now mixed with relief, and a little hope. "I will earn the Xhosa's friendship, I promise. This is very valuable information, George. The Allies will be grateful, and it may save many lives."

"Not Boer lives, I hope." Nconganwe grinned, then left. He had many kilometers to go before dawn.

Dworski and Griffith looked at him. Their smiles were of frank admiration and of those sharing good news.

"Get me a runner," Hawkins ordered. "I have to send a message to Mantizima. Then we'll go over to the communications hut. I have another message to send."

USS *MOUNT WHITNEY*, IN DURBAN HARBOR

Craig and his staff examined the map of Natal. Ladysmith was an old town, with a history of past battles. It lay along National Route 3, the route picked by Craig and his forces as the best path of advance through the mountains.

Best was a relative term, though. They had lost lives and time fighting through those passes. At times, Craig had wondered if they would lose the campaign here. Taking Ladysmith could change all that.

Ladysmith lay beyond the mountains, in the low foothills on the western side. Beyond the town, the country changed to the veld, open country perfect for mobile warfare.

It was also the supply center for the South African forces in the area and occupied an excellent blocking position. The South Africans had kept it well garrisoned, with a strong air-defense network.

Part of that network was an air surveillance radar. Parked on any of the hills surrounding the town, it gave early warning of any enemy approach. Jet fighters had attacked it several times, with little effect. Like many modern tactical radars, it was mobile and could move quickly from place to place. It couldn't radiate on the move, but each attacker would find it in a different place. Now, it appeared the South Africans were running a bluff.

Taking Ladysmith would change the Drakensberg Mountains from a South African fortress into a prison.

Craig had already started planning the assault on Ladysmith, but that had been from the south, up the highway. He'd thought of it as their graduation exercise, the last battle before the breakout. Now, if they could take the town by storm, it would cut a week off the campaign and maybe win the race for Pretoria.

Normally, sending helicopters into an established air-defense network was military idiocy. The air defenses that could engage a jet fighter made short work of the "slow movers." If that radar was down, though, a fast-moving assault force could appear and attack before the defenders knew they were there.

Craig turned to the divisional commanders assembled before him. "Greg, how much of your 101st is unloaded?"

"One brigade and one aviation battalion, sir. Elements of the second brigade are being off-loaded now." The demolitions in Durban's harbor still allowed only a few ships to unload at once. Engineers were working to clear the obstructions, but progress was measured by the week, not the day.

The 101st Air Assault division used helicopters to move its men, which paradoxically made it hard to move from place to place. Aircraft were light, but took up a lot of room, and thus required many ships to carry them. The division's Aviation Group could lift an entire brigade at once.

Even the forces already landed had a lot of men and immense firepower. The combined formation, about a third of the 101st's strength, could deploy over ninety troop-carrying helicopters carrying twenty-five hundred men. The vulnerable troop carriers would be screened by Kiowa scout and Apache attack helicopters.

Craig couldn't wait for the other two brigades and didn't think it would be necessary, if they moved fast. The South Africans were moving units out of Ladysmith, sending them north. Those troops were probably headed for Pretoria and the Cubans. More importantly, it told him what the enemy was thinking. The other side expected him to be bogged down in the mountains for some time to come. They were wrong.

"Greg, I want you to land at Ladysmith tomorrow at dawn." The general's surprise and concern were mirrored on his face. "Take everything you can scrape together, but don't wait an extra minute for gear from the ships."

The general nodded, and Craig said, "Do it however you have to, but take and hold Ladysmith until the ground forces can link up."

The 101st's commander, a lean, tanned soldier, saluted and said, "In that case, sir, I hope you'll excuse me. We've got a busy night ahead of us."

Craig returned the salute. "Thanks, Greg. We're trading your sleep for lives and time. Make it count."

JANUARY 2—OUTSIDE DURBAN

The 101st Air Assault division was based just to the north of the city. Space was at a premium along the coastal plain, but a helicopter didn't need a lot of room to take off.

Part of a two-lane asphalt road had been turned into a runway, while fields and shacks on either side had been bulldozed flat to make way for rows of sand and green helicopters. The Africans displaced by this had wisely been housed in some of the prefab accommodations brought along for the division.

"Camp Zulu" was growing rapidly, with the engineers busily making plans for water and electrical utilities, security fences, and the other things that kept a military community running. They were very distressed when they were told to drop everything and help load stores onto the division's sole operational brigade.

Mechanics had worked all night under harsh floodlights, assembling and inspecting helicopters, repairing what was wrong, and scrounging for parts that were still "on the water."

Many helicopters, having been declared unfixable in the short time allowed, had been "canned" or cannibalized, their functional parts removed and installed to make some other aircraft flyable. A single helicopter could make three or more other aircraft functional by donating an engine to one, a part of the instrument panel to another, and so on. There would be time to restore the gutted hulk later.

The confusion at the airfield was only amplified when Marine helicopters, some of them also needing maintenance, arrived to reinforce the 101st's machines. Marine pilots were quickly taken aside and in one-on-one briefings, taught Army procedures by their opposite numbers.

Even as the brigade's transport and attack helicopters were frantically readied, the division, brigade, and battalion commanders quickly built the necessary elements into the attack plan. Even with a straightforward movement to objective and an assault, a hundred details, on which lives depended, had to be decided, checked, and then passed down the line.

Maj. Gen. Greg Garrick, the division commander, had finished the basic attack plan while riding in a helicopter from the *Mount Whitney* back to his base. The brigade commander, Col. Tom Stewart, had been waiting with the rest of the division staff. By midnight they had fleshed out Garrick's plan into a brigade assault, coordinating it with naval and Marine air support, a logistics plan, communications and intelligence procedures, air defense plans, chemical warfare plans, down to the locations for helicopters to land once they had delivered their loads.

This detail-oriented procedure was complicated by a sketchy intelligence picture, and a changing list of the forces available. Halfway through the planning session, the maintenance officer came in with the news that enough helicopters were available to lift a fourth battalion. This was good news, but many plans had to be reworked.

The battalion commanders were summoned at midnight and in a two-hour brief, filled in on their roles in the operation. Planning had been so hurried that no name for the assault had been picked, and someone had suggested Next-Day Air. Garrick had finally agreed to Air Express.

The battalion commanders took their orders, expanded and implemented them for their own situations, and summoned the company commanders at three. The company commanders briefed their platoon leaders at four, and the squad leaders were finally given their orders at four-thirty.

At five the lead helicopters took off.

The noise and confusion inside the base drew the attention of the local citizenry, who stood outside the hastily erected fences and watched the lights and machinery and listened to the sounds of jet engines. The display of resources and technology was almost overwhelming, and frightening to many. What would these foreign conquerors want?

Standing near the flight line, General Garrick saw the spectators outside the fence, but was more worried about the security aspect than their impressions. His grandmother's cat could have figured out by now that the division was making an assault. Their salvation lay in speed. By the time a Boer spy sent the news to his superiors and they analyzed the report, his men and machines would be over the objective. He hoped.

He watched, along with the spectators outside the fence, as the first rank of helicopters lifted off. The troop carriers, UH-60 Blackhawks and CH-47 Chinooks, took off first. They were the slowest and would set the pace for the rest of the formation. In twos and threes they used the improvised runway to make rolling takeoffs, compensating for their heavy loads. As soon as one group had cleared the runway, another taxied on and repeated the maneuver.

The sound of hundreds of jet engines and rotor blades filled the air, and even with ear protectors, Garrick found it difficult to think. The citizens outside the fence could be seen backing up, trying to balance their curiosity against the blast of sound. A hot wind filled the air with dust, and the smell of burnt metal. By the time the force had lifted off, it would be ten degrees warmer in camp.

The last of the troop carriers had lifted off, and Garrick could now see the scouts and attack birds going. The sleek OH-58s contrasted sharply with the long, angular Apaches. The faster machines would quickly overtake the "slicks" and assume positions in the van and the flanks.

"It's time, sir." Garrick's aide, a captain, escorted him over to the door of a waiting Blackhawk. The door gunners ignored him. Their faces hidden by helmets and visors, the two men seemed already intent on their task.

While Colonel Stewart ran the battle from his forward ground headquarters, Garrick intended to see the assault himself. As a division commander, he would normally have to coordinate the actions of three brigades, but with only one in the field, this was a rare opportunity to see the fight firsthand and at the same time stay out of Tom's way. He had a radio link both to Stewart and the division staff, located nearby.

Belting himself in, he donned a headset, and even as he was checking the circuit, the command helicopter lifted off. More lightly loaded than its fellows, it would easily be able to follow the action.

Garrick moved forward, through the cabin, so that he could stand near the cockpit and look out the forward windscreen. Stretched out ahead of them like a cloud of insects was an entire brigade. Elite troops, they were moving at a hundred-plus knots toward their objective.

They were headed west, away from the sun, but as they climbed, the morning light illuminated each aircraft enough to show its location. His command chopper continued to climb, and as he watched, the last stragglers assumed their positions.

The troop carriers, "slicks," each with a squad of infantry aboard, flew in trail formations, strings of four machines separated by a hundred yards and staggered at different altitudes. The larger Chinooks carried heavier weapons and supplies. On either side, teams of scout and attack helicopters served as "pouncers," ready to attack any ground-based threat that appeared. In front, a wedge of gunships, all fully armed, slowly pulled ahead. They would hit the area just before the slicks landed and provide support to the attacking troops.

Garrick knew that other aircraft ranged farther out. Marine AV-8Bs and Air Force F-16s, now based at Durban, would hit the target while a solid cover of F-15s would cover the entire assault force from South African fighters.

Looking to the left, Garrick saw the mountain escarpment that marked the borders of Lesotho. The cliffs rose two miles above sea level on the side he faced. Below him was rugged, mountainous country. His admiration for the "straight-leg" infantry increased. If they were fighting their way through stuff like that, then this was the way to go to war.

The cool morning air minimized the chance of downdrafts, and the assault force carefully picked its way along a river valley that ran to the northwest. In about half an hour, they would turn right and head through a mountain pass, flowing down like water onto the city below.

LADYSMITH

Commandant Korster hugged the ground under the radar van and watched as another flight of needle-nosed fighters roared overhead. This wasn't the first time that the Americans had hit the town, but they seemed very serious about it today. Could they know about the radar?

Korster was responsible for Ladysmith's air defenses. Besides a battery of Cactus SAM launchers, he had some captured Russian antiaircraft guns and two batteries of South African twenty- and forty-millimeter guns. Only the SAMs were radar directed.

He had been inspecting the radar van, talking to the technicians who were trying to somehow coax the balky electronics back to life. It was difficult enough to keep one of these things working in normal times, and these times were anything but normal.

Their discussion had been interrupted by the sound of an explosion directly overhead, and the van had been rocked by a thousand hammers beating on the roof. Several holes had been punched through, and the zinging fragments had ruined several pieces of equipment and wounded the senior technician.

Everyone had piled into the emplacement dug for the wheeled van, but Korster had taken one moment to look at the shredded antenna, tilted crazily off the vertical. A failed relay was now the least of its problems.

They had been hit by an antiradar missile, and without the radar to warn them of the missile carrier's approach, they had been unable to turn it off in time. It appeared the Americans had called his bluff.

The radar was dug in on a small hill that not only gave it excellent coverage, but now afforded a ringside seat on the attack below. Jet aircraft, in pairs or flights of four, appeared over the ridges and hills. Rolling inverted as they passed over the crest lines, they would approach from different directions, sometimes separated only by seconds, it seemed.

Korster watched as they bombed the equipment parks and antiaircraft sites. The SAM launchers seemed to be getting special attention from the fighters. He saw one or two missiles launched, probably in optical mode, but they failed to hit anything, and that was all the response the unready crews could muster.

The man-made storm lasted about fifteen minutes. Korster waited two or three minutes to see if there were any later waves of attackers, but finally decided that the raid was over. He looked over the town. A gray haze covered large sections, the still morning air holding the smoke overhead. Several fires burned, and he could see two of his precious SAM launchers lying on their sides. Scattered figures wandered around, still in a daze.

He had to get down there and see what was left. Turning to the senior technician, he saw that the man, a beefy sergeant, was sitting upright, being bandaged by one of his coworkers. Korster started to tell the sergeant to check the radar van for new damage when he heard a chattering sound to the southwest.

It sounded as if his antiaircraft guns were firing again, and he was ready to dive for cover again when one of the men pointed.

OVER LADYSMITH

General Garrick watched the assault from five thousand feet up and two miles back. It was close enough, with effort, to see individual men through his binoculars.

His headset, tuned to the frequency of the attack aircraft, allowed him to follow the aircrafts' preparatory attacks, as well as their escape without casualties. The first wave of gunships had been timed to hit within a minute of the last jet's attack, and for the most part, they made it.

Coming in low, the Apaches raced toward prebriefed targets that had been found on the reconnaissance photos. The South Africans were recovering quickly, he noticed. Flak emplacements sent streams of tracers up, forcing the gunships to jink and dive. One gun, opening up on the flank of the oncoming choppers, caught a machine and slammed several rounds into the tail boom. Its antitorque rotor out, the aircraft spun twice then slammed into the ground.

Returning fire with rockets, missiles, and chain guns, the gunships suppressed any location that opened fire. Garrick had heard the assault commander declare the LZ "cold," and still in formation, the slicks started coming in. The Apaches and scout helicopters moved off to predetermined areas, covering both the landing zone and the town itself.

"General, we're at bingo fuel." The voice in his headphones pulled him back from the landing zone to his noisy metal perch. Helicopters could not stay airborne forever, and the pilot had a long way to go.

"Right. Take me to the division's forward command post, please." Garrick sighed. Oh, well, once the men were out of the slicks there would be little to see from the air anyway.

LADYSMITH

Korster and his technicians watched the landing and the fight from their hilltop. Since the initial attack on their position, the enemy had not molested them, and Korster and the others had maintained a low profile. Three more R4 rifles and a pistol were not going to influence events below.

The small group hugged the earth and watched as wave after wave of American helicopters landed and disgorged soldiers and heavy equipment.

The firing in town started almost immediately, with Korster listening on the field telephone to the surprised garrison commander's orders to dig in and hold in place.

The South African defenders numbered no more than a weak battalion, but they knew the town and refused to budge from a building until they were blown out or killed in place.

Korster visualized the Americans advancing up Poorte Street, and he heard his colonel radio the order to abandon the Royal Hotel, one of the buildings being used to billet the men. He waited, hoping that the defenders would somehow hold, but it was clear who the eventual victor would be. The *kommandant* gave them another hour at most.

He stood up suddenly, surprising the other men. "Come on, we have work to do."

The technicians looked at him with amazement. They had followed and discussed the progress of the American attack. They had seen gunships and other helicopters fly directly over the ruined van. What did he think he was doing?

"The sergeant needs to have his wound tended. I want every document shredded and piled in the center of the radar van. We will burn them and the van with them and deny both to the enemy."

For him, the fighting was over. He'd see what the Americans could do with this land.

CHAPTER 37

Death Trap

JANUARY 2—44TH PARACHUTE BRIGADE REACTION FORCE, NEAR SKERPIONENPUNT

Maj. Rolf Bekker burrowed farther under the camouflage awning he'd rigged over his foxhole and then lay motionless—imitating other animals he'd seen survive the desert's bone-dry air and sun-drenched heat. Movement meant sweat. Sweat was lost water. And water was life.

His watch alarm beeped softly. Time for another drink.

He uncapped his third canteen and took a careful swig, swishing the body-temperature liquid around the inside of his mouth before swallowing. Despite the flat metallic tang imparted by the canteen itself, the water tasted good. And it felt good trickling down his parched throat. He recapped the canteen and hooked it to his web gear.

Still thirsty, Bekker settled back to wait. It was ironic, though a self-imposed irony. While he and his three hundred paratroops rationed their precious water mouthful by mouthful, one of South Africa's two significant rivers, the Oranje, lay only eight kilometers away—flowing northwest on its way toward the Atlantic. Eight kilometers south, that was all. Only a brisk two hours' walk, perhaps less.

Right now, though, the river might just as well have been on the far side of the moon. His own strict orders kept his men under cover in their fighting positions.

There was a good reason for that. Bekker's northernmost outposts were already reporting dust rising in the distance. Henrik Kruger's renegade battalion was coming south down the only road he'd left open and apparently unguarded. In reality, the men of the 20th Cape Rifles were being lured right into a killing zone.

The Afrikaner major studied his handpicked battlefield through slitted eyes. If anything, the brown, barren valley seemed even more suited to his purposes now than it had when he'd ringed it on the map.

Bordered by the rugged foothills of the Langeberg to the east and an only slightly less rugged ridge to the west, the valley sloped gently downhill from the Kalahari Basin before falling away sharply into the Oranje River basin. An unpaved secondary road ran down the eastern edge of the valley—flanked by a long, low hill topped only by small patches of brush and three solitary, stunted trees.

Bekker's two infantry companies were posted along that hill, carefully dispersed in six camouflaged platoon strongpoints surrounded by thin, hastily emplaced minefields. To give his infantry a stronger long-range punch, he'd attached a Carl Gustav 84mm recoilless rifle team to each platoon. Indirect fire support would come from the two sections of four 81mm mortars in place behind the hill—their crews crouched ready and waiting in shallow pits scraped out of the dirt and sand. And finally, he had his two Puma gunships on standby several kilometers away.

His battle plan was simple. Use HE from the mortars to kill Kruger's truck-mounted infantry. Hit the enemy's APCs with rounds from the Carl Gustavs. Finish any vehicles left moving with 30mm cannon bursts from his helicopter gunships, and then mop up with his rifle- and machine gun–armed paratroops. Bekker smiled to himself. Simple, yes.

And also damned effective. That was what combat experience taught you. Simple things worked. Complicated plans or weapons usually looked good on paper and then got you killed.

His radio crackled softly. "Rover Foxtrot One, this is Tango Zebra Three." Tango Zebra Three was the call sign for his northernmost observation post.

Corporal de Vries passed the handset across the foxhole. "Go ahead, Three."

"Enemy scouting force in sight. Four Land Rovers ahead of the main column."

Bekker propped himself up against the lip of the foxhole and raised his field glasses. The lead Land Rover leapt into view—dented, travel stained, and armed with a heavy machine gun on a pivot mount. Four men in South African uniforms rode in the vehicle—a driver, gunner, and two others. He lowered the glasses and pressed the transmit switch. "Keep your heads down, Three. Let them pass."

"Roger your last, Rover One. They're rolling by now. Out."

Bekker felt himself start to sweat. The next few minutes were critical. He was gambling that Kruger's recce units wouldn't spot his carefully prepared ambush. Ordinarily he wouldn't have risked it. An alert scout commander would be too likely to send a team up the hill for a look-see. But Kruger's men had been on the run for more than two weeks now—traveling for hours on end each day through empty deserts and desolate mountains. And Rolf Bekker was willing to bet that they'd lost some of their edge.

COMMAND RATEL, 20TH CAPE RIFLES, NORTH OF SKERPIONENPUNT

Even with the hatches closed and the air-conditioning going full blast, the Ratel's crowded interior was still almost unbearably hot. Ian Sherfield sat across a narrow fold-down mapboard watching Commandant Henrik Kruger methodically charting their course. The South African's calm, cool appearance made Ian even more conscious of the sweat stains under his own arms and across his back.

The Ratel bucked suddenly, and he grabbed a strap with one hand, hanging on tightly as the APC lurched over a bump in the rock-strewn track the South Africans called a secondary road. The sight of Kruger's grease pencil skittering randomly across the plastic map overlay made him feel a little better. Even Emily van der Heijden's old fiancé could lose his grip from time to time.

Ian's eyes roved around the crowded Ratel. Emily and Matthew Sibena sat wedged in one corner, next to wall clips holding assault rifles and mesh bags full of canteens and spare rations. He met her eyes and nodded ruefully toward the table. She just smiled slightly and shrugged as though to indicate her exclusion didn't really matter.

But he knew it did matter—especially to her. By rights, he thought, Emily should be up here with them talking over their next move. But it had become clear that Kruger felt uncomfortable when she tried to take an active part in their conferences.

His gaze moved on around the Ratel, studying his fellow passengers. Three young staff officers occupied the folding seats on their commander's side of the vehicle. One stood beside a machine gunner in the turret, holding a radio headset pressed to one ear—monitoring reports from the scouts probing ahead of the column. All of them looked tired. Sunlight streamed in through eight small firing ports—four on each side.

Kruger finished his work and sat back. He raised his voice to be heard over the APC's powerful engine. "We're making good time today." He tapped a spot on the map. "We should be across the Oranje by noon."

Ian nodded. "What then?"

"Depending on what's up ahead, we push on to Kenhardt and Brandvlei. After that?" Kruger shrugged. "That we must talk about, Ian."

The South African put his pencil on the tiny town labeled Brandvlei. Ian mentally measured the distance from there to

Cape Town—less than five hundred kilometers. Maybe a two-day drive at their present speed. "What's the problem?"

"Your country has aircraft based at Cape Town, true?"

Ian nodded. They'd caught bits and pieces of Voice of America news broadcasts en route. Enough to follow major developments in the war. Both the U.S. and Great Britain were still staging troops and air units through the Cape Town area.

Then he realized what was worrying Kruger. What would any red-blooded U.S. pilot do if he spotted a battalion-sized column of trucks and APCs rolling south toward the city? He'd strafe or bomb the hell out of it, that's what. Ian looked up. "Are you saying we run a risk of becoming jet bait?"

"Jet bait?" Kruger hesitated briefly, obviously puzzled. Then his face cleared up as he mentally translated the slang phrase. "Yes, exactly. We cannot move beyond Brandvlei until we've made firm contact with either your nation's forces or those of the provisional government."

"Well, what's so hard about—"

The lieutenant manning their radio interrupted. "Excuse me, sir, but the recce troop reports they have the Oranje in sight! No enemy contacts."

REACTION FORCE

Maj. Rolf Bekker held his breath as the long column of canvas-sided trucks and wheeled APCs drove straight down the road into his killing zone. De Vries's manpack radio lay beside him, with its whip antenna poking above the foxhole's camouflage awning.

Bekker keyed the mike. "All units, this is Rover Foxtrot One. Stand by. Hold fire. Wait for my order."

The lead Ratel rolled past a cracked and weathered boulder in line with Bekker's foxhole. Fifty or so vehicles were strung out behind it at twenty-meter intervals. They were in range. "Now! Fire! Fire! Fire!"

Two explosions rocked the desert floor—both within meters of the road. Hit by shrapnel, a five-ton truck slewed out of control, slammed into a boulder, and rolled over. Dazed survivors staggered out of the wreck and toppled over, hit repeatedly by rifle and machine-gun fire. Near the tail end of the column, a Buffel APC blew up in a spectacular rolling ball of flame, hit broadside by a single Carl Gustav round. Human torches, men on fire, threw themselves screaming over the sides and then crumpled as the paratroopers put them out of their misery.

Bekker's men had spent most of the preceding day zeroing in their weapons. Now their hard work was paying off. "Papa Charlie One, this is Rover One. On target! Fire for effect!"

In seconds, eight more mortar bombs burst near the road —spraying fragments up and down the line of trucks and personnel carriers. Several vehicles were on fire, some while still moving. Other lay canted at odd angles, their drivers dead or disabled.

Bekker showed his teeth in a quick, wolfish smile. Kruger's traitorous battalion was being cut to pieces by his textbook-perfect ambush.

COMMAND RATEL

A nearby explosion rocked the Ratel, sending maps, pencils, and loose gear flying. Fragments rattled off its side armor.

"Christ!" Henrik Kruger staggered forward through the confusion and grabbed the radio headset from the pale, frightened lieutenant. Panicked, garbled voices poured over the airwaves.

"Taking fire from the hill . . . Arrie's hit! My God, I'm hit! . . . Got to get out. . . . Estimate four, maybe five guns . . ."

Another shell slammed into the road just ahead of them. Kruger heard his driver swearing as he swerved off onto the shoulder to avoid ramming a truck stopped dead and on fire. As they roared by the blazing vehicle, a single sheet of furnace-hot flame washed over the turret and commander's cupola. Then they were past.

He swung round in a quick circle, trying to see what was happening to his battalion through his cupola's narrow vision slits. Burning vehicles and sprawled corpses littered the barren landscape in every direction. They were being massacred.

Kruger squeezed the transmit button. "This is Kruger. Wheel left and pop smoke! Pop smoke!"

The Ratel slewed over in a hard left turn. As it spun around to face the enemy-held hill, the machine gunner beside him triggered the APC's four turret-mounted smoke dischargers. They coughed in sequence, firing four smoke grenades out through a fifty-meter-wide arc.

Other Ratels were doing the same thing, creating an instant smoke screen to hide themselves from the heavy weapons on the hill above them. Sand and dirt sprayed high near the APC's right flank as another shell ploughed into the ground.

Kruger grimaced. The smoke gave them a temporary respite from direct fire, but those damned mortars didn't need to see their targets to hit them. They only had to pour bombs onto preregistered firing points to be sure of killing something.

Conscious of precious seconds slipping by, he scanned the terrain behind them. Nothing. No cover at all. Just flat, bare rock, packed dirt, and tufts of dead grass. They'd have to break this ambush the hard way. He clicked his mike again. "All units. Attack! Attack immediately! Our objective is the hill!"

As the Ratel bounced forward, accelerating through its own smoke screen, acknowledgments flowed in from his surviving company and platoon leaders. The men and vehicles of the 20th Cape Rifles surged ahead, charging uphill toward their enemies.

REACTION FORCE

Bekker scowled at the puffs of dense white smoke dotting the ground below the hill. His Carl Gustav teams were having trouble finding targets in all that muck. Another mortar bomb salvo landed—bright flashes rippling through the thickening haze of smoke and dust. Directed by forward observers, his gunners were walking their fire back and forth along the road, pounding the enemy's stalled vehicles and dismounted infantry.

"Major!" De Vries grabbed his shoulder and pointed downhill. Shapes were emerging from the smoke. Turreted Ratels, open-topped Buffels, and even trucks were advancing on his positions at high speed.

For a second, Bekker's confidence slipped. Kruger was doing exactly what he himself would have done under the same circumstances. And he was doing it fast.

Clang. Hit by a Carl Gustav round, one of the oncoming APCs shuddered once and stopped moving. Flames spewed out of the gigantic hole punched through its thin front armor. Nobody got through its buckled hatches.

But the recoilless rifle's backblast hovered over its firing position like a billboard advertising its existence. Bekker caught a last glimpse of the Carl Gustav's two-man crew hurriedly reloading before two Ratel turrets whined round and fired repeatedly—pumping 20mm cannon shells into the foxhole until it vanished in a spray of sand and dirt.

More vehicles were hit and burning, but the rest were still coming on—their guns chattering wildly, traversing right and left to lay down a curtain of suppressive fire across the hilltop.

Bekker dove for the bottom of his hole as a machine-gun burst tore through the air all around him. Corporal de Vries wasn't fast enough. A 12.7mm bullet caught him at the base of the throat and ripped his head off. The radioman's decapitated corpse fell backward against the lip of the foxhole, still spouting bright-red arterial blood.

The major grabbed his R4 and snapped its safety off. Damn it. Where were his gunships? The helicopters were his ace in the hole.

PUMA GUNSHIP LEAD

Capt. Harry Kersten brought his helicopter up out of the Oranje River basin and then dropped its nose to gain speed for forward flight. Rotors clattering, the Puma surged ahead—closing on the battlefield at eighty knots. He squinted through the haze, looking for targets.

Pillars of black smoke curled skyward above burning trucks and armored personnel carriers. Others lay tilted over, evidently abandoned. All the signs of a successful and bloody ambush. Then he saw boxy shapes moving up the side of the hill and frowned. The renegade battalion's vehicles were almost right on top of Bekker's infantry. Target selection was going to be a bitch.

Kersten spoke over the intercom. "You with me back there, Roef?"

"Sure, Captain." His door gunner had to shout over the noise of the slipstream howling in through his open door.

"Good. Now listen up. We're going in now—nice and low so you can see who you're shooting, right? And you only shoot the vehicles, okay?"

"Understood."

"Great." Kersten half-turned his head to catch a glimpse of the other Puma pacing them just off the desert floor. "You copy that, Hennie?"

His wingman acknowledged.

Kersten took a quick breath and brought the helicopter around in a gentle, curving arc. They'd cross the battle area at an angle to bring their door-mounted 30mm cannons to bear. He came out of the turn and dropped the Puma's nose again. Airspeed crept up slowly—climbing from eighty knots to one hundred and twenty. The other gunship settled into formation behind him.

Now they were hurtling straight for the hill, two helicopters flashing past isolated clumps of brush and jagged boulders, one right after the other. The battlefield seemed to leap closer in seconds. Distant specks expanded suddenly into individual vehicles. Ratels with their distinctive turrets. Open-topped Buffels crammed with white faces staring up at him from under helmets. Land Rovers weaving over the ground at fantastic speed. Even a few trucks, which seemed sadly out of place among the fighting vehicles.

The Puma's 30mm gun opened up with a rattling, jackhammer roar.

Kersten pulled the gunship's nose up sharply, following the rising terrain. He and his crew were blind for an instant as the Puma clattered through the thick, oily smoke billowing from a burning vehicle, and it shuddered violently—caught in a sudden upsurge of superheated air. Then they were through and on the other side of the hill, howling away at high speed.

"Two of them! I got two of the bastards!" his door gunner shouted over the intercom, caught up in a wild mix of ecstasy and relief. "They fireballed! I got them, Captain."

"Great, Roef." Kersten yanked the Puma around in a tight, spiraling turn. "Look sharp now. We're going in again."

The two South African gunships flew south and west in an arc that would bring them back over the hilltop battlefield.

RATEL ONE SIX

LCpl. Mike Villiers ducked as a mortar round exploded several dozen meters behind his APC. Spent fragments and pieces of dirt pattered down over its deck armor and off his helmet. He raised his head and gripped his ring-mounted light machine gun even tighter. Christ. He hated riding facing backward like this, and he hated standing in an open hatch with half his body exposed outside the Ratel's armor. Still, somebody had to do it. Kruger's decimated battalion needed whatever antiaircraft defenses it could muster.

The three burning vehicles to his left were proof of that. They'd been shredded from end to end by 30mm cannon shells—gutted like fish. Smoldering corpses hung half in and half out of hatches. Villiers had no desire to end up dead like those poor sods, so he watched the sky with renewed intensity.

A fast-moving blur near the horizon caught his eye. "Here they come! Three o'clock low!"

He squeezed the trigger convulsively, feeling the machine

gun kick back against his upper arm and watching his glowing tracers reaching out for the incoming blur. Other tracer streams were rising from nearby Ratels, all aimed at the lead helicopter flying barely a hundred feet off the ground.

Trying to hit a target moving at more than one hundred miles an hour while riding a bucking, lurching platform moving at nearly twenty miles an hour itself would ordinarily seem an almost impossible task. Even a machine gun's ability to fire hundreds of rounds per minute merely lowers the odds against success from the astronomical to the wildly improbable. But sometimes you get lucky.

LCpl. Mike Villiers got lucky.

PUMA GUNSHIP LEAD

Four 7.62mm rounds hit the Puma. Three simply tore inconsequential holes in its fuselage and hurtled onward, tumbling through empty air. The fourth did catastrophic damage.

It ripped into the Puma's starboard engine at an angle that took it straight through a fuel line and into the turbine blades. One blade shattered instantly—spewing white-hot fragments in every direction. The turbine engine seized up, died, and then erupted in flame.

Capt. Harry Kersten barely had time to notice the glowing red fire-warning light before his helicopter lost power, dipped too low, and slammed nose first into the hill. The Puma flipped end over end twice and then exploded—spraying burning fuel and sharp-edged fragments over hundreds of meters.

The second gunship veered wildly away from the rising fireball and vanished over the hill. It reappeared moments later, flying southeast—away from the battle. With Kersten dead and their potential targets already in among the defending strongpoints, the second Puma's crew saw little reason to stay and fight.

Maj. Rolf Bekker had just lost his ace in the hole.

REACTION FORCE

The 44th Parachute Brigade's paratroopers were dying hard. They were taking their enemies with them, but they were dying. Rifles and machine guns were no match for armored personnel carriers mounting 20mm cannon and coaxial machine guns. A well-placed Carl Gustav round could turn any APC into a shattered wreck, but most of their recoilless rifle teams were only getting off one or two shots before being spotted and knocked out.

Burning APCs and trucks dotted the hillside, but enough made it through unscathed to overrun Bekker's platoon-strength strongpoints. And once Kruger's men were inside each defensive ring, the paratroops were wiped out foxhole by foxhole—killed by soldiers firing from inside their Ratels, by point-blank cannon shots, or by dismounted infantry charging forward behind a barrage of grenades and automatic weapons fire.

COMMAND RATEL

Ian Sherfield hung to his seat strap for dear life as the Ratel canted upward, grinding uphill at more than twenty miles an hour. His ears were numb—deafened by the constant chatter of the APC's heavy machine gun and by bullets spanging off its armor. Smoking, spent shell casings rolled back down the metal floor toward the rear.

Kruger's staff officers crouched behind the vehicle's firing ports, ready to open fire with their R4 assault rifles the moment they had targets. Emily and Sibena were still in their seats, though only just barely. They both looked almost as scared as he felt.

The front end of the Ratel dropped downward as it roared over the crest.

And then the world blew up.

At first Ian was only aware of the blinding white flash that started outside the driver's compartment and then rippled backward down the length of the Ratel. Then a shock wave punched the air out of his lungs and threw him out of his seat. The sound came last—a tremendous clanging, discordant thunderclap that tore conscious, coherent thought to shreds. As he blacked out, he felt the Ratel being lifted upward, twisting sideways in midair.

He came to on his knees, tangled in fallen gear and still-hot shell casings. The Ratel lay tilted on its left side, no longer moving. Foul-smelling smoke eddied in from the outside. Coughing and groaning men lay in heaps all around him.

Emily! Ian shook his head to clear it and regretted it right away. He must have slammed into something hard and unforgiving when the APC tipped over. He staggered upright and looked around.

There she was. Emily sat upright in a loose pile of canteens, medical kits, and assault rifle magazines. She seemed dazed but unhurt. His heart started beating again.

"You are wounded?" Kruger had to scream it into his ear to be heard. The Afrikaner officer had a ragged, bleeding cut over one cheekbone, but no other apparent injuries.

"No!" Ian shouted back. "What happened?"

"We hit a mine." Kruger coughed as a thicker tendril of smoke curled in through the viewslits in his commander's cupola. It smelled very much like burning oil. His eyes widened. "We must get out! We're on fire!"

Oh, shit. Ian whirled and lurched through the debris toward Emily. Sibena scrambled to his feet beside her. Behind him, he could hear Kruger rousing the rest of his crew and staff.

"Ian, thank God . . ." She clutched at his arm as he helped her up.

"Yeah." He turned to Sibena. "Matt! Hit those clips!" He pointed to the metal locking bars holding the rear hatch shut.

"Right." Sibena spun them up and away. Ian put his hand on the hatch handle and then felt someone grab his shoulder in a strong grip. He turned to see Kruger.

The South African had an assault rifle slung over his own

shoulder. His staff officers and vehicle crew crowded behind him with their own weapons. "Let my men go first. We have enemies out there."

"You got it." Ian, Emily, and Matt squeezed to one side of the battered Ratel—allowing the six men by.

The soldiers shoved the hatch open and threw themselves through the narrow opening one after the other. Staying low, they fanned out in a semicircle around the wrecked APC. A lieutenant stayed by the door to help the others out. Smoke and blowing sand cut visibility to meters at best.

Ian's hearing was coming back. He wasn't sure what sounded more dangerous—the staccato rattle of automatic weapons fire outside or the steady crackle of the flames now engulfing the Ratel driver's compartment.

The young officer standing outside signaled him frantically. "Come on, man. Pass her through. I'll get her to cover."

Ian guided Emily through the hatch and turned to motion Sibena forward—

And an assault rifle opened up from somewhere close by, spraying rounds at full automatic. Several punched into the hatch door and howled off into the surrounding smoke.

Ian whirled round in horror. His vision darkened and then cleared. Emily and the lieutenant lay tangled together on the ground, bright blood staining the sand around them.

"No!" Without thinking Ian dived through the hatch.

She was still alive, though bleeding badly from one shoulder. The staff officer was dead. He'd taken most of the burst.

Ian scrabbled through the dead man's gear looking for his medical kit. He needed bandages to stop the bleeding. He never even thought to look up.

Ten meters away, Staff Sgt. Gerrit Roost rose from his foxhole, cradling his R4 assault rifle. He yanked out the empty thirty-five-round clip and shoved in a full magazine. This one would be an easy kill. He started to raise his weapon, sighting straight at the kneeling civilian's chest.

Three separate hammer blows knocked him off his feet. Astonished, Roost strained to raise his head and saw the ugly, red-rimmed holes torn in his chest and stomach. Then he saw the man who'd shot him. His mouth dropped open. A kaffir! He'd been killed by a damned black!

The Afrikaner sergeant died with that look of shocked, unbelieving surprise frozen on his face.

Matthew Sibena let go of the trigger he'd squeezed and held down, threw the dead lieutenant's rifle from him as far as it would go, and ran to help Ian.

EMERGENCY AID STATION, ON THE HILL NEAR SKERPIONENPUNT

Henrik Kruger stood looking at a scene straight out of his worst nightmares. Wrecked trucks and armored personnel carriers were strewn up and down the road and across the hillside in almost every direction. Most were still on fire, sending greasy plumes of smoke billowing up to stain the sky. Bodies sprawled beside the vehicles, some in heaps, others alone. Others littered the hilltop.

Stretcher parties wandered through the carnage, looking for wounded they could carry up to the aid station behind him. He smiled bitterly. Aid station. That was an impressive-sounding name for what was only a patch of bare rock and sand covered by a hastily rigged tarp.

Dozens of seriously injured men lay in rows behind him. His lone surviving surgeon and handful of corpsmen were completely swamped by sheer numbers. As it was, they were still frantically engaged in triage—the gruesome, though essential, task of sorting those who were sure to die from those who might be saved with the limited gear and supplies on hand.

Kruger clasped his hands tightly behind his back, trying hard not to hear the low, sobbing moans rising from the rows of wounded. Tears rolled slowly down his face, stinging as they dripped into his torn cheek. This isn't a battlefield, he thought. This is a butcher's yard. For both sides.

"*Kommandant!*"

Several of his men waved him over to a foxhole not far from his wrecked Ratel. He sighed, wiped his face roughly, and moved in that direction.

They'd found the paratroop commander. Maj. Rolf Bekker lay crumpled near the bottom of his foxhole—wounded and only semiconscious, but still alive. Kruger stared down at the man. From the look of things, the paratrooper had taken a faceful of grenade fragments, been shot, and then left for dead when Kruger's infantry overran this part of the hill.

The South African felt a cold rage building up inside him as he looked at Bekker. This was the bastard who'd murdered his battalion. The man whose soldiers had shot Emily. Kruger's fingers brushed the 9mm pistol at his side. Revenge would be so simple. So easy. Too easy. He shook his head. There'd been enough killing.

He straightened up. "Take him to the aid station and have him patched up. I want this bastard to live."

The *kommandant* turned and walked away, heading for the small cluster of officers awaiting their next orders. Orders? What orders could he give?

Ian Sherfield intercepted him. The tall American looked gaunt and completely exhausted. "Henrik, I need one of your Land Rovers and a driver."

Kruger stared at him for a moment, taken aback by the sudden request. Then he sighed and nodded. "I understand, Ian. With luck, you and Emily can still reach Cape Town." He motioned to the wreckage strewn around them. "I gather it's pretty clear that the rest of us have come as far as we can. I'll arrange for extra supplies and cans of petrol."

"No, you don't understand." Ian shook his head in exasperation and smiled tightly. "I just want a ride into the nearest town with a phone. I think it's time we tried to scare up some help."

The American's thin smile faded as a high-pitched scream rose from the aid station. "God only knows, Henrik, but I think we could sure use some right now."

OPERATIONS CENTER, D. F. MALAN AIRPORT, CAPE TOWN

More than a dozen U.S. Air Force technicians and radar consoles crowded the darkened room. Calm, quiet voices rose and fell as they controlled the movements of incoming and outgoing C-5s and C-141s crammed with troops, equipment, and supplies.

"Major?"

Irritated at the interruption, the Operations Center duty officer glanced up from the argument he'd been having over the availability of JP-4 and JP-5 fuel stocks. "Yeah. What is it?"

The enlisted man manning their phone line held up the receiver. "I've got kind of a strange call here, sir. Some reporter named Sherfield wants to talk to whoever's in charge."

Another reporter. Swell. The major snorted and said, "Look, turn the bozo over to Public Affairs . . ." He stopped in midsentence. Sherfield? Why did that name ring a bell?

Then he remembered. Sherfield was the TV reporter whose reports had helped break this mess wide open. The guy who was missing. The major whistled softly. "Well, I'll be a sorry son of a bitch." He moved toward the man. "Gimme that phone. Now!"

JANUARY 3—EVACUATION POINT, ON ROUTE 64, NEAR THE ORANJE RIVER

Emily van der Heijden and Ian Sherfield stood close together, watching as a lumbering C-130 Hercules dropped out of the sky, touched down precisely on the centerline of the road, and rolled past them with its props howling and brakes screaming. Two more turboprop transports were visible orbiting slowly in the distance—waiting for their turn on the improvised runway.

The C-130 taxied to a stop and several uniformed officers

emerged, blinking in the bright sun. They moved to meet Henrik Kruger as he stood rigid by the side of the road.

Despite her obvious pain and a shoulder swathed in bandages, Emily refused to lie down. "I can walk perfectly well, and you know it, Ian." Her stern gaze softened. "Besides, there are too many others who must be carried. So many others who have been so terribly hurt."

Ian gave up. "Okay, but at least let me help you down. As a sop to my manly pride. Deal?"

She smiled at that. "Deal." She looked up. "Henrik wants us."

Kruger had insisted on meeting the Americans by himself first. He wants to end his part in this war with honor, she realized sadly. Even though he had rebelled against Pretoria, this was still a form of surrender for him. She hoped he could live with that.

They moved downhill toward the tiny knot of South African and U.S. Air Force officers. With a tightly controlled, emotionless voice, Kruger introduced them to the ranking officer, a Lieutenant Colonel Packard.

Packard stepped forward with an outstretched hand and a broad, toothy smile. "Mr. Sherfield, I'm damned glad to meet you!" He lowered his voice to a level slightly below a booming shout. "I hope you don't mind, but we've arranged a small press conference for your arrival at the airfield. I guess I don't have to tell you this is gonna be big news back in the States!"

Emily hid a sudden smile of her own as Ian leaned in close and whispered in her ear, "Oh, my God. A press conference. Now I know we're in trouble."

CHAPTER 38

Last Stand

JANUARY 4—U.S. EXPEDITIONARY FORCE HEADQUARTERS, DURBAN, RSA

It was part of his job, but General Craig found it hard to hide his contempt for the junketing politicians who kept appearing at his headquarters. As soon as the U.S. forces had expanded their toehold into a beachhead, and then broken out from the Drakensberg, a group of congressmen, bureaucrats, and even some state officials had decided to visit South Africa on a "fact-finding" mission. It didn't hurt that while it was winter in Washington, it was summer in South Africa.

A few were sincere. They were easy to spot. They knew the background, had read up on the forces involved, and had even taken the time to look at a map. The rest were idiots. Their idea of preparation was to watch a tape of *Zulu*.

Craig begrudged the time, the stupid questions, and their long trips to the beaches of Durban and to Table Mountain in Cape Town. They walked over the battered mountain's landscape as if it were an old Civil War battlefield. One had actually asked why there weren't any park rangers!

Craig endured. He was savvy enough to know that these men wielded real power in Congress, and they would remember the red-carpet treatment the next time they voted on defense appropriations. It reminded him, though, why he detested politics and politicians.

Most of the group had taken the afternoon off to attend to "personal business," which Craig knew meant sun and surf along the Golden Mile. Two members of the party, though, had asked to see Ladysmith. Craig had long ago marked them as the good ones, and he decided to escort them personally.

Ladysmith was a lot more recent battle than Table Mountain, and it showed in the gutted vehicles and burned-out buildings. Even with surprise on their side, the 101st had taken over 15 percent casualties in the lead battalion, 10 percent in the brigade overall.

Their helicopter had followed the same path as the assault force, and the very real door gunners in the aircraft had given the congressmen the feeling of taking part—exactly what Craig had wanted.

As instructed, the pilot made an assault landing near the original LZ, and they had toured the town, the new Army base nearby, and the field hospital, which treated not only the casualties from Ladysmith, but from the entire Drakensberg campaign.

Craig had warned the hospital staff in advance, and they had tracked down any patients from the congressmen's states. A military photographer was standing by and caught the scene as they visited their constituents in the field.

It was good stuff, and Craig had caught himself smiling in spite of himself. These two cared, and he didn't mind helping them out. He also wanted to be around when those double-damned pleasure seekers found out they'd missed a "photo opportunity."

The two officials had eaten lunch on the ride back, trying MREs for the first time. "Meals ready to eat" were vacuum-packed meals meant to be carried by soldiers in the field. Some were good, some not so good. Craig told the senators they were a definite improvement on the old tinned C rations, but the troops called them "meals rejected by Ethiopians."

The small group was now about to take part in Craig's daily afternoon intelligence brief. This would put the politicos in the picture as much as he was, Craig thought, plus would let them feel they had the inside scoop. Congressmen automatically had the security clearances necessary to see this stuff, and he was pretty sure these two would not blab it around.

The briefing was always given in one of the conference rooms at the Durban Hilton. The hotel's convention facilities had easily been converted to serve as Craig's headquarters, and the staff had simply treated the Allied soldiers as another set of conventioneers.

A detailed map of South Africa covered one wall. The position of each division, and each brigade within the division, was marked, as well as their progress over the past two days and their objectives for the next twenty-four hours.

Information on enemy forces was also displayed, but this was much less well defined. Not only was the intelligence fragmentary and possibly wrong, but there was more than one enemy.

Still, it was gratifying to look at the map. It clearly showed the speed and sweep of the Allied advance, radiating out from Ladysmith in several directions.

As they settled into their seats, the J-2, or intelligence officer, detailed new data on each of the belligerents. The Cuban forces were still consolidating their hold on Naboomspruit and had successfully repelled a weak counterattack by the Boers. It had probably been launched quickly, to try to knock them out before they dug in.

The Boers themselves had units scattered all over the map. A line of infantry and armor stretched in front of Pretoria, screening the capital from the Cuban advance, while a second appeared to be forming in front of Johannesburg to the south. Anchored on Vereeniging and the mountain west of it, it would guard the biggest city in South Africa from the advancing Allied army.

Other Boer units continued to try to suppress the rebellion, either garrisoning mines and cities or chasing rebels around the countryside. Craig was glad to see so much of South

Africa's fighting power distracted, but it cut two ways. After his troops occupied the area, he would be responsible for civil law and order.

Finally, there were the commandos. A cross between militia and guerrillas, they operated behind American lines and tied up troops and time chasing them down. Data on them was sketchy.

As much for the senators as for Craig, his J-2 summarized the situation. "Although U.S., British, and rebel South African forces now hold the RSA's major port cities and coastal lands, much of the interior, the 'deep north,' remains in the hands of Vorster and his AWB cronies. This is his heartland, the source of his political strength, and much of the population would support him against any outsider.

"Even worse, the Cuban invasion force holds two of South Africa's most important minerals complexes and is closer than we are to Pretoria and Johannesburg."

The J-2 pointed to Naboomspruit. "The nearest Cuban forces are about a hundred and ten kilometers away from Pretoria. Based on reconnaissance photos and other intelligence, they will not be ready to advance for another two days."

The officer moved his pointer to the south. "Leading elements of the Twenty-fourth, advancing up National Route Three, arrived in Warden this morning. That puts them one hundred and eighty kilometers from Johannesburg."

Craig chimed in, "And to get there, we will have to swing around the Vaal River dam complex and punch through the line at Vereeniging. Then we take the city itself, fight our way over the Witwatersrand"—he sighed—"and then we can go after Pretoria."

The two senators looked questioningly at the general. "Then we can't beat the Cubans to Pretoria?" one asked.

"Not at the rate we're going, sir." Craig smiled ironically. "Vega had one hell of a head start on us."

Craig continued, "Given the time, we could build up enough forces to take on the enemy positions with excellent odds of success, and use those odds to hold down casualties. My supply line is long, though, and as you've seen, not completely secure. As it is, I'm pressed for time and have taken risks, like Ladysmith, to keep the offensive moving. Remember that when you see the casualty lists back home."

The two congressmen nodded. One asked, "If you can't get to Pretoria in time, why spend those lives pushing so hard?"

"Because I still need to be in Pretoria as quickly as possible. I don't want the Cubans dug in deep." He paused, looking at the map. "And there's always the uncertainty of war."

"And until you take Pretoria and drive the Cubans out, South Africa will be bloody chaos."

"You now understand the situation in South Africa, Senator."

PRESIDENT'S OFFICE, THE UNION BUILDINGS, PRETORIA

Another meeting had ended. Though perhaps *meeting* was the wrong word, Karl Vorster thought wearily. Once again, he'd been forced to lecture a cabinet that resembled a flock of helpless sheep more than anything else.

Depressed and angry, he'd left his generals and deputies arguing over the map while he retreated to his private office. He slumped in his leather-backed chair, feeling his age and a few years more. None of those idiots had anything useful to contribute. Instead, they bickered and squabbled, interfering with every political and military step he took.

Some were traitors, Vorster knew. A few were actively in league with the enemy, and others would rather serve themselves than South Africa. Most of his advisors, though, were simply fools, unable to see with his vision or act with his daring. Panicked, they waffled and wailed while their nation was being shattered simultaneously both from within and from without.

Cut off from outside supply, invaded by Cuban and Allied armies, and with rebels and guerrillas running wild inside its borders, South Africa was on the verge of complete defeat.

Vorster scowled. He had no allies left. Even his most trusted political supporters counseled abject surrender.

Still, he had faith that his nation would rise again. Defeat by foreign armies was part of the Afrikaner heritage, but his people, the sturdy Boer farmers, had always survived and ultimately triumphed. It was the farmer, the man of the earth, who had always saved South Africa.

Vorster frowned. The mines with their diamonds and gold and platinum had been a source of power, but now they were attracting the hyenas. The republic stood like a wounded lion at bay with the scavengers closing in. The lion might put up a heroic fight, but it would fall in the end.

He glanced at the small, but beautifully detailed, map of South Africa hung on his office wall. It showed every major road, city, and industrial center. It didn't show the territories captured by the advancing enemy armies—but it didn't have to. Those lines were burned in his very brain. The Cubans, the Americans, and the British were all closing in like a vise around the Witwatersrand and its rich mineral resources.

His hands tightened into clenched fists. If he and his followers went down in blood and flame, he only hoped his enemies would choke on their newfound wealth. God grant that they would fight over the mines and smelters until only a wasteland remained. . . .

Karl Vorster stopped there, suddenly struck by an idea breathtaking in its very boldness. South Africa's fate had seemed sealed, its future dark and grim. But now he saw a new road, a new option—one aimed squarely at the heart of his enemies' plans.

STATE SECURITY COUNCIL CHAMBER, PRETORIA

Vorster's cabinet meetings always started quietly. This day's afternoon session was no exception. The intelligence briefer, an SADF major, gave the assembled group the latest batch of bad news in a steady monotone, his body subconsciously poised for flight. The President's rages were legendary, and even the carefully filtered data he saw was often enough to send him into orbit.

Today, though, Vorster sat quietly, almost calmly. He seemed preoccupied by the document in front of him, and utterly uninterested in the briefer's recitation of battlefield disasters and guerrilla attacks. He only nodded as the major finished and hastily excused himself.

Then Vorster looked up and smiled, an expression that seemed almost frightening on his haggard face. "I bring good news, my friends. God himself has shown me the way to defeat our foes and save our people."

What? He's done it, thought Gen. Adriaan de Wet, he's finally retreated completely into his world of fantasy. The general quickly studied the faces of the surviving cabinet members. Working with Karl Vorster forced one to develop a poker face, but he could read them well enough.

Marius van der Heijden looked troubled, but seemed the least affected. The minister of law and order even seemed ready to believe the President really had found an answer to their problems. The rest showed their disbelief in a dozen different ways. Many of the military men on de Wet's staff stared down at the map, looking for some operational scheme that they had overlooked.

"The solution to our present situation is clear if we go back to basics. Our enemies are not attacking us for political reasons, but for economic ones." Vorster rose from his chair, towering over his assembled followers. "The West gladly suffered our existence for forty years. The communists attacked us verbally and sent black guerrillas to terrorize us, but they did not move openly. Behind the scenes, the Soviets were very happy to make joint agreements on gold and diamond sales."

De Wet and the others nodded, a little impatiently.

Vorster continued, "As long as the gold and platinum and chromium and all the rest were produced in steady stream, the world was happy. But at the first sign of trouble in the mines, they turned on us. The world's two biggest power blocs, with everyone else cheering them on, have attacked our nation—nearly tripping over each other in their greed."

Vorster smiled again, even more grimly this time. "So what we must do is clear. We must threaten to destroy what they hold so dear. We will send an ultimatum to our enemies, threatening to render these mines useless unless they leave our lands immediately."

De Wet's puzzlement was so strong that he forgot to mask his feelings, but his expression was mirrored around the table.

Vorster swept his arm around the room, his voice filled with excitement. "Can't any of you see it? Think! The world's financial markets have been frightened by a temporary disruption of the resources we hold. Think of how much pressure those money-grubbing bankers will put on their governments if they think the supply will stop altogether."

De Wet could not wait any longer. "But how? We can dynamite some of our mines, but they could always be reopened. And most are nothing more than vast open pits—impossible to destroy."

Vorster nodded. "True enough, General. But the answer is not dynamite. It is radioactive dust—the wastes produced by our reactors." If he noticed the instinctive horror on the faces around him, he didn't show it.

"Our threat will be simple and credible. Unless the attacking armies cease fire immediately and withdraw from our territory, we will scatter radioactive waste over every mine and smelter under our control."

De Wet found himself intrigued by the idea. The high-level radioactive wastes produced by South Africa's two nuclear reactors could contaminate the surfaces of the mines and other industrial facilities for hundreds, if not thousands, of years. Decontamination would be both fantastically difficult and prohibitively expensive. What Vorster had in mind would be a powerful threat to the world's strategic minerals supplies.

De Wet looked up. "But what do we do, Mr. President, if they call our bluff?"

Vorster's face reddened and he shouted, "It is not a bluff! If they continue to advance, we will wreck these mines!"

He paused and spoke more calmly, almost pleading. "Don't you see? We have never truly needed this wealth to survive as a pure society. It has been a source of endless trouble—of Uitlander speculators and unruly black laborers. The trekboers and early farmers built our nation. And when these mines are gone, our farms will remain."

De Wet nodded slowly in agreement. The South Africa they all knew was dying anyway. Perhaps it was better to rob their enemies of the fruits of victory than to go down to defeat whimpering in despair. He started, suddenly aware that Vorster was speaking directly to him.

"General, I need every engineer you can muster, and a list of every mine we still possess."

De Wet nodded, turned to his officers, and started issuing the orders needed to prepare South Africa's economic suicide.

CHAPTER 39

Acceleration

JANUARY 6—HEADQUARTERS, ALLIED EXPEDITIONARY FORCE, DURBAN

Lt. Gen. Jerry Craig held two message slips in his hand. One read, *Do not believe Vorster has political control or resources to carry out his threat. Recommend continuing offensive operations.*

The second telex said, *Expert consultants have advised us that Vorster's claim is credible. Suggest you halt operations and use time to consolidate position until way is found to clear demolitions from mine sites.*

One was from CIA, the other from the State Department. The third message he'd received was the one that counted—ostensibly a secure voice call from the chairman of the Joint Chiefs of Staff, but actually reflecting the President's own opinion. Ten minutes of talk that boiled down to, "We rely on your estimate of the situation and will back whatever judgment you make." Well, he would have resented anything else, but it still left him the man on the spot.

Every senior and junior staff officer in the Allied headquarters packed the briefing room. Officers of two nationalities and every service filled the chairs and lined the walls. Christ, Craig thought, I don't know half of these people. And that bothered him. Part of the problem of holding higher-level command was that you had to rely on the abilities of men and women you would never know as more than slots filled in on an organization chart.

As more and more officers streamed in, Craig sat, conferring with Skiles and the division commanders. There were always operational matters to discuss, and he was so wrapped up in the 24th's supply situation that he almost didn't feel the tap on his shoulder. Sergeant Major Bourne loomed over him, tall, barrel-chested, and every inch the Marine's Marine. "Sir, it's time."

Craig glanced at his watch. "Thank you, Sergeant Major."

He glanced behind him at the packed room and listened to the near-deafening buzz of conversation. He knew what they were talking about. Any headquarters was a rumor mill, and Vorster's last-ditch threat had provided fertile ground for speculation. Some of the rumors about planned Allied action were entertaining, others were just flat-out wrong. "Let's get things rolling."

Bourne nodded and strode to the front of the room, facing the assembled group. Ignoring the microphone on the podium nearby, he called in a parade-ground bellow, "Attention on deck!"

The voices stopped as if turned off by a light switch, replaced by the momentary thunder of hundreds of boots hitting the floor.

Craig strode up to the podium and turned to scan the erect, silent crowd—a sea of upturned faces. "Seats, ladies and gentlemen."

He paused while they settled in again. Then he started, careful to keep his voice hard, incisive, and confident. This was a pep talk more than a briefing. Some commanders forgot that staff morale was sometimes just as important as frontline morale. He wasn't one of them.

"You've all heard Vorster's promise to destroy the mines if we don't withdraw unconditionally from South Africa. A threat that he's made to the Cubans as well." Craig nodded toward Skiles and the rest of his immediate staff. "I want you to know that we are taking him seriously, although I admit that can be hard to do at times."

That prompted a light wave of laughter. Vorster's nickname at headquarters was Gonzo. Good. Everyone's attitude had been a little too grim for his liking.

Craig let the laugh die away before continuing. He wanted every man and woman in the room to hear exactly what he had to say next. "Serious or not, I don't intend to let this bastard slow us down. We will continue to advance as far and as fast as we can. Right now, our forces have the momentum—to stop now and try to regain that momentum later would cost time and lives I will not waste."

He studied the faces in front of him. They looked serious and grimly determined. Good. "Frankly, Vorster's political situation seems so unstable that we're not sure he can persuade his own military to go along with this demolition threat. There's a maxim of warfare that you tend to overestimate an enemy's capabilities. Well, we don't want to fall into that trap here."

Heads nodded around the room.

"Nevertheless, we will be conducting intensive reconnaissance of mines and other important industrial facilities as we move forward. And I want all troop commanders to make sure their people know their NBC procedures from front to back."

More heads nodded. With warning and the proper equipment, men could live and fight in a radioactive or chemically contaminated environment. But it took constant training and refresher courses to ensure that the warning and the gear would be put to good use.

"Now, there's no question that our job's just gotten tougher and more complicated." He smiled grimly. "No question at all. Unfortunately, nobody's civilized enough these days to fight in straight lines on nice, open battlefields. But we take the enemies we get. And Vorster is what we've got."

Craig spoke flatly. "One thing's certain. Vorster and his fanatics are desperate. This latest threat proves that. We have them on the ropes. So let's keep them off-balance and go in for the knockout." He'd opted for boxing terminology at the last moment. His British officers might not have understood the football comparisons that had first popped into his mind. "Fourth and goal" didn't mean anything in soccer. "That is all, ladies and gentlemen. Carry on."

He nodded to Bourne.

"Attention!" The staff rose to their feet as one. As Craig stepped down from the podium, the sergeant major whispered, "Your press conference is set up in the London Room, sir."

Craig sighed. He begrudged the time, but he had to give the media something to chew on. Reporters abhorred a vacuum more than nature, and if they didn't have hard information, they'd take the soft stuff. Every rumor and whisper his staff had started would be amplified a hundredfold. At least when his officers speculated, it was informed speculation. "Tell them I'll be there in five minutes, and tell General Skiles I want my immediate staff assembled for a meeting in half an hour."

Craig looked at Skiles and the others in his office, sitting, perched on the edges of desks, or standing. "All right, gentlemen, the troops have been given the gouge, and the press has received a distilled dose of the same. Now what the hell are my options?"

Nobody even considered advising him to halt or slow down. Offensive pressure was more than a military decision. It was an extension of their commander's personal desire to end this war as quickly as possible.

His J-2, the officer in charge of intelligence, cleared his throat. "I don't know about options exactly, General, but I do have more information from the JCS. They have nuclear and mining engineers talking to each other. Apparently, what Vorster wants to do is possible."

Craig nodded. That only confirmed his basic assessment. It was always easier to wreck something than to build it, and Vorster had already shown he was an expert at tearing things apart.

Skiles looked thoughtful. "I've been working on the time factors involved, General. I don't think Pretoria would have made this threat public unless they already had at least one site wired. On the other hand, they'd be stupid to wait until the job was completely done."

"Makes sense."

"Okay." Skiles doodled a quick series of numbers on a pad while he talked. "I put some of our engineers and some Navy people with nuclear-power training on this. Now, based on the number of targets and some very rough estimates of South Africa's transportation capabilities, they don't believe the Afrikaners could prep a significant part of the Witwatersrand before the eighth or ninth at the earliest. Maybe even later than that."

The chief of staff looked up from his doodling. "It also gives us another reason for pressing the attack. The more pressure we put on Pretoria, the fewer troops the Afrikaners can release for transport and demolition work."

"Then let's keep the pressure on," Craig said, "but let's face facts. Even at forty-plus klicks a day, we're still not going to be close enough to the mines before they're rigged and ready to blow."

His Air Force liaison leaned forward. "Hell, we have total air superiority. Why not grab these places by air assault like Ladysmith? We've got the helos and the manpower."

Craig shook his head. He liked his officers to think aggressively. But sensible planning had to be firmly grounded in reality. "I'm afraid that's a nonstarter."

The intelligence officer amplified Craig's reasoning. "There are literally hundreds of shafts and pits in the Witwatersrand, John. Every one of them would have to be hit by surprise and cleared simultaneously. It's just not possible."

"Yeah. I get the picture." The Air Force brigadier general lapsed into a gloomy silence.

The faces around the room mirrored his uncertainty and frustration.

Craig let the silence drag on for several seconds. Then he

leaned forward. "We're looking at this situation the wrong way, gentlemen. We've been looking from the bottom up instead of from the top down. How do we capture the mines? How do we block half a dozen channels of possible communication? How do we stop Afrikaner demo teams from setting off their charges?" He shook his head. "The fundamental problem we face isn't tactical—it's strategic. So we need a strategic solution. A head shot, not more body blows."

They stared back at him. Skiles got it first. "You mean Vorster."

"Right." Craig's voice was cold. "Once Vorster gives the word to contaminate the mines, there's nothing we can do to stop it from happening. So we have to take him out before he can give that order."

JANUARY 7—LOUIS BOTHA INTERNATIONAL AIRPORT, DURBAN

Two men wearing South African Army uniforms stepped down out of the U.S. Air Force C-141 Starlifter and walked across the pitted tarmac toward the terminal building. The Air Force security troops on guard detail stiffened in surprise until they saw the red-white-and-blue armbands marking the men as Cape Province regulars. Both also had passes countersigned by the Allied commander at Cape Town.

None of the MPs were especially surprised when the pair asked for directions to the Special Warfare compound at one end of the airport. Everybody knew the Rangers and the SAS had dealings with all sorts of unusual people.

Col. Robert O'Connell sat behind his desk with his hands folded together in front of him. He was pleased to note that they weren't shaking—at least not much. That one week's enforced leave on Cape Town's beaches might have been worth it after all.

The remnants of O'Connell's 1/75th Rangers were back in the States enjoying a well-deserved rest and an outpouring of public and media adulation. With Geller dead, the Pentagon brass had frocked him to the rank of full colonel and put him in command of the whole Ranger regiment. They'd expected him to handle that job from the U.S. Instead he'd taken his promotion and volunteered for immediate service in South Africa. Part of that was pure cussedness, or maybe just stupidity, he thought. But mostly it was sheer professional pride. The war was still on. This Marine general Craig had the 2/75th under his orders now. And no Ranger regimental commander worth his pay could possibly run the show from a comfortable stateside berth while his men went into combat.

O'Connell smiled slightly, remembering his irritation when Col. Paul Geller had said much the same thing to him. He shook his head. Geller had been right. Things did look different from the other side of the desk.

A polite cough from one of his guests brought him back to the present. He looked up at the three men seated across from him. He'd gotten to know Brig. Chris Taylor pretty well during several meetings in Cape Town. Maj. Oliver Cain served as both the commander of the British Special Air Service squadron attached to the Allied force, and as O'Connell's deputy in the Joint Special Warfare HQ set up to coordinate the Ranger, Green Beret, SAS, and SBS units operating in South Africa.

The third man, though, was someone he knew only by reputation. Commandant Henrik Kruger's trek through hostile territory had made headlines around the world. O'Connell sat up straighter. "So you're that sure of this guy Coetzee? You don't think he'd get cold feet and back out at the last minute?"

Kruger shook his head. "I would trust Deneys Coetzee with my life. What he says he will do, he does." He suddenly bared his teeth. "In fact, Colonel O'Connell, I will trust him with my life, quite literally. Take me with you if this operation I propose is approved. If he betrays us, you can kill me yourself."

O'Connell studied the South African officer closely. Christ, he'd thought Brave Fortune was crazy. But what this man Kruger was suggesting was pure, unadulterated insanity. On the other hand, what options did they really have? General Craig was right. They had to get Vorster and get him fast. The Air Force wanted to bomb, but bombing made martyrs. And bombing was never a sure thing.

He shrugged mentally. Kruger's idea might just be harebrained enough to work. Anyway, it sure as hell couldn't hurt to explore it further.

He picked up the phone on his desk. "Bill? Patch me through to the chief of staff's office. I want to talk to Skiles himself, understand?" He waited for a few minutes, his fingers drumming on the desktop in impatience as he listened to static.

Finally, a familiar voice came on the line, harried but still friendly. "Good to hear from you, Rob. What can I do for you?"

Time for the plunge. O'Connell sat up straight in his chair. "I need an appointment with General Craig, sir."

Skiles sounded doubtful. "I might be able to get you in sometime this afternoon . . ."

Hell, in for a penny, in for a pound. O'Connell gripped the receiver tighter. "No, sir, you don't understand. I need to see General Craig now."

HEADQUARTERS, CUBAN EXPEDITIONARY FORCE, NABOOMSPRUIT

Gen. Antonio Vega cursed the Afrikaners and their fanaticism. They were willing to destroy their entire economy in order to deny it to their enemies. This was scorched earth on a new scale.

He knew what Vorster and the other Boer leaders thought. They would return to basics, to the simple farming life that they had known in the past. They were fools. Cuba had been trying to climb out of the very trap they wanted to climb into for half a century.

Colonel Suarez knocked on the door. "Comrade General, your car will be ready in five minutes."

Vega nodded heavily. It was time for him to visit the remnants of his once-proud First Brigade Tactical Group now encamped fifty kilometers down the road at Warmbad—only one hundred kilometers from Pretoria itself. Their final offensive would begin tomorrow, and as was his custom, he planned to inspect the assault units and say the encouraging things generals were always expected to say on such occasions.

There was a bittersweet feeling to this attack. He'd never doubted that there would be a last battle and a final victory. He had even acknowledged that it might be much harder than originally planned, and it had been. But if the Afrikaners carried out their monstrous threat, it would snatch the prize away moments before it became his.

Under his breath, Vega cursed Vorster again, but he also wondered if he might not have done the same thing under similar circumstances. The temptation to rob a hated enemy of victory must be overpowering.

He buried the thought and rose to follow Suarez. He and his troops had only one option left to them—charge hard for Pretoria and hope for the best.

Both Havana and Moscow had sent messages exhorting him on. They were reassuring, especially the Soviet Union's promise of expanded logistic support, but also late and unnecessary. He'd scheduled this final Cuban push for tomorrow in any case. Karl Vorster and his cronies would soon learn that their threats could not deter Antonio Vega.

South Africa's rulers had made one mistake in their calculations. They'd assumed that both the Cuban and U.S. forces would stop rather than risk loss of South Africa's mineral reserves. Vega didn't know the American commander Craig's mind well enough to guess what he would do, but for Vega there wasn't any dilemma at all.

If he captured Pretoria and seized the mines intact, he won. The Afrikaner regime would be destroyed and the West would lose its essential resources. On the other hand, if the mines were contaminated, Cuba and its allies would lose, but so would the Afrikaners and the West. And that, too, was good enough for him.

JANUARY 8—DURBAN

The planning session had been going on since before breakfast. The scattered remains of a hotel meal still littered the table. For security reasons, the kitchen staff weren't allowed in, and Craig refused to have his enlisted men acting as busboys.

"They can do it, sir." Craig's intelligence officer sounded both sure of his facts and distressed by them. "JCS has confirmed the new message from Vorster's government this morning. It's all there: materials, methods, everything needed to prove they have the capability."

That eliminated some of the uncertainty, although there had never really been any doubt. Craig had been hoping for a miracle, some sign that the Afrikaners were bluffing. Miracles were hard to come by down here.

The colonel continued, "JCS has also revised their time estimates. There's no question that Pretoria has at least half its mining facilities wired already." He frowned. "And they'll have the rest done by the end of the day."

In response to Craig's questioning look, the colonel explained, "Our original estimates included complete coverage of each mine by several explosive devices, all connected to a central control point and one alternate. It appears all the Afrikaners are doing is dropping one waste canister on the end of a wire into each mine and leaving one or two men behind to monitor it."

Craig nodded. One canister of high-level radioactive waste would be enough to poison a site for decades, maybe even centuries. They could always beef up the demolitions later, if they wanted to.

The discussion broke off as a sergeant came in hurriedly, clutching a sheaf of papers and photographs. He handed the material to the colonel and whispered briefly with him.

"The Cubans are moving." The staff stirred in their seats at the half-expected, half-dreaded news. Craig swore silently to himself.

With one hand, the J-2 cleared away some of the papers and dishes littering the table. Spreading out a line of photographs, he examined each one. "These were taken this morning by reconnaissance aircraft from *Vinson*." The photos, taken by advanced cameras and digitally enhanced, were clear. Long lines of vehicles, some tanks, clogged every road south of Warmbad.

One photograph had managed to catch a skirmish between the Boers and the Cubans. The orderly columns were in disarray, and several smudges of smoke could indicate burning vehicles, or perhaps the explosions of artillery shells.

Clearly, the Afrikaners were still fighting, but the Allied staff had already seen the orders of battle for each side. Craig agreed with the common wisdom: the Cubans could be in Pretoria in three days, four at the outside.

They studied the pictures in silence for several minutes. Then Skiles spoke up, obviously expressing the unstated opinion of the whole Joint Staff. "Unless we do something fast, General, we're screwed."

Craig nodded. "True. It's a win-win situation for Cuba, and this guy Vega knows it. He's turned into a spoiler, and we've got to stop him." He turned to the naval commander. "Move *Independence* and *Vinson* up the coast, Admiral. Start launching airstrikes against the Cuban forces immediately. Don't attack South African ground forces unless they get in the way, but shoot down anything that flies."

Rear Adm. Andrew Douglas Stewart arched an eyebrow. "What about Washington, General? Will the President approve an escalation like this?"

Craig pointed to the photos. "My original orders cover engaging the Cubans, if it becomes necessary. Don't worry about D.C., Andy. By the time they've spent five minutes looking through these, they'll be howling for action."

Many of his staff nodded in acknowledgment, but Skiles looked troubled. "General, why not use just one carrier? That would slow them down some and still leave one ship to support our own advance. Our air cover is still a little thin."

Craig shook his head. "No, George, send them both. We're gonna have to depend on land-based air, and the Cubans are going to need a lot of stopping." He looked as if he had a bad taste in his mouth. "I hate to look like we're defending the Afrikaners, but if Vega reaches Pretoria, the show's over. We'd wind up doing nothing but fighting over Vorster's dead body and the ashes of South African industry."

He looked off into space for a brief moment, silently calculating the kind of delay the Navy's air strikes could impose on Cuba's armored columns. The answer he kept coming up with was unpalatable and equally undeniable. Some, but not enough. He lowered his gaze to the small group of waiting staff officers. "All right, gentlemen. We've run out of sensible options. It's time to go for broke. We have to authorize Quantum."

First Skiles and then the others reluctantly nodded.

Craig dialed a single-digit number preprogrammed into his command phone.

It was answered on the first ring. "O'Connell."

"Rob, this is Jerry Craig. Listen carefully. Your operation is a go. You have forty-eight hours to prepare."

PRETORIA

Brig. Deneys Coetzee looked up sharply as the phone in his downtown flat buzzed repeatedly. That wasn't his normal line. That was the second phone. The one he'd had installed covertly and with an unlisted number known only to a special few.

He raced to answer it. "Yes?"

"Deneys? This is Henrik."

Coetzee sat down abruptly. Kruger. This was incredible. He chuckled suddenly. "My God, man, but you gave me a shock there."

Kruger laughed softly with him. "I thought I might." He turned serious. "Tell me, can you speak freely?"

"I can. What's up?"

As Kruger told him, Coetzee began to feel hope for his nation for the first time in months. Despite what he'd always been taught and believed, these Americans and British had guts.

CHAPTER 40

Checkmate

JANUARY 10—QUANTUM STRIKE FORCE, OVER SWARTKOP MILITARY AIRFIELD, PRETORIA

From the outside the C-130 Hercules looked exactly like one of the three such planes left in South Africa's inventory. U.S. Air Force maintenance crews had worked round the clock repainting the aircraft with the right camouflage colors and insignia. One of Brig. Deneys Coetzee's conspirators inside the SAAF had even given them the side number for a real South African C-130, currently undergoing emergency repairs at Upington Military Airfield—more than eight hundred kilometers from Pretoria. The impostor was considerably closer than that, now just two minutes' flying time from Swartkop's main runway.

The ninety grim-faced men riding inside the Hercules were also flying under false colors. All of them wore South African uniforms and carried South African weapons—weapons and clothing provided by Cape Province units. Beneath their uniforms they were a mixed bunch—a reinforced Ranger rifle platoon, a British SAS troop, and several Afrikaans-speaking volunteers from Henrik Kruger's 20th Cape Rifles. They had much in common, though: physical and mental toughness, superb combat skills, and a driving determination to carry out their mission at any cost. Their commanders shared those same attributes.

From his seat near the C-130's rear ramp, Col. Robert O'Connell checked the magazine on his R4 assault rifle and slid it back in place. His hands still shook, but only slightly. Not enough for anybody not looking closely to notice. He kept his hands busy by checking the rest of his gear: a pistol with a separate, concealed silencer, a sheathed knife, and two colored-smoke grenades for signaling purposes. Somehow it didn't seem like enough. Then he shrugged. Even in battle dress, a South African officer couldn't go waltzing about Pretoria looking like a walking arsenal.

Satisfied that he was as ready as he'd ever be, O'Connell glanced at the men seated to either side of him. Capt. David Pryce, the tall, mustachioed SAS officer he'd picked as his XO for Quantum, was making the same kind of last-minute personal inspection.

Major Cain, the senior SAS man in South Africa, had kicked and screamed to come along, too. But Craig had vetoed that on the sensible grounds that the Joint Special Warfare units being readied at Durban needed an experienced and battle-tested commander.

If Quantum failed, General Craig would need every Ranger team and SAS patrol he could lay his hands on. Those in-country were already prepping for what would almost certainly be a series of desperate and abortive commando raids on South Africa's radioactive-waste-rigged mining facilities. O'Connell's mind shied away from imagining what a bloody shambles those attacks were likely to be. Then he laughed inwardly. If Quantum failed, he wouldn't be around to see it all happening.

Beside him, Commandant Henrik Kruger wore a headset plugged into the Hercules's intercom system, listening as a former South African Air Force lieutenant handled the C-

130's cockpit conversations with air traffic controllers on the ground. As O'Connell watched, Kruger slipped the headset off with a decisive gesture. "We've been cleared to land. One minute."

The whining clunk of the aircraft's gear coming down confirmed Kruger's statement.

O'Connell sat back in his seat, trying to clear his mind of any thoughts or worries outside this mission. Total concentration on the job helped keep his fears at bay.

Touchdown. Coming in low and fast, the C-130 bounced once on Swartkop's bomb-damaged runway and braked just enough to stay on the ground—rolling rapidly toward a small group of trucks and other vehicles parked at the far end. Once there, it braked still more, slowing as it swung through a 180-degree turn so that its nose pointed down the runway again.

Still in his seat, O'Connell felt a final shudder as the aircraft came to a complete stop. He unstrapped himself and stood up in a single fluid motion with his assault rifle gripped in his right hand. The men around him were doing the same thing.

A sliver of daylight appeared, growing larger as the C-130's rear ramp whined open. It dropped onto the runway and locked in place. Slinging his rifle, the Ranger officer trotted down the ramp with Kruger by his side. The assault force followed him in a column of fours—emerging into a whirling chaos of turboprop-blown sand and dust.

Three uniformed Afrikaners stood waiting for them at the foot of the ramp, each holding his peaked cap on his head against the howling, artificial windstorm. Kruger went straight up to the shortest of the three and shook his hand, shouting to be heard over the noise. "Deneys, man, you're a sight for *blery* sore eyes!"

"You expected somebody different, maybe?" Brig. Deneys Coetzee grinned. At Kruger's gesture, he turned to O'Connell. "You are the American commander?"

O'Connell nodded.

"Good. I have the vehicles you need here." Coetzee jerked a thumb at the ill-assorted collection of military trucks and jeeps visible behind him. "I suggest you get your men aboard and we'll talk later. In some place safer. Right?"

"Definitely." O'Connell turned and waved his arm toward the waiting convoy. His troops scattered by squads, each jogging toward a different truck.

The group of six officers—the four South Africans, O'-Connell, and Pryce—trotted after them at a slightly more sedate pace. The American kept his eyes open. The last time he'd seen Swartkop, it had been dark and most of the base had been on fire.

He was glad to see that the airfield still showed signs of the damage inflicted by his Rangers. Swartkop's control tower stood silent—a burned-out, blackened ruin. Piles of twisted steel girders and warped aluminum siding were all that were left of maintenance hangars and storage sheds. For now, flight operations were being handled out of a small cluster of camouflage-draped tents set up next to a mobile radar van.

O'Connell frowned. Fuel trucks and ground crews were already rolling across the cratered tarmac—heading for the C-130. That was bad. The Hercules looked fine from a distance. Up close might be a different story. He checked his watch. Three minutes had passed since they'd landed. So where were the F-15Es the Air Force had promised?

They were right on time.

Sirens started wailing, their eerie howling rising and falling all across the air base. In seconds the fuel trucks and ground crews were racing away, heading for cover. A lone South African Air Force officer pounded across the tarmac toward the C-130. "Air raid! Clear the field! Get off the ground! Go!"

The aircraft's still-spinning props blurred as it lumbered down the runway, picking up speed fast. With plenty of runway left to spare, the Hercules roared off the ground and into the air.

Coetzee turned around to see him smiling. "Your idea, Colonel?"

"Yeah." O'Connell trotted ahead and glanced back. "Keep moving, Brigadier. Our flyboys won't be too choosy about what they drop bombs on."

The South African chuckled and waved him aboard the lead Land Rover. Its driver shifted into gear and pulled out onto the airfield's access road while O'Connell was still struggling into a seat.

As they drove, he felt a mixture of fear and satisfaction. Swartkop was a hive of confusion and activity as its occupants took shelter. He could sense their fear though, and some of it was communicated to him. They had to get off the base quickly.

The sentries at Swartkop's main gate waved them through without even a cursory glance at their papers. Nobody bothered with formalities under air attack.

As the small column of five-ton trucks, jeeps, and Land Rovers turned north into the capital, explosions rumbled in the distance behind them. Twin-tailed fighter-bombers flashed across the sky. Smoke and flame boiled up into the air. In all the confusion, Swartkop's security forces completely forgot the small group of soldiers who'd landed only moments before.

O'Connell and his raiders were past South Africa's first defenses.

OUTER SECURITY POST, THE UNION BUILDINGS, PRETORIA

They ran into trouble just a few hundred yards short of their objective. A security checkpoint manned by Brandwag brownshirts blocked the tree-lined road winding uphill to Pretoria's massive governmental complex—the Union Buildings.

"Show me your papers . . . *Kaptein*." The cold-eyed Brandwag officer added the honorific only at the last minute and with obvious reluctance.

"Of course." Henrik Kruger handed over the documents Coetzee had forged for them without any hesitation.

The South African *kommandant* had taken his apparent demotion in stride. Now wearing the three stars of a captain he sat beside the Land Rover's driver. O'Connell and a big Ranger sergeant named Nowak occupied the seat behind them, carefully eyeing the five sentries clustered around the guardhouse and barricade. Six canvas-sided trucks and two jeeps packed with Rangers, SAS troopers, and renegade Afrikaners sat idling behind the Land Rover.

One man was missing. They'd dropped Deneys Coetzee off at the Ministry of Defense before driving on to the Union Buildings. The South African brigadier still had work to do to make Quantum pay off.

"These appear to be in order." The Brandwag lieutenant tapped the papers in his hand and then glanced suspiciously at the line of vehicles stretching down Church Street. "But why wasn't I notified of this troop movement? And why would General de Wet add so many men to our guard force here?"

Kruger shrugged. "How should I know, Lieutenant? Perhaps he's worried about a possible enemy attack." He smiled thinly. Then his smile disappeared. "In any case, I do not question my orders."

The other man still looked worried. "I will have to confirm this with my superiors, Captain."

"Naturally." Kruger waved him away nonchalantly.

As the Brandwag officer turned around, O'Connell frowned. He didn't speak Afrikaans but he could recognize danger when he saw it. He watched the man walk toward the guardhouse and its phone through narrowed eyes. "Sergeant."

"Ready." The big Ranger bent over, reaching for something on the Land Rover's floorboards.

"Now." O'Connell's silenced 9mm pistol "popped" three times.

The Brandwag officer staggered and then fell facedown on the pavement, hit in midstride. Bright red stains spread quickly across the back of his tunic.

In the same moment, Sergeant Nowak reared upright and opened fire on the rest of the startled guards. His silenced Heckler and Koch MP5 submachine gun stuttered briefly and then stopped. Thirty rounds tore paint and wood off the barricade and slammed into the five Afrikaners. They toppled over, dead before they hit the street and sidewalk.

Kruger was already out of the Land Rover, sprinting forward to open the barricade. Other men jumped down out of the lead truck and began hauling bodies into the flower gardens surrounding the checkpoint. In seconds, only a few blood stains were left on the road—drying fast in the hot sun.

"Do we post any guards here?" The South African *kommandant* hopped back into the vehicle.

"No." O'Connell pulled the partially used clip out of his pistol and snapped another home. "They'd never make it out with the rest of us. We go in together."

He leaned forward and tapped their driver on the shoulder. "Okay, let's get this done."

They roared up the road toward the red-roofed Union Buildings.

None of their briefings or maps had done much to convey the sheer size of the complex. With its three-story-high, semicircular colonnade added in, the whole massive pile of rock and marble stretched more than seven hundred and fifty feet on its long side. Clearing the internal maze of offices and corridors would have required a full battalion of commandos—not just ninety men. Fortunately, the Allied raiding party had been given both a more limited objective and very detailed information.

O'Connell hopped out of the Land Rover while it was still slowing and ran up the steps leading to the building's east-wing entrance. Kruger and Nowak followed, weapons out and ready. The rest of their troops were scrambling down out of their trucks and jeeps as they pulled up. From here on, speed was life.

Breathing heavily, O'Connell reached the top of the steps and kept on going—heading for a pair of wood-and-glass double doors behind a wide portico. He drew his pistol as he ran. Booted feet clattered up the steps behind him.

A Brandwag officer wearing major's insignia and carrying

a clipboard pushed through one of the doors, still talking to someone inside. He looked up in astonishment. "What in God's—"

O'Connell shot him twice and jumped over the body. The door slammed shut in his face and he bounced off it with a sore shoulder. Sergeant Nowak reached the entrance in the next second and rammed into it with teeth-rattling force. The big man stepped back, shaking off the impact—

Three close-spaced shots fired from inside threw the Ranger noncom back in a spray of blood and shattered bone. Pieces of broken glass and splintered wood cascaded across O'Connell.

"Back!"

He threw himself to one side as Kruger opened fire—systematically emptying his assault rifle's magazine in a long, tearing burst through both doors. Agonized screams rose above the gunfire and then faded.

O'Connell, Kruger, and half a dozen Rangers and SAS troopers shoved the broken, bullet-riddled doors open and poured through into a marble-floored entrance hall. Several bodies sprawled in an untidy heap right behind the doors—Brandwag and Army guards who'd been caught by the South African *kommandant*'s burst. More men flooded in from outside.

O'Connell caught a glimpse of movement down a side corridor and whirled around. One of the Brandwag sentries was still very much alive. The man was inside an antique telephone cabinet—the kind with wood-paneled walls and a light that came on whenever the soundproofed sliding door was closed. The light was on now, and O'Connell could see the Afrikaner yelling energetically into a phone.

Without time for conscious thought, the Ranger colonel brought his pistol up, aimed, and fired. The glass door shattered and the brownshirt fell against the wall-mounted telephone before sliding down to the floor. The receiver itself fell out of the dead man's hand and swung back and forth in a slowly diminishing arc.

Damn. So much for surprise.

MAIN GUARDROOM, OUTSIDE THE STATE SECURITY COUNCIL CHAMBER

The Brandwag captain plucked the phone away from his ear. An expression of disgust warred with one of puzzled concern and won. "Idiot."

"Something wrong?" His closest subordinate looked up from the newspaper he was reading.

"I doubt it." The captain shrugged. "Well, maybe." He chewed his lower lip for several seconds. "One of the morons upstairs said there were intruders in the building. Then he hung up before I could ask him anything! And now they're not even bothering to answer their *blery* phone."

"Should we tell the President?"

The captain snorted. "Are you crazy, man? Interrupt a war briefing just because some door guard might be spooked by the sight of a kaffir janitor?" He waved a hand at their magazines, water cooler, and upholstered furniture. "Maybe you want to go fight Cubans, but I know a plush assignment when I see one.

"Let's find out what is going on before we look like fools. Take Jaap and Dirk. It'll do them some good to get off their fat behinds for a change. You go, too, and don't take all day doing it."

His subordinate chuckled and rose to his feet, buckling on a pistol holster over a slight paunch. He was getting a little bit heavyset. Maybe they'd take the stairs for a change. . . .

QUANTUM STRIKE FORCE

"Pryce!"

O'Connell's British XO stopped beside him. "Here, Colonel."

"They know we're coming. Put eight men on the door here. The rest with me!"

The SAS captain nodded and whirled away, shouting for two of his sergeants. "Jenkins! McRae!"

O'Connell paused long enough to holster his silenced pistol

and unsling the R4 dangling from his shoulder. Firepower was more important than stealth now. He ran down the hall, heading for the staircase marked on Coetzee's hand-sketched map. Rangers and SAS men followed on the double.

Behind him, squads and fire teams peeled off as they ran past connecting corridors and other staircases—setting up blocking positions to bottle up the Afrikaner bureaucrats and security guards in this wing. By the time he reached the right set of stairs going down, he had twenty men left.

O'Connell skidded to a stop on the marble floor. "Grenade."

Kruger passed him a fragmentation grenade from one of the SAS troopers. Automatic rifle fire echoed down the hall from behind them. The Afrikaners were starting to wake up.

He took a quick look down the stairs. Not good. About fifteen stairs down to a landing and a sharp bend to the right. Terrific. A blind corner.

O'Connell took a quick, deep breath, let it out, and started down the stairs slowly, moving one step at a time. He stayed close to the right wall. Two men dropped prone at the top of the staircase, ready to nail anybody coming around the bend.

Sweat trickled into his eyes despite the cooler air inside. Every sense he had seemed fine-tuned beyond normal human perception. He could hear every man behind him breathing heavily. He could see the tiniest strands of color running through the marble stairs ahead. He could even smell the coppery scent of the blood he'd tracked through back at the doors. Some inner core of dry humor and common sense told him that maybe he should have let one of the others go first.

Voices drifted up the stairwell from around the bend. Christ! O'Connell froze where he was and yanked the pin out of the grenade. . . .

The Brandwag lieutenant stopped at the bottom of the stairs. What was that sound echoing down from upstairs. Gunfire? A prolonged rattling burst from somewhere above them transformed uncertainty to certainty. He turned to yell a warning back to the guardroom.

Something clattered and bounced down the stairs, rolling

right under his feet. The overweight Afrikaner looked down just as the grenade exploded.

"Go! Go! Go!" As the echoes faded, O'Connell took the stairs two at a time, charging through a fog of drifting, acrid smoke. Contorted shapes writhed on the floor—men who'd been scythed down by the fragments from his grenade. Rangers and SAS men passed him and burst out into the corridor leading to the State Security Council Chamber.

Assault rifles chattered from somewhere farther down the corridor. Stray rounds flashed and sparked off the walls and floor—whining down the hallway. Several Allied soldiers spun round and fell. Others advanced, firing back from the hip.

"Come on!" O'Connell ran forward toward the door just a few meters away. He saw a wounded brownshirt fumbling for his weapon and shot him. None of the other Afrikaner guards heaped on the floor were still moving.

STATE SECURITY COUNCIL CHAMBER

Trapped inside the soundproofed Council Chamber, Gen. Adriaan de Wet stood next to Karl Vorster, listening in appalled silence as the tall, grim-faced man gloated again over his plans to destroy his own nation's wealth for centuries to come. This is not war, he thought, this is raw madness.

"Seventy percent . . . can you believe that, General? Seventy percent of our remaining resources are already prepared for demolition." Vorster laughed harshly as he leaned over the map, tracing out the largest concentrations of mines and mining facilities. "The rest will be wired before these bastard Uitlanders can come within a day's march of the Witwatersrand."

South Africa's President nodded toward the secure phone in the corner. "After that, one word from me and *phfft*"—he snapped his fingers—"both the damned West and the communists go watch their precious fruits of conquest glow in the dark."

De Wet roused himself. He had to make one more effort to make his leader see some kind of sense before it was too late. "Mr. President, we know that American carrier aircraft have been attacking Cuban forces along the N1. Couldn't we try to make a separate peace . . ." His voice faded away as Vorster's face darkened with rage.

"I did not think to hear such treason from you, General de Wet." Vorster's voice was menacing. "You know, I have other officers who would be more than happy to take your place."

Suddenly the door rattled nosily—literally vibrating back and forth under dozens of sharp, thumping impacts. De Wet stared in shock at the sound. Bullets? Here?

Men in torn, bloodstained South African uniforms crashed into the chamber, their assault rifles aimed straight at the small group of men clustered around Vorster. *"Freeze! Freeze! Get your fucking hands up! Up!"*

One of de Wet's military aides grabbed for a phone and died in a hail of gunfire. Inside the small room, the noise was terrifying, deafening. What was left of the officer's body thudded onto the floor.

My God. De Wet put his arms up, palms out and open. The other men standing around the map table imitated him. All but one. All but Karl Vorster.

The general felt Vorster scrabbling with the flap on his pistol holster and spun away sharply, careful to keep his own hands high in the air. "You fool! Can't you see we've lost?"

Soldiers pushed into the crowd and yanked Vorster out, throwing him roughly against the table. A burly corporal wrenched the President's arms behind his back and snapped police-issue handcuffs around his wrists. Others prodded de Wet and the others into a rough line against the bullet-scarred wall.

De Wet felt his knees trembling. Were they all going to be shot out of hand? He closed his eyes briefly, then opened them to find a man wearing captain's insignia standing in front of him.

"Where is the minister for law and order?"

For a moment, de Wet could only stare in amazement. The

man before him was Henrik Kruger. Then who were the rest of these men?

Kruger took the safety off his assault rifle. "I asked you a question . . . General."

"In his private office upstairs!" De Wet licked his lips that suddenly felt dry and cracked. "I swear it. He's upstairs!"

Kruger swung away contemptuously. He spoke in English to a shorter, dark-haired man wearing sergeant's stripes. "I need a fire team, Colonel. Van der Heijden's in his office."

The other man nodded. "You got it. Collins! Take your guys and go with the *kommandant*."

De Wet stared from one to the other. A colonel? In sergeant's clothing? And an American colonel, too, from his accent. He swallowed hard against a sudden urge to vomit.

Two soldiers hauled Vorster to his feet and held him there, ashen faced and shaking. South Africa's President had gone from absolute ruler to abject, broken prisoner in seconds.

PRIVATE OFFICE, MINISTER OF LAW AND ORDER

Marius van der Heijden wasn't surprised when the door to his outer office broke open. He'd heard the sound of automatic weapons fire echoing through the Union Buildings for several minutes. Attempts to get through to either the Ministry of Defense or to his own security forces had proved useless. Whoever was attacking them had collaborators inside Pretoria—collaborators who'd been able to cut off phone service.

Any attempt to escape seemed likely to prove equally futile. He could see several bodies scattered in the gardens below his window. Van der Heijden looked down at his own short legs and prominent belly and smiled grimly. No, he wouldn't get far trying to run away.

Which left one honorable option open to him. Just one. And that was why he waited behind his desk holding a loaded Browning Hi Power pistol. Waited for someone to appear in the open doorway.

"Marius?"

The voice took him by surprise. Kruger? Henrik Kruger? He shook his head. It hardly seemed possible. He stayed silent.

"Marius, I'm coming in. I don't want to hurt you, so I ask you, don't do anything foolish. Right?"

Van der Heijden found his voice. "Come ahead, Henrik. But slowly, you understand?"

Kruger eased around the doorjamb, holding an assault rifle in both hands. There were other men in the doorway behind him. "I have come to take you prisoner, Marius."

"A prisoner? For which side?" Van der Heijden kept his pistol out of sight, below the desk.

Kruger smiled sadly. "For the Americans and the British, my old friend. And for those who have rebelled against this unlawful government."

"You have fallen far, Henrik. You keep strange company for an Afrikaner of the old blood."

"Maybe." Kruger kept his rifle pointed toward the floor. "I have seen your daughter, Marius."

Van der Heijden kept his face rigid. He'd heard the American propaganda broadcasts and secretly praised God for his daughter's safe deliverance. Of course, he'd cursed her very name publicly to avert Vorster's suspicions. "She is well?"

"Yes . . ." Kruger seemed about to say more and then stopped himself. "Surrender to me now and you will see that for yourself."

For a brief moment, van der Heijden relaxed his grip on the pistol. It seemed a priceless gift. To see his daughter again, despite all the hurtful words and deeds that had passed between them . . .

He straightened up in his chair. He could not surrender. As a prisoner, his name would always come before hers. She would never escape the shame of it. No, it was better by far to lie buried and forgotten.

Marius van der Heijden looked up from his desk with a sad, worn expression on his face. "I am sorry, Henrik, but I cannot. You understand?"

Kruger nodded slowly, his own face somber and suddenly much older than his years would warrant. "I understand."

"And you will tell her that I . . ." Van der Heijden choked on the words.

"Yes."

"Thank you, my friend." South Africa's minister for law and order raised the Browning Hi Power and slowly aimed it at Kruger's chest. "Then I tell you I refuse to surrender."

Kruger stood motionless, his own weapon still aimed at the floor.

Van der Heijden sighed. Despite everything, it was clear that his old friend and hoped-for-son-in-law could not bring himself to kill a man he'd once respected. So be it, he thought, then we shall both die together.

Van der Heijden tightened his finger around the trigger . . . and felt himself knocked backward out of his chair by several sledgehammer blows. For what seemed a long time he stared up at the ceiling, surprised that being shot wasn't more painful. And then he died.

Henrik Kruger sighed and turned away from the old man's corpse.

Beside him, Sgt. Asa Collins slowly lowered his assault rifle. "I'm sorry, Mr. Kruger. I really am. I didn't want to kill him. But that guy would have shot you."

Kruger nodded sadly. "Don't worry about it, Sergeant. This was what he wanted."

QUANTUM STRIKE FORCE

Col. Robert O'Connell crouched low beside the ground-floor window. A radioman lay beside him, holding his radio's antenna out the window. "X-ray Tiger One, this is Quantum One. Touchdown. I say again, touchdown. Over."

Touchdown was the code word indicating that they had successfully captured Vorster and were ready for pickup. Whatever else happened, the order to poison the mines would never be given. O'Connell knew that the message would be flashed around the world at the speed of light. In less than a minute, Washington would get it and celebrating would begin.

Of course, O'Connell and his men still had to get out of Pretoria alive.

A voice crackled over the static-clogged channel. "Roger that, Quantum One. Pickup ETA is five minutes. Say status of LZ. Over."

A sudden burst of machine-gun fire hammered the window frame above them, spraying O'Connell with tiny bits of wood, granite, and marble. He clicked the mike button. "LZ is hot, X-ray Tiger. Fucking hot. Hostiles in platoon strength hold the gardens approximately one five zero meters north."

"Understood." The voice faded and then came back on channel. "Injuns en route. ETA three minutes."

"Roger, out." O'Connell tossed the mike to the radioman and belly-crawled away from the window back down the corridor. Kruger and Pryce squatted near their prisoners. "Any trouble here?"

"None." Pryce flashed a quick smile. "I told the bastards I'd kill the first one who so much as blinked wrong. They seem to know I meant it."

O'Connell grinned back. He studied the row of dejected men sprawled on the marble floor. Except for Vorster, all had their hands tied with silver duct tape. And all of them had their mouths taped shut. Lightweight, cheap, and convenient, he thought. South Africa's whole wartime military and political leadership all wrapped up in one neat package.

More firing echoed down the hall. The Afrikaners outside were definitely getting restless.

He checked his watch. One minute left. He turned to the two men. "Get 'em on their feet and ready to go. We've got company coming anytime now."

They nodded and started moving among the prisoners, hauling them roughly to their feet. Most still seemed to be in shock. Good. That would make them easier to handle on the ride back—always assuming any of them lived that long.

O'Connell moved back to the window. He could see several black specks on the horizon now, growing bigger as they drew closer to the Union Buildings.

"Quantum One, this is Red Chief One. On station. Pop smoke to mark your position."

No shit, O'Connell thought. Even in the building he could hear the clattering, eggbeater sound of several rotors closing fast. O'Connell readied one of his two colored-smoke grenades. He pulled the pin and lobbed the grenade through the open window out into the courtyard beyond. Wisps of purple mist began wafting upward almost immediately.

"I have violet smoke, Quantum One."

"Confirm violet," replied O'Connell.

"Coming in."

O'Connell turned to face his men crowding the corridor. "The gunships are coming in now! Get ready to move and move fast!"

Two AH-64 Apaches popped over the trees at the far end of the Union Buildings' botanical gardens. Both vanished in brief clouds of smoke and flame as they ripple-fired salvos of 2.75-inch rockets into the Afrikaner troops holding the gardens. Explosions rocked the whole area—shredding plants, trees, and men alike. A stuttering, buzz saw–like roar signaled that the two gunships were also firing their belly-mounted 30mm chain guns—each pouring more than six hundred rounds a minute into the same area.

Before the smoke even started to drift away, more helicopters were visible—a long line of ten UH-60 Blackhawk troop carriers flaring in to land in the courtyard one at a time.

O'Connell scrambled upright. "Kruger! Pryce! First ten! Move 'em!"

Five Rangers and SAS troopers dragged and shoved five bound prisoners—Vorster and de Wet among them—out the door and hauled them up into the first waiting helicopter. The Blackhawk lifted off immediately, going nose down to pick up speed as soon as their gear cleared the ground.

Like clockwork, the second troop carrier came in. More prisoners and troops ran out and loaded aboard as it waited, rotors howling through the air.

Load after load. Chopper after chopper. By the fifth or sixth, those Afrikaner security troops who'd survived inside the Union Buildings were beginning to take potshots at the groups of American or British troops racing for safety. Men who'd almost made it home were being killed or wounded. Not many, but some.

O'Connell watched in anguish. There wasn't anything he could do. They couldn't use the gunships without killing many of the hundreds, maybe even thousands, of civilians who were pinned down in their offices inside the government complex. There were snipers in only a very few of those offices. And rockets and chain guns didn't offer the kind of pinpoint accuracy needed to deal with the bastards.

"Colonel! This is it! Last bird!" Pryce shouted in his ear and pointed behind them. Except for the last eight Rangers and SAS troops, the corridor was empty.

"Right." O'Connell rose and moved to the door. He gripped his assault rifle hard. Any second now.

The last Blackhawk came in low and flared out just meters from the doorway.

Now! O'Connell and his men raced outside, bent over low to stay beneath turning rotors. He saw a flash just ahead of him as a bullet slammed into the pavement and ricocheted away. Damn it!

The man running in front of him suddenly grunted and collapsed. O'Connell and Pryce each took an arm, hauled the wounded man to his feet, and then half-dragged, half-carried him over to the waiting helicopter. Crewmen in flak vests and goggled helmets helped them aboard.

The Blackhawk surged off the ground and raced ahead, skimming Pretoria's rooftops as it flew south.

MINISTRY OF DEFENSE, PRETORIA

Brig. Deneys Coetzee stared out his window, watching the tiny black specks carrying Kruger, the Allied commando force, and Karl Vorster vanish in the distance. My God, it bloody well worked, he thought, seeing the last traces of dirty-gray smoke drifting away from the Union Buildings.

He swiveled round in his chair and picked up the phone. "Colonel Doorne, this is Coetzee. They did it. Execute Plan Valkyrie immediately. Yes, that's right. Immediately."

He hung up and went back to the window. Within an hour, soldiers commanded by officers heartily sick and tired of Vorster's insane regime would begin fanning out through the capital. Within two hours, most of the AWB's now-leaderless fanatics and Brandwag party troops would either be dead or in custody. By nightfall, Deneys Coetzee would head the only viable government in what little was left of South Africa's territory.

And by daybreak on the eleventh, he planned to be deep in hurried negotiations with Lt. Gen. Jerry Craig—trying desperately to save something of his people's self-respect and sovereignty.

CHAPTER 41

Fait Accompli

JANUARY 10—WARMBAD

Night had not brought any relief from the air attacks. The American aircraft could see in the dark better than his men could. In addition to the continuing damage, the aerial pounding was denying his men any sleep, or a chance to recover from the day's raids.

It was near midnight now. Gen. Antonio Vega had spent the hours since sunset moving from unit to unit, gathering information, issuing orders, and reassuring his troubled men. Veterans of dozens of South African air raids, the men were unready for the volume and strength of the American attacks.

Instead of four Mirages dropping a ton of bombs each, four Intruders would drop four or five times that amount, and they would be preceded by two Hornets armed with antiradiation missiles and cluster bombs. Only after the fighters had worked over his flak and SAM sites would the heavily loaded attack aircraft arrive.

The first raiders had come at dawn and had continued to attack throughout the day. In pairs, fours, and once in an entire squadron, they had come, and his carefully prepared advance had slowly ground to a halt. Right now he was trying to rally his men and see how they could get moving again.

Vega's next stop was one of his antiaircraft batteries. In the darkness with just a quarter moon and no headlights, only his driver seemed to know the way, guiding him safely to the spot.

The battery had been deployed on an open patch of ground five hundred meters east of the town. This gave its guns clear arcs of fire and separated them from some of the more obvious targets.

Vega's approach was unannounced, and he'd actually climbed out of the jeep before a lone sentry came forward, his weapon at port arms. He started to challenge the general, then recognized him and called for the sergeant of the guard. Vega continued to stride toward the guns, returning the sentry's salute and listening as word of his arrival was passed along.

In less than a minute a stocky, hook-nosed captain came trotting up, still wiping grease from his hands. He stopped a few paces away and saluted. "Captain Rudolfo Morona, commanding B Battery, ready for your inspection, sir." The general noticed an ironic smile creeping onto the captain's face and fought back the urge to reprimand him for impertinence. It looked as if the man was doing his job.

"What is your status, Captain?"

"Four guns of the six are working, with a fifth under repair. We should have it working in about half an hour. The sixth is total loss."

"How about the radar?" the general asked.

Morona shook his head. "Not a chance, sir." He gestured with an arm. "This way please, General. You can see for yourself."

The two officers approached the radar, located on the edge of the antiaircraft site. The entire battery consisted of six S-60 57mm guns, reliable weapons that provided protection against low- and medium-altitude attackers. They were an older design, though, towed by trucks and unarmored. Laid out in an evenly spaced circle, each weapon was connected by a cable to the SON-9 gunfire-control radar, code-named Flap Wheel by NATO.

The radar was simple enough in appearance. A square-sided van, mounted on four wheels, it carried a small parabolic dish on top. Again, it was an older design and had been in service for twenty years.

As they approached the van, Vega could see its shape in the moonlight. It looked undamaged. As they got closer, though, the general could see that the van's surface was covered with spots, giving it a mottled appearance. Then, looking up, he saw jagged, irregular holes in the radar dish.

Morona shone a red flashlight onto the van's side, and Vega could see dozens of fist-sized holes. "The roof and the rear of the van are just the same," Morona reported. "We were hit by an antiradar missile. It detonated twenty or thirty meters up, off to this side and behind the radar. One man saw a streak of light, almost too fast for him to see. Most of them heard a *whoosh-boom* and the radar was showered with these."

The captain offered Vega a handful of metal lumps. Taking them, the general could see that they were cubes, some deformed by their impact. "Those were in the missile's warhead. They littered the area after the explosion, and we have found over fifty inside the van—and its crew." Morona paused.

"I lost five men in that attack, sir, and another seven are wounded. We are working to get the optical backup on the van working, but even if I had the parts to fix the radar, I wouldn't want to turn it on. We'd probably just attract another missile like this one."

Vega shook his head. This was a dangerous attitude. Even if Morona's statement held a ring of truth, there was an acknowledgment of the enemy's strength that he didn't like. Still, this man had shown he could do his job. B Battery had accounted for two American planes today, one of them in the same raid as the missile attack.

"Captain, I understand your reluctance—"

A shrill siren cut through his words, and both men realized the meaning of the sound. Another air raid was approaching.

"General!" Morona shouted. "You have to get back to headquarters!"

Vega shook his head and also raised his voice over the alarm. "Headquarters may be the target again." It had already been bombed, moved, and bombed again. "I'll stay here."

"Into the command trench, then, sir." Morona's imperative, almost an order, made perfect sense, and the two men sprinted for the dugout, Vega following the captain's lead.

Other men were running, dozens of them, as the gun crews settled into position. Phone circuits were hooked up and tested, and Vega saw gun barrels elevate and swivel as the aimers checked their mechanisms.

The two officers reached the command trench, little more than a six-foot-deep rectangular hole. The field phone operator shouted to Morona as he leapt in, "At least eight aircraft, from the east!" Normally the report would have included altitude and speed, but Vega suspected this warning was based on a visual or sound sighting. The mobile air-search radar had also fallen victim to an antiradar missile. Not only did this deny them information about the attacking aircraft, but also warning time. Those aircraft will be here any moment, Vega thought.

Morona picked up his own headset and listened briefly. Speaking into his microphone, he ordered, "Barrage pattern, one hundred meters altitude." Picking up a pair of field glasses, he scanned the night sky, looking for any sign of the oncoming raid.

Without taking his eyes from the sky, the battery commander spoke to Vega. "With both radars out, General, we cannot aim at individual aircraft, especially at night. All we can do is lay a pattern of fire in the sky at the right altitude and let them fly through it."

"Why one hundred meters?" Vega asked.

"Because the American pilots like to come in low, and that is the lowest they fly."

The captain continued to scan with his binoculars and suddenly pointed to the southeast. "Tracers! Troops on the ground are firing at the aircraft!" Pressing his mike switch, Morona said, "Center sector on one three five. Barrage pattern! Commence!"

Half a second after he spoke, the four working guns of the battery opened up, filling the air with a rapid-fire roar. In addition to the guns themselves, Vega could hear the sound of the motor drives whirring and stopping, and the even higher-pitched sounds of the empty shell casings spilling from the guns. Fragments of shouted orders filled the small open spaces between the guns' firing as men scurried to supply the guns with ammunition.

The S-60 can pump out seventy rounds a minute. The four in combination seemed to pour a stream of shells skyward, each one glowing and increasing in size as it flew. A few hundred meters up and about a kilometer away, the shells converged in a pattern of lines, hopefully intersecting the approaching aircrafts' flight path. Even with aimed fire, it took thousands of rounds to get a single hit. Vega could only watch the display and hope.

"How many rounds do you have?" Vega shouted at Morona.

"More than two hundred rounds per gun ready," he replied. Morona seemed to be almost leaning into the guns, as if the continuous muzzle blasts created a strong wind. Vega wished for six guns instead of four, and a functioning radar, then realized he was being foolish. He might as well wish for Pretoria. His business was facts, and the hard reality of combat.

A high-pitched scream appeared behind the barking of the guns, and Vega saw a group of angular shapes appear to the southeast, crossing his field of view left to right. They were low and appeared only in silhouette against the moonlit sky. It was hard to tell their type, but they were almost certainly Intruders or Hornet attack jets. They seemed to approach slowly, even though he knew their speed must be a thousand kilometers an hour.

Yes! Their path was taking them through the flak barrage, and some of the tracer streams wavered as the gunners attempted to track the fast-moving aircraft. As they neared, their apparent speed increased until they flashed past, gone before Vega had time to count them or guess their target.

"Down!" Hands grabbed his shoulders and roughly dragged him to the floor of the trench. As he started to protest, a deafening roar filled the air above, spilling over into their shelter. The roar ended in a popping, crackling sound that was even louder. As he fell full length to the dirt floor, fragments zinged around them, and choking dust filled the trench. Vega felt a burning sensation in his left leg.

Shaking his head to clear it, Vega looked over at Morona, who stared back at him. "I saw them coming in from the north while we tracked the first group of planes. Two aircraft. They were headed straight for us." The captain took a breath and nodded toward the lip of the trench. "I think they just cluster-bombed the battery."

The general started to stand up and suddenly sat down as his left leg gave way beneath him. He realized he couldn't move it.

Morona leaned over him and took one look at the leg. His eyes widened, and he shouted, "The general's been hit!"

Vega was curious about the damage to the battery and was insisting on trying to stand up as a medic appeared and began tearing at his pants leg. The general tried to help him, but suddenly felt dizzy and weak. As he leaned forward to look at the wound, the night spun around him and he remembered nothing else.

JANUARY 11—WARMBAD, VEGA'S HEADQUARTERS

The third and latest headquarters was located in an anonymous-looking row of shops off a side street in town. Since they communicated solely by runners and field telephone, there was none of the exterior bustle and activity that marked it as a headquarters. There were no vehicles to spot, no radio traffic to detect. It was harder to do business, but they were still alive.

Vega had chosen a small bookstore for his own office, one

of the prerogatives of command. Propped up in an easy chair from one of the apartments above, his leg elevated so that he was almost lying down, he didn't feel foolish only because of the throbbing pain.

"The Russians have promised to replace our antiaircraft guns and send more and newer missiles to improve our defenses." Suarez handed Vega the message slip.

Vega reached for the paper, then weakly waved it away. "How many SAMs will it take to protect us from two aircraft carriers, Colonel? Who will provide the advisors and training for the new equipment?" The general scowled. "It will help, but in addition to air-defense equipment, ask for smoke generators and more dummy equipment."

Suarez nodded, smiling. "That will serve two purposes: provide them with more targets, and fool the South Africans and Americans as to our real strength."

Vega shook his head and smiled. "I'd rather they both thought we were weaker, not stronger. It's clear that South Africa is concentrating their remaining forces against us.

"We can beat them. What are the casualty figures this morning?"

"Roughly ten percent of our armored vehicles are lost, another ten percent damaged but repairable, especially with cannibalization from the destroyed ones. The figures are double that for specialist units: artillery and air defense units have been especially hard hit."

Vega nodded soberly, remembering B Battery. They were reduced to two guns now and had suffered over twenty dead in last night's raid. It gave sober reality to Suarez's cold statistics.

"In return for that, we shot down seven aircraft and damaged another ten," Suarez reported.

Vega had learned long ago not to trust completely enemy body counts. "How many wrecks have we found?"

"Three, sir. The other four were seen to be trailing smoke and in trouble as they left the area."

The general shook his head. "However many there were, I think they will lighten up now. We can still expect attacks, but not at the level of the past twenty-four hours. From now on, we will conduct major movements at night. If we pay more attention to proper dispersal and concealment, we can continue with minimal casualties."

Suarez tried to sound hopeful. "As long as they don't attack the airheads in Mozambique and Zimbabwe, we will still receive supplies."

"The Americans don't need to attack the airheads. The supply line is long enough for them to hit it between here and the border. The risk of hitting Russians or other foreign citizens is too great, just as the risk of losing a cargo aircraft or its crew is too great for the Russians to land here." Vega remembered the airfield at Naboomspruit. It could easily handle large transport planes, but the Soviets had insisted on landing at the original airfields, now a hundred kilometers away. He understood their reasoning, but it didn't keep him from hating them.

Vega had been half-sitting up, but suddenly fell back in the chair as all the strength left him. Lack of sleep and a hole in his thigh that had needed thirty stitches could not be ignored. Suarez was worried. The general had been pushing himself before the wound. Now he was pale, and obviously on the brink of exhaustion. Tired men don't make good leaders.

"I'll send in the medics and some lunch, sir. You should rest and heal."

"So should the rest of the Army," Vega replied.

A mild painkiller and some food had relaxed and refreshed him, and his chief of staff let him sleep until dinnertime. That gave Suarez time to organize the Army and the disrupted supply lines.

The general woke from his long nap, and while he was still pale and thin, he spoke more energetically and was much less defeatist. As they ate dinner, Vega issued a dozen directives, all designed to help deal with the American air attacks and the problems of night combat. He railed against the loss of half a day, and Suarez smiled. He would gladly spend half a day's advance to get his general back.

Evidence of the American attacks was everywhere when

the command group went forward to their observation position. Suarez was visibly uneasy, but Vega had insisted on observing the first night attack personally. None of them had any experience in large-scale night attacks, and Vega said that he needed to learn faster than anyone else in the Army, and hopefully faster than the South Africans.

Gomez parked the jeep in a gully formed where a dry streambed cut into the side of a hill. Although there were several groups of trees nearby, the Cubans' first lesson had been to avoid prominent terrain features. Instead, they sheltered it against the gully's side, then moved forward slowly to the top of the hill.

The command group, consisting of Vega, Vasquez, Gomez with the radio, and two bodyguards, settled down to wait for the opening moves. Suarez would run the battle from headquarters. In fact, Vega thought, Suarez was shaping up nicely. Certainly, when the next list of generals was announced, Suarez should be on it. The man should have his own division. . . .

A rippling group of explosions woke Vega with a start. "How long have I been asleep?"

"About half an hour, sir. There's been nothing to see, and you needed the rest. The artillery barrage is just beginning."

"Good." Initially afraid that he'd missed something, his relief was mixed with irritation. Was everyone in the Army going to nursemaid him now? Vega was lying on his back and rolled over, grabbing his field glasses.

Only the general outlines of the landscape could be made out. Scattered clouds blocked some of the starlight and a very new moon. A classic example of the veld, or savannah, making up much of northern South Africa, it appeared flat, covered with scrub brush and tall grass.

Off to the left, he could see a glow and hear the explosions made by artillery shells as they landed. They had probably started a few fires in the grass, hopefully among the South African defenders.

The deceptively flat terrain was laced with dips and rises, some of them large enough to conceal an armored vehicle.

With time to prepare, vehicles could be dug in so that only their turret and gun were exposed, forming an excellent defensive position. Their slow progress had given the Boers more than enough time.

This battle was to regain the initiative. The South Africans had rebuilt their defenses, and Vega was going to have to knock them back on their heels. His wound notwithstanding, the general felt the old drive again. He knew he could blow these damn Boers out of their holes, and the artillery was just the first step.

The barrage ceased, and Vega knew that kilometers back, the gun crews were hurriedly bringing the guns out of battery and moving them to their second firing position. He would lose the battery for half an hour, but better that than losing them forever.

Vega lay on the rise and watched, waiting. It was quiet again, and in the darkness, the only sound he could hear was a faint rumbling, far to the rear. Some part of his forces was being bombed, and Vega could only hope that Suarez could deal with the extra confusion.

The second phase was late, or seemed to be, and Vega felt himself displaying uncharacteristic nervousness. He was almost ready to reach for the radio when he heard the crack of high-velocity cannon, off to the left. There were no new lights, but as the tank cannon fired, he could see streaks of light fly forward and land all along the South African line. The T-62s probably wouldn't hit anything, Vega decided, but they would get the Boers' attention, and certainly their respect.

After a few shots, Vega saw streaks of fire going back the other way. There was no sign of the source, or its effects, and he could only hope his men were giving the best part.

The general scanned the rest of the battlefield. Good. No lights, no sounds, no other sign of activity. Fifteen minutes had passed since the barrage had stopped, and the general nervously counted each one, hoping that his artillery would be redeployed in time.

They didn't get the chance. A popping noise heralded a harsh, white, flickering light. Vega noted that the flares were fired over the right side of the battlefield and knew that his plan had been detected.

The magnesium light illuminated row after row of tanks and personnel carriers, advancing on the right toward the Boer lines. Somebody must have heard engines and called for flares. It had to happen eventually, but like all generals, Vega had wanted them to get a little closer before they were discovered.

The firing on his left had been by no more than a handful of tanks, picked for their cranky engines, but functional guns. Combined with a preparatory barrage, Vega's feint had not only drawn the enemy's attention but hopefully their reserves as well.

Vega watched his lines of armor advance. They were speeding up now, sacrificing neat formations to close quickly with the enemy. Breaking standard doctrine, they would not fire until they had a target, which would hopefully be at short range. As it was, they were only a kilometer or so from the Afrikaner line.

It only took a few seconds for the enemy to see the advancing battalion and realize their danger. Their positions erupted in tracers, bathing the advancing Cubans in explosives. There were a few hits, but the dark, moving targets held their fire and kept advancing.

Vega started to get up, but almost as soon as he stirred, he felt Vasquez's hand on his shoulder, urging him to stay. "You won't see anything if you get closer, sir. It would just increase the chance of you getting hit again, and we might not be as lucky."

The general nodded and returned to his prone position. His urge to get closer was natural, but even at close range, a night battle was no more than a confused mix of sound and images. His best vantage point was up here, getting the "big picture," even if it was a little dark.

The general shook his head a little. Normally he would have dismissed an impulse such as that without giving it a second thought. Vega could only wonder if his wound had weakened him, made him more emotional. He resolved to consider his actions carefully.

The storm of fire suddenly doubled, and Vega realized that his battalion must be close enough to see the Boer positions clearly. Fire was starting to come in from the left and center as well now. The general smiled as he imagined the confusion behind the enemy line—first sending units over to its left, then frantically trying to shift them as the true danger was revealed. Vega loved the chaos and confusion of battle—as long as it was behind the enemy's lines.

Gomez spoke up. "Battery commander reports ready for second fire mission."

Vega felt his spirits lift a little more. "Tell him to execute as planned," he ordered the radio man. He listened to Gomez relay his order as he studied the battle.

More of his tanks and APCs were burning now. The progress of the battalion could be followed by a widening wedge of flickering fires, and Vega knew that for every burning vehicle there were probably two more that had been knocked out.

He hoped the men had escaped from their metal traps. More importantly, he hoped they would have the wit and the will to advance in the right direction in the swirling, lethal confusion.

A whooshing roar was followed by a hollow crump sound. His artillery was shelling the Afrikaner line, but the shells were smoke, not high explosive. Landing at right angles to the Boer positions, and lying across the center, the smoke would make the dark night darker, effectively isolating one-third of the battlefield from the rest. It would not block all of the Boer fire, but it would reduce its effectiveness and slow any movement to that area.

The artillery stopped, and Vega knew they were moving again. American air power, even if not directed by the South Africans, was driving his tactics. Like weather or terrain, it had to be considered, but it could be dealt with.

"The assistant battalion commander says that his tanks have penetrated the line and are swinging left!" Gomez's report was almost a cheer, and Vega was glad that the darkness hid his grin. Then he stopped worrying about it.

With the tanks behind them and on their flank, the South

Africans would have to quickly retreat or face utter destruction. Vega almost hoped they didn't. He imaged the panicked Boer infantry, turning their heads to see shadowed steel monsters emerging from the smoke almost on top of them.

Still, it had not been without cost. Obviously the battalion commander was unable to report. His tank was in the front rank, and Vega could only hope that his vehicle's problems were limited to a broken radio.

The trick now was to seize the Afrikaner positions, dig in, and be ready for the morning light and a new round of air attacks. By the time the Americans knew he was here, he wanted his men secure.

He stood up slowly, weakly, but victorious. He was a heartbeat away from Pretoria. He and his men had survived nuclear weapons, guerrilla attacks, American air power, all in addition to a dangerous enemy and a harsh landscape. Nothing could stop him.

JANUARY 13

Vega slept in that morning, unusual but quite reasonable. He was used to rising early and liked attacking difficult problems first thing, but that was before his wound, and before his forces had shifted to their new nighttime pattern.

His room, a former office in the back of the bookstore, was dark when he awoke. In his disorientation, for a moment he thought it was still before dawn, but he felt rested. Then, panicking, he thought he had passed the whole day asleep. There was another night attack to organize, and when he caught Suarez, he was . . .

He heard voices out in the front rooms, saw sunlight streaming through the shuttered windows, and finally looked at his watch. It was eleven o'clock. He'd slept for eight hours, and even though his leg hurt like hell, he felt better than he had in weeks. It was time to plan the next battle, before the South Africans had time to dig in too deeply.

Vega dressed himself quietly, carefully, favoring his leg. He missed Gomez's presence, but the corporal was now needed for other tasks at headquarters and could not be spared for orderly duty.

Drawing himself upright, he opened the door and stepped out into the main room, which was a common office for the headquarters staff.

Vasquez, Suarez, and several of the reconnaissance platoon officers were engaged in a heated, although not angry, discussion. Books and maps were scattered everywhere. They were so intent that they did not notice Vega's presence until he was almost next to them.

Vasquez sensed his presence first and turning, gasped when he saw the general standing over him. The rest of the staff, embarrassed and a little frightened at not noticing Vega's entrance, quickly came to attention.

The general responded to their muttered good mornings and gratefully sat down in the chair offered to him. Rustlings behind him soon resolved into a breakfast of bread and jam, some tinned meat, and strong coffee. As they handed him the plate, Vega remembered that fancy dinner in the Strand Hotel. It seemed as if it had been years ago, but he remembered the elegant food clearly. He liked this much better.

"What is our situation, Colonel?" asked Vega as he picked up his coffee cup.

"Based on prisoners and other information, we believe the battalion we faced last night was a composite of several understrength units. They suffered at least twenty-five percent casualties, based on the bodies and destroyed equipment we have found."

Suarez added, "Our casualties were closer to fifteen percent, including Colonel Oliva."

Vega nodded somberly. Night actions were always fought at close range, which meant a lot of hits and a lot of casualties. All the maneuvering and preparation in the world finally resolved into a hugger-mugger encounter where a bayonet was as good as an antitank missile. He was willing to sustain those losses, though, if he could reach Pretoria. A big victory would force the Russians to shorten his supply lines, pull in more of the socialist world as allies . . .

He realized he was drifting. Vasquez had gone on to describe the next most likely Boer position, the town of Temba. A small mining settlement, scouts following the retreating South Africans had seen them retreat into it. A minor road junction, it had the added complication of lying across a small river. The terrain was definitely tricky.

Vasquez pointed to a sketchy map, which had been heavily annotated. "Although the setup is more complex, I have reconnaissance personnel scouting the terrain for dead zones and potential approach routes. They should be back in this afternoon. We are also trying to build up a picture of the enemy's order of battle, but"—the colonel, paused, hesitating—"we are having some difficulty doing so."

Vega nodded, a little impatiently. Vasquez had done well in a job that had grown harder and harder. Reconnaissance assets had been scarce to begin with, and now American aircraft made any movement dangerous. The chance of any aerial reconnaissance was also nil, especially after two of his precious reconnaissance aircraft had been shot down by carrier-based fighters.

Still, everyone knew the problems, and also the solutions, or the best ones that could be found. He looked at the colonel. "Well?"

"We are seeing massive movement, not only in the town but on the roads leading to it."

"That only makes sense," Vega countered. "It is the South Africans' next defensive position, and we are getting closer to the capital all the time. It's only natural—"

"Sir, my worst-case estimate for the Afrikaner defenses was a composite battalion of armor, two understrength infantry battalions, and two batteries of artillery." Everyone on the staff who heard the list winced. Such a strong defense would make Temba nearly impossible to take.

"We have hard information about two battalions of armor, both stronger than we expected. One of them appears to be made up exclusively of tanks!"

"What?" Vega's look of puzzlement was natural. The entire South African Army didn't have a complete battalion of tanks left anywhere.

"We've had several reconnaissance vehicles killed at long range, in excess of three thousand meters, by antitank missiles. The launchers were masked, but appeared to be deployed around the flanks of the town."

The intelligence officer continued, "We are also seeing helicopters operating near Temba. They are not approaching close enough for us to make them out, but my scouts cannot recognize the type."

Vega was intrigued. "What do you think they are up to, Colonel?"

"We can only conclude that it is a last-ditch effort, sir. We are much closer to Pretoria than the Americans, and the Boers have always put the bulk of their forces in against us. The American front to the south has been quiet in the last few days. It may be that they have run into the same kind of supply problems we have faced, but their supply-hungry army cannot operate as well on short rations.

"My assessment is that they have been stripping the American front of every unit they can, and especially after our victory last night, have committed their national reserves from Pretoria."

The general said, "Other possibilities?"

"I see none, sir. We had very good information on their strengths before we started the war, and there are simply no other units left. If we don't include the units fighting the Americans and British, this brigade is the last major South African force in existence."

"Then let's start planning. If we can organize another night attack, concentrating on only one portion of the brigade, we can do to them what we did to that battalion last night." Vega's voice was full of energy, and it galvanized the entire staff. They could take on a dug-in force almost as large as their own, and win.

Vega and his officers were clustered around the map, trying to take it apart and visualize the terrain, when the radio operator interrupted them.

"Sir, one of the scouts reports a jeep moving north from Temba under a white flag."

Vega, already deep in his element, took this development as one more piece of a very interesting puzzle. What could the Boers want from him? What was in the commander's mind?

"Halt them at the edge of our defenses, but do not molest them," Vega ordered.

The general grabbed his hat and battered uniform coat. "Come on," he said. "I will not meet the Boers in the middle of a bookstore. We will meet them at our front lines."

The party climbed into a GAZ jeep and drove south at high speed. An escorting party of soldiers barely had time to pile into another and follow them.

The road south to Temba cut through a line of low hills, the same ones that had held the Boer defenders but now held Cuban soldiers.

The command group approached the spot, and Vega noticed a strange-looking vehicle parked under one of the few trees in the area. It was an American jeep, neatly painted in sand and green colors. A small knot of men lounged or sat in the vehicle, under extremely heavy guard.

As their own jeep neared the scene, the men stood up and appeared to be speaking to each other. The circle of guards tightened, as if to prevent any sudden treachery.

Vega's group was now close enough to see them clearly, and his mask of calm was nearly shattered by the sights of not only a South African officer, but what looked like American and British officers as well. What in the world were they doing here? Witnesses? Observers?

Regaining control, he stepped out as the jeep slowed to a stop and then waited patiently as his staff also climbed out and assembled themselves.

He let Vasquez take the lead, and they crossed the ten meters or so to where the enemy officers stood, waiting. Vasquez spoke English, and so would act as interpreter. Vega spoke only Spanish and Russian.

The colonel approached the South African, who appeared to be a brigadier, or one-star general. "I have the honor to be Colonel Jaume Vasquez of the Cuban Revolutionary Ground Forces. I would like to present General Antonio

Vega, supreme commander of the Socialist Armies in Africa." Vega nodded politely.

The South African returned Vasquez's salute, although he managed to do it in such a way that the colonel could feel the man's hatred. The brigadier's tone was cold, and stiff, and the clipped English only accented his anger. "I am Brigadier Deneys Coetzee, chief of staff of the South African Defense Forces and provisional head of the South African government."

Vasquez's reaction was so obvious that Coetzee smiled. They'd had no idea. News of Vorster's fall had been suppressed, easy to do in the tightly controlled media Vorster's regulations had created. That had given Coetzee and the Americans valuable time to consolidate, and more importantly, to prepare a rude surprise for the Cubans.

Coetzee allowed the colonel just enough time to translate this introduction for Vega before introducing the other two men. "This is Major General Samuel Weber of the United States Army, and Colonel Nigel Moore, of the British Army."

Vega as well as Vasquez recognized Weber's name from the intelligence reports. He commanded the American 24th Mechanized Division. Late reports had placed it on National Route 3, fighting its way north toward Johannesburg. Vega felt a wave of cold creeping up his spine.

Coetzee spoke again. "Tell your general that the South African government has ceased hostilities with the American and British governments and has now asked for their assistance in repelling the communist forces that have invaded our territory."

Vasquez bristled slightly, but translated the sentence. Vega maintained his impassive expression, but from the expressions of the rest of his staff, the information hit home.

Vega said, "Ask him what happened to Vorster." Vasquez translated the question.

Coetzee replied, "That is none of your business, but since it will soon be public knowledge, we can tell you that he is under arrest and will soon be indicted, under South African law, on several counts of murder."

When this was translated, Vega's cold chill now turned his heart into a block of ice. He could almost feel it in his throat. Vorster would never have made peace with the Americans. He was ready to destroy his country before he'd loosen his grip. If Vorster was really gone, then the Americans and British had a free hand.

The American walked two steps forward, facing Vasquez. Weber said, "I'm not going to mince words. If your intelligence people are on the job at all, you know who I am." Without thinking, Vasquez nodded.

Jerking his thumb back behind him, Weber said, "I've already deployed a full battalion of M-1 tanks in that town back there, and I'm bringing up another two battalions of one of my brigades sometime soon. I won't tell you boys exactly when, but you can assume the worst."

He leaned closer to Vasquez, so that they were almost nose to nose. "The other two *brigades* will be along presently." He pointed to the British officer. "That gentlemen there also has some units he controls, and there are other officers that couldn't make it to this little meeting. Vaquez noted in passing that the British officer wore a red beret, which could only mean that he commanded a battalion of paratroopers.

"In short, Colonel, you tell your general back there that instead of facing a divided South African Army, he faces the combined forces of South Africa, Britain, and the United States."

Vasquez started to translate, but Weber cut him off. "And tell General Vega that we are fresh as fucking daisies. I've been fighting South Africans for a while, and I haven't enjoyed it too much. Now that Vorster's been taken care of, I'd love to kick some Cuban ass."

Vasquez, controlling his temper, transmitted a paraphrase of Weber's speech to Vega, which even in summary caused him to drop his mask of detachment and take one step toward the American.

Coetzee said, "We offer you these terms: Withdraw from South African territory immediately, using the same routes you came in on. You will be escorted along the entire route, but not molested. Once you have returned to Mozambique and Zimbabwe, you will evacuate all national forces. On the Namibian front, we will institute an immediate cease-fire, followed by a mutual phased withdrawal with the purpose of restoring Namibian sovereignty.

"You have two hours to organize your forces and begin the retreat. If we have not seen you comply with our terms at the end of that time, we are going to blow you to hell."

The jeep ride back to Warmbad was absolutely quiet. All of them had their own thoughts and recommendations, but if the general wanted them, he would ask for them.

Vega's own mind was on fire—calculating, considering, discarding. He had no intention of giving in limply to the threats of the South African and his Western friends.

Vorster was gone, and presumably any of his sympathizers as well. What did that mean for the South African government? They were obviously the creatures of the Americans and British, but it had always been that way.

If the Americans were moving into Temba in strength, then they already held Pretoria. Vega guessed that his threat to the mines was over, and with it the Cuban forces' role as a spoiler.

The general kept trying to fit the pieces together, to reduce the situation down to its basics. Could he still take Pretoria? Not likely. Not with his present forces and supply situation.

Could he hurt the West? Probably, if he could ruin the mines. Vega knew that simply by remaining in South Africa, the economies of many Western nations were being threatened.

That was a goal he could fight for.

The jeep pulled up in front of his headquarters and Vega got out more slowly, favoring his sore leg. "Send a message to Havana. Tell them about the new situation and request reinforcements. We will need an increased level of support from the Russians. Tell Castro that 'the capitalist forces have united themselves against us, and it is time for the socialist forces to match them. This is the great confrontation.' "

Vasquez ran off to compose the message. Vega made no

immediate move to speak, and finally Suarez asked, "Then we are not retreating?"

"Yes, we are, Colonel, but only as far as Warmbad. Pass word to all the commanders that we are taking up defensive positions in town." He saw their stares and added, "We have been advancing, which means that we were on the wrong end of the three-to-one equation.

"If we dig into Warmbad and let them come to us, we can easily hold off a division-sized attack. After we give them a bloody nose, we will launch limited counterattacks, concentrating on holding ground and killing his troops. No advances, no offensives. They will have to come to us, and we will make them bleed.

"By the time they can bring up enough forces to overwhelm us, Havana and Moscow will have sent us the additional reinforcements we so desperately need."

Suarez nodded. It was a good plan, but he was still worried. "What about the American air attacks?"

"We have seen what their air power can do. We can ride it out if we are ready. Start pulling our men back right away. Make it obvious and noisy, then dig them in around the town. Dig hard and deep."

JANUARY 14—DEFENSE COUNCIL MEETING, THE KREMLIN, RSFSR

Vega's message asking for additional reinforcements was under intense discussion. It was not an argument, because everyone in the council was agreed: Vega had done the impossible and was only inches short of his goal. The question was, how much more aid should be provided?

The council was also in complete agreement about the Cuban's request to shorten the supply lines. It was dismissed out of hand. Transport aircraft landing in South African territory would certainly force a direct confrontation with the Americans. The Cubans would have to make do.

Marshal Kamenev, chief of the general staff, looked pale

and haggard after a night with his planners. The Defense Council had been unable to reply to Castro and Vega without hard numbers, and his job had been to find them.

Distilling the situation to its basics, Kamenev said, "Vega now faces forces not only of greater strength but of higher quality. His T-62s and Sagger missiles will be facing M-1s and TOWs, as well as attack helicopters and high-performance fighters."

Everyone nodded in agreement. Although only the defense minister and Marshal Kamenev were military men, all of them could understand the advantage of first-line equipment over twenty-year-old castoffs.

"It is also clear that we can no longer plan on seizing the South African capital. The Americans and British have won that race, installing their own puppet government. Instead, we must plan on a strategy of economic denial. If Cuban forces can reach the Witwatersrand, they can dig in and hold on indefinitely."

Kamenev's aides started passing out copies of a thick document to each council member.

"This is a list of equipment we will have to make available if Vega is to fulfill his role as spoiler: advanced antitank missiles, artillery, air defense equipment, and especially more aircraft."

The foreign minister interrupted. "I have been in communication with several of our socialist allies. They are not prepared to offer more material assistance, but would welcome the chance to give their pilots combat experience. They will all make commitments to the fight, if we do."

The President nodded. There was a political stake here. If the Soviets abandoned their socialist ally now, they would bear the blame for Cuba's defeat. He looked around the table, and there was no sign of dissension.

"Then we are agreed to supply the material." Turning to Kamenev, the President said, "When can you start?"

"We will begin staging transport aircraft immediately. With luck, we can have the first supplies down there by tomorrow night. The ships will take longer, of course."

The President nodded, then swept the entire group with

his gaze. "Understand, this means turning a short war into a long one."

The foreign minister said, "Yes, Comrade President—one that will tie the West's economy into knots. We are not risking Russian lives, only spending a little that will cost the West much more."

WARMBAD

In the growing light, Vega inspected the command bunker, dug out and concealed by the headquarters group, with the assistance of the engineers.

Built in the basement of a collapsed house on the outskirts of town, the roof was alternating layers of wooden beams and earth almost two meters thick. The entire bunker, including the signs of its construction, was carefully camouflaged. The general had even given permission for a dummy transmitter to be set up, in hopes of drawing enemy attention away from the real headquarters.

It had been a welcome relief to find out that they had the whole night to prepare. Initial plans had revolved around a hasty improvement of the existing positions, but when the sun disappeared with no sign of the enemy, Vega had taken a risk and ordered more extensive preparations. Outside of a few enemy overflights, probably reconnaissance aircraft, they had not been molested.

The entire Army had dug frantically all night, knowing what lay in store with the dawn. The general was proud of his men. Exhausted from a series of night battles, underfed and understrength, they had still dug in with a will, sweating now to avoid bleeding when the enemy came.

Vega hadn't left it entirely to his men, though. He had drafted every remaining able-bodied citizen of Warmbad to assist in digging the emplacements, under the direction of his engineers. White or black, they had worked under the guns of his men until near dawn, when they had been released, fleeing into the countryside.

He didn't blame them, Vega thought. You didn't have to

be a military genius to see that the Cubans were preparing for trouble.

Vega was still inspecting the exterior of the bunker when the radio operator called out, "Captain Morona reports incoming aircraft."

Vega hustled toward the entrance. He'd been caught by surprise once, but would not make the same mistake again. He'd been lucky the first time, but wanted to save his good luck for more important things.

The newly installed field-telephone network allowed Vega to reach all of his battalion commanders, the forward outposts, and the air defense sites. There were alternate lines, and critical lines had been buried so they wouldn't accidentally be cut.

A muffled rumbling could be heard through the bunker's heavy door. Putting his hand on the cement wall, he could feel the vibrations, the slamming sensation of explosions against the earth.

"All posts report," he said.

The switchboard operator relayed his order, then listened, relaying the words as they came in. "Twenty-fifth battalion reports no attacks. It sees aircraft bombing targets in town, though. They are engaging with small arms and machine guns."

Vega nodded approvingly. Standing orders directed every soldier to fire his weapon straight up as enemy aircraft passed overhead. An entire company or battalion of men, all firing up, was a threat no airplane willingly accepted.

The other three battalions gave similar reports, and his artillery was similarly untouched. What became clear, though, was that the aircraft were concentrating on the air defenses—in huge numbers.

"Outpost five reports at least six jet aircraft attacking B Battery." The switchboard operator paused, then tried to call the battery directly. "No answer."

Again and again reports came in of heavy air attacks, all concentrating on the air defense units. Vega had three batteries of 57mm guns, and three of 23mm weapons. While they had been carefully dug in, they were not supposed to stand this kind of pounding.

Normally aircraft would evade antiaircraft units or settle for suppressing them, since the idea was to bomb the target, not the target's defenders. His combat units were virtually untouched, though.

After twenty minutes of aerial bombardment, Vega challenged his staff directly. He had his own opinion, but he wanted their evaluations. "What is the enemy planning, gentlemen?"

Vasquez spoke first. "It is a calculated plan to first destroy our air defense, then concentrate on the rest of our forces."

Suarez agreed. "They may have underestimated the strength of our emplacements. It costs them less in blood to pound us from the air. We may be in for a morning of air raids, then a ground attack later in the day."

Vega nodded. He hoped they were right.

After a full thirty minutes of aerial attacks, Vega sensed it was time for a shift. None of the antiaircraft batteries responded, and the outposts and other units that could see them reported no signs of movement. A volunteer runner from a nearby emplacement had risked a dash to B Battery and back, only to report heavy casualties and many wrecked guns.

Vega had to concede, although it made no difference to the Americans overhead, that his air defenses were gone.

"Outpost three reports more aircraft approaching from the east."

A little irritated, Vega demanded more information. "Tell Three they can do better than that. We need numbers, type, altitude."

The operator relayed Vega's criticism and then listened, eyes widening. "Three says about ten aircraft, that they are very large, and are at high altitude. They cannot make out the type."

"I can," said Vega, and grabbed a pair of binoculars. Opening the bunker's door, he stood in the opening and scanned the sky. Suarez and the rest of his staff held looks of puzzlement or confusion. What were the Americans doing now?

Vega knew, or thought he did. He had been an observer in Vietnam. He was looking up, but raised the glasses still more. There. The aircraft were almost too high to be seen, but even at that altitude, the long, thin wings and fuselages were unmistakable.

The instant of recognition galvanized him. Spinning and slamming the door, he said, "American B-52 bombers. Grab something and hold on."

Setting an example, he tucked the binoculars in the space between the desk and the wall, then sat down, bracing himself. His staff quickly followed his example.

Inside the bunker, they couldn't hear the high-altitude jets. The first sound they heard was the bombs landing.

Four cells of three B-52Gs had been launched from Diego Garcia five hours before. The order to launch had actually come before nightfall, South African time, but it had taken time to fuel the eight-engine monsters and load each plane with fifty-one 750-pound bombs.

The bombers came over in level flight and tight formation. A squadron of F/A-18s provided close escort, and one of F-14s ranged farther out. After three squadrons of attack aircraft had pounded the ground defenses, no real opposition was expected from them, either.

The bomber laid a perfect, tight pattern on top of Warmbad.

The sound of the explosions swelled quickly, so quickly that it was overhead before they could measure its approach.

What had been a distant rumbling became a nearby thunderstorm and then a cascade of explosions that Vega thought would tear the bunker open. The sound grew still more, into a nauseating concussion that threw him away from the wall, and finally to a single, continuous, deafening roar.

At first, the inside of the command bunker filled with airborne dust, all of it created by the vibrations from the bombs dropping outside. Loose gear started to rattle and fall over, but the men inside hung on as they looked at the ceiling and hoped it would hold.

In seconds, the crescendo of sound and vibration rendered thought impossible, and those unable to hold on literally flew across the room, slamming into anything in their way.

Vega was literally bounced out of his corner, and he collided with the switchboard operator, who either from duty or confusion had stayed seated at his panel. Now the equipment lay in a jumble of wires, and only the cabling that attached it to the wall kept it from flying around as well.

The lights went out, and Vega could hear yells and thuds as people and equipment collided in a room that seemed more and more mobile. For one moment, he thought the entire bunker had somehow become detached and was tumbling end over end, but he knew that the concrete-block walls could never survive that.

In the confusion of the tumbling men and darkness, Vega hardly noticed that the explosions had stopped. Coughing in the murky, dust-choked air, he fumbled to stand upright. Succeeding, he bumped his head on the ceiling. Crouching as he rubbed the sore spot on his skull, the general remembered being able to stand upright in the bunker.

They had to get out, and quickly. Where was the door? The dust was so thick that it was impossible even to see the walls, but in the darkness, Vega could see a glow and stumbled toward it.

The wooden door was off its hinges, broken, then crushed when the frame surrounding it buckled. A concealing pile of lumber had been blown clear, and the general climbed up the ramp and out into the open.

The air outside was only a little better than that inside. Trying to breathe, he almost choked and bent over in a spasm of coughing.

It had to be a little clearer, though, since he could see some distance, almost a hundred meters. The town looked fairly intact, and he had begun to have some hope before he turned around and looked over where the 25th battalion should have been located.

Vega's bunker was on the outskirts of Warmbad, on the northern side. He had deployed his battalions in a circle around the town, each of the four occupying a ninety-degree sector. Dug in on the flat, treeless landscape, the battalion should have been seen only as series of low mounds, and the turrets of its dug-in armored vehicles.

Instead, the uneven, churned-up earth showed no sign of plant or animal life, or anything of human construction. The smoke and dust cleared a little more, and Vega could see the individual craters made by the bombs. They were huge, each almost a dozen meters across. More disturbingly, in the near distance he could see the shattered remains of an AK-47.

Vega heard voices behind him—exclamations, gasps, a few shouted orders. His staff was also emerging from their barely adequate bomb shelter. Ignoring them, he started to walk toward the 25th's command post, a few hundred meters away.

A mild breeze was moving the dust, clearing the air. As it did so, the outlines of the landscape became harsher, and more details, all of them horrible, were visible.

Vega had taken no more than a few steps past the shattered weapon when he found a leg, half-buried in the dirt. The exposed hip joint was covered with dust. Moving forward more slowly, the general found more body parts, whether from the same man or another it was impossible to tell.

Vega had to pick his way carefully. A layer of loose earth, perhaps half a meter deep, covered everything. He remembered walking in freshly plowed fields back home, and this dirt had the same consistency.

He stepped and felt something solid under the surface. A rock, a man, or some piece of equipment, it was impossible to tell. Carefully picking his way in the uncertain footing, he almost bumped into the metal side of what had been an armored personnel carrier.

The vehicle was fairly intact, but was nearly covered with loose dirt. Lying on its side, it was at least fifty or a hundred meters from the nearest spot APCs could have been emplaced.

Vega reached for a hatch, intending to check the crew, then dropped his hand. There was no point.

His staff found him there five minutes later. Looking out to the west, he made no move to turn to face them as they approached. When they stopped, sharing his silence, he said, "Send a messenger to the South Africans."

He turned to face them. "We're going home."

CHAPTER 42

Retreat

JANUARY 14—CLOSE-UP FLIGHT, OVER NATIONAL ROUTE 1

"Ice" Isaacs fought his instincts and flew straight and level, following the road. Below him stretched the entire Cuban Army, or the remains of it, at least.

Lacking anything else to do, Ice checked on Spike Faber. His wingman was in position, and when he saw Ice turn his head to face him, he waved cheerfully, then slow-rolled his Hornet in place.

Isaacs fought the urge to give him at least a mild chewing out. Acrobatics such as that on a combat mission were strictly forbidden, for good reason, but this was like no combat mission he'd ever flown.

Thousands of armed Cubans passed beneath his wings, and then the road was empty. Isaacs continued north, extending the distance before his turn.

At three hundred feet and slow speed, every detail of the column was visible. The trucks, the long lines of men on foot, some of them limping, and best from his point of view, not a weapon raised against them.

Isaac pulled the Hornet up in a long, graceful curve, taking the time to enjoy the sensation. This was no five-g turn designed to bend the airplane onto a new course as quickly as possible. There was no hurry, and nothing more dangerous than the afternoon thermals to occupy his attention.

Lieutenant Isaacs was a little relieved, actually. He had of course been briefed that the Cubans would not fire, and that they were expecting close overflights, but there was always the chance some hothead would take a potshot at them. He smiled. Maybe the flight of A-6 Intruders a thousand feet up and a mile off to the left had cooled any hot tempers.

Ice finished his turn and lined up on the road again. The long shadows were going to make the photo interpreters' lives a lot easier. In a few hours headquarters would have an excellent idea of the retreating Cubans' strength.

He triggered the cameras and started a second pass.

General Vega looked up at the jets, sure the pilots were laughing at him and his men. The urge to shoot, to lash out at his enemies, was almost as great as his shame, but the certainty of death was too great.

He was proud of his men, and his sole goal was to ensure that they all reached home successfully. The thought of Cuba pulled him forward, even as the American tanks and troops pushed from behind.

The enemy had been generous. Victors can afford to be. He and his men, stunned from the massive bomber raid, had spent the morning digging out survivors, then at noon had started out on the long march home.

Along the way, they would meet supply convoys, en route before the great reversal. Like a snake eating its own tail, Vega's army would march back unopposed, but unassisted.

JANUARY 15—DEFENSE COUNCIL, THE KREMLIN, RSFSR

Marshal Kamenev stood before the council, holding the message as if were news of a loved one's death.

Tumansky, the foreign minister, asked, "Is there no action we can take, no promise that will make him stop this retreat?"

Kamenev shook his head. "I have met General Vega and have read his messages over the months. I know him. He is beaten."

Reading aloud, the marshal said, " 'The correlation of forces is too great for any conceivable force to overcome. Even with Cuba's whole armed forces, I could not stand against the Western alliance.' "

Kamenev looked up from the paper. "He rebukes us, comrades. He is implying that he stands alone against the West, and that Cuba cannot stand, but that we could."

"Could we, comrade?" Tumansky's face was a mask of concern. "Our goal was clear. The socialist forces fought a real enemy, the last capitalist power in Africa. World opinion was on our side."

"More importantly," the President added, "we could have put a noose around the Western economies' necks, while ours grew strong." He turned to Kamenev. "What military options are open to us?"

The marshal sighed. "If we wish to continue fighting, we would have to land Soviet troops, in division strength, in Mozambique and Zimbabwe. Vega's men are finished. We would have to provide the forces ourselves. Once secure airheads had been established, we could then begin advancing south, along the same routes used by Vega's forces."

The chairman of the KGB nodded. "The prize might be worth a risk of war with the Americans."

The President and other members of the Defense Council did not appear to share his feelings. "How long to execute such a plan, comrade?"

"I could have airborne forces moving in twenty-four to forty-eight hours." The marshal's positive words did not match his reluctant tone. "Category A divisions could be taken from the strategic reserve. It would take a minimum of two weeks to build up, then a campaign of several months before we would reach Pretoria, if at all.''

The President prompted, ''And the chance of success?''

''Very poor, sir. American and British forces are already in place in the area. We could expect to be bombed by carrier- and land-based aircraft as soon as our troops started appearing. They would undoubtedly bring in more units, matching our buildup. Our interventions might trigger other Western countries into joining the Americans. We would be fighting an armed and ready enemy, on ground of his choosing, far beyond our normal reach. It could take much longer than several months.''

Tumansky said, ''A long war would be a disaster. If we can move quickly, outpace world opinion—''

Kamenev interrupted him. ''We do not have the initiative, Minister. A wise man picks his fights carefully. This is not the time.''

The foreign minister was silent.

''Then we have no options?'' The President's question was accompanied by a long look around the table. The other Defense Council members remained silent.

''Comrade President. With your permission, I will start ferrying Cuban troops back to Luanda, and then to Havana.''

The President sighed. ''Approved.'' It would be a long time before they'd risk another ruble in Africa.

JANUARY 16—ALLIED EXPEDITIONARY FORCE HEADQUARTERS, DURBAN

The visitor from the State Department looked out of place, his suit and tie clashing with the drab camouflage colors surrounding him. General Craig had half-dreaded and half-expected his arrival.

Normally, a military government was set up in the conquered territory until order could be restored and a civilian government established. Craig knew he could do the job.

In this case, though, the civilian government was already

established. In this day and age, too, Washington would want to maintain much closer control over the situation.

Craig sighed. He'd spent a lot of time in the Pentagon and the Navy Annex, but that didn't make him an insider. Washington would want one of their own men in charge.

With the State Department in the act, his job would be over. What would happen to him next? A staff job for the commandant? He smiled, remembering the current assignments. If they could stash him somewhere for a few months, the assistant commandant's slot would open when Bud retired. . . .

Edward Hurley was special ambassador to South Africa, reporting directly to the secretary of state. A small, professorial type, he looked the part of an academic right down to a neatly trimmed beard and mustache, and tortoiseshell glasses. The general had heard Hurley's name mentioned during the crisis, always favorably. Obviously, he'd done well and was now reaping the reward—a top diplomatic post.

Craig thought that he looked young for the job—only in his late thirties or early forties. Still, he'd need the energy. He was welcome to the headaches.

They had been exchanging pleasantries for several minutes now, and Craig was impatient to get on with the meeting. Stories about the weather change and the gossip in Washington only delayed the inevitable.

Finally, Craig broke in. "I'm grateful that the State Department has sent you personally, rather than just sending me a new set of orders."

"I wanted the chance to introduce myself and make sure that we could work together." Hurley's tone toward the general was respectful, something he didn't hear from a career bureaucrat that often.

"I take orders pretty well, Mr. Ambassador. I'm sure there won't be any trouble."

Hurley smiled. "I think we'd better take care of the paperwork before we go any further, General." He reached into his briefcase and withdrew an envelope. "This should clarify our relationship."

Craig accepted what had to be his orders with a feeling of

resignation, and a little apprehension. Every military man feels a little uneasy tearing open the envelope. It still wasn't too late for a booby prize.

The Marine tore open the envelope and pulled out the two sheets of paper, both from the Joint Chiefs of Staff. The first page appointed Gen. Jerome D. Craig, USMC, as military governor of South Africa, responsible for preparing for the restoration of civil government. . . .

Craig looked up at Hurley. "Then I'm to be left in charge?"

"As head of a military government until the South Africans establish their own."

"But there is a government. Brigadier Coetzee . . ."

"Has absolutely no power, except what you give him. And too many people in Washington are unhappy with the idea of a 'military junta' taking Vorster's place. TransAfrica wants us to hand everything over to the ANC, the conservatives in Congress want guarantees that the government will not have any socialist elements, and so on."

Hurley held both hands, open, in front of him. "Don't get me wrong. The State Department would love to have much more 'direct participation' "—Hurley smiled—"which translated, means running things itself. The problem is that it's just too hot a political issue right now. Any move made by the State Department will be criticized. The consensus is that a military transition government will be seen as apolitical."

"Unpolitical is more like it," Craig grumbled. He didn't bother to protest the order or try to evade it. Craig was puzzled, though. "What is your role?"

"That's on the next page," Hurley answered.

Craig turned to the second of the two sheets. Special Ambassador Hurley was assigned as a political advisor to the military governor of South Africa, and official U.S. representative to the new government.

As he finished the page, Hurley added, "I'm going to try and take the heat on some of the political questions, General. Washington wants you in charge, though. You're a popular man. You won the war. Did you really think your job was finished?"

"The Cubans are shattered, Mr. Ambassador, and the civil war is over."

"There are still bands of guerrillas, both black and white, all over the country, General. Some of them are no more than bandits. Those that we can't persuade to surrender will have to be . . . dealt with."

Craig noticed Hurley's distaste at the idea of hunting guerrillas. They both remembered the Vietnam experience.

Then the ambassador smiled. "Besides, General, your political skills have been underrated. Your settlement of the Cape Town question—"

"All I did was stall."

"Which is at least half of politics, and not always the bad half," Hurley countered. "And sir, I hope you can just call me Ed."

Craig smiled, but kept most of it inside. So he was still in charge. No man likes to hand over the reins, but the easy job in South Africa was over. From now on, it would be politics and more politics. Part of him shuddered. He'd take war over politics any day.

Craig reached out and shook Hurley's hand again. "Welcome aboard, Ed."

The Marine turned to General Skiles, standing nearby. "George, we need to get Ambassador Hurley an office—right next to mine."

Skiles nodded and left.

"As long as you're here, Ed, here is a list I've been working on. It's the 'easy stuff.' I'll pass this by you, before I go any further." He handed a sheet of paper to Hurley, who took it and started to read. "If you don't have any comments, I'm going to turn that over to our military lawyers and let them draw it up."

Hurley's eyebrows raised, Craig hoped approvingly. Good intentions were all well and good, but this was the test. Could they work together, and who really was the boss in the political sphere?

Hurley was reading, half to himself, half aloud. "Legalization of all political parties except any advocating racial superiority. Removal of all AWB members from any public office. Release of any prisoner held for political crimes only. Freedom of the press. Labor unions. Integrating the armed forces. Prison reform."

Craig was following the list in his mind, and Hurley paused for a moment. "You don't mess around, General."

"Call me Jerry, Ed. I might as well tell you. I move fast, and I view these as just preliminary steps. It buys us time with the black opposition groups, and the white conservatives can blame us, instead of the new government, for those moves."

Hurley smiled admiringly. "Jerry, I foresee a brilliant future for you in politics." He then returned to the list.

The last item was guaranteed to be a shocker. "Total replacement of the police force?" Hurley's voice was hard to read, but Craig knew it deserved some explanation.

"The civil war's shattered their organization. They'd have to overcome their own mutual distrust as well as the distrust of the black population. After some of Vorster's excesses, even the whites don't trust the police.

"I'm bringing in every Military Police unit we and the British can find. I've already got my civil affairs people in place. We can do the job until the new constabulary is formed. That's not a problem."

Craig leaned forward, pressing his point home. "I want the South Africans, black and white and in between, to think like we do: if you get in trouble, you call a cop. That's the last thing a black does. We'll have new personnel, new uniforms, and a new set of rules."

"Okay, Jerry, I see your point and agree. But what rules will they enforce?"

"That's the hard part."

JANUARY 21—ON NATIONAL ROUTE 1

Nxumalu Mchwenge was a Xhosa. He was also an ex-member of the ANC, the South African Defense Forces, where he had been a spy, and of Vega's army. Mchwenge had gladly acted as a scout for the Cubans. They had promised to drive the Boers out, to bring about the socialist paradise that he had always dreamed of.

Then had come Potgietersrus. Thousands of black civilians had been gassed, shocking all of the native Africans working with the Cubans. A delegation sent to Vega's chief of staff had been turned away, and two men who had protested more vigorously had been arrested, never to be seen again.

So Mchwenge had acquired another enemy. They had fled the Cuban column and joined the army opposing them. His army had no name, but with others, they had bombed and raided the Cuban liberators-turnedinvaders. Sometimes, they had even worked with white farmers to attack the Cuban soldiers, but that had been an exception, not the rule.

The war was over between the Cubans and the Boers now, but they were still his enemies. The Americans and British were probably his enemies as well, even though they had ended the war. Mchwenge had decided that he had a very short list of allies.

Now Mchwenge lay in a small rock pile fifty meters from the highway. The small, stocky black was used to the heat and discomfort, especially on a mission such as this. He had been tracking the retreating Cuban column for days, watching and thinking. Finally he had picked his spot. Preparing carefully, he had quietly lain since before dawn, easily evading the patrols that covered the highway. Now he clutched the controller and waited.

Headquarters was the back of a truck. Its canvas cover provided protection from the summer sun, and its bed was more than ample for the few functions Vega's staff still had to perform.

Gen. Antonio Vega, Liberator of Walvis Bay, sat easily on a camp stool in the moving truck, reading a summary of the previous day's casualties. The truck was moving slowly, out of deference to the thousand-plus men who still had no transport.

Facing to the open rear, he looked out and saw the entire column laid out behind him. Vega's truck was first, not only to avoid the dust but to make him easy to find. Even with the lead position, the dust and the heat had become more than irritating, almost intolerable.

Twin lines of men filled the road, with trucks interspersed among them carrying the column's wounded, as well as its food, water, and other supplies. There were nowhere near enough trucks to carry all the men. Virtually all of Vega's own transport had been destroyed on that terrible morning. These were supply vehicles that had been en route from the north, their original cargoes dumped or consumed.

His men were suffering in the heat. A week on the road had weeded out the weak or infirm, but even the strong were tested by the midday sun and the dust. There was nothing to do but march, though.

The enemy had stopped molesting his supply line and had virtually given over National Route 1 for his exclusive use, as long as he marched north. A company of American and British military police preceded him, clearing the road and making sure none of the Cubans strayed. A similar unit followed, picking up any stragglers. They had also picked up more than a few deserters—"defectors" in Western idiom.

It angered him that all the men under his command did not share his desire to return to Cuba. Even with Castro's wrath to look forward to, the general's only impulse was to get home. So far, his demands for the deserters' return had been ignored. Of course, it's easy to ignore a beaten general.

His leg still hurt, his clothes were filthy, and he ached in a hundred places. The rigors of life in the field seemed to be no different from before, but now there was no purpose to them, nothing else to occupy his mind.

Nothing except the casualty list, he thought, returning to the paper. No deaths, he was grateful to see, but more casualties to heatstroke, foot-related injuries, and two men who were hit by a truck.

They would last, though. Without any enemy assistance, he would march his forces out of South Africa and onto the airplanes in Zimbabwe. The Americans and British had prohibited any landings by Soviet aircraft or personnel in South

Africa, and no amount of paint would ever convince them that the Cuban Air Force had suddenly acquired Il-76 cargo planes.

More trucks would arrive over the next few days. Once his entire column was mounted, they would move ten times as fast. He allowed himself a faint anticipation. Even with delays, General Vega knew he would be home in a week.

Mchwenge felt the column's approach in the ground beneath him, then saw the dust plume. Finally, almost an hour after the first warning of its approach, the column's head appeared on the horizon.

They were slow, walking at the pace of an infantryman's tired stride. The same slowness that had made it easy to pace and scout the Cubans now maddened him, filling him with impatience.

The Xhosa picked up the controller, then put it down, then picked it up again, checking the settings on its simple controls. He put it down again, almost throwing it, and fought the urge to pick it up again and check for damage.

The rock pile was waist high and had been altered slightly by Mchwenge to provide overhead concealment, as well as shade. Gaps at various points allowed him to peer out, and his comrades, checking the day before, had assured him that he was invisible from more than a meter away.

Mchwenge lay in the dark heat and waited, watching the steady progress of the column. His original plan had been to sneak looks occasionally, remaining completely concealed to minimize the risk of detection.

When the trucks had actually appeared, though, he had found it impossible to tear his eyes away, as if from half a mile's distance they could suddenly zoom past the spot before he could react.

So he had watched through the gaps and waited, and finally, after half a morning of waiting, he reached for the controller again.

The small black box had a wire running from it. He looked it over carefully and again fought the urge to fiddle with its insides. He had put in fresh batteries that morning and so limited himself to one press of the test button. The yellow test light came on, and Mchwenge knew he had a circuit.

He had placed a small stone twenty meters from the spot, and as the lead truck's tires passed, he lifted a cover on the controller's box and flipped a toggle switch up. A red light next to the yellow one came on. The circuit was armed.

The actual spot was easy to see. The metaled road had been torn up here, by weather or fighting. Even tracked vehicles crossing it could have created the break, but it was just what he had needed.

It was no different from a hundred other gaps, but it was close to the crash site and had made their trip relatively short. Besides, why should the Cubans be suspicious? The fighting had stopped.

There was no sign of any reaction in the column, just a slow, steady march north that took them right over the break in the road.

A few miles from here, a South African jet had crashed, a forced landing by the looks of it since the airframe was still intact. The pilot had died on landing. Mchwenge's comrades had found his dessicated body, still gripping the stick.

The plane's ordnance load had also survived, or almost. Two five-hundred-pound bombs had been found near the wrecked plane, and one was adjudged safe enough by ordnance experts to be moved.

As the truck rolled over the gap in the metaled road, Mchwenge pressed the firing button, sending an electric pulse through a buried wire to five pounds of C4 plastic explosive. It detonated, serving the same purpose as the bomb's damaged fuze. Two hundred pounds of Minol detonated exactly under the lead truck's center.

Colonel Vasquez saw the explosion. He had gotten out to walk for a while, not only to give the general a little room but to think about his own future, personally and professionally. Castro was not a tyrant, shooting people at whim, but they had failed their leader, and he would need scapegoats. What would be their fates?

He was looking at Vega, sitting in the back of the truck,

when a bright flash and a roar knocked Vasquez over, stunning him. He had one brief impression of the surprised general, unable even to lift his eyes from the paper, before the entire vehicle was enveloped in smoke and flame.

Vasquez came to a moment later as a soldier dragged him away from the fire. A thick column of greasy smoke rose from the blackened, shattered remains of a Russian-built ZIL heavy truck.

Panic filled Vasquez, and he grabbed at the arms pulling at his. He looked up into the soldier's face and shouted, "Did anyone get out? Where is the general?"

"He is gone, Comrade Colonel. Nobody escaped."

Vasquez refused to give up. "Maybe someone was blown clear." Maybe that someone was Vega.

"No, Comrade Colonel, the explosion was too great. They were all killed instantly."

The soldier, absorbed in their conversation, was still dragging the officer. Vasquez shook off the man's hands and stood up unsteadily. His uniform was torn and blackened from the blast, and he saw, but did not feel, blood trickling from a few small cuts.

He took one unsteady step back toward the wreckage, then another, until he could clearly see that only the bare metal skeleton of the vehicle remained. The wooden flooring had a four-foot hole blown in the center, and the frame was twisted, as if it had been softened by the heat and then dropped. He could see no sign of any bodies and knew that any human remains that might be found would be in pieces too small to identify.

Vega was gone, and Suarez, and Gomez, who had been driving, and perhaps others he would have to search for. His sadness was mixed with relief for his comrades. At least they would not have to make the long journey home to face Castro's anger.

"Colonel, what should we do?" One of the lieutenants nearby, in charge of a group of men that had once been a company, looked to him for orders. Vasquez was almost certainly the senior officer in the force now. He looked again at the wreckage of Vega's truck. It was one post he had never wanted.

The lieutenant repeated the request. "Colonel, what can we do now?"

Vasquez pointed ahead and to the side of the road. "Bear left and keep marching."

CHAPTER 43

Settlement

FEBRUARY 15—CNN HEADLINE NEWS

In many ways, the televised images from Cape Town carried even more meaning than the reporter's spoken commentary.

Pockmarks were still visible on the graceful columns fronting the Houses of Parliament. Sections of its iron rail fence were missing, warped, or shattered by shell bursts. Most of the century-old oak trees that once shaded Government Avenue's gravel walk were also gone—blown down during the fighting and now replaced by newly planted saplings.

There were even more dramatic changes among the somber faces of the men and women filing slowly in past temporary metal and bomb detectors. Most wore business suits and many carried bulging leather briefcases. Unlike past gatherings in South Africa's legislative chambers, however, those assembling for this first, full working session of the new Constitutional Convention represented all of the nation's varied races and ethnic groups. Some were lawyers and politicians. Others were farmers or doctors or teachers or businessmen, people with no experience in government. Despite their obvious differences, they had one important thing in common. All had opposed Vorster's regime at the risk of imprisonment or death.

"Although innumerable problems remain to be settled, one thing is clear: apartheid in South Africa is a thing of the past.

"With so many of the extremists on all sides dead or in prison, the way may finally be clear for others to lead South Africa's separate peoples toward a better future together. The political settlement that emerges from this convention's closed-door conference rooms is unlikely to be perfect, but it just might be workable.

"For CNN headline news, this is Tom Stavros, reporting from Cape Town, South Africa."

The camera cut away to show the network's Atlanta studios and anchorwoman. "In other South Africa–related news, reports that Witwatersrand mining operations were back to fifty percent of prewar levels sent commodities prices tumbling at exchanges around the world. Commerce Secretary Reid hailed the news as a 'firm signal that the battered global economy is on the mend.' "

MARCH 23—HEADQUARTERS, ALLIED PEACEKEEPING FORCE, DURBAN

Both Gen. Jerry Craig and U.S. special ambassador Edward Hurley had kept their offices and headquarters in Durban instead of moving them to either Cape Town or Pretoria. Part of their rationale for that was military common sense. After all, Durban was a central strategic point. Ships arriving at the city's deepwater port supplied the U.S. and British units stationed throughout South Africa.

But their biggest reason for staying put was political. Both men were determined to avoid even the slightest appearance that the American and British military presence in South Africa meant they were dictating every last word of the country's new political framework. Periodic plane trips between

Cape Town and Durban were a small price to pay for making it clear that South Africa's ultimate fate rested in the hands of her own people.

"Hot off the fax machine, Jerry—a genuine historical document." Edward Hurley couldn't hide his excitement or his relief. He plopped a mass of thin papers on Craig's desk, threw himself into a chair, and exhaled loudly. He looked more as if he'd run a race instead of just walking over from his office.

Craig arched an eyebrow. "The Convention's over?"

Hurley grinned. "Christ, no. I expect they'll be squabbling over the fine print for months yet. But that pile there"—he pointed to the document on the desk—"shows the broad outline of what they've already agreed on."

Unable to restrain his curiosity any longer, Craig flipped randomly through the pages, scanning boldfaced headings. " 'Powers of the Central Government. Powers Reserved to the Provinces. Rights of the Individual' . . ." He looked up. "So what's the gist?"

"Fundamentally?" At Craig's nod, Hurley leaned back in his chair, looking even more professorial than ever. "Not quite one man, one vote, but they're headed there. For now, a lower house elected by popular vote, but with an upper house where every group has an equal voice. They're trying to set up a system where everybody participates, but no one dominates."

Craig chuckled softly. "Good luck to them making that work."

Hurley nodded, agreeing. "Yeah. It is sort of like trying to figure out how many angels can dance on the head of a pin."

The ambassador pointed to the section headed "Rights of the Individual." "What's in there is more important than the rest, anyway. Guaranteed freedoms of religion, speech, assembly, and all the rest. Equal pay for equal work. Plus equal access to education through integrated schools and universities. The whole idea's to shift more power to the individual—no matter what his skin color or tribe is."

"No trace of apartheid?"

"None at all. After your setup in January, nobody even said boo when they proposed stripping away the last vestiges. I'll say it again, General, you can come over to the State Department whenever you want. We need good diplomats."

Craig just smiled. He knew the ambassador well enough now to know that no insult had been intended. "What about all that socialist doctrine the ANC people were spouting earlier? Nationalizing key industries and the rest?"

Hurley laughed. "They were pretty quiet about it. Seems like their experiences with Cuban-style 'fraternal socialism' soured a number of them on good old Marx and Lenin. Plus they've had a close look at what's left of Eastern Europe and the Soviet Union. There's even talk of breaking up existing state-run industries."

Craig breathed a little easier. His biggest fear had been that the Constitutional Convention would fall apart while squabbling over economic ideology. Maybe the sheer chaos and horror of the past several months had knocked some sense into South Africa's inhabitants.

Hurley continued, "Even the basic political framework they've picked makes imposing socialism or any other ism more difficult. They're moving toward a weaker federal government presiding only very loosely over stronger provincial and local governments. Plus they'll have just one federal capital—Johannesburg."

He smiled again. "No more of this crazy shuttling back and forth. Can you see our government moving between D.C. and San Francisco every six months?"

Craig winced at the thought. Things ran badly enough when the government just sat still in Washington. "Why Johannesburg?"

Hurley shrugged. "Lots of reasons. Politically, Pretoria generates too many bad memories, and picking Cape Town seemed like a step backward toward the days of British colonial control. Johannesburg's never been a capital city before. Racially? Well, Jo'burg's population distribution's pretty close to the national average. Both Cape Town and Pretoria are too white."

The ambassador shook his head. "Anyway, the location

doesn't matter as much because the whole federal government won't matter as much. After what they went through under Vorster and his predecessors, it'll be a long time before anybody in this country lets a central government have much power at all."

Craig frowned. "That could mean trouble someday. They might need a tougher federal government to impose reform on individual provinces if they go back to apartheid. Hell, a lot of our early civil rights rulings had to be enforced by federal troops."

"Maybe. All we can do is help them get started." Hurley tapped the sheaf of documents Craig was still slowly shuffling through. "And that's not a bad start."

"Yeah." Craig flipped a page and stopped suddenly. "What in God's name are these?" He held out an inset map showing proposed boundaries for two "Reserves"—one labeled the Oranjewerker Staat, the other the Azanian People's Republic.

Hurley grinned. "Now those are two of the most bizarre ideas I've ever heard seriously proposed in a serious political setting." He shook his head in disbelief. "And the strangest thing of all is that they may actually make a certain amount of sense—at least sense South Africa style.

"The idea's to create a couple of places of last resort for the holdouts on both sides. White diehards can try their cherished whites-only, rural lifestyle in Oranje. And black separatists can enjoy their own company in the APR. Inside each enclave, they'll be free to live however they want. But outside them, they'll have to obey the laws of the Federal Republic."

Craig laughed. "Yeah, and we'll see how long that lasts. The old folks may believe in apartheid of one sort or another, but their kids will start asking some hard questions when they see the rest of the country sorting itself out."

"Not all the true believers will be in the reserves," Hurley reminded him. "Nobody in this damn country knows what it's like for different races to live together. It took seventy-plus years for Soviet-style communism to fade. It could take that long for South Africa to recover fully from this mess."

Craig nodded. Hurley's warning was valid. South Africa's racial and political problems wouldn't vanish overnight or even in one or two generations. People were too stubborn and contrary to expect overnight brotherly love. Far from it.

Still, at least South Africans of goodwill and common sense now had a decent chance to pull their country together. That was more than most of them had ever expected. Craig smiled down at the draft constitution on his desk. With that as a framework, they might even succeed.

APRIL 12—PROVISIONAL SUPREME COURT, FEDERAL REPUBLIC OF SOUTH AFRICA, JOHANNESBURG

Television cameras had carried the week-long trial into homes throughout South Africa and around the world. Tens of millions watched a story of ambition, blind hatred, and treachery unfold—piece by sordid piece.

Despite earlier predictions, the case hadn't been tried before an international war crimes tribunal. The eleven justices, the prosecutors, and the defense attorneys were all South Africans. Even the laws being applied—though stripped of all racial references—were South African. In many ways, this trial was the first test of the new nation's ability to handle its own problems.

In the end, an overwhelming tide of undeniable evidence produced the only possible verdict—guilty on all counts.

"The prisoner will rise."

Helped by his barrister, Karl Vorster staggered to his feet and stood wavering. Few would have recognized him as the man who'd once held South Africa in an iron grip. Stooped shoulders and lost weight made him appear smaller and much older—an impression strengthened by his gaunt, haggard face, trembling hands, and sunken, red-rimmed eyes. He'd aged twenty years in barely half as many months.

South Africa's acting chief justice spoke flatly. "Karl Adriaan Vorster, you have been found guilty of high treason, murder, and conspiracy to commit murder. Have you anything to say before this honorable court passes sentence on you?''

With a visible effort, Vorster raised his eyes from the table in front of him and tried to square his shoulders. His enemies might have him in their clutches now, but soon his memory would inspire other, younger men to carry on his work. ''I refuse to acknowledge the authority of this illegal government or this puppet court. Kill me if you will. But only God Himself may judge me or my actions.''

A low murmur of outrage raced through the spectators and witnesses seated behind him.

The chief justice simply waited until silence returned. Then he folded his hands. ''Know then, Karl Adriaan Vorster, that this court sentences you to life imprisonment at hard labor. You will have all the days that God grants you to contemplate your crimes and the wickedness of your ways.'' He gestured to the pair of waiting policemen—one white, the other black. ''Remove the prisoner.''

Vorster felt his shoulders sag. Despair flooded in, burying that last flicker of hope and bitter defiance. He had lost everything—even the chance for martyrdom.

APRIL 21—PELINDABA, THE PLACE OF MEETING

Col. Robert O'Connell stood motionless watching the crowd of military and civilian dignitaries drift away across Pelindaba's manicured lawns and gardens. It didn't look anything at all like the war-ravaged, corpse-strewn compound he'd last seen. In the months since the end of the war, work crews had worked night and day bulldozing slit trenches and demolishing machine-gun bunkers. Even the wrecked uranium enrichment building had been torn down—its existence now marked only by a solitary metal plaque.

But the five long, low weapons storage bunkers were still there—ominous even in the bright fall sunshine. The earthen mounds would stand forever behind the simple granite column they'd dedicated that day. An American flag flew overhead, snapping back and forth in the crisp, cool breeze.

O'Connell silently read the memorial's deeply incised inscription: *FORTUNE FAVORS THE BRAVE. In honor of the valiant soldiers and airmen of the Armed Forces of the United States of America who gave their lives here so that others might live. "No Greater Love Hath Any Man."*

His gaze wandered down to the list of names below—a list that seemed far too long. Each conjured up a familiar face or voice. His vision blurred briefly and then cleared as he blinked rapidly.

O'Connell glanced down at the ribbons on his uniform. Along with several of his Rangers, he'd been awarded the Congressional Medal of Honor for his actions during the attack on Pelindaba. The 1/75th Rangers itself had won another Presidential Unit Citation to add to its many battle honors. Memories of the cheering crowds, the military marching bands, and the President's firm handshake and kind words drifted through his mind.

He looked up again at the monument erected by South Africa's new government. In a way, that simple stone column meant more than any ceremony or piece of colored ribbon. While it stood, the men who'd fought and died at Pelindaba would never truly be forgotten.

"Colonel?"

O'Connell turned. Brig. Henrik Kruger, South Africa's new chief of staff, stood waiting for him. He forced a smile. "Sorry for the woolgathering, Henrik. An old soldier stuck in the past and all that."

Kruger laughed softly. "Not so very old, my friend. And not so very stuck, I think." He nodded toward his staff car. "But come, I have a bottle of very old and very good Scotch in my quarters. Let's drink to those we've lost and to all that we've won. That would be the right thing to do, true?"

O'Connell felt his smile firming up. "Amen to that, Brigadier. No real Ranger lets good liquor go to waste."

Together, the two soldiers strolled toward their waiting car. The afternoon sun cast their shadows behind them.

MAY 1—NEWSROOM, THE *JOHANNESBURG STAR*

Emily van der Heijden stared unhappily at the story on her computer screen. She punched the cursor keys, running backward and forward from paragraph to paragraph. The writing wasn't bad. Not bad at all.

No, she thought moodily, the story she was working on had nothing to do with her present gloomy frame of mind. The depression came from within.

Emily gave herself a solid mental shake. She shouldn't be so sad. It was ridiculous. After all, here she sat—a rising young reporter on South Africa's largest-circulation daily newspaper. Her long-held dreams were finally coming true. So what could be so wrong?

A treacherous corner of her brain whispered the answer. Ian Sherfield was what was wrong. Or rather, his absence.

Right after the war ended, he'd been called home to America by his network. She hadn't minded that so much. After all, he deserved the awards and accolades he'd said they'd showered on him. Besides, he'd wanted to see his parents and brothers and sisters. Nothing could be more normal.

But he hadn't come back. Oh, they'd exchanged cards, letters, and even a phone call or two—but the intervals of silence had steadily grown longer. Now she hadn't heard anything from him for more than two weeks. He hadn't answered any of the messages she'd left in various places.

Emily shook her head, impatient with her own feelings. What else could she have expected? They came from two different worlds and now their two different worlds were even farther apart. Ian was well on his way to being a top-ranked newsman in America. She knew what that meant. No matter what his wishes were, there would always be another assignment, another crisis that would keep him busy and away from South Africa. Time and distance would do the rest—gradually burying love under a growing pile of new experiences, new friendships, and everyday worries they couldn't share.

She stabbed keys with even more vigor, ripping apart a perfectly good piece of prose for no particular reason.

"I hope you've got that keyboard insured, Emily van der Heijden. Didn't anybody ever tell you how expensive computer gear is?"

Emily spun around in her seat, stunned by the familiar voice. Ian Sherfield stood behind her, grinning down at her startled face.

"Ian!" She jumped up and into his waiting arms. Her staring colleagues, her computer, and her current assignment could all go hang.

"Mmmm." He pulled his lips away briefly. "So aren't you going to ask what I'm doing here?"

She touched his lips. "Don't be an idiot, idiot. You are kissing me."

Ian laughed. "True. No, I mean here. In Jo'burg."

"Then tell me."

He sat down in a nearby chair and she pulled her own seat up close.

Ian's story tumbled out in excited words that almost got tangled up with one another. Practically as soon as he'd landed in New York, his network bosses had begun giving him everything he'd considered his heart's desire—an overdue vacation, a big pay raise, and the promise of a plum assignment on Capitol Hill. It had taken several weeks for reality to sink in. Being back on the "fast track" didn't seem to matter very much when you weren't sure you wanted the prize waiting at the finish line.

At the same time, he'd begun realizing that, back in the States, he was just another sharp-eyed reporter—one of hundreds all chasing the same stories, following the same leads, and coming up with pretty much the same angles. In South Africa, he'd actually come to believe his work had meaning. Even more important, he'd come to realize just how much Emily meant to him—and just how big a void her absence left in his life and heart.

She interrupted him there. But once she let him up for air, Ian kept going with what he obviously considered the most important part of his tale.

"So I told the guys in New York they could take their new job and . . . give it to somebody else." He grinned. "My two weeks' notice expired a couple of days ago, so I hopped the first available plane out here."

Emily was shocked. "You quit your job? For me?"

"Well, not exactly . . ." He had the grace to appear slightly shamefaced. "I'm going free-lance. I did a little checking around and it seems that the other networks and Sunday-morning news shows think I'll have some kind of edge over here. Or anywhere in Africa for that matter. So they're all willing to pay me for footage—maybe even some commentary or documentary pieces."

"But that's wonderful! Truly wonderful! You will be your own master."

"Yeah." Ian smiled at her. "Besides, there's always that book we were talking about writing together."

He leaned over to kiss her again.

A second familiar voice broke them apart. "Hey, Ian! I heard some big news over the police radio. A madman is saying he will blow both himself and the Voortrekker Monument to tiny pieces unless his demands are met. I have the car around front already."

Emily stared at Matthew Sibena. The young black man stood in the doorway to the newsroom—practically staggering under the weight of the camera, sound gear, and other equipment slung over his thin shoulders. He smiled shyly at her. "Hello, miss."

Ian grinned at her surprise. "I need a cameraman, don't I?" He rose. "Well, gotta go. The news waits for no man."

"Or woman." Emily thumped him in the ribs.

"I yield." He raised his hands in mock surrender. "Take my story, but give me your heart."

She scooped a notebook, pen, and tape recorder off her crowded desk. "Don't be silly, Ian Sherfield, you have them both."

GLOSSARY

A-6E Intruder—A twin-engine attack plane, the Intruder is one of the few planes that can strike a target in any weather. It is launched from carriers and has a prodigious payload. The crew of two sits side by side, and although the copilot has no flight controls, he can fly the plane by telling the plane's computer what to do.

AA-2 Atoll—The first Soviet heat-seeking air-to-air missile, it is a direct copy of the 1950s-vintage AIM-9B Sidewinder. Like the early model of this missile, it can attack targets only from the rear. It has a range of about two miles.

AA-7 Apex—A Soviet radar-guided missile of mediocre performance. It has a range of about twenty miles.

AA-10 Alamo—An advanced Soviet radar-guided missile. It has a better seeker and a higher speed than the Apex.

AA-11 Archer—A Soviet short-range, heat-seeking missile. It has a range of about four miles, and most importantly, the ability to engage enemy aircraft from the front.

Afrikaans—Along with English, one of South Africa's two official languages. Afrikaans is a variant of Dutch mixed with French and German. It also includes words brought from Malaya and Madagascar by slaves.

Afrikaner—Term used to described white South Africans descended from Dutch, German, and French Huguenot settlers first arriving in the seventeenth and eighteenth centuries. Often referred to as Boers, the Dutch word for "farmer," they now dominate both South Africa's politics and its economy.

AFV—Armored Fighting Vehicle—This abbreviation is used to describe any military vehicle that can shoot and expects to be shot at.

AH-64—An American armored attack helicopter, it carries both laser-guided antitank missiles, rockets, and a 30mm chain gun.

AIM-7M Sparrow—The standard U.S. radar-guided missile, its twenty-five-mile range is shorter than that of the AIM-54C Phoenix, but much longer than that of the Sidewinder or any other heat-seeking missile. It has gone through many improvements. Although the initial versions used in Vietnam were poor performers, the later makes are considered very effective.

AIM-9M Sidewinder—One of the most effective and successful missiles ever made. After launch, it homes in on the heat given off by an aircraft and explodes. Unlike earlier models, or other similar missiles of other countries, it does not need to see the hot tailpipe of a jet aircraft, but can even lock onto an aircraft from the front. It has a range of about ten miles.

AIM-54C Phoenix—A U.S. radar-guided missile, it is linked to the F-14 Tomcat's AWG-9 weapons system. This huge weapon has a range of over one hundred miles and a speed over five times the speed of sound.

AK-47—A Russian-designed assault rifle, this simple, effective weapon has been widely exported and copied by many nations. A 7.62-caliber rifle, it can be fired either in semi or full automatic. It weighs about ten and a half pounds, and has a thirty-round magazine.

AKM—A newer and slightly lighter version of the Soviet AK-47 rifle.

ANC—First established in 1913, the African National Congress is the largest and most prominent black political group opposing apartheid. It has always had socialist leanings and is closely allied with the South African Communist Party. Its military arm is Umkhonto we Sizwe—"spear of the nation."

Apartheid—An Afrikaans word literally meaning "apartness" or "separation." A political philosophy espoused by Afrikaners and first articulated between World War I and World War II. Implemented as government policy after the National Party electoral victory in 1948. Apartheid was intended to ensure continued white control by geographically and socially separating racial groups as much as possible. Unlike the American concept of segregation—"separate but equal"—apartheid included as one of its explicit assumptions the superiority of the white race.

APC—Armored Personnel Carrier—A general term used to describe vehicles designed to ferry infantry across the battlefield. Their light armor provides protection against artillery fragments and small-arms fire.

AWB—Afrikaner Weerstandbeweging, or Afrikaner Resistance Movement. A political movement and paramilitary group, it could be compared to the Ku Klux Klan, or the Minutemen in America, except the Armenian groups are too liberal. Its entire political philosophy is based on white supremacy and the use of violence to maintain white rule. The AWB believes that armed resistance to the liberalizing trend of the South African government is necessary.

Battalion—A large ground unit made up of three to five companies. A battalion will have about one thousand men.

If it is a tank or an armored-infantry battalion, it will also have about fifty armored fighting vehicles.

Brigade—A ground unit of three or more battalions, with smaller specialized units attached. Sometimes an ad hoc formation, brigades combine available units for a specific task. A fast, mobile brigade might consist of one tank battalion, two motorized-infantry battalions, an artillery battalion, and an antiaircraft company.

Broederbond—Afrikaans for "band of brothers." A secret society established in 1918. Members had to be both ideologically and racially pure Afrikaners, committed to the reestablishment of "Afrikaner culture" and the imposition of apartheid as a governmental system. Broederbond cells permeate Afrikaner political parties, businesses, schools, and churches. Until recently, only Broederbond members held political or party office inside South Africa's ruling National Party.

BTR—*Bronetransportr*—A Russian term for a series of armored personnel carriers.

BTR-60—An eight-wheeled armored personnel carrier, it first appeared in the early 1960s. The first of a long series of similar designs, it has a boat-shaped hull and can carry fourteen men. One flaw in this design is its two gasoline engines, located behind thin armor. This was corrected in later versions.

Buffel—A wheeled personnel carrier, it is arguably the ugliest armored vehicle ever built. Specially designed to be mine resistant, it can carry a squad of infantry and is often used by South African paramilitary or police forces.

C4—The designation for a type of plastic explosive used by the U.S. Army and others. It can be worked like modeling clay, burned, or dropped, but will not detonate without an igniter.

C-5 Galaxy—The largest aircraft in the U.S. inventory, this monster can carry 110 tons of cargo. It can also carry troops, but is usually used to carry items too bulky or heavy for the C-141 Starlifter.

C-130 Hercules—An American four-engine turboprop cargo plane, this successful design is used by dozens of countries around the world.

C-141 Starlifter—This four-engined transport is the standard cargo plane for the U.S. Air Force. It can carry over two hundred troops or thirty-five tons of cargo.

Cactus—A South African version of the French-designed Crotale, Cactus is a short-range surface-to-air missile system designed to protect high-value installations from air attack. It consists of a wheeled launcher vehicle with four missiles and a guidance radar, and separate command vehicle and search radar. It has a range of about five miles. Although never used in combat, the system has a good reputation.

Carl Gustav—A man-portable antitank weapon, this Swedish-designed weapon is used by many countries. It is lighter and cheaper than an antitank missile, but has shorter range and less hitting power. It can be used to attack targets other than tanks and still packs a respectable punch. In the 1982 Argentine invasion of South Georgia, British troops nearly sank a frigate with two hits from the weapon.

Chain gun—A form of automatic cannon, the gun takes its name from the fact that a bicycle chain forms part of the drive mechanism. These rapid-fire, medium-bore cannon pack a terrific punch and are often capable of defeating lightly armored vehicles.

Claymore mine—Most land mines are buried in the ground and are tripped when a vehicle or soldier passes over them. The Claymore is different. Spikes hold it upright on the surface of the ground. It is tripped electrically, on command, and sends out a fan-shaped pattern of steel balls that shred anything in their path. It is called a "directional" mine.

Company—A ground unit of one hundred to two hundred men, made up of three or four platoons of three or four squads each. Normally three platoons will be of the same type—infantry or armored vehicles, while the fourth platoon is made up of heavy support weapons or other specialized equipment. In the cavalry, a company-sized unit is called a troop.

Division—A large ground unit, often containing three brigades or nine maneuver battalions, plus separate support units—engineers, artillery, supply and maintenance personnel, and others. A division will have between ten and twenty thousand troops, hundreds of vehicles, and dozens of helicopters.

Eland—An older armored car still in service with the South African Army. Designed and built in South Africa, it is based on a 1950s-vintage French design and mounts a 90mm, high-velocity gun on a very small chassis. Like all armored cars, it is lightly armored, but its wheels make it faster over flat terrain than many tanks.

F-14 Tomcat—A twin-engine, two-seat, swing-wing fighter used by the U.S. Navy for fleet air defense. It carries a powerful radar and very long range missiles.

F/A-18 Hornet—A twin-engine, single-seat jet designed to replace the A-7 Corsair II. The F/A-18A is a multirole aircraft intended to be equally adept as either an attack aircraft or an air-superiority fighter. Very maneuverable, it is designed to be launched from carriers.

G-5 guns—The best artillery piece in the world, the G-5 was designed and built in South Africa using technology stolen from several sources, including the United States. It can fire a 155mm (six-inch) shell twenty-four and a half miles with phenomenal accuracy. The G-5 is towed behind a truck or logistics vehicle. The related G-6 mounts the same gun on a six-wheeled, lightly armored chassis.

Gun—Artillery pieces are classed as either "guns" or "howitzers." Guns have longer barrels, which give them higher velocity and longer range, but at a cost in weight. A howitzer has a shorter range, but can also fire at higher angles of elevation, making it possible to drop shells into "dead zones" behind obstacles that a gun could not hit.

Homelands—An integral part of the 1948 apartheid plan, each major tribe in Africa was assigned a geographic area that was ostensibly its traditional region. For the most part, they have little to do with the actual location of the tribe and are often on barren, undeveloped land. Every black in South Africa was assigned a tribe, and thus a homeland, of which they were automatically a citizen.

The fact that an individual had never seen their particular homeland and had no desire to live there was irrelevant.

HUD—Heads Up Display—Projects important information onto a clear plastic plate directly in front of the pilot's eyes, making it possible to avoid going "heads down" to look at cockpit instruments. The HUD is a vital aid during a fast-moving air combat. The data displayed on the windscreen includes speed, altitude, weapons status, g forces, target data, and fuel status.

IFF—Identification Friend or Foe—An airplane or ship sends a coded electronic signal out to an unknown contact. A black box on an aircraft, if it receives the proper code, responds with a signal of its own, telling the observer that the aircraft is friendly. Aircraft without the proper codes are the enemy. The codes are changed daily.

Il-76 Candid—An Ilyushin-designed cargo plane, it is the Soviet analogue to the U.S. C-141 Starlifter. It has four engines and a rear cargo ramp, like the Starlifter. It can carry about forty metric tons.

Inkatha—A political party made up almost entirely of Zulus, with the majority of its members in Natal Province. Inkatha is the primary rival of the ANC, another black opposition group within South Africa. Some of this rivalry is based on political differences, the rest on centuries-old tribal enmity.

IP—Initial Point—Refers to the geographic location used as the start point for an approach to a target.

Kukri—A heat-seeking missile designed and built in South Africa. While not as advanced as first-line missiles, it does have one advantage. When mounted on the Mirage F.1, the pilot can use a special helmet-mounted sight to lock the missile's seeker on targets off to one side. This is a tremendous advantage in a dogfight, since the plane's nose must no longer be pointed exactly at a violently maneuvering enemy.

LAW—Light Antitank Weapon—A 66mm rocket in a fiberglass tube, this one-shot, throwaway weapon weighs about five pounds. It has a short range and limited penetrating power, but gives the individual soldier a powerful onetime "punch" against lightly armored vehicles, bunkers, or buildings.

LCAC—Landing Craft, Assault Cargo—A large Hovercraft used to ferry troops and equipment from naval ships to the beach. Because of its Hovercraft design, it can move at eighty knots and does not have to stop at the water's edge.

M-1 tank—Arguably the best tank in the world, if the most expensive, the M-1's main advantage over other first-line fighting vehicles is its tremendous speed. While the exact figure is classified, the tank can easily move at fifty miles an hour or more over uneven terrain and is even faster on a road. It is heavily armored and its 120mm gun (in the latest models) is controlled by an advanced fire-control system that allows first-round hits even while the tank is moving at high speed.

M16—The standard U.S. Army infantry weapon, it is much lighter and smaller than its predecessor, the M14 rifle. The M16 weighs eight and a half pounds.

M60 machine gun—The standard U.S. Army machine gun, it is actually derived from a World War II German design, the MG 42. It weighs twenty-three pounds and is normally fired from a bipod.

Mark 82—One of a series of low-drag bombs used by the United States and other countries. The Mark 81 weighs 250 pounds, the Mark 82 weighs 500 pounds, the Mark 83 1,000 pounds, and the Mark 84 2,000 pounds.

Mi-24 Hind—An armored gunship developed by the Russians, it carries a powerful rocket, missile, and gun armament. Although not as new or sophisticated as the Apache, it has a good record in Afghanistan.

MiGs—*MiG* stands for "Mikoyan and Gureyivich," whose aircraft designs have been produced since World War II. Other design bureaus have also produced fighter designs, but the MiG series has been the most famous and the most successful. All Russian aircraft have been assigned code names by NATO, since the Soviets do not give their aircraft names such as "Falcon" or "Eagle." Fighter code names always begin with *F*, bombers with *B*, and special-purpose aircraft with *M*.

MiG-21 "Fishbed"—The MiG-21 is a single-engine, single-seat fighter designed by the Soviets, but widely distributed to their allies. Though an older design, it is still a fairly maneuverable aircraft and a dangerous opponent in a close-in dogfight. It carries a primitive radar and heat-seeking missiles in addition to a cannon.

MiG-23 "Flogger"—The MiG-23 is a single-engine, swing-wing, single-seat fighter also distributed by the Soviets. Very fast, it is a notoriously poor dogfighter. It does have a fairly effective radar and radar-guided missiles to compensate for that fact.

MiG-29 "Fulcrum"—A first-line Soviet fighter that has been heavily exported to their allies. It is easily a match for American types such as the F-16 and F/A-18. It is equipped with a good radar and missile armament.

Mirage F.1—A single-seat, single-engine fighter, the Mirage F.1 is an inexpensive, if mediocre, fighter first produced for France and now widely exported. Customers included South Africa, Iraq, Libya, and other third-world countries. In South African service, it is armed with air-to-ground ordnance or Kukri air-to-air missiles.

National Party—A South African political party closely allied with the Broederbond and the concept of apartheid. First coming to power in 1948, its officials established the network of laws that constituted apartheid in South Africa. It has now mellowed somewhat in its outlook and is moving very slowly toward reform. Even this minor liberalization has spawned right-wing political groups totally opposed to change. These include the Conservative Party and the Heerstige (reconstituted) National Party, which is even more conservative than the Conservative Party itself.

NSC—National Security Council—A special committee made up of cabinet members, military officers, and other U.S. government officials. Its role is to provide information and advice to the President regarding issues that could affect national security.

Olifant tank—A testimony to the effects of arms embargoes on the South African Army. Originally purchased in the 1950s as British Centurion tanks, the vehicles have been upgraded and improved, since South Africa does not have the ability to build her own and cannot buy any more abroad. Although not up to modern standards, their 105mm guns and well-trained crews are a match for anything the South African Army can reasonably expect to encounter.

OP—Observation Post—A small, often concealed, position occupied by one or two men whose mission is to provide early warning of enemy movement.

Osprey—A new aircraft under development by the military. Although it appears to be a propeller plane, it can rotate its wing surfaces to the vertical and take off and land like a helicopter. It can carry troops or cargo and is being considered for a variety of uses, most importantly carrying assault troops from amphibious ships to the beach. In this configuration, it could also be used as a commuter transport.

PFC—Private first class.

Puma—A French-designed troop-carrying helicopter, it has been widely exported, including to South Africa. It is also used as a gunship by the South Africans, mounting a stabilized

30mm gun in the troop door. In its infantry-carrying role, it can carry sixteen to twenty troops.

R4—The standard South African infantry weapon, it is patterned after the Israeli Galil assault rifle. It weighs ten pounds and fires a 5.56mm bullet from a thirty-five-round magazine.

Radar-guided missiles—All air-to-air missiles have some sort of guidance mechanism to help them find the target. The two most common types are infrared, or heat-seeking, systems, such as the AIM-9L Sidewinder, and radar-guided systems, such as the AIM-7M Sparrow. Essentially, radar-guided missiles home in on a target "painted" by a friendly radar. They are longer-ranged than heat-seeking missiles and can usually attack a target from any angle. They are also more complex and cost more to build.

Rangers—Although they are sometimes confused with paratroopers or other Army units, U.S. Rangers have a specialized, demanding mission. They are tasked with striking targets deep behind enemy lines, in battalion or larger strength. This is usually done by parachute, but can be done by other means. Their targets are always strategic, critical to the outcome of a campaign.

RANKS:

U.S. Army	**South African Army**	
	AFRIKAANS	ENGLISH
2nd Lieutenant (2nd Lt.)	*Tweede Luitenant*	2nd Lieutenant
1st Lieutenant (1st Lt.)	*Luitenant*	Lieutenant
Captain (Capt.)	*Kaptein*	Captain
Major (Maj.)	*Majoor*	Major
Lieutenant Colonel (Lt. Col.)	*Kommandant*	Commandant
Colonel (Col.)	*Kolonel*	Colonel

Brigadier General (Brig. Gen.)	*Brigadier*	Brigadier
Major General (Maj. Gen.)	*Majoor Generaal*	Major General
Lieutenant General (Lt. Gen.)	*Luitenant Generaal*	Lieutenant General
General (Gen.)	*Generaal*	General

Ratel—This boxy, six- or eight-wheeled armored personnel carrier comes in many variants, equipped for troop or cargo transport, command, or fire support. It is used by the mechanized infantry units of the South African Army.

Renamo—Portuguese acronym for "Mozambique National Resistance." Created in 1976 as an anticommunist guerrilla organization, it is dedicated to the overthrow of the Mozambican Frelimo government.

Rooikat—An armored fighting vehicle designed and built in South Africa. *Rooikat* is Afrikaans for "lynx." The vehicle itself is lightly armored, with a high-velocity, 76mm gun and an advanced laser fire-control system, including gyrostabilizers. It is a match for second-line and older tanks.

RPG—Rocket-Propelled Grenade—Russian designation for a series of simple antitank weapons. The most common is the RPG-7, which is a shoulder-fired weapon with a short range.

RPK—A Russian designation for a light machine gun of mediocre performance, especially when compared to the U.S. M60 machine gun. It weighs a little over twelve pounds.

RSA—Republic of South Africa.

RTO—Radio Telephone Operator—Any soldier assigned to carry and operate a unit's radio. He is usually found within arm's reach of the officers.

S-60—The designation for a single-barreled 57mm antiaircraft gun. It is normally deployed in batteries of six or regiments of twenty-four. The guns are radar guided.

SA-8 Gecko—A newer, mobile antiaircraft missile, it can engage aircraft at low and medium altitude. It is completely self-sufficient, with the radar and missiles mounted on an amphibious wheeled vehicle.

SAM—Surface-to-Air Missile—A general term applied to any missile used to shoot at aircraft.

SAR—Search and Rescue—The use of aircraft and specialized rescue teams to search for and recover aircrews downed behind enemy lines.

Sarin—One variety of "nerve gas." Sprayed over enemy troops, it kills by inhalation or skin contact. An extremely small dose, measured in milligrams, is lethal. It works by interfering with the nervous system.

T-62A—The successor to the T-55 tank, the T-62A first appeared in the 1960s. It mounts a 115mm gun and improved fire-control system. It has thicker armor, but compares poorly with its U.S. equivalent, the M60 tank.

T-72 tank—A modern Russian design, the T-72 mounts a 125mm gun and improved armor. It has several flaws, notably its fire-control system and a cranky automatic loader. Nevertheless, the T-72's heavy armor is still hard to penetrate, especially from the front.

TOW—Tube-launched, Optically-tracked, Wire-guided missile—A large, long-range antitank missile that first saw service in Vietnam and was a spectacular success. Since then it has been improved and is now the standard U.S. heavy antitank weapon. It has a range of 3,750 meters.

UH-60 Blackhawk—A troop-carrying helicopter used by the U.S. military. It can carry a squad of infantry and is also used for special warfare missions, and for sub-hunting by the U.S. Navy.

ZU-23—A Russian twin 23mm cannon on a ground mounting, it has a small chance of hitting a jet aircraft, but has the advantage of being cheap and numerous. It can also be used against ground troops.